ALSO BY SUSAN HOWATCH

THE DARK SHORE *1965*
THE WAITING SANDS *1966*
CALL IN THE NIGHT *1967*
THE SHROUDED WALLS *1968*
APRIL'S GRAVE *1969*
THE DEVIL ON LAMMAS NIGHT *1970*
PENMARRIC *1971*
CASHELMARA *1974*
THE RICH ARE DIFFERENT *1977*
SINS OF THE FATHERS *1980*
THE WHEEL OF FORTUNE *1984*
GLITTERING IMAGES *1987*
GLAMOROUS POWERS *1988*
ULTIMATE PRIZES *1989*
SCANDALOUS RISKS *1990*
MYSTICAL PATHS *1992*

ABSOLUTE TRUTHS

ABSOLUTE TRUTHS

A NOVEL BY

Susan Howatch

ALFRED A. KNOPF

NEW YORK 1995

THIS IS A BORZOI BOOK
PUBLISHED BY ALFRED A. KNOPF, INC.

 Published in the United States by Alfred A. Knopf, Inc., New York, and simultaneously in Canada by Random House of Canada Limited, Toronto. Distributed by Random House, Inc., New York.

Owing to limitations of space, acknowledgements for permission to reprint previously published material may be found on page 563.

Library of Congress Cataloging-in-Publication Data

Howatch, Susan.
Absolute truths : a novel / by Susan Howatch.
— 1st ed.
p. cm.
ISBN 0-679-41206-9
1. Church of England—England—Clergy—Fiction. 2. Cathedrals—England—Fiction. 3. Bishops—England—Fiction. I. Title.
PR6058.O912A3 1994
813'.54—dc20 94-27510
CIP

Manufactured in the United States of America
First Edition

THIS BOOK is dedicated
to all my friends among the clergy
of the Anglican Communion
(and in particular
the Church of England)
with thanks for their support and
encouragement. My special thanks
also goes to Alex Wedderspoon
for his great sermon preached in
Guildford Cathedral in 1987
on the eighth chapter of St. Paul's
Epistle to the Romans,
verse twenty-eight.

Contents

PART ONE

TRADITION AND CERTAINTY

"Absolute truth is a very uncomfortable thing when we come into contact with it. For the most part, in daily life, we get along more easily by avoiding it: not by deceit, but by running away . . ."

REGINALD SOMERSET WARD
(1881–1962)
Anglican Priest and Spiritual Director
TO JERUSALEM

I

"No doubt it would be more suitable for a theologian to be absolutely pickled in devout reflection and immune from all external influences; but wrap ourselves round as we may in the cocoon of ecclesiastical cobwebs, we cannot altogether seal ourselves off from the surrounding atmosphere."

AUSTIN FARRER
Warden of Keble College, Oxford, 1960–1968
SAID OR SUNG

I

WHAT CAN be more devastating than a catastrophe which arrives out of the blue?

During the course of my life I have suffered three catastrophes, but the first two can be classified as predictable: my crisis in 1937 was preceded by a period of increasingly erratic behaviour, and my capture by the Germans in 1942 could have been prophesied by any pessimist who knew I had volunteered on the outbreak of war to be an army chaplain. But the disaster of 1965 walloped me without warning.

Ten years have now passed since 1965, but the other day as I embarked on my daily journey through the Deaths Column of *The Times,* I saw that my old adversary had died and at once I was recalling with great clarity that desperate year in that anarchic decade when he and I had fought our final battle in the shadow of Starbridge Cathedral.

"AYSGARTH, Norman Neville ('Stephen')," I read. "Beloved husband of Dido and devoted father of . . ." But I failed to read the list of offspring. I felt too bereaved. How strange it is that the further one journeys through life the more likely one becomes to mourn the loss of old enemies almost as much as the loss of old friends! The divisions of the past seem unimportant; we become unified by the shrinking of the future.

"Oh God!" said my wife, glancing across the breakfast table and seeing my expression. "Who's died now?"

Having answered her question I turned from the small entry in the

Deaths Column to the many inches of unremitting praise on the obituary page. Did I approve of this fulsome enactment of the cliché *Nil nisi bonum de mortuis est?* Summoning all my Christian charity I told myself I did. I was, after all, a retired bishop of the Church of England and supposed to radiate Christian charity as lavishly as the fountains of Trafalgar Square spout water. However, I did think that the allocation of three half-columns to this former Dean of Starbridge was a trifle generous. Two would have been quite sufficient.

"What a whitewash!" commented my wife after she had skimmed through this paean. "When I think back to 1965 . . ."

I thought of 1965, the year of my third catastrophe, the year Aysgarth and I had fought to the finish. Bishops and deans, of course, are not supposed to fight at all. Indeed as senior churchmen they are required to be either holy or perfect English gentlemen or, preferably, both.

How we all hanker after ideals, after certainties—and after absolute truths—which will provide us with security as we struggle to survive in the ambiguous, cloudy, chaotic world which surrounds us! Moreover, although in a rapidly changing society ideals may appear to be swept away by a rising tide of cynicism, the experience of the past demonstrates that people will continue to hunger for those ideals, even when absolute truths are no longer in fashion.

Society was certainly changing with great speed in the 1960s, and when I was a bishop I became famous for defending tradition at a time when all traditions were under attack. I had two heroes: St. Augustine, who had proclaimed the absolute truths till the end, even as the barbarians advanced on his city, and St. Athanasius, the bishop famous for being so resolutely *contra mundum,* against the world, as he fought heresy to the last ditch. By 1965 I had decided that I, like my two heroes, was being obliged to endure a dissolute, demoralised, disordered society, and that my duty was to fight tooth and nail against decadence. A fighting bishop unfortunately has little chance to lead a quiet life, but I decided that was the price I had to pay in order to preserve my ideals.

In the 1960s there were three years which now stand out in my memory. The first was 1963, when I clashed with Aysgarth over that pornographic sculpture which he commissioned for the Cathedral churchyard; it was the year Bishop John Robinson wrote his bestseller *Honest to God,* a book which rocked the Church to its foundations, and the year I wrote in rebuttal *A Modern Heresy for Modern Man.* That was when I ceased to be merely a conservative bishop, underlining the importance of preserving the accumulated wisdom from the past, and became a fighting bishop *contra mundum.* The second year which I remember vividly is 1968. That was the year young Nicholas Darrow, my spiritual director's son, was finally ordained after what I suspected was a very shady interval in his private life. It was also the year my son Charley became engaged and my son Michael was married yet despite these family milestones, 1965 remains the year which is most clearly etched in my memory. Not 1963. Not 1968. But 1965.

Let me now describe the man I was before my third catastrophe felled me, the catastrophe which arrived out of the blue. I had been the Bishop of Starbridge for eight years and despite a tentative start I had become highly successful. My sons were both doing well in their chosen careers, and although in their different ways they still worried me, I had come to the conclusion that as a parent I must have been doing something right; at the very least I felt I deserved a medal for paternal endurance. I was on happier ground when I considered my marriage, now almost twenty-eight years old and a perfect partnership.

In short, I was not ill-pleased with my life, and stimulated by this benign opinion of myself I travelled constantly around my ecclesiastical fiefdom, spoke forcefully on education in the House of Lords, held forth with confidence on television discussion programmes, ruled various committees with an iron hand and terrorised the lily-livered liberals of the Church Assembly. I also had sufficient zest to maintain my prowess on the golf course and enjoy my wife's company on the days off which she so zealously preserved for me amidst the roaring cataract of my engagements. Occasionally I felt no older than forty-five. On my bad days I felt about fifty-nine. On average I felt somewhere in my early fifties. In fact I was as old as the century, but who cared? I was fit, busy, respected, pampered and privileged. Frequently and conscientiously I thanked God for the outstanding good fortune which enabled me to serve him as he required—and what he required, I had no doubt, was that I should fight slipshod thinking by defending the faith in a manner which was tough-minded and intellectually rigorous. St. Augustine and St. Athanasius, I often told myself, would have been proud of me.

I was proud of me, although of course I had far too much spiritual savoir-faire to do other than shove this secret opinion of myself to the very back of my mind. By 1965 I was too preoccupied by my current battles to waste much time visualising my future obituary in *The Times,* but on those rare moments when I paused to picture my posthumous eminence, I saw long, long columns of very dense newsprint.

God stood by and watched me for some time. Then in 1965 he saw the chance to act, and seizing me by the scruff of the neck he began to shake me loose from the suffocating folds of my self-satisfaction, my arrogance and my pride.

2

IN ORDER to convey the impact of the catastrophe, I must now describe what was going on in my life as I steamed smoothly forward to the abyss.

1965 was little over a month old, and we were all recovering from the state funeral of Sir Winston Churchill, an event which had temporarily united in grief the members of our increasingly frivolous and fragmented society. For people of my generation it seemed that one of the strongest ropes tethering us to the past had been severed, and "The old order changeth, yielding place to new" was a comment constantly in my thoughts at the time. Watching that winter funeral on television I shuddered at the thought of the inevitably apocalyptic future.

However, I had little time to contemplate apocalypses. As one of the Church's experts on education, I was required to worry about the government's plans to scrap the 11-plus examination and establish comprehensive schools; I was planning to make a speech on the subject in the Church Assembly later that month, and I was also framing a speech for the House of Lords about curbing hooliganism by restricting the hours of coffee-bars. My involvement in current events of this nature required in addition that I brooded on racism—or, as it was called in those days, racialism—and marvelled at the state of a society which would permit a play entitled *You'll Come to Love Your Sperm-Count* to be not only performed in public but actually reviewed by an esteemed magazine.

I remember I had begun to think about my Lent sermons but Easter was late that year, Good Friday falling on the sixteenth of April, so the sermons had not yet been written. In my spare time I was working on a book about Hippolytus, that early Christian writer whose battles against the sexually lax Bishop Callistus had resounded throughout the Roman Empire; at the beginning of my academic career I had made a name for myself by specialising in the conflicts of the Early Church, and before my accession to the bishopric I had been Lyttelton Professor of Divinity at Cambridge.

At this point may I just rebut two of the snide criticisms which my enemies used to hurl at me? (Unfortunately by 1965 my fighting style had earned me many enemies.) The first was that academics are unsuited to any position of importance in what is fondly called "the real world." According to this belief, which is so typical of the British vice of despising intellectuals, academic theologians are incapable of preaching the faith in words of one syllable to the proletariat, but this is just crypto-Marxist hogwash. I knew exactly what the proletariat wanted to hear. They wanted to hear certainties, and whether those certainties were expressed in monosyllables or polysyllables was immaterial. Naturally I would not have dreamed of burdening the uneducated with fascinating theological speculation; that sort of discourse has to be left to those who have the aptitude and training to comprehend it. Would one expect a beginner at the piano to play Mozart? Of course not! A beginner must learn by absorbing simple exercises. This fact does not mean that the beginner is incapable of intuitively grasping the wonder and mystery of music. It merely means he has to take much of the theory on trust from those who have devoted their lives to studying it.

Now that I have demolished the idea that I am incapable of communicating with uneducated people, let me go on to rebut the second snide criticism hurled at me during my bishopric. It was alleged that as I had spent most of my career in an ivory tower I was ill-equipped for pastoral work. What nonsense! The problems of undergraduates sharpen any clergyman's pastoral skills, and besides, my years as an army chaplain had given me a breadth of experience which I would never have acquired in ordinary parish work.

I have to confess that I have never actually done any ordinary parish work. The training of priests was more haphazard in my youth, and if one had the right connections one could sidestep hurdles which today are *de rigueur.* In my case Archbishop Lang had taken an interest in me, and I had spent the opening years of my career as one of his chaplains before accepting the headmastership of a minor public school at the ridiculously young age of twenty-seven. Not surprisingly this latter move had proved to be a mistake, but even before I returned to Cambridge to resume my career as a theologian, I felt that an appointment to a parish was merely something which happened to other people.

I admit I did worry from time to time in the 1930s about this significant omission from my *curriculum vitae,* but always I came to the conclusion that since my path had crossed so providentially with Archbishop Lang's it would have been wrong to spurn the opportunities which in consequence came my way. I was still reasoning along these lines in the 1950s when I told myself it would have been wrong to spurn a bishopric merely because I had sufficient brains to flourish among the ivory towers of Cambridge. (Indeed if more bishops had more brains, the pronouncements from the episcopal bench in the House of Lords in the 1960s might have been far more worthy of attention.)

I did not turn my back on my academic work when I accepted the bishopric. Indeed as I toiled away in Starbridge I soon felt I needed regular *divertissements* to cheer me up, and this was why I was nearly always writing some book or other during my spare time. I dictated these books to a succession of most attractive part-time secretaries, all under thirty. In 1965 my part-time secretary was Sally, the daughter of my henchman the Archdeacon of Starbridge, and I much enjoyed dictating the fruits of my researches to such a glamorous young woman. It made a welcome change from dictating letters on diocesan affairs to my full-time secretary Miss Peabody who, although matchlessly efficient, was hardly the last word in glamour. My wife quite understood that I needed a break from Miss Peabody occasionally, and always went to great trouble to recruit exactly the right part-time secretary to brighten my off-duty hours.

My wife and Miss Peabody kept me organised. I had two chaplains, one a priest who handled all the ecclesiastical business and one a layman who acted as a liaison officer with the secular world, but Miss Peabody guarded my appointments diary and this privilege gave her a certain amount of power over the two young men. I classed this arrangement as prudent. Chaplains can become power-mad with very little encouragement, but Miss Peabody ensured that all such delusions of grandeur were stillborn. Miss Peabody also supervised the typist, recently hired to help her with the increased volume of secretarial work, and organised the book-keeping.

In addition I employed a cook-housekeeper, who lived out, and a daily cleaner. A gardener appeared occasionally to mow the lawns and prune any vegetation which acquired an undisciplined appearance. From this list of personnel it can be correctly deduced that Starbridge was one of the premier bishoprics, but if I had not had a private income to supplement my episcopal salary I might have found my financial circumstances tiresome, and we were certainly a long way from those halcyon days before the war when my predecessors had lived in considerable splendour. Alex Jardine, for instance, had kept twelve indoor servants, two gardeners and a chauffeur when he had been Bishop in the 1930s. He had also lived in the old episcopal palace, now occupied by the Choir School, but despite the loss of the palace I could hardly claim I was uncomfortably housed. My home was a handsome Georgian building called the South Canonry which also stood within Starbridge's huge walled Close, and from the upstairs windows we could look across the Choir School's playing-field to the tower and spire of the Cathedral.

"I'm glad the trees hide the palace from us," Lyle had said on our arrival at the South Canonry in 1957. She had lived at the palace before the war as the paid companion of Bishop Jardine's wife, and the experience had not always been a happy one.

Lyle was my wife, and I must now describe just how important she was to me by 1965. Before the war people had joked that she ran the diocese for Jardine in addition to his palace, and I sometimes thought she could have run the diocese for me. She was the perfect wife for a bishop. She solved all household problems. She appeared in church regularly. She excelled in charity work. She controlled numerous committees. She controlled the chaplains. She even controlled Miss Peabody. She monitored the wives of the diocesan clergy so skilfully that I knew about any marriage trouble among my priests almost before they were aware of it themselves. She also read the Church newspapers to keep me informed of any serpentine twist of Church politics which I might have been too busy to notice.

In addition she ensured that I had everything I needed: clean shirts, socks, shoes, every item of my uniform—all appeared as if by magic whenever they were required. Bottles of my favourite whisky and sherry never failed to be present on the sideboard. Cigarettes were always in my cigarette-case. I was like an expensive car tended by a devoted mechanic. I purred along as effortlessly as a well-tuned Rolls-Royce.

The one matter which Lyle never organised for me was my Creator. "You deal with God," she said. "I'll deal with everything else." I did talk to her about God, particularly when I needed to let off steam about the intellectually sloppy antics of various liberal-radical churchmen, but although she listened with sympathy she seldom said more than: "Yes, darling" or: "What a bore for you!" Once I could not resist saying to her: "I sometimes feel troubled that you never want to discuss your faith with me," but she merely answered: "What's there to discuss? I'm not an intellectual."

The truth was that Lyle was no fool, but a skimpy education had given her an inferiority complex about intellectual matters with the result that she always played down the knowledge of Christianity which she had acquired through her copious reading. I knew her faith was deep, but I knew too that she would never be one of those clerical wives who gave talks on such subjects as "Faith in Family Life." Her most successful talk to the Mothers' Union was entitled: "How to Survive Small Children," and faith was barely mentioned at all.

But by 1965 Lyle had become profoundly interested in prayer. She had even formed a prayer-group composed entirely of women, a move which I found remarkable because in the past she had seldom had much time for her own sex. My spiritual director was most intrigued and said the formation of the group was a great step forward for Lyle. I was equally intrigued and wanted to ask questions, but since my advice was never sought I realised my task was merely to provide tacit support. I did enquire in the beginning what had triggered this new interest but Lyle only said in an offhand voice: "It was my involvement with Venetia. When I had that lunch with her in London I realised there was nothing more I could do except pray for her," and I saw at once it would be tactful not to prolong the conversation. Venetia, a former part-time secretary of mine, had been Lyle's protégée. I had seen that Lyle was becoming too involved, regarding the girl as the daughter we had never had, and I had several times been tempted to utter a word of warning, but in the end I had kept quiet, preferring to rely on the probability that Lyle's hardheaded common sense would eventually triumph. Such pseudo-parental relationships often dissolve unhappily when one party fails to fulfil the psychological needs of the other, and it had been obvious to me that Venetia, a muddled, unhappy young woman, had been looking not for a second mother but for a second father, a quest which had had disastrous consequences. By 1965 she had moved out of our lives, but the prayer-group, her unexpected legacy to Lyle, was flourishing.

Our younger son Michael had commented during the Christmas of 1964: "The prayer-group's Mum doing her own thing," but our other son, Charley, had said with his customary lack of tact: "Cynical types don't usually become mystical—I hope she's not going nuts." I gave this remark the robust dismissal it deserved, but it did underline to me how uncharacteristic this new deep interest in prayer was. I also had to admit to myself that although Charley had been tactless in describing Lyle as cynical, he had not been incorrect. "I always believe the worst," Lyle would say, "because the worst is usually true"—a philosophy which was repugnant to me, but no matter how often I was tempted to criticise this attitude, I always remembered her past and abstained. A disastrous love affair in the 1930s had left her emotionally scarred. In the circumstances I felt it was a wonder she had any faith left at all.

And now, having disclosed the disastrous love affair which Lyle had endured, I must disclose just how far we were from being a conventional ecclesiastical family. Lyle had been pregnant at the time of our marriage, and our elder son was not, biologically, my son at all.

3

I HATE to speak of this skeleton in the cupboard, but as I am engaged in painting a picture of my career, marriage and family life in order to set the scene for 1965, I can hardly leave a large central section of the canvas unpainted. If I did, the events of 1965 would be to a large extent incomprehensible.

So let me now turn, with great reluctance, to the skeleton.

We had a code-name for this lover who had nearly destroyed Lyle. It was Samson, a man ruined by his involvement with the wrong woman.

I had chosen this sobriquet in a rush triggered by my loathing of the entire subject and had only afterwards reflected that the choice automatically cast Lyle as Delilah, a lady who has never received a good press. However, when I had voiced my misgivings Lyle had said bleakly: "And what right have I to receive a good press?"—a question which had taken me back to the harrowing early days of our marriage when she had been recovering from the most destructive aspects of the affair.

Lyle was my second wife. I had been married for three years in my twenties to a pleasant, innocent girl called Jane whom nowadays I could recall with only the smallest twinge of anguish. We had been fond of each other but unsuited, and our difficulties had been unresolved at the time of her death in a car crash. Fortunately I had managed to come to terms with this tragedy before I journeyed again to the altar in 1937, but although I realised Lyle was curious to know more about her predecessor I felt no desire to pour forth a torrent of information. Perhaps it was fortunate that back in 1937 Lyle was far too bound up with her own unhappy past to spare much time to speculate about mine.

Lyle's affair with Samson had been conducted with fanatical secrecy because he had been not only a married man but a distinguished married man. In fact—and I hate to admit this but I do need to explain why he was so vulnerable to scandal—he was a clergyman. Of course clerical failures have always existed and of course one must do one's Christian best to be charitable to those who break the rules, let the side down and drag the Church through the mud, but I have to confess that Samson reduced my stock of Christian charity to an all-time low. I knew I had to forgive him for the damage he had inflicted on Lyle, but unfortunately forgiveness cannot be turned on like a supply of hot water from a well-stoked boiler, and this particular act of forgiveness had remained frozen in the pipes of my mind for some time.

It was not until I returned from the war that I managed to forgive him. At least I assumed I had forgiven him because I realised I had reached the point where I was seldom troubled by his memory. By that time he was not merely tucked away behind a pseudonym, categorised theologically as a sinner who had to be forgiven and thereby rendered as harmless as an exhibit in a museum; he was also dead, a fact which meant the affair with Lyle could never be resurrected. Occasionally his name—his real name—came up in ecclesiastical circles, but not too often, and as the 1940s drew to a close I realised I had consigned him to the compartment in my mind which housed other obsolete images from the previous decade: Edward VIII abdicating the throne, Jack Buchanan singing, Harold Larwood bowling and Shirley Temple dancing. The point about these people, as I told my spiritual director, was that I could think of them without pain; therefore, I reasoned, if I had relegated Samson to this harmless group, I must on some deep psychological level have forgiven him. The hallmark of forgiveness is that it enables the forgiver to live painlessly with the forgiven.

Certainly by 1965 I was satisfied that I had not only forgiven Samson but managed to convert his malign memory into a benign force in my ministry. Indeed it was arguable that my reputation as a bishop tough on sexual sin was the direct result of being obliged to pick up the pieces after a catastrophic adulterous liaison. The 1960s might have been the age of the permissive society, but thanks to my encounter with Samson at Starbridge in 1937 I was going to preach against immorality until I dropped dead or my tongue fell out. After all I had endured, nursing Lyle back to a normal life, no one could have expected *me* to endorse promiscuity—but no one still alive knew now what I had endured in the early days of my marriage, no one except Lyle herself and my spiritual director, Jon Darrow.

I had had no trouble forgiving Lyle for this affair which had already run into difficulties by the time I met her. It is easy to feel compassion for someone one loves, particularly when that someone is emotionally wrecked and verging on the suicidal. What I did find hard to endure was the fact that after we were married she could not love me as much as I loved her. This gradual realisation that she was still far more bound up with Samson than she was willing to admit became so hard for me to bear that I was more than willing to escape from my marriage once the war came. Naturally I told everyone that I was volunteering to be an army chaplain because I wanted to have a hand in Hitler's defeat—and this was no lie—but the whole truth was rather less palatable. Nowadays, I dare say, I would have wound up in the divorce court. So much for the permissive society! Young people refuse to acknowledge that there can be rewards for enduring the dark days of a marriage; happiness is always supposed to be instantaneous and any deferral is regarded as intolerable. Was there ever such a flight from reality? No wonder the young resort to drugs to ease their disorientation! They have never been taught to face reality and endure it—or in other words, they have never been taught how to survive. The permissive society is a phantom utopia which promises perfect freedom and yet has all its adherents in chains on Death Row.

The mention of chains reminds me of the three years I spent as a prisoner of war. That experience certainly taught me some lessons about how to survive adversity, and when I returned home in 1945 I found the rewards of my long endurance were about to begin. Samson was dead, Lyle was at last ready to be devoted to me and a new era in my marriage had dawned. With relief I prepared to live happily ever after, but did I? No.

I had had a tough time as a prisoner and I returned home with my health damaged. I did manage to reconsummate the marriage, but our efforts to produce another baby failed and tests revealed my poor health was to blame, a diagnosis which did nothing for either my marriage or my self-esteem. Now it was Lyle who endured, Lyle who battled on, Lyle who was not loved as she should have been. She was saved from despair by the doctors' belief that I would make a full recovery, but I languished, suffering a reaction from my long ordeal and reduced to apathy by the well-known syndrome of survivors' guilt. Finally an old friend of mine, a doctor called Alan Romaine, took me aside and said: "You *will* get better, Charles, but you've got to work at recovery—it's no good just sitting back and waiting for it to happen." He gave me a diet-sheet, listing all the unrationed, nutritious foods I could eat, and he dragooned me into taking up golf again, but I think I was eventually cured not so much by exercise and good nutrition as by his care and compassion.

Did Lyle and I then have our much-wanted third child and live happily ever after? No. Lyle was by this time approaching the menopause and our daughter continued to exist only in our imaginations. Lyle became increasingly upset. I became increasingly upset. Meanwhile the two boys were big enough to be perpetually fighting, yelling and smashing everything in sight. The marriage limped on.

The reward for our endurance of this apparently endless ordeal finally arrived when Michael followed Charley to prep school and Lyle and I found ourselves on our own for two-thirds of the year. It was then that the terrible truth dawned: we were happiest as a childless couple.

I was so shocked by this revelation, contrary as it was to all the modern Christian thinking on family life, that for a long while I found myself unable to speak of it, even to Lyle, but eventually I forced myself to discuss the matter with my spiritual director.

Jon reminded me that family life had not always been a Christian ideal. He also suggested that my duty was to be myself, Charles Ashworth, not some ecclesiastical robot who mindlessly toed the fashionable Church line on domestic matters.

I felt obliged to say: "But I can hardly preach on the joys of being a childless couple!"

"You could preach on the heroism of those who feel called to bring up other people's children."

I denied being a hero, but when Jon answered: "You are to Charley," I was comforted. Charley's idolising of me ranked alongside Lyle's devotion as my reward for all I had had to endure in the early years of my marriage. Moreover this hero-worship by my adopted son went a long way towards compensating me for the difficulties I experienced with my real son, Michael.

And now, having exposed the less palatable side of my marriage, I must nerve myself to describe the effect on my sons of the skeleton in the family closet. I need to explain why and how they became the young men they were at that time in February, 1965, when we were all steaming forward towards the abyss.

4

OF COURSE I thought of Charley as my son. Of course I did. I had married Lyle in full knowledge of the fact that he already existed as a foetus, and I had accepted full responsibility for him. I had brought him up. I had made him what he was. He was mine.

Yet he was not mine. He was unlike me both physically and temperamentally. I understood early on in his life why many adopting parents go to immense trouble to find a child who bears some chance resemblance to them. They need to forget there are no shared genes. A benign forgetfulness makes life easier, particularly when the child has been fathered by one's wife's former lover. Even after I believed Samson to be forgiven, living harmlessly in the nostalgia drawer of my memory alongside Edward VIII, Jack Buchanan, Harold Larwood and Shirley Temple, I could have done without the daily reminders of that past trauma, but I taught myself to overlook Charley's resemblance to Samson and see instead only his resemblance to Lyle.

The bright side of Charley's inheritance lay in the fact that he possessed Samson's first-class brain. This was a great delight to me, particularly when Charley became old enough to study theology, and it made us far more compatible than we had been during his childhood when his volatile temperament had persistently grated on my nerves.

It had grated on Lyle's nerves too. Lyle was not naturally gifted at motherhood, and although she loved the boys she found it difficult to manage them when they were young. This lack of management meant the boys became hard work for anyone determined to become a conscientious parent—but I have no wish to blame Lyle for this state of affairs; after all, life was hard for her during the war, particularly during those years when I was a prisoner, and no doubt she was not alone in finding it difficult to be the sole parent of a family. If I appear to criticise her it is only because I need to explain why, when I returned home after the war, I soon discovered that parenthood was no picnic. Probably one of the reasons why we both became so keen to celebrate the new beginning of our marriage by producing a daughter was the belief—almost certainly misguided—that a little girl would be all sweetness and light, a compensation for the barbarity of our sons.

Another fact which exacerbated our complex family situation was that Lyle was ill-at-ease with Charley. No doubt all manner of guilty feelings were at work below the surface of her mind, but the result was that she tended to escape from this unsatisfactory relationship by idolising Michael. Charley resented this behaviour and to prevent him being hurt I found myself paying him special attention. This in turn upset Michael, who became abnormally demanding. Again, I have no wish to blame Lyle for triggering these emotional disorders; she could not help feeling guilty about Samson and muddled about Charley, but nonetheless the situation was one which even the most gifted of fathers would have found challenging.

The final fact which aggravated our troubles was no one's fault at all and can only be attributed to the lottery of genetics. Michael resembled me physically but his intellect was dissimilar to mine, and the older he grew the more incomprehensible he became to me. It was not that he was stupid. He was just as clever as Lyle, but as he grew older we found we had nothing in common but a fondness for cricket and rugger. I minded this more than I should have done, and when he embarked on a phase, common among the sons of clergymen, of rejecting religion, I minded fiercely. Meanwhile nimble-witted, intellectually stimulating, devoutly religious Charley was ever ready to compensate me for Michael's shortcomings. Was it surprising that I welcomed this development? No. But Michael became jealous. He began to misbehave, partly to grab my attention and partly to pay me back for favouring the cuckoo in the nest. Michael thought he should come first. I greatly regretted that he knew Charley was only his half-brother, but once Charley had been told about Samson it had proved impossible to keep Michael in ignorance.

I knew all adoption agencies recommended that an adopted child should be told the truth at an early age, but I could never bring myself to tell Charley. I had convinced myself that the truth, an example of extreme clerical failure, was too unedifying to be divulged to a child, but I knew that eventually I would have to speak out and I knew exactly when that moment would come. Samson had left Charley his library, the gift to take effect on Charley's eighteenth birthday. Samson's widow was still alive, so Charley did not inherit the money until later, but the books were in storage, waiting to be claimed. Possibly I could have explained away this legacy as the generous gesture of a childless old man, but there was a letter. I knew there was a letter because Samson's solicitor had spoken of it; he was keeping it in his firm's safe for presentation along with the storage papers. Lyle said I had to get hold of the letter and give it to Charley myself. The solicitor hesitated, but after all, we were a clerical couple who could be trusted to behave properly. The letter arrived.

"Steam it open," said Lyle, confounding his expectations.

We were at Cambridge at the time. It was 1956, the year before I was offered the Starbridge bishopric, and I was still the Lyttelton Professor of Divinity. Charley was away at school but due home on a weekend exeat in order to celebrate his birthday. We were breakfasting in the kitchen when the letter arrived. I remember feeling sick at the sight of Samson's writing on the envelope, and this reaction startled me. A communication from Edward VIII, Jack Buchanan, Harold Larwood or Shirley Temple would never have induced feelings of nausea.

Meanwhile Lyle had refilled the kettle and was boiling some more water for the steaming operation.

I did manage to say strongly: "It's quite unthinkable that I should steam open this letter," but Lyle just said: "If you won't I will," and removed the letter from my hands. I was then told that after all I had done for Charley I had a right to know the contents, and somehow I found myself unable to argue convincingly to the contrary. Nausea is not conducive to skilled debate. Neither is fear, and at that point I was very afraid that my relationship with Charley—that just reward for my past suffering—would be damaged beyond repair by this potentially devastating assault from the past.

Lyle read the letter and wept.

I said: "It's quite unthinkable that I should read a single word of it." But I did. I read one word. And another. And after that I gave up trying to put the letter down. As I read I automatically moved closer to the sink in case I was overcome with the need to vomit.

"It's all about how wonderful you are," said Lyle, unable to find a handkerchief and snuffling into a tea-towel.

"How very embarrassing." This traditional public-school response to any situation which flouted the British tradition of emotional understatement was utterly inadequate but no other phrase sprang to mind at such an agonising moment. The grave, simple, dignified sentences skimmed past my eyes and streamed through my defences so that in the end I was incapable of uttering a word. I could only think: this is a very great letter from a very Christian man. But I had no idea what to make of this thought. I could not cope with it. Vilely upset I reached the signature at the bottom of the last page, dropped the letter on the draining-board and waited by the sink for the vomiting to commence, but nothing happened.

"Well, you don't have to worry, do you?" I heard Lyle say at last. "Everything's going to be all right."

I suddenly realised that this was true. Weak with relief I picked up the letter and read it again. Samson had made no paternal claims. My role in Charley's life was affirmed, not undermined. The writer assumed all responsibility for the past tragedy and said he quite accepted that he had been unfit to play any part in Charley's upbringing, but he still hoped that Charley would accept the books and later the money as a gift. They came with no obligation to respect the donor. The writer realised he had no right to demand any benign response. He wanted above all to stress how immensely grateful and happy he was that Charley should have been brought up by . . .

I stopped reading, folded the letter carefully and put it back in the envelope. I did not want his praise. I did not want him offering Charley the kind of selfless love which expected nothing in return. And above all else I did not want him making my wife cry and reminding us both unbearably of the past.

"Very nice," I said. "Very sporting of him not to upset the apple-cart." The dreadful middle-class banalities sounded hideously false but at least they were safe. The next moment I said: "He's got no business coming back like this. He should stay locked up in the 1930s where he belongs." That was not safe at all. That was a most dangerous thing to say, indicative of some convoluted state which could never be allowed to see the light of day, but Lyle was coming to my rescue, Lyle was saying: "We'll lock him up again. Once all this is over we'll put him back in the 1930s where he belongs."

And that was that.

Or was it?

5

I TELEPHONED my spiritual director. In 1956 Jon had yet to become the recluse who refused to have a telephone in his home.

"It occurred to me," I said, "that there's a sound moral argument for destroying the letter. For the good of the family—and to save Charley distress—"

"This is a very bad line," said Jon. "Could you say all that again? I don't think I can possibly have heard you correctly."

A long silence followed before I said: "I'm in such a state I can't think straight. What on earth am I going to say to Charley?"

"Believe me, I do understand how hard it will be for you to master all your ambivalent feelings."

"What ambivalent feelings?"

A second silence ensued. At last I said: "I don't feel ambivalent towards Charley. He's my reward now for responding to that back-breaking call from God to bring him up. I'm devoted to Charley. I'm proud of him."

"Then trust him to work out what he owes and to whom."

"But how much of the truth should I tell him?"

Jon said nothing.

"Must I tell the whole truth?" I said. "The absolute truth?"

"I'm sure you know at heart what the answers to all those questions are, Charles."

I put down the receiver.

6

OF COURSE I forgot every word of my set speech. I discovered that my most important need was to keep talking—to impart the same information in a variety of different ways so that the sheer brutality of the truth was cocooned and smothered in excess verbiage. While I was speaking I was conscious that Charley, who was small and slim and looked younger than his eighteen years, was becoming smaller and slimmer, almost as if he were returning to the childhood he had so recently left. I half-thought he would interrupt me—in the end I was yearning for him to interrupt me and express all the normal emotions of incredulity, amazement and horror—but he said nothing. It was as if his volatile temperament had been frozen by the blast of an icy wind. Pale and still, he regarded me blankly with his lambent, amber eyes.

". . . and naturally you'll want to know more about him. That's why"—I heard the lie coming but found myself powerless to stop it—"I'm glad he's written you this letter." I managed to hold out the envelope with a steady hand. "Let him speak for himself," I said, "and then I'll answer all your questions as truthfully as I can."

Despite this dubious conclusion I believe in retrospect that my speech was very far from disastrous. I had reassured Charley about my feelings for him; I had said nothing adverse about Samson, and I had paved the way for the necessary question-and-answer session. However unfortunately Charley was not at that moment interested in Samson. He was much too busy trying to digest the fact that his parents had spent eighteen years deceiving him about a fundamental aspect of his identity.

Ignoring the letter which I was holding out to him he said in a voice which shook: "I should have been told from the beginning."

At once I tried to adjust my approach. "I'm very sorry. I assure you we did consider it. But the trouble was—"

"How could you have allowed me to believe a lie? *You!* The man who always preaches the importance of truth!"

"I know how you must feel—I know how it must look—but—"

"I think you and Mum have behaved absolutely disgustingly and I just want to go away and be sick!"

That concluded the conversation. Scarlet with emotion he rushed upstairs to his bedroom where he locked the door and refused to speak to either of us. Eventually Lyle lost her nerve and shouted: "I don't care how vile you are to me but don't you dare be vile to Charles after all he's done for you!" but when even this unwise reproof produced no response she turned to me and demanded, tears streaming down her face: "Where's that letter? He's got to read it."

That was when I realised this harrowing scene must have been clearly visualised by Samson who had then done all he could to give us a helping hand. Or in other words, the clerical failure had behaved like a wise, compassionate priest, setting his own feelings aside in order to try to ensure the survival of the family, whereas I . . . But I could not quite work out how I had behaved. I only knew that I had always acted towards Charley with the very best of intentions.

"The kind that pave the road to hell," muttered Lyle, shoving Samson's letter under the locked bedroom door.

More agonising minutes passed. We went away. We waited. We returned. We banged futilely on the panels. We took it in turns to beg him to let us in. At last, egged on by Lyle and feeling nearly demented with anxiety, I fetched a screwdriver, opened up the lock and forced my way into the room. It was empty. Charley had made a rope of sheets and escaped through the window. The letter was lying unopened on the floor.

No mere words could describe the sheer horror of the next few hours, so I shall merely record our ordeal as tersely as possible. First of all I hauled up the sheets before they could be spotted by our neighbours. Then we began our search, but enquiries at the station and bus terminal proved fruitless.

At one stage I was in such despair that I said: "Supposing he's tried to kill himself by jumping into the Cam?" but Lyle, hiding her terror behind an ice-cool facade, answered: "If he leapt into the river he'd make damn sure there were plenty of people around to haul him out."

We returned home to sweat blood and plot our next move, but we could think of nothing to do except wait by the telephone. It seemed too soon to notify the police. However as the hours passed and no contrite call came I was obliged to notify the headmaster that Charley would not be returning to school that evening. I was tempted to lie by saying he was ill, but I knew I had to tell a story which bore some resemblance to the truth in case the absence lasted some time, so I said that Charley had run away after a family disagreement. When the headmaster had recovered from his astonishment he was so kind that I had difficulty in sustaining the conversation, but I did say I would take his advice to call the police.

More appalling conversations followed. The policemen clearly felt they were being troubled unnecessarily and said they were sure Charley would turn up, probably sooner rather than later. No sooner had they departed than a neighbour dropped in, saw the uneaten birthday cake in the kitchen and demanded an explanation. The grapevine began to hum. The local paper got hold of the story. Garish headlines screamed: PROFESSOR'S SON VANISHES, SUICIDE OR SNATCH? We fobbed off our friends' enthralled enquiries by saying we needed to keep the telephone line open, but some of them still insisted on calling in to commiserate with us. The *schadenfreude* generated by a clergyman's son who goes off the rails is massive indeed.

I was just thinking how very pleasant it would be to spend a week in the nearest mental hospital, far from this repulsively madding crowd, when Jon rang from his home near Starbridge and said: "He's here. He's unharmed. Be sure you bring the letter when you come to fetch him."

I drove through the night with the letter in my breast pocket, and when I reached Jon's home the next morning I found Charley sitting on the steps of the porch as he waited for me. Halting the car I jumped out and rushed over to him and when he muttered: "You didn't have to drive through the night," I shouted: "What the hell else did you expect me to do?"—not the mildest of replies, but I was almost passing out with relief. At that point Charley broke down and began to whimper, but I grabbed him and held him so tightly that both of us were unable to do more than struggle for breath. Eventually Jon appeared and announced, rather in the manner of a tactful butler, that breakfast was available in the dining-room.

When Charley and I were alone together he told me he had completed the long journey by walking and by thumbing lifts. Having little money he had slept under hedges and survived on a diet of Mars bars. "The whole journey was hell," he concluded morosely, "but I wanted to see Father Darrow. I thought he'd know about everything and I'm sure he does, but he said you could explain it all better than he could." He hesitated but added: "He also said I should read the letter because letters from the dead should be treated with respect."

I handed over the letter. Charley pocketed it and embarked upon his breakfast. He ate two fried eggs, a sausage, three rashers of bacon and a fried tomato while I toyed with half a piece of toast. Eventually I withdrew to the cloakroom where I at last achieved my ambition to vomit. On my departure from the dining-room I had heard the faint noise of tearing paper as Charley at once opened the envelope.

When I rejoined him I found that the envelope had disappeared.

Charley's careful comment was: "That was an interesting letter. I might let you read it one day."

Not surprisingly, I found myself unable to reply.

"I was thinking," said Charley, "what a useful thing it was that Mum took me to see him—I mean *him*—back in 1945 when I was old enough to remember him properly. If I hadn't seen him, I might always have wondered what he was like."

I managed to agree that this was quite possible.

"He seemed to like you a lot," said Charley at last. "Of course he took the blame for everything, and that was right, wasn't it? You were the hero of the story and he was . . . well, what was he exactly? I can't quite make him out. Was he a villain? Or a fool? Or a tragic figure felled by hubris like Charles Stewart Parnell? Or . . ." His voice trailed away.

The pause lengthened.

Eventually Charley said in a rush: "Of course if you'd rather I didn't ask any questions—"

"But of course you must ask questions!" I said, finally summoning the strength to behave as I should. "And of course I must answer them as truthfully as possible!"

But I think I knew, even as I expressed this admirable intention, that the absolute truth about my wife's lover was still quite beyond my power to articulate.

II

"Bad pride is negative; it blinds us to truths of fact or even of reason . . ."

AUSTIN FARRER
Warden of Keble College, Oxford, 1960–1968
A CELEBRATION OF FAITH

I

I SHOULD much prefer to say no more about this dreadful scene with Charley, but unfortunately I have to go on to record what a hash I made of it; the consequences were so far-reaching.

"It would be uncharitable to call him a villain," I said to Charley as I embarked on this doomed attempt to depict Samson in the light of truth, "and it would certainly be inaccurate to describe him as a fool. One could, perhaps, acknowledge a resemblance to Parnell, but only a superficial one. After all, Parnell was not a clergyman of the Church of England who broke the vows he made at his ordination." As I spoke I insisted to myself that I should speak the truth. I also insisted that I would not let the truth be distorted by my anger. I told myself fiercely: I shall *not* lie.

"He was a gifted man who had weaknesses which made him vulnerable," I found myself saying. "I felt sorry for him. At the end of his life he could be considered a pathetic figure, a man ruined by the flaws in his character—but I mustn't judge him too harshly. That wouldn't be right."

I drank some tea. Eventually I said: "It was a tragedy that those inherent weaknesses wrecked his life and wasted his talents."

"When you say 'weaknesses,' do you mean—"

"I mean primarily his weakness for women. It clouded his judgement. His disastrous marriage was quite obviously an example of a sexual attraction which had soon faded . . . but I don't want to be too harsh on him."

There was a pause. As I waited for the next question I saw with dismay that Charley had lost his brave air of nonchalance. His face had a pinched look.

"I don't want to be too harsh on him," I repeated hurriedly, trying to put things right. "Anyone can make a mistake." But before I could stop myself I was saying: "It was just a pity his mistakes were so crucial. His weakness for women was compounded by a tendency to drink too much. Certainly he enjoyed a luxurious style of life which was quite unsuitable for a priest, and in the circumstances it was hardly surprising that his moral will was sapped so that he was unable to resist the temptation which your mother presented . . . although of course I don't mean to pass judgement on him for what he did to her. All judgements must be left to God."

Charley said unevenly: "I just don't understand how Mum could ever have—"

"Oh, the whole episode was entirely his fault. She was an innocent young woman corrupted by a sophisticated older man," I said, but I knew at once I could not let that statement stand unmodified. Furiously I told myself: *I will not lie.* "No, let me rephrase that last sentence," I said rapidly. "By using a cliché I've made the affair sound simple and it wasn't. It was complicated." But even as I spoke I was thinking: Charley wants simplicity, not complexity; he wants certainties, not ambiguities; it really would be kinder to him to sketch the story in black and white.

"But never mind all that," I said even more rapidly. "The rock-bottom truth is that he was older than she was and should have known better. Of course I'm tempted to blame him for putting her through hell, but in fact it's futile to assign blame since our prime task is to forgive. As I keep saying, I don't mean to pass judgement on him for what he did." Realising that I was becoming convoluted, once more passing judgement and rescinding it in the same breath, I made a mighty new effort to be clear and simple.

"You don't have to worry," I said. "I've brought you up. I've made you what you are. So long as you model yourself on me you'll never have to worry that you'll make a mess of your life as he did."

Charley by this time seemed to be barely breathing. His pallor had a faint greenish tinge.

"Upbringing's the important thing," I said at top speed. "You needn't worry about your heredity. I often think how like me you are, sharing so many of my interests."

"All I ever wanted," said Charley painfully, "was to be just like you."

"In that case there's no need for you to give this man"—I could not name him—"a second thought. I mean, of course you'll give him a second thought"—I was tying myself in knots again—"but there's no need for you to become obsessed by him. We'll give him a code-name," I said, fastening on the device which enabled top-secret matters to be referred to with discretion, "and then he can be filed away. He won't be lost or forgotten. He'll merely be out of sight unless we choose to recall him."

But Charley was already worrying about something else. "Should I refuse to accept the legacy?"

"Certainly not!" I was startled by this question and also, at some profound level, distressed. I remembered the sacrifice implicit in that letter, the love given without hope of any return.

"I just want to do what you want, and if you think it would be safer for me to reject him altogether—"

"No, no, that wouldn't be right at all! If you reject the legacy you're really passing judgement on him, but our business is to forgive, not to condemn."

It was all true, of course. Yet it was all, subtly, false. Later I tried to work out how I could have eradicated the distortion, but I was never able to decide where the distortion had come from and how I could have eradicated it. Later still I did think to myself: one day Charley should know just how selflessly that man loved him. But the thought vanished, pushed aside by my enormous relief that the crisis was past. Charley had emerged from his ordeal more devoted to me than ever while I was now free to rebury Samson in the nostalgia drawer of my memory.

Telephoning Lyle five minutes later I told her we were all set to live happily ever after.

2

DID WE all live happily ever after? No. As soon as Charley had returned to a stable state Michael began to cause trouble.

I told Michael about the skeleton in the family cupboard as soon as he returned home for the half-term holiday. I had had no choice. Charley's escapade, now public knowledge, had to be explained, and with dread I steeled myself for yet another parental ordeal.

Michael, who was then sixteen and still more interested in cricket than in girls, listened with astonishment to my brief recital of the facts and afterwards appeared to be too nonplussed to offer any comment. I did stress that Lyle had been a mere innocent victim but I soon discovered that his mother's consent to the affair was not what was puzzling him. "She's still Mum no matter what she did," he said commendably before adding: "But why didn't she go to hospital and have Charley removed when he was no more than a blob?"

I was considerably shocked by this reaction, unmodified as it was by anything which resembled a Christian morality, and as a result I found myself discussing the ethics of abortion, but Michael was uninterested in generalities, only in his mother. "She must have been mad to have wanted a baby in those circumstances," he said. "The older I get the more peculiar I think women are." And before I could comment on this verdict he asked: "If Charley's not your real son, why do you spend so much time slobbering over him?"

"I don't slobber over him!"

"Oh yes, you do! Mum says it's because Charley's small and plain and needs encouragement, but why should I be penalised just because I'm tall and good at games and okay to look at?"

"Nobody's penalising you! You mean just as much to me as Charley does!"

"Why don't I mean more? If you're not his father—"

"For all practical purposes," I said, trying to remain calm, "I *am* his father, and anyway, regardless of who his father is, he's still your brother and I'm sorry that you make so little effort to get on with him."

"I don't care who he is, I think he's a louse."

"That's the most unchristian thing to say!"

"So what? Lots of Christians are unchristian—look at Charley's real father! He didn't exactly behave in a very Christian way, did he, and he was a clergyman!"

"Well, of course he was a clerical failure. I'm not denying he was a disgrace to his profession and I'm not denying that the Church, like any large organisation, has the occasional rotten apple in its barrel, but Christians in general do at least try to live decent lives, and—"

"Too bad they so seldom succeed!"

At that point I lost my temper and Michael lost his. The scene ended shortly afterwards when he yelled: "Bloody hell!" and bolted straight to his mother to complain that I had been unfair to him. Lyle was livid. We had a row. She accused me of getting up on my Christian soapbox and pontificating; I retorted that I had a duty to draw the line when Michael started slandering the Church. Lyle then accused me of short-changing Michael; I then accused her of spoiling him rotten. Lyle said the whole grisly episode, beginning with Charley's running away, reminded her of the parable of the prodigal son, and what a pity it was that Jesus had never recorded the feelings of the prodigal son's mother. I said that Jesus had had no need to record the feelings of the mother in order to make his theological point, and Lyle shouted that she hated theological points and hated theologians who pulled out all the intellectual stops in order to win an argument and make their wives feel miserable. Seconds later I was deafened by the slamming of the door as she stormed out of the room.

I did look around for something to smash but fortunately no suitable object lay invitingly to hand and anyway after nearly nineteen years of marriage I knew there were better ways of resolving marital quarrels than behaving like a Cossack. I allowed Lyle time to cool off. Then I followed St. Paul's admirable advice ("Let not the sun go down upon your wrath") and made the required gesture of reconciliation. During the cooling-off period I consumed one very dark whisky-and-soda and meditated on my heroes of the Early Church, those titans who had been obliged to abstain from marriage. How would St. Athanasius, a bishop popular with the ladies, have adjusted to the wear and tear of married life? His energy reserves might well have been so seriously depleted that he would have been unable to dredge up the enormous strength required to be *contra mundum,* with the result that the Arian heresy would have prevailed—but no, heresy never prevailed in the end because always truth was "the daughter of time." With a sigh I absolved the imaginary wife of Athanasius from ensuring the triumph of Arianism.

Later that evening Charley obliquely expressed his new anxiety about our relationship by saying to me: "I'm worried about Michael. Supposing he thinks you just took me on because you wanted to marry Mum? Supposing he thinks you don't really like me at all and that secretly you regard me as a ghastly reminder of the past?"

"He couldn't possibly think anything so ridiculous! I decided to take you on from the moment I knew you existed. I regarded it as a very special and quite unmistakable call from God."

"And later you didn't privately moan and groan and regret the whole thing?"

"Oh, don't be so melodramatic and absurd!"

"But—"

"All right, no, I didn't. What an idea!"

"And you're sure I don't remind you of him all the time?"

"Of course I'm sure! As I've already said, you often remind me of myself."

"And you're sure that if I go on modelling myself on you everything will be all right?"

"Absolutely certain," I said, now so exhausted by the demands of family life that I barely knew what I was saying, and so it was that we set off along the path which was to end so cataclysmically nine years later in 1965.

3

THE INTERVAL between 1956 and 1965 seemed to pass with extraordinary speed, possibly because I had reached that point in middle age when the years go by faster and faster, but certainly because my change of job thrust me into a frenetic new world in which there never seemed to be enough time to do all that needed to be done.

In 1957 I was offered the Starbridge bishopric.

My first thought was that this was the one bishopric I could never accept. How could I take Lyle back to the scene of her disastrous love affair, and how could I myself face returning to the place which I always associated with my first catastrophe, the spiritual crisis which had almost brought my ministry to a very sticky end? Then slowly, with mounting dismay, I realised I had been manoeuvred into a position where the bishopric was the one job I could not refuse.

At first I thought the manoeuvring was being done by the Devil—or whatever one chooses to call the dark underside of creation which gives God so much trouble in achieving his plans for humanity. Then I thought the manoeuvring was an illusion and that I was the victim of blind chance. But in the end I decided that blind chance alone could never have ensured the snug fit of the metaphorical straitjacket in which I now found myself encased, and I had to acknowledge that God was touching my life in the manner of a potter reshaping the clay on his wheel—if I may cite the analogy drawn by my Oxonian friend Dr. Farrer. For some reason I was to be plucked from my ivory tower, where I was so comfortable, and dumped back in a city where I had been very uncomfortable indeed. This was such an unwelcome truth that I was reluctant to believe it, but when I realised I could not decline the appointment without incurring the wrath of that tough disciplinarian Archbishop Fisher, I accepted with a sinking heart that I was going to have to leave Cambridge. Ecclesiastical Starbridge begged, the Archbishop ordered, the letter from Downing Street arrived and the Queen smiled. I was doomed.

I had already turned down two bishoprics. Contrary to what many laymen think, not all clergymen aspire to high office, and because of my lack of parish experience and my success in academic life I had had no trouble accepting the idea that I would spend the rest of my working life as a divinity professor. However a call from God is a call from God, and since my duty was to serve my Maker, not to sulk impertinently, I made a big effort to regard the radical rewriting of my future in a positive light.

The diocese lay in the south of England, in the half of the country where I belonged, so I knew I could settle there without feeling like a foreigner. (I have never been at ease north of Cambridge.) Starbridge was set in beautiful countryside yet was only an hour and a half by train from London. There was a seat immediately available in the House of Lords, a fact which ensured I had an influential platform on which to expound my views on education, and there was even a theological college crying out in the Cathedral Close for reform by a divinity professor. (This was the main reason why I was considered uniquely suited for the job and why Archbishop Fisher told me brusquely to "stop bleating on and on about Cambridge.") Indeed the bishopric was far from being an unattractive prospect and I could see the job would provide me with an exciting challenge. Yet still my misgivings remained.

"You don't want to go back there, do you?" I said to Lyle when I was agonising about the decision, but Lyle stunned me by replying: "Why not?" Apparently she was now unperturbed by memories of her love affair. "The 1930s are another world," she said, "and we don't live in that world any more." She also admitted she was only too keen to leave behind the twittering gossips of Cambridge who had thrived on the scandal of Charley's birthday brainstorm.

". . . and then there's the matter of the curtains," she added as an afterthought.

"What curtains?"

"I ordered the curtains for Carrie when the Jardines moved from Radbury to Starbridge in 1932. I remember fingering the material in the shop and dreaming that *I* was the Bishop's wife, ordering the curtains for my very own episcopal palace—and isn't it nice to think my dream's finally going to come true?"

I was amazed. I could quite see that there was a certain pleasure to be derived from the fact that Lyle would be returning in triumph as the Bishop's wife to the Cathedral Close where she had once been no more than a paid companion, but I was still so taken aback by her unambivalent enthusiasm that I could only say: "We won't be living in the palace where you lived with the Jardines."

"Yes, isn't that fortunate! No poignant memories of Alex and Carrie to make me weepy—and anyway the palace was hell to run. The South Canonry will be much easier."

I retreated into a baffled silence.

"It's a bit odd, isn't it?" I said to my spiritual director during an emergency conference with him.

"Is it, Charles?"

"Well, she seems to have forgotten everything—except that she can't have done because she talks of finally exorcising the past."

"I think we can acquit her of amnesia. Perhaps the truth is that she herself has come to terms with the past and hopes that in Starbridge you'll be able to come to terms with it too."

"But I came to terms with it years ago! It's all tucked neatly away in the nostalgia drawer alongside Edward VIII, Jack Buchanan, Harold Larwood and Shirley Temple!"

The conversation closed.

4

I CONFESS I took some time to adjust to being a bishop. In fact I even went through a phase of thinking I had made an appalling mistake and that my manipulation out of Cambridge had been the work of the Devil after all, steering me into a deep depression which would render me useless to God. I did recover from this neurotic suspicion and I did eventually settle down, but for a long while I pined for Cambridge, particularly for the intellectual companionship of my colleagues.

However, there were compensations. I found that in my new life there was less venom directed at me and more respect—in fact there was no venom at all. Although arguments between Christians can be extremely heated, people do usually refrain from being venomous to a bishop. In the bitter feuds which periodically ruffle the surface of academic life, no one is exempt from venomous attack, least of all professors of divinity whose very existence represents an affront to the atheists.

This lack of venom in my new job made committee work less tiring. I was also soothed by the deference shown to me whenever I ventured into the palace of Westminster to attend the House of Lords or whenever I made a visit to one of the parishes in my diocese. But being a revered figurehead can be a lonely business and the dark side of all the deference was the isolation. Looking back I can see that this was when my marriage entered a new phase of intimacy and interdependence: increasingly I found that in my daily life I could only be my true self, relaxed and at ease, with Lyle. Of course I could also be myself with my spiritual director, now only twelve miles away in the village of Starrington Magna, but Jon had become a recluse after his wife's death in 1957, and although I did visit him regularly he never came to Starbridge. Apart from my wife I was on my own in that gilded cage of a Cathedral Close.

At last I pulled myself together. Realising that moping for Cambridge and bewailing my loneliness was all very self-centred, spiritually immature behaviour, I managed to stop thinking about myself and start thinking instead of how I could best serve God—a move which meant I poured myself into my work as I embarked on a massive programme of reform.

I started with the Theological College. It had begun life in the nineteenth century as an independent institution, cushioned by an endowment which permitted only modest fees to be charged, but in the twentieth century mismanagement and rising costs had brought it under the control of the diocese, and the bishop was always one of the governors. I not only increased the diocesan grant which supplemented the now almost worthless endowment, but I also pushed the diocese into taking out a loan so that the premises could be improved and expanded. My fellow-governors, long accustomed to dozing at meetings of the board, were stunned by my activities but no one dared oppose me; they realised that no bishop of Starbridge had ever been so well qualified as I was to pump new life into that place, and besides, when I produced the evidence that showed the institution had become a moral disgrace they were so shocked that they almost fell over themselves to give me carte blanche.

I took a similar line with the diocese itself, which was also in a most sluggish and decayed state. My predecessor as bishop, I regret to say, had reputedly died of inertia. In the 1930s Alex Jardine had set the diocese alight with his dynamism, but after his retirement the authorities had taken fright and appointed mild-mannered nonentities to the Starbridge bishopric with the inevitable, enervating results. Dr. Ottershaw, Dr. Jardine's successor, had at least allowed himself to be organised by an efficient archdeacon, but Bishop Flack, my immediate predecessor, had made a disastrous archidiaconal appointment and the diocese had become slothful. How quickly men become demoralised when their leaders fail to be crisp, conscientious and hard-working! At least my years in the army had taught me that particular lesson. Having woken everyone up by shaking them, metaphorically speaking, until their teeth rattled I embarked on a plan of radical reorganisation.

All this took much time and kept me very busy. I appointed a suffragan bishop to manage Starmouth, the large port on the south coast, and I streamlined the diocesan office in Starbridge by pruning the bureaucracy which had mushroomed during the days of Bishop Flack. In addition to all this high-powered executive activity, I had to find the time to visit parish after parish in the diocese in order to preach, confirm and tend the flock in my role as spiritual leader. And as if all this activity were not enough to fell even St. Athanasius himself, I was soon serving on committees at Church House, the Church of England's London headquarters, and toiling at sessions of the Church Assembly. The last straw was when my turn came to read the prayers every day for a short spell in the House of Lords.

Dashing up to London, dashing around the diocese, dashing from committee to committee and from parish to parish, I began to wonder how I could possibly survive, but propped up by a first-class wife, a first-class spiritual director, two first-class archdeacons, a first-class suffragan bishop and a first-class secretary, I finally learnt how to pace myself, how to delegate, how to spend most effectively the time I allotted to private prayer and, in short, how to avoid dropping dead with exhaustion. After a while, when I began to reap the benefits of a more efficient diocese, life became less frenetic. But not much. No wonder time seemed to pass so quickly. Sometimes the days would whip by so fast that I felt as if I could barely see them for dust.

This arduous professional life, which became increasingly gratifying as I earned a reputation for being a strong, efficient, no-nonsense bishop, was punctuated by various awkward incidents in my private life, but fortunately Lyle and I, now closer than we had ever been before, managed to weather them tolerably well. Charley was no longer a problem. He recovered sufficiently from the agony of his eighteenth birthday to do well in his A-level examinations and I did not even have to pull a string to ensure his admittance to my old Cambridge college. He then decided to defer his entry until he had completed his two years of National Service. At first he loathed the army, finding it "disgustingly Godless," but soon he was saved by his ability to speak fluent German, and he wound up working as a translator in pleasant quarters near Bonn. Having survived this compulsory diversion, he at last began to read divinity at Cambridge. Here he was ecstatically happy. Glowing reports reached me, and after winning a first he proceeded to theological college—but not to the one in Starbridge; I was anxious that he should have the chance to train for the priesthood far from the long shadow I cast as a bishop. To my relief his desire to be a priest never wavered, his call was judged by the appropriate authorities to be genuine and eventually he was ordained. It was a moment of enormous satisfaction for me and more than made up for the fact that I continually found Michael a disappointment.

Michael had not wanted to move to Starbridge. He thought it was the last word in provincial boredom, and we were obliged to endure sulks, moans and tart remarks. Later he developed an interest in popular music, already a symbol of rebellion among the young, and began to attend church only mutinously, complaining how "square" it all was. Recognising the conventional symptoms of adolescent dislocation I kept calm, said little, endured much and waited for the storms to pass, but to my dismay the storms became hurricanes. Michael discovered girls. This was no surprise, particularly since he was a good-looking young man, and all sensible fathers are glad when their sons discover that girls are more fun than cricket, but I was concerned by the girls in whom he chose to be interested and even more concerned when he showed no interest in drinking in moderation.

He managed to do well enough at school to begin the training to be a doctor, but before long he was asked to leave medical school, not because he was incapable of doing the work but because he was incapable of avoiding fornication and hard drinking. Naturally I was concerned. I was also, as Lyle well knew, furious, shocked, resentful, embarrassed and bitter. She somehow managed to stop me becoming wholly estranged from Michael, and she somehow persuaded him to promise to reform. Jon suggested that I might make more time to talk to Michael, since such a move would make it unnecessary for him to behave badly in order to gain my attention, but I disliked the idea of being bullied by bad behaviour into reorganising my busy timetable, and I thought it was up to Michael to pull himself together without being pampered by cosy little chats.

"My father never pampered me," I said to Jon, "and if I'd ever behaved as Michael's behaving he'd have disowned me."

"But I thought you realised long ago that your father had actually made some unfortunate mistakes as a parent! Do you really want to treat Michael as your father treated you?"

I was silenced. Eventually, working on the theory that Michael was a muddled, unhappy young man who needed every possible support as he struggled to find his balance in adult life, I told him he was forgiven and promised to do all I could to get him into another medical school, but Michael merely said he now wanted to be a pop singer in London.

Unfortunately by this time National Service had been abolished so I could not rely on the army to knock some sense into his addled head. I tried to control my fury but failed. There was a scene which ended when Michael announced, "Right. That's it. I'm off," and headed for London with the small legacy which he had been left by my old friend Alan Romaine, the doctor who had ensured my physical recovery after the war. Lyle extracted a promise from Michael that he would keep in touch with her, so we were able to tell everyone truthfully that he had gone to London to find a job and we were looking forward to hearing how he was getting on.

"I'm sure it'll all come right," said Lyle to me in private. "What he's really interested in is the stage, and he's so handsome that he's bound to become a matinée idol."

I was too sunk in gloom to reply, but Lyle's prediction turned out to be closer to the mark than I had expected. Michael became involved with a suburban repertory company and quickly decided that his talent was for neither singing nor acting but for directing and producing plays. He stayed a year with the company but then announced that the theatre was passé and that television was "where it was at" (a curious American phrase currently popular among the young). To my astonishment he succeeded in getting a job at the BBC.

"You see?" said Lyle. "I told you it would all work out in the end."

I found it so pleasant to be able to tell all my friends that my younger son now had a respectable employer that I decided the time had come to wave the olive branch of peace, and writing Michael a letter I offered to take him out to lunch at the Athenaeum when I was next in London. A week later I received a card in reply. It said: "Athenaeum = Utter Dragsville. Take me to that bar in the House of Lords, food not necessary, I drink lunch."

I did not like this card at all but Lyle said Michael was only trying to shock me and there was no reason why he and I should be unable to down a couple of sherries in the House of Lords bar while we tried to make up our minds whether we could face lunching together in the dining-room.

We met. Michael, who had clearly been drinking, ordered a double dry martini. I let him drink one but drew the line when he demanded another. He called me an old square and walked out. After that, relations remained cool between us for some time.

"He can't last long at the BBC," I said to Lyle. "He'll get sacked for drink and wind up in the gutter."

"Nonsense!" said Lyle, and once again she was right. Michael continued to work at the BBC and even obtained promotion. Obviously I needed to give our battered olive branch of peace another wave. By this time we had reached the end of 1964 and I invited—even, I go so far as to say, begged—him to spend Christmas with us. I had hoped he might telephone in response to this fulsome invitation, but another of his terse little cards arrived. It said: "Xmas okay but don't mention God. Will be arriving on Xmas Eve with my bird, the one Mum met when she snuck up to London to see my new pad. Make sure there's plenty of booze."

"Oh *God!*" said Lyle through gritted teeth when she read this offensive communication.

Making a great effort to seem not only calm but even mildly amused I said: "I don't understand the ornithological reference."

"It's his latest ghastly girl. She's American."

"You never mentioned—"

"She was too ghastly to mention."

"Well, if he thinks he can bring his mistress here and bed down with her under my roof—"

"Darling, leave this entirely to me."

Michael did spend Christmas with us at the South Canonry, but the girl was ruthlessly billeted by Lyle at one of the local hotels. Michael wore no suit. He did not even wear a tie. He was never dead drunk but he was certainly in that condition known to publicans as "nicely, thank you," an inebriated state which fell short of causing disruption but was still capable of generating embarrassment. My enemy Dean Aysgarth, on the other hand, was constantly accompanied to a variety of services by a veritable praetorian guard of well-dressed, immaculately behaved, respectable and charming sons. If I had not had Charley to cheer me up I might well have expired with despair.

However, Lyle had been working hard behind my back, and on Boxing Day Michael sidled up to me with a penitent expression. "Sorry," he said. "I just want you to know that my new year's resolution will be not to get on your nerves. Can we bury the hatchet and drink to 1965?"

We drank to the coming year.

"I've decided that 1965's going to be a great time for the Ashworth family," said Michael, coming up for air after downing his martini. "I prophesy no fights, no feuds and absolutely no fiascos of any kind."

Michael had many gifts but I fear prophecy was not among them.

III

"I am going to set before you one of those standing themes that always ought to be preached about: the relation between the sexes . . . And if we achieve no other aim, we shall at least show sympathy with those who are concerned to manage the most baffling and the most ungovernable part of their instinctive nature."

AUSTIN FARRER
Warden of Keble College, Oxford, 1960–1968
SAID OR SUNG

I

HAVING COMPLETED this portrait of myself, my family and my professionally distinguished but privately turbulent life—having, in other words, set the scene for my third catastrophe—I now feel it is time to describe the crises which battered me in rapid succession towards the edge of the abyss.

"Do you remember," said Lyle, taking the telephone receiver off the hook one afternoon early in the February of 1965, "how miserable we were when we were forced to face the fact that our third child was never going to exist?"

"Vividly." I was in an excellent mood for it was a Monday, and Monday was my day off. As Lyle severed our connection to the outside world, I sat down on the bed to remove my shoes.

"And do you remember," pursued Lyle, drawing the curtains and plunging the bedroom into an erotic twilight, "how you said God might know what was best for us better than we did, and I was so angry that I hurled an ashtray at you?"

"Even more vividly."

"Well, I just want to say I'm sorry I hurled the ashtray. We would never have survived a third child."

"Does this belated enlightenment mean you'll stop feeling queasy whenever anyone cites the quotation: 'All things work together for good to them that love God?' "

"No, I still think that's the most infuriating sentence St. Paul ever wrote—which reminds me: why have you taken to writing it over and over again on your blotter?"

"It calms me down when someone rings up and wastes my time by drivelling on about nothing."

"It wouldn't calm me down," said Lyle, removing the counterpane from the bed as I stood up. "I'd just want to grab a gun and shoot St. Paul."

Whenever possible on my day off I played golf, but on this occasion bad weather had ensured that I stayed at home. The winter so far had been very cold. There had been blizzards in January, and although a dry spell had now been forecast there was as yet no sign of it beginning in Starbridge. I had spent the morning working on my new book about the early Christian writer Hippolytus and the sexually lax Bishop Callistus, and my glamorous part-time secretary Sally had taken dictation for an hour before returning home to type up her notes. Sally had been wearing a shiny black coat, which she had told me was made of something called PVC, and tall black leather boots which had appeared to creep greedily up her legs towards the hem of her short purple skirt. After viewing this fashion display the sexually lax Bishop Callistus would undoubtedly have dictated some weak-kneed thoughts about fornication, but since I was anticipating an intimate afternoon with my wife, I had been able to say to Sally with aplomb "What an original ensemble!" and deliver myself of some intellectually rigorous thoughts about Hippolytus's theology. There are times when I really do think the case for a celibate priesthood is quite impossible to sustain.

Lyle and I were now alone in the house. Our cook-housekeeper had gone home at one o'clock; the chaplains had disappeared to their nearby cottages after a quick glance at the morning post to ensure there was no crisis which needed my attention, and Miss Peabody, who shared my day off, was no doubt doing something very worthy elsewhere. The house was not only delightfully quiet but delightfully warm as the result of the recent installation of a central heating system, an extravagance paid for out of my private income and now periodically triggering pangs of guilt that I should be living in such luxury while the majority of my clergy shivered in icy vicarages.

"Isn't the central heating turned up rather high?" I said conscience-stricken to Lyle.

"Certainly not!" came the robust reply. "Bishops need to be warm in order to function properly."

I thought Hippolytus would have made a very acid comment on this statement, but of course he had not been obliged to endure the numbing effect of an English February. Fleetingly I pictured Bishop Callistus toasting himself without guilt in front of a brazier of hot coals as he planned his next compassionate sermon to adulterers.

Our bedroom at the South Canonry faced the front of the house, and from the windows we could see beyond the huge beech-tree by the gate and across the Choir School's playing-field to the southern side of the Cathedral: the roof of the octagonal chapter house was clearly visible above the quadrangle formed by the cloisters, and beyond this roof the central tower rose high above the nave to form the base of the spire.

"Why are you gazing glassy-eyed at the curtains?"

"I was thinking of the Cathedral beyond them. Since you've just apologised for throwing the ashtray at me all those years ago, let me now apologise for wanting our bedroom to face the back garden when we moved here."

"Thank you, darling. But of course I realised that was because you were slightly neurotic about Starbridge at the time. Imagine wanting to face a boring old back garden when you had the chance to face one of the architectural wonders of Europe!"

I laughed dutifully at the memory of this foolishness.

In contrast to the tropical temperature generated by the new heating system the bedroom presented a cool, austere appearance. The modern furniture was white; my wardrobe and tallboy, inherited from my father, stood in my dressing-room next door. Lyle had chosen the white furniture, just as she had chosen the ice-blue curtains and the wintry grey carpet. At first I had thought: how cold! But soon I had realised that the coldness became erotic when it formed the background for Lyle's collection of nightwear. Lyle had never adjusted her wardrobe to her advancing years. Having kept her figure she had no trouble buying exactly what she liked, and what she liked had changed little since I had first met her. During the day she wore simple, elegant suits and dresses in chaste, muted colours and looked like a very exclusive executive secretary—or perhaps like a grand version of the lady's companion she had been in the 1930s when she had run the palace so efficiently for the Jardines. But at night the air of propriety was discarded and amazing creations foamed and frothed from the ice-white wardrobe. Then indeed my pity for the celibate bishops of the Early Church knew no bounds.

"What would I do," I said as I slid between the sheets, "if you weighed twelve stone and wore flannel nightgowns and had hair like corrugated iron?"

"Die of boredom. And what would I do if you were bald and paunchy and looked like an elderly baby?"

"I'm sure you'd find some stimulating solution."

An amusing interlude followed. I find it curious that it should be so widely believed that no one over sixty can possibly be interested in sexual intercourse, and I find it well-nigh scandalous that so many people today still believe that Christianity is against sex. Christianity has certainly experienced bouts of thinking that there are better ways of occupying one's time—in the Early Church, for instance, when the end of the world was believed to be imminent, procreation was inevitably regarded as a self-indulgent escape from the far more urgent task of saving souls—but today it is generally recognised among Christians that sexual intercourse is good. It is the *abuse* of sexual intercourse which causes all the problems and which prompts Christians like me to speak up in the hope of saving people from being exploited, tormented and wrecked. At Cambridge my undergraduates had nicknamed me "Anti-Sex Ashworth," but no sobriquet could have been more inappropriate. I may be an ardent moralist but I put a high value on sex—which explains why I am an ardent moralist. I detest the fact that this great gift from God is regularly devalued and degraded.

"St. Paul should have had sex regularly," said Lyle later as we lit our cigarettes.

"Why have you got your knife into St. Paul all of a sudden?"

"He was beastly to women and queers."

"That's a highly debatable statement. If one takes into account that some of the epistles weren't written by him—"

"What would St. Paul have said to the woman in my prayer-group who broke down last week and told us her son was deeply in love with another man?"

"I'm sure he'd have been extremely kind to her."

"But she doesn't want mere kindness, Charles, least of all for herself! She wants her son to be accepted, particularly by the Church. She says: is it right that a promiscuous homosexual can confess to an error and receive absolution while two homosexuals who practise fidelity in a loving relationship are barred from receiving the sacrament?"

"She's mistaken in assuming that a promiscuous homosexual would automatically receive absolution. I certainly wouldn't absolve anyone I thought intended to continue committing buggery in public lavatories."

"Yes, but—"

"Also I don't think you should lose sight of the law of the land. Homosexual acts are illegal. You surely can't expect the Church to condone law-breaking *en masse!*"

"But what are ordinary, law-abiding homosexuals supposed to do, Charles, if they have no gift for chastity? After all, most heterosexual men find chastity quite beyond them—how would you yourself manage if I ran off and left you on your own?"

"I'd run after you and haul you back."

"What fun! But seriously, Charles—"

"Oh, I freely admit I'd hate to be celibate. But that doesn't mean God's incapable of calling me to such a life and it doesn't mean either that I'd be incapable of responding to such a call if it came. By the grace of God—"

"—all things are possible. Quite. But Charles, are you really saying that the Church has nothing to say to these people except that they should regard their homosexual inclinations as a call to celibacy?"

"The Church has plenty to say to everyone, regardless of their sexual inclinations. And let's get one point quite clear: the Church is not against homosexuals themselves. Indeed many homosexuals do excellent work as priests."

"Yes, but they're the celibates, aren't they? What I want to know is—"

"My dear, I have every sympathy for anyone, heterosexual or homosexual, who's severely tempted to indulge in illicit sexual activity, but the Church can't just adopt a policy of 'anything goes'! Any large organisation has to make rules and set standards or otherwise, human nature being what it is, the whole structure collapses in chaos!"

"Yes, I quite understand that, but you still haven't answered my question. What happens to the people who just can't fit into this neat, orderly world designed by the Church? I mean, have you ever thought, really *thought,* about what it must be like to be a homosexual? Your problem is that you haven't the slightest interest in homosexuality and you have no homosexual friends."

"Surely those are points in my favour!"

"Charles, I'm trying to have a serious conversation with you! Now stop being so frivolous and just try to be helpful for a moment. How would you, in your professional role, advise my prayer-group to pray for my friend's homosexual son who's living discreetly with his boyfriend in a manner which has absolutely nothing to do with a promiscuous career in public lavatories?"

I sighed, ground out my cigarette and to signal my resentment that I was being dragooned into playing the bishop I reconnected us to the outside world by replacing the telephone receiver with a thud. "Excuse me," I said, "while I put on my cope and mitre."

"No, don't you dare sulk! I've always been very careful not to bother you about the prayer-group, and yet now, on the very first occasion that I've actually paid you the compliment of asking for your advice—"

I slumped guiltily back on the pillows just as the telephone jangled at my side.

2

"*I'LL ANSWER* it," said Lyle, slipping out of bed.

"No, let it ring." I was already regretting that I had slammed back the receiver in a fit of pique.

"If we let it ring you'll crucify yourself imagining a suicidal vicar screaming for help," said Lyle tartly, and moving around to the table on my side of the bed she picked up the receiver and intoned in her most neutral voice: "South Canonry."

A pause followed during which I wondered whether to light another cigarette. Contrary to Lyle's fears I thought it was most unlikely that some suicidal vicar was screaming for help in an icy vicarage while his bishop lounged in a centrally heated haze of post-coital bliss, and having made the decision to light the cigarette I turned my thoughts instead to Lyle's prayer-group, those middle-aged, middle-class, churchgoing ladies who seemed so unlikely to want to discuss unnatural vice. It occurred to me that the kindest advice I could give them was to pray for the wholesome family life of their married friends and leave any deviant relations to God.

"Just a moment, please," said Lyle, bringing the silence to an end. "Let me see if my husband left a number where he can be contacted." Sitting down on the edge of the bed she muffled the receiver in the eiderdown and whispered to me: "It's the chaplain at the hospital. Desmond Wilton's been beaten up in his church. He's unconscious, he needs an operation and the chaplain thought you ought to know about it."

Crushing out my cigarette I began to struggle out of bed.

"Yes, I can get in touch with him straight away," said Lyle. "Either he or the Archdeacon will be with you as soon as possible." She hung up. "Charles, surely Malcolm can cope with this?"

"I couldn't possibly palm such a disaster off on my archdeacon."

"Trust Desmond Wilton to get himself beaten up on your day off!"

"Darling—"

"What was he doing anyway, getting himself beaten up? I just hope there's no sinister explanation."

I was appalled. "But Desmond's been leading an exemplary life ever since he came to Starbridge! If we hadn't been discussing homosexuality, it would never have occurred to you to make such a remark—and I refuse to believe there's any truth in it!"

"Dear Charles," said my wife, slipping into a black silk negligée. "Such a very Christian nature."

"It's got nothing to do with any Christian nature I might have," I said, very heated by this time, "and everything to do with the fact that Desmond made a complete recovery from that spiritual breakdown he had in London. All right, I know you think the Bishop of London palmed him off on me, but even the best priests can have breakdowns and I absolutely defend my decision to give him a job in the diocese as soon as he'd recovered!"

"I know you'll always defend it—and how good it is for me to be reminded that despite all my advanced liberal thoughts about homosexuals you're still so much more compassionate and Christian towards them than I am! If I were a bishop nothing would induce me to employ a pathetic old priest who'd been beaten up while soliciting in a public lavatory . . . Shall I try and track down Malcolm for you?" she called after me as I headed for the bathroom.

"Yes, he ought to be told straight away, but say there's no need for him to cancel everything and rush to the hospital. The chaplain and I'll sort things out."

Five minutes later, dressed in a black suit with a purple stock and pectoral cross, I emerged from my dressing-room to find that Lyle had picked up from the floor the casual, off-duty clothes which I had discarded earlier, made the bed and tracked down my archdeacon. "He's making a visitation at Upper Starwood," she informed me, "but I've left a message at the vicarage there."

"Good." I turned to leave but on the threshold I hesitated and looked back. "I'm sorry I took evasive action when you started to talk about the prayer-group," I said. "I really would like to hear more about it. Maybe later—when I'm in neither a rush nor a post-coital torpor—"

"Of course. Later."

I hurried away to the hospital.

3

WHEN I had visited Starbridge in 1937, the year I had met and married Lyle, I had thought it more than lived up to its reputation of being the most beautiful city west of the Avon. In my mind's eye I could still see it shining in the hot sunlight of that distant summer; I could remember how enchanted I had been by its medieval streets, flower-filled parks and winding, sparkling river, how mesmerised I had been by the Cathedral, towering above the walled Close on a mound above the shimmering water-meadows. "Radiant, ravishing Starbridge!" I had exclaimed to myself more than once during that crucial time, but that was all long ago, and Starbridge was not the city it had been before the war.

Why must unspoilt county towns inevitably change for the worse? Those Starbridge parks remained flower-filled in summer but now they were litter-strewn as the result of the huge increase in tourists and the slovenly habits of the young. Most of the medieval streets still existed but a number of them south of Mitre Street had been bulldozed to make way for a hideous invention, a "multi-storey car park" which was attached to something called a "shopping centre." This new development was so ugly that I felt hot with rage whenever I saw it. Fortunately the Mayor who had encouraged this act of vandalism had dropped dead so I was no longer obliged to be polite to him, but the city council members lingered on, a sore trial to my Christian patience. More concrete horrors were rising on the outskirts of the city where a by-pass (on stilts!) was being constructed, but this innovation I was prepared to tolerate since its purpose was to eliminate the city's traffic jams.

The Starbridge General Hospital, a Victorian building, was unchanged on the outside despite being constantly modernised within. It stood near Eternity Street on the river which flowed swiftly, fed by two tributaries, through the heart of the city. As I arrived that afternoon the rain was hardening into sleet and a bitter north wind was blowing. From the car park the tower of St. Martin's-in-Cripplegate, my archdeacon's church, could be seen standing palely, as if numbed with cold, against a yellowish, snow-laden sky.

For a moment I thought of those radiant sunlit days of 1937, and suddenly I heard a much younger Lyle say in my memory: "I'm Miss Christie, Mrs. Jardine's companion . . ." I hurried into the hospital but the memories pursued me and I heard Bishop Jardine himself exclaim: "Welcome to Starbridge!" as he made a grand entrance into his drawing-room. It occurred to me then that I was on the brink of remembering Loretta, but that was one episode from 1937 which I always willed myself not to recall, particularly since I had become a bishop. Blocking it at once from my mind I entered the hospital's main hall.

A dreary interval ensued. I asked for Desmond but was told he was in the operating theatre. I asked for the chaplain but was told he was not in his office. I asked for the hospital almoner and/or the doctor in charge of the case, but was told to take a seat. Evidently I was becoming tiresome and needed to be disciplined.

Since I was not wearing my formal uniform of frock-coat and gaiters, and since my overcoat hid my purple stock and pectoral cross, I was not immediately recognisable as a VIP. I did toy with the idea of opening my coat and flashing my chest at the lacklustre receptionist, but I thought better of it. No degree of impatience can excuse vulgarity.

I managed to kill my annoyance by telling myself the woman was probably worn out by long hours and low pay, and having thus transformed myself from a cross old buffer into a charitably inclined bishop (a process which I found more than usually exhausting), I received my reward: the almoner arrived to look after me, and I was taken speedily down a chain of cream-coloured corridors to meet the doctor in authority. The almoner even called me "my lord." For one golden moment I could imagine we were both back in those sunlit days before the war.

My spirits rose even further when the doctor told me that although the injuries were unpleasant, Desmond's life was not in danger. A series of heavy kicks had cracked a couple of ribs; a series of heavy punches had battered his face, which was now being stitched up; the main problem was the shock sustained, and Desmond would need to be in hospital for at least forty-eight hours, possibly longer, while his progress was monitored. Since he was an elderly man, not robust, a period of convalescence would be advisable once he left the hospital. Meanwhile he could be allowed no visitors until the following morning.

Having thanked the doctor for all this information I was taken by the almoner to her office in order to deal with certain bureaucratic formalities relating to the admission. She did try to contact the chaplain on the internal telephone and when there was still no reply from his office she arranged for a message to be broadcast on the public address system, but he appeared to have vanished. Not wishing to delay the almoner further I said I would wait for him in the main hall, but this decision proved to be a mistake. No chaplain appeared, despite yet another summons on the public address system, but two cold-eyed men in raincoats entered the building and immediately collared me.

With dismay I found myself in the hands of the police and confronting the possibility of scandal.

4

I KNEW Inspector Parker. Indeed I knew all the top men on the Starbridge force and I was on good terms with the Chief Constable, but to know a policeman formally as the result of one's public position is one thing; to be interviewed by him during his investigation of a crime is quite another. Too late I wished I had brought my lay-chaplain to the hospital.

Roger was an old hand at dealing with worldly matters which had the potential to be awkward for a bishop.

Assuming my most confident manner I said to Parker, "How glad I am to see you!" and without hesitation offered him my hand. I then both took control of the interview and underlined the power of my position by demanding: "Please tell me exactly what happened."

I could see Parker was thinking what a tiresome old smoothie I was, but he said civilly enough: "Mr. Wilton was found in the church by one of the lady members of the congregation, and judging from the loss of blood we think he may have been lying there for some time. He was unconscious when the ambulance arrived but we're here in the hope that he can be interviewed."

"He's in the operating theatre."

"Then when he comes out my sergeant here can sit at his bedside till he recovers consciousness."

I thought it prudent to leave all comment on that plan to the doctor. What I really wanted to hear was information about why Desmond had been attacked, but I did not want to appear too curious for fear of arousing Parker's suspicions. I decided to try to float the most likely explanation in the hope not only that it was true but that I might learn something from Parker's reaction.

"It's disgraceful for a priest to be beaten up in his own church!" I exclaimed, playing the outraged old buffer. "I assume Father Wilton interrupted a thief who was in the act of robbing the alms-box."

"No, sir, from our preliminary investigation it appears that nothing was taken."

I noted that I was addressed as "sir" instead of "my lord" or "Bishop," and suspected that this was a move to grab control of the interview by cutting me down to size.

"Then I assume," I said, refusing to be reduced, "that the culprit was a vandal bent on sacrilege."

"No, sir, nothing was disturbed or damaged."

"Then I can only conclude that this outrage was perpetrated by a lunatic. Well, Parker"—by this time I had decided that I quite definitely did not want to answer any questions about a possible motive for the attack—"I wish you every success in your investigation and I hope you'll keep me informed of all developments. And now, if you'll excuse me—"

"Just a moment, my lord." Parker had decided it was worth bending over backwards a fraction in order to stop me dead in my tracks. "Would you be so good as to tell us a little about Mr. Wilton? In this sort of case the personality of the victim is often of the first importance when it comes to solving the crime."

Having lost control of the interview I realised that my task now was to appear so immensely distinguished that my opinions could not easily be doubted. "Father Wilton," I said, again giving Desmond the title which as an Anglo-Catholic he preferred yet this time contriving to infuse it with an air of sanctity, "is sixty-four years old and has been vicar of St. Paul's church in Langley Bottom since 1960. He's an extremely devout and conscientious priest, and is greatly respected by his congregation."

"Has this kind of thing ever happened to him before?"

"To the best of my knowledge," I said with perfect truth, "Father Wilton has never in his life been beaten up by a thug in his own church." But I could see where this line of questioning was going and the destination was gruesome. "What exactly are you implying?" I demanded, taking the split-second decision that attack was the best form of defence.

"I was just wondering how accident-prone he was. Some old gentlemen do suffer more than others from this sort of mishap," said Parker, still very civil, but at that point his sergeant interposed brutally: "Not married, is he?"

I drew myself up to my full height and allowed a blistering pause to develop before announcing in my grandest episcopal manner: "Father Wilton is called to celibacy."

In the silence that followed I reflected how far removed the scene was from that popular television series about the policeman with the heart of gold, "Dixon of Dock Green." The oafish sergeant was bright-eyed, his lips moist where he had licked them in his excitement; he reminded me of one of the more disagreeable carnivores—a rhinoceros, perhaps—who had just scented food. In contrast Parker was as cool and still as steel in ice. Refusing to be intimidated by my grand manner he said levelly: "I'm sure you understand, my lord, that since there was no robbery or vandalism, the likelihood is that he was attacked by someone he knew. May I ask your permission to search the vicarage? A desk-diary, for instance, would reveal if he had an appointment to see someone at the church this afternoon."

I was still trying to conceal my horror at this potentially ruinous request when deliverance arrived in the form of my henchman, the Archdeacon of Starbridge. No detachment of the United States cavalry could have been greeted with more relief in the final reel of a Hollywood western than Malcolm Lindsay was greeted by his bishop as he swept into the hall of Starbridge General Hospital that afternoon.

"Ah, there you are, Bishop!" he exclaimed, deceptively jovial. "I thought I'd better look in here as soon as I'd finished my visitation—good heavens, it's Inspector Parker! And Sergeant Locke! Nice to know the police have their best men on the trail. Now, Bishop, off you go to pray for poor Desmond—I'm sure Inspector Parker will quite understand that you shouldn't be detained from your spiritual duties a moment longer."

Parker allowed himself to look baffled by the concept of spiritual duties, but recovered himself sufficiently to say: "I've no wish to detain the Bishop, Mr. Lindsay, but there are one or two questions—"

"Address them to me!" said Malcolm, still relentlessly exuding bonhomie. "I'm the one who has direct supervision of Father Wilton, so I know much more about him than the Bishop does."

"But I need the Bishop's permission to search the vicarage. In my opinion—"

"Oh, the Bishop couldn't possibly give such a permission! I see you're unfamiliar with the concept of the 'parson's freehold,' Inspector—that house is at the moment, to all intents and purposes, Father Wilton's, and in the absence of his permission I'm afraid you must obtain a search-warrant, but that won't be difficult, will it? In the circumstances I'm sure it'll be just a formality . . . Off you go, Bishop."

I escaped, bathed in cold sweat.

Outside the sleet was still falling from that heavy, yellowish sky and the gloom had thickened. Scrambling into my black Rover I switched on the headlights and drove straight to Desmond's vicarage in the working-class city parish of Langley Bottom.

5

THERE WERE two police cars parked outside the church and a young constable was on guard in the porch, but the adjacent vicarage was not yet besieged by either the police or the hound from the *Starbridge Evening News.* Parking my car in the forecourt of the bleak Victorian house I rang the front doorbell and waited, eyeing with dismay the state of the woodwork, which needed a coat of paint, and the windows, which were caked in grime. Eventually I was admitted by the daily housekeeper, a dour woman who conceded with unprecedented animation that the news had given her "ever such a turn." Also present in the hall was the elderly parishioner who had found Desmond lying in a pool of blood when she had entered the church to perform her weekly chore of dusting the pews. Various other members of the small, aging congregation were twittering in the front reception room as I looked in.

I was unsure how quickly the police would be able to pick up a search-warrant, but knowing Malcolm would delay them as long as possible I thought I had at least an hour in which to prove or disprove the worst. Willing myself to betray no trace of impatience, I singled out the one male in the group and asked him to escort home the woman who had found the body; luckily the woman lived across the street so I was not obliged to waste time giving them a lift in my car. Then I dismissed the remainder of the gathering by assuring them that there was no need for anyone to linger at the vicarage for news; the churchwardens would be issued with regular bulletins which would be posted in the church porch. As the front door closed after the last parishioner I got rid of the housekeeper by requesting some tea and finally invaded Desmond's study, a large dim dusty hole where the temperature hovered uncertainly above freezing.

I need hardly say that by this time I was exceedingly worried. Of course there might still be an innocent explanation for the attack: a parishioner might have had a brainstorm or a passing tramp might have succumbed to psychosis, but Desmond's past did mean the attack was capable of a seamy explanation. After the attack upon him in the public lavatory in London he had been arrested for soliciting. The charge had later been dropped but the Bishop of London's archdeacon, taking charge at the vicarage as Desmond languished overnight in hospital, had to his horror discovered a cache of pornographic magazines in the study. Homosexual behavior combined with a taste for pornography could well have led to imprisonment. Desmond had been lucky to escape and had no doubt been spurred on by gratitude when he had made the best of his rehabilitation, but if he were now in the midst of a second breakdown, the possibility that his old weaknesses had resurfaced was strong.

I knew I had to search his study. I had no wish to impede the police in the execution of their duty but what drove me on was the dread that the police might uncover material which was irrelevant to their enquiry but of immense interest to the press. I thought it unlikely that Desmond would have managed to acquire the kind of hard-core pornography which would render him liable to prosecution on a pornography charge alone, but even a soft-core collection could prove disastrous if Sergeant Locke chose to make a caustic comment to the hound from the *Starbridge Evening News.* The hound's scoop would tip off Fleet Street and then all hell would break loose.

I glanced around the study. At once I noticed that the desk was in chaos, a sinister sign indicating a disorganised mind unable to cope with the daily routine, but the upper layers of paper contained nothing more sensational than unpaid bills and copies of *The Church Gazette.* I looked at the desk-diary. The page for the day contained—to my relief—only two morning appointments, but it did occur to me that an afternoon appointment might still have existed even though Desmond had chosen not to write it down. Opening the drawers of the desk I found that although they were crammed with an extraordinary variety of rubbish ranging from candle-stubs to undarned socks, no pornography lay waiting to be revealed. The cupboards below the bookshelves were similarly innocent, and the books themselves were unimpeachable, displaying a respectable, orthodox, old-fashioned taste in both English literature and theology. The fact that the volumes were so neatly arranged on their shelves, however, suggested that they had not been read for some time.

I concluded that although I had discovered evidence of a priest fraying at the seams, there was nothing to suggest that he had actually fallen apart. Sitting down in the chair behind the desk I reached for the telephone and dialled the South Canonry.

"It would take a week to go through the study properly," I said to Lyle after I had given her a rapid resumé of events, "but at least there's nothing frightful lying around."

"Well, of course there isn't, not after that Archdeacon in London went looking for an address-book and instantly uncovered horrors! Wake up, darling! This time there'll be a hidey-hole designed to outwit any archdeacon—try the bedroom."

"I couldn't."

"Why not?"

"Only private detectives invade bedrooms."

"And the police! Darling, do you really want Desmond to hit the headlines in the *News of the World?"*

There was a pause while I wrestled with my middle-class upbringing, my public-school *mores* and my Christian duty as a bishop to look after a wayward member of my flock. "If you only knew," I muttered at last, "how much I wish I was back in Cambridge—"

"Charles, this is not the time to wallow in a pointless nostalgia. Think of the Church—think of the diocese—"

"If only I'd never taken him on! Of course I knew it was a risk but the Abbot-General absolutely swore Desmond was fully recovered as the result of that long retreat with the Fordite monks—"

"Darling, stop fluttering around in a purple panic and *search that bedroom.* Or do I have to come over and do it myself?"

"I must say I think this is a singularly distasteful conversation for a bishop to have with his wife!"

"Don't waste any more time thinking, Charles—ACT!"

"Very well." I replaced the receiver, marched out of the room and almost collided with the housekeeper who had been approaching with my tea. Thanking her profusely I returned to the study, but as soon as the tray had been deposited on the desk and the housekeeper had once more retreated to the kitchen, I made another swift exit into the hall.

As I padded silently upstairs I was aware of the size of the house, built for a large Victorian family with several servants, and it occurred to me that this size was enhanced by the interior dilapidation which underlined the high ceilings, the wide staircase and the long corridors. I suspected the housekeeper neither dusted nor swept, probably because Desmond had never noticed whether she did so or not. Upstairs the cold intensified. Stooping over the floor in one corner of the landing I flicked open my lighter and saw the mice-droppings beside the hole I had noticed in the wainscoting. The notorious lines of the well-known hymn flared in my mind: "The rich man in his castle, the poor man at his gate; God made them high and lowly, and ordered their estate." I thought of my comfortable home and felt not only guilty but angry and ashamed.

I told myself that something should be done for the parish, but I knew the problems it presented were intractable. The diocesan board of finance had already classed the church as a white elephant which required too much money too often. The congregation had dwindled to a remnant. It was hardly surprising that the vicarage was now a mere sordid niche for a man whom no other bishop would employ, but how I hated that long decline from Victorian power to mid-twentieth-century enfeeblement! It made me despair of the future of the Church.

But then I remembered St. Athanasius, battling on *contra mundum,* never giving up, never sinking back into despair, and it occurred to me that I should stop bewailing the present in disgust and pray for the future with hope. So I said in my head to God: "Breathe new life into this parish—resurrect it from the dead!"—an outrageous demand indeed and I hardly hoped for it to be met, but no attempt to align oneself with God can ever be futile, and perhaps the result of my prayer would be that in future I would take more interest in this dying parish, a move which would produce beneficial results for the congregation.

To finish off my prayer I added my current mantra, " 'All things work together for good to them that love God,' " and feeling fractionally calmer—or was I in fact more depressed than ever?—I resumed my journey to Desmond's bedroom.

6

IN CONTRAST to the chaos in the study, this room was uncluttered. It was as if Desmond had created a small, austere space where he could escape from a world which demanded too much of him. The narrow bed had no counterpane and no eiderdown and the top blanket looked as if it had come from an army surplus store. A dressing-gown, frayed at the cuffs, hung from a hook on the back of the door, but all his other clothes had been consigned to the wardrobe. Beside the bed I saw the Missal of the Fordite monks—Jon's old Order—stacked with the Bible and the Book of Common Prayer. An alarm clock nearby was so weathered by the vicarage climate that the metal had rusted at the base.

I noted the prie-dieu by the window, the crucifix above the bed, and suddenly as the aura of a devout life permeated my consciousness I felt as if Christ himself were watching me from some corner of the room which lay just beyond my field of vision.

Immediately I asked myself what Jesus would have thought of this shoddy episcopal invasion of a devout man's monk-like cell, but my task at that moment, as Lyle had so forcefully reminded me, was not to think but to act. I picked up the Missal and shook it but no pornographic photograph or incriminating letter fell from the pages. Desmond had wanted to be an Anglican monk long ago, but when the Fordites had turned him down he had decided he was called to parish work after all. But had that decision of the Abbot-General been correct? Perhaps if the Order had accepted him . . . But I was wasting time in thought again. Setting down the Missal, I shook the Bible and the prayer-book with equally unproductive results and opened the drawer of the bedside table, but I found nothing there except indigestion tablets. I examined the drawers inside the wardrobe but the majority were empty. Desmond had even fewer clothes than I had imagined.

However I noticed that in the section of the wardrobe where his one suit and spare cassock were hanging, a tin box was sitting on the floor alongside a down-at-heel pair of shoes. It was the sort of box, about fifteen inches high, in which people kept personal memorabilia such as old letters and family photographs, but when I tried to raise the lid I was unable to do so. Kneeling on the threadbare carpet I flicked open my lighter again and confirmed that although the hasps were unfastened a lock was holding the lid in place. I told myself that it was not unnatural for Desmond to wish to keep his personal memorabilia from the housekeeper's prying eyes, but the locked box bothered me and I became even more bothered when I was unable to find the key.

I felt along the top of the wardrobe but my fingers encountered nothing but dust. I stood on a chair so that I could see the top of the picture-rail and door-frame, but no trace of metal glinted among the cobwebs. I lifted up the box and looked underneath but found nothing. It was certainly possible that Desmond kept the key with him at all times, but priests in charge of large churches usually have quite enough keys on their key-rings without further burdening themselves with one which was not in daily use.

I stood motionless for a moment in the centre of the room while I tried to identify the one place which the housekeeper would never touch. My glance finally fell on the crucifix. Removing it from the wall I found, to my utmost dismay, that a small key had been taped to the back.

I now began to feel distinctly queasy. In truth I had not expected to find the key hidden in such an abnormal place. A key hidden on top of the wardrobe or picture-rail would have indicated a normal desire for privacy; a key hidden behind a crucifix suggested nothing less than a guilty desire to be secretive. Very carefully I detached the key in such a way that the sticky tape could be reused, and tried the lock. It yielded, and as I raised the lid my last faint hope that the box contained innocent memorabilia expired. I found myself plunged into an episcopal nightmare.

Removing the magazines I found the photographs. If I had still been an army chaplain, working among men from all social backgrounds, I could have taken the discovery in my stride, but in that room, so quiet, so still, so redolent of a devout life, I was appalled. I had knelt on the floor again to open the box, but now I sank back on my heels and wiped the sweat from my forehead. Gradually the shock faded and the anger streamed through me, anger with Desmond for jeopardising the good name of the Church, anger with the Bishop of London who had palmed him off on me, anger with the Abbot-General of the Fordite monks who five years ago had pronounced Desmond fit for service, anger with the decadent spirit of the age which encouraged pornography to flourish—anger with anyone or anything other than with me and my bishopric. But at last I pulled myself together, flicked through the photographs to make sure none of them showed Desmond himself in unspeakable circumstances, and confirmed that there were no letters in the box. I then considered the implications of my discovery.

It seemed clear that although I had uncovered evidence that Desmond was in serious spiritual trouble, there was no evidence either of blackmail or of a pornography ring; in addition to the absence of letters, there was no list of addresses, no indication that the collection had ever been shared. Moreover, although I was no expert on pornography I suspected that both the magazines and the photographs could be purchased without too much trouble in the shadier shops of Soho, and if this suspicion was correct the police would be unlikely to press charges. Desmond might indeed have been beaten up as the result of an illegal homosexual encounter, but there was no proof that the assailant had provided the pornography and no proof either that Desmond had been conducting anything which could be described as an affair. I decided I could purloin the box without worrying that I was obstructing the police in the investigation of the crime.

Removing the sticky tape from the back of the crucifix I fastened the key to the inside of the lid and secured the box by pulling down the hasps. The crucifix I returned to its place on the wall. My next step was to swathe the box in the malodorous dressing-gown which hung on the back of the door; the anonymous bundle could be passed off if necessary to the housekeeper as items which Desmond required in hospital. I turned to survey the room for the last time. All was in order. Switching out the light I padded downstairs, slipped outside to my car and stuffed the bundle in the boot. Then I sped noiselessly back indoors, drank the cold tea waiting for me in the study and summoned the housekeeper to say that the Archdeacon would be in touch with her shortly. As I finally made my escape I noticed that the two police cars were still parked outside the church and the young constable was still on duty in the porch.

I drove erratically home to the Cathedral Close.

7

"CAN I take a peep?" said Lyle in a voice which suggested she expected the answer "yes," and when I refused to open the box she even had the nerve to exclaim: "Oh darling, don't be so Victorian!"

"If being Victorian means wanting to protect someone I love from a vile experience, then yes, I'm a Victorian and proud of it!"

We were standing in the drawing-room of the South Canonry while my indescribable haul from the vicarage sat on the coffee-table between us. Lyle had removed the malodorous dressing-gown and incarcerated it in the washing machine. Around us the comfortable armchairs and sofa, all newly upholstered, seemed so luxurious that I wanted to close my eyes to blot them out. Guilt gnawed at me again as I remembered the furnishings of Desmond's slum, and I said more violently than I intended: "Pornography degrades the human spirit—literally de-grades, drags it down to a subhuman level. Desmond's a good man. I've just witnessed his degradation, and I don't want you to share that experience."

"All right, I understand—but don't get so upset that you lose sight of the main issue! Is this stuff connected with the assault or isn't it?"

"It's only connected in the sense that an indulgence in pornography could lead on to the desire for a sexual encounter. But in my opinion . . ." I delivered myself of the opinion that there was no other connection before speculating: "I think I can guess what happened. Desmond goes up to London every couple of months to see his spiritual director at the Fordite HQ, and I suspect that when he became overstrained he started visiting the wrong kind of bookshop. After all, he knew where to go. He'd trodden that road before."

"So much for spiritual directors! Obviously this one was dozing."

"They can't always get it right, and if Desmond was too guilt-ridden to talk honestly—"

The telephone rang.

"That'll be Malcolm," I said at once and grabbed the receiver before Lyle could reach it. "South Canonry."

"Hullo, Dad!" said Charley brightly in London. "Enjoying a quiet day off?"

"Oh yes! Savouring every moment!"

"Who is it?" Lyle was muttering at my side.

"Charley. Darling, could you mix me a very dark whisky-and-soda? I feel I need reviving."

". . . utterly stupefied," Charley was saying at the other end of the line.

"Sorry, I missed the first part of that sentence. Could you—"

"I said I'm utterly stupefied because old Aysgarth seems to have gone round the bend."

"Good heavens, not again!" This mention of my old enemy certainly diverted me from Desmond. "What's he been doing?"

"He rang me up this morning, said he was going to be in London for the day and invited me to have lunch with him."

"But how extraordinary!" The Dean and I were hardly in the habit of taking each other's sons out to lunch.

"Wait—it gets even odder. Once we were swilling away at the Athenaeum he said he wanted to see me because it was Samson's birthday."

"What?"

"I know, I was stunned too, nearly fell off my chair. I didn't think he knew anything about me and Samson."

"But he doesn't!"

"Well, he certainly thinks he does. He told me that when he visited Samson on his deathbed in 1945, Samson asked him to look after not only me but Michael too—that was when you were still a POW, of course, and Mum was going through her phase of thinking you were dead. Now just you listen to this: Samson told Aysgarth that Mum was his—Samson's—*daughter!* I nearly passed out. I did try to speak but all that came out was a strangulated grunt—which was probably just as well as I was so pole-axed that I might have blurted out that Mum was Samson's mistress, not his daughter—or could she conceivably have been both? For one ghastly moment I found myself wondering—"

"No, of course Lyle wasn't his daughter!"

"But then why did Samson tell that whopper on his deathbed?"

"He wanted to make sure there was a man who would take a paternal interest in you if I failed to come home from the war. That meant he had to explain why he was so involved with your welfare, but naturally he couldn't bear Aysgarth to know you were the product of his adultery. So with your mother's connivance he cooked up this story that she was his illegitimate daughter, the result of a wild oat sown before he was ordained, and that in consequence you and Michael were his grandsons. What exactly did you say?"

"I stammered: 'Honestly, Mr. Dean, it's a subject I never discuss,' and he said soothingly: 'I've never discussed it with anyone myself, but I just wanted you to know that I knew.' He said he'd meant to have a chat with me ever since my ordination, but because you and he were on bad terms he'd never got around to it. Then he got sentimental—he went on and on and on about how wonderful Samson was—"

"They were good friends. You must allow him his rose-tinted spectacles." To my extreme relief the doorbell rang in the distance. "Hold on," I said, and added to Lyle who was approaching with my whisky-and-soda: "I'll answer that—it's bound to be Malcolm. Have a word with Charley."

"Not if he's talking about Stephen Aysgarth and that idiotic lie I let myself condone back in 1945."

The doorbell rang a second time.

"I'll phone you back," I said to Charley and hung up. Grabbing the glass from Lyle I took a large gulp of whisky and headed into the hall where I set down the glass on the chest before flinging wide the front door.

But it was not my archdeacon whom I found waiting in the porch.

"Surprise!" chorused my uninvited visitors, and to my dismay I found myself confronting not only Michael but his American girlfriend, Miss Dinkie Kauffman.

8

MICHAEL WAS by this time almost twenty-five. During the 1960s he wore his curly hair longer and longer, and by early 1965 it had begun to crawl well below his collar at the nape of his neck. Having curly hair myself I know that it has to be kept short if one wishes to appear tidy, and

Michael looked, in my opinion, a mess. I had hoped his employers might order him to the barbers, but recently there had been abundant evidence that the BBC had lost its nerve and succumbed to the anarchy of the *zeitgeist;* one hardly expected all shows to be as innocuous as the film *Mary Poppins* but recent satirical programmes had been both tasteless and unpleasant while experimental drama had reached the point where all such experiments should have been terminated at birth.

On that evening I thought Michael's hair was more of a mess than ever and I detested the way he underlined the mess by sporting sideboards. Lyle had said recently that they made him look sexy. I had said they made him look like a spiv, but I knew I could not voice this opinion to Michael for fear of triggering a row—and since the fragile truce engineered by Lyle the previous Christmas, we were all supposed to be living happily ever after.

Michael had dark eyes, shaped like his mother's, and he also had her resolute, subtle mouth. Our voices had once been so similar that we had often been mistaken for each other on the telephone, but at some time during the early 1960s his voice had acquired mid-Atlantic inflections which had been enhanced when he had started to "go out" with Dinkie. (How I detest euphemisms for immorality!) When I had complained about the sheer phoniness of these vocal affectations I was told I was a typical middle-class dinosaur who had become a father too late in life to understand anyone under thirty. This could well have been true but no active man on the wrong side of sixty likes to hear himself described in such disparaging terms. However, Michael had promised Lyle last Christmas that he would never call me a dinosaur again.

It was a pity he had not also promised to end his association with his American mistress. Miss Kauffman, whose first name (I cannot describe it as Christian) was Lurlene, had called herself Dinkie at an early age as the result of misunderstanding the slurred speech of her inebriated mother. The latter was supposed to have held out her empty glass with the plea: "Dinkie darling!" and her offspring, obediently refilling the glass with gin, had not realised until much later that the word "dinkie" had referred to the drink. One always had to remember, when contemplating Miss Kauffman, that her early life had been far from ideal.

As she stood on my doorstep on that February evening in 1965 she could have been any age between eighteen and thirty, although she had taken care to tell Michael she was two years his junior. She had a figure which she was careful to expose in all weathers, and as soon as she took off her coat I saw that the hemline of her tight black skirt lay well above her knees while the V-neck of her tight black sweater plunged recklessly in the direction of her navel. In short, she looked like the tart she was, and Michael had been keeping her for some months at his flat in London. I had assumed in the beginning that he had picked her up on the street, but had learnt later to my astonishment that he had met her through his friend Marina Markhampton, the notorious young socialite whose grandmother, Lady Markhampton, was one of my neighbours in the Cathedral Close. Apparently Dinkie had once had a temporary job in the art gallery where Marina worked, and Marina, spotting someone who would amuse her fast set, had taken a fancy to her.

After the job in the art gallery had ceased, Dinkie had made no attempt to find other employment. Uneducated, culturally illiterate and vulgar beyond belief, she walked as if parodying Marilyn Monroe and spoke in a purring voice which injected even the most innocent statement with a sexual innuendo. Michael, of course, thought she was quite wonderful.

"Hot news!" he was exclaiming to Lyle, who by this time had joined us in the hall. "And I've gone AWOL from the Beeb for twenty-four hours to break it to you!"

"We would have called you," purred Miss Dinkie, "but we wanted it to be a lovely, lovely surprise!"

I saw Lyle's smile freeze. I myself was aware of shivering lightly, like a tree ruffled by a Siberian breeze, and as the chill of understanding smote me, Michael slipped his arm around Dinkie's waist and announced in triumph: "We're going to get married!"

I could almost hear Lyle thinking: over my dead body. But all she said in an emotional voice was: "Darling!" This struck me as an immensely clever response, astonished, affectionate but committing her to nothing.

"Well, well, well!" I said, aching with rage behind my most charming smile. I tried and failed to utter some other banality, and Lyle, seeing I was in difficulties, immediately made the decision to ease me from the scene.

"Well, don't just stand there, Charles!" she said to me. "Plunge down into the cellar and get the champagne! Now, Michael, take Dinkie into the drawing-room to get warm while I go into the kitchen to inspect the deep-freeze. We must all have a lavish dinner!"

This cunning manoeuvre enabled us to wind up together within seconds behind the closed kitchen door.

"What on earth are we going to do?" I was in despair.

"Don't worry, leave this entirely to me."

"I just can't understand how he could possibly—"

"There are two explanations: either he's doing it to drive you round the bend—which doesn't seem likely since you've done nothing lately to infuriate him—or else she's got her claws sunk so deeply into him that he can't work out how to shake her off and he's come down here for help."

"You mean she might be pregnant?"

"Good heavens, no, that type would never put her figure at risk! But she might have made Michael think she was."

"I suppose it's just possible that she could be genuinely in love with him—"

"Love? That sort of cheap floozie wouldn't even know the meaning of the word! She'd think it meant having sex three times a day."

"But could Michael perhaps be genuinely in love with her?"

"Don't be idiotic, Charles—how could he be when he's lived with her long enough to exhaust her very limited possibilities? Now don't panic—this is what we do: first of all we serve champagne and exude charm. Then once the champagne's disappeared I'll bear Dinkie off to my sitting-room and—oh good heavens, there goes the doorbell again!"

"That really must be Malcolm. Shall I—"

"Yes, you whisk Malcolm into your study and I'll tackle the love-birds single-handed. On second thoughts I can probably handle them better if you're not there."

We parted, she descending the cellar steps to fetch the champagne, I hurrying back across the hall. Once more I flung wide the door to welcome my archdeacon, and once more I found myself receiving a far from pleasant surprise.

My next visitor proved to be Dido Aysgarth, the wife of my enemy, the Dean.

9

NO ONE knew why Aysgarth, a clergyman riddled with ambition, had jeopardised his career in 1945 in order to marry an eccentric society woman whose one talent was to offend the maximum amount of people in the minimum amount of time at any social gathering burdened by her presence, but Lyle had long since decided that he had been temporarily unhinged by sex. However, I had never been satisfied by this prosaic explanation because I had never been able to regard Dido as sexually attractive. She had a flat chest and legs like matchsticks; it was fortunate that she was now too old to risk following the current fashion of revealing the knees. Her bumpy nose, broken as the result of a hunting accident in her youth, was set in a face where other irregular features conjured up images of nutcrackers and hatchets. But having catalogued her bad points, I must hastily add that she dressed in excellent taste and always looked exceedingly smart. Let me also add, to do her justice, that her brain, although untrained by a formal education in a school, was razor-sharp. Finally I must praise her loyalty to her husband and admire the fact that even in the most adverse circumstances her devotion to him had never wavered.

"Charles my dear!" she exclaimed, sweeping over the threshold before I could even open my mouth to invite her in. "Do forgive me for dropping in on you without warning, but as soon as I heard the ghastly news about Desmond Wilton—that peculiar woman Miss Baines phoned me to say she found the body—well, no, to be strictly accurate I must confess it was Tommy Fitzgerald she phoned—you know she's his charlady—but I happened to be calling on Tommy at the time to discuss the arrangements for feeding the visiting choir after the 'St. Matthew Passion,' and as he was making tea when the phone rang I answered it—the phone, I mean—and of course Miss Baines recognised my voice because I sorted out her varicose veins with the hospital after they tried to tell her there was a two-year waiting list—"

"Come into the study, Dido. Can I offer you a drink?"

"No, no, quite unnecessary, thank you—was that Michael's car I saw parked in the drive?"

"Well, as a matter of fact—"

"I can't imagine why young men like sports cars, so draughty in winter, but Michael's only twenty-four, isn't he—or is it twenty-five?—and still has quite a lot of growing up to do, I daresay, particularly in regard to women—and quite frankly, Charles, if I may be absolutely candid—and as you know, I'm famed for my candour—if one of my stepsons was mixed up with a foreign drug-addict I'd put my foot down in the firmest possible way—but of course you're trying to be Christian, aren't you, which is always so terribly difficult, just as Browning says in the poem. Well, as I was saying—"

"Do sit down, Dido."

"No, I won't stay, Charles, I mustn't interrupt your family gathering for more than a minute, but I felt I simply had to tell you, as soon as I heard the news about poor dear Desmond, that I have it on the best authority from a very good friend in London that she saw Desmond at Piccadilly Circus on a Saturday night last month, and of course you know what that means, don't you, because no respectable person would normally be seen dead in Piccadilly Circus on a Saturday night."

"In that case what was your friend doing there?"

"She'd just left a theatre on Shaftesbury Avenue."

"Maybe Desmond was also emerging from an evening at the theatre."

"Not with a young man in black leather, my dear. And my friend, who only wears glasses for reading and who met Desmond years ago when she did charity work for his East End mission—my friend tells me they were less than fifty yards from the public lavatories."

"My dear Dido!"

"I'm only speaking with the welfare of the Church in mind, Charles, and of course we all know Desmond was thrown out of the London diocese after being convicted of soliciting in a public lavatory—"

"He was not convicted. He was arrested along with the drunk who took a swipe at him, but he wasn't charged and the incident isn't generally known. I don't know who could have told you about it, but—"

"Oh my dear, we all know, I can't think how you convinced yourself that you could ever keep *that* kind of fact a secret, and to be absolutely candid, Charles, I can't imagine how you ever dared take him on, particularly since you're so rabid on the subject of homosexuals—"

I tried to repudiate this slander but there was no chance. Dido had merely paused to draw a quick breath and had no intention of being interrupted.

"—but of course I do realise how soft you are on clergymen who have had nervous breakdowns, and the softness is your way of compensating, isn't it, for that utterly *ruthless* line you take on immorality—no, no, don't think I'm criticising you, my dear, quite the reverse, thank God at least one bishop takes a strong stand against immorality, that's what I say! I've no time for all this silly permissiveness, and I said right from the beginning that Bishop John Robinson was up the creek when he spouted all that rubbish about a New Morality and gave silly young girls the scope to wreck their lives and go down the drain—and talking of going down the drain, I do hope poor dear Desmond can be eased into retirement as soon as possible, because choirboys will be the next step, won't it, and then you'll wish you'd acted as soon as you knew he'd been seen in Piccadilly Circus on a Saturday night with a young man dressed in black leather. And talking of black leather—"

The door of the study opened and in walked Lyle.

"Dido!" she exclaimed. "I heard your voice as I came out of the kitchen—how sweet of you to call, but you must excuse Charles now because Michael's paid us a surprise visit and they're dying to talk to each other."

Almost panting with relief I escaped into the hall only to realise that the last person I wanted to face at that moment was Michael. I was still inwardly shuddering as the result of Dido's reference to a "foreign drug-addict," for I had long lived in fear that Michael, moving in Marina Markhampton's fast London set, would dabble in drugs and wreck his respectable future with the BBC. I wondered what evidence Dido had for labelling Dinkie a drug-addict, but unfortunately I could not reassure myself with the thought that this was another remark generated by Dido's taste for exaggeration. Dido could well know more about Dinkie than I did. Her two eldest stepsons—the sons of Aysgarth's first marriage—also belonged to Marina Markhampton's set, and although they were both now married they often visited their father's home and could well have talked frankly about Marina's less presentable friends.

I was still trying to convince myself that Michael was no more likely than Christian or Norman Aysgarth to dabble in drugs, when the doorbell rang yet again. Hardly daring to respond I eased the door open six inches and peered out to identify my next visitor.

It was Malcolm.

"Thank God!" I said sincerely, and scooped him across the threshold.

10

"WHAT HAPPENED with the police?"

"It's all right, everything's under control. Heavens, Charles, you look shattered! What's going on here?"

"Oh, nothing special, just all hell breaking loose. Quick, come into the kitchen before you get buttonholed by Dido Aysgarth—she's just told me that Desmond's been seen near the Piccadilly Circus public lavatories on a Saturday night in the company of a young man dressed in black leather."

"That woman's round the bend!"

"I only wish I could be as certain of that as you are. Drink?"

"Make it a double."

We withdrew rapidly to the kitchen where I took a new bottle of scotch from the crate on the larder floor and extracted two glasses from a cupboard.

"Charles, you don't believe this ridiculous story of Dido's, do you?"

"I'm trying my hardest not to, but you know what a nose she has for scandal. She even told me everyone knew about the disaster which ended Desmond's career in the London diocese."

"Who's 'everyone'?"

"I dread to think. The Dean and Chapter?"

"At most, I'd say. No one knows in that parish, Charles—if they did, I'd have had people coming to me to express their anxiety. And how on earth could the story have reached the Dean and Chapter? Do you think some gossipy monk at the Fordite HQ spilled the beans to Tommy Fitzgerald during one of his retreats?"

"I'm sure no Fordite would ever have been so indiscreet. Much more likely that someone in the Bishop of London's office talked and the word got back to Aysgarth through his former colleagues at Westminster Abbey and Church House. After all, apart from the Fordite monks only the Bishop's office knew—the Bishop nipped the scandal in the bud."

"It was a brilliant piece of nipping. If he hadn't been sitting next to the Police Commissioner at that Mansion House dinner—"

"Talking of the police, how did you tame Parker and Locke?"

"Oh, that was no problem at all! I became very earnest and confidential, swore Desmond was a most devout Anglo-Catholic and assured them that I'd be among the first to know if he hadn't always lived a blameless life. (Well, I was, wasn't I?) Of course Parker and Locke believed me—the great advantage of telling the truth is that one's so much more likely to sound convincing."

"But did the police then decide it was a motiveless crime?"

"Yes, they started speculating that the attacker was a Langley Bottom lout stoned on LSD."

"Surely LSD hasn't reached Starbridge!"

"Oh, nothing's sacred nowadays! Anyway I fed that theory to the hack from the *Starbridge Evening News* who turned up at the hospital just as I was leaving and he was thrilled, said he'd do an exposé on the Starbridge drug scene—"

"But there *is* no Starbridge drug scene!"

"There will be tomorrow. Anyway, I'd just finished making the hack's day when the chaplain turned up—apparently he'd been collared on one of the wards by some bereaved relatives and by the time he'd sorted them out—"

"I wondered where he'd got to. Did you tell him to watch Desmond?"

"Like a hawk, yes, and he said he'd arrange for the nurse on duty to contact him as soon as Desmond recovers consciousness, but luckily they've left a woman police constable at the bedside, not that thug Sergeant Locke, so at least Desmond won't be browbeaten as soon as he opens his eyes. At that point I finally managed to tear myself away from the hospital and rush to Langley Bottom, but the housekeeper had gone home so I was unable to get into the vicarage. Did you manage to get in earlier, and if so—good heavens, Charles, what is it, what have I said?"

"Ye gods and little fishes!" I shouted, leaping to my feet. "I've left that unlocked box in the drawing-room with Michael and Dinkie!"

As if on cue Lyle entered the kitchen with the box itself in her hands.

11

"I HID it in the dining-room when you went to answer Michael's ring at the door," she said, setting the box on the kitchen table as I slumped down with relief on the nearest chair.

"Dare I ask what's inside?" enquired Malcolm, eyeing the box with dread.

"Desmond's bedtime reading," said Lyle, confirming his worst fears.

Malcolm went so pale that the freckles stood out starkly across his cheekbones.

I had first met Malcolm after the war on a course designed for army chaplains who were returning to civilian life. I had been asked to give a lecture on the theology currently fashionable, and afterwards Malcolm proved to be the truculent member of the audience who sat at the back and asked awkward questions. At that time he had red hair and an impudent look. Later in the canteen he apologised, explaining that he was only taking the course because he had been ordered to do so by his bishop and that he considered it a waste of time to listen to theology when he could be out and about preaching the Gospel. I liked both his honesty and his zeal. Not everyone is born to be a theologian, and certainly not everyone is born to appreciate the Neo-Orthodox theology of Karl Barth.

Word reached me by chance in the early 1950s that Malcolm had raised some market-town from the dead in the Starbridge diocese, but I never dreamed our careers would intersect. Then in 1957 I accepted the bishopric and found I had inherited an unsatisfactory archdeacon. As soon as I had freed myself from this millstone, I offered the archdeaconry to Malcolm.

The archdeaconry was attached to the city parish of St. Martin's-in-Cripplegate, but Malcolm had curates to help him run the parish while he roamed his section of the diocese on my behalf. The archdeacon is by tradition "the bishop's eye," the henchman who keeps watch on all the clergy and churches in the archdeaconry and tells the bishop everything he needs to know. The diocese was divided into two archdeaconries, but the other archdeacon lived in the port of Starmouth forty miles away so I saw less of him, particularly since I had appointed a suffragan bishop to supervise the south of the diocese for me. Meanwhile Malcolm patrolled the north. The exercise of power had made him a trifle bossy in his manner, but he remained devout, diligent and efficient. I relied on him in my professional life almost as much as I relied on Lyle in my private life, and considered him one of my most successful appointments.

"Am I right in thinking," he was saying morosely "that the parish of Langley Bottom has finally driven its vicar completely round the bend?"

"I hate to intervene at this point," said Lyle, "but Charles, we're all waiting for you to join us for a drink. If you could just leave Malcolm alone for ten minutes to browse through the box—"

"I'll be along in a moment."

Lyle withdrew, trying not to look exasperated.

As soon as we were alone Malcolm heaved up the hasps, flung back the lid and demanded: "How bad is it?"

"Appalling."

"Within the meaning of the Act?"

"Not being a legal expert on pornography, I'm not sure. What do you think?"

Malcolm efficiently inspected the cover of each magazine and flicked through the collection of photographs. His final verdict was: "No children or animals. All this might set the *News of the World* alight, but it's not going to raise any eyebrows among the vice-squad."

"I certainly don't believe the police would have any interest in prosecuting an elderly man who has no connection with a pornography ring and no interest in corrupting minors. But could there be a connection between all this stuff and what's just happened to Desmond?"

"Where's the link?"

"Exactly. There isn't one, so in my opinion there's no need to turn the box over to the police, but—"

"Good heavens, no—quite unnecessary!"

"—but it's absolutely vital that in our desire to protect Desmond and the Church we don't wind up obstructing the police in the execution of their duty. We've got to be very careful here."

"Of course, but if there's nothing in this box which links Desmond with any particular man, the odds are that the criminal's a lunatic and has no connection with Desmond's sex-life whatsoever. Let's just wait, Charles, and see where the police get to. If you ask me, we're in the clear: we're not withholding evidence that Desmond knew his assailant."

This opinion certainly chimed with mine, but I found I was still worried. "The trouble is there's still a possibility that he was being blackmailed. Maybe he just didn't keep the letters in this box—maybe they're hidden away somewhere else in the house—"

"I doubt it. Charles, I'd be very surprised if Desmond was being blackmailed and I'll tell you why: he'd crack up almost straight away as the result of the strain and by this time I'd have received reports from the churchwardens that Father Wilton was no longer able to celebrate mass. Desmond just doesn't have the emotional stamina to sustain a double-life with a blackmailer."

This assessment had the ring of truth. I finally began to relax.

"I'll take this stuff home," said Malcolm as he closed the box and stood up. "The sooner it's burnt the better."

Automatically I said: "No, you can't burn it."

Malcolm's long nose quivered as if he scented trouble. "Why not?"

"Because this is Desmond's property, taken from his house without his permission, and we have no right to destroy it. What I have to do is confront him with the box, explain exactly why I felt obliged to search his bedroom, and apologise for the invasion of his privacy. Then I must make it clear I trust him to do the burning himself."

"But my dear Charles, I can see that's a magnificent example of Christian behaviour, but is it really appropriate for a bishop? No, wait a minute—hang on, just let me rephrase that—"

"Please do." I started to laugh. I suppose I was finally suffering a nervous reaction to the crisis.

"Well, what I'm trying to say is this: of course you have to behave like a Christian, but do you necessarily have to behave like an English gentleman with an overdeveloped sense of fair play? A bishop has to show compassion for sinners, we all know that, but don't let's lose sight of the sin! Personally I think you should be quite tough with Desmond here and feel no obligation to treat him with kid gloves. After all, supposing the police had found this box? We'd all have been up to our necks in scandal!"

"But they didn't. And we're not. And I don't see why you should think I'm glossing over the sin by giving Desmond a soft option—it's not a soft option at all. His punishment will lie in the fact that I know what's been going on."

"Very well," said Malcolm with reluctance, "but meanwhile what are you going to do with the box? You can't leave it lying around the South Canonry! Supposing Miss Peabody finds it?"

"By all means let's protect Miss Peabody from a potentially heart-stopping encounter, but isn't there an equal risk that your wife and daughters will stumble across it at the vicarage?"

"In my study there's a cupboard which locks and only I have the key." Malcolm was always prepared for every archidiaconal emergency. "The most urgent question," he said as he tucked the box under his arm, "is what we're going to do with that church while Desmond's incapacitated. I can rustle up poor old Father Pitt to celebrate a daily mass, but he's half-blind now and so lame that he almost has to be carried to the altar—I couldn't ask him to substitute for Desmond for more than a week and the Sunday services might well finish him off altogether. And what are we going to do with that parish in the long run? The whole place is a nightmare."

Before I could reply Lyle returned to the room again. "Charles, I really don't think you can postpone Michael any longer but at least you don't have to face Dinkie at the moment—she's upstairs waiting for me to begin our tête-à-tête in my sitting-room."

"But what do I say to Michael?"

"Oh, anything—ask him about the BBC. He's working on a production of *The Cherry Orchard.*"

"Is that the play where everyone goes around sighing: 'Moscow! Moscow!'?" said Malcolm, temporarily diverted from the nightmare of Langley Bottom.

"No," I said. "That's the *Three Sisters*—which reminds me of the three witches in *Macbeth*—which in turn reminds me of Dido. Has she gone?"

"Yes, ages ago. Awful woman! No wonder Stephen Aysgarth drinks like a fish."

"Well, at least we don't have to worry about Aysgarth at the moment," said Malcolm. "All quiet on that particular front. Lyle, I do apologise for interrupting your family party, but with any luck I'll be your last interruption tonight."

As if to confound him the telephone began to ring again.

"I'll answer that," I said at once, seizing any excuse to postpone my conversation with Michael, and ignoring Lyle's exasperated expression I hurried from the kitchen to my study.

12

"SOUTH CANONRY," I said into the receiver as I sat down in the chair behind my desk.

"Hullo, old boy, it's Jack!"

I was so disorientated, both by the Desmond disaster and by Michael's arrival, that I suffered a moment of amnesia. "Jack who?"

"My God, the Bishop's gone senile! Charles, it's your distinguished friend of far too many years' standing, the editor—"

"—of *The Church Gazette.* Sorry, Jack—temporary aberration. I hope you're not planning to cancel our lunch tomorrow."

"Far from it, old chap, calling to confirm—and to say that I've got the most shattering piece of gossip for you. Order a brandy in anticipation if you arrive at the Athenaeum before I do."

"What gossip?"

"Oh, I couldn't possibly reveal it over the phone! I just wanted to make sure you rushed panting to London."

"Does it have anything to do with Piccadilly Circus?"

"Piccadilly Circus? No, I seem to have missed that one. Hang on while I find a pencil and paper—"

"See you tomorrow," I said. "Sorry—got to dash." But having replaced the receiver I found I still could not face the ordeal of confronting Michael. For some minutes I lingered, speculating about Jack's piece of gossip and then brooding on Desmond's disaster, but finally I remembered I had promised to call Charley back. At once I put through the call.

"It's me again," I said as he answered on the first ring. "Sorry about the interval. Are you all right? I hope Aysgarth didn't upset you with all that talk of Samson."

"No, but I admit I'm bothered about something else. Are you by any chance going to be in London this week?"

"I'm lunching with Jack Ryder tomorrow before chairing a committee meeting at Church House. Why don't we meet for tea at four-thirty downstairs at Fortnum's?"

Charley was pleased by this suggestion and seemed to think this marked the end of the telephone call, but I hung on, unable to resist the temptation to delay my interview with Michael. "Any other news?" I enquired hopefully.

"No—except that I've just heard the most awful piece of gossip about Michael. I bumped into Eddie Hoffenberg today and he told me that Venetia had told him that Marina had told her that Michael was actually talking of *marrying* that ghastly tart of his! Could he really be so fantastically unhinged?"

The door of my study crashed open and Michael stormed into the room.

IV

"It is extraordinary how we betray our friends. Or (as we think in our conceited minds) it is not extraordinary at all: for we, of course, are superior persons, viewing mankind from a great height, and awarding our acquaintances praise and blame with poetic justice, if not with justice, anyhow with such charm, that even malice ought to be forgiven us."

AUSTIN FARRER
Warden of Keble College, Oxford, 1960–1968
A CELEBRATION OF FAITH

I

AS THE door shuddered on its hinges I said quickly into the telephone: "Sorry, got to go—see you tomorrow." Meanwhile Michael had swept to my desk and was standing in front of me with his fists clenched and his arms held rigidly at his sides as if he were barely able to restrain himself from aiming a punch at my jaw.

This was clearly a situation which demanded all my pastoral skills, but I had long since discovered that during confrontations with Michael my professional experience was of no use to me; Michael knew at once when he was being treated as a pastoral "case" and became more unpleasant than ever. On the other hand all my attempts to treat him affectionately as a son fell on stony ground. It was as if Michael was never satisfied until he had needled me into losing my temper, and the more I slaved at the task of keeping calm the more he slaved at the task of provoking me.

I repressed the urge to bolt from the room and shout in despair for Lyle.

"Have you quite finished?" said Michael.

"I'm sorry, it's been chaotic here tonight—"

"I bring my fiancée down here to announce our engagement and you can't even find the time to drink a glass of champagne with us!"

"I really am very sorry—"

"I don't want you being sorry! I just want you to do something halfway decent such as saying: 'Congratulations!' If it had been Charley who had arrived here with his fiancée, you'd have been beside yourself with excitement!"

"Not if the fiancée were Dinkie," I said before I could stop myself, and as Michael showed signs of extreme rage I said very rapidly: "Now calm down and be sensible—you must realise that this kind of aggressive behaviour does neither of us any good. What happened to your new year's resolution to reform?"

"You've just wiped it out by continuing to disapprove of everything I do! There's no pleasing you, is there? I live in sin with Dinkie and you storm and rage until Mum shuts you up, but when I try to do the moral thing and marry, you sulk and skulk in corners!"

"If I'm lukewarm about your news it's only because I don't think she can make you happy."

"If you married a pregnant woman, why shouldn't I do the same?"

"Are you trying to tell me—"

"Yes. She's pregnant."

"Are you sure?"

"God, what a *bloody* thing to say!"

"I'm merely trying to uncover the truth!"

"The truth is that I'm in the process of saving Dinkie just as you saved Mum! Dinkie's had an awful life, she's vulnerable, she's lonely, she needs a lot of love and security—and by living with her and looking after her, I've actually *done her good.* So if you think I'm just an immoral bastard screwing her for kicks—"

"Does she take drugs?"

"Of course not!" But the denial was too fervent to be plausible, and when he saw I was unconvinced he added quickly: "Not hard drugs. Just pot occasionally. But everyone does that nowadays."

"Everyone most certainly does not! And I won't tolerate any drug-taking under this roof!"

"You don't tolerate anything under this roof!"

"I don't tolerate self-destructive behaviour, and you wouldn't respect me if I did!"

"I'd respect you if you could admit the truth—which is that by living with Dinkie I've actually done her good!"

"If you really wanted to do that pathetic young woman good," I said, "you'd love her without exploiting her. Obviously you need to justify your immorality by seeing yourself as a hero, but Dinkie's not marrying you because you're heroic—she's marrying you because you're the first man who's ever been fool enough to propose!"

Lyle walked into the room just as Michael began to hurl unprintable abuse at me.

2

"IT'S SUDDENLY occurred to me," she said to Michael as he at once fell silent, "that it might be better if you dined out. In fact I believe Dinkie's now keen to do so. We've just finished our little talk together in my sitting-room."

Michael was confused. "But what did you say to her?"

"I pointed out that a meal from the deep-freeze would be rather an anti-climax after champagne and I told her about the wonderful food at the Crusader. No, don't worry about money—dinner's on us, of course, and your father will pay for your night at a hotel too."

"But Mum—"

"Darling, it was wonderful to see you but let's be absolutely clear-eyed for a moment, shall we? You know you can't stay the night here—you'll want to share a room with Dinkie and that would be wrong because your father's forbidden it and since it's his house he's entitled to make the rules. So you'll have to go to a hotel anyway, and although I could give you both dinner I'm not sure that would be a wise move. Just think: if you and your father are quarrelling now, after only five minutes together, how on earth could you survive a full hour in the dining-room? So darling, bearing in mind all these awful truths, don't you think it would be much nicer for Dinkie if you dined at . . . no, not the Crusader. Too square. How about a romantic candle-lit dinner at La Belle Époque in Chasuble Lane? Go up to my sitting-room to have a word with her about it."

"Okay, but—"

"And never forget, darling, that your father and I both desperately want you to be happy. Don't we, Charles?"

"Yes," I said.

Michael ignored me, gave her a look in which suspicion and relief were fleetingly intermingled, and withdrew from the room without further argument. I promptly collapsed into the nearest chair and covered my face with my hands.

"Where's your current drink, Charles?" said Lyle briskly. "So far I've found one in the hall and one in the kitchen, neither of them finished. Are there any more?"

"No." I let my hands fall. "What happened between you and Dinkie?"

"Oh, she was no trouble at all. I dealt with her very quickly."

Sheer admiration enabled me to exclaim: "How?"

"I said: 'How wonderful of you to want to marry Michael even though he'll never have a penny more than he earns as a producer—such a shame the BBC are so stingy to their employees!' and she said: 'But he'll have lots of money in the end, won't he, because the Bishop's rich.' At which point I said: 'Oh no, my dear, we don't even own our own house, and as the Church is even stingier than the BBC the Bishop's constantly worrying about how to make both ends meet.' "

"But my capital—my private income—Michael must have told her—"

"Oh, I just said it was almost all gone. All right, I know that was a fib, but if the Jesuits can say 'the ends justify the means' I don't see why I can't do the same—"

"But what end did you eventually reach?"

"The one we want. After I'd trapped Dinkie into revealing her mercenary motive I said kindly: 'If I were you I'd take an interest in Robert Welbeck. He's much the richest young man in Marina Markhampton's set, and has an income which I happen to know is over twenty thousand pounds a year.' I paused to let that sink in and then I added: 'Net.' "

I was so dazed that all I could say was: "Is that true or false?"

"True. Dinkie was stunned. 'Gee, I had no idea!' she said, and I answered with immense sympathy: 'I'm afraid in England gentlemen don't talk about their incomes. So tiresome of them, isn't it?' We ended up sitting on the sofa together and chatting like lifelong friends."

Words finally failed me.

"Of course she tried to tell me she was pregnant," said Lyle as an afterthought, "but I soon got her to admit the pregnancy is mere wishful thinking. The situation's simply this: she's in her mid-twenties, time's ticking on and she knows she's got to get a husband before the eligible men start regarding her as a has-been. I think she does like Michael, I'll say that for her, and I'm sure she's grateful that he's given her free lodgings for so long, but the truth is she's exploiting his idealistic infatuation, and I'm sure that if he thinks she's been faithful to him, he's deceiving himself. God knows what she gets up to when he goes away on location to shoot the outdoor scenes for his dramas, but of course poor Michael, welded to his idealism, would have overlooked all the signs of infidelity."

"If she's been seeing other men while living with Michael she must be very disturbed." For the first time I caught a glimpse of Dinkie not as a stereotype but as a complex human being whose behaviour was more of a mystery than I had ever bothered to imagine. "I hope she doesn't start taking hard drugs when things don't work out as she wants," I said troubled. "I hope this isn't the beginning of a road to disaster."

"Oh, don't be so stupid, Charles, of course it isn't! The girl's a classic gold-digger, tough as old boots, and in the end she'll nail a rich husband

and live happily ever after. No chance of *that* one ever dying young of an overdose of heroin!"

I made no attempt to argue because by that time my thoughts had returned to Lyle's Machiavellian machinations. "Wait a moment," I said. "Isn't there something you've forgotten? How's Michael going to forgive you for pointing Dinkie at Robert Welbeck?"

"Very easily because I'm now ninety-nine percent sure that I was right and he came down here panting to be rescued from the whole ghastly mess. His idealistic dream of 'saving' Dinkie proved impossible to endure in reality . . . Charles, if you're going to light that cigarette you'd better do so before you tear it to pieces."

I took off my clerical collar before flicking open my lighter. "But if what you say is true," I said at last, "why was Michael so angry with me for opposing the marriage?"

"Because he knew you were right and he couldn't stand it."

"But why couldn't he have talked to me honestly?" I was in despair. Finally I said: "I just don't understand where I've gone wrong with that boy."

"Oh God."

"I've tried so hard to be a good father—"

"Look, you need a drink—and for heaven's sake don't abandon this one when it's only half-finished. Come and sit in the kitchen with me while I cook dinner."

I stood up obediently but I was still grappling with despair. "If only I could understand what it all means—"

"Darling, it means absolutely nothing except that parenthood can be hell and young men can make damned fools of themselves over tarts." She paused to give me a kiss. "It'll all come right," she said at last, and added with unexpected fierceness: "I'll *make* it all come right."

We were just embracing each other as if to crush out my misery when yet again the telephone started to ring.

3

THE HOSPITAL chaplain was ringing to let me know that Desmond had awoken from the anaesthetic but could remember nothing about the assault; the policewoman stationed at his bedside had departed and the doctor had again recommended that my next visit to the hospital should not take place until the following morning.

"I feel like murdering that instrument," said Lyle, eyeing the telephone as I replaced the receiver. "Leave it off the hook while we have dinner."

Before I could answer, Michael and Dinkie descended from Lyle's upstairs sitting-room and announced their intention of dining at Jock's Box, the local lorry-drivers' café, before departing for London—a statement which drew a wail of protest from Lyle who begged him to leave the long drive until the following day.

"I'd like to," said Michael, "but all I can afford is Jock's Box and the petrol to take us home. I'm not going to let Dad buy me off with a flash of his cheque-book after giving us such a bloody awful reception."

At that point I decided it would be best for all concerned if I withdrew from the scene so I retired to the cloakroom and did not emerge until I heard the front door close. Returning to the kitchen I demanded: "Did he allow you to write the cheque?"

"No, but as soon as you were out of the way dinner at La Belle Époque became affordable and he said they'd bed down at the nearest guest-house . . . Where's your drink?"

Retrieving my glass from the cloakroom I sat down again at the kitchen table and drank in a morose silence while Lyle cooked a mixed grill.

Afterwards as she washed up I distracted myself by switching on the television and staring at the news. Mr. Kosygin had received a cool welcome in Peking. Frightful things were happening as usual in Vietnam . . . I dozed, but it was hardly surprising that I was exhausted. Sexual intercourse was not, for a man of my age, the wisest activity to indulge in before trying to survive a diocesan disaster and a family débâcle.

"Worn out?" said Lyle as we toiled upstairs to bed.

But unfortunately my brief doze had revived me and my brain was active again. "I'm so worried about Desmond," I confessed. "I forgot to tell you that according to Dido he was seen recently in Piccadilly Circus with a young man in black leather."

"What absolute poppycock—a sexy young man in black leather would never look twice at poor old Desmond!"

"Poor old Desmond . . . There'll be a terrible interview when he's well enough to discuss the future—if I'm not careful he'll wind up utterly pulverised."

"Being pulverised is the least he deserves and I can't see why you should wallow in agony about it. Just offer him a full pension and boot him out on the grounds of ill-health. Personally I think he'll be damned lucky. In the old days he'd have been tried in the ecclesiastical courts and booted out with nothing."

"But I can't help feeling I've failed him in some way—"

"Rubbish! You took him on, didn't you, when no one else would touch him? If anyone's failed Desmond it's Malcolm, never noticing that Desmond was coming apart at the seams!"

"And who's responsible for Malcolm?"

"Charles, you *cannot* blame yourself for this disaster, I absolutely forbid it! Malcolm slipped up, that's all, but anyone can make a mistake, even a first-class archdeacon. Now stop agonising, stop thinking about wretched Desmond and *switch off.* Shall I run your bath for you?"

"Thank you," I said dryly, "but I think I still have enough strength to turn on the taps."

I had a long hot bath and repeated over and over to myself my mantra: "All things work together for good to them that love God." Then I tried to think about Hippolytus and the sexually lax Bishop Callistus, but the thought of sexual laxness only reminded me of Michael and the moral wasteland of the 1960s and the horrible changes which were being made in the name of progress. Abolishing the grammar schools, ignoring coffee-bar hooliganism, showering publicity on gangsters like the Kray brothers, turning bad singers into idols, embracing American culture without discrimination (and what on earth was America getting up to in Vietnam anyway?), permitting mass-mockery of distinguished institutions, encouraging the destruction of moral standards, campaigning for the legalisation of homosexuality . . . I started thinking of Desmond again. Hauling myself out of the bath I opened the medicine cabinet to retrieve my indigestion tablets.

In my dressing-room I said my prayers and tried to meditate on a paragraph written by St. Augustine, but my attention soon wandered. How would St. Augustine have dealt with Desmond? No full pension rights in those days, no financial sop to offer a fallen brother-in-Christ, but would St. Augustine have flinched from the prospect of a fearsome interview? Certainly not. Fortified by God's grace and supremely confident in his ability to administer a Christian justice he would have faced Desmond without turning a hair.

Feeling episcopally inadequate I returned to the bedroom.

"What was your meditation piece tonight?" asked Lyle.

"I chose a paragraph from *The City of God.*"

"Splendid! That must have cheered you up," said Lyle with relief, and returned to her library-book, a sex-offering by Françoise Sagan.

I picked up *The Rector of Justin* by Louis Auchincloss and began to toy with the fantasy of replacing the box in Desmond's wardrobe so that he would never know I had discovered his pornography.

"Can you really read that book upside down?" enquired Lyle with interest.

"No." I reversed the book before adding: "In the bath I was thinking about Hippolytus and Callistus. No doubt Hippolytus would have urged that Desmond be drummed out of the Church while Callistus would have made some excuse to keep him in."

"Callistus reminds me of Bishop Robinson being soppy about sex in *Honest to God.* Incidentally one of the women in the prayer-group said that excruciatingly boring book actually brought her to Christianity. Yet another example of how God moves in mysterious ways."

I said vaguely; "I must hear about that prayer-group sometime," and putting aside my book I switched off the light on my side of the bed. "If Callistus were alive today," I remarked, "he'd be like that new Bishop of Radbury, Leslie Sunderland. He has such an optimistic view of human nature that he believes everyone can be brought to Christian perfection by a rational outlook, a decent wage and the National Health Service. In fact when I see him tomorrow at my committee meeting I'm sure he'll—" I broke off and sat bolt upright in bed. "Ye gods and little fishes! I haven't looked at those graphs which I have to present to the committee!"

"Darling, SWITCH OFF. Leave all that until tomorrow—you can perfectly well study the graphs on the train to London. Do you want one of my sleeping pills?"

But I distrusted sleeping pills. They made me feel sluggish the next morning, and I needed my brain to be crystal clear from the moment I woke up. I tried to calm myself by another silent recitation of my mantra.

But I never derived much benefit from mantras. Too often I allowed my mind to drift away down theological avenues, and that night I started thinking of St. Paul, writing "All things work together for good" in his letter to the Romans—which had prompted Karl Barth to write his great commentary—which had led to Neo-Orthodox theology—which was a reaction to the liberal theology which had been prevalent before the First War—in which so much idealism had been destroyed—with the result that the atmosphere at the start of the last war had been very different—as I had realised when I had volunteered to be a chaplain—who had been captured at the fall of Tobruk—which had led to that POW camp—and to the concentration camp—which reminded me of Desmond—everyone degraded—cut off from God—in hell . . .

I slept.

4

IN MY dream I was back in the concentration camp. A naked Desmond was being flogged by Nazi guards while I stood by, powerless to stop them and hating God for not saving me from this undeserved and unbearable ordeal. After my capture at Tobruk in 1942 I had been confined to an ordinary POW camp, but in 1944 after I had assisted several men to escape I had been transferred to a far harsher environment. I had consoled myself at the time by thinking that at least I had not been summarily shot. Later I had come to believe that a quick death would have been preferable to dying by inches. But I had not died. The Allies had arrived and my ordeal had ended. The liberators had all looked so fleshy and pink. I could still see their appalled expressions.

I had wanted to thank God for the deliverance but the words had refused to come; he had been absent so long—or so I had thought—that I had forgotten how to talk to him, although of course I had always put up a front and gone through the motions of being a priest. That was what the army had required of me and that was what I had to do to the end, regardless of whether my faith was shattered or not. Later I had realised that this obstinate, distorted sense of purpose had helped to keep me alive, and later still I had seen that God had not been absent at all but had instead been speaking to others through the medium of my battered self, but these insights had not been immediately apparent to me.

After the war I had made sense of my suffering by classifying it as a "showing"—not of God but of the Devil. Or, to put the matter in less emotive terms, I had seen it as an unforgettable demonstration of what happened when men turned aside from the truth in order to embrace a false ideology. Indeed it was this sojourn in a world born of absolute lies which had made me resolve to battle all the harder for the absolute truths. Such a battle, I had reasoned, would justify my spared life, neutralise my survivor's guilt and simultaneously enable me to align myself with God as he worked to redeem all the suffering which people had inflicted on one another during the war.

So every time I now took a tough line on sin I felt I was in some small way redeeming the horror and agony I had witnessed in the past. My experiences in Starbridge in 1937 had given me a particular horror of sexual sin, but it was the concentration camp which had given me a horror of all evil. "The only thing necessary for the triumph of evil," Burke had written, "is for good men to do nothing." No one was ever going to catch *me* doing nothing. Mocking criticism in the press might hurt, television debates might inwardly reduce me to pulp, the scorn of the younger generation might continually sear me, but all that was of no consequence. What did such trivial distress matter when I recalled the appalling suffering of those who had died in the concentration camps? To whine that I hated being mocked for my views was unthinkable. The fact was that I had lived while others had died, and my job now was to bear witness to the truth no matter how much it cost me to do so.

In my dream the Nazi guards stopped flogging Desmond and began to castrate him. Sweating with horror I awoke just in time to stop myself shouting out loud and waking Lyle. In my dressing-room I switched on the light, sat down and began to shudder repeatedly with revulsion.

After a while I stopped shuddering but my distress, as memories of the camp streamed through my mind in an unstoppable tide, was so acute that I could only ease it by pacing up and down. I was just beginning to think I would never be able to dam this terrible cataract when Lyle looked in.

Before I could apologise for waking her she said severely: "All this pacing's very bad for you. Come back to bed instead and tell me how ghastly you're feeling."

Staggering into her arms I allowed myself to be steered back between the sheets.

"Which nightmare was it?"

"The flogging-castration. But this time the victim was Desmond."

"That wretched Desmond! Poor darling," said Lyle, giving me a lavish kiss.

I at last began to relax. Glancing at the clock I remarked: "I can hardly believe that only twelve hours ago we were here enjoying my afternoon off with no thought of either Desmond or Dinkie."

"I detest that girl."

"So do I. I can't understand why Michael finds her so attractive."

"Can't you, Charles? Honestly?"

"Honestly. I've never been attracted to stupid women."

"That's because you're reacting against your mother."

"Nonsense! It's because I want more from a woman than just sex!"

"How much more?"

I laughed.

Lyle gave me another lavish kiss and said: "That was a sterling performance you gave this afternoon."

"At my age I probably won't be able to repeat it for at least two weeks. I can't tell you how geriatric I felt this evening when I was watching the news."

"Then don't. Words like 'geriatric' bore me. And anyway, if you're really so enfeebled why were you pacing up and down just now like a sex-starved tiger at the zoo?"

"More like a mangy old lion in the first stages of senility!"

"All right, if you're really so past it, even after several hours' sleep, let's just blot out your nightmare by having a friendly cuddle."

"What a loathsome phrase!"

"I'd never have uttered it if you hadn't behaved as if you were ripe for a coffin! Honestly, British men are the limit sometimes—any Frenchman would be absolutely panting to demonstrate his vitality by this time!"

I tried a pant or two. I do in fact have some French blood flowing in my veins as the result of a Victorian indiscretion unrecorded in the Ashworth family tree, and Lyle had said once that if I had been born in France and escaped my middle-class English upbringing I might have become one of those Frenchmen who drink for hours in raffish Parisian cafés and supplement their long-suffering wives with a succession of pretty mistresses. My comment on this fantasy had been: "I'd have missed my golf and cricket," but Lyle had retorted: "No, you wouldn't—you'd have been much too busy elsewhere."

But I could not quite imagine a life in which I was not a clergyman of the Church of England, and I suspected that if I had been a French layman I would have long since expired as the result of sexual exhaustion and liver failure.

"You're better off married to an Englishman," I said to Lyle.

"I know, but I always adore being convinced."

I forgot Desmond and Dinkie, just as Lyle had known I would. I forgot the pornography in the present and the putrefaction in the past. I forgot I was a bishop. I even forgot I was a clergyman. I had entered a world in which only Lyle and I existed, a comforting cocoon in which I could feel secure and cherished, enfolded by a love which excluded all pain, all anxiety and all the baffling complexity of my current existence.

Later Lyle said: "I can never resist seducing you when you get as haggard and tormented as a nineteenth-century poet."

"I must try and be haggard and tormented more often."

We laughed, stubbing out our cigarettes, and gave each other one last embrace before falling asleep.

But I had not reached the end of the exhausting stream of crises which had been battering me towards the abyss, and in fact the worst crisis was still to come.

5

FOLLOWING MY usual routine I rose at half-past five and made myself some tea which I took to my dressing-room. No matter how crowded my timetable was for the day ahead, I devoted at least the first hour to being myself, alone with my Maker; I was recharging my spiritual batteries. While I drank my tea I focused my mind on the coming day and recalled, item by item, all I had to do. Then I prayed that I would do everything in a manner acceptable to God and I prayed for God's grace and God's help. Afterwards, if I had no plans to attend a service of Matins, I said the office before moving on to my reading.

I read the leading books as recommended by the most important theological and ecclesiastical journals, but this was no chore because I was being myself, indulging in one of my favourite pursuits. I enjoyed a book if I agreed with its propositions, and if I disagreed with them I enjoyed the book even more because I had the opportunity mentally to tear it to pieces. I loved demolishing a slipshod theological construct, just as a counsel for the prosecution loves demolishing the case for the defence in a court of law. I was often asked to write reviews, and my cool, lucid little paragraphs had earned me bitter enemies. Periodically my opponents tried to soothe their wounded egos by demolishing my own books, but this was an uphill struggle for them because I applied to my theology a logic and scholarship which my enemies, if they had any professional integrity, were reluctantly obliged to acknowledge. Revelling in these academic battles I found each clash greatly stimulating.

My spiritual director was keen that I should read exactly what I liked during this period of early morning solitude. I often thought another spiritual director would have queried this self-indulgence, but Jon realised that the more eminent I became in public life the more I needed to have this time to exercise my intellect, my special gift from my Creator. So on that particular morning I read just as I always did, my brain skipping from concept to concept in an ecstasy of intellectual satisfaction, and when I had finished this treat I washed, shaved and dressed before setting off to the Cathedral for Matins.

In accordance with tradition, the Cathedral offered the full range of services every day. During the week and on Saturdays these consisted—at the very least—of Matins, Holy Communion and Evensong, the latter being usually a service sung by the Choir, and on Sundays this weekday programme was elongated into a sung Matins and a sung Communion in addition to the sung Evensong. (In 1965 the Dean was still refusing to convert the sung Communion into the main Sunday service and refer to it as the Eucharist.) I never cease to be amazed by the idea, prevalent among the unchurched masses, that nothing now happens in cathedrals except the occasional royal wedding, but perhaps this misunderstanding arises from the fact that apart from the chaplain, the guides and the flower-arrangers, no devoted local supporter of the Cathedral would dream of visiting it between ten and four when the tourists rule the roost. The twentieth-century revival of our cathedrals as places of pilgrimage must certainly be welcomed as a manifestation of the Holy Spirit, but the swarming hordes can be disconcerting to anyone in search of peace and quiet.

Leaving the South Canonry on that cold, dank winter morning, I took the short cut across the Choir School's playing-field and began the short walk up Palace Lane towards the wall of the cloisters. The Cathedral, invisible at first in the darkness, began to take shape as I approached so that I was reminded of a sculpture emerging mysteriously from a block of stone. A masterpiece of English perpendicular architecture, built within the short space of forty years with no later additions, its eerie perfection so dominated its surroundings that it seemed to wear the darkness with the nonchalant elegance of a beautiful woman modelling a long black velvet gown. As I drew closer I fancied that the dawn, which was about to break, was making the Cathedral vibrate in anticipation. Beyond the wall nearby birds had begun to sing in the branches of the ancient cedar-tree in the cloister garth.

A bishop need have little to do with his cathedral; the running of the building is not his business, even though he remains ultimately responsible for the spiritual welfare of all who work there. However, although tradition required that I should keep a certain distance from those who did run the Cathedral—the Dean and the three residentiary Canons who formed the Chapter—I had felt driven in the early days of my episcopate to set the pace in the matter of daily worship. That was because of the shortcomings of my enemy, the Dean.

Let me say at once that Aysgarth did have virtues: he had a good brain, a talent for administration, a genius for fund-raising, a not inconsiderable gift for forceful preaching and a certain range of social skills which made him popular in Starbridge. A self-made man, he had a chip on his shoulder about his origins in Yorkshire where his father had been in trade. This inferiority complex manifested itself in frequent references to the fact that he had read Greats at Oxford. (He was a scholarship boy, of course.) Not having a degree in theology he was hostile to those who had, but I must in all fairness concede that he was a sincere Christian. Unfortunately, after an upbringing among the crudest kind of Non-Conformists and an intellectual reaction in which he had embraced the wildest forms of

Liberal Modernism, his theological outlook was, to put it kindly, confused.

When he became Dean—at the same time as I became Bishop; a testing stroke of providence—he made no secret of the fact that he disapproved of the habit of receiving the sacrament more than once a week, and that he thought auricular confession was Papist poppycock. One simply *cannot* go around making those sort of statements if one is the Dean of a great cathedral in the middle of the twentieth century. I concede that one may be allowed to think them; after all, in our broad Church Protestants and Catholics are equally welcome, but such thoughts should be kept private and balanced by a determination not only to be tolerant of the other side but to learn from it. The older cathedrals in England are shrines to the pre-Reformation Catholic tradition and are now witnesses to our famous Anglican "Middle Way" where the Catholic theology of the sacraments embraces the Protestant theology of the Word; in consequence a dean has no business making inflammatory statements in the manner of some Non-Conformist fanatic who bawls out: "No Popery!" whenever he sees a statue of the Virgin Mary.

Fortunately Aysgarth was no fool and he soon realised he had to modify his stance in order to avoid giving offence to a great many people. He backtracked on auricular confession, although he refused to hear penitents himself, and he swore devotion to the cause of ecumenism, the reconciliation of the different branches of the Church, although his statements were strangely silent on the subject of Rome; I suspect he confined his ecumenical yearnings to union with the Methodists. But despite this improved behaviour he still failed to show up regularly at the early morning weekday services, and during the months when he was officially "in residence" he constantly delegated the saying of Matins and the celebration of Communion to one of the minor Canons. (Lyle said Aysgarth needed the extra time in bed in order to recover from his hang-overs, but this charge was not evidence of Aysgarth's drinking habits but of Lyle's dislike.)

The upshot of all these abstentions from public worship was that I soon felt obliged to give the residentiary Canons the spiritual lead which he was apparently unwilling to provide, so I started turning up more regularly at the Cathedral's early services. I was careful not to exaggerate my response. I did not turn up every day. But I appeared at least twice during the week and often three times.

That made Aysgarth reform with lightning speed. His competitive nature ensured that he could not bear to be outshone by me, particularly on his own territory, and the embarrassing absences ceased.

This tense game of spiritual one-upmanship, with all its revolting worldly implications of rivalry, dislike and distrust, was played between us for six years in an atmosphere which, despite repeated clashes of opinion, we managed to keep tolerably civilised. By that I mean we never actually had a row, although we often came close to one. Then in 1963, as Jon put it in his old-fashioned way, "the Devil wriggled into the Cathedral and caused havoc." It is not my purpose now to describe the events of 1963, but this was the year when Aysgarth commissioned a pornographic sculpture for the Cathedral churchyard.

I regret to say that there was even more going on than this row over the sculpture (the commission was eventually cancelled), but I still cannot bring myself to write about what Aysgarth was getting up to on his days off. Some forms of clerical misbehaviour really do have to be buried six feet deep for the good of the Church. I think I may divulge, however, without going into lurid detail, that his two most dangerous habits at that time were a tendency to drink too much and an inclination to be undignified with women many years his junior.

Naturally I wanted to sack him, but I had no power. The Deanery was a Crown appointment, made by the Prime Minister on the Queen's behalf, and although I could have threatened to make a considerable fuss in high places in an attempt to extort his resignation, it had seemed clear that my duty was to conceal the scandal, not risk exposing it. In the end I took the pragmatic course, aiming for rehabilitation by forcing Aysgarth to pray about his situation with Jon's guidance, and fortunately by that time Aysgarth was so shattered by the consequences of his aberrations that he did not even have the strength to whisper: "No Popery!" when compelled to seek help from an Anglo-Catholic spiritual director.

Jon patched him up until he was once again capable of running the Cathedral with dignity. Then Jon began the task of patching up me. I was the Bishop, and in the manner of Harry Truman I could have kept on my desk a sign which read: THE BUCK STOPS HERE. There could be no denying the fact that the cathedral of my diocese was in a mess, and like Aysgarth I had to kneel before God, confess my part in the disaster and pray for the grace to do better. It was only after this ritual had been performed that Jon and I tried to work out how to cleanse the poisoned atmosphere and mend the fractured community.

Jon never held a session which Aysgarth and I both attended, but he suggested to each of us that the Bishop, Dean and Chapter should all make a habit of praying together, and when he judged that the moment was right I held a meeting at the South Canonry. Here it was agreed that for six months all five of us would attend Matins daily and all five of us would participate together in the early service of Holy Communion at least once during the week. I also suggested that once a month we all meet at the South Canonry to discuss any contentious issues in a calm atmosphere over coffee.

Life improved. The coffee-meetings were a failure, since everyone was so nervous of a quarrel that nothing contentious was ever discussed, but at least afterwards the Canons were more willing to confide in me whenever Aysgarth drove them to distraction. Meanwhile the daily attendance at weekday Matins had become a successful routine and we all stayed on for Communion on Wednesdays. This agreed pattern of worship should have meant that Aysgarth and I were free to abandon our game of spiritual one-upmanship, but I noticed that whenever I chose to exceed the agreed pattern and stay on for an additional Communion service, he usually stayed on too. However I thought it best to try to believe this was because of changed spiritual needs and had no connection with our old rivalry.

I must at this point give credit where credit is due and admit that Aysgarth worked just as hard as I did to eliminate the spiritual decay which had affected our community. He kept himself sober, behaved immaculately with young women and worked hard to raise money to restore the Cathedral's crumbling west front. It was then I realised that Aysgarth's principal talent, the one which outshone all the others, was for survival.

It would be untrue to say we became friends, but we did make elaborate attempts to be pleasant to each other. "And bearing in mind our temperamental incompatibility," I said to Jon, "even elaborate attempts to be pleasant must represent some sort of modest spiritual triumph," but Jon immediately became very austere.

"I agree it's a triumph," he said, "but it's certainly neither modest nor spiritual. It's a gargantuan triumph of the will fuelled by pride and self-deception, and all that's really happening is that you're passing off a spurious affability as a Christian virtue. Phrases such as 'temperamental incompatibility' and 'modest spiritual triumph' actually fail to describe or explain anything that's going on here."

I was baffled. "But Aysgarth and I *are* temperamentally incompatible!"

"I see no evidence of that. You're both intelligent men capable of strong passions and deep commitment. In fact I don't see you as incompatible at all, temperamentally or otherwise—you've actually got a lot in common. You're both well-educated men in the same line of business. You both enjoy fine food, good wine and the company of attractive women. You're both devoted to your children."

"Yes, but—"

"Your present attitude to Aysgarth says a great deal about your desire to behave like a good Christian, but very little about your desire to take the essential Christian journey inwards and examine your soul to work out what's going on there. Perhaps if you were to take another look at the writings of Father Andrew, who was not only a modern master of the spiritual life but a man of immense humility and psychological insight . . ."

I did meditate on the passages Jon marked for my attention, but I regret to say I did not like Aysgarth any better afterwards. I could only redouble my efforts to treat him in the most Christian way I could devise.

It had been arranged that we should take the short service of Matins together on that particular morning in February, I reciting the office and leading the prayers, he reading the assigned passages from scripture, and when I entered the vestry of the Cathedral shortly before half-past seven I found he was waiting for me. I assumed that the three Canons had already taken their seats among the congregation in St. Anselm's chapel.

"Hullo, Charles! Tiresome sort of weather, isn't it?"

"Very dreary. I hope it doesn't snow and disrupt the trains."

"Going anywhere special today?"

"Just nipping up to town for a committee meeting at Church House."

"Rather you than me!"

This concluded our opening round of pleasantries and was, as a golfer might say, par for the course. Aysgarth smiled at me benignly. When I had first met him long ago in 1940, he had been reserved, serious and not unappealing in his appearance despite that lean and hungry look which is always supposed to indicate an oversized ambition. Now, many double-whiskies and many sumptuous dinners later, he was stout and plain with a racy social manner which bordered constantly on frivolity. Being short, he was probably grateful for his thick hair which added a few precious tenths of an inch to his height. The hair was off-white and untidy, calling to mind the fleece of a bedraggled sheep. His blue eyes were set above pouches of skin in a heavily lined, reddish face, and his thin mouth, suggesting obstinacy, aggression and a powerful will, marked him as a forceful personality, someone who had no hesitation in being ruthless when it suited him. For some reason, which must remain one of the unsolved mysteries of sexual chemistry, women consistently found this tough little ecclesiastical gangster attractive. The phenomenon never ceased to astonish me.

As I took off my coat I carefully embarked on a second round of innocuous conversation. "How very kind of you, Stephen," I said, "to give Charley lunch yesterday."

"Not at all," said Aysgarth, following my example and toiling to be agreeable. I had thought he might make some comment on the lunch and perhaps even mention Samson, but he asked instead: "How's Michael? Dido told me he came down to see you yesterday."

I quickly moved to protect my Achilles' heel. "Oh, Michael's fine, couldn't be better!" I said, taking care to exude the satisfaction of a proud parent. "How's Christian?"

Christian, Aysgarth's eldest son and the apple of his eye, was a don up at Oxford.

"Oh, doing wonderfully well!" said Aysgarth at once. "I'm so lucky to have sons who never give me a moment's anxiety!"

Instantly I grabbed hold of my temper before I could lose it, but it was still difficult not to shout at him: "Bastard!" I knew perfectly well that Aysgarth was remembering Charley, running away from home, and Michael, being flung out of medical school, while the Aysgarth boys had journeyed through adolescence without ever putting a foot wrong. Aysgarth had four sons from his first marriage, all of whom were highly successful and utterly devoted to him.

"Is Christian working on another book?" I enquired politely, but I was unable to resist adding the barbed sentence: "I hope I'll find it more original than his last one."

"Ah, but the influence of classical Rome on medieval philosophy isn't quite your subject, is it, Charles?" said Aysgarth, delivering this lethal riposte without a second's hesitation. "If you'd read Greats up at Oxford, as I did, you'd find that Christian's scholarship was more within your intellectual reach."

The worst part about Aysgarth, as I had discovered to my cost in the past, was that he was a killer in debate. One entered an argument with him at one's peril, but of course, as Jon would have instantly reminded me, I had no business getting into an argument with Aysgarth at all.

Fortunately the entry of the verger put an end to this serrated conversation, and when I was ready we were led silently through the Cathedral to the chapel where the daily services were held.

I could not help thinking that my visit had begun on a singularly unfortunate note.

Much depressed I prayed for an improvement.

6

THE CONGREGATION stood up to greet us as we entered St. Anselm's chapel, and I saw that all three residentiary Canons were in the front row. The most senior was Tommy Fitzgerald, who had once confessed to me that Aysgarth was the only man he had ever wanted to punch on the jaw, and next to this normally unpugnacious Anglo-Catholic stood Paul Dalton, who had once told me he hardly knew how to face a Chapter meeting without having a nervous breakdown. On the far side of this normally stable churchman of the Middle Way was the newcomer to Starbridge, Gerry Pearce, whom I had selected for his staying-power after his predecessor, a crony of Aysgarth's, had decamped to London as a direct result of the 1963 crisis. Gerry was a moderate Evangelical who had spent some years as a missionary in an unpleasant part of the world before returning to England for the sake of his growing family; I had poached him from the Guildford diocese where he had passed five arduous years persuading the affluent middle-classes that there was more to life than making money in London. Coming from an affluent middle-class area of Surrey myself I was in a position to appreciate his achievement.

I did not care greatly for Tommy Fitzgerald, an unmarried fusspot who in his own way could be just as pigheaded as Aysgarth, but I liked Paul Dalton, who had read divinity long ago at Cambridge, just as I had, and who was so devoted to cricket that he seldom left his television set when a test match was being broadcast. Apart from a tendency to wander off the point in diocesan committee meetings, Paul's most tiresome habit was to complain how difficult it was to remarry. Since his wife's death he had tried hard to find a suitable replacement, but he had never found anyone who matched his rigorous specifications. Lyle said he did not want to remarry at all but merely felt driven to go through the motions of pretending that he did, but having been obliged to listen to Paul's confidential opinions on the subject I knew that unlike Tommy Fitzgerald he was not happy as a celibate.

Beyond the three Canons who were gathered in the chapel that morning I recognised the Vicar of the Close, who conducted the day-to-day pastoral work for the Dean, and in the same row I noted three retired clergy and my two chaplains, all of whom lived nearby. A couple of devout laymen from the diocesan office and half a dozen equally devout elderly women formed not only the remainder of the congregation but the loyal core of the Cathedral's band of regular worshippers.

I was about to conclude my quick inspection of those present when I saw there was a stranger among us. This was very unusual. As I have already indicated, few people chose to attend a weekday "said" Matins on a dark winter's morning, and usually the Starbridge visitors who attended church during the week preferred to pass up Matins in favour of Holy Communion at eight. I gave the stranger a sharp look, and as if sensing my interest he raised his head to stare straight into my eyes.

I blinked, taken aback. He was a priest, but a sinister one: swarthy, blunt-featured and built like a pugilist. His remarkable eyes, black and hypnotic, were set deep in shadowed sockets, and as soon as I had registered their potential power to cast a spell I found myself thinking: that man's big trouble. And I wondered which bishop had the ordeal of keeping him in order.

The service started. When Aysgarth read the first lesson I stole another glance at the visitor and wondered if my instinctive distrust had been unjustified. He was conservatively dressed in a well-cut suit. His clerical collar was thick enough to look old-fashioned and his black stock was adorned with a small gold cross, hinting at an Anglo-Catholic churchmanship. The extreme respectability of his clothes formed a bizarre contrast to his sinister countenance and his curious aura of . . . But I could not quite define the quality of the aura. I could only think again: that man's big trouble. And I could imagine not only all the women in his home congregation being disturbed by his powerful presence, but far too many of the men as well.

Towards the end of the service I briefly mentioned Desmond's disaster and proposed that we all observe a moment of silence to pray for his recovery. Intercessions were usually made at the Communion service, but I felt that Desmond's case should be presented to that tightly knit Matins congregation. With the exception of the stranger we all knew each other and we all knew Desmond. In such circumstances I thought my request would call forth a particularly solid shaft of prayer.

After the service I adjourned to the vestry with Aysgarth for the short interval between Matins and Communion, and soon we were joined by the three Canons.

"Who was that man?" demanded Tommy Fitzgerald.

But no one knew.

I asked: "Did no one introduce themselves?"

"He gave us no chance," said young Gerry Pearce. "He stayed on his knees and kept praying."

"An Anglo-Catholic," said Aysgarth neutrally. "I noticed the pectoral cross."

"Talking of Anglo-Catholics," said Paul Dalton, "what a shocking piece of news that was about poor old Desmond . . ."

Desmond was discussed in suitably muted tones for a couple of minutes. Then since it was not the morning when we all attended the Communion service, the group dispersed. Gerry and Paul drifted away to their homes for breakfast. Tommy, who was that month the Canon "in residence," responsible for the services, wandered off to make sure the new verger had set out the right quantities of wine and wafers. Only Aysgarth lingered, waiting to see what I was going to do. "Staying on,

Charles?" he enquired casually after Tommy had disappeared. "What about that train to London?"

"I'm not leaving until I've seen Desmond." Making an enormous effort I forced myself to say: "I'm afraid our conversation earlier wasn't one of our best efforts. I'm sorry."

"No need to apologise. Entirely my fault. I'm sorry too."

How hard we were both trying to be Christian! And what a stilted, awkward job we were both making of it! In despair I wondered if I was even fit to receive the sacrament, but I knew this descent into gloom was unjustified. I repented of my earlier burst of anger; I wanted to attend Communion; I needed the comfort of the sacrament as I faced the long, arduous day which lay ahead.

In silence I returned to the chapel, and in silence Aysgarth, not to be spiritually outdone, padded along by my side.

I wondered what Jon would have said, but decided I was much too depressed to want to imagine.

7

THE STRANGER nipped out so smartly at the end of the service that he still managed to avoid introducing himself, but everyone had noticed him and everyone wanted to know who he was.

"Any news?" said Lyle, bringing me my eggs and bacon as I finally reached the dining-room.

"Stephen and I bared our teeth at each other."

"That's not news, that's just history repeating itself. Did you tell Paul that I've found yet another possible wife for him?"

"I'm afraid I forgot. I was diverted by an unknown priest who looked like an English version of Elmer Gantry."

"How exciting!"

"Not for the bishop who has to mop up the inevitable mess."

I began to skim through *The Times.* Lyle filled my coffee-cup at intervals and provided hot buttered toast at exactly the right moment. "I do wonder what's happened to Michael," she said after refilling my cup for the second time. "Will Dinkie break off the engagement straight away or will she wait until she has her claws into Robert Welbeck?"

But I did not want to think of Michael. Instead I retreated to the office where Miss Peabody, already informed by Lyle of my approaching visit to the hospital, was waiting to tell me how appalled she was by the news of Desmond's assault. The typist had not yet appeared, but from the window I could see my chaplains pausing by the gate to finish their conversation before they turned up for work. At once I glanced at my watch, but they still had five minutes to spare before they were due to cross my threshold. Mentally shelving my standard lecture on punctuality I said to Miss Peabody: "Anything interesting in the post?"

"Nothing urgent." Miss Peabody, a large woman of indeterminate age whose favourite colour was navy-blue, adjusted her pince-nez before adding: "But there's the most unusual letter from a divorced priest in the Radbury diocese who wants to work in Starbridge. He's been in a mental hospital for some time."

"Draft a letter telling him kindly that I license neither divorcés nor lunatics."

"Oh, he wasn't a patient, Bishop! He was in the mental hospital as a chaplain, but he says he feels he's now being called to establish a healing centre in a parish setting."

"I don't license charismatic wonder-workers either," I said, and then reflected with horror that this description could be applied to Jesus Christ. Rapidly I added: "Just tell him the Bishop has a policy of never licensing divorced priests."

"But Bishop," said Miss Peabody, whose resolute nature could sometimes lead her to sound like a nurse telling her charge that "Nanny knows best," "he has the most glowing reference from the Abbot-General of the Fordite monks."

This was indeed surprising. The Fordites were Anglican-Benedictines who represented the apex of the High Church wing, and I would have expected their leader to be as opposed to divorced clergymen as I was. "Never mind the Abbot-General," I said, the recalcitrant charge determined to "talk back" to Nanny. "Where's the reference from the man's bishop?"

"There isn't one."

"Exactly. The man's obviously been sacked for improper conduct and is now trying to wriggle into another diocese by reviving an old connection with the Fordites. Write to him at Radbury, Miss Peabody, and—"

"Oh, he's not at Radbury now, Bishop! He's here in Starbridge and staying at the Crusader."

"Camping on my doorstep," I said, "will get him nowhere. In fact—" I broke off as I put two and two together and made an astonishing four. "Wait a moment," I said slowly. "Wait a moment . . ."

Miss Peabody waited obediently, but so mesmerised was I by the notion that an English version of Elmer Gantry might be attempting to invade my diocese that when I spoke I could only produce a completely irrelevant question. It was: "How on earth can an unemployed priest afford to stay at the Crusader?"

"I don't know, Bishop—he doesn't divulge his financial circumstances," came the unfalteringly serious reply. (Nothing a bishop said was ever judged irrelevant by Miss Peabody.) "But the letter is literate and suggests that he's a gentleman."

Ignoring this romantic notion that literacy and good breeding invariably coexist, I said abruptly: "I can't possibly see him. It would be a waste of my time, particularly as it would be out of the question for me to license a divorced priest for parish work. Think of the comments I should get from the Mothers' Union! No, no, Miss Peabody, write to the man and—"

The telephone rang. I was still so bemused by the manifestation of an Elmer Gantry in my diocese that I picked up the receiver before Miss Peabody could take the call.

"Charles?" said the Suffragan Bishop of Starmouth, startled to speak to me without being delayed by an intermediary. Nigel Farr had by that time been assisting me in the south of the diocese for six years, and although I gave him a free hand to run Starmouth as he thought fit we kept in close touch and he always consulted me over problems of behaviour among the clergy. On that particular morning he was worrying about a curate who had been preaching sexual liberation behind his vicar's back while running the parish youth club.

" . . . and according to the enraged vicar there's now an anonymous letter accusing the curate of flirting with a fourteen-year-old moppet."

"Almost certainly the product of another fourteen-year-old moppet who fancies the curate herself," I said, "but anything's possible. What's the vicar been doing while his curate's run amok? Obviously their relationship has broken down—see the pair of them, reintroduce them to each other and drill it into that curate's head that it's his business to fight the permissive society, not to join it. No clergyman sanctions immorality in *this* diocese," I concluded, adding some familiar words out of habit as I glanced at my watch and shuddered at the prospect of my interview with Desmond. I suddenly remembered that the petrol tank of my car was almost empty—which would mean a stop on the way to the hospital—which in turn meant I had less time than I had thought. Truncating the conversation with Nigel I promised to phone him back later and replaced the receiver.

Immediately the phone rang again. This time Miss Peabody pounced. Meanwhile my chaplains had arrived and were milling around like a couple of dogs who needed to be taken for a walk. "Bishop, if I could just have a word with you about your visit to the alms-houses . . ." "Bishop, if I could just see you about your meeting today at Church House . . ." As I listened to this chorus with half an ear I suddenly realised

Miss Peabody was saying: "Just a moment, Archdeacon, I'll see if he's available."

I grabbed the receiver. "Malcolm?"

"Good news, Charles. The police have arrested a man for the attack on Desmond. He's a lunatic, just released from mental hospital, who's got a phobia about Roman Catholic priests. When he walked into the police station this morning to confess, he told them he thought that St. Paul's was an RC church and that Desmond was one of the Pope's flock."

"So he was quite unknown to Desmond?"

"No previous connection whatsoever."

"Thank God. Talk to you later." I hung up and immediately, as my chaplains began to mill around me again, Miss Peabody said in her firmest voice: "Time for you to go to the hospital, Bishop." The typist had arrived red-nosed and was busy sneezing over everyone. Edging out of the room I promised my chaplains they would have my full attention on my return, and on reaching the hall I found that Lyle was already waiting with my hat and coat.

I said distractedly: "The car's nearly out of petrol."

"No, it isn't. I put some in while you were at the Cathedral."

In the office the telephone was ringing again, and for one poignant moment I pictured myself back in Cambridge with nothing to do all morning but write about Hippolytus and Callistus.

"Off you go, darling," said Lyle propelling me outside, "and don't get bogged down with Desmond. It's bad for your blood pressure when you fall behind in your timetable."

I hurtled away down the steps to my car.

8

THE SUN was now shining but the air was still cold and the Cathedral had a hard, dense, sculpted look as it rose from the frozen grass of the churchyard. Above the central tower the spire narrowed to a pinpoint against an ice-blue sky. Leaving the Close by the main gateway I drove with dread to the hospital.

I had no doubt whatsoever that Desmond would have to be sacked, although obviously the sacking would have to wait until he had recovered from his ordeal. One simply cannot keep priests who persist in hoarding pornography and in consequence risk embroiling the Church in scandal. I would do my best to help Desmond overcome his problems; I would arrange the best medical care, the best spiritual direction, the best possible form of early retirement. But there was no question of allowing him to continue at St. Paul's. I was all too aware that Malcolm and I had had a very lucky escape from disaster. To let Desmond remain in his job would have been the height of foolishness.

It was precisely because I knew Desmond had to be sacked later that this visit to the hospital promised to be such an ordeal for me; I knew I had to conceal the decision to sack him in order to offer him something which resembled pastoral care, and as I reluctantly prepared to hide behind the public persona which Jon called my glittering image, I found that shame was mingling with my dread. Dissimulation is not a comfortable course for a bishop to take, even when the purpose is to be kind to a sick man in hospital.

On arrival I was directed to a distant ward and found Desmond in a long room with a dozen other patients. The nurse on duty had warned me that because of the injuries to his jaw he was unable to talk, but despite this warning I was still shocked when I saw him. Heavy bandages hid most of the bruises but the flesh around his eyes was dark and swollen. Normally Desmond had rosy cheeks which in combination with his round blue eyes and lack of hair gave him a resemblance to an affable baby. The brutal destruction of this innocent appearance seemed unforgivably cruel. I found it hard not to flinch.

"How very sorry I am to see you like this, Desmond," I said, drawing up the visitor's chair and sitting at his bedside. "What a terrible thing to happen." And I took his hot, damp hand in mine.

His eyes filled with tears, and at once I found the scene so distressing that I hardly knew how to endure it. I realised he was reminding me of my POW days and the men who had been beaten up, but I realised too that I had to blot out all thought of the past in order to deal with the present. Tightening my grip on his hand I said quickly: "It's all right, I know you can't speak and I know you can remember nothing about what happened. I've just called to tell you the man was a mental patient who had never met you before, so there's no need to torment yourself with the thought that you were attacked by someone you knew who had a grudge against you."

Desmond was now struggling to blink back his tears, and I found this pathetic attempt to keep a stiff upper lip for his bishop almost intolerably touching. Speaking more rapidly than ever I said: "And don't worry about the parish. The Archdeacon will see that mass is celebrated every day—and yes, we do realise that Father Pitt is only fit enough to take the occasional service. I intend to seek Bishop Farr's help in finding a locum—Starmouth is more of an Anglo-Catholic stronghold than Starbridge, as you know." I realised as I spoke that I had forgotten to mention the problem to Nigel when we had discussed the fourteen-year-old moppet, so I made a mental note to telephone him as soon as I returned home. "The point is," I heard myself saying, "that you must have all the time you need to get fit again, and your prime task now is to focus on making a good recovery."

A single tear trickled down Desmond's cheek as he lost the battle to beat back his emotion. I suspected guilt was now mingling with all the pain and shock, guilt that he was not worthy to receive kind words from his bishop. Repressing a shudder at the thought of the pornography and somehow keeping my voice calm despite the hellish level to which the scene was sinking, I asked: "Does the chaplain know you like to receive the sacrament every day?"

He shook his head.

"I'll make sure he's told. Now . . . shall we take a moment to pray?"

He achieved a nod. I then had the task of framing some appropriate sentences, but I was in such a state of distress by this time that my creative powers failed me and I found myself falling back on a prayer I had used as a POW. This upset me still further, but with an iron will I clamped down again on the harrowing memories and followed the prayer with a recitation of the Matins Collects. I was wondering if I should offer the laying-on of hands. Many sick people find this sacramental gesture comforting, but I had my doubts about whether I should attempt it in this case. Jon was keen on the laying-on of hands but always said it should never be attempted in a situation where there was a marked ambivalence of feeling. This was because the darker side of the ambivalent emotions would block the healing power of the Holy Spirit, with the result that only the negative feelings of the ego would be communicated.

In the end I thought: better safe than sorry. So I made no sacramental gesture, but still my anxiety remained at a high level. I was now wondering if Desmond was seeing the attack as a punishment for his sins, and I knew I should take time to demolish this superstitious dread. God, after all, hardly requires someone else to beat us up. We are only too busy beating ourselves up by committing wrong acts which have unpleasant consequences.

"Desmond," I said after concluding our prayers, "I can't leave without making sure you don't misinterpret this appalling crime. First, although we can't deny that God has created a world in which random violence takes place, we can be certain he never wills this random violence to happen. And second, we can be certain that because he never wills suffering he'll strive always to redeem it by bringing good out of—" I broke off. I had realised that for Desmond good was not going to come out of evil because as the result of the assault he was going to lose the job which constituted his entire life. But now was obviously not the time for a complex meditation on the mystery of suffering. Now was the time for a good bishop to speak with confidence in order to reassure Desmond as he deserved. I had to offer certainties, not doubts. "—by bringing good out of evil," I concluded firmly. I stood up as I added: "Forgive my hesitation, but I was thinking for a moment of your suffering and feeling upset." I might have said more, but when I saw Desmond's eyes were shining with tears again I gave him my blessing, promised to visit him later and fled.

Outside the hospital I sank down in the driving-seat of my car and grappled with the horrible thought that despite all my efforts I had been a pastoral failure, but there was no time to grapple for long. Raggedly I drove home for the next segment of my obstacle race.

By the time I arrived at the South Canonry I had reviewed what I had to do before leaving for London. I had to tell Edward, my priest-chaplain, to talk to the chaplain at the hospital and make sure Desmond received the sacrament daily. Then I had to phone Nigel in Starmouth to tell him to dredge up an Anglo-Catholic locum. Then I had to have a conference with Roger, my lay-chaplain, about the Church House meeting and get him to explain the graphs which I had failed to look at yesterday. Then I had to remember to take my formal uniform to London—I broke off to wonder if my favourite frock-coat had come back from the cleaner's.

Halting the car with a screech of the brakes I leapt out, hared up the steps to the porch and flung wide the front door.

But the next moment I had stopped dead.

Standing stock still in the middle of the hall was none other than the sinister priest who had reminded me of Elmer Gantry.

V

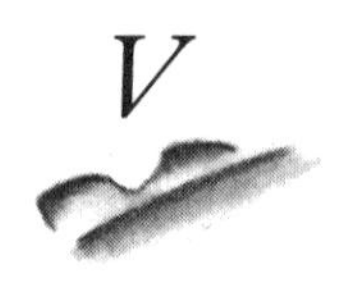

"Nothing blinds us to the true and living image of God except the false man-made idol, worldliness."

AUSTIN FARRER
Warden of Keble College, Oxford, 1960–1968
SAID OR SUNG

I

WHEN I had the chance to observe him at close quarters I saw that he was merely a plain man in his early forties with a thickset figure which would have profited from regular exercise on a golf course. His nose was too large, his jaw too square and his mouth too thin for his features to be judged other than irregular. At a loss to understand why he should be planted in my hall when he had no appointment to see me, I gave him my chilliest stare and waited for Miss Peabody to rush from the office to my rescue.

But the priest was clearly not a man who let the grass grow under his feet. Moving forward he held out his hand and said warmly in a courteous voice: "Good morning, Bishop! My name's Lewis Hall."

Finally detaching my feet from the threshold I closed the front door and allowed my hand to be gripped. But before I could utter a word Miss Peabody erupted from the office. "Oh Bishop"—I had seldom seen her so flustered—"this is the gentleman from Radbury whom we were discussing earlier. I did explain that it was quite impossible for you to see him, but when I mentioned that you'd gone to the hospital to visit Father Wilton he asked if he could wait for your return so that he could hear the latest news."

This was a move which contrived to be both thoroughly Christian and immensely cunning. As Miss Peabody quivered vanquished before me and I found myself registering a reluctant admiration for the man who had outwitted her, the stranger saw the chance to build on his success by cornering me for conversation.

I clearly remember thinking to myself: this man shall not pass the threshold of my study.

Meanwhile the man was saying soberly: "I do hope Father Wilton's progress is satisfactory. I was very struck by the way you spoke of him at Matins."

I could not recall saying anything in particular about Desmond himself; I had merely announced that he had been the victim of an attack. Confused by the discrepancy I became fatally hesitant. "Well," I began, but that was all I was allowed to say.

"Since you referred to him as Father Wilton, I assume he's an Anglo-Catholic," said my visitor, "and if you're now looking for a locum, may I volunteer for the job? I'm an Anglo-Catholic myself, and Miss Peabody confirms that you have my reference from the Abbot-General of the Fordite monks." He gave Miss Peabody a radiant smile.

Miss Peabody turned pink, in the manner of a wallflower suddenly asked to dance by the beau of the ball, and babbled: "I did mention the reference to you, Bishop, and if you want me to fetch it—"

I held up my hand. She stopped. I opened my mouth to take control of the conversation. "I thank you for your kind offer, Mr. Hall," I said. "I shall forward it to the Archdeacon. And now I have a train to catch shortly. If you'll excuse me—"

"Yes, of course, Bishop. I'll be only too happy to come back at a more convenient time."

This assurance was not what I wished to hear at all. In a moment of fury I repeated to myself: this man will *never* cross the threshold of my study.

"Mr. Hall," I said, "I'm aware that you feel called to establish a healing centre and certainly I wish you every success. However, I feel bound to say that in this diocese I have a policy of never licensing—"

"I want to specialise in priests who have suffered a spiritual breakdown."

Silence fell upon us all, but now I no longer saw the stranger, still as a statue, or Miss Peabody, fluttering in the background. As the memories of 1937 cascaded through my mind I saw only Loretta on that Surrey hillside and Alex Jardine removing the decanter from me when I had been so very drunk at his episcopal palace—although I never thought of those incidents nowadays, never, they were all buried so deep in my mind that I never had to think about them—indeed I never had to think about any incident from that spiritual breakdown, my first catastrophe, but now I was thinking, now I was remembering, and I could hear my younger self reciting the words of the General Confession to Jon, who had helped me survive.

". . . spare thou them that confess their faults . . . restore thou them that are penitent . . ." I remembered how I had been spared and restored. I remembered how conscious I had been of the healing power of the Holy Spirit as it moved ceaselessly through the world to raise up and renew all that was broken and cast down. I remembered that I had not always been a strong, successful bishop, battling *contra mundum* to preach the absolute truths.

My worldliness and my sophistication, those two hallmarks of a civilised man at the top of his profession, abruptly dissolved; it was as if a curtain had been rent from top to bottom by an unseen hand so that light could pour into the darkened room beyond. Acting instinctively—because for one mysterious moment my entire intellect had been bypassed—I turned, gestured to the door of my study and said to the stranger: "Come in."

Then I myself led the way over the threshold which seconds ago I had sworn he would never cross.

2

I SHOULD make it clear that I did not immediately think: ah, this is the Holy Spirit in action and I must give this man everything he asks for. I merely wish to explain why I let Hall cross the threshold of my study when I had resolved to refuse him admittance. In fact one has to be most cautious about detecting the presence of the Holy Spirit. It is all too easy to be driven, by either mental stress or psychological peculiarities or faulty reasoning, to make a mistaken identification, and I knew as soon as I had recovered from my moment of impulsiveness that I would have to be very careful what I said next. It was more than possible that Hall's invasion of the South Canonry had nothing to do with the will of God at all. Indeed one could just as easily argue that the Devil was pushing this man into my diocese to cause disruption, and that the memories of my spiritual breakdown had reduced me to a state of addle-headed incompetence.

Having thus flogged myself back within the boundaries of common sense, I said abruptly to Hall: "What's so special about the Starbridge diocese that you should feel called to work here?"

"You."

"Me?"

"Yes, my friends among the Fordite monks said you took a special interest in priests who had suffered breakdowns. They mentioned no names, but they told me about one priest who'd been kicked out of the London diocese after an incident in a public lavatory. No one else would touch him but you gave him a second chance."

I found I was too overwhelmed by the irony of this latest twist of the conversation to reply. My decision to give Desmond a job—a decision which had just been proved disastrously unsound—was now being presented to me as a powerful Christian action which was still having important consequences. So confused did I feel at this point that I had to make a considerable effort to concentrate on what Hall said next.

"I was intrigued by this story," he was adding, "because it was so contrary to your popular image as a bishop tough on sexual sin. That was when I realised you had to be a far more subtle and complex character than your enemies were willing to believe. I decided to find out more about you, and soon I realised how much I respected your attempt to uphold traditional moral standards, your advocacy of spiritual direction, your friendly attitude to both wings of the Church and your unusual ability to be both a highly qualified theologian and a gifted spiritual leader. I felt then that you were exactly the Bishop I was looking for—and after the recent change of bishops at Radbury I assure you I was looking hard. I got on well with Derek Preston, but Sunbeam leaves me cold."

I emerged from my stupefied silence. "Sunbeam?"

"Leslie Sunderland, the new Bishop of Radbury. Surely you know that his clergy call him Sunbeam! It's a tribute to his radiant liberal optimism."

Recognising my obligation to be loyal to a brother-bishop, even a radically liberal brother-bishop, I suppressed my amusement and said austerely: "I did notice that you enclosed no reference from Bishop Sunderland with your letter."

"I confess I never wasted time asking for one, but the Fordites will speak up for me. You know the Abbot-General, don't you?"

"Well enough to be surprised that he hasn't told you my policy on the licensing of divorced priests."

"He did tell me, but of course I knew that an exceptional bishop like you would always know when to be flexible about applying those sort of rules. After all, why should you wish to penalise me for the fact that my wife ran off with another man? With your happy marriage you'd be much more likely to offer me sympathy."

"I certainly wouldn't hesitate to be sympathetic, but—"

"And of course you'll have grasped that as an extremely conventional Anglo-Catholic I don't believe remarriage is an option for a divorced priest. In fact I shall never embarrass you either by remarriage while my wife's still alive or by any other unsuitable behaviour," said Hall firmly, and added, looking me straight in the eyes: "I consider myself called to celibacy."

After a pause I said in my most neutral voice: "Really." But before I could say more we were interrupted—to my relief—by the buzzer of the intercom.

"You must leave for the station in twenty minutes, Bishop," intoned Miss Peabody, "and don't forget that you still have to talk to Roger about the government's education graphs."

"Thank you." I replaced the receiver. "Well, Mr. Hall," I said, rising to my feet. "I confess this has been an interesting interview—and certainly, despite your marital status, I wouldn't object to engaging you on a temporary basis as a locum, but—"

"Thank you so much, Bishop, I knew I could rely on you to be flexible. Now, I'd only need about twenty minutes to explain my plans for the healing centre, so it shouldn't be too difficult to find a slot for me in your diary, particularly since I can come back here at any hour of the day or night—"

There was a tap on the door and Lyle peeped in. "Excuse me, Charles, but Michael's here again. Could you have a quick word with him before you rush off to London?"

I immediately wanted Hall to expound for twenty minutes on his healing centre.

Meanwhile Hall himself was saying rapidly: "I'll see Miss Peabody, shall I, to fix a time when I can come back?"

As I heard myself consenting docilely to this suggestion, it occurred to me to wonder if I had been hypnotised.

3

"WHO WAS that extraordinarily sexy priest?" muttered Lyle, reappearing after I had parted from Hall at the front door.

"Today's English version of Elmer Gantry. He tells me the clergy in the Radbury diocese call Derek's appalling successor Sunbeam."

Lyle was still laughing when my lay-chaplain sped out of the office to waylay me. "Bishop, about those graphs—"

"He'll be with you in a moment, Roger," said Lyle, instantly becoming ruthless. "He has to have a word with Michael." And as I found myself being propelled towards the drawing-room door she added to me *sotto voce:* "Dinkie broke off the engagement this morning, thank God, and poor Michael felt so wretchedly upset that he came straight here for consolation after putting her on the train to London."

"You mean he really did want to marry her after all?"

"No, no, no, of course he didn't! Deep down he's sick with relief that it's all over, but just think for a moment how *you'd* feel if you'd taken endless trouble to try and 'save' someone only to have her kick you in the teeth at the end of it! He's absolutely mortified that he could have been so idiotic as to practise his idealism on a money-grubbing tart—apparently in the end she just said straight out that he wasn't rich enough for her. Imagine that! I suppose she was simply too stupid to find a tactful excuse—oh, and talking of stupidity, don't mention the phantom pregnancy. It turned out he colluded with that lie because it was the only reason he felt would justify the marriage."

"But if he didn't want to marry her anyway—"

"Well, of course for his pride's sake he had to pretend that he did! Otherwise he'd have had to admit he'd been a perfect fool and allowed his idealism to lead him up the creek!"

"But isn't he having to admit that now? Surely he's too humiliated to want to face me!"

"That's not the point. The point is that because he's at such a dreadfully low ebb you have the golden opportunity to forge a new relationship by being kind and sympathetic and understanding, and if you dare slink off to London now without seeing him—"

"All right, all right, *all right!*"

Terminating this feverish conversation, which had been conducted almost entirely in whispers, I resigned myself to my fate and ventured reluctantly into the drawing-room.

Sprawled on the sofa Michael was drinking black coffee and looking hung-over. I noted that his long hair was uncombed, his face was unshaven and he wore no tie. My own father, presented with such a challenge to his standards, would have exclaimed: "What a debauched, decadent and downright disgraceful sight! Disgusting!" but I thought my old friend Alan Romaine would have said gently: "You look a trifle wrecked, old chap. Anything I can do to help?" I tried to keep Alan's memory in the forefront of my mind as I faced Michael, but it had been Eric Ashworth, not Alan Romaine, who had brought me up and I found it very hard at that moment not to react like a strict Victorian father.

I cleared my throat. "You look a trifle wrecked, old chap," I said, carefully uttering the right words, but as I spoke I realised with horror that every syllable vibrated with insincerity. The worst part of this débâcle was that I was genuinely desperate to show kindness, sympathy and understanding. It was just that I was quite incapable of articulating it.

"Oh, you needn't pretend you're not thrilled to bits!" said Michael exasperated. "God, how I detest the hypocrisy of the older generation!"

I struggled to repair my error. "Sorry," I said, finally managing to sound sincere. "I didn't mean to hit such a false note. And yes—it's true I'm glad the engagement's off, but I'm genuinely sorry you're upset."

"Balls! You're delighted that I've got my comeuppance after months of fornication!"

"I'm much more worried about the mess she may have left you in. Are you in debt?"

"Well, I had to spend a bit of money on her, didn't I? She always said money was the only thing that made her feel secure, money never let her down like people did. You see, when her parents' marriage broke up she blamed herself and—"

"How much do you owe?"

"—and she's been in a mess ever since really, okay, I know she was as dumb as a lobotomised kitten but I was prepared to overlook that because I thought she was really rather sweet underneath all her bloody awful hang-ups, and I thought that if only I could show her there was at least *someone* who cared, *someone* who was prepared to stand by her, she'd stop being so money-fixated but—"

"I don't want you getting bogged down in debt. If things are really bad—"

"—but it turned out she'd only shacked up with me because she thought we were millionaires—she saw you as an aristocrat with a big house and a seat in the House of Lords and it never occurred to her that you were just an ordinary middle-class chap who lived rent-free in a Church house and only got the seat in the Lords as a perk which went with the job! Why do the Americans never understand the English class system?"

"Look, Michael, I think you'd better tell me how much you owe and then—"

"You're not listening to me, damn it! You never listen, do you? You never listen!"

"I do listen, but all I hear is a lot of romantic adolescent drivel about how you made a fool of yourself in the worst possible way with a girl who was quite unworthy of you! Now answer my question: *how deeply are you in debt?"*

"Your problem," said Michael furiously, "is that you can't forgive me for having sex with her! Just because you haven't had sex for years and have never in your life been lucky enough to make love to a steamy American sexpot—"

Lyle walked back into the room.

"Darling," she said to Michael, "I'm so sorry your father keeps saying the wrong thing, but I assure you he does understand how horribly upset you feel now that Dinkie's rejected all your heroic efforts to care for her. You do understand that, don't you, Charles?"

"Yes," I said.

"What your father really means, Michael—although he's too worried about you to make himself clear—is that he hates to think you may be in debt as the result of all your praiseworthy idealism, and he wants to do all he can to help. That's what you want, isn't it, Charles?"

"Yes," I said.

"But Mum—"

"Hold on, darling, I must get your father launched on the journey to London. Charles, you must have a word with Roger about those graphs—thank you so much for insisting on seeing Michael before you left."

Battered and baffled I retreated to the hall.

Instantly I was waylaid by my lay-chaplain with a sheaf of papers. "Bishop, I really am worried by these graphs I got from the Education minister—I can't make sense of them at all, and although I've had them Xeroxed for the committee, I honestly think it might be better to leave them out. On the other hand, if you leave them out paragraph 19(b) of the report becomes incomprehensible, so—"

"I'll sort everything out on the train," I said, relieving him of the papers as Miss Peabody appeared at my elbow.

"Oh Bishop, I do apologise for Father Hall's invasion, but he was so persuasive and so obviously a gentleman—"

"I thought he looked like an assassin," said Roger, unable to resist taking a swipe at Miss Peabody's cast-iron snobbery.

"I thought he looked like Heathcliff," said the typist, passing by with a mug of coffee.

Edward my priest-chaplain erupted from the office. "Bishop, I've got Lord Flaxton on the phone—he says he's discovered that the new vicar of Flaxton Pauncefoot is a member of the Campaign for Nuclear Disarmament, and he wants to know how you could have licensed a pacifist to work in the diocese. He says the man's probably a KGB agent."

"Don't get diverted, Charles," said Lyle, emerging from the cloakroom with my hat and coat.

Edward, who was new to his job, demanded wildly: "Is Lord Flaxton nuts?"

"Eccentric," said Lyle, stuffing me into my coat.

"But what shall I say to him, Bishop? He's absolutely livid—breathing fire—"

"Suggest he has a drink with me at the House of Lords next week."

"Here, Bishop," said Roger, taking the papers back from me, shoving them into my briefcase and thrusting the briefcase into my arms all within the space of five seconds.

"Togs for Church House," said Lyle, passing me the bag containing my formal episcopal uniform. "Darling, I'll drive you to the station—you don't have time to search for a parking space."

"I've got a feeling there was something else I had to say to Edward . . ."

"He's gone back to be beaten up by Lord Flaxton," said Roger before I could digest that Edward had vanished from the hall. "Do you want him to visit Father Wilton in hospital?"

"Ah—Desmond, yes, that was it—tell Edward to get hold of the hospital chaplain and explain that Desmond likes to receive the sacrament daily—"

"Bishop, you've run out of time," said Miss Peabody, and for one bizarre moment I felt I had been sentenced to a most unpleasant eternity. "You must leave at once."

But another thought had occurred to me. "—and tell him to phone Malcolm Lindsay to say we may not need to trouble Bishop Farr about a locum for St. Paul's—"

"Come *on,* Charles!" Lyle was chafing by the front door.

But still I hesitated, my mind refastening on Desmond as it belatedly occurred to me that he might be in no fit spiritual state to receive the sacrament. I told myself firmly that he would always repent of his sins and pray for the grace to do better, but still I was gnawed by doubt. A repentance which did not include confessing his renewed taste for pornography could hardly be construed as acceptable . . . I started to worry that in my desire to be a compassionate pastor I had been inexcusably sentimental and slack as a father-in-God.

"Do you have a locum in mind, Bishop?"

"That man Hall who was here earlier. Tell the Archdeacon—no, on second thoughts I'd better tell him myself—"

"Charles," said Lyle, "do you really want to miss both your train and your lunch with Jack at the Athenaeum?"

She finally managed to detach me from the South Canonry.

4

REACHING WATERLOO station at half-past twelve I took a taxi to the Athenaeum and retired to the cloakroom in order to change into my uniform. By 1965 senior churchmen were abandoning this traditional ensemble of frock-coat, apron and gaiters, and I was certainly willing to travel in a plain black suit which guaranteed that the other occupants of the train did not waste time staring at me, but I was meticulous in wearing my uniform at any ecclesiastical gathering. I felt that in an age which was marked by declining standards and rampant iconoclasm, bishops should be resolute in respecting the symbols which pointed to traditional values.

The thought of declining standards and rampant iconoclasm depressed me, but I cheered up when I found the editor of *The Church Gazette* hunched cosily over a pink gin.

Lyle had once said that Jack Ryder reminded her of Babar the Elephant, and although I had pointed out that he was much more fun than the serious, innocent Babar, I had had to concede that Jack was indeed very large with small, narrow eyes and unusual ears. We had been up at Cambridge together. He too had taken a degree in divinity but had decided not to be ordained, and for a time it had seemed that our careers would take us in different directions. Then shortly after he had obtained his first job as an ecclesiastical journalist, I had become one of Archbishop Lang's chaplains.

Firmly linked again by our involvement with the Church of England, we found our friendship had continued and now after forty years I had to acknowledge, to my surprise, that Jack was my oldest and closest surviving friend. I write "to my surprise" because Jack and I had little in common except the Church, a subject about which he knew even more than I did. His memory for obscure scandals was prodigious and his nose for ecclesiastical gossip unerring. At one time he had written a series of sound freelance articles on theology for the serious secular press, but since he had become the editor of *The Church Gazette* he merely reviewed the occasional important biography.

By 1965 he was married to his third wife, but since he had been twice a widower and never a divorcé these matrimonial ventures had been entirely respectable. It was true that his third wife had been his mistress for some years while his second wife was dying of disseminated sclerosis, but he had behaved with great discretion and never mentioned the matter to me. I had only heard about it from Lyle and Lyle had only heard about it from Dido Aysgarth, that dangerous woman who always knew the gossip before anyone else had dreamed it could exist. Sometimes I wondered if Jack's refusal to confide in me meant that I had failed him in some way, but when his friendship never wavered I came to the conclusion that he had merely been afflicted by a typically British reticence about his private life. Englishmen, after all, would rather discuss cricket than adultery.

"How's the family?" I said to him that day at the Athenaeum after we had exchanged greetings and I had ordered a Tio Pepe.

"No idea, old chap, haven't seen any of the offspring lately, but no news is good news . . . How are your boys?"

"Oh, fine . . ." Having written off our offspring, we established that our wives were well and agreed that the weather had been dismal. At that point the waiter arrived with my drink and Jack proposed a toast in the slang of the 1920s. This was all very soothing and kept my depressed thoughts about the 1960s at bay.

"How's the west front?" inquired Jack, referring to the ailing section of Starbridge Cathedral. "Still standing?"

"Just. But according to Aysgarth, the Appeal's coming along remarkably well."

"How *is* Aysgarth? Still swilling?"

"No, no—he's got all that quite under control. In fact the Cathedral seems to be running very smoothly at the moment."

"Think so?"

My heart automatically produced an extra beat. "What do you mean?"

"Oh my God," said Jack to his pink gin. "He doesn't know."

"What on earth—"

"I did suspect during our brief phone conversation that you were still in a state of blissful ignorance, but I clung to the romantic hope that against all the odds you had that gangster at the Cathedral under control. You know I told you to brace yourself for a shattering piece of gossip?"

"Yes, but I assumed that was mere journalistic hyperbole. Are you trying to tell me—"

"I had a drink yesterday with a young antiques dealer who used to take out my younger daughter before she was so foolish as to ditch him in favour of the chap who's now my son-in-law. You almost certainly know this young man—not only is he the grandson of one of your neighbours but he's also the brother of your Michael's friend Marina."

"Douglas Markhampton."

"Precisely. Now, Douglas has a new girlfriend who works at Christie's—and when I say 'works' I don't mean she's just a typist. She's one of those wonderful American girls who can be tremendously high-powered while still looking radiantly sexy—"

"I didn't know you liked that type."

"Admire it from afar, old chap—too terrified to do anything else. Well, this American girl, whose name I can't quite remember but I think it's Marilyn or Merrilee or maybe even Mary-Lou, told Douglas that since his grandmother lived in the Close at Starbridge, she might be interested to hear that a number of rare books from the Cathedral library were coming up for auction."

"What?"

"Wait, it gets worse. Douglas was sure Mary-Lou had made a mistake, so he phoned another chum of his at Christie's who said yes, it was true but the story was top secret at present and Mary-Lou should be shot at dawn for pillow-talk. Douglas then phoned me out of sheer curiosity to ask if I'd heard anything on the ecclesiastical grapevine—with the result that I rushed hotfoot to his antiques shop in St. James's, lured him to White's and plied him with drink until finally he divulged the most top-secret top secret of the lot: according to this other chum of his at Christie's, the star turn at the auction is going to be none other than that fabulously rare manuscript which you always get so sentimental about—the one containing the margin-painting of the cat with a mouse in its mouth."

"Great Scott, the St. Anselm masterpiece!" I sprang to my feet.

"Whoa there, Charles, calm down—"

"But Aysgarth can't possibly sell that! Good heavens, if he's trying to sell off the Cathedral treasures behind my back, I'll—"

By this time Jack had flagged down a passing waiter. "A brandy for the Bishop, please."

I just managed to remember my afternoon committee meeting and amend the order to a second sherry. Jack ordered another pink gin and begged me to sit down again before I had apoplexy.

Sinking back into my chair I said: "I simply can't believe Aysgarth would do this."

"No? But if he's strapped for cash—"

"If the Cathedral's so strapped for cash that he needs to sell the St. Anselm manuscript, I should have been told there was a major financial crisis. Why, it's as if the Queen had decided to sell off the Crown Jewels in order to repair the Tower of London! What on earth can be going on?"

"Maybe Aysgarth's being blackmailed by some gorgeous popsy with the result that he's embarked on a criminal career to make ends meet."

I tried to smile but failed. I could only manage to comment: "I'll say this for Aysgarth: he's no fool. Or in other words, I don't believe he'd ever get in a financial mess which could be described as embezzlement, and I don't believe he'd ever cultivate a friendship with the sort of woman who's capable of blackmail." I stood up again. "I must get hold of Malcolm."

"I do wish you'd have a brandy, old chap. No bishop should try to survive this sort of crisis on sherry alone," said Jack solicitously, but I was already rushing off in search of a telephone.

Malcolm proved to be out. I phoned Nigel Farr in Starmouth but he was out too. Finally I tried to speak to Lyle but without success. In frustration I returned to my host.

"Maybe I should talk to Christie's and try to arrange for the books to be held back," I said. "When's the auction?"

"I don't know, but it can't be imminent because Mary-Lou's still working on the catalogue. Look, toss back the Tio and let's eat before you pass out as the result of shock and lack of nourishment."

We took our places in the dining-room. In the interval between the mulligatawny soup and the roast beef I retired to the telephone again and this time I found Malcolm at home.

"It can't possibly be true," was his reaction to the news.

"I'm afraid Jack's sources really do suggest this isn't just a preposterous rumour. What do you think's going on?"

"A financial mess a mile high, but what beats me, Charles, is how Aysgarth imagines he can get away with this scheme! Does he really think he can sell the St. Anselm manuscript on the quiet? As soon as the catalogue's issued, all the art correspondents will be trumpeting the news in the press!"

"Meanwhile I'm baffled by the Canons' silence. Do you think they know nothing of this? I mean, is such ignorance by a Chapter actually possible?"

"Must be. If they knew, they'd have tipped us off."

"But how can he keep them in ignorance when under the Cathedral statutes he can't do anything without their consent?"

"Oh, he wouldn't let the statutes bother him! Think of how he commissioned that pornographic sculpture single-handed in 1963—the sculptress only had to bat her eyelashes at him over the dry martinis, and immediately all memory of the Cathedral statutes was wiped from his mind! The truth is Aysgarth's quite capable of acting on his own and then bullying the Canons into ratifying his actions later."

"At least there's no woman involved this time."

"What makes you so sure?"

The operator intervened to ask for more money. "Talk to you later," I said to Malcolm, and replaced the receiver.

Returning to the dining-room I found the roast beef waiting for me alongside a glass of claret. "Sorry," I said to Jack. "I'll now stop wrecking our lunch."

"I rather think I was the one who did the wrecking. How many strokes did the Archdeacon have?"

"He somehow managed to stay conscious. Look, Jack, can I ask you to sit on this story for a day or two while I find out exactly what's going on? I suppose it's always possible that there's an innocent explanation."

"You mean maybe there's no financial mess and that Aysgarth's merely taken a dislike to priceless medieval manuscripts?"

"I mean," I said severely as he shook with laughter, "that Douglas's chum at Christie's could have got hold of the wrong end of the stick. Someone might have said to him: 'Forget the St. Anselm manuscript,' and he might have thought the sentence was: 'We'll get the St. Anselm manuscript.' Maybe the Dean and Chapter are only disposing of a few books of minimal importance."

"All right, old chap, check the story at your end, but make sure you keep me posted—and make sure you don't delay too long or you'll have all the hounds of Fleet Street baying at your door. Much better for you and everyone else connected with the Cathedral if those vulgar beasts are tastefully scooped by *The Church Gazette.*"

But before he could sketch further details of this nightmare, I diverted the conversation into another channel.

5

MY AFTERNOON committee meeting should have been of interest to me because it concerned my special subject, religious education, but by that time I hardly felt capable of concentrating on it. The committee's title was the Church of England's Working Party on Education in Theological Colleges, known as CEWPET (even as CUPID by the facetious new Bishop of Radbury) and I was the chairman. The meeting that day was to discuss an interim report which I was due to make to the Church Assembly later that month, and I intended to announce my unswerving belief that the purpose of theological colleges was to train men for the priesthood by giving them a thorough grounding in Christian history, doctrine, literature and liturgy so that they could proclaim the Gospel cogently and conduct a well-ordered service of worship. This aim might seem very obvious to an outsider, but within the Church fierce debates raged about reforming the traditional syllabus. It was all part of the general debate about how far the Church should modernise itself in order to speak intelligibly to twentieth-century man.

My opponent that day was inevitably going to be that most tiresome of my liberal opponents, the new Bishop of Radbury, whom I now knew was called Sunbeam, and I was far from surprised when, true to form, he made a shamefully florid speech in response to my opening remarks. As far as I could judge, he seemed to be advocating that we should all return to the educational standards of first-century Palestine.

". . . and why not abolish all exams? What's the point of ordinands cramming their heads with facts which are irrelevant to this day and age? Who cares now about the quarrels of the Early Church? Would Our Lord Jesus Christ have passed the university exams in theology? Would he even have passed Religious Knowledge at A-level? Why, I bet he wouldn't even have wasted time sitting the exam! He'd have been out there in the world caring for people, relating to them, sympathising with them about poverty—political oppression—sexual injustice—oh, and while we're on the subject of sex, I think we should bear in mind the inevitable ordination of women and put an end to this nonsense about making the theological colleges into single-sex ghettos like the colleges at Oxford and Cambridge. It's my firm belief that women—"

"No, really, Leslie," I interrupted, reflecting that Lyle would have been worrying by this time about my blood pressure, "before you start putting cooking and needlework on the curriculum, I'm going to rein you in. We're still a long way from ordaining women, and fascinating though it may be to picture Our Lord wearing jeans and kicking the educational system in the teeth, I think we should face the fact that if Our Lord were here today he'd preach the Kingdom of God, just as he did two thousand years ago—he'd preach the absolute truths which never change, not the current fashions which are ephemeral. Now, if we can turn to the statistics showing the decline in candidates for A-level—"

"Excuse me, Bishop," interposed the one woman on the committee, a thin woman draped in purple, "but I find these graphs confusing."

"Women can never understand graphs," I said, in such a state of irritation by this time that I failed to think before I spoke. "I've noticed that before."

"I must say, Bishop, I find that a surprisingly offensive remark, particularly coming from a man of your distinction!"

"I do apologise, Miss Drew . . ." I was indeed horrified to realise I had been discourteous to a lady.

"Now, Charles," said that abominable Bishop of Radbury, "if you'd had sociology lessons during your own training for the priesthood, you'd have overcome the deficiencies of your public-school education and achieved a more enlightened attitude to women—with the result that such a remark would never have passed your lips!"

"If by an 'enlightened attitude' you mean a belief that men and women are interchangeable," I said, "that's nonsense. Truth is truth, and I've noticed that women on the whole are less comfortable with mathematical information than men. Of course I was wrong to say they can never understand it, and I apologise unreservedly to Miss Drew for that, but men and women are complementary, not identical—equal before God but nonetheless dissimilar—and it's a liberal delusion to assume otherwise."

"Okay, fine," said Sunbeam brightly. "Why don't you exercise your complementary masculine powers by explaining the graphs to Miss Drew? I'm sure we'd all welcome a shaft of enlightenment from our chairman."

Very fortunately I had heeded Roger's warning about the graphs and had managed to work out on the train a way of dismissing them when the subject of A-level statistics was under discussion.

"To avoid controversy," I said at once, "and to ensure this meeting doesn't last longer than the allotted time, why don't we pass over the graphs altogether and turn to the statistics on page . . ." I somehow succeeded in extricating myself from this tight corner, and the meeting ground on until I had the majority of the committee on my side at a quarter past four. After taking care to say a tender goodbye to the offended Miss Drew I retired with relief to the lavatory but faltered at the sight of Sunbeam at the urinal.

"You know, Charles," he said with an unexpected seriousness, "as a brother-bishop who wishes you well, I think you should ask yourself why you're so keen to cling to these absolute truths of yours which keep you in such a conservative straitjacket. Personally I feel liberated by the modern view that everything's relative and that there are no absolutes any more—but could it be that for some reason you find the idea of such liberation threatening?"

"My dear Leslie, liberals like you can be as dogmatic as any conservative, and since relativism is simply an ideology like any other, maybe you should ask yourself why you're treating it as one of the absolute truths you profess to despise! Why do you feel driven to rebel against order by embracing chaos?"

"Good point!" said Sunbeam cheerily. "You answer my question and I'll try to answer yours!"

"Obviously we must call this skirmish a draw," I said, satisfied that I had won it by pointing out to him that intellectually he was behaving like an adolescent. "By the way, before I rush off I must just ask you this:

what can you tell me about a priest from your diocese called Lewis Hall?"

"Hall," mused Sunbeam, adjusting his ill-cut, off-the-peg suit. (Naturally he refused to wear the traditional uniform.) "Hall, Hall—oh, *Hall!* Yes, he's left the Radbury diocese now, much to my relief—he's one of those embarrassing types who fancy exorcism. Apparently my predecessor Derek Preston gave him a bit of leeway but when I let it be known that I wasn't standing for any of that kind of hanky-panky, Hall realised he had to seek fresh woods and pastures new . . . Don't tell me he's wound up in Starbridge!"

" 'Passing through' will probably be the final description of his activities. Was there any scandal attached to him?"

"Isn't any modern clergyman who dabbles in exorcism a scandal of unenlightenment?"

"No, I meant—"

"Oh, I know what you meant! No, Charles, he's not a homosexual, and if he does run around with women on the quiet he takes care not to commit the ultimate sin of being found out. Did he tell you he was divorced?"

"Yes."

"In that case I'm surprised you're sufficiently interested to ask me about him—although in my opinion the Church should welcome a divorced clergyman even if he was the guilty party and even if he's remarried. We should welcome homosexuals more warmly too. I mean, are we Christians or aren't we? Shouldn't one love and accept people instead of persecuting and condemning them?"

I said: "Of course we must love people no matter what they've done, but we mustn't forget that love should include justice for those who have been wronged by the sins of others—you can't just pretend that sin doesn't matter! Sin hurts people, sin destroys lives—haven't you yourself ever suffered as the result of the wrong acts of others?"

Leslie Sunderland carefully finished drying his hands on the towel. Then he turned to face me and said: "Yes. But I've forgiven them."

In the silence that followed I had the odd impression that someone was listening to us, but when I turned to look at the closed door no one was there.

"Well, never mind!" said Sunbeam, casting aside his moment of extreme sobriety and becoming cheery again. "Someone on the bishops' bench has to worry about sex, I suppose, but thank goodness it isn't me because I'd rather worry about the Bomb and South Africa and the starving millions in India. So no hard feelings, old fellow—God bless . . ." And he pattered off in his cheap slip-on shoes in order to be radically liberal elsewhere.

Having changed swiftly back into my Savile Row suit, I left Church House and took a taxi to Fortnum's to meet Charley.

6

I WAS late when I reached the restaurant but there was no sign of him waiting to greet me. Wondering what had delayed him, I sat down at a table.

Charley's church, St. Mary's Mayfair, had been the centre of a rich, plush parish before the war, but now it stood in an area where many of the grand houses had been converted to commercial use with the result that the vicar's ministry was mainly to the tourists, hotel staff and office-workers who swarmed daily through the neighbourhood. Charley was the curate. He had tried working in the East End of London but had disliked it, so when my friend the Earl of Starmouth had mentioned to me one day in the House of Lords that there was a vacancy for a curate in his local parish I had encouraged Charley to apply for the job. After all, one can hardly get further from the East End than Mayfair.

Charley had quickly settled down. His aptitude for languages had proved useful with the tourists and hotel staff. His youth and energy had attracted the office-workers. His theologically conservative outlook had proved popular with the vicar and the few remaining aristocratic parishioners. Soon I had told myself that I no longer needed to worry about his career—and yet I had continued to worry, and I worried still. This was because although it was obvious to me that Charley had great gifts as a priest, he showed no sign of developing a mature personality which would enable him to use those gifts to the full.

He was now heading for his twenty-seventh birthday, but his lack of control over his volatile temperament still suggested an adolescent secretly ill-at-ease with himself. All too often he was high-handed, didactic and tactless. Strong on oratorical fireworks and teaching the faith, he was weak on empathising with others and far too rigid in his theological views—but of course the ability to empathise with others and to be a flexible thinker without compromising one's integrity are the fruits of maturity. Too often Charley seemed to me more like sixteen than twenty-six.

When I had expressed my worry to Jon he had pointed out that some men take longer to mature than others, but I had begun to think that in Charley's case the delay was abnormal. After all, I reminded myself, he had done two years of National Service and spent three years as an undergraduate; he had been out and about in the world for some time, so what was now holding him back? But although I often asked myself this question I found I never arrived at a satisfactory answer.

For a moment I recalled this mystery when Charley erupted into Fortnum's that afternoon and hurried over to the table where I was waiting for him; slim and small, he looked so much younger than his years. I cheered myself with the reflection that at least he was mature enough to dress properly and avoid looking a mess. His short dark hair was combed and smoothed. His pale brown eyes blazed with energy. He was breathless, an indication of how hard he had tried to arrive on time, but he was smiling, delighted to see me.

"Dad! So sorry I'm late, but . . ." After he had produced his very acceptable excuse for keeping me waiting we shook hands, sat down and ordered tea. I then asked him about his work, and when he began to talk about the Lent sermons he was planning I became so interested that I quite forgot about my arduous meeting at Church House. I even forgot to enquire why he was so anxious to see me, but eventually, after the waitress had deposited our tea on the table and promised to return with the hot buttered crumpets, I remembered to ask what was troubling him.

"Well, the first thing I want to talk to you about is Michael's behaviour," said Charley, grabbing a sugar-cube to stave off his hunger-pangs. "But please don't accuse me of telling tales behind his back. I'm acting solely with his welfare in mind, and the truth is his ghastly girlfriend hasn't been faithful to him. So if he's crazy enough to marry her—"

"He isn't. The engagement's off."

"Oh, thank goodness! Actually I didn't think he could possibly be serious since I hear on good authority that he hasn't been faithful to her either. He's been secretly plunging around with yet another girl from that awful Marina Markhampton's dreadful set—"

"Charley, repeating gossip really isn't a suitable occupation for a priest."

"I know, but Michael's such a chump about girls that I can't help feeling concerned—and it's Christian to be concerned, isn't it?"

"Yes, but—"

"And if I tell you everything you can pray for him too, and that must be better than just me praying alone. Anyway, this new girl he fancies is called Holly Carr, and as a matter of fact she's rather nice—I met her at that party Venetia gave last November—so maybe Michael will marry her, who knows, but *he shouldn't sleep with her first.* It's quite wrong to treat a nice girl with such absolutely unbridled contempt."

I said nothing.

"Well, aren't you going to condemn Michael for carrying on with two girls at once?"

"Since you know my views on such behaviour I hardly think it's necessary for me to repeat them." Telling myself that Charley's unedifying behaviour sprang from his insecurity as an adopted son and that any attempt to reprove him for being a priggish sneak would only make that insecurity worse, I made a big effort to change the subject.

"Talking of Venetia," I said, "have you seen her since she was kind enough to invite you to that party in November?"

"It was her husband who invited me—Venetia herself always behaves as if she finds me repulsive, and every other girl I meet reacts in the same way. It makes me want to bang my head against the wall in sheer despair."

With dismay I realised that I had given him yet another opportunity to dramatise his insecurity. Charley had never had what was nowadays described as "a steady girlfriend." I regarded it as another symptom of his immaturity. "Don't talk such nonsense!" I said, trying to sound robust. "You may not be classically handsome, but—"

"Actually my utter failure with women brings me to the second thing I want to talk to you about. I think I'm being called to be a monk."

The waitress chose that moment to arrive with our plate of hot buttered crumpets.

7

FEW BISHOPS could have claimed to be a more loyal supporter of the monks and nuns in Anglican orders than I was, but it is a fact of life that parents want their children to marry and procreate. This is obviously such a deep-rooted human desire that one might call it a biological absolute truth, and it explains the surge of disappointment felt by parents when for whatever reasons their children abstain from marriage. I know there are Roman Catholic cultures where parents consider it an honour if their child chooses a celibate life, but I have noticed that the child is usually one of a large family and can be spared without too great a sense of loss. I did not have a large family of children. I had two sons and I wanted neither of them to be cut off from the complex dimensions of human fulfilment which I had experienced as a husband and father.

Indeed the fact that Charley was my adopted son only made me more anxious that he should wind up a married man with two-point-three children—or whatever current statistics rated the norm for a middle-class Englishman in the mid–twentieth century. If he deviated from this norm I knew I would feel that despite all my efforts I had failed to bring him up properly—and I did not want to think I had failed in any way with Charley. I needed Charley to be a success. It justified all the hardship I had endured in the early years of my marriage. Like his hero-worship of me, his success was part of my reward.

Telling myself that this new crisis was merely a manifestation of his continuing immaturity, I fought back my panic and toiled to appear mildly surprised. I said: "Isn't this a trifle sudden?"

"Yes, but it's abundantly clear to me now that I've no hope of serving God properly unless I'm in an all-male environment and soaking myself in asceticism." Apparently unconscious of any irony he took a most unascetic mouthful of hot buttered crumpet.

Still immaculately courteous I enquired: "But what's driven you to abandon all hope of marriage?"

"The realisation that I'm desperately in love with a married woman who finds me repulsive."

"You mean—"

"Yes. I'm besotted with Venetia," said Charley, again referring to the young woman who had been Lyle's protégée. "I think of her constantly. I dream of her. I toss and turn in bed every night until I'm drenched in sweat—"

Much relieved to receive this new evidence that Charley was sexually normal I said dryly: "How very inconvenient."

"Inconvenient! Dad, I can't tell you—words fail me—it's impossible for me even to begin to describe the quality of my erections—"

"Dear me."

"—and they always come at exactly the wrong moment! Never in all my life have I experienced such—"

"I'm sure they're most remarkable. But Charley, I suspect the real question here is not why you should have fallen in love with Venetia but why you should always be falling in love with women who are unavailable for marriage. After all, Venetia isn't the first of these hopeless passions of yours, is she? There was the married lady-dentist when you were up at Cambridge—and then there was that nun who gave those lectures on the mystics—"

"Those were just adolescent infatuations. This is the real thing—and what slays me, Dad, is that I could have married her when she was single back in 1963! If only—"

"You weren't sufficiently interested or you'd have done something about it. Obviously it wasn't meant that you and Venetia should marry."

"Well, I couldn't possibly marry anyone else, and since all women are now a torment, reminding me of what I can't have, what other choice do I have but to become a monk as soon as possible?"

"If you're called to be a monk I'll eat my mitre, but don't listen to me, I'm just a married bishop. I'll ask Jon if he'd be willing to see you."

Charley groaned and sighed and bit deep into his second crumpet, but this suggestion seemed to satisfy him and I realised he was much happier now that he had acted out his feelings in such an exasperatingly self-indulgent manner. I felt wrecked, of course, but I had long since discovered that feeling wrecked was an occupational hazard of parenthood, nothing to get excited about. I assumed I would eventually recover.

I was still trying to calm myself by predicting my inevitable recovery when Charley said in a low voice: "If I don't go into a monastery I might wind up making a mess of my private life," and I heard at last the genuine cry for help which in my distress I had failed to recognise earlier.

At once I said: "Of course you won't make a mess of your private life! I've brought you up, you've modelled yourself on me, you're going to be fine."

Charley looked relieved, as if I had recited a magic incantation guaranteed to keep all disastrous futures at bay, but I was aware that a shadowy uncertainty was trying to rise from some burial-ground deep in my mind. I could not analyse this uncertainty. It merely hovered for a second in my consciousness before I blotted it out.

Pouring myself some more tea, I began to calculate which train I could catch from Waterloo.

8

AT WATERLOO I telephoned Lyle. "I'm getting the six-fifteen," I said. "Have a stretcher waiting at the station."

"Did you murder that ghastly Bishop of Radbury?"

"Not quite. But I feel in the mood to murder our Mr. Dean."

"Don't tell me Jack's prize piece of gossip involved Stephen!"

"Imagine the worst and multiply by ten. Darling, I've got to see Jon before I explode with the force of an H-bomb and devastate the diocese. Can you ask Edward or Roger to take the Rover to the station so that I can drive straight to Starrington?"

"Oh Charles, don't overdo it! You've been rushing around all day long—"

"I'll have a nap on the train. Oh, and phone the Community at the Manor, would you, to tell them I'm coming—I want to make sure the door in the wall is unlocked."

The operator came on the line to demand more money. Hastily I said to Lyle: "See you later," and hurried away on my journey to the one man who was always able to restore my sanity whenever I wanted to retreat to the nearest lunatic asylum.

VI

"Oh God, save me from myself, save me from myself . . . this masterful self which manipulates your creation . . . this self which throws the thick shadow of its own purposes and desires in every direction in which I try to look, so that I cannot see what it is that you, my Lord and God, are showing to me. Teach me to stand out of my own light, and let your daylight shine."

AUSTIN FARRER
Warden of Keble College, Oxford, 1960–1968
SAID OR SUNG

I

I HAD met Jon in 1937 at the time of my first catastrophe, an event which I have discreetly alluded to as a spiritual breakdown. I judge it unnecessary to describe this episode in detail here, so I shall merely say that although I never lost my faith I became for a time incapable of functioning as a priest. This nightmare was the result of various psychological conflicts which Jon helped me to resolve. He was then still a monk, the abbot of the Fordites' Grantchester house where I made a prolonged retreat in order to master my problems.

At the time of my second catastrophe—my capture by the Germans at Tobruk—Jon had left the Fordite Order and was living in the Starbridge diocese with his second wife. It was here, in 1945, that he again played a vital role in steering me back to spiritual health, and since I owed him so much it was not surprising that I tended in those days to view him through rose-tinted spectacles. But as the years passed I realised that although he was a most gifted priest he was not without his problems and failings.

Jon did not leave the Order because he wished to remarry. His departure, approved by his superior, was in response to a call from God to return to the world in order to use his gifts on a larger stage, and after many trials and tribulations he was led to the Starbridge Theological College which he ran most successfully in the years immediately after the war. (It was only after his retirement that the College descended into the mess which I had to mop up when I became bishop in 1957.) This post-war career of Jon's primarily exploited his gifts as a leader and teacher, and it was not until he retired from his position as principal that he was able to concentrate solely on his favourite work: spiritual direction.

Let me now say something about the qualities which made Jon such an original priest. He was a mystic—by which I mean he was one of that army of people, existing in all religions, who understand themselves and the world in the light of direct experiences of God. Such people do not fit easily into conventional ecclesiastical structures, as their individuality is at odds with institutional life, but the best Christian mystics, the ones who have been able to explore their special knowledge of God to the full by attaining a holy, disciplined life, are always those who have managed to integrate themselves into the institutional life of the Church. The mystic who insists on steering his own course runs the risk of isolation, self-centredness and delusions of grandeur, and this is never more true than for those mystics who are psychics. Not all mystics are psychics and not all psychics are mystics, but there is a degree of overlapping between the two. Both groups tune in to the unseen, but mystics do not necessarily experience the paranormal phenomena which are considered by all spiritual masters to be more of a hindrance than a help to those following the spiritual way. I should stress that neither psychic powers nor mystical inclinations guarantee spiritual health. Any gift can be prostituted; or as Jon would say, anyone can dedicate their gifts to the Devil.

Jon was one of those mystics who are also psychic, but he had long since dedicated his psychic gifts to God's service and he kept a firm grip on them by operating within a strict framework of Anglo-Catholic religious practice. Before I met Jon I did not believe in psychic powers. I still do find it hard to believe some of the things that appear to go on in defiance of rational expectations, but since I had become a bishop I had learnt that pastoral help is consistently sought by people whose lives have been made miserable by paranormal phenomena, and that although most of the cases prove capable of a rational explanation, there remains a group for which no explanation is possible. As an academic theologian I am not at all keen on this state of affairs, but unfortunately the phenomena do not depend for their existence on whether or not I happen to be keen on them. Jon helped me to keep an open mind and restrained my urge to retreat into a furious scepticism.

His own psychic speciality was telepathy, which stood him in good stead in his counselling, and he was also a clairvoyant, occasionally experiencing visions. He never spoke of these gifts to me until we had been friends for at least twenty years, although I had suspected from the start that his insight into my problems hinted at the existence of rather more than a well-developed intuition. For a brief time in the 1940s he had been involved in the ministry of healing and deliverance, but this had ended in disaster and he had always refused to take an active part in helping me solve paranormal problems.

As an academic theologian of the twentieth century I do not, of course, believe in the classical ministry of deliverance which involves the rite of exorcism, but unfortunately—yet again—the need for it exists whether I happen to believe in it or not. Over the years I have come to the reluctant conclusion that a little holy water sprinkled by my representative in a "haunted" place can do no harm and often produces a more peaceful state of mind in those who have complained about the disturbance to their local clergyman. (Naturally one never lets the story get to the press.) On the exorcism of people I have more negative views, but luckily the demand is so rare that my natural distaste has seldom been put to the test. Psychiatric treatment for those tormented is obviously the best solution, but honesty compels me to admit there are cases where the practitioners of orthodox medicine have no effect whereas a skilled exorcist, backed up by a prayerful Christian community, can achieve a healing. Jon regarded this as such an obvious truth that it hardly needed stating, and became very irritated with me when I tried to work out explanations involving theories of multiple personality and the power of hypnosis.

He was twenty years older than I was, so in that February of 1965 he was three months short of his eighty-fifth birthday. His health was excellent, and he lived alone in a small cottage which had been built for him after his second wife's death. The cottage stood in the grounds of her manor house at Starrington Magna. Both the house and the grounds were now run by a small Anglican community, founded by Jon to preserve the inheritance for his son Nicholas, the only surviving child of the marriage.

I find it hard to give a thumbnail sketch of someone so unusual as Nicholas, so I shall simply say that he was a psychic like his father and a very odd young man indeed. He seemed popular with his contemporaries, who were apparently fascinated by his oddness, but he never had a special friend. He told me once that he did not need a special friend because he had his father. Lyle thought that he and Jon were much too bound up together and that it was a great burden for a young man to have such an ancient parent. She also said that Jon had made the greatest possible mistake by embarking on parenthood again when he was over sixty, but Lyle was always rather tart about Jon. I suspect it was because he was one of the few men who had always found her wholly resistible.

Jon had not been altogether successful in his attempts to forge partnerships with women. His first marriage, made when he was a very young priest, had been a failure but his wife's death had released him from it, and as soon as the two children of the marriage were grown up he had abandoned his work as a prison chaplain in order to embark on a career as a monk.

When he left the Order seventeen years later, he had quickly—much too quickly, we all thought—plunged into matrimony again; I can see now how difficult life must have been for him as he tried to adjust to the world, and how the loss of his brethren's support would have created a disorientating emotional vacuum. His new wife, Anne, was a sensible, down-to-earth, competent woman, very "county," who ran her family estate and always behaved as if she had never heard of the word "psychic" and never wanted to. She was twenty-eight years Jon's junior and had extremely good legs. Jon adored her; she adored him; Lyle prophesied darkly that it would all end in tears. Much irritated I told her not to be such a cynic, but as time passed I realised that the marriage was indeed under stress, chiefly because Jon had only the haziest idea of how to live as a married man. He told me once that his parents had lived separate lives beneath the same roof, and I realised then that he had grown up in a home where marriage had been seen not as an integrated partnership but as an association between two people who had never become interdependent.

Pursuing his career at the Theological College after the war, he began to follow a policy of cramming far too many commitments into every twenty-four hours. His wife often complained and he promised to reform, but he never did. In fact after his retirement from the College in 1950 he became busier than ever as a spiritual director. Why did Jon overwork like this? Lyle said there was something wrong with the marriage and that he was using his work as an escape. I merely thought he found his work so rewarding that he had a hard time tearing himself away from it, but eventually I did begin to wonder if Lyle's diagnosis was more accurate than mine. Elderly men who have young wives should expect to encounter problems as the years advance, and at last I wondered if Jon was frightened of impotence; I asked myself whether his immersion in his work, where he was confident his powers would not let him down, was his way of blotting out his fear of a physical decline.

Then in 1957, when his wife was only forty-nine, she suddenly died and he had to face up to the difficult truths which he had tried so hard to evade. Overnight he changed into a recluse. Probably a profound guilt that he had neglected his wife mingled with an equally profound guilt that he was glad to return to the celibate life, and the two produced intolerable feelings of shame and failure. Probably too one could say that he associated this failure with his life in the world and could only come to terms with the former by rejecting the latter. Certainly from a spiritual standpoint one could theorise that God, taking advantage of that compulsion to atone for past mistakes, had then given Jon his final call: to be a hermit, devoting his life to prayer.

It is one of the many unattractive features of the twentieth century that anyone who wishes to lead a solitary life is generally considered to be either wholly deranged or at the very least psychologically disabled. Christians, I regret to say, are not exempt from holding this fashionable view, although anyone who has studied the history of the Church knows there is a strong eremitical tradition in Christianity. The great question to be asked when confronted by a would-be hermit is this: is the withdrawal from society made so that he can be self-centred, freely indulging his neuroses without benefit to anyone else, or is it made so that he can become God-centred, using the drive to solitude as a means of serving others with fruitful spiritual results? Jon eventually became God-centred, continuing his spiritual direction by letter, still counselling a few of his oldest friends and constantly praying for the welfare of others, but for some months after Anne's death I thought he was stuck fast in a self-centred groove. Indeed I was seriously worried about his mental health when his guilt-induced depression showed no sign of lifting, and no one was more relieved than I was when he began to recover his spiritual equilibrium.

No doubt he owed a considerable debt during this time to his friends among the Fordite monks who provided strong support and took special care of young Nicholas, then a pupil at the monks' public school, Starwater Abbey. I tried to supplement this care as well as I could and we often had Nicholas to stay, but he was like a puppy pining for his master and he always seemed happiest when he was on his way home. Charley and Michael were very good, treating him as a younger brother, and I think he liked them in his cool, detached way, but I noticed that he never made any marked effort to maintain their friendship.

At that time in 1965 Jon had been separated from his beloved Nicholas for longer than they had ever been separated before, and the result was that the master was now pining for the puppy. Having come down from Cambridge with a degree in divinity, Nicholas had decided to do two years of voluntary work in Africa before proceeding to theological college to train for the priesthood. He had now been away for five months. Cool, laconic little letters would arrive regularly at the Manor, and Jon would pore over every one of them in a fever of quite unnecessary anxiety. Often I was shown the letters and asked for an opinion, but no matter how hard I tried I was unable to allay this somewhat neurotic paternal concern. Once I did say gently; "He *is* twenty-two. I think you must give him a little leeway now to make mistakes and learn from them," but poor old Jon, my former superhuman hero, remained beset with the problems arising not only from parenthood at an advanced age but from a recluse's over-fearful view of the outside world.

When I arrived at Starrington Manor that night I drove past the main entrance and followed the boundary of the grounds for another mile until I reached a door set in the wall. This was the quickest way to Jon's cottage, much quicker than following the path through the grounds from the main house, and Lyle's call earlier to the Community had ensured that the door was unlocked when I arrived. Jon had no telephone at his cottage, not even a private line which would connect him to the Manor and those who looked after him.

Having parked the car on the verge I opened the door and began the short walk to the dell where Jon's cottage had been built beside the family chapel. It was dark among the surrounding trees and the air was very cold; I was relieved to step beneath the light which shone above the front door.

"Jon—I've arrived!" I called in order to avoid startling him by a sudden thump on the panels, and the next moment I was face to face, just as I had been in 1937, with my spiritual director, friend and mentor, Father Jonathan Darrow.

2

JON HAD been very tall, well over six foot, but he had begun to stoop so that we were now almost the same height; I have yet to shrink from six foot one. Apart from the stoop he had changed remarkably little since I had first met him. He possessed one of those lean, well-proportioned frames which age well, and although his grey hair was thinner it was not scanty. He had an unusually pale complexion, and this pallor made the shadows created by the angular bone structure of his face more striking. His eyes, very clear, very grey, always giving the impression of seeing everything there was to see, were quite unchanged from that day in 1937 when he had introduced himself to me at the Fordites' house in Grantchester.

"Take the chair by the fire, Charles," he said after he had ushered me across the threshold. "It's cold out there tonight."

"I do apologise for dumping myself on you outside normal visiting hours, but . . ." The few people whom Jon consented to see without an appointment were expected to arrive between four and five in the afternoon and stay no more than half an hour. When I was consulting him professionally instead of merely paying a social call to see how he was, I would make an appointment to meet him earlier in the day, and although Jon had always told me that I could call upon him at any time and without prior warning, I was careful not to abuse this privilege. Normally I would never have visited him in the evening.

Generously waving away my apologies, Jon pottered off to his kitchen to make tea.

He lived in one large room. Bookcases flanked the stone fireplace where logs were burning; a bunk-bed with a built-in wardrobe and drawers occupied one wall; a small table with two chairs stood by the window. Usually there were no pictures anywhere, but in recent months Jon had taken to displaying a photograph of his absent Nicholas on the chimney-piece. A crucifix hung on the wall above the bed. The wooden floor was uncarpeted apart from a rug on the hearth, and on this rug a large tabby-cat sat gazing at the flames. Jon was a cat-lover. I preferred dogs and could never quite understand this passion of Jon's, but I accepted it as one of his idiosyncrasies. Unlike most cat-lovers he never behaved in a frivolous fashion with the animal but always treated it as if it were an intelligent child who could be relied upon to behave impeccably. This particular cat had been around for some time but had been preceded by other tabbies, all displaying an uncanny empathy with their master.

When he returned with the tea I offered him the armchair into which I had collapsed on my arrival, but he refused, saying he was sure I needed the comfort more than he did. Once the tea was poured out he drew up a chair from the table and sat facing me across the hearth.

At last I felt able to relax. Having taken a sip from my cup I said: "Can you guess what's happened?"

"No, of course not! How many more times do I have to tell you that I don't experience telepathy on demand?"

I laughed. "But you've always predicted trouble on this particular front!"

"In that case I suppose you've had another row with Aysgarth."

"Not yet. But I feel angry enough to want to beat him up." Every bishop—indeed every clergyman—should have at least one person to whom he can express feelings which are utterly unacceptable when expressed by a man who is supposed to epitomise all the Christian virtues. As soon as the words were spoken I felt a great easing of my tension, as if a painful boil had been lanced.

"Hm," said Jon, putting aside his cup of tea in order to pick up the cat.

When I had first met him I had been so debilitated that he had been obliged to take a strong lead in our conversations; a spiritual director's primary task when working with those who seek his guidance is to develop and nurture the life of prayer in accordance with the unique needs of each soul, but when a person is in pieces, unable to pray at all, the spiritual director's first task is necessarily to glue the pieces together by reintegrating the personality—that is to say, by regrounding the soul in God. In my own case this had been achieved when I had first sought his help in 1937, and over the years as I had developed as a priest I found that during our meetings Jon said increasingly little while I said increasingly more. We had now reached the stage where I did most of the talking. I would set out my problems as bluntly as I liked (lancing the boil), examine them with as much detachment as I could muster (applying the antibiotic) and try to work out how I could solve the problems in a way which would be acceptable to God (healing the wound by a continuing care and attention). Jon, puncturing my monologue with the occasional sentence, would help me organise my thoughts; he would shine a spotlight on possible options, make recommendations about prayer and at the very least try to ease me along the path which led to a more enlightened perspective on my problems.

Continuing in my initial task of lancing the boil, I now embarked on a monologue. Jon listened and nodded and eventually tucked the cat under his arm as he stood up to pour me some more tea.

". . . and what am I supposed to do?" I demanded after I had told him of Aysgarth's current negotiations with Christie's. "The man's a disaster for the Cathedral, for the diocese—and for me as the bishop. Obviously there's a financial mess. Maybe he's drinking too much again as well, and maybe—though heaven forbid!—there's some woman involved. The truth is I should have battered him into resigning back in 1963—well, I would have done if I hadn't been so afraid of the damage to the Church resulting from a scandal. Perhaps he thought I was soft and stupid, letting him get away with it. Maybe I *was* soft and stupid. More fool me. Bishops have got to be strong and adroit. If we were in the secular world . . . Yes, I know we're not, but nevertheless I'm a senior executive in a big corporation and I just can't afford not to crack down on a manager who threatens to blacken the corporate image."

"Hm," said Jon.

"All right, all right, all right, I know you're thinking that drawing a parallel with big business is inappropriate! But I'm talking now about the way things are, not the way things ought to be—I'm talking about the real world, the world I have to work in every day, and the truth is that people expect a strong lead from bishops. People want certainties, they need to feel that the bishops haven't abandoned tradition and still have high standards of moral behaviour—and of course I mean 'moral' in the widest sense of the word, I'm not just talking about sex. That new Bishop of Radbury—the one who succeeded my friend Derek Preston—said today he welcomed the doctrine of relativism which says there are no absolutes, he said he found it liberating, but how could he be so spiritually blind? If everything is relative, even moral standards, then we descend to the law of the jungle in double-quick time—and that means pain and suffering for innocent people. What are the authorities doing, appointing a man like that to a bishopric? It's so bad for the Church! All this liberalism's a disaster. The whole decade's a disaster. Let me tell you that unless we stand firm and stick to traditional moral values, we'll all be swept down the drain into hell."

"Hm," said Jon, stroking the cat behind the ears.

"Radbury—Leslie Sunderland—was spouting a lot of drivel which implied sexual permissiveness doesn't matter. Sometimes I think those liberals don't know anything about real life at all. Treating sex as no more than a handshake—and saying deviant behaviour should be regarded as normal, even when statistically it can never be normal, never be more than the preference of a small minority—well, it's all so unreal, such a distortion of all the truth I've ever witnessed. When I think of Lyle and what she went through . . . How can people say sexual sin is unimportant? How can they say it doesn't matter? I've seen people laid waste by it. It does matter. It matters horribly. All suffering matters, whether it's the gross kind which exists only in concentration camps or the everyday kind which exists in human relationships. Don't tell me suffering doesn't matter! All this liberal-radical blindness to pain makes me sick . . .

"And talking of sexual sin, I've got an appalling problem which has just blown up concerning Desmond Wilton—remember me telling you about Desmond who was booted out of the London diocese after a lavatory disaster? Well, it now turns out that Desmond's been keeping pornography again, and that ghastly woman Dido Aysgarth's going around bleating about . . ." I outlined the Desmond fiasco. ". . . and the oddest thing happened this morning after I'd returned home from the hospital," I said, as the cat put both paws on Jon's chest and gazed up at him adoringly. "Just as I was worrying about finding a suitable locum, this extraordinary priest turns up—early forties, divorced, quite obviously big trouble—and tells me not only that he's willing to be an Anglo-Catholic locum but that he's set on muscling his way into my diocese to start a healing centre! Imagine that—a shady wonder-worker on the loose! But do you know what I do? Do I say 'no thanks' and dismiss him in double-quick time? No, I don't! I tell him to come back for another interview! How could I conceivably have been so soft and stupid? The only possible answer is that the Desmond crisis had temporarily deranged me, because of course I can't possibly do what he wants, it's out of the question. He says he's a celibate, but he's exactly the sort of priest who'd have a sex-life on the quiet when he wasn't cavorting around exuding charisms in a cassock.

"It's all Desmond's fault. If he hadn't upset me so much—yes, yes, yes, I know he couldn't help being the victim of random violence, I know I mustn't be angry with him, but I was so shattered by that pornography—I mean, what can one do with a priest who keeps that sort of stuff, what can one do? Obviously he'll have to go away and have the appropriate treatment, but I can't take him back, I just can't, it's too much of a risk, and anyway I have to keep up the standards among my clergy, I can't tolerate that sort of behaviour, it's letting the side down in the biggest possible way, it's too devastating for the Church. So I'll have to sack him, but oh, the strain of it all, the sheer *hell* of being a bishop sometimes—it all makes me wish yet again that I'd never left Cambridge—all right, I know Cambridge was a narrow, back-biting community in some ways, but I could always escape there into my histories of the Early Church, and here I can't escape, I hardly ever get the time to write about Hippolytus and Callistus, and I just get angrier and angrier with all these frightful people who seem determined to drive me completely up the wall . . . Jon, stop making love to that cat and SAY SOMETHING, for heaven's sake, before I have an apoplectic fit and drop dead!"

Jon carefully set the cat down on the floor. Then he looked me straight in the eyes and said one word. It was: "Forgive."

"Oh good heavens . . ." I had been sitting on the edge of my chair but now I sank back against the upholstery with a groan. "It's all very well for you to say that! You're a hermit, but I'm out there in the real world and I just can't afford—"

"Christianity is, of course, a very costly religion," said Jon, "but I'm sorry to hear you're finding it too expensive."

I groaned again, but in fact I welcomed this austere rebuke, found it bracing—as Jon had known I would. I needed a strong rod to flog me out of the pit of despair. A flimsy switch would have been of no use at all.

I took a deep breath. The boil had been lanced and the time had come to apply some antiseptic ointment. Calmer now that I had expelled my anger I began my attempt to regard my problems with detachment.

"Very well," I said, "we'll set Desmond aside for the moment. There's a hellish interview in store for me there but at present my task is simply to be a good pastor and ensure he's properly looked after. I suppose I might just manage to achieve that if I can stop being so self-centred that all I think about is not Desmond's welfare but my own discomfort. And we'll set aside the wonder-worker for the moment too; if I employ him as a locum it doesn't commit me to any fantastic scheme for a healing centre. The really intractable problem is—as usual—Aysgarth. What on earth do I do about that drunken menace at the Deanery?"

"Why don't you start by referring to him in a manner which reflects his reformed drinking habits? And perhaps you might take a moment to remember that even if he was the worst drunkard in Starbridge he'd still be a member of your flock."

"All right, what do I do about that stone-cold-sober old sheep who's been gambolling in the Cathedral library with such unfortunate results?"

"This sounds so obvious that I hardly like to mention it," said Jon apologetically, "but why don't you have a friendly chat with him and simply ask what's going on?"

"Because we're beyond friendly chats where the Cathedral's concerned. No, I can see I'll be driven to make a visitation—I'll have to bring in the lawyers and haul him over the coals in the chapter house."

"You'd look a big fool if he's got a satisfactory explanation."

This pithy realism had the required effect: I struggled to think more profitably. After a moment I said: "Maybe it would be best if I dealt with him through the Archdeacon. At least if he has a row with Malcolm he won't be having a row with me."

"That's certainly a pragmatic suggestion," conceded Jon, adopting a milder tone as he realised I was making a big effort to be constructive, "but I wonder if you've allowed sufficiently for Aysgarth's psychological peculiarities. If you send in the Archdeacon, Aysgarth's inferiority complex will get the better of him and he'll think you're being intolerably grand and stand-offish. Is it really so impossible for you to invite him informally to the South Canonry for a glass of sherry?"

"He'll brag about all his brilliant, successful sons and I shan't be able to stand it. No, sorry, forget I said that—I'm being self-obsessed and negative again—"

"Why the new outburst of envy on the subject of Aysgarth's sons? How are Charley and Michael?"

"Oh, don't ask! Michael's just become engaged and disengaged to that frightful American tart and continues to regard girls as nothing but animated mattresses. As for Charley, he's just told me he wants to be a monk, but of course it's not a genuine call—he's merely expiring with frustration because of his compulsion to admire women who are unobtainable. I had to eat hot buttered crumpets with him at Fortnum's today while he wailed about the extraordinary nature of his erections."

"But how wonderful that he could be so frank with you!" said Jon encouragingly. "I'm sure I never talked to my father about such matters!"

"I'm sure I never talked to mine about them either, but the young seem to talk about anything these days—Michael even tried to tell me he was saving Dinkie by fornicating with her! I've begun to think it's impossible for the two of us ever to have a conversation which doesn't end in a row."

"It reminds me of what I went through with Martin," said Jon, referring to his son by his first marriage. "The normal channels of communication had become so blocked that all we experienced when we met was pain."

"How did you finally unblock them?"

"I accepted him as he was."

This was not the answer I had expected. I had thought he might say: "Martin eventually became mature enough to behave better," or: "Once Martin had conquered his alcoholism I was able to see him without getting upset." After a pause I ventured the comment: "I'd be doing Michael no favours if I accepted him as he is, locked in a self-destructive pattern of behaviour."

"But what is he trying to say to you by behaving in this particular way?"

"I told you years ago. He's saying how furious he is that I don't spoil him rotten, just as Lyle does."

"I'm sure that's at least partly true. But should one really be content with a mere partial truth?"

"What do you mean?"

"Is that the only reason why Michael should be angry?"

"Well, obviously he's also jealous of his brother, but he's just got to learn to grow up, that's all, because I'm not altering my relationship with Charley. That's my one big success as a family man—and my reward for all I went through in the past."

Jon said nothing.

"It's not as if I neglect Michael," I insisted, more irritated than disturbed by this silence. "I've always tried to do my very best for him, even though the only reward I get is bad behaviour."

Jon picked up the cat again. The animal, delighted, patted his cheek with its paw.

"That cat'll talk to you one day," I said, finishing my tea.

Jon smiled, moulded the cat into a motionless mass of fur and began to speak of prayer.

Later, after we had prayed together, I was able to tell him I felt better. I knew my problems had not magically melted away, but I was more at peace, more accepting of my tasks as a bishop, more confident that I would be granted the grace to exercise my responsibilities as I should. Having thanked Jon whole-heartedly I declined his offer of more tea and moved at last to the door.

"By the way," I said, hesitating with my hand on the latch, "I quite forgot to tell you—this divorced wonder-worker, who's trying to wriggle into my diocese, has a reference from the Abbot-General of the Fordites."

"That fails to impress me," said Jon, very chilly. "I don't approve of the present Abbot-General."

I knew why. The present Abbot-General, who in fact was a decent enough fellow, educated at all the right schools, had closed the Fordites' house in Yorkshire where Jon had spent his happiest years as a monk. Jon had disagreed vehemently with this decision and said it showed an inexcusably supine spirit, but in common with the Roman Catholic orders, the Fordites were declining in numbers, and the Abbot-General had had little choice but to shed one of his four houses. It had been yet another sign of the depressing times in which we lived.

"But don't you think it's odd," I persisted, "that the Abbot-General's prepared to recommend a divorced priest?"

"Well, of course in my young day it would have been unthinkable. Certainly Father Darcy would have said . . ." And as he so often did, Jon began to speak about the hero of his monastic years, Father Cuthbert Darcy, who had died in 1940 but had subsequently taken up residence in Jon's head as a golden memory. However, halfway through the Darcy anecdote (which I had heard at least twice before) Jon broke off and said abruptly: "Forgive me—I'm keeping you from Lyle and you must go. How is she, by the way?"

"Wonderful. Best wife in all the world. Don't know how I'd ever manage without her."

Jon smiled again. Then he said: "I'll continue to pray for you and Aysgarth."

We parted. I was on my own once more but ready (or so I thought) to face whatever horrors lay ahead, and as I headed down the track through the woods I noticed that far above me in the cold night sky the stars had started to shine.

3

I CROSSED the threshold of the South Canonry as the grandfather clock began to strike ten in the hall.

"Darling!" I shouted, just as I always did when I finally regained my safe harbour after an exhausting day sailing on the ecclesiastical high seas. It was as if I were announcing my presence to the pilot who would then guide me to the right berth.

"Coo-ee!" called Lyle from upstairs, revealing that she was waiting for me in her little sitting-room.

I steamed forward with alacrity across the hall.

When I entered the room I saw she had the whisky bottle and the soda-siphon waiting for me alongside a plate of sandwiches covered by a glass dome. She had turned up the central heating, and I was immediately aware, amidst all the welcoming warmth, of a vast relief that I was at last safe in my own home with the wife I loved. I found myself thinking ardently: thank God! as I realised how very fortunate I was despite all my troubles, and how very greatly blessed.

"Feeling better?" said Lyle, putting aside her sewing. She had been mending the sagging hem of one of my favourite golfing shirts.

"Much better. I don't think I'll murder Aysgarth just yet," I said, moving forward to give her a kiss.

Lyle stood up. I have this very clear memory of her standing up. I have not described Lyle apart from mentioning that she had kept her figure, but I shall now add that she was small and fine-boned and that she had dark hair, smooth and thick, which she wore drawn back from her face and gathered in a bun at the nape of her neck. Her hair had once had a reddish tinge but this had disappeared along with her first grey hairs towards the end of her forties. Her dark eyes appraised the world coolly from behind rimless spectacles which heightened the impression of an efficient employee, devoted to her job. Her poise, her graceful movements, the hint of a strong sexuality held ruthlessly in check behind that faultlessly proper facade—all combined to create the air of mystery which was as fascinating to me in 1965 as it had been in 1937 at our first meeting. For me indeed she was "beyond compare," not merely a devoted wife but a loyal friend and an exciting companion, and I knew that so long as we were married no day would ever seem too hard to endure.

I saw her stand up. She was wearing an olive-green wool dress, perfectly plain, and the diamond brooch I had given her on our silver wedding anniversary. In the soft light from the lamps she looked very young. I shall always remember how young she looked at that moment, how alluring, how indestructibly beautiful.

I saw her stand up. I was still crossing the room towards her. She put aside her sewing and she stood up. In my memory I can see that scene happening over and over again.

She was smiling as she rose to her feet. I can still remember how she smiled. Then suddenly without warning she lost her balance and staggered to one side.

"You've been hitting the gin!" I teased her as she righted herself, but she only said in confusion: "But I haven't had a drink all day! So why—"

The clot of blood cut off her voice.

The clot of blood cut off her breath.

The clot of blood cut off her life.

My third catastrophe had arrived out of the blue.

PART TWO

CHAOS

"How then can a lifetime be described in the language of absolute truth? . . . It seems to me that it is a good thing to have constantly in mind the shortness of our life on earth."

REGINALD SOMERSET WARD
(1881–1962)
Anglican Priest and Spiritual Director
THE WAY

VII

"Crosses and wreaths can be made to order, and that is a very comforting thought; for when something so un-made-to-order *as death turns up, it is a pathetic sort of consolation for us to switch our attentions on to something that can be made to order."*

AUSTIN FARRER
Warden of Keble College, Oxford, 1960–1968
SAID OR SUNG

I

DIMLY I began to realise that I was quite alone.

All my employees were absent from the house so no one heard me when I shouted Lyle's name over and over again, and no one saw me when I crawled off my knees after the failure of my attempt to revive her. For some time I sat on the edge of the sofa where she had been waiting for me. Wholly disabled by shock I could do nothing else. The silence in the room became profound.

At last I realised I had to summon the doctor, but the act of making a telephone call seemed beyond my power to accomplish. I stared at the bottle of whisky, standing beside the sandwiches which Lyle had made for me, but I was unable to pick it up. The terrible silence went on and on and on.

In the end a primitive psychological mechanism, an antidote to shock, began to operate in my mind. I denied the death. Telling myself that Lyle could be revived in hospital I found I was able to summon not only my local doctor but an ambulance. Then I poured myself a small whisky. My hand was quite steady.

The silence closed in on me again as I waited, and after a while I knelt down by Lyle's body again to see if she showed signs of recovering from her unprecedented fainting fit. I even took her hand in mine as if to escort her back to consciousness. When she still failed to revive I knew I was on the brink of panic but I decided to calm myself by reciting my current mantra. Then I would be in control of my emotions, in control of my surroundings, in control of all I had to be in control of, in control of the uncontrollable.

" 'All things work together for good,' " I said aloud, " 'to them that love God.' "

The silence instantly consumed the words but they remained echoing obscenely in my consciousness.

All things work together for good . . .

I looked down at Lyle's body and thought: what good can ever come out of this? But God did not answer; God had slipped over the edge of the horizon; God had been driven away by the immense darkness which now surrounded me on all sides.

I had moved from shock to denial, but now my denial dissolved into rage.

All things work together for good—

"No!" I shouted. "No, *no,* NO!" And seizing the bottle of whisky I hurled it with all my strength at the nearest wall.

2

OF COURSE I cleaned up the mess straight away. I cleaned it up before the ambulance arrived, of course I did; after all, I was the bishop, I had to behave in a certain way, the tradition had to be upheld and I had to set an example to my community. I knew that. I knew it as I swept up the broken glass, I knew it as I scrubbed the carpet with a floor-cloth, I knew it as I held the electric iron close to the wall to dry out the wallpaper. I knew it as the ambulance men arrived, I knew it as I explained that in the shock I had spilled a little whisky, nothing much, sorry the room smelled like a public bar, all such a shock, but never mind, I was sure they quite understood. "I suppose she's in some sort of coma," I said, slipping away from reality again as I struggled to endure their presence, and I thought of the story of Jairus's daughter and how the Liberal Modernists had speculated that she had been not dead but deeply unconscious when she had been healed by Jesus all those years ago in Palestine. Then I heard one of the ambulance men suggest that I should have a brandy and I realised with dismay that I was presenting a disordered image to these strangers who were being so helpful.

"I'm all right," I said. "Don't need brandy. Didn't have it when I was a POW, shan't have it now. Just get her to hospital and put her in an iron lung or something to help her breathe." And as I spoke I was remembering the concentration camp where chaos had reigned and God had appeared absent and I had never known from one day to the next whether I would survive. Then my memory spun backwards beyond the war—both wars—to my childhood when again I had lived with uncertainty and never known from one day to the next if my strict father would decide to beat me in order to bring me up properly. One had to have certainties otherwise life became hideous, painful, terrifying. Order had to be promoted and defended with tenacity. It was a question of survival.

"I'm all right," I said later to my doctor—and indeed to everyone who flocked to my rescue. "It's a terrible shock, but I've got everything under control."

I was floundering around in reality now, that violent world where death tore gaping holes in the fabric of life, but fortunately my position as bishop meant that I knew how to reduce it to order. There were rituals to be observed, tradition to be embraced, standards to be maintained.

Clinging to the formalities like a limpet I began to plan a faultless funeral.

3

SO MANY people kept interrupting me. I behaved perfectly, saying all the right things, but I wished the people could be somewhere else. I was surprised how fatigued I became by all those devoted Christians, caring for me and trying so hard to help. "See how those Christians love one another!" the pagans had marvelled in the days of the Early Church, but I discovered I did not want hordes of Christians loving me. I wanted one special Christian loving me, but she was no longer there.

I went on behaving perfectly. I talked about how wonderful everyone was being. I even made theological remarks about the outpouring of grace which can result from a tragedy. No one would have guessed how alienated I felt, how dislocated, devastated and adrift. No one except Jon.

Emerging from his hermitage to see me he said: "You're reminding me of how you were in 1937 when we first met," but I refused to understand and when he saw I could not face this truth he did not press it. Meanwhile everyone was expressing admiration for my courage in adversity and I felt pleased that I was managing to have such a well-ordered bereavement—but of course it was not my true self who was acting the bereaved bishop to perfection. It was the malign alter ego which back in 1937 at the time of my spiritual crisis I had called my "glittering image." No wonder Jon had been reminded of the past! The shock of Lyle's death had caused such psychological disruption that now once more the glittering image ran my life while I—*I,* the real Charles Ashworth—remained dumb and paralysed in his shadow.

"I'm quite capable of working," the glittering image said to my suffragan and both archdeacons after they had arrived at the South Canonry to devise a plan for managing the diocese while I was disabled. I even smiled at them, but no one smiled back and I found their expressions unreadable. Finally my suffragan said in a tone which I could not quite classify: "At least leave everything to us until after the funeral. You must have so much to do."

The glittering image recognised at once that it would be wrong to sound ungracious. I heard him say: "Very well, if you insist, but do please consult me whenever it's necessary."

Meanwhile the sympathy letters were arriving in such abundance that I found I had no time to read them, so I told Miss Peabody to prepare a file which I could browse through later. That was the moment when I realised I was worried about Miss Peabody. She seemed so hushed and docile, not herself at all.

I thought what a relief it was that in contrast to everyone around me I had my feelings so absolutely in control.

4

THE FUNERAL ran as smoothly as a royal pageant. At first I had thought I might ask one of my Cambridge friends to give the address, but I decided in the end that an academic might be too cerebral. I felt I wanted someone who was well accustomed to funerals, someone who had spent his working life as a parish priest, so I turned to one of my oldest friends, Philip Wetherall, whom I had met in my twenties. Philip had once been the vicar of Jon's parish, Starrington Magna, and was now in charge of two rural parishes in the north of the diocese after resisting all my attempts to promote him. At the beginning of our careers we had drifted apart, and when I had become Archbishop Lang's chaplain I had even been arrogant enough to pity Philip as he toiled in his obscure curacy, but those days were long ago and now I could see so clearly that he was fulfilled and happy, being exactly the kind of priest he had been designed to be. In fact occasionally I wondered if the wheel had turned full circle and he was the one gripped by pity as he saw me endure so much wear and tear in my bishopric.

I asked Philip not merely to give the address but to conduct the entire service in the Cathedral. As I was concentrating so hard on playing my part I only heard the occasional phrase, but I knew the address must be excellent because the silence among the mourners was so intense. Philip was white-haired now and wore glasses, but I could still look at him and remember him as he was in the 1920s when we had drunk beer together and debated the Modernist heresies of Bethune-Baker, Hensley Henson and Hastings Rashdall on those long, hot summer evenings so many years ago.

I was aware of women crying, but their grief did not disturb me; women are allowed to cry at funerals. Adult males closely related to the deceased are also allowed a quick tear or two, provided that the tears are shed with discretion, but Michael, unlike Charley, remained dry-eyed throughout the service. Judging from the odour of brandy which enveloped him, I assumed he was too inebriated to be much aware of his surroundings.

I myself had drunk no alcohol since Lyle's death. Bishops never relied on alcohol as a prop. Bishops merely drank as part of the social ritual: a small glass of Tio Pepe here and there, a little claret at the Athenaeum, a single whisky at the end of a long day. A bishop had to be perfect, perfect, perfect, a model for his flock, a Christian hero on a pedestal—never "letting the side down," as we used to say at school, always "playing the game."

The glittering image—being perfect, perfect, perfect—listened to Philip reciting the traditional words about resurrection and thought: quite so. But I—*I,* the real Charles Ashworth—thought: what do I really believe about life after death?

Yet this was an unacceptable question because it implied uncertainty and uncertainty implied a disordered mind, something which could not be permitted if I wanted to survive that funeral. I had to think clear, simple, well-ordered thoughts from which all doubt had been completely eliminated. That was the best way to manage myself, the best way to lead the flock, the best way to serve God at this particular time.

God?

In a moment of panic I looked around the Cathedral as if I could prove his existence by glimpsing him among the mourners—what a descent into crude anthropomorphism!—but all I saw were white strained faces registering various degrees of grief. Later I looked around the cemetery, but there was no hint of his presence there either and I saw only bare trees, winter skies and frozen grass. Then I remembered how although God had seemed to be absent from my world during the war, Aysgarth had said to me on my return home: "He couldn't have been absent if you, a man of God, were there." And as I remembered those words I realised I was watching Philip as he finished conducting the service. He was a man of God and he was undoubtedly there—which meant that God was undoubtedly there too, but how interesting that he should be manifesting himself not in the Bishop who was so busy "playing the game," not in the worldly leader who was so much at home in the ecclesiastical corridors of power, but in a humble, elderly country priest—and yes, there was a message for me there, I could see there was, but I was too damaged to grapple with it. I could only think of those words of Christ which Philip had recited: "I am the Resurrection and the Life, and he that believeth in me, though he be dead, yet shall he live . . ." And for one profoundly disorientating moment I felt as if *I* was the one who was dead and *I* was the one being called to life—only that was a mad thought, not rational, and had to be shoved to the back of my mind where it could be forgotten.

The last clod of earth fell on the coffin.

Michael finally shed a tear.

I did put my arm around him, but he pushed it away and turned aside.

5

HOURS LATER when my sons were in bed and I was alone in my study, I opened the file of sympathy letters which Miss Peabody had prepared and found on the top a note attached by a paperclip to a sealed envelope. The note, written on paper embossed with the Deanery's address, read: "Dear Miss Peabody, I enclose a letter of condolence for the Bishop. Please could you see that it is passed unopened to him. Yours sincerely, STEPHEN AYSGARTH."

Reluctantly, not in the least anxious to know what kind of sympathy letter he had concocted but realising that the communication had to be faced, I broke the seal of the envelope and extracted the contents.

"My dear Charles," I read. "I was very shocked to hear of Lyle's death. I felt that an important strand in a complicated pattern had been lost, yet at the same time I wondered if the inevitable alteration of the pattern can in some way reweave the threads which became so unfortunately entangled after the war. If that could be accomplished, then we would be witnessing not a diminished present but a past redeemed.

"You may well think that I act in execrable taste by using a sympathy letter to recall that part of the past which we have both tried so unsuccessfully to bury, but since death is the point where we all have to face the realities of life, I venture to hope that you will see my action not as an embarrassing faux-pas by someone who never received your social and educational advantages, but as the gesture of a Christian who believes passionately in the power of Christ to heal those who are alienated from each other, and in the power of the Holy Spirit to redeem all that has gone wrong.

"Of course I send you my deepest sympathy on your loss. But I also send you my deepest apology for my wrong action in 1945, and I hope that if you respond, as I pray you will, we shall finally be able to set to rest that part of the past which has poisoned the atmosphere between us for so long.

"Yours most sincerely, STEPHEN."

I shuddered. Then I tore the letter into fragments which I burnt in the ashtray.

I sat looking at the ashes for some time, and at last it occurred to me that I was no longer "playing the game." Bishops never burnt sympathy letters in revulsion and harboured unchristian thoughts about men they detested. I realised I ought to feel ashamed of myself.

But I felt no shame. I was unsure what I did feel, but shame was certainly not among the emotions jostling for pride of place in my mind. I knew I was very upset and I thought I was also very angry, but I was so shattered that it was hard to be sure.

Then I realised that I could take a rest from "playing the game." The funeral was over. I was on my own. There was no one left whom I had to impress.

I had a double-brandy.

I did try and read some of the other sympathy letters but the words failed to register and after five minutes I closed the file, went to bed and sank into an exhausted sleep.

I felt as if I had managed to survive a nightmare. But of course the real nightmare, the real ordeal of bereavement, was now about to begin.

6

SOME HOURS later I found myself sitting in my study after taking the boys to catch the early train to London. Neither Miss Peabody nor my chaplains nor Malcolm had yet appeared, but all were due to arrive within the hour. At eleven Nigel would arrive from Starmouth and the work would disappear, like dust vanishing before a Hoover. David, Malcolm's opposite number in the south of the diocese, was left behind in Starmouth to hold the fort while Nigel performed the Herculean feat of attending to the needs of the whole diocese, but how long my suffragan should be obliged to continue in this heroic fashion was open to debate. I told myself that now the funeral was over I should return to work straight away.

The telephone began to ring as I sat torpidly at my desk and contemplated the short journey to the office. After a while I realised I was gazing at the dust which had accumulated on my desk. No one had dusted anything lately. No one kept an eye on the charwoman, who seemed to spend her time drinking cups of tea with the cook-housekeeper and saying what a tragedy it all was. The cook-housekeeper now devoted her time only to shopping and serving tepid meals. No one polished my shoes or picked up my suits from the cleaner's or filled my cigarette-case or put petrol in the car. Streams of devoted ladies, who were affiliated in some way with the Cathedral, offered soup, cakes and even meals which could be stored in the new deep-freeze, but I could hardly ask any of these worthy neighbours to fulfil the duties of valet, chauffeur and personal assistant. Besides, the glittering image had been giving everyone the impression that the Bishop was more than capable of dealing with humdrum chores. Bishops did not sink into a helpless inertia, no matter how grave the circumstances; helpless inertia was not the done thing at all.

I sat, helpless and inert, and listened to the ringing of the telephone.

It rang and rang. In the end it was sheer irritation which drove me to lift the receiver and murmur: "South Canonry."

Jon said: "Congratulations."

I was so astonished to hear his voice that I failed to grasp why I was being praised. Jon liked to be quite alone in the mornings after he had celebrated mass in the family chapel by his cottage. The fact that he had not only abandoned his routine but walked up to the main house to make a telephone call made me realise he had something very serious to say. Struggling to concentrate I said: "Jon?"

"Who else would be telephoning to congratulate you on your magnificent performance? Charles, I'd like to see you this morning, and when I say you, I mean *you,* the real Charles Ashworth. That other person is to be left behind at the South Canonry."

I was so dazed by this plain speaking that I could only say: "What other person?"

"The glittering image," said Jon crossly, annoyed that I should be so obtuse, and replaced the receiver with a thud.

7

I LOOKED at the clock. I had missed Matins in order to take the boys to the station, and although I had planned to go to Communion in order to keep up appearances I had been too overwhelmed by inertia to leave my study after I had returned home. I had not read the office. I had done no spiritual exercises, no theological reading. I had been entirely preoccupied by the task of behaving properly in front of my sons and driving them to the station without having an accident. These tasks had consumed my last reserve of energy so that now all I could do was think: yes, I shall drive to Starrington to see Jon. But as the minutes passed I made no move.

Eventually the thought of the Communion service which I had missed reminded me of the Cathedral, and the thought of the Cathedral reminded me not only of Aysgarth but of his letter.

I started to recall the incident to which he had referred, the incident which Lyle had told me about long ago in 1945. After a while I found I could even hear her voice.

"Neville Aysgarth was there . . ."

Neville was Aysgarth's real name. It was not until some time after his second marriage in 1945 that people began to follow his new wife's example and call him Stephen. Dido had declared that the name Neville had been irrevocably ruined by Mr. Chamberlain and that the name of an early Christian hero was much more suitable for her husband, but Lyle and I—and I suspect other people too—had had so much trouble seeing Aysgarth as a Christian hero that we had never wholly achieved the adjustment which Dido had demanded of us. This was why he was so widely known as "Aysgarth." Caught between the discarded "Neville" and the inappropriate "Stephen," many people found that the surname was the most comfortable way of referring to him in his absence.

"Neville Aysgarth was there," Lyle said in my memory. She had been talking about the funeral of her former employer, Bishop Jardine. The service had been held at the Oxfordshire village to which Jardine and his wife Carrie had retired.

"Neville Aysgarth was there . . ." I could hear her voice so clearly now that I flinched. "It turned out we'd both been invited to stay with Carrie, but after the funeral she went upstairs to rest so Aysgarth and I were on our own. We were in such a state—I thought you were dead, his honeymoon with Dido had been a disaster, and we'd both been demolished by the funeral. So we started to drink. I was supposed to be preparing dinner. I was standing by the kitchen sink with a gin-and-tonic the size of a goldfish bowl while Aysgarth sat at the kitchen table with a triple-whisky, and then suddenly—*suddenly*—Dr. Jekyll became Mr. Hyde. It was so odd that it's hard to describe what happened next . . ."

Lyle's voice flowed on, urgent and unstoppable. By that time I had left the chair behind my desk. I was pacing up and down the room as the memory streamed through my mind.

"You remember how serious he was when we first met him at the Darrows' wedding in 1940? You remember how we wrote him off as prim and proper? Well, he wasn't prim and proper. We got him wrong. He wasn't prim and proper at all . . ."

The study made me feel claustrophobic. Blundering out into the hall I groped in the cloakroom for my coat.

". . . and he made a pass at me—I mean a heavy pass—and I was just so startled that I was a bit slow off the mark in fighting him off—although I did fight him off, of course I did, I fought him tooth and nail, but I had to fight pretty hard, and in fact I think if he hadn't been a clergyman he would have gone even further than he did—but then, thank God, he pulled himself together and there was no harm done—well, no, I can't quite say that, because he went to bed with the whisky bottle while I spent the night sicking up the gin, but at least we did agree the next morning to treat the entire episode as if it had never happened . . ."

I was opening the front door but I had forgotten my hat. I usually wore a hat when I went out, usually but not always, and indeed I had realised only the other day that I was wearing a hat less and less. Lyle had said the biggest change in men's fashion since the war had been the mass abandonment of hats.

". . . and I did decide I wouldn't mention it to you, but now that you know I was at Alex's funeral it's obviously best that you should also know exactly what went on there, but you needn't worry, darling, because it was just one of those stupid, humiliating incidents which actually mean nothing at all in the long run, and now much the best thing to do is to forget about it. After all, we're hardly going to be seeing Aysgarth every day in future, are we?"

Having retrieved my hat I opened the front door again but realised I had left no note to explain my absence. In the office I pencilled a few words to Miss Peabody.

". . . and the truth is I never want to see him again so you needn't waste any energy feeling jealous—oh darling, I'm so sorry, don't be upset, I love you so much . . ."

I suddenly realised I was sitting in the driving-seat of my car and searching for my key. Several seconds passed before I saw it was already in the ignition. I had no memory of putting it there.

Rain spattered the windscreen as I drove past the Cathedral, and the west front, shrouded in scaffolding, looked mutilated. Above the central tower the spire was lost in heavy cloud.

"I hate that man," Lyle's voice said in my head as my memory spun forward to 1957, the year I accepted the bishopric and Aysgarth accepted the Deanery and we all wound up living in the Close at Starbridge. "Every time I look at him I see the Jardines' kitchen and that gin-and-tonic the size of a goldfish bowl."

"But surely if nothing of importance happened—if you fought him off so furiously—"

"Oh yes, yes, yes, don't listen to me! I'm just temporarily knocked silly by living alongside the Aysgarths, but I'll get over it, I'll survive . . ."

I had reached the main gateway of the Close but I could not remember where I was supposed to be going. The windscreen wipers were labouring beneath a torrent of rain and beyond the medieval arch the traffic lights of Eternity Street shone a dull red in the gloom.

I heard myself say to Jon back in 1957: "Lyle's bothered by Aysgarth, I can't think why, he always behaves immaculately towards her, but now she even says she hates him. Bearing in mind that nothing truly unspeakable happened between them all those years ago, don't you think her behaviour's a trifle extreme?"

But Jon had said calmly, soothingly, in reply: "Now that Lyle's the Bishop's wife she's no doubt excruciatingly embarrassed that she once got dead drunk with the man who's become the Dean. I'd say that was a very natural reaction in the circumstances . . ."

A horn sounded behind me. I suddenly realised that the car was stationary in front of green traffic lights, but at least I could now remember where I was supposed to be going.

Turning left into Eternity Street, I crossed the hump-backed bridge over the river and headed rapidly north from the city to Jon's home in Starrington Magna.

8

"I TRUST you left your alter ego behind," said Jon as soon as he opened the door of his cottage.

"I believe he's finally faded away out of sheer exhaustion."

Crossing the threshold I almost collided with the cat who was heading in the opposite direction; striped fur hurtled past my ankles and disappeared outside. Jon produced tea. We sat down together at the table by the window. He was wearing a spotless clerical suit, carefully pressed, and looked, I was sure, very much smarter than I did. He had once told me that old age should be no excuse for scruffiness.

"Forgive me for ordering you over here," he was saying, "but I could no longer bear the thought of that glittering image ruling the roost at the South Canonry."

"It was a relief to be ordered around for once."

We drank some tea in silence. Jon made no effort to rush me into speech, but I managed to say before the silence became too prolonged: "It was a good funeral, wasn't it?"

"Very fitting."

"It was kind of you to come."

"Not at all."

Conversation ceased again. I was unable to strike anything which sounded like the right note. Mutely I sat at the table and waited to be rescued.

"What else has been going on?" said Jon, taking pity on me at last.

"I'm not sure. It's all a bit of a blur. Nigel's running the diocese for me."

"Ah."

"The major problems have all been temporarily frozen. Desmond Wilton's out of hospital and spending a convalescent holiday at Allington Court. Malcolm had to tell him I'd found the pornography—Desmond might have had a heart attack if he'd found it had vanished from his wardrobe—but Malcolm said we'd sort out that problem later and that his first task now was to get well. Meanwhile that itinerant exorcist has grabbed the job of locum; it really did seem the easiest way out of the Langley Bottom dilemma, although of course I can't possibly allow him to work permanently in the diocese. And as for the Cathedral . . . well, Nigel's tackled Aysgarth about the plundering of the library but Aysgarth obstinately refuses to discuss the matter with anyone but me. However, he's suspended the Christie's transaction, so at least the books are safe for the time being."

"Good. But Charles, I don't want to hear about the activities of your archdeacon and your suffragan. I don't even want to know, fascinating though it may be, about the latest move made by your itinerant exorcist. I want to know what's been happening to you."

"Well, of course it's been a harrowing time, but one can hardly expect the aftermath of one's wife's death to be a picnic. The good news is that Michael brought Holly, his new girlfriend, to the funeral and she's a great improvement on Dinkie even though she's at present sharing a flat with that dangerous girl Marina Markhampton. Thank God Charley keeps himself aloof from that set—and talking of Charley, there's more good news because he's going to make his Lent retreat with the Fordites at Grantchester and I'm sure Father Wilcox will sort out this pseudo-call to the cloister."

"Splendid. Now Charles, I can see you're trying hard to have an honest conversation with me so I shan't be cross with you, but I really think you ought to do better than this. How's your life of prayer? When did you last receive the sacrament? Apart from the funeral, have you been able to face going to church?"

I drank my tea and stared down at the grain of the table as I tried to frame a sentence which was truthful but not too shaming for a bishop to utter.

"Sorry," said Jon at last. "My fault. Too many questions. Let's just choose one: have you been able to face going to church?"

"I went to weekday Matins a couple of times and I went to the early service last Sunday." I forced myself to add: "I felt I had to keep up appearances."

"I see. So it was the glittering image who went to church. Has he also been doing your praying for you?"

"No. I haven't really been able to pray at all."

"I'd rather hear that than hear your alter ego has been going through the motions. Are you at least able to read your theology?"

"I can't even read a newspaper."

"Had any whisky lately?"

"Not a drop. I did have a soupçon of brandy last night, but I felt I'd earned it for enduring the funeral."

"What exactly is a soupçon?"

"A smidgin." We laughed. Then I said: "A double. But I shan't do that again."

"What makes you so certain?"

"I was reacting to something which won't recur—and I'm not just talking about the funeral. I had the most nauseating letter from Aysgarth."

"What was wrong with it?"

"Everything."

"How curious! I've heard that Aysgarth has a considerable talent for letter-writing. Did you bring the letter with you?"

"No, I burnt it."

" 'Curiouser and curiouser,' as Alice would say! Are you going to tell me more or does it defy your powers of description?"

"He dragged up that incident in 1945 when he pawed Lyle and she boxed his ears—he talked as if there was a hatchet to be buried. Oh, the whole thing was the most revolting exercise in bad taste! No wonder I was tempted to knock back the brandy."

"How will you answer him?"

"I'll just pen a line saying the entire incident's long since been forgiven and forgotten. I can't think why on earth he chose to bring it up. Anyone would think they'd actually been to bed together."

There was a pause. Jon looked down at his folded hands.

"Well, of course," I said, "I know they didn't. But I did always wonder if there was rather more to the incident than Lyle was willing to admit."

Jon never moved.

"I think there was a moment when she found him sexually attractive," I said. "That was why she was slow off the mark in fighting him off, that was why the memory of the incident disturbed her so much and that was why she hated him—only it wasn't really Aysgarth she hated; she was projecting on to him the hatred she felt for herself for not finding him immediately resistible. It was all mixed up with that trauma she went through in the 1930s. Her susceptibility would have frightened her and awakened all the bad memories—I understood all that," I said, speaking with increasing speed. "I understood that sometimes it was better just to love her and not ask questions. She didn't want to be questioned further about that incident with Aysgarth, so I didn't. And I'm sure I was right. It was a question of trust. I trusted that she would never have gone to bed with him. I trusted that she would never have betrayed me like that."

Jon nodded and waited.

"And if Aysgarth thinks for one moment," said my voice furiously, "that I'm nursing some unchristian grudge against him for something I know never happened, he couldn't be more mistaken . . . Did Aysgarth ever talk about this to you?"

"Yes."

"Did he say . . . no, of course you can't tell me. It would have been a confidential conversation, but oh God, if only I knew exactly what happened, if only I knew why Aysgarth obviously felt so *guilty*—"

"Isn't his guilt sufficiently explained by the fact that he, a clergyman, got so drunk that he lost control of himself and made a pass at another man's wife?"

"I don't know, I can't decide, I'm in such a muddle—I just feel that if only I knew for certain, one way or the other—"

"I think you should have faith in Lyle," said Jon.

Tears of relief burnt my eyes. I had not wept since Lyle's death because I had been too afraid of losing my grip on the fragile order I had established, but now at last I was able to say in despair: "How am I ever going to live without her?" And leaning forward on the table I buried my face in my arms.

VIII

"The Christian sufferer need not know why the blow was struck. He wants to discover what God is doing in the face of it . . ."

AUSTIN FARRER
Warden of Keble College, Oxford, 1960–1968
LOVE ALMIGHTY AND ILLS UNLIMITED

I

WHEN I had pulled myself together I managed to say: "It would be easier to bear if I could see meaning in the chaos. It's meaningless suffering which is unendurable."

"So you said after the war when we were talking of your experiences as a POW. And I suggested, if you remember, that since God never wills suffering but works always to redeem it, the perception of meaning is an important part of the redemptive process."

"Well, I don't see any meaning here and I can't imagine such a disaster being redeemed. Since my life's been permanently diminished—"

"Your life has been permanently changed. Whether it remains permanently diminished is up to you. You actually have three options here. One: you can be passive and give God no help whatsoever. Two: you can be active by putting up a front and bustling around until you crack up with sheer exhaustion. Or three: you can be active by being yourself (which is, after all, what God wants) and trying to re-establish contact with God through prayer so that you can at least make some attempt to assist in the redemptive process. The more you align yourself with God, the greater chance the Holy Spirit has of flowing into this situation and redeeming it in ways neither of us can at present imagine."

"I hear what you say. I understand what you say. I know intellectually that what you say is right. But"—despair overwhelmed me again—"all

I can think at the moment is: why did this have to happen to me, it's not fair, I want her back, I didn't deserve this, I've had enough pain in my life, I'd earned the right to a happy old age with the woman I love—loved—" I could not go on.

"Well, don't just say that to me, Charles! Say it to God! Shout with rage like the psalmist! Put aside that glittering image and let God know how the real Charles Ashworth feels! And then in the silence that follows I think not only that he'll speak to you but that you'll be able to hear him again."

But all that happened when Jon finished speaking was that another kind of silence began, the silence of a wet dark morning in winter, the silence of desolation, the silence of hell.

I covered my face once more with my hands.

2

JON STOOD up and moved his chair around the table so that he could sit beside me. More time elapsed but at last I said: "Tell me what to do to get myself into a state where I can pray properly."

"Charles, I don't have a magic wand to wave and I'm not going to dictate to you. I'm no longer so spiritually strong-willed and over-confident as I was when we met in 1937—or at least I hope I'm not—"

"I want you to dictate to me. I want you to take over, get the disaster under control, reduce it to order before I go off my head—"

"Naturally. How useful that would be! But that's the magic wand solution and it doesn't exist because this is *your* disaster, *your* bereavement, *your* tragedy, and you're the only person who can triumph over it—I can't triumph over it on your behalf and transmit the triumph to you by some flashy use of psychic power. Now, let's try and be practical for a moment. Can you drop everything, leave home and come to stay here at the Manor for two weeks? I fear your most immediate problem is isolation combined with the apathy which stems from despair."

"Yes, but for the moment I've got to stay at the South Canonry."

"Is that because you don't trust Nigel and Malcolm to hold the fort?"

"No, it's because . . ." But I found I could not quite put my reason into words.

"Is it possible for you to come here on a daily basis? If you were to arrive in time for Matins and mass in the chapel, for instance, and leave after Evensong—"

"Yes, I could manage that."

"But you have to get back to the South Canonry every night?"

"Yes, it's because . . ." I hesitated again but finally succeeded in finding the right words. "It's because I haven't yet said goodbye to Lyle."

"Too busy organising the funeral, being the Bishop and doing the done thing?"

"Exactly. So what I've got to do now is say goodbye in my own time in my own way and to do that I have to be close to her at night, I need to remember her in the rooms where she lived. It's part of the process of grieving."

"It's certainly part of the process of grieving but it doesn't seem to have much to do with saying goodbye. It sounds much more as if you're trying to hang on to her."

I said mulishly: "It's something I have to do. I can come and see you every day, but at night I have to get back to Starbridge."

"Very well."

Instantly I was suspicious. "You think that's the wrong decision. Why? Do you have some sort of premonition of disaster? What do you think's going to happen?"

"I think that if you try to struggle on alone at the South Canonry at the moment you'll wind up very unhappy, but that prediction's so obvious that it requires no psychic power whatsoever to produce it. But maybe I'm wrong. Or maybe I'm right but you actually need to be very unhappy in order to see the correct way forward. Who knows? I certainly don't . . . Anyway, at least we've agreed that you'll spend tomorrow here and arrive for Matins. Let's just take one day at a time."

In an effort to appease him for my obstinacy I said: "I'll make a new effort to pray. I'll attend Evensong in the Cathedral tonight, and—"

"Oh no!" said Jon at once. "You stay away from that Cathedral!"

I stared at him. "Why?"

"At the moment that's where you put up a front; that's where the glittering image takes control. And besides . . . I didn't care for the Cathedral's atmosphere when I attended the funeral. The whole place needs to be prayed for—and talking of prayer, we should pray for you before you leave. Or if you feel unable to pray, perhaps you can at least listen while I say a prayer on your behalf."

I asked no more questions but sank to my knees, and when he had finished praying I was able to say: "I feel better now I've got a plan of action. Thanks for helping me see my way through the fog." And as I remembered his own crippling bereavement some years earlier, I added: "I do realise things could be worse—at least my grief's uncomplicated by guilt. Lyle and I had our problems in the beginning but we couldn't have been closer or happier at the end."

Jon opened the door and picked up the cat who was sitting on the doorstep. All he said to me was: "I'll look forward to seeing you in the chapel tomorrow morning."

"I'll be there, I promise," I said at once.

But it was a promise I was destined to break.

3

AS I drove home I made up my mind to fight apathy by answering some sympathy letters so as soon as I arrived I retrieved the file and retreated upstairs to Lyle's sitting-room where I knew no one would interrupt me. But I never uncapped my pen. Sitting on the sofa I retreated into my imagination. I had been doing this now for some days. I began by imagining the conversation we might have had if the catastrophe had never happened and then I would visualise other scenes, holidays we might have shared, public engagements, private moments. They all seemed so real, so possible, waiting ahead in that future which would never happen. By savouring them one by one as if they were inevitably going to take place, I was able to rest from the ordeal of my bereavement.

At one o'clock the housekeeper called out that lunch was ready so I went downstairs and consigned the entire meal to some delighted birds beyond the dining-room window. Then it occurred to me that as the boys had now returned to London I could take a rest also from the housekeeper, whose presence was increasingly grating on my nerves, so I explained to her that I was going to be out every day for two weeks and that she could take paid leave during that time. I also told Miss Peabody to give the charwoman similar instructions.

After that I retired to the bedroom, where I managed to escape into unconsciousness for a while. Later I opened the wardrobe, and time passed not unpleasantly as I pictured Lyle in a variety of outfits at numerous occasions in the imaginary future. When I realised the time was four o'clock I decided to brew myself some tea, but on reaching the hall I found the time was not four but six. My watch had stopped. In my growing disorder I had forgotten to wind it.

I was now alone in the house, but that was a relief because I no longer had to worry about meeting people accidentally and trying to think of the correct thing to say. Returning to Lyle's sitting-room I resolved to make a new assault on the sympathy letters, but as soon as I opened the file I was paralysed by the memory of the letter I had burnt. Obviously it was best to reply to Aysgarth straight away so that I could forget about him. Overcoming my inertia by an enormous act of will I sat down at

Lyle's desk and wrote: "My dear Stephen, Thank you for your kind expression of sympathy. I assure you that in my memory the incident to which you refer requires neither a wrathful response on my part nor a guilty supplication on yours. Therefore you may consider the matter entirely closed. Yours sincerely, CHARLES."

After I had placed the envelope in Miss Peabody's out-tray I realised that the effort involved in constructing this brief communication had exhausted me. Then I remembered that I had skipped lunch. Possibly I would feel less exhausted if I had something to eat. Returning to the kitchen I inspected the contents of the larder but decided I had to be revived before I could face food. In the drawing-room I mixed myself a whisky-and-soda.

It was odd that the telephone should be so silent. People had obviously decided to leave me in peace to recover from the funeral. Perhaps Charley would ring later. There was no chance that Michael would—but I could not bear to think of Michael. How were he and I ever going to manage in future without Lyle constantly negotiating reconciliations?

I drank a second whisky and reached for the decanter to pour myself a third, but I thought better of that idea and returned to contemplate the larder shelves again. In the end I opened a can of sardines. Fish were nutritious. Eating fish would be a sensible, well-ordered thing to do. I would eat fish.

I glanced into the open can but as soon as I saw the slimy slivers within I experienced a twinge of nausea. I withdrew to my study and made a sensible, well-ordered list of things to do, but I did none of them; I merely returned to Lyle's sitting-room and resumed my position on the sofa, but this time I found I was unable to escape into the imaginary future. I began to think of the sympathy letters, those stark reminders of reality, and slowly it dawned on me that in penning those few lines to Aysgarth to seal up the past I had opened a window onto a future which I was unable to face. Lighting a cigarette I began to pace up and down the room.

I had just reached the door for the third time and turned to face the sofa when the memory of Lyle's last moments replayed itself so vividly in my mind that I halted. Now indeed reality had me by the throat; I was in the grip of that traumatic reaction which is common among those who have suffered a severe shock. Making a great effort to keep calm, I glanced around for something which would distract my attention and moved towards Lyle's desk, which I had closed after completing the letter to Aysgarth.

I pulled down the lid again and remembered at once how I had opened the desk on the day after her death, not to find her will, which I knew was with our solicitors, but to see if there were any unanswered letters which needed a prompt response. There were not. Lyle, efficient as always, had been up to date with her correspondence and the contents of the desk were arranged with extreme neatness.

I stared at those contents again: the couple of non-urgent letters from old friends, a bill not due for payment until the end of the month, the files relating to her charity work, the catalogues from Marshall and Snelgrove, the stationery, the address-book, the paperclips, pencils and Parker fountain pen. Shutting the lid of the desk I began to open the drawers beneath—any action seemed preferable to doing nothing and laying myself open to a further assault by traumatic memories.

In the drawers I found mementos: photographs of the boys and a selection of their letters from school, photographs of ourselves—and press-cuttings about my activities—all carefully pasted into a scrapbook. The collection of cuttings was not comprehensive; Lyle had merely selected the ones she liked best, and I began to turn the pages to see what new additions she had made to the scrapbook since I had last seen it. As I did so, an envelope fell out and fluttered to the floor.

The envelope contained a letter from Marian Lindsay, Malcolm's wife, who had enclosed a cutting about a visit which I had recently made to my old school. Marian had written: "Lyle dear—thought you might like to see this, it comes from my godson, the one I told you about who's now in the sixth form. He said Charles made a terrific impression on the boys and they loved the fact that he knew so much about cricket and rugger! See you at the prayer-group tomorrow—can't wait! Love, MARIAN."

I saw the words "prayer-group."

I remembered how I had meant to ask Lyle about it but had postponed the task until another time. I remembered how Lyle had tried to talk to me about it on the day of Desmond's disaster, but how I had neither listened nor taken her seriously.

The letter crumpled as I clenched my hand.

Guilt began to ooze from some sudden split in the fabric of my mind. I said desperately: "I'm sorry, I'm sorry . . ." But the only words which echoed in my mind in response were: you'll never hear her talk about that prayer-group now.

In shame I thought: maybe there's a file somewhere, maybe she made notes, maybe there's something I can read which would enable me to share the experience with her in some small way. Dropping Marian's letter in the wastepaper basket, I searched the remaining drawers of the desk and when I found nothing I went to the bedroom. I knew now exactly what

I was trying to find. Before going overseas in the war I had given Lyle a leather writing-case for her birthday and I knew she would never have thrown it away.

I was just thinking that I would have to wade through the junk in the box-room when I found the case under a cashmere shawl in the chest of drawers.

The case was locked. Back I went to her sitting-room where her handbag was still lying beside the sofa. I found the key-ring straight away.

Inside the case were some very old letters, written by Lyle's father who had been killed in the First War, and also a cheap exercise book, the kind one can buy at Woolworth's. Opening the pale blue cover I found that the first page was headed: JOURNAL.

Automatically, not even pausing to think twice, I sat down and started to read.

4

"THIS IS a spiritual exercise," Lyle had written with her fine-nibbed fountain pen. "Clergymen used to keep journals as a spiritual exercise. I remember Alex telling me about his journal soon after he had employed me to be Carrie's companion. How long ago it seems now since I lived with the Jardines! When Alex told me about his journal he was Dean of Radbury and the glamorous years as Bishop of Starbridge were still in the future, but even then he lived in a style which would be unthinkable for a senior cleric today. When he did become a bishop he lived like a prince. All those indoor servants—and the chauffeur-driven car—and the vast quantities of claret in the cellar . . . Funny to think that all the while Alex was bucketing around as a great prince of the Church, he was secretly scribbling away in that journal—and making a hash of it. He told me once that in the end his journal bore no relation to what was actually going on in his life, and of course that was why his awful autobiography, based on the journal, was such a travesty.

"Poor Alex! Starbridge demolished him in the end, ploughed him under, I can see that now. It overwhelmed him with too much wealth, too much glamour, too much mind-numbing beauty. Deep down, Alex was always the self-made man trying to compensate himself for that hellish childhood which was so dark and dreary and impoverished, and he just didn't have the inner stability to withstand an appointment such as the Starbridge bishopric. It cut him off from God, cut him off from himself, cut him off from the truth so that his journal became fiction.

'Flawless, fairytale Starbridge!' I can remember him saying as he gazed dotingly at the Cathedral. 'So beautiful!' But it finished him. Savage, sinister Starbridge! A fairytale, perhaps, but not an innocent little fable from Hans Christian Andersen. More like some gruesome concoction of the Brothers Grimm.

"But I'm not going to let Starbridge plough me under and I'm going to write a journal that's true. Why do I have to do this? Several reasons: (a) I feel that we're very mixed up as a family and that we're now wandering around in such a fog of illusion that it's about time someone made the effort to discern the truth; (b) I'm seriously worried about Charles, but because he's the Bishop I don't dare discuss him with anyone and so confiding in a journal is the only safety valve available to me; (c) I'm pretty damned fed up, but again I daren't say so (bishops' wives aren't allowed to be fed up) and anyway I'm not exactly sure why I'm so cross, but I think if I write down my thoughts I might eventually have a better grasp of what's going on; and (d) today, 15th November, 1963, I had lunch with Venetia in London and it was a disaster. I'd really looked forward to seeing her again, but I could tell the meeting was too painful for her. That's because I remind her of Starbridge—demonic, destructive Starbridge!—and a lot of memories which she now longs to forget.

"I understand but I'm upset. I want to help her but I don't know how. All I could think on the train was: I can do nothing more for that girl now except pray for her. But the trouble is I'm not very good at praying. In fact I'm spiritually pretty stupid. What an awful confession for a bishop's wife to make! But there—I've said it. Or rather, I've written it down. And I feel a bit better, so I think I must be on the right track. I'll keep writing things down and see where I get to.

"MEMO TO GOD: Please excuse my spiritual stupidity and show me the way forward. But make sure you spell the way out to me very clearly because otherwise I shan't understand."

* * *

"16th November, 1963. I've reread what I wrote yesterday. What a muddle! And God must have thought me rather impertinent at the end. Never mind. Soldier on. I've just tried praying for Venetia, but I can't believe it'll do her any good. However, *I* feel better. Interesting. I suppose if one's powerless any activity, even prayer, is better than doing nothing, and—wait a moment. I'm not just powerless to help Venetia. I'm also powerless in regard to my other problems. Perhaps I should pray about them too. Of course I'm always praying for Charles and the boys and our life as a family, but that's routine, like brushing my teeth, and I'm not really *praying,* not actively trying to open up my mind and will to God and begging for enlightenment so that the situation can be seen in the light of truth and changed. If you name the demons you gain power over them, as they used to say in the old days. So (metaphorically speaking, of course) I have to uncover the names of the demons here so that they can be conquered and cast out. Or in other words, I have to uncover the truth because the truth will give me power over all the illusions—the truth will set me free.

"MEMO TO GOD: It looks as if you're calling me to pray, but I can't help thinking this is very eccentric of you as I have no obvious gift for prayer. Make it very clear, please, if I'm on the wrong track, because I don't want to waste either your time or mine."

* * *

"17th November, 1963. I keep thinking about prayer, although I can't decide whether this is an indication that I'm going senile or that God's sending some sort of signal. When I passed that brute of a Cathedral today I thought: Perhaps I should pray for it. (I'll be praying for everything at this rate!) Why should I have this urge to pray for the Cathedral? I was thinking of Stephen and Charles and their hopeless relationship as Dean and Bishop, and suddenly I wondered if the Devil had got into the Cathedral back in the 1930s, when poor Alex was Bishop, and had never been permanently ejected—with the result that every so often he (the Devil) comes back and creates havoc, chewing people up left, right and centre.

"Do I really believe in the Devil? No. But I do believe in the dark forces of the human mind and how they can be projected outwards to blight other people. Can these forces also blight buildings? And even if they do, is it really possible to cleanse such buildings by prayer? That sounds a bit dubious to me. I can see prayer working when humans pray for humans; it's a sort of mind-over-matter, extra-sensory-perception activity, which is why that awful old monster Jon Darrow's so good at it. But how can prayer affect a building, which has no mind? But maybe buildings have spirits. No, that's animism. It's humans who have spirits. But humans do inhabit buildings. And if all creation is a unity . . .

"No, I really must be going peculiar, speculating about such odd things. I do hope it's not the onset of senility, but at least it can't be the onset of the menopause. (Thank God for large mercies.)

"MEMO TO GOD: I'm praying away but I still can't quite believe this is what you want me to do—and when I say *me* I mean ME, Lyle, not Mrs.

Bishop, the fabulous clerical accessory, and not Mum, the fabulous clerical mother. If each human being is created for a special purpose in your plan, then by all means show me what my purpose is at this stage of my life so that I can do it, but can it really be prayer? Honestly? Surely I'm better equipped to do something more interesting and rewarding?"

* * *

"18th November, 1963. No reply from God, of course. But what did I expect? A telegram on a silver salver borne by an angel?

"Acting on the principle that I should soldier on, since it's better to do something than nothing, I made the decision to get up early so that I can do my praying while Charles is reading his theology. I don't like getting up early but it's the only time when peace and quiet are guaranteed, and if I'm going to soldier on with the praying I must at least try to do it properly.

"I'm still thinking about Venetia and wishing for the umpteenth time that I had a daughter—which is so silly, I know, because I couldn't have coped with a third child and anyway I'm sure I'd have been madly jealous of her later when she was flouncing around being gorgeous and attracting droves of young men. Also, being incorrigibly sentimental about young girls, Charles would have pampered her to death, just as he's pampered Charley, under the mistaken delusion that pampering means you're a good parent.

"I know why Charles does this. It's because he doesn't think *he* was pampered enough by his father when he was little, but actually my sympathies lie entirely with Eric, trying to give Charles a sensible upbringing while that awful Helen, who I thought was the last word in mindless femininity, spoilt him rotten.

"The irony is that if you dig deep enough into Charles's convoluted psyche, you realise that he found his mother very tiresome once he was grown up but Eric he respected and admired. Yet Charles is so gripped by this compulsion not to make Eric's 'mistakes' that he's lost sight of the fact that Eric did a tremendous job in difficult circumstances. After all, if he hadn't, Charles would hardly have made this huge success of his life; he'd be lying on a psychiatrist's couch and sobbing that Helen had converted him into a 'mother's boy,' but anyone less like a 'mother's boy' than Charles, who's a tough, brave survivor, is hard to imagine. Good old Eric. He was a tricky old bastard in some ways, but I quite liked him.

"I prayed for Charles today. I mean, I didn't just say: 'Please, God, bless my husband,' like some lobotomised clerical wife. I shouted in my head: 'HELP HIM, HELP HIM!' And I thought about this ghastly relationship with Charley—yes, CHARLEY, not Michael—and I tried to set it out neatly before God, but it was all such a muddle I gave up.

"How do I tell Charles that if you love a child wisely you don't pamper it? Answer: I can't. He'd get upset at the implication that his love for Charley is out of alignment, in some hidden way not ringing true. Charles thinks *I'm* the one who doesn't love Charley properly just because I don't smother him in gooey behaviour, but Charley's so emotional that the last thing he needs is a parent being emotional back. I know I'm austere with Charley, but that's not because I don't love him properly; it's because I do. He often irritates me enormously, but all children irritate their parents sometimes, that's normal. What's not normal is for the parent to be forever radiating sweetness and light no matter how much the child plays up. I adore Michael, but even Michael I never allowed to get away with bad behaviour when he was young.

"I actually think that in my own peculiar way I'm a good mother. It nearly killed me, bringing up those two boys, but if there were exams for parenthood I'd pass them. Charles, I know, thinks I'm not really cut out for motherhood just because I don't slop around being sentimental and effusive like *his* mother, but he's blind to the truth—which is that *he's* the one who'd have a hard time passing the parenthood exams. Can I ever tactfully point this out to Charles? No. He'd never believe me.

"The ironic part is—more irony—that although Charles and Michael don't get on at the moment and although Charles thinks *this* is the relationship which has gone profoundly adrift, the truth is that the two of them deep down—DEEP down—are comfortable with each other. By that I mean they have a relationship that's real, not phony. It doesn't matter that Charles yells and screams at Michael and Michael yells and screams back—or at least it does matter, it's frightful, especially for me, but it doesn't alter the fact that they have a blood relationship which can't be broken, they'll always be deeply connected, and one day, if Charles doesn't wreck everything by being so utterly STUPID, they'll wind up being friends.

"But Charles and Charley don't have this real relationship. I don't quite know what they do have, but it's not *real.* No, wait a moment, maybe it *is* real, but it's got nothing to do with fatherhood. Charles behaves like a supremely over-indulgent godfather, or perhaps like some ultra-benevolent Victorian guardian (e.g. John Jarndyce in *Bleak House*). But what does Charles really think of Charley?

"That's the sixty-four-thousand-dollar question, and I don't know the answer. Maybe Charles doesn't know the answer either. Charles is so convoluted sometimes, and the whole problem is compounded by the fact that we never talk about Charley's natural father apart from alluding to him casually every now and then, just to reassure ourselves we can mention him without flinching—he's been swept under the rug, otherwise known as the pseudonym, and covered up. I don't approve of all this covering up—we ought to discuss him freely among ourselves, but Charles says Charley would get upset. I feel like saying: 'Oh yeah?' although of course I never do. The truth is that Charley only gets upset because he senses Charles gets upset—or in other words, it's Charles who can't cope with this skeleton in the family cupboard, and we're all, in our different ways, reflecting his convoluted, unacknowledged emotions.

"How can I ever begin to tackle Charles about this? He'd simply deny everything and think I was round the bend. Sometimes I feel I'd like to discuss him with the old monster, but Jon, I'm sure, would plead the secrecy of the confessional and avoid a discussion. Or maybe Jon too would think I was round the bend. I can never quite decide whether Jon's a spiritual genius or a complete charlatan—maybe he's capable of being both. He certainly glued Charles together in 1937 and he certainly helped Charles back to a normal life after the war, but maybe Charles would have got better anyway, regardless of who was around to help him. The trouble is I don't like Jon and he doesn't like me. Don't know why. It seems to be just one of those irrational antipathies—or maybe sex is at the bottom of it somewhere. What a wrecker he must have been when he was young, mesmerising women with those cold grey eyes of his but never fundamentally committing himself to anyone but God! Nasty. But never mind the past. The situation in the present is that I can't ask him for help here and he wouldn't give it to me even if I asked. Forget him.

"MEMO TO GOD: Please grant Charles more self-knowledge somehow. I don't know if my prayers for him will do any good, but at least I can hope that they will, and so long as I can hope, I can beat back that terrible feeling of powerlessness. So I shall go on praying, but please send me instructions about how I can pray as effectively as possible."

* * *

"25th November, 1963. I haven't written anything here for a week, but I've been so busy. I've done a little praying every day, but it seems futile and I can't see any results. That's why I'm giving myself a holiday from prayer this morning and writing something in the journal instead.

"Looking back I see I was writing about Samson and I realise more clearly than ever that Charles isn't at peace with him. I am, though. Or am I deceiving myself? No. I'm free now. I was freed when Charles came home from the war and I knew I was madly in love with him at last. Absence makes the heart grow fonder, and I'd come to realise how wonderful he'd been to me and how lucky I was to have him. No more Samson. I was cured, healed, entirely restored to sanity. Poor Samson, losing me and missing out on Charley! I can look back at him today with compassion.

"But Charles can't. That's clear to me now, but maybe subconsciously I've known it for a long time. After all, didn't I think of our return to Starbridge as an exorcism of the past? I must have thought there was something that needed to be exorcised, but the exorcism hasn't happened. Quite the reverse. Starbridge, I find with horror, has stirred everything up. Charles could forget about Samson in Cambridge, but he can't forget about him here, in Starbridge, where we acted out the great crisis of 1937. Samson lives on in Starbridge even though Charles pretends he doesn't. Charles pretends too that he's got over his antipathy to the Cathedral which was so marked when we came to live at the South Canonry—maybe he found that the best way to suppress the undigested, unaccepted past was to go through the motions of falling in love with the place all over again. 'Radiant, *ravishing* Starbridge!' sighs Charles, gazing at that horribly eerie hulk just as dotingly as Alex ever did, and I can feel my blood run cold as I repress a shudder.

"How do I exorcise this subterranean river of demonic memories? No idea.

"I can't help wondering if Samson would have been easier to exorcise from our family life if Charley had been a girl who looked just like me. Yes, I think that *would* have made a difference. Charles would simply have blotted Samson right out and adored her in that sentimental way he has with young girls. But Charley—so like Samson, such a constant reminder . . . Of course Charles always says the resemblance doesn't bother him, always insists that he actually liked Samson, bears him no ill will, and so on and so on. This is the way things ought to be, I agree. But is that the way things really are? No. Charles, wrapped up in his public-school ethos, can't see the way things really are, won't see it, daren't see it. It's easier for him in such an agonisingly complex situation to take refuge in a world where people say things like: 'No hard feelings, old chap!' and 'Keep a stiff upper lip, play the game and don't let the side down!'

"Phony, phony, phony . . . But Charles doesn't know. He's not insincere, just mixed up, and I don't know how to unravel him.

"Supposing I took the bull by the horns and said: 'Your problem is that you're a jealous man and you can't bear the thought that any other man's ever had me.' No, that wouldn't work. He'd just laugh and say: 'I know you love me now—why should I bother to be jealous, as if I were someone who can't stop being emotionally insecure?' And I'm not sure I know the answer to that question. I just know that Charles can't bear me to look at another man and that he's never really satisfied unless I'm devoting myself to him 100%. That's why, of course, the best years of our marriage came after the children had grown up. It wasn't because I couldn't cope with motherhood. It was because Charles couldn't cope with sharing me. No wonder he was always so keen on sex! It was his way of re-establishing himself at the centre of my world.

"No, that's unkind to Charles. Obviously he also wanted sex because he loved me. But in the beginning—when he was so insecure—when he sensed I didn't love him half as much as I loved Samson—yes, of course he felt jealous, it was only human to feel jealous in those circumstances, and he was very jealous and very insecure indeed.

"Perhaps the insecurity goes back even further too; perhaps it goes all the way back to his childhood. That doting mother, devoting herself to him 100%—or trying to, but of course he had to share her with his father—a fact which made him feel insecure and jealous—particularly since Eric was so strict that Charles no doubt came to feel he needed every ounce of Helen's devotion as compensation . . . Yes, one could make out quite a Freudian case to explain why Charles is the way he is, but even if that's all rubbish (and I can't say I'm terribly keen on Freud) one can't get away from the fact that Charles has a jealous streak in his nature and he can't forgive any man who makes the fatal error of finding me too attractive.

"That's at the bottom of the whole Aysgarth mess, although it's more than my life's worth to mention it. If I drag the subject up again now and have another go at proclaiming that intercourse never happened, Charles will immediately suspect out of sheer jealousy that it did happen, and then the whole agony will begin all over again. It's much better just to let him know regularly how much I detest Stephen—which I do. When I think of what happened this summer—that pornographic sculpture—and the ensuing rows which put Charles under such strain—and then all that other utterly dreadful behaviour which—but no, it's no good thinking about that now. Charles buried the scandal six feet deep for the good of the Church, and that's that.

"Or is it? Everything's festering underground, that's the trouble. In Charles's eyes Stephen committed the sin of 'letting the side down,' and in Stephen's eyes Charles is 'the man who knows too much'—with the result that the more Charles bends over backwards to be Christian in order to 'do the done thing' and allow Stephen to make a fresh start, the more humiliated and resentful Stephen must feel. If only Stephen would resign! But he'll cling to power like a limpet, he'll ride out the pain and the humiliation, he's tough as old boots. And meanwhile the bad feeling goes on and on and on . . . No wonder the Cathedral's looking sinister nowadays. By this time it must be stuffed with a sort of demonic sludge. Maybe I *should* pray for it—or maybe I should pray for Stephen, but no, I can't, I'm not holy enough to pray for a man I detest. Well, let's be honest! I'm not holy at all.

"I'll pray some more for Venetia instead. Oh, I did like her! I'm not good at liking women, but I liked *her.* She was my kind of person. Clever. Amusing. Interested in sex. Fun. I shall keep praying for her—and for Charles—but not for Stephen, bloody Stephen, turning on the sexual power when I was at my most vulnerable, when I was dreading so much that Charles wasn't coming home—oh God, I can still see that gin-and-tonic the size of a goldfish bowl, no, don't think of it, wipe it out, think of something else, start praying.

"MEMO TO GOD: I don't really have to pray for someone I loathe, do I? I mean, how can one do such a thing and remain sincere?"

* * *

"26th December, 1963. Another long interval has elapsed during which I've written nothing, but Christmas really is an impossible time of year to do anything except try to keep sane.

"Darling Michael's given me a book token and I'm just wondering if I should drop into the SPCK bookshop and invest in a tome on prayer. The trouble is that I'm such a Protestant at heart that I don't like people giving me orders or advice on my spiritual life and getting between me and God. The very phrase 'spiritual director' makes me recoil, but maybe that's because I always associate it with the monster at Starrington. Selfish old eccentric! Imagine going off into the woods to live as a hermit when you've got a fourteen-year-old son to look after! No wonder Nicholas is so peculiar, even now he's in his twenties and grown up.

"But I must stop ranting about Jon, and perhaps I should also stop being too proud to seek advice on prayer. After all, since I'm so ignorant and stupid about praying, shouldn't I at least make *some* effort to improve my almost non-existent skill? If I really feel called to pray, should I be content with merely muttering inefficiently to God for a short time every morning? But maybe the whole call's a gigantic delusion and I'm just playing psychological games with myself. I do wonder sometimes, especially when I'm depressed. I feel depressed now, exhausted by Christmas. No wonder the suicide rate soars at this time of the year, but no, I don't want to cut my throat, I just want to put my feet up and not talk to anyone in the Church of England for at least twenty-four hours.

. . .

"MEMO TO GOD: If you really want me to go on with the praying you'd better say so—and SAY IT CLEARLY. I've been praying in this new serious way for some weeks now but as far as I can see there have been no positive results and I'm getting discouraged. I do still have this vague urge to pray and I offer it to you again, even though it's so feeble and inadequate, but if the whole thing's a delusion LET ME KNOW so that I can do something more rewarding instead. I'll give you till Easter.

"(I'm sure one's not supposed to give God ultimatums, but what the hell, I'm fed up.)

"An afterthought: at least I haven't turned my journal into fiction yet. I suppose that must rank as some sort of modest achievement."

* * *

"2nd March, 1964. I might have known I'd never keep up a journal regularly. Over two months since my last entry! Hopeless. All I can say in my own defence is that I've kept up with my early morning prayers. Still no visible results, but I'm going to go on till Easter before I chuck it in.

"I did buy the book on prayer but I couldn't get on with it. This was a real disappointment because for some reason I was convinced that buying the book on prayer would lead to a big break-through—in fact I was so sure of this that I was even beginning to believe God himself had planted the thought in my brain. How stupid of me! How sentimental! And how utterly self-centred! I'm sure God has better things to do with his time than to go around planting fantastic hopes in the minds of clerical wives who are trying to kid themselves they have a special call to pray.

"On the advice of the man at the SPCK bookshop I waited until the Lent books started to be published before making my dud purchase, and I did read all the right reviews in *The Church Gazette,* so it wasn't as if I bought the book without the proper care and research. Well, I suppose anyone can make a mistake—or would I find any book on prayer peculiar and dull? Maybe books on prayer are written for peculiar, dull people. What sort of people are interested in prayer anyway?

"But the answer to that question appears to be: all sorts, some of them most unexpected. Eileen Pearce, the new Canon's wife, who's smartly turned out and not obviously churchy, asked me today if there was a women's prayer-group she could join. Imagine it! Sitting around with a bunch of women and praying *en masse*! I wouldn't mind sitting around with a bunch of men—but if I did, I doubt if I'd keep my mind on my prayers.

"Anyway I don't like the idea of praying in a group. I'd much rather pray on my own. (I've found I don't really *pray* at church services, I just go through a praying ritual—which I'm sure can be perfectly adequate, but I find praying at home less distracting.) I suppose, if I'm to be fair, praying at home in a group might have its interesting side—getting together with like-minded people usually does—but how could I ever tell anyone why I have to pray so hard for Charles?

"I'm increasingly worried about Charles. He took a real hammering from those atheists on that beastly TV show. He's tough and brave to face them but he's sensitive underneath and they hurt him, I know they did. If only he could retire to Cambridge for two weeks and write some wonderfully erudite monograph on the Early Church! Then he'd feel better. I really wish now that we'd never left Cambridge. Sometimes I feel he's still not happy as a bishop. Sometimes I think he's still expending far too much energy on 'keeping a stiff upper lip' and 'playing the game.'

"Oh God, please help Charles, he's really not cut out to be a militant bishop, and being any kind of bishop's so difficult, he's always in a rush, there's never enough time (how the pace of episcopal life has speeded up since Alex's day!) and I think he's really getting very troubled by it all, particularly since the *Honest to God* fuss in all the secular press when he felt called to speak out against the 'New Morality.' I have this horrible feeling that Charles is being driven down a blind alley where he'll be endlessly beaten up—a vile image but an apt one.

"What can I do to make things easier for him? Devote myself to him 100%. Fine. But where does that leave me—*me,* Lyle? Where it always does nowadays—powerless but praying. God, I can see now why I get so fed up! I feel there's no *me* at all, the true me has been squeezed out by this clerical automaton called Mrs. Bishop who hovers constantly at Charles's elbow to ensure he has everything he wants . . . Poor Charles, I'm so worried about him, I do wish I could talk to him properly, but I can't, he wouldn't understand, he'd just get upset, and I mustn't make him upset, he's upset enough by being a bishop, and I mustn't make matters worse.

"All I can do is pray. Funny about Eileen Pearce, bringing up the idea of a prayer-group. I wouldn't have thought she was the type at all—too young, too busy. She even has a part-time job—she's a secretary in a firm which has *nothing to do with the Church.* Only Wednesdays and Fridays, but she says it's so nice to have a little life of her own. Her mother takes care of the children when they come home from school. Her husband doesn't seem to mind. Of course they're much younger than us, a different generation. Charles would mind, but then he needs me to devote myself to him 100%. Oh God, what am I going to do about Charles . . .

"And there's me too, isn't there, I can see that dimly now. What am

I going to do about *me?* I'm not happy, my life's somehow out of alignment, it's as if we've all been dislocated in some way by forces we don't understand and can't control.

"MEMO TO GOD: Cracks seem to be opening up in my consciousness and when I peer into them I don't like what I see. Is it that prayer has somehow opened my mind so that I can see farther than I ever did before? Or am I simply going mad? Please, *please* don't let me have a nervous breakdown—it would make life even more awful for Charles."

* * *

"8th March, 1964. An astonishing thing's happened and it's all tied up with that purchase which was a complete failure, that dreary book I bought at the SPCK.

"Eileen Pearce, aged under forty and looking so unlined I could slap her, arrives at the South Canonry this morning to say she'd been thinking what a pity it was that there was no women's prayer-group because in Gerry's last diocese there'd been a wonderful woman of great spiritual power who . . . etc., etc.

"I listen with glazed eyes and think how exhausting Evangelicals can be. Finally I'm allowed to say: 'But Eileen my dear, unfortunately in this Cathedral Close we've no women of great spiritual power who could lead a prayer-group.' I thought that would close the conversation as tactfully as possible, but no, she's shining-eyed and unstoppable. 'Oh, but Mrs. Ashworth,' she says, '*you* could be our leader! That nice man in the SPCK bookshop mentioned yesterday that you'd bought a book on prayer not long ago, and as soon as I heard him say that I thought: YES! *There's* the woman who could do it! You're so admired, Mrs. Ashworth, and such an example to us all! Everyone thinks you're the perfect wife for a bishop!'

"I thought: my God, if only she knew.

"I'll have to get out of it, although I don't quite see how. Sitting around with a bunch of women all talking about motherhood and exchanging recipes when they're not offering up embarrassing prayers—no, it would be intolerable.

"MEMO TO GOD: Get me out of this, it isn't what I want at all, I can't do it, can't cope."

* * *

"14th March, 1964. Marian Lindsay arrives hotfoot from St. Martin's vicarage and says she's heard I'm starting a prayer-group for women and she does hope it isn't confined to the Cathedral Close because she'd love to join. By coincidence she'd been thinking of starting a prayer-group at St. Martin's, but naturally I'd be better at it than she could ever be because she'd never bought a book on prayer in her life whereas Eileen Pearce had told her I'd been to the SPCK bookshop and . . . etc., etc. 'And of course,' she concludes, quite pink with enthusiasm by this time, 'everyone admires you much more than me because you're so clever and efficient as well as being such a devout Christian—all your committees, all your charity work, and yet you always find the time to give Charles such tremendous support . . .' And so on and so on.

"I really wonder sometimes whether anyone knows anything about anyone else at all. To buy myself a little time to recover from this extraordinary onslaught I say vaguely: 'What does Malcolm think of the idea?' but to my surprise Marian just laughs and says she hasn't told him. 'He'll be the last to know!' she says cheerfully. 'Men are always so condescending when women try to do something important together—and you know how all clergymen secretly think churchwomen are only good for arranging flowers!'

"And suddenly, when she said that, I had a revelation, it was as if God had finally given me a blast on the trumpet, *I saw it all.*

"I thought: this is my chance to be me. In this context I wouldn't be just a perfect clerical accessory with no life of my own and an identity which is being subsumed by my husband's job. This would be me being ME. God created me to be this special person at this particular time in my life, and I'm going to be her. I'm like a lump of wax which is being called to life—I feel as if my Creator has finally reached out and taken me in his hands to reshape me—I feel overcome by excitement and hope.

"Or at least I did, when I had that conversation with Marian some hours ago, but now that I've come down to earth I'm wondering how the hell I'll ever run a prayer-group since it's so absolutely not my cup of tea. But never mind, it doesn't matter, I'll manage somehow, I *shall* do it, I SHALL! Churchwomen of the world unite—join a prayer-group and cast off your chains!

"MEMO TO GOD: I hope you're having a big laugh about all this somewhere."

* * *

"1st April, 1964. I break the news to Charles that I'm starting a prayer-group. He thinks it's an April Fool. I assure him that I'm serious.

"He's most surprised and asks very politely, like the gentleman he is, how I got the idea. I tell him about the overtures from Eileen and Marian, and add that I became interested in prayer as the result of Venetia moving out of my life. He says, ultra-courteous: 'I see,' and comments kindly: 'I think it's a very good idea, if you have the time.' That's a hint that I'm not to neglect him, but a bishop has to encourage anyone who wants to pray, so he's decided that the new prayer-group can exist as Lyle's Little Hobby. Probably he finds it all rather charming. How smooth Charles is sometimes, but he's not insincere. He genuinely wants to be kind to me.

"I'd actually like to ask his advice, but I'm not going to. I don't want a professional treating us as amateurs with the result that we feel foolish and inferior. We don't need any clergymen here anyway because God will look after us. Do I really believe that? Yes. Have I finally gone round the bend? Possibly, but I don't think so.

"No, of course I haven't gone round the bend! God's simply made himself clear at last, and about time too.

"MEMO TO GOD: Please use me in such a way that I don't let the prayer-group down."

* * *

"7th April, 1964. A nasty moment: Dido Aysgarth arrives saying she's heard about my prayer-group and it's all too, too divine. With mounting horror I wait for her to announce that she intends to join us, but finally she reaches the peroration of her monologue which is: '. . . and I'm *devastated* that I can't take part, but I have to devote *all* my time to darling Stephen and the children—and really, life's simply too *frantic* at present—but don't worry, Lyle my dear, because I'll offer up my own prayers for you all and make sure I'm with you in spirit!'

"Ghastly woman! Why does everyone go on and on speculating about why she and Stephen ever got married? The answer's as plain as a pikestaff: they were *made* for each other.

"MEMO TO GOD: Thanks for saving us from Dido. Or should I be regretting her absence and sparing a prayer for her? But again—how can one pray for people one detests without being hopelessly insincere? Answer this one, please. It's beginning to bother me."

* * *

"14th October, 1964. I really did mean to keep up this journal to chart the progress of the prayer-group, but I haven't. I can only conclude that it's been more important to pray than to write about it.

"It all turned out rather differently than I anticipated. I'd thought some hefty recruiting would be needed and a certain degree of organisation, but no, people just appeared, word travelled around just as it always does in this kind of community, and in the end all I had to do was set aside a room at the South Canonry, provide coffee and make some sort of introductory speech which wasn't a complete failure. To my surprise I was very nervous—*me,* after all my committee work!—but I shrieked silently to God: HELP! And the next moment I was opening my mouth and gabbling: 'Look, let's forget I'm Mrs. Bishop, let's forget who our husbands are, I know nothing about this sort of thing, but I'm willing to learn, and let's all start by calling each other by our Christian names, because we're all equal before God, all special in his sight, and this is about us being US, talking to God as our true selves and hoping he can use us effectively in some way which we may find difficult to visualise at present but which by his grace will become increasingly clear to us.'

"It was surprising how well that went down. People sagged in relief and said they didn't know much about prayer either—and the ones who kept silent, of course, were the ones who did know something, so straight away I was able to pinpoint who the natural leaders were.

"But I soon discovered that leading doesn't mean the same in this context as it means at a committee meeting. One has to mop up the idle chatter occasionally, but most of the time one leads by taking a back seat and encouraging others to step forward. A paradox.

"One or two people dropped out but others came in and finally we decided ten people were quite enough. We start by having ten minutes' silence so that we can collect our thoughts and 'tune in,' as it were. Then we embark on some general prayers which focus on three or four categories in turn—like the intercessions in church, except that there are no words, someone just names a category—the poor, the sick and so on—and we all pray in silence. At the end of that phase we do talk—we discuss the special subjects we want to pray about, and people reveal their problems. For example, someone's sister-in-law is dying of cancer, how could God allow this to happen, and so on. Of course it's not all on that level, but even the minor problems can be intriguing. Eileen's little boy suffers from bed-wetting. Someone suggested that might be because she goes out to work. Eileen was furious. Everyone hastened to pour oil on the troubled waters and I was asked what I thought, but I wasn't sure. Something might be adrift in the family, but possibly the little boy just has a weak bladder. In the end I just said with deep feeling: '*All* families have their problems,' and everyone looked at me gratefully. They know Charley ran away from home and Michael was chucked out of medical school, and—bizarrely—this is now an advantage to me, as if weakness had been converted into strength. People know I've sailed through murky domestic waters, they know I can empathise with them.

"After the discussion we pray about each problem and the people who are affected by it. More silence, but this is the most intense because it's easier to focus on specific people than on huge groups such as the poor. If this silence were a noise it would be deafening. Ten people together can make so much more noise than one person shouting.

"The most surprising thing about the group is that many of my preconceived notions about the participants have been overturned. For example, my chum Marian Lindsay, who I thought would make the whole enterprise bearable, is often a source of irritation—she can't concentrate for long, and if you give her a chance she'll start talking about her hysterectomy. But Emma Granger, who I always thought was so quiet and mousey, has shown great wisdom and strength. And what about me—*me,* Lyle? Now here's another paradox: I'm becoming more me by thinking less of me. I'm getting involved with these people. My fundamental problems remain unchanged, but *I'm* changing. Does that mean the fundamental problems will change too? Surely it must! If I'm a number in a sum, any change in me will affect the other numbers in that we'll all add up to a different answer.

"At the beginning I used to think to myself: do our prayers work? Are we a success? But now I know that these are the wrong questions to ask, they're irrelevant. It's not for us to judge how successful we are—and anyway what does 'success' mean in this context? To be successful is to do what God wants—and I know that what God wants for us at these times is to *be,* lining ourselves up with him so that he can use us to batter away at the suffering in the world. If we can only *be,* then he can use us and arrange us in the right patterns so that we're playing an active part in his creative purpose, an active part in his redemptive love.

"Emma Granger has lent me the latest edition of the *Revelations* of Julian of Norwich, a work which in the old days I found unintelligible and repulsive. It's odd how interesting I find that book now. Dame Julian and her 'showings' . . . Masses of people used to go to Norwich and talk to her in her cell. I wish I could go and talk to her about Charles, but I'm several hundred years too late.

"Charles never asks about the prayer-group. I can't make up my mind whether his silence arises from misguided tact and a commendable desire not to intrude, or whether he's like Rhett Butler and doesn't give a damn. Never mind. It doesn't matter.

"What matters is that Charles's problems don't get any better. But what's happened is that I understand them better—in fact the more I pray about him the more I realise that he's got himself trapped in a theological blind alley and that this is blighting not just his life but my life and the boys' lives too. I'm not supposed to know anything about theology, of course. Well, I'm the first to admit I couldn't write a learned article about that pig-headed old fanatic St. Athanasius, but I can certainly say with conviction that this hard-line, ultra-conservative stance which Charles has found himself compelled to adopt isn't making him happy—and that's primarily because it doesn't reflect his true nature. Charles does indeed have conservative leanings—and why shouldn't he? Most men of his age do—but he's actually a flexible thinker, quite capable of taking on board new ideas (look how he reorganised the diocese by using the very latest secular theories about management!) and he's also more than capable of a deep, non-bigoted compassion on ethical issues (look how he rescued that ninny Desmond Wilton from London!), but all this intellectual flexibility and moral compassion have been lost in a thundercloud of righteousness as he proclaims his absolute truths with the vigour of an Old Testament prophet—or with the pig-headed fanaticism of his Early Church heroes.

"The truth is he's become a caricature of himself, with the disastrous result that the press delight in pillorying him, and Charles in defence gets driven deeper and deeper into this fierce dogmatic role which he's not at heart equipped to play. Of course it goes without saying that the press have got everything wrong when they mock him as a sex-hating old misery, but the question which I'm increasingly asking myself is: has Charles got everything right? And I don't think he has, not by a long chalk. Of course he has to condemn immorality and uphold tradition, but why is everything getting so distorted and strained in consequence? I find myself asking: can this really be what God requires from the Bishop of Starbridge?

"I wish I could talk to Charles about it, but I can't. He'd be upset—and I think he'd be angry too that I was criticising him in his work. No, my job is simply to keep him going and not bother him when he's under such stress doing what he honestly believes is God's will. But I shall pray for him. I shall pray and pray and pray.

"MEMO TO GOD: Next time Jon Darrow tunes in to you, tell him to get off his bottom and *do* something about Charles. Why doesn't Jon make Charles question himself more? I mean, what the hell's Jon doing out there in Starrington? But perhaps Jon's saying all kinds of things which Charles simply can't hear—or maybe he hears but prefers not to understand because it's too difficult, too painful, too frightening. Anyway there's a limit to what Jon can do. He can't forcefeed Charles information which Charles isn't ready to accept. Maybe Jon, like me, is gnashing his teeth and muttering to himself: 'All I can do for Charles is pray for him.'

"Dear God, in the name of your son Jesus Christ, HEAR OUR PRAYERS. Amen."

* * *

"28th November, 1964. Today I broke down and told the group how much I hate Michael sleeping with that awful Dinkie and how miserable it made me when Charles was so beastly to Michael about it. Everyone was *so kind.* I just didn't know it was possible for women to be so kind to one another. We prayed that Michael would learn how to treat women with genuine love and respect, and we prayed that Charles would be more understanding and forgiving. Emma said: 'Perhaps we should pray for Dinkie too.' And then the most extraordinary thing happened. As everyone else looked horrified at the idea of praying for this slut, this 'lost girl,' this 'fallen woman' who had been shamelessly living with a man who wasn't her husband, I—*I,* not Mrs. Bishop but *I,* Lyle—*I* said: 'Yes, of course we must pray for her.'

"So we prayed for Dinkie, whom I detest—but why do I detest her so fiercely? Not just because I think she's messing up Michael; Michael will survive. Not just because she makes Charles so angry that the trouble between him and Michael is exacerbated; I can stand that if I have to. It's because I see in her what I detest in myself—or rather, I'm projecting on to her my painful hated memories of that time long ago when *I* was a 'lost girl,' sleeping with a man who wasn't my husband, a course of action which nearly destroyed me and did in the end destroy my lover.

"Today at last I prayed with genuine feeling for someone I detest, except that I didn't detest her any more then. I felt nothing but the tangled-up pain—her pain, my pain, it was all one—and I saw I had to forgive her as I'd forgiven myself, because in the end we all need to be forgiven, all of us, and 'he that is without sin among you, let him cast the first stone.'

"I saw then too so clearly why Charles is beastly to Michael. It's all connected with this business of projection—of projecting on to another what you hate or fear in yourself and then condemning it in order to make yourself feel safe. Charles would like to have lived in the 1920s as Michael lives today, but of course he can't admit, even to himself, how much he would have enjoyed bedding lots of pretty girls and living in sin with a voluptuous tart. That's such a dangerous truth that it has to be buried instantly, alongside the fact that Charles spent a lot of his youth feeling sexually frustrated. Perhaps if he'd been truly upper-class and truly rich he could have cottoned on to a wild set when he was an undergraduate and sown some really lavish wild oats, but he was just a middle-class solicitor's son from the Stockbrokers' Belt on limited funds, and Eric would have clamped down at once on any high living. Things are so different today, so much more egalitarian. Now even the working-classes can sow lavish wild oats, thanks to the ability of pop singers to earn millions. So Charles doesn't just condemn Michael for the sexy, wild streak which he daren't acknowledge in himself; he condemns him because he's jealous of Michael living in the sexy, wild 1960s and having all the fun he never had.

"Yet this is an over-simplification of the truth, I realise that. For instance, I know Charles is also against Michael's promiscuity for very good, sound reasons, reasons of which I entirely approve—he's not motivated merely by dark promptings of the psyche. Indeed surely anyone with any experience of the world can see that when men treat women like Kleenex tissues—use once and dispose—women wind up degraded and the whole selfish activity ultimately debases both sexes. But there's a right and a wrong way to be anti-fornication, and if you go about it in the wrong way (aided and abetted by convoluted feelings in your psyche) you're heading for trouble. It's no good being dictatorial and dogmatic, crashing around in outrage that people should so wilfully refuse to 'play the game' and 'stick to the rules.' That just sends people rushing naked to the nearest bed to affirm their freedom from tyranny. No wonder Michael sleeps around—it's his way of expressing his individuality. It's the wrong way, I hardly need add, and one day he'll learn there are more mature ways of being grown up, but meanwhile Charles gives him no chance to grow up because he positively drives him into promiscuity.

"Meanwhile Charley, cunningly taking advantage of the Dinkie affair in order to curry favour, is being insufferably virtuous and churchy. I bet he spends hours masturbating. If Charley really feels so secure with Charles, why is he forever creeping around trying to curry favour? It's as if he can never relax sufficiently to be himself because he's never sure what Charles really thinks of him. (Or is it that he never dares be himself because he's all too sure what Charles will think of him?) But whatever it is that's really going on, it's a disaster.

"If only I could talk to Charles about this! But he has to believe he and Charley have a successful father-son relationship. That's his reward, he says, for all he went through. But how good is it for Charley to go through life bearing an invisible placard which proclaims: I AM CHARLES ASHWORTH'S REWARD? God, I get so worried about it all sometimes . . .

"Never mind, at least I can talk to the group. Can't tell them everything, of course, but at least I can tell them something, and I really do feel now that so long as I have the group supporting me it doesn't matter that I can't talk to Charles any more.

"MEMO TO GOD: I've been demanding and demanding things from you, often quite rudely, in fact often very rudely, like an ill-bred spoilt child, but I think prayer must have made me better-mannered or perhaps it's helped me grow up a little and now I should like to say politely: 'Thank you very much'—not just for staying with me no matter how unpleasant I was, but for actually moving closer and surrounding me with people who care.

"An afterthought: How curious it is that all those sayings of Jesus which one learns by rote an an early age—sayings that become so familiar that one never thinks deeply about them—are now all chiming and making sense, like a great poem leaping up from the printed page to hit the reader between the eyes. I find myself thinking about Jesus more and more, which is so odd because I've never thought much about Jesus except as a historical figure, very interesting, of course, and greatly to be respected but not exactly the sort of person you'd see walking across the Cathedral sward at Starbridge. Yet the strange thing is that now I think he *was—is—*the sort of person who might turn up in Starbridge, and sometimes when the group meets I look at the closed door of the room and remember how he moved through the closed door after his death to be present with his disciples, and then I—no, I'm writing like a religious maniac and I must stop.

"Another afterthought: Would Charles recognise Jesus if he appeared in the diocese? Would any of those powerful, worldly clerics who 'play the game' and 'do the done thing'?"

* * *

"1st December, 1964. Advent's started. All the awful pressures of Christmas are looming on the horizon, and the biggest problem is that Michael's still insisting on bringing Dinkie down for Christmas Day. I'm really looking forward to the next meeting of the group, it's such a life-line, I wonder now how I ever managed without it. How lonely I was before! How isolated, adrift and confused! What's the purpose of all this prayer, I used to ask—I suppose I had some high-flown, self-centred notion of playing the heroine and saving people, but what's happened is that God's saved me. By grounding myself in him and turning outwards towards the world I'm losing my fixation with myself as I care for others and am cared for by others in return. 'For whosoever will save his life shall lose it,' said Jesus, 'but whosoever will lose his life for my sake, the same shall save it.' Such a paradox, but I feel I'm experiencing what he meant. How did Jesus know so much when he was only in his early thirties? Extraordinary! I wish I could have talked to him, but no, I've missed him by centuries again, just as I've missed Julian of Norwich.

"Or have I? I've missed him in the flesh, certainly. I'm not pottering around in Palestine two thousand years ago. But in the spirit . . . 'For where two or three are gathered together in my name,' said Jesus, 'there I am in the midst of them'—and there we all are, gathered together in his name, all supporting one another, all joined together in prayer, and this tiny, faltering, initially almost pathetic activity by a group of middle-aged and elderly women—a group most men would have instantly written off—has become a huge, powerful, dynamic, meaningful enterprise which has enriched all our lives. Back and back Christ comes to us, again and again and again—and the life and light he brings is God in action, it's a miracle, it's nothing less than the saving power of the Holy Spirit—

"THANKS BE TO GOD!

"How I wish I could share all this with Charles, but he's so busy and I mustn't bother him.

"MEMO TO GOD: Thank you for this wonderful 'showing' which has changed my life. I hardly like to ask for anything when you've given me so much, but please give me a helping hand through Christmas."

* * *

"29th January, 1965. Well, I got the helping hand and survived Christmas. No time to write the journal, but never mind, no one will read it anyway. In fact now that my life's been so transformed I'm not sure I need to write a journal any more to give vent to my bottled-up feelings, and perhaps I should destroy it in case I fall under a bus. I wouldn't want Charles to read it. He'd be upset to find out there was a whole side of me he never knew. He'd think he'd failed me—and perhaps he has, but poor Charles, this damned bishopric is twisting him into such a tortuous pattern and he can't help being so self-absorbed.

"How I wish we'd never come to Starbridge!

"How I wish too that I could discuss him in depth with the group, but some subjects really are *verboten.* I just can't dissect the Bishop and invite the group to pore over the pieces. I must be content with the general support, but it torments me that I'm no nearer solving Charles's problems. I always wind up thinking: he's absolutely right to condemn immorality and uphold tradition, yet at the same time he's absolutely wrong. And I know I can never say that to him—well, let's face it, I know I can never say anything important to him at all.

"MEMO TO GOD: Please show me how to help Charles solve his problems before something frightful happens. He's under such strain that I'm beginning to wonder how much longer he can keep going without breaking down."

* * *

"9th February, 1965. Ghastly goings-on—so ghastly that I'm driven to take refuge in my journal to work off my horror and despair. Yesterday Desmond Wilton was beaten up and Charles found pornography in his (Desmond's!) bedroom. Dido Aysgarth swooped in screaming about men in black leather. Poor Charles was absolutely at the end of his tether and Malcolm was drinking scotch as if it were lemonade. To cap it all, Michael and Dinkie arrived to announce their engagement.

"Mess after mess after mess! Naturally 'Mrs. Bishop' and 'Mum' have to ride to the rescue, and I get fed up all over again with these two cardboard cut-out heroines who are so far removed from the real me. (I note this self-centred, bolshie reaction just to remind myself that even though the prayer-group has wrought a miracle in my life I'm still a long way from being [a] a saint, and [b] a noble, self-sacrificing Christian wife and mother.)

"Anyway, I sorted out the tart, Michael and Charles. At least I didn't have to sort out Desmond. I wonder if Marian managed to sort out Malcolm. (I wonder what *he's* like in bed. I find it hard to imagine a red-haired man being erotic, but that's just my personal blind-spot. Maybe Malcolm's an absolute dynamo—or does he work off all his dynamism roaring around the diocese? I must say, if I had to listen daily to Marian reminiscing about her hysterectomy, I'd roar around the diocese too.)

"Talking of sex, thank God Charles can still (a) 'get it up,' as they say in those large American novels which I peep at discreetly in the library, and (b) do something with it after it's been upped. I'm sure this triumph in the face of advancing years is entirely due to the fact that I look after him so carefully, not overfeeding him and always ensuring that he's well exercised both in the bedroom and on that silly old golf course—although actually, what a bore all that sex was last night, I could hardly have been less in the mood to play the siren, but poor Charles, he was in such a state that I had no choice but to rush to the rescue.

"However, I've come to think I'm rushing to the rescue much too much where Charles is concerned, and that this situation where I devote my whole life to keeping him going isn't healthy for our marriage. We've now reached the stage where I even have to put petrol in his car for him. What does he think I am, a robot who does all the chores at the touch of a button? I clean his shoes, fill his cigarette-case, organise his wardrobe, run his house, control that trout Peabody, protect him from all the churchwomen who adore him passionately, make sure he has nourishing meals at the correct times, listen to his moans and groans—and provide sex on demand. Do I ever get any thanks? No. He takes me for granted. It's not right, Charles, it's not right! I know you love me, but you've lost sight of me, lost touch, and now we don't talk any more.

"But at least I can still pray for you. I pray that somehow you're going to get out of this dreadful blind alley you're in. I pray that one day you and Michael will be friends. I pray that one day all our painful family problems will be resolved. I pray and pray, but just recently I've begun to feel nervous, even frightened, and I'm not sure why—it's as if this awful mess with Desmond Wilton is the harbinger of some really catastrophic mess which will shake everyone to the foundations. I looked at the Cathedral today and its windows seemed so black that when it looked back at me I thought of the monsters Behemoth and Leviathan in the Book of Job—and I was reminded again of the Devil, slipping into Starbridge in the 1930s and never being properly cast out. Then I thought: he's not only back, infesting the Cathedral—he's exuding a thick black poisonous miasma which is going to destroy us all.

"All neurotic fantasy, of course. I don't really believe that. But what I do believe is that I'm describing in symbolic terms the chaos which is lurching around on a psychic level at the bottom of our unconscious minds, and I've got to pray and pray to God for help. How I wish Jesus could walk across the Cathedral churchyard and say to the demons: 'BE GONE!' Jesus was the greatest healer and exorcist who ever lived, reaching right down into the bottom of everyone's unconscious minds to iron out all the kinks and twists caused by guilt and pain so that each soul became smooth and clean, and every distorted personality became straight and true, lined up right with God and set free to realise its full potential. 'I am come that they might have life,' he said, 'and that they might have it more abundantly.'

"MEMO TO JESUS: Give us life! We're all so crippled at the moment that we can't function properly. Heal Charles, heal us all, make us whole.

"MEMO TO GOD: *Save Charles!* Or rather, help me to save Charles, tell me how to say all that has to be said, I'll do anything to save Charles, anything, I love him so much that I'd even lay down my life to save him, I've been so lucky to have him all these years, especially when I didn't deserve such happiness, he saved me when I was *in extremis*—give me the chance now to save him. Amen.

"Afterthoughts: Oh God, please don't let Starbridge destroy Charles as it destroyed Alex. Please, *please,* PLEASE.

"We should never have come here, never, never, never.

"Fatal, lethal Starbridge.

"Demonic, destructive Starbridge.

"So vilely, so *hideously* beautiful.

"I HATE IT."

* * *

5

THERE WAS no more. The remaining pages were blank. I closed that small, cheap exercise book and at once it slipped through my shaking fingers to the floor.

My voice was saying: "Oh my God." My voice appeared to be operating independently of my will and it said "Oh my God" over and over again. Dimly I remembered that when the black box is recovered after a plane crash, the pilot's last words invariably consist of expletives. It was the instinctive reaction to a horrific and overwhelming shock.

After a while I had another instinctive reaction: I wanted to burn the book. I even picked it up and fumbled for my lighter. The thought that Charley and Michael might one day know how deeply I had failed Lyle by all my omissions, insensitivity and neglect was unbearable, but the next moment I knew there could be no incineration. I knew that as surely as I knew I had to read that journal again.

I stumbled into my dressing-room and sank down on the easy-chair where on the mornings before the catastrophe I had read my theology.

Later, after I had again reached the last line of the final page, I realised why the journal had to be preserved; I realised that in Lyle's fragmentary record of her great spiritual journey, the journey I had never bothered to uncover, there lay the truth—the absolute truth—about the woman with whom I had lived for so long. Although I disagreed with her on a number of matters (had to disagree, had to, how could I live with myself if I were to agree with every word she had written?) my disagreement was irrelevant. What mattered was that in her words, accurate and inaccurate, biased and unbiased, discerning and undiscerning, lay the fact that she had offered herself to God and that in consequence her life had been transformed. This complex woman with her chequered past, her continuing cynicism, her persistent bitchiness on the subject of her own sex, her sharp-clawed, feline personality—and yes, I knew all Lyle's faults as well as all her virtues—this most unlikely woman had been singled out by God for a special prayer-life and she had not failed him. It was as if God had seen straight past the tough layers of her personality which had accumulated over the years as the result of her unhappy childhood, her impoverished youth and her disastrous love-affair, and had shone light on the true self which had been hidden beneath all the layers of scar-tissue from the past wounds. I saw her finally as Christian, questing, humble and brave.

I knew I had glimpsed this true self repeatedly during the years of our marriage, but in the end I had done nothing to help her foster it and achieve fulfilment. I had been too busy with my theology and my bishopric. I had been too busy with my absolute truths. I, the strong, militant Christian leader whose business it was to steer the members of my flock towards the destiny to which they had been called by God, had allowed the person closest to me to struggle on alone towards her own special fulfilment of the spirit. I had been so preoccupied with laying down God's laws that I had been blind to the work of the Holy Spirit which had been going on under my nose.

I wanted to resign my bishopric.

My fingers tightened on the journal. How despicable that I had wanted to destroy this testament of truth because I had feared it would diminish me in my sons' eyes! And as I glimpsed this unhealthy preoccupation with my self-image, this unhealthy dread of facing unpalatable facts and this unhealthy urge to preserve my pride, I knew myself to be spiritually debilitated, unfit even to be an ordinary clergyman. It was hard to know how to endure such a recognition of my inadequacy.

I remembered how I had said to Jon: "At least my grief's uncomplicated by guilt." And I remembered too how Jon had looked away, avoiding comment.

The full horror of my bereavement's new dimension finally hit me. Staring down at the final page of the journal I again confronted the words: "I'd even lay down my life to save him," and in a paroxysm of rage, heightened by my unendurable guilt, I shouted out loud to God: "How dare you take her at her word!" But no, that was wrong, I knew that intellectually, I knew it was not God who had killed Lyle but the blood clot. God had merely invented a world in which such hazards happened; they were side-effects of the creative process, part of the mechanism of continuous change which enabled the world to avoid atrophy and to develop.

"How dare you invent such a world!" I said to God, but that was a crazy remark, quite inappropriate for a theologian, and I knew I had to clamp down on any inclination to talk like an uneducated lunatic. I told myself I was now encountering a phenomenon which we theologians called "the mystery of suffering." We wrote articles about it. We propounded theories. My Oxonian friend Dr. Austin Farrer had delivered a whole series of lectures on the subject and published them under the title of *Love Almighty and Ills Unlimited.* I too had planned to publish such a book, but I had never found the time to do more than sketch out a few avenues to be explored: the concepts of determinism and free will, the possibilities of spiritual growth in adversity, the perceptions about the teleology of the divine will, and so on and so on. I had found it soothing to reduce the mystery of suffering to an intellectually rigorous, well-ordered pattern.

But no intellectual rigour was of any use to me now.

"It's not fair!" I shouted to God. "It's not just! It's not right!" Shoving the journal away from me I blundered downstairs. "Why couldn't I have found the journal when she was still alive . . . why couldn't you have kept her alive long enough for me to say I was sorry . . . why couldn't you have shown me earlier that I'd taken a wrong turn . . . why did she have to die like that . . . why, why, why . . ."

In the drawing-room I found that the bottle of whisky was a quarter full. I started to drink.

Goodbye to sanity. Goodbye to a well-ordered world.

Chaos had come again.

And darkness.

And no light shone.

I drank.

IX

"Pain, grief, and every sort of discontent put a drag on action and drain the colour out of enterprise. Merely to resist the deadening influence, and go on with life at all, may be an effort almost too great."

AUSTIN FARRER
Warden of Keble College, Oxford, 1960–1968
LOVE ALMIGHTY AND ILLS UNLIMITED

I

IT IS hard to find the words to describe my terrible awakening the next morning. I was fully dressed, except for my jacket, and clutching my pectoral cross in the manner of a baby clasping a rattle. The cross banged against the basin as I vomited. It jarred against my chest as I slumped back upon the bed. It juddered against the bedside table as I scrabbled to read the dial of the electric clock. I was now quite beyond thinking about "the mystery of suffering." My whole being was focused on the fact that I was in a desperate state and that no one must know about it. It had to be concealed in order to preserve not merely my reputation but the good name of the Church. I could not—*could not*—be seen to be suffering from alcohol poisoning. I had to recover swiftly and silently with no fuss whatsoever. That was my absolute moral duty as a bishop, and I was going to do my duty or die in the attempt.

I did wonder vaguely if I would die, but then realised with horror that death was a luxury I could not afford, since an autopsy would reveal the scandalously high level of alcohol in my blood. The cross and I journeyed to the basin again for another round of retching, but there was nothing left to bring up. I cursed myself for eating so little the day before and thus compounding the current torture. I started to drink water. I drank and drank. I found the Alka-Seltzer and mixed the stiffest permissible potion. I endured diarrhoea. I drank still more water. I held my head under the cold tap and finally I took a cold shower.

By this time it was nine o'clock and I could hear Miss Peabody moving about, but that was all right, Miss Peabody was no threat, she was hardly going to come upstairs and root me out of the bedroom. I shaved, dressed carefully in fresh clothes and brushed my hair so hard that afterwards it was almost straight. I had already brushed my remaining teeth and cleaned the five false ones on their plate, but I was worried in case my breath might provide a clue to my over-indulgence, so I swallowed some toothpaste in the hope that its peppermint flavour would neutralise all odours. The sheer sordidness of these manoeuvres overwhelmed me. It was a relief to escape downstairs.

As I crept across the hall I thanked God I had given the cook-housekeeper and the charwoman two weeks' holiday; their absence meant I could clear up after myself, and having returned the open bottle of whisky to the sideboard I headed for the back door with the bottle I had emptied. Only when this was safely buried beneath a pile of other rubbish did I begin to breathe more easily.

I had brought the journal downstairs and now I locked it in one of the drawers of my desk. Moving back to the kitchen I had to pause to retch by the sink, but fortunately Miss Peabody was closeted with the typist in the office and could not possibly have heard me. I just had time to make a large pot of tea before Malcolm arrived. As I hid behind the kitchen door I heard him say in the hall "How's the Bishop?" and Miss Peabody, who had emerged from the office to meet him, replied: "He isn't down yet, Archdeacon. Such a good thing he's at last able to rest."

So far so good. Tiptoeing to my study with the tea I sat down again. I was trying to work out whether the pain in my head was more unpleasant than the queasiness in my stomach, and some time passed as I tried to resolve this most distressing puzzle.

I had just finished the tea when I remembered my promise to Jon to attend the morning services at Starrington Manor's chapel.

"Bloody hell!" I muttered, too battered to mind my language. I looked at the clock. Mass would long since have finished and Jon would no doubt be worrying that I had had an accident. Telephoning the Manor I asked one of the members of the Community to tell Father Darrow at once that I had been unavoidably detained in Starbridge but would be in touch with him again soon.

I was so exhausted by this attempt to sound normal that several minutes passed before I realized how disturbed I was by the thought of my next meeting with Jon. Naturally I would tell him the truth; naturally I would confess that I had temporarily lost control over myself and indulged in a drinking bout; naturally I would tell him all that. But after careful reflection I did not think I would tell him just yet. I needed to recover my equilibrium. I needed to prove that I had not gone irrevocably to pieces. I needed to reassure myself that I was still capable of displaying the sort of behaviour which a bishop ought to display no matter how adverse the circumstances. I decided I would behave impeccably for the remainder of the day. Then on the morrow I could go to Jon and say: "Look, I've been a complete fool and behaved disgracefully, but I've pulled myself together and now, by the grace of God, I'll be all right."

Very edifying.

Or was it? Wouldn't Jon immediately say: "Why didn't you come to me straight away? Why did you have to save face by demonstrating your strength of character for the remainder of the day? Hasn't this in fact been a classic demonstration of pride?"

But I would reply: "Yes, you're quite right, I'm sorry, I've been very proud and even more stupid than I thought, and I'll say as much when I make my confession." Then everything would be all right.

Or would it? No, not really. I was twisting around in a bog of shame and cowardice, I could see that just as clearly as I could see that I couldn't face Jon that day, couldn't, not when I was so hung-over and humiliated, not when I felt so devastated by Lyle's journal, not when all I wanted to do was crawl into the nearest corner and speak to no one.

But crawling into the nearest corner and speaking to no one represented yet more luxuries I could not afford, because I had to keep fighting my hang-over. Dragging myself from my study I grabbed my overcoat and slipped out of the back door into the icy air of that February morning.

2

MY AIM was to weaken the hang-over further by taking a brisk walk, but although I achieved the extraordinary feat of escaping from the Close without encountering anyone I knew, I soon felt unsteady and realised I had to eat. There were numerous tea-shops in Starbridge, but I was afraid of meeting the Cathedral ladies, who would inevitably patronise such establishments at that hour of the morning. Fortunately my gaze then alighted on Woolworth's which, so I had heard, had recently been equipped with a restaurant counter in imitation of an American drugstore. Relief seized me as I realised that no one I knew would ever be found eating at such a plebeian place. A minute later I was sitting at the counter and asking in my plainest BBC accent for coffee and a Bath bun.

Food revived me. I ordered more coffee and some scrambled eggs. Finally the waitress, who called me "dear" but was very obliging, presented me with a bill which was so cheap that I thought she must have made a mistake in the addition. I foresaw the restaurant would prosper.

Returning to the Close I found that the Cathedral had a glassy, jagged, ravaged look as the melted frost ran damp fingers down its walls, but it seemed to me now to be more jaded than sinister. Still hoping to avoid chance encounters I cut through the churchyard, but this turned out to be a mistake because as I passed the Dean's door, the clergy's private entrance on the north front, the Dean himself emerged from his Cathedral.

Startled by this malign coincidence we initially could do no more than exclaim each other's names. "How are you?" added Aysgarth, mercifully ending the absurd pause which developed afterwards.

"Oh, fine! And you?" I said, trying to work out how long I needed to sustain a conversation in order to be judged normal.

"Oh, splendid! Any plans to go away now the funeral's over?"

"No, no," I said at once, overcome by the urge not to appear disabled in any way. "I'm sure it's best if I pick up the reins again as soon as possible."

"I hope you're not saying that just because of all that idiotic confusion about Christie's and the West Front Appeal! In fact if the Christie's affair is bothering you, let me hasten to set your mind at rest—why don't you drop in at the Deanery after Evensong tonight for a tot of Tio Pepe?"

The very thought of alcohol was enough to make me feel nauseous, but naturally I could not allow myself even the briefest of winces. If Aysgarth realised I was recoiling from a single glass of Tio Pepe, he would instantly put two and two together to make the most humiliating four.

"Why don't you come to the South Canonry?" I said, grasping with lightning speed the fact that on my own territory I could pass off a ginger ale as a whisky-and-soda. "I'd be delighted to see you."

"Well, if you're sure that's all right . . ."

We expended some additional time slaving to be nice to each other. Then beneath the scaffolding of the west front we parted, he moving away across the sward to the Deanery while I headed south down the path to Palace Lane. I knew I had made a mistake; I was hardly in a fit state to interview Aysgarth about a matter which would no doubt demand all my episcopal skills, but I was unable to work out what other course, at that particular moment, I could have taken. I did realise I had been trapped by shame into putting up a front—"hiding behind the glittering image," as Jon would have phrased it—but it would have been a big mistake to appear vulnerable to the toughest clergyman in the diocese.

By the time I reached the South Canonry I had made the pragmatic decision to accept the challenge which the interview represented and make the best of it. There was always the possibility that getting back to work really was the best course for me to take, and if the interview went well I could say to Jon: "I behaved idiotically when I hit the bottle, but at least afterwards I managed to pull myself together, get back into harness and sort out the Christie's mess."

Still entranced by this day-dream which showed me in such a flattering light, I entered my house and prepared to demonstrate my normality to my employees.

3

EVERYONE BEGAN by treating me with intense kindness and concern, as if I were suffering from an illness which was unspeakable but not quite terminal. This attitude had in fact been noticeable since Lyle's death, but since I had been so immersed in organising the funeral I had been only dimly aware of how I was being treated. Now, gripped by my obsession to appear normal, I felt obliged to adopt a hale and hearty manner in order to rebut all suggestion of infirmity.

"Put away those kid gloves!" I ordered. "No need to handle me with care! I've decided my best course is to get back to work straight away—where's Nigel?"

"He's been delayed but he'll be here this afternoon." Miss Peabody sounded confused by my energy. The chaplains were gazing at me as if I were a very peculiar pastoral case. Even the typist was boggling at me beneath her beehive hair-do.

Finally my archdeacon took control of the scene by suggesting that he and I should retire to my study so that he could bring me up to date on the major issues, but as soon as the study door was closed he said: "Honestly, Charles, wouldn't it be best if you took some more time off? You've been running around non-stop ever since Lyle died, and you've almost certainly got to the stage now where you don't even realise how exhausted you are."

"I'm fine."

"Well, you don't look it! Listen, I understand if you can't face going away anywhere, but why don't you hole up with us at the vicarage for a few days? You could be very secluded, I promise—Marian would guard you like a tigress from unwanted callers."

"That's most kind, but—"

"As a matter of fact Marian would love to look after you—she'd see it as something she could do for Lyle. Incidentally, they're all praying for you, you know."

"Your congregation?"

"No—well, yes, of course we're all praying, but I meant Marian and that funny little prayer-group. Actually I'm surprised it hasn't broken up by this time—you know what women are like when they all get together!—but of course I do see it's nice for the girls to have something to do other than arrange the flowers in church."

There was a silence. To my horror I felt a lump form in my throat. I had sat down behind my desk but now I stood up and moved to the window. I wanted to extol the prayer-group, but I did not trust myself to speak.

"Well, never mind all that," said Malcolm hastily, realising that the mention of the prayer-group had reminded me much too painfully of Lyle. "Let's get down to business. If I start at the top with the diocesan board of finance and work downwards to Langley Bottom . . ."

He embarked on a monologue. I tried to listen, but found it impossible to concentrate. After a while I managed to wipe my eyes surreptitiously with my fingers. The need to do this appalled me but Malcolm, talking busily, appeared not to notice. A bishop shedding tears in front of his archdeacon! Hardly able to believe I was capable of such a shameful lack of self-control, I sent a fraught, furious prayer to God for the grace to behave properly.

". . . sodomy and bestiality," said Malcolm.

My prayer was answered. Forgetting my emotion I gave a galvanic start and swung to face him. "I'm sorry, I was thinking of something else. Could you—"

"I was saying that Lewis Hall was telling me about a Devil-worship group he uncovered on the Fens near Radbury—the members used to meet in an isolated church to commit sodomy and bestiality."

"What did Hall do?"

"Ran amok with a crucifix and emerged triumphant. He talked about it exactly as you would talk about a round of golf."

"But why should he have been talking to you about it at all?"

"I'd had a confidential word on the phone with the Archdeacon of Radbury who said Hall was useful enough at mopping up any mess which no decent clergyman would touch with a barge-pole, but that he was opinionated, bolshie and very much too interested in the paranormal. So I thought I'd better read Hall the Riot Act and make it clear that no exorcisms take place in this diocese without your permission, but he said he'd always sought his bishop's permission before—and that was when we got on to the subject of the Satanists."

"I see." I had to struggle to digest this. "But surely there's no need to be too anxious? So long as Hall's only working here on a temporary basis, he's going to be on his best behaviour in order to impress me."

"Well, don't be too impressionable, that's all I can say! You mark my words, that man's Trouble with a capital *T*—the average age of the female congregation is sinking like a stone and he's already got them doing everything he wants—"

"What on earth do you mean?"

"Oh, I don't mean he's started a harem! But he's got them all producing flowers—*flowers!* In the depths of winter!—and the church is now so stuffed with them that the scent even blots out the reek of the incense! Whatever next, I ask myself, but never mind, at least we've got St. Paul's ticking over until we can sack Desmond and close the church—and in my opinion we've no choice but to close it; the place is an unjustifiable drain on the diocesan purse and we're never going to get a dynamic young Anglo-Catholic priest who'll revitalise it, not in this day and age. Nigel objects to closure, I have to tell you, but of course he doesn't know the place as I do—and by the way, Charles, talking of Nigel, I must say he has a very hazy idea of the correct relationship between a suffragan bishop and an archdeacon! Of course I've suspected for some time that poor David's remorselessly ground down in Starmouth, but if Nigel thinks he can grind *me* down—"

"I'm sure he wouldn't be so stupid." Suddenly I felt so exhausted that I knew my performance as a fit executive could no longer be sustained. "We'll talk about Nigel later," I said. "And now if you'll excuse me . . ."

I got rid of him but realised afterwards that I had forgotten to disclose the news of my approaching interview with Aysgarth. Perhaps I was going senile, but no, the most likely explanation was that I was simply too worn out to think properly.

Staggering upstairs I slumped on to my bed and plummeted into unconsciousness.

4

WHEN I awoke it was half-past five and Miss Peabody was still in the office. I said to her: "Could you phone the Dean, please, and ask him if he would mind postponing our drink until tomorrow?" Miss Peabody made the call and reported that the Dean did not mind in the least.

This postponement was undoubtedly the wisest decision I had made all day and underlined to me how idiotic I had been to pretend that I was now fit for work. "I think perhaps I might not pick up the reins just yet after all," I said to Miss Peabody. "You can tell the Archdeacon and Bishop Farr tomorrow that I've changed my mind."

Miss Peabody said she thought I was being very sensible.

I was still feeling groggy after my prolonged sleep, so I brewed myself some tea and drank it in the kitchen. Miss Peabody eventually went home. Taking some bread and cheese to my study I wrote a list of things to do and tried to eat, but I had no appetite. After a while I opened a bottle of claret. I was surprised that I could face drinking alcohol, but I knew how important it was that I should eat and I thought a single glass of wine might stimulate my appetite.

The bread and cheese disappeared. So did the single glass of wine. I had no intention of drinking more but then I started to remember Malcolm talking about the prayer-group and I thought another glass of wine might induce amnesia.

It did not. I poured myself a third glass. And later I poured myself a fourth. Dimly I realised I was frightened, and not just of my painful memories but of everything which awaited me in that still, silent house. I was frightened of opening the file of sympathy letters and feeling unbearably distressed. I was frightened of receiving no solace if I tried to calm myself by retreating to Lyle's sitting-room. I was frightened in case sleep now proved impossible because I could no longer ignore the emptiness of the bed. I was frightened of the future. I was frightened of the present. I was frightened by the sheer vastness of that terrible landscape of bereavement which had begun to open up in front of me as far as the eye could see.

I finished the bottle of claret.

And finding myself still conscious, I opened another.

5

I AWOKE feeling like a piece of elderly rope, bedraggled and frayed at the edges, but this time I was not seriously unwell; I had only drunk a little of the second bottle, the wine had been of good quality and I had not been drinking on an empty stomach. I decided I had behaved regrettably but not disastrously, and by avoiding whisky I could even be said to be improving. I boosted my morale with this fable for some time. Then I looked at the clock and saw that yet again I had missed mass at Starrington. That was certainly not what I had intended to do, but when one drinks oneself into a stupor the possibility of failing to set an alarm clock is high.

Determined to make amends for my idiocy by behaving as if I were completely well, I consumed a cooked breakfast and departed in my car for the golf course. I took no clubs; I did not delude myself that I was fit enough to hit a ball effectively, but I saw no reason why I should not go for a long, brisk, bracing walk on the fairways. Unfortunately, however, I was so busy planning what I should say to Jon to explain my second failure to attend mass, that I missed the turning which would have led me through the suburb of Parson's Mill to the golf club. Hardly able to believe I could have made such an extraordinary error, I made a couple of right turns in an attempt to get back on course, but all that happened was that I found myself in a new system of one-way streets, and I was still fuming as the result of this navigational débâcle when I realised I was crossing the parish boundary into Langley Bottom.

I forgot my plan to take a bracing walk on the fairways. I glimpsed the forlorn hulk of the church rising above the shabby terraces which flanked the railway yards, and suddenly, gripped by an impulse which I made no attempt to analyse, I realised I had to see for myself that former ecclesiastical desert which was now so improbably filled with flowers.

6

OF COURSE it seems obvious now that the flower-filled church constituted the perfect diversion from everything I was too afraid to face, but at the time I could think only of the message implicit in a dark wasteland penetrated by light. Assuming the church would be locked I went to the vicarage to obtain the key, and seconds later Hall himself was opening the front door.

He was wearing a black V-necked jersey with no vest or shirt so that the dark hair on his chest was displayed in a manner which I found most inappropriate for someone whose profession required him to look seemly in public. Around his neck he wore a gold chain, and dangling from this flashy item was a florid crucifix of the type which makes a Protestant like Aysgarth want to yell: "No Popery!" and become empurpled. Even I, a tolerant representative of the Middle Way, found myself blinking at this unquestionably Romish style of adornment. But this was not the only reason why I blinked. I had noticed to my horror that he was also sporting denim trousers, sandals and a complete lack of socks.

"Good morning, Hall," I said appalled.

"Good morning, my lord," he said, sufficiently shocked to fall back on the old-fashioned style of address. I was hardly about to object, however, to being called "my lord." That terrible new Bishop of Radbury encourages everyone, even the junior clergy, to call him by his Christian name. Sometimes I think the Church really is going to the dogs. What purpose can such a false intimacy possibly serve? To treat a stranger as a close friend of many years' standing is quite simply unreal; there are far more Christian ways of showing concern for a person than to indulge in a phony manner which ignores social realities. In my youth one called all males by their surnames unless either they were members of one's family or one had known them for a long time. My one concession to changing times was that I was willing to address my clergy by their Christian names if I had known them for more than three years. But they, naturally, knew better than to dare address me by mine unless I had given them express permission to do so.

"Do please come in," Hall was saying, surreptitiously tugging down his jersey as if driven to cover up as much blue denim as possible. "The kitchen's the warmest room in the house, but if you'd prefer the morning-room—"

"By all means let's be warm," I said, very chilly.

Hall gave a nervous cough. As I followed him down the passage into the area which had once been the servants' quarters, I noted that his hair was growing below his collar and he appeared to be cultivating sideboards. "I trust you intend to visit the barber soon," I said, "and by 'soon' I mean within the next twenty-four hours."

"Yes, Bishop. I do apologise, but I've been so busy that I've hardly had time to comb my hair, let alone cut it . . . May I offer you coffee?"

"Since you're so hard-pressed, I scarcely like to trespass on your time."

"Oh, the coffee's already made for elevenses! I believe one has a religious duty," said Hall firmly, "to keep up one's strength by eating regularly."

I thought the consumption of elevenses bore a closer resemblance to self-indulgence than the performance of a religious duty, but I preserved an austere silence.

We entered the cavernous kitchen which was smelling so markedly of disinfectant that I wondered if Hall had scrubbed not only the floor but the walls. This odour of chemical purity mingled oddly with the scent of coffee which was wafting from a smart modern percolator on the dresser.

"Milk and sugar, Bishop?" said Hall, very solicitous. I realised he was recovering his equilibrium.

"No thanks. And before we leave the subject of your appearance I feel I should make it clear that in this diocese priests are required to dress as priests except on their days off—and even on their days off they're required to dress with good taste and discretion."

"I quite understand, Bishop. But I'm only dressed informally because I was about to put in an hour working on Father Wilton's study. I'm repainting it."

"You mean you dressed informally when you got up this morning? You mean you celebrated mass in sandals? And *without socks*?"

"Oh no, no, Bishop—good heavens, what a horrifying thought! No, I wore black shoes and socks for the service, of course I did, but I shed them along with the cassock when I arrived home. I find I paint better in sandals."

"Indeed." There seemed little else to say in the face of such eccentricity, so I sat down at the kitchen table, a large item of furniture which was covered with an eclectic array of objects. I noted a half-mended pair of trousers with the needle still sticking in the seam, an iron, an open jar of honey, a bag of apples, a copy of the *Daily Mail*—very light-weight reading for a priest—a packet of cigarettes, a ball of string, a letter in childish handwriting beginning "Dear Daddy" (that gave me a jolt; Malcolm had either failed to uncover evidence of fatherhood or else had forgotten to pass it on), two half-crowns, a book of stamps and a box of candles. My glance had just returned with disapproval to the newspaper when Hall set down a cup of coffee in front of me and said with a panache I could not help but admire: "You'll be surprised to see the *Daily Mail,* I daresay, but I must have a newspaper I can read in five minutes. Otherwise I waste too much time." Opening a biscuit-tin he offered me the contents. "Flapjack?"

I declined but commented: "I see the ladies of the parish are already baking for you!"

Hall looked wary at the mention of ladies but answered equably enough: "People like to rally round in a crisis. For example, when I asked for volunteers to clean the church I was amazed by how many people responded."

I forgot my disapproval. "You saw the cleaning as therapy?"

"Yes, I did. People were very shocked by the violence to Father Wilton—even the non-churchgoers were shocked. It's a close-knit community."

"Who suggested bringing the flowers?"

"I did. It was all part of the ritual of cleansing and renewal . . . Who told you about the flowers?"

"The Archdeacon." I paused, but since I always believed in giving praise where praise was due I added: "I congratulate you. You must have worked very hard, making yourself known to so many people in such a short time and enabling them to express their feelings in a way which was psychologically and spiritually effective."

Hall made a commendable attempt to look modest.

There was another pause, and it seemed to me then that although the interview had begun so inauspiciously we were now at ease. Indeed it was as if we had reached a point where my rank and his eccentricity were no longer sources of friction but of harmony, as if each in some mysterious way complemented the other. I was reminded of the way in which two apparently unrelated pieces in a huge jigsaw can suddenly slot together in a perfect fit, and no sooner had this thought entered my head when Hall said: "I knew you were the right bishop for me." And he added, speaking with increasing speed: "I'm sorry about your wife. Obviously this is quite the wrong moment to talk to you about my plans, but that's all right, they'll keep, and meanwhile I'm quite happy just to be working here in your diocese."

I knew I should signal to him that there was no possibility that I would allow him to work in the diocese permanently, but all I said was: "I'm sorry you have to work in a church which is so run-down and unprepossessing."

"Unprepossessing?" said Hall astonished. "But it's magnificent! A Victorian masterpiece! The space, the light, the stonework, the glass—"

"And now the flowers?"

Hall stood up, reached for the keys which were lying on the dresser and said: "You came to see the flowers, didn't you?"

"How did you know?"

"I can see they have meaning for you. Let me take you over to the church straight away."

Pushing aside my cup of coffee, I followed him from the house.

7

WINTER FADED and spring seemed close once I saw the flowers. They were everywhere: hardy weeds from the water-meadows; snowdrops, crocuses and even daffodils from the little back gardens of the Victorian terraces; innumerable varieties of chrysanthemums from the local florists. I wandered around touching the blooms as if I could not quite believe they were real, and after a while I became aware of the transformed church itself, the scrubbed floor, the polished pews, the shining brass; even the Anglo-Catholic accoutrements, which can so easily with lack of care degenerate into a ramshackle mess, seemed stylish, glittering, sumptuous. All the tarnish had vanished. So had the elderly candle-stumps. The holy water stoup was pristine. And beyond all the renovated furnishings, beyond all the flowers, the great cross glowed in the multi-coloured light which streamed down on the high altar, a numinous sign pointing beyond itself to the eternal cycle of suffering, death, resurrection and renewal.

I sat down in one of the pews and Hall sat down beside me. At last I said: "I must be honest with you. This can only be a temporary renewal. There's no money to finance a healing centre anywhere, least of all here. The diocesan board of finance—"

"This needn't cost you a penny."

I assumed that either he had misheard me or that I had misunderstood him. "What needn't cost me a penny?"

"The healing centre. For a start, I wouldn't take a salary, I don't need one. And second, there's no reason why a healing centre shouldn't be funded by charities and private individuals. The Fordite monks would set it up."

"The Fordite monks?"

"Why not? Now that their numbers are reduced, they hardly know what to do with all their money, it's an embarrassment to them—just think of all the loot they got when they sold off the Ruydale estate!"

"But surely a remote Yorkshire sheepfarm wasn't worth much?"

"The Abbot-General laughed all the way to the bank."

"But—"

"Every river was stuffed with fish and every moor was groaning with grouse! The international estate agents even printed a special colour brochure to make sure that the price was pushed into the stratosphere, so don't worry about the money, Bishop, I'll get the Abbot-General to launch a new charitable foundation, he'll love it, it'll give him a new interest in his old age."

I struggled to comment but words failed me.

"One day," said Hall, "one day when you're free to grapple with the problems of St. Paul's Langley Bottom, please do allow me to explain my plans to you in detail. St. Paul's is actually the perfect place because it has that very large, bone-dry crypt yet there are hardly any corpses in it—I suppose that's because the church is comparatively new and in the old days most of the parishioners wouldn't have been able to afford an expensive interment. So although we'd have to do a certain amount of reburying, I don't regard that as a major obstacle, and once all the bones have been transferred to the cemetery . . ."

I ceased to listen. I was thinking: there must be an ecclesiastical law which I can invoke to extricate myself from this fantastic scheme, but the next moment I was remembering Lyle, writing in her journal about the sayings of Jesus, and into my head came the words: "The letter killeth, but the spirit giveth life."

Before I could stop myself I said to Lewis Hall: "Come and dine with me this Saturday."

X

"The pressure of immediate sufferings may unhinge, indeed, the balance of judgement. Our derangement may be wholly pardonable, but it must not be allowed to pass for sanity."

AUSTIN FARRER
Warden of Keble College, Oxford, 1960–1968
LOVE ALMIGHTY AND ILLS UNLIMITED

I

NOW IT was Hall's turn to be astounded. I watched while he searched for the words to thank me but I did not wait till he had found them. Assuming his acceptance of the invitation I said: "Come at seven-thirty and we'll dine at eight." Then, unable to restrain my curiosity, I remarked: "You seem on very familiar terms with the Fordite monks!"

"I was at school at Starwater Abbey and because of unfortunate family circumstances I spent several holidays at the monks' London house. The Abbot-General took an interest in me."

"Was that Father Ingram?"

"No. Father Darcy."

"Darcy! How his reputation comes echoing down the years! My spiritual director often speaks of him . . . Did you ever meet Father Darrow?"

"Unfortunately our visits to the London house never coincided."

"Ah, that would explain why Jon hasn't mentioned you . . . And did you never think of becoming a monk yourself?"

"I made the mistake of believing my life would be more comfortable as a married priest."

"Valuable experiences aren't always the most comfortable ones."

"I'm afraid this particular valuable experience was very uncomfortable indeed. But it did teach me a lot. And it did produce my daughter Rachel."

"How old is she?"

"Seventeen."

"You see much of her?"

"Not as much as I'd like—although by coincidence she's coming down to Starbridge for a visit this weekend."

"In that case please bring her with you to the South Canonry on Saturday night." I stood up and moved into the aisle but when I realised he had remained motionless in the pew I said to him: "Is there some difficulty about bringing her?"

"None at all. Forgive me, but I was just very surprised—I didn't expect you to be so hospitable to a divorced priest."

"I may be hospitable towards a divorced priest," I said, "but as you've already discovered, I'm not at all kindly disposed towards an ill-dressed one. I trust, Hall, that I shall see you suitably attired on Saturday night—and don't forget to make that visit to the barber's." I thought it wise at this point to show him that although I had been as soft as butter for some time, I was still capable of being a tough disciplinarian.

"Yes, Bishop," said Hall, faultlessly meek.

We parted in amity.

2

I DID think of driving on from the church to Starrington, but I decided it would be more sensible to go home for lunch, rest and then visit Jon in the early evening. Accordingly I returned to the South Canonry where Miss Peabody informed me that Charley had telephoned; he had obtained additional leave and would be returning to Starbridge on the morrow to spend the weekend with me. I said that would suit very well, since Mr. Hall was coming to dine with his young daughter on Saturday, and could Miss Peabody please arrange for the cook-housekeeper to return to work for a few hours to produce an unpretentious three-course meal for the occasion.

Thinking of food reminded me that I had to eat again, so I wandered into the kitchen to inspect the larder. My devoted Cathedral ladies were still busy ensuring that I did not die of starvation—so busy that I had already ordered the chaplains to eat all perishable food which lingered on the shelves longer than twenty-four hours. (In the pantry the new deep-freeze was almost bursting at the seams, but at least frozen food did not spoil.) After much thought I removed from the larder a single scotch egg before making myself a mug of instant coffee. It was only after I had retired with this modest lunch to my study that I realised I had no desire to see Charley at all.

I dialled the number of his flat in Mayfair.

Delighted to hear from me, Charley at once began to talk about his coming visit. ". . . so I can be with you by tomorrow evening and stay all Saturday—I'm only sorry I can't stay on after that, but I'm preaching at Matins on Sunday."

I was finally allowed to speak. "Charley, it's not necessary, you know, for you to come down—in fact as you've already taken time off this week for the funeral I shall quite understand if—"

"But of course it's necessary for me to come—you need to be looked after! Now, don't worry about anything, Dad, I'll be with you tomorrow and—bother, there goes the doorbell, sorry, got to rush—" And the line went dead.

I fidgeted with the scotch egg but abandoned it to dial the BBC. Michael was out. After leaving a message asking him to telephone me, I went to the office where Miss Peabody was working through her lunch-hour.

"I'm expecting a call from Michael," I said. "Be sure to let me know when it comes through. But I don't want to speak to anyone else."

Miss Peabody made a conventional response to these instructions but was obviously preoccupied by another matter. "Bishop, I'm terribly sorry, but this morning I found another sympathy letter at the bottom of the in-tray—I can't think how it managed to wind up there and not in the special file, but . . ." The apology was prolonged.

Meanwhile I was discovering that the letter was from someone called Sheila who lived in Guernsey Street, Pimlico, an area of central London which was almost unknown to me. "Who's this?" I said baffled.

"I tracked her down in the Christmas card list," said Miss Peabody, pleased to redeem her error by flaunting her efficiency. "It's Mrs. Preston, the wife of the late Bishop of Radbury."

"Derek's Sheila . . . yes, of course." After pausing to remember Sunbeam's predecessor, who had been a good friend of mine, I drifted back to my study and began to read the letter.

"My dear Charles . . ." It was a conventional expression of sympathy, but it was perfectly done, the handwriting clear and elegant, the sentiments framed with unflawed good taste. Reflecting that it was exactly the kind of letter that I would have expected from a woman who had made a great success of being a bishop's wife, I thought: I must show this to Lyle.

The letter slid from my fingers as my memory lurched into action a second later.

Sinking down in the chair behind my desk I covered my face with my hands.

3

EVENTUALLY I pulled myself together. I made another call to the BBC and left another message. Then I wondered whether it was time to drum up the energy to drive to Starrington but no, now I had to wait for Michael to telephone. I waited and waited, and waiting proved to be such an exhausting occupation that I had to go upstairs to lie down.

But I was in such a state at the thought of conversing with Michael that I found I was unable to sleep. I also found I had to drink some claret to calm myself. My nervousness was exacerbated by the fact that I had no idea what I was going to say to Michael. I only knew I had to talk to him because of what Lyle had written in the journal—but I knew too that I could not face the journal again without Jon's help—and I could not go to see Jon because I had to stay at home to wait for Michael's call.

Round and round my thoughts went in an increasingly confused pattern of circles, and more and more claret disappeared from the bottle I had opened the previous evening, but instead of calming me down the alcohol this time seemed to stir me up so that I found myself moving beyond inertia into a thickening fog of grief.

I said to myself: "This is a phase of bereavement. It's all perfectly normal. It'll pass." But I felt more distracted than ever, and in panic I returned to Lyle's sitting-room to escape into that imaginary future which seemed so natural, so credible, so absolutely waiting to happen in a parallel world where blood clots never formed.

Eventually, when there was no more claret in the bottle, I did sleep a little for I was lying down on my bed again by that time and it was easier to feel drowsy. But I was awake before Miss Peabody shut the front door with a bang at a quarter to six. I lay on my back and watched the ceiling and eventually the grandfather clock chimed six in the hall.

I had just emerged from the bathroom and was on my way downstairs to make yet another attempt to speak to Michael, when the front doorbell rang.

I froze, my grip tightening on the empty bottle of claret.

The doorbell rang again.

I debated whether to do nothing but I found I had to know who the caller was. Michael did have a front door key but he was always losing it and he certainly had not had it when he had arrived with Dinkie to announce his engagement. In a sudden burst of hope I hurried downstairs, thrust the empty bottle out of sight in the case of the grandfather clock and flung open the front door.

On the doorstep, keeping the engagement which I had postponed from the previous evening, was none other than my enemy, the Dean of Starbridge.

4

AGAIN I found myself presented with a diversion from my bereavement. My initial dismay was followed quickly by relief, and in my relief I made a bad decision: I invited him in.

"Are you all right?" said Aysgarth, hesitating on the threshold.

"Absolutely fine. Good to see you."

"When no one answered the door I wondered if—"

"Sorry for the delay. Lavatory."

"Ah. I just wanted to say that if you still don't feel like a drink—"

"Can't wait for the Tio Pepe!" I had quite forgotten my intention of passing off a ginger ale as a whisky-and-soda.

We entered the drawing-room and when I invited him to sit down he settled himself in one of the chairs by the fireplace. "How are you getting on?" he said as I concentrated on wielding the decanter as if no alcohol had passed my lips for twenty-four hours.

"Well, I go through a bad patch every now and then, but that's normal, isn't it?" I had realised that if I continued to insist that I was absolutely fine I would be behaving like a psychopath.

"Just because it's normal doesn't mean it isn't frightful. Thanks," he added as I handed him his drink.

I sat down opposite him. My guest then chose to adopt that quiet attentiveness which the bereaved usually prefer to a torrent of conversation, but I felt driven to say: "No need to be pastoral. How's your family?"

"Very well," said Aysgarth, at once picking up the hint that I needed some trivial conversation before we broached the subject of the Cathedral. "Pip's got the leading solo in the Choir's Easter concert, and Elizabeth's top of her form in every subject as usual." Elizabeth and Pip were the children of his second marriage.

"Splendid!" I said, regretting that I had given him the chance to brag but unable to work out how to avoid the next question which was: "And how are all your other children?"

"Oh, doing wonderfully well!" said Aysgarth, delighted to be able to chronicle the remarkable achievements of the adult children of his first marriage. "Christian and Katie are happier than ever, and Norman and Cynthia have just moved to the most beautiful mews house in Chelsea so they're happier than ever too. As for James, he's still going from strength to strength in the army—no marriage on the horizon yet, but I've always pictured James marrying late, perhaps when he's reached the rank of brigadier. Sandy's decided to do a doctorate—no problems there at all—and back in Starbridge my wonderful Primrose is busy making a huge success of marriage and motherhood, so there's no cloud on the horizon there either."

After a slight pause I managed to utter a single syllable. It was: "Good."

Aysgarth smiled placidly and took another sip of sherry. His small, thick-fingered, brutal hands looked incongruous as they clasped the delicate, elegant curves of the Waterford glass. Leaning back in his chair he crossed one leg over the other to signal how relaxed he was, how self-confident and self-possessed, just as a successful self-made man should be in even the most trying of social situations. Aysgarth had short legs and wore trousers which were never quite the right length. Many were the times when I had longed to refer him to my tailor.

The pause lengthened. Suddenly Aysgarth uncrossed his legs, leaned forward in his chair and made another, far more radical attempt to be pastoral. "Look, Charles," he said, "I can see this isn't the right moment to discuss the Cathedral. I know you're keen to get back to work and of course that's very commendable, but—"

"Why are you trying to sell off the Cathedral treasures?"

Aysgarth leaned back in his chair, recrossed his legs and sighed. Then having signalled that he was quite unintimidated he replied mildly: "Who told you I was negotiating with Christie's?"

"Jack Ryder."

To my amazement Aysgarth laughed. "I swear Jack will even get wind of the Day of Judgement in advance! But I hope he takes more trouble then to get his facts right."

Incredulously I demanded: "You're saying Jack's been misinformed?"

"Well, of course he has! You don't seriously think I'd flog the St. Anselm masterpiece, do you?"

"But in that case what on earth—"

"It was all a magnificent stunt to gain publicity for the West Front Appeal! As soon as the catalogue was published I planned to give a press conference, wring my hands and bemoan the crisis which was apparently driving me to take such desperate action—I'd even got a blown-up photo of Puss-in-Boots for the TV cameras—"

"Puss-in-Boots?"

"Well, he doesn't actually have any boots on, but you know the Puss

I mean—it's that margin-drawing of the cat with the mouse in his mouth. Think how sentimental the English are about animals! They might have resisted the plea of an elderly dean, but once Puss-in-Boots had flashed on to their TV screens the money would have come rolling in! The climax would have come when I snatched the manuscript back, saving Puss for England. Think of the drama in the tabloids!"

"But surely that's extraordinarily unethical behaviour! Christie's would have been livid once they realised how they'd been used!"

"Nonsense—free advertising for them, and anyway I'd have let them sell a few unimportant books to keep them happy—"

"No book in that library's unimportant! What's gone so wrong with the Appeal that you have to stoop to such highly questionable behaviour?"

"Charles, I know you're only two years older than I am, but you're sounding like a real old buffer in an old people's home. This is not 'highly questionable behaviour'! This is modern fund-raising, using the power of television! And nothing's gone wrong with the Appeal—we've merely reached the point where we need a final burst of publicity in order to reach our target in a blaze of glory!"

"But if you were on course to reach the target anyway—as you always assured me you were—I simply don't see why you need to behave like some vulgar executive in an advertising agency. This is the Church of England, not Madison Avenue!"

"Now calm down, Charles, and do try not to be so over-emotional—"

"I must say, I deeply resent your patronising tone!"

"Your tone to me is consistently patronising," said Aysgarth, the killer in debate, "and it's particularly patronising when you imply I'm not a gentleman just because I've got the guts not only to welcome modern marketing techniques but to use them! Now look here, Charles. I'm the Dean, I have autonomy where the Cathedral's concerned, and I'm well within my rights in taking whatever decision is necessary for the preservation of the fabric."

"Well, if you think I'm going to stand by and allow the library to be plundered—"

"I do hope we're not going to have a serious quarrel about this, Charles. I always find it so very unedifying when a bishop tries to undermine the authority of the Dean and Chapter by behaving in a manner which is inconsistent with the dignity of his office."

At once I knew there was only one way of ending this interview which I had so disastrously mishandled. Rising to my feet I walked to the door, opened it and said: "Obviously we both need to pray about this very difficult matter before we attempt to continue our discussion."

Aysgarth set down his glass with a thump and stood up. "I'm sorry I've upset you," he said. "You certainly don't need any further distress at this time, but you must realise that most deans don't have to put up with such consistent interference from their bishops."

"Most deans don't try to sell off their cathedral treasures!"

"I'm not selling off any treasures. I admit I was thinking of selling a few old books which no one would miss, but—"

"I shall miss them! Posterity will miss them! Every book in that library is a precious legacy from the past and must be preserved for the future!"

"If you're so interested in dead relics, run a museum," said Aysgarth, delivering his final devastating riposte, "but I've better things to do with my Cathedral than seal it in a glass case until it's crumbled into dust."

And he walked out, slamming the front door.

5

HAVING LIT a cigarette to calm my nerves I telephoned Malcolm at his vicarage in the centre of the city.

"I've just tackled Aysgarth about Christie's, and I regret to say the conversation became very acrimonious indeed."

"Confound the man! What was his explanation for the Christie's shenanigans?"

I managed to summarise the interview without disclosing that Aysgarth had made me look old-fashioned, stupid, snobbish, arrogant and—most intolerable of all—impotent. In conclusion I added: "The worst part is that there's nothing more I can do."

"Oh yes, there is! Make a visitation!"

"But that's such a double-edged sword! The publicity, the gossip, the scandal—"

"It needn't be as bad as you think. Don't forget the entire enquiry can take place behind closed doors and you have control over the final report."

"Even so—"

"Charles, take a deep breath and go for the jugular. How else are we going to find out what's going on?"

"You really think the Appeal's in a mess?"

"What else can one think? One moment he's swearing to us that everything in the garden's lovely and the next moment he's behaving like a shady confidence trickster and planning to sob over that cat on television!"

After a pause I said: "I need to pray about this."

"Well, of course I shall pray too. But in my opinion—"

"I don't think either of us can have a worthwhile opinion until we've prayed. I'll talk to you tomorrow," I said, ending the conversation.

As I replaced the receiver it occurred to me that Malcolm had become too bossy. Why had I never noticed before that he was talking like an over-zealous secular executive? All archdeacons risk falling in love with the power their position confers on them, but their bishops should make sure that a mild flirtation never becomes an *amour fou.* I wondered if I should have a quiet word with Malcolm's rural deans to discover if they were on the brink of mutiny, but before I could reach any decision the telephone rang.

Immediately, certain the caller was Michael, I grabbed the receiver.

"Charles my dear," said Dido Aysgarth almost before I had announced: "South Canonry," "I've just heard from Miss Peabody who dropped in here to give the Bible Reading Fellowship Notes to Miss Carp that you're starting to go out and about again, driving off in your car this morning and disappearing for hours, and I thought that was so brave of you as the more you sit around and mope the worse it gets, as I know all too well, I found that out when my sister Laura died, and believe me, it's action plus the determination to build a new life that keep one going in terrible times—so when I heard from Miss Peabody that you were going out and about again, I thought *poor* Charles, *so* brave, and I knew straight away that I was being called to invite you to dinner."

"How very kind," I said, rigid with horror, "but please don't feel obliged—"

"My dear, it's not a question of obligation, it's a question of doing one's Christian best, and although Stephen and I have left you alone till now, we only did so because we didn't want to intrude on your grief. As I said in my sympathy letter—and although it's so terribly hard to write a sincere sympathy letter I do hope it was obvious that I wrote straight from the heart—for after all, I'm famed for my candour—well, as I said in my sympathy letter, Stephen and I were devastated by Lyle's death and Stephen was especially shocked because he knew how he would feel if he lost *me.*"

By this time I was beyond speech.

"And anyway, Charles my dear, do come and dine tomorrow night—I'm having a little dinner-party for sixteen and it'll all be very quiet, just the family and nice people like Lady Markhampton—who has a brilliantly clever woman staying with her, I don't quite know who she is and I can't remember her name, but Lady Markhampton said she'd been doing research in Cambridge—her friend, I mean, not Lady Markhampton—and it suddenly occurred to me how delightful it would be for you to talk to an intellectual woman who knows Cambridge—although please don't think I'm trying to marry you off because obviously you won't remarry for at least a year. However—oh, here's Stephen, back from the South Canonry! I do hope you enjoyed your sherry together—Stephen! Stephen, I've got Charles on the phone and I've asked him to come to dinner tomorrow!"

"Just a moment, Dido," I said as I pictured Aysgarth's appalled expression. "I've got Charley coming down tomorrow evening, and—"

"Lovely—bring him too!"

Now it was Charley's appalled expression which flashed before my eyes. I seemed to be floundering deeper and deeper into the most lethal of social quicksands. "I rather doubt if his train will arrive early enough to ensure—"

"What a pity but never mind, he can wait for you at home, we won't keep you late. Oh, hang on, here's Stephen, simply bursting to have a word with you!"

At this stage I felt so pulverised that I wondered why I was not spreadeagled unconscious over my desk.

"Charles," said Aysgarth as I marvelled that I was still upright in my chair, "I do apologise—I know Darrow would say I'd let my fighting streak get the better of me. Come and dine tomorrow—please!—and let's bury the hatchet."

The unreserved apology, the reference to Jon, the knowledge that I would look intolerably churlish if I now refused the invitation—all combined to make me realise I had no choice but to accept. "Very well, Stephen. Thank you," I said, trying not to sound too enfeebled, and I heard Dido screech: "Seven-thirty for dinner at eight!" before Aysgarth exclaimed: "Splendid!" and ended the call.

6

I REMAINED sitting at my desk as I thought of Aysgarth, and the more I thought of him the more convinced I became that he had issued his winning apology because he knew I would be toying with the idea of a visitation. Visitations are usually friendly; archdeacons make them all the time when they inspect churches to ensure that all is in the proper ecclesiastical order, and in the vast majority of cases no hard feelings are generated. In theory there is no reason why an episcopal visitation should not be equally benign, but in practice the word "visitation" too often has a sinister ring because it signifies the one occasion on which an autonomous dean can be compelled to answer directly to the Bishop about the affairs of the cathedral, and no bishop embarks lightly on such a potentially explosive procedure.

In the secular world potentially explosive procedures can be described in the language of power-politics and regarded as normal within a corporate structure; that is to say, the situation can be acknowledged without embarrassment and guilt. In the Church, on the other hand, it is not "the done thing" to talk of personality clashes and power struggles and boardroom battles. This does not mean that these unpleasant events never happen; it simply means that they are described in different language and dressed up in a variety of disguises. And this in turn does not necessarily mean that the churchmen are being hypocritical. The purpose of the different language and the multiple disguises is to enable the protagonists, who are mere fallible men beneath their cassocks, to have as much chance as possible to behave like Christians instead of like cut-throat corporate monsters.

The secular world too is better equipped to deal with the fall-out of a corporate explosion; the chairman has the power to fire the crooked and the incompetent as the result of a boardroom investigation, and so although violence takes place in the form of sackings there is more scope for healing after the victims have gone. But I, as the Bishop, had no such powers when I made a visitation. No matter what iniquity I uncovered I could not sack the Dean or any member of the Chapter; I could make recommendations in my report, but the Dean and Chapter were not obliged to accept them. I could not imagine Aysgarth resigning even if I were to recommend that he should do so. That meant the only result of the visitation would have been the laundering of a lot of dirty Church linen in public. And how long would the shattered Cathedral community take to heal afterwards? There might be years of further division and strife.

I had just finished thinking along these depressing lines when it occurred to me that I was going to great lengths to persuade myself not to make a visitation. In fact the picture in this particular case was not as black as I was trying to paint it because if the worst came to the worst and some profound iniquity was uncovered, I was sure I could enlist the support of the Archbishop of Canterbury to extort Aysgarth's resignation. I could not seriously imagine even Aysgarth having the nerve to defy Dr. Ramsey, and once a new dean had been installed the Cathedral would be on the road to recovery.

Why then was I so determined to view the prospect of a visitation with reluctance? I began to suspect that it was because I did not want to confront Aysgarth either in the chapter house during a visitation or anywhere else, and in a flash I saw that Aysgarth had become one of those topics which could only be explored with Jon. It seemed the journal had converted my old enemy into a taboo subject even before my quarrel with him that evening.

The thought of Jon reminded me that I wanted to go to Starrington but was pinned to the South Canonry by my desire to hear from Michael. I put in yet another call to the BBC but was told he had left for the day. I telephoned his flat but no one answered. In frustration I took a sheet of writing-paper and scribbled: "My dear Michael, I have come to realise I have not in the past been as helpful as I should have been in our attempts to resolve our difficulties. I'm very sorry about this and hope I can be more constructive in future. Perhaps you and"—I had a moment of amnesia during which I was unable to remember the name of the new girlfriend, the one Charley had grudgingly admitted was "rather nice," but fortunately the moment passed—"Holly can have dinner with me when I'm next up in town. I should so much like to see you. Blood really is thicker than water, and—"

I stopped writing. Such a sentence was absolutely *verboten* and I had been unhinged to write it. Supposing Michael showed the letter in triumph to Charley? Tearing the letter up I prepared to begin again but found I had run out of energy.

I went to the kitchen and ate the scotch egg which I had tried to eat at lunch and which someone (Miss Peabody, no doubt) had returned on its plate to the larder. By this time I had realised that the letter to Michael was in reality a letter to myself, my first faltering attempt to rebut, negate, neutralise or merely assimilate some of the more distressing statements Lyle had made. But I knew I could not start thinking about the journal until I was with Jon.

Instead I ate another scotch egg and tried to read the latest issue of *The Church Gazette* which had arrived that morning. The Church Assembly was in progress; I had earlier sent my apologies that I was unable to attend, and now as I glanced at the speeches about suffragan appointments I felt guiltily relieved that I had been spared hours of boredom. Turning the page I read that some woman professor had allegedly found the bones of St. Peter. I spared some sympathy for the Pope, required to comment.

Shoving the paper aside in a spasm of irritation I returned to the drawing-room to watch the television news but I switched channels as soon as I heard the syllables "Vietnam." Nothing on ITA appealed so I turned off the set, and when I glanced at my watch I saw it was too late to go to Starrington. I poured myself a double-whisky. Then I retrieved *The Church Gazette* and again settled down to wait for the call which I felt sure now would never come.

Two double-whiskies later I returned to my study, took another sheet of paper and wrote rapidly: "My dear Michael, I know you think I don't understand about sex, but I do, and believe me, I'm not jealous because you lead the kind of life I couldn't lead as a young man, I couldn't be, because in truth for a short time when I was up at Cambridge in the days before my ordination, I did live a little fast on the quiet, and even later when I was a clergyman I wasn't quite as chaste as I should have been but that was because I was mixed up, and in fact during my spiritual breakdown in 1937 before I married your mother I met an American woman called Loretta who was just as sexy as your Dinkie, and—"

It suddenly dawned on me that I was writing like a lunatic. In horror I burnt the letter in the ashtray.

Having realised that I was no longer capable of writing sense I went to bed, but there more horrors awaited me because writing about sex had made me think about sex, and having thought about sex I wanted to make love to Lyle.

At two o'clock in the morning I went downstairs and drank as much scotch as I needed to pass out.

It was the worst night I had so far experienced as a widower.

7

SOMEONE WAS saying quietly: "Charles?" and as I plummeted painfully back to consciousness I was aware of a hand pressing on my wrist. Someone was feeling my pulse. Evidently I looked like a corpse. Opening my eyes I found the Suffragan Bishop of Starmouth stooping over me.

"Sorry, Charles," said Nigel, removing his hand from my wrist at once, "but when you didn't appear downstairs we were concerned."

"Give me ten minutes."

"If you'd rather stay in bed—"

"Ten minutes."

Nigel fled.

I took a quick look around the room, but I had done my nocturnal drinking downstairs and afterwards hidden my dirty glass in the case of the grandfather clock alongside the empty bottle of claret, so there was no evidence of disorder to betray me. To my horror I saw the time was ten past eleven. Trying not to feel as if I were trapped in a downward moral spiral, I went through the usual anti-hang-over routine and managed to shave without cutting myself. Shortly afterwards, washed, brushed and dressed, I descended to the office to prove to my staff that I was still alive. Ignoring their anxious expressions I asked the typist to bring me coffee, told Miss Peabody that I wanted to see Lewis Hall's reference and invited Nigel to accompany me to the study.

"Where's Malcolm?" I said, trying not to look exhausted after this performance.

"He's not here this morning—he had a visitation to make in the north. Charles, is there anything I can do? I'm worried that I'm not doing enough for you at the moment."

"But you're running the entire diocese!"

"I'm not talking about professional help. I'm talking about help on a personal level. And please don't think I'm just producing a pastoral manner out of a sense of duty. I'm genuinely concerned for you as a friend."

I began to panic because I found his sincerity moving and I did not want to be moved; it was vital that I kept my emotions on a tight leash.

"How very good of you," I said, somehow managing to speak evenly, "but I've got Charley coming down this evening for the weekend, and I shall also be visiting Jon Darrow. I'll be all right."

There was a pause while Nigel tried to decide whether to press the matter further and I watched, with a detached interest, to see how he would handle the situation. Nigel was tall and a trifle stout, with some scanty greyish hair, every strand combed smoothly into place, and he possessed glasses which he continually put on and took off during his well-prepared, smoothly delivered public speeches. He had pale eyes, a sensitive mouth, a pleasant smile, an adroit social manner and smooth, pale, well-kept hands which had never attempted to hold a golf club. Although I greatly respected his ability and found him agreeable company, we had nothing in common except the Church and rarely saw each other except on business. That was why I admired him all the more for making an effort to address me on a personal level. He was several years my junior, and although he always appeared at ease with me I suspected there were times when he found me intimidating.

"Well, I've no wish to be intrusive, Charles," he said at last, "but I thought you should know how deep my concern is and how willing I am to do something to help. Please feel you can call on me at any time."

It was a smooth little speech but, again, it was not insincere and I was able to thank him without hesitation. It was only when I said: "And now if we may turn to other matters . . ." that I sensed how relieved he was to be spared any further attempt to be personal.

The typist delivered my coffee and after her departure I summarised my conversation with Aysgarth.

"Very spivvish behaviour," was Nigel's terse comment. Reminding me that he normally had nothing to do with the Cathedral's hidden problems, he asked: "How much do you know for certain about the progress of the Appeal?"

"I know only what I'm told by the Dean and Chapter. The Appeal's entirely in their hands."

"Isn't the diocesan office sent the accounts as a courtesy?"

"Good heavens, no! Relations between the Cathedral and the diocesan office have been strained for years."

"Isn't there even a cosy relationship between the two sets of accountants to ease things along?"

"I'm afraid not. The Cathedral's accountant, Bob Carey, is terrified of Aysgarth and Aysgarth wouldn't approve of such a cosy relationship at all."

"So what are you going to do?"

"What do you advise?"

"Extreme caution. The innocent explanation is that Aysgarth's just trying to save face. Having bragged to you about how well the Appeal was going he was embarrassed to discover reality wasn't measuring up to his expectations, so he planned the Christie's coup to boost not only the coffers but his self-esteem."

I was so struck by the plausibility of this theory that it took me several seconds to pose the next question. "So you think I should do nothing?" I felt limp with relief.

"Well, not quite *nothing,*" said Nigel warily. "I think you should continue to demand that he withdraws all the books from Christie's, not merely the St. Anselm manuscript. After all, you'd be setting a dangerous precedent if you turned a blind eye while he pilfered the library."

"True." My relief ebbed. Reluctantly I asked: "Do you see a case for a visitation?"

"Oh, there's certainly a case for it! When a dean starts behaving in a spivvish way, a bishop's got the right to give him a good fright, but since Aysgarth's such a formidable opponent you don't want him to wriggle off the hook for lack of evidence. Much better to wait until you have a watertight case . . . What does Malcolm say?"

"He favours an immediate assault on the Cathedral with all our six-shooters blazing."

Nigel allowed himself the thinnest of smiles and said in the dryest of voices: "Malcolm can be a trifle headstrong sometimes."

I kept quiet and prayed that this deadly little comment was not the harbinger of further criticism. Meanwhile Nigel was adjusting his pectoral cross and smoothing a small crease from his stock. I was just daring to hope that I was to be spared further evidence of friction between my suffragan and my archdeacon when he said in an indulgent tone, rather as if he were discussing the wayward antics of a bunch of children: "Of course archdeacons do tend to have an inflated sense of their own importance which can feed the temptation to behave like a secular executive . . . I hear Malcolm has quite a reputation in the rural deaneries."

I inwardly cringed but managed to remain outwardly calm. "I suspect," I said, "that we all suffer sometimes from the temptation to behave like a secular executive."

"True. But we don't all give in to it."

To my immense relief I was then saved by the sound of a car in the drive. "Who's that?" I demanded at once, trying not to sound too thankful. "I'm not in the mood for visitors."

Nigel stood up and glanced out of the window. "You'll be in the mood for this one," he said. "It's your son Charley."

That was the moment when I realised that the day had started badly and was going to get worse. Moving to the window so that I could see Charley's unexpectedly early arrival with my own eyes, I felt as if I were lurching from one ordeal to the next with no hope of rescue.

I could only wish I felt less exhausted and hung-over.

8

"I WAS determined to get here before noon!" Charley announced in triumph as his taxi drove away and I emerged from the house to meet him. "As soon as you said yesterday that it wasn't necessary for me to come down, I knew you were longing to see me as soon as possible!"

Unable to frame a reply I found myself becoming the object of a most exhausting pastoral care. I was given the traditional brief Anglo-Saxon hug which is permitted between males who belong to the same family, but was then pinned by the forearms and subjected to an anguished scrutiny at the end of which I was told I looked "wiped out." I was then propelled into the drawing-room and eased into the nearest armchair as if I were eighty and mentally deficient. At that point I was told with religious fervour: "Relax—the Church is taking care of you!"

I did open my mouth to query this masterful assault on my independence, but before I could utter a word Charley retrieved his luggage from the front doorstep and produced a bag containing my favourite delicacies from Fortnum's.

"You haven't been eating, have you?" he said. "But I intend to rescue you from starvation—I'm going to whip up a feast which you'll be quite unable to resist!"

I followed protesting as he marched to the kitchen, but he paid no attention and I wound up confronting a plate of pâté de foie gras on toast. He even produced a bottle of something called "tonic wine," and when I declared with horror that I was not an invalid he merely laughed as if I had made a joke.

"Now, tell me all that needs to be done and I'll do it!" he said brightly, sitting down beside me at the kitchen table and helping himself generously to the pâté. "Have you suits to be picked up at the cleaner's? Socks to be washed? Do you want cigarettes? A new library book? More lavatory paper? The chaplains said you'd temporarily banished Mrs. Perkins and Mrs. Potts so I'm sure you must be running out of everything, but don't worry, I'll soon have you organised again!"

"How very kind of you," I said, "but—"

"Never mind, we can sort that out later. I think at present I should devote myself entirely to hearing you talk—and you'd like to talk, wouldn't you? You'll be amazed by how good I've become at listening, especially to the bereaved, so please feel you can tell me *anything*! Naturally I realise that you've been too numb to talk much, but now the shock will be wearing off and you'll want to talk non-stop—oh, I know how it is, believe me, I've seen it all! When I was counting up all the funerals we've had at the church this year, I—"

"Charley."

"Yes?"

"Just shut up for a moment, there's a good chap."

"Oh, you want silence! Okay, I'll stay as quiet as a mouse," said Charley, biting so deeply into his toast that the sound of his munching crackled around the room.

At last I managed to say: "It's extremely good of you to go to such trouble and please don't think I'm unappreciative, but to tell the truth I had a bad night and all I want to do is rest." I saw his disappointment and at once felt guilty. "I really am delighted to see you," I added in haste. "I haven't been finding it easy here on my own."

"The chaplains realised that—they were very worried about you when I spoke to them yesterday . . . Dad, do you think it might be a good idea if you saw your doctor?"

"No."

"But—"

"Oh, for heaven's sake stop fussing around as if you were my mother!" I cried in a paroxysm of irritation, but instantly I was stricken by remorse. To lose my temper with Charley, particularly when he was trying so hard to be kind to me, was detestable behaviour. "I'm sorry," I said desperately. "I'm very sorry—I'm not myself at the moment, and—"

"Things aren't going to change between us now she's dead, are they?"

I was so appalled by this question that I could only say: "What on earth do you mean?"

"I was worrying about it all last night. I hardly slept a wink. In fact that was the reason why I felt I had to come down this morning—I couldn't wait till the evening. When you said it wasn't necessary for me to come down, I almost thought for a moment that you didn't want to see me—and then I started to worry in case you felt—"

"Oh, stop talking such melodramatic drivel! Of course I wanted to see you!" I exclaimed, but even as I spoke I was struggling to my feet to escape from him, and after insisting again that I had to rest I hurtled upstairs to my bedroom.

9

I WAS so physically exhausted and so mentally drained that I fell asleep within seconds of slumping down on my bed. Several hours passed. When I awoke I again felt guilty that I had failed to see Jon, but I knew the rest had been essential and I was just planning further rest in the form of a mindless evening in front of the television set when I remembered that I was due to dine with the Aysgarths.

"Surely they'd understand if you cancelled!" Charley protested when I dragged myself downstairs and revealed my approaching fate.

"Unfortunately the situation between me and Aysgarth is at present so awkward that if I cancel he might well take it as a declaration of war." I switched on the television and sat down in front of it as if determined to sample the leisurely evening I was to be denied. "Blue Peter," the children's programme, was being broadcast. I began to watch avidly.

"Can I get you a drink?" said Charley at last.

"Tea would be nice," I said. "Thanks." Just in time I remembered to add: "Sorry I flaked out like that but I was exhausted."

Charley said he quite understood.

As soon as he had withdrawn to the kitchen, the word "drink" resonated in my brain and I remembered the empty bottle and dirty glass which I had hidden in the case of the grandfather clock. Supposing Charley, busily buzzing around, decided to wind the clock in order to save me the trouble? Abruptly switching off "Blue Peter" I crept into the hall, extracted from its hiding-place the sordid evidence of my drinking bouts and bolted to my study where I locked both the bottle and the glass in my desk. As I did so I noticed two items waiting on the blotter for my attention. Miss Peabody had attached a note to each. The first read:

"As requested, here is Father Hall's reference from the Abbot-General," and the second read: "This letter came by second post. As the postmark is Starrington Magna and the handwriting is Father Darrow's, I felt you would want to see it."

Guilt ensured that I dropped the letter as if it had scalded me; in an attempt to distract myself, I began to read Hall's reference.

"My Lord Bishop," the Abbot-General had written. "It is without hesitation and with considerable pleasure that I recommend to you Lewis Hall from the diocese of Radbury. I have known Father Hall for many years and can testify that he is a devout and conscientious priest with a range of unusual gifts which render him peculiarly suited to the ministry of healing and deliverance. This is the ministry which he has followed for the past ten years, and during this time he has come to my house regularly for spiritual direction.

"Father Hall has a family connection with the Order, but for various reasons he prefers neither to discuss this nor to trade upon it in any way. That is one of the reasons why it is such a pleasure for me to be able to recommend him on his own merits. I think I may add, however, without straying beyond the boundaries of what he would wish me to reveal, that both my predecessors, Father Darcy and Father Ingram, thought very highly of him.

"I regret to record that his marriage was not a success, but the divorce was not of his choosing and I do beg you not to hold it against him. He sincerely believes that he is now called to the celibate life, and I assure you he has the very highest moral standards.

"In conclusion I hope not only that he may be of service to God in your diocese but that you yourself may find him an interesting and stimulating acquaintance. As always, my dear Bishop, I have the honour to be your affectionate brother-in-Christ . . ." The letter trailed away into an elaborate signature.

Much soothed by the Abbot-General's epistolary style which reminded me so strongly of those golden days before the war, I found that my curiosity now outweighed my guilt and I was able to break the seal of the envelope which Jon had marked PRIVATE AND CONFIDENTIAL.

"My dear Charles," he had written neatly in black ink on white paper, "you are much in my thoughts. I know you are a wise priest, but bereavement can distort a man's wisdom and lead even the most devout priest down the darkest of spiritual alleys. I have no wish to nag you to visit me. That would not be right. You must come here only when you are ready. I write now merely to set down a few thoughts which you might find helpful to consider if you can spare the time.

"One: be very mindful of your major weaknesses, even those—perhaps especially those—which you feel sure you have conquered. Take time to consider each one in turn and remind yourself as you do so of an occasion when that specific weakness cut you off from God so that you acted contrary to your true nature.

"Two: ask yourself why you have not come back to see me yet, and be very sure you arrive at the right answer. There may be an acceptable explanation, in which case I beg your pardon for raising the matter, but if you have any doubt about your motives, you can be sure the explanation is not acceptable.

"Three: consider afresh how you might mend matters with Michael so that you may give each other the proper support at this difficult time. (One of your most debilitating problems, as I mentioned after the funeral, is likely to be isolation—an emotional isolation arising from the fact that extreme shock has made you unable to respond to all offers of help. Reaching out to Michael might ease this trauma.)

"You will remember that I told you how I eventually put matters right with my own son. I omitted to tell you that I began this task by writing Martin a short, simple letter. It ran something like this: 'My dear Martin, I should so like to see you. Please come. You could cheer me up by telling me some of your amusing theatrical stories.' I did not mention either his unsuitable friends or his way of life but implied acceptance of his profession and delight in one of his most attractive features, his sense of humour. He was on my doorstep in twenty-four hours. At that point we never mentioned his shortcomings at all. Instead I told him all about mine. He was most surprised. He had never understood me before. I was surprised too; once I started talking honestly I could see the mistakes I'd made. In the end I apologised and that was that. He did try to apologise too for not being exactly the son I wanted, but I said that what mattered was what God wanted, and since God had evidently designed him to be an actor, his task in life was not to please me by being something he was not, but to please God by being the very best actor he had it in his power to be.

"Interestingly, once Martin realised that I loved and accepted him as he was, even though I might still disapprove of some of the things he did, his private life immediately took a turn for the better. That was when he finally conquered his alcoholism. I must be quite honest and say I still wish he was not a homosexual, but as he said to me the other day, if he were not a homosexual he might well not be such a good actor. By that he meant that he had come to terms with being different, one of a widely despised minority, by converting all the pain and tension into a powerful, positive creative force. You and I, of course, would see this as an example of the redeeming work of the Holy Spirit. So perhaps one might argue that our task as priests is not primarily to condemn sinners but to facilitate the work of the Spirit so that all suffering, merited and unmerited, may be redeemed. Then indeed we would be able to say with St. Paul: 'All things work together for good to them that love God.' What a hard saying that is, and how easy it is to pay it lip-service in the name of piety while side-stepping the task of expending blood, sweat and tears to make it a living truth.

"I must now close this letter. I shall of course continue to pray for you daily, and until we meet again I can only assure you that I remain always your most devoted friend, J.D."

I had just finished reading this letter in which Jon handled me with kid gloves while trying to keep me on the spiritual rails, when Charley arrived with my tea.

"Are you going to drink this in here?"

"Yes, there's a letter I want to write," I said without thinking, but a second later I realised he wanted me to drink the tea with him in the drawing-room. "It won't take long," I said hurriedly. "I'll be with you in a minute."

He trailed away without a word.

Quickly I locked up Jon's letter in the desk alongside the bottles, took a sheet of paper from the top drawer and wrote: "My dear Michael, I should very much like to see you. If you were to visit Starbridge soon it would mean a lot to me. Perhaps you could cheer me up by telling me some amusing stories about your friends." But at this point I stopped. Michael would know I was being insincere. I detested his friends, that fast set presided over by the dangerous Marina Markhampton, and I found no story about their excesses in the least amusing. I considered substituting "the BBC" for the words "your friends," but decided the letter would still sound insincere. Apparently Jon's approach was not one I could use.

But when I read Jon's letter again I saw he was recommending not a slavish imitation but an attempt to be plain-spoken and honest. Then I began to think not of Jon but of my father. I myself had come from a troubled family, although after many years my father and I had resolved our difficulties—and as soon as I remembered the resolution of those difficulties in 1937, I remembered too the letter which had been waiting for me when I had come back from the war.

"My dear Charles," he had written shortly before his death early in 1945, "in case we never meet again I wish to commit the following thoughts to paper: (1) I am exceedingly pleased that you have turned out well. (2) The fact that you haven't gone to the dogs convinces me that I was right to be strict with you when you were young, but I regret that this led to a certain amount of mess and misunderstanding. And (3) I'm sorry we took so long to get everything straight between us. But at least you know now that I was, am and shall always be your most devoted father, ERIC ASHWORTH."

I thought: he put everything right in the end.

Grabbing a fresh sheet of paper I wrote: "My dear Michael, your mother thought—" I broke off, shying away from the memory of the journal, but suddenly I saw that by drawing on the journal I was joining Lyle at last on her great spiritual journey, and although I had let her travel alone at the end of her life I was now being given the chance to show she had not travelled in vain. "Your mother thought," I wrote, "that I'd behaved very stupidly towards you for a long time. I'm sorry. Having spent so many years in academic life I know very well that clever men can behave like complete fools when they embark on a basic human endeavor such as fatherhood, but I do now want to behave more intelligently. I know there's so much I haven't got right, but after I'm dead I'd like you to think that despite all my mistakes I did manage to put everything straight at the end. Can we meet? Name the time and the place and I'll be there. Your most loving and devoted father, CHARLES ASHWORTH."

I folded the paper, crammed it into an envelope and wrote the address before dropping the letter into the out-tray. By this time my tea was tepid. Having poured it down the drain in the kitchen I reluctantly rejoined Charley in the drawing-room, but fortunately he was watching the television news so I was spared the task of sustaining a conversation.

Staring with unseeing eyes at the screen I tried to steel myself for the dreaded dinner-party at the Deanery.

10

DIDO AYSGARTH'S "little dinner-parties for sixteen" were occasions to be avoided by those anxious to escape indigestion. The cooking was erratic, the company eclectic and the conversation extraordinary. At the last dinner I had attended, some inebriated youth had tried to tell me that the Beatles were greater musicians than Beethoven; that was the moment when I knew beyond doubt that the 1960s had finally parted company with reality.

Dido's "buffet-lunches for sixty" were preferable to her "little dinner-parties for sixteen" because one had more chance of meeting an interesting guest. Her other form of hospitality, her "intimate suppers for eight," was fortunately confined to her dearest friends who, so I was told, always had to endure a recital by her children; her daughter Elizabeth would play the piano and her son Pip would sing. How those two children ever survived their mother must remain a mystery, but Pip was a mild, pleasant child with excellent manners while young Miss Elizabeth was as charming as she was pretty. She had recently caused chaos at the Theological College when two ordinands had fallen in love with her, and there was even some story that she had been smuggled into the College after midnight as a "dare," but I did not believe this wild rumour. My ordinands would not have risked falling short of the high moral standards I demanded, and besides, it was impossible for me to imagine a schoolgirl from a clerical family behaving in a manner which would have been so very improper. Her half-sister Primrose, the daughter of Aysgarth's first marriage, had been one of the most proper young women I had ever met, although Lyle had said this was because Primrose was so plain that she never had the opportunity to be anything else.

In my opinion Lyle's protégée Venetia was just as plain as Primrose, but Lyle had claimed that Venetia's keen interest in sex gave her the potential to be a *femme fatale*. Primrose's only interest, on the other hand, was in power—or so Lyle had always insisted. Before her marriage Primrose had worked in the diocesan office and had become known as the Archdeacon's Axe-Woman. Malcolm always spoke very highly of her organisational skills.

When I arrived at the Deanery that evening I was pleased to see Venetia's parents among the guests. Lord Flaxton, the eccentric peer who had telephoned me on the day of Lyle's death to complain about the local vicar, was over seventy and inclined to favour a vapid Victorian agnosticism, but he was at least capable of intelligent conversation. I was relieved to discover that he had decided in a burst of unprecedented tolerance—generated, perhaps, by a desire to be kind to me in my bereavement—to overlook the unfortunate vicar's devotion to the Campaign for Nuclear Disarmament.

After my spirits had been raised by the sight of the Flaxtons, they were instantly lowered by the sight of Sir Miles Calthrop-Ponsonby, a bachelor whose family had long been connected with the Cathedral Close. Sir Miles seldom spoke but was immensely rich; I guessed at once that Aysgarth was cultivating him in the hope of extracting yet another donation to the West Front Appeal Fund.

Beyond the dour figure of Sir Miles I spotted one of Dido's Scottish cousins, now senile, and beyond this unpromising guest I glimpsed sixteen-year-old Miss Elizabeth, leaning very prettily against the piano. Someone, I noticed, was trying to hide behind this instrument, but Dido hauled him out and offered him to me for inspection with the news that he was Elizabeth's latest young man. Meanwhile I had recognised him as one of the ordinands at the Theological College—but not one of the pair who had been rivals in love. The boy evidently feared I might make all the wrong deductions from Dido's description of him, so I smiled to signal that I was far from opposed to ordinands paying a respectable attention to the opposite sex. At the same time his extreme nervousness made me look at little Miss Elizabeth with new eyes. Could there conceivably have been an element of truth in those wild rumours? "No smoke without a fire," Lyle had commented predictably at the time, but Lyle had been so cynical. Hastily, not wishing to consider the possibility that I might become disillusioned with little Miss Elizabeth, who was always so charming to me, I moved on towards her half-sister Primrose.

It will be clear already that I did not care for Primrose, but fairness obliges me to state that she had become an admirable wife and mother after relinquishing her duties as Malcolm's axe-woman at the diocesan office. Whether she was at heart suited to this conventional role, however, was open to question, since she was a rampant feminist and had already upset the Mothers' Union (who to their dismay had found they could not do without her superb organisational skills). Being a Christian and, I hope, not an unjust man, I can see it was right to give women the vote and I firmly believe they should be paid the same wages as men when they do identical work, but as I had tried to make clear to my committee on the day of Lyle's death, men and women were not created by God to be interchangeable and it was simply a distortion of reality to pretend otherwise.

I was so busy feeling annoyed by the memory of Primrose's strident feminism that I could not even remember the name of her husband and had to glide past him as swiftly as possible. He was a nonentity who taught at the Choir School.

Regaining my equilibrium with an effort, I reflected that the dinner-party was looking even more unpromising than I had anticipated, and my dismay was in no way allayed when I came face to face with the next guest: Aysgarth's favourite son, the eldest offspring of his first marriage.

Unfortunately I found Christian Aysgarth almost as uncongenial as his sister Primrose. Why? I hoped—even prayed—that I was not swayed by jealousy that Aysgarth should have had such an outstanding son. Perhaps the trouble was that there was something a little too familiar about that glittering image which Christian presented to the world; perhaps, looking at him, I saw a reflection of my younger self, the tormented, divided self which Jon had helped me to acknowledge, accept and assimilate during my spiritual crisis in 1937.

Christian was in his late thirties. Tall, dark, elegant and charming, he was one of the few people who were capable of discussing my books intelligently with me. Up at Oxford he had taken a first in Mods, a first in Greats and had then crowned this academic triumph by taking a first in theology. Declining ordination he had become an Oxford don specialising in the unrewarding subject of medieval philosophy. I knew I ought to find him excellent company but in fact I found him superficial, arrogant and spoilt, and it annoyed me that with one exception everyone doted on him. The one exception was Dido, a fact which I found very intriguing because although I disliked Dido I had to admit she was a shrewd judge of character and a lynx-eyed observer of her acquaintances. No wonder she was so lethal as a gossip! Beneath the hyperbolical statements there nearly always lurked a hard core of shattering accuracy—which is why even to this day I can never entirely dismiss the possibility that Desmond Wilton really was seen at Piccadilly Circus on a Saturday night in the company of a young man in black leather.

With Christian was his wife Katie, who was the grand-daughter of a very old friend of mine, the late Lady Starmouth. Before the war Lady Starmouth had been famous for her benevolent interest in promising young clergymen, and both Aysgarth and I had been counted among her protégés.

I noted that Katie was heavily pregnant and that unlike many women in that condition she looked neither radiant nor well. She had inherited something of her grandmother's dark good looks, but unfortunately nothing of Lady Starmouth's wit and style. I often thought Christian might have preferred someone more animated than this pale quiet girl—and indeed it was common knowledge that he enjoyed the company of the dangerous Marina Markhampton—but one cannot deny that the grand-daughter of an earl is a great catch for a young man whose grandfather was a Yorkshire draper.

Beyond Katie I encountered an old friend of Christian's, a young man called Palmer who worked in the Foreign Office, and beyond this unremarkable civil servant I was delighted to see Lady Markhampton, grandmother of the dangerous Marina. Recently widowed, Lady Markhampton lived in the Close, and although now over eighty was still sharp, bright and nimble.

"My dear Bishop!" she exclaimed warmly, putting a be-ringed little paw into my outstretched hand. "What a splendid surprise! I had no idea you were to be here tonight, but how glad I am to see you moving among us again after such a very tragic time."

While she spoke I was aware of a stranger sitting beside her and realised this was the woman who was supposed to keep me amused by talking about her recent intellectual activities in Cambridge. To my surprise a quick glance convinced me she was American. The tanned, lined, rather leathery skin, the excessive use of costume jewelry, and the extraordinary clothes—a pastel-pink trouser-suit—all convinced me that I would hear an American accent as soon as she opened her mouth. She wore glasses which were almond-shaped, very modish. Her thick silver hair was immaculately waved and styled. Good-looking, smart and obviously sophisticated, she could have been any age between fifty and sixty-five.

". . . and now let me introduce you to one of my oldest friends," Lady Markhampton was saying with enthusiasm. "This is Professor Loretta Staviski from America. Loretta my dear, may I present the Bishop of Starbridge, Dr. Charles Ashworth?"

I nearly had a stroke.

There was a pause which seemed to endure a full minute but which probably lasted no more than five seconds. Then Loretta said with magnificent panache: "The Bishop may not remember, but we met very briefly back in 1937."

A smooth voice which I was amazed to realise was my own replied: "The Bishop remembers very well." And I somehow managed to clasp her rock-steady, outstretched hand.

XI

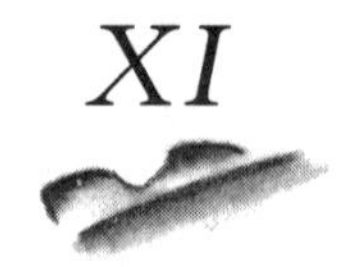

"God works everything into his further purposes, for his work never ceases; and he always goes on from the actual situation into which things have come. Everything gets worked into God's further purposes. So God brings good out of much evil; much good that we cannot recognise, but a considerable range that we can."

AUSTIN FARRER
Warden of Keble College, Oxford, 1960–1968
A SCIENCE OF GOD?

I

I COULD hardly have been more shocked and stupefied if Lady Markhampton had hit me over the head with a croquet mallet. Memories from 1937 streamed through my mind like a mighty cataract. Feeling as if my feet had been cemented to the handsome Persian carpet I tried frantically to think what I could say next, but before I could reach any conclusion I became aware that contrary to my worst fears, no one was apparently wondering why the Bishop was now as immobile as a block of wood. Aysgarth was saying "Tio Pepe, old chap?" and thrusting a glass into my hands. Dido, armed with a large platter of hors d'oeuvres, was announcing to her guests: "My dears, I know these look perfectly ghastly but they taste simply wonderful." And Lady Markhampton was exclaiming astonished to Loretta: "But you never told me you'd met the Bishop!"

"Met the Bishop?" said Dido, fastening instantly on this fascinating item of information with the skill of the gifted gossip.

"Met the Bishop?" echoed Aysgarth, pausing in his peregrinations with the sherry decanter.

"Loretta says she met the Bishop in 1937!" said Lady Markhampton, equally enthralled.

"It was so long ago that I'm surprised Dr. Ashworth remembers," said Loretta, and added, referring to my late benefactress Lady Starmouth: "I was staying with Evelyn at the time."

"When I first met Lady Starmouth in 1937," I said, contriving to sound as if I were indulging in an innocuous reminiscence, "she invited me to call on her, and I met Professor Staviski on a visit to Starmouth Court."

"There was some sort of lunch, I seem to recall," said Loretta, "and a little walk afterwards. I know I found it all very entertaining."

"Wait a minute," said Dido as I wished I could be instantly transported to Timbuktu. "I'm all at sea. How did you know Lady Starmouth, Loretta?"

"Her mother and my mother were at school together in America. When I came over to England following the break-up of my marriage, Evelyn looked after me—which was a brave thing to do in those days when divorced women were considered beyond the pale—and eventually she introduced me to Enid"—she indicated Lady Markhampton—"and to her other great friend, Sybil Welbeck."

"Sybil, Evelyn and I were all united by our devotion to dearest Bishop Jardine," explained Lady Markhampton to Dido, and added as an afterthought: "You liked him too, didn't you, Loretta?"

"Adored him," said Loretta, fitting a cigarette into a very long black holder.

"Alex Jardine and his 'Lovely Ladies'!" drawled Aysgarth's son Christian, joining our group. "Maybe we should all pause now to mourn the passing of the 1930s when bishops lived in palaces, swilled claret by the case and romped through the drawing-rooms of Mayfair whenever they weren't hamming it up in the House of Lords!"

"My dear Christian!" said Lady Markhampton indulgently. "Dr. Jardine certainly knew how to enjoy the wealth and position he had attained through his great gifts as a clergyman, but I assure you he was always the soul of propriety."

"As morally beyond reproach as our present bishop!" said Aysgarth gallantly, slaving away at the task of being a genial host.

"I can't say I remember Bishop Jardine ever campaigning against fornication as our present bishop does," said Dido, choosing the worst possible moment to flaunt her famous candour, "but then Charles campaigns with such exceptional vigour. No wonder you're known as Anti-Sex Ashworth, my dear," she added to complete my devastation. "You've really only yourself to blame."

"Anti-Sex Ashworth?" murmured Loretta in the mildest of voices as she finally raised the cigarette-holder to her lips. "Well, well."

As Christian and his father both sprang forward to give her a light, I drank my entire glass of Tio Pepe straight off.

"Dear Charles," said Dido, "you're looking a little pale—I do hope all this isn't too much for you, *so* brave of you to come, but don't be afraid I won't look after you—I know where my duty as a hostess lies, and although I have my faults no one can say I'm not attentive to my guests. Come over and talk to Elizabeth—I know you find her enchanting, so sad you and Lyle never had a daughter—oh, Perry"—she thrust my empty glass at Christian's friend from the Foreign Office—"fetch the Bishop another Tio Pepe, would you—come along, Charles my dear, just relax and let me look after you."

This sinister command reduced me to a renewed state of helplessness. Utterly silent, too stunned to attempt even the smallest gesture of rebellion, I allowed myself to be led back to her daughter Elizabeth.

2

SLOWLY I achieved a recovery. Little Miss Elizabeth was so charming that I soon felt certain that all the gossip about her was baseless. She declared how "super" I was on television and how "fabulous" I looked in my formal uniform and how "groovy" gaiters were, much nicer than the purple cassocks which Archbishop Ramsey favoured, and had anyone ever told me that when I was in uniform I looked just like the hero of an eighteenth-century novel.

This was all so pleasant that I temporarily forgot the horror latent in Dido's "little dinner-party for sixteen," but soon my hostess was returning with the information that she had specially rearranged the placing of the guests so that I could be seated next to "dear brilliant Loretta, so intellectual." Barely had I recovered from this sledge-hammer blow to my equilibrium when Venetia's father Lord Flaxton cornered me and began to talk about how the country was going to the dogs. Making a supreme effort I managed to say "yes" and "no" when required.

At the dinner-table Aysgarth, very deferential, invited me to say grace and for three appalling seconds I thought I was going to be unable to string the appropriate words together. Fortunately my memory staged a recovery before people could wonder if I was suffering from the onset of senility, and we all sat down to consume our soup. I found myself unable to identify the soup's principal ingredient. It could have been mushrooms but it might possibly have been chicken. The liquid was pale, thick and tepid.

"Well, Bishop!" said Loretta on my left after we had recovered from this affront to our tastebuds. "What a surprise it is to see you again!"

"Astounding," I said, effortlessly achieving a note of deep sincerity, and paused to examine the silver-mark on my soup-spoon.

"But perhaps I'm only surprised because I didn't think you'd be accepting dinner invitations at the moment. After I'd re-established contact with Enid I did realise it wasn't beyond the realm of possibility that we might meet again."

I said cautiously: "You'd lost touch with Lady Markhampton?"

"Long ago, yes. After all, I was very much younger, I lived three thousand miles away and I never knew her as well as I knew Evelyn. But once we'd met again at Evelyn's funeral we began to exchange letters—and then one thing led to another—"

"—and now here you are."

"Here I am," she agreed dryly. "Fun, isn't it?"

"White or red, Charles?" enquired Aysgarth, who was circulating with the wine bottles.

Resisting the impulse to reply: "Both," I said: "White, please." Hock promptly splashed into my glass.

"Loretta?"

"I'll try the claret, Stephen. I feel in the mood for something smooth, European and interesting."

"If Englishmen considered themselves Europeans I could make the most dashing reply to that remark!" declared Aysgarth, unable to resist sinking into flirtatiousness. He poured the wine and moved on.

"Cute, isn't he?" said Loretta amused. "I guess I never did get over my weakness for Englishmen." And as I nerved myself at last to look at her directly, she smiled straight into my eyes.

The people around us were already talking with animation. Lord Flaxton was saying: "In my young day . . ." while Christian was declaring: ". . . and as soon as I saw that production of *Lysistrata* I realised . . ." And Dido was bawling across the table to Lady Markhampton: ". . . and at Harrods I saw the most divine dress which I knew I *had* to have, and so I rang up my sister Merry who just so happened to be staying at Claridge's, and I screamed at her: 'My dear!' I screamed. 'Come and see this absolutely divine . . .' " And Primrose was saying: "Well, of course the Greeks treated women as subhuman, everyone knows that, and if you ever analyse the work of Aristophanes you'll find . . ." And Aysgarth was enquiring: "White or red?" as he paused by the morose Sir Miles Calthrop-Ponsonby, and Sir Miles Calthrop-Ponsonby growled: "No damned German rubbish for me, Dean, and that damned claret gives me indigestion."

But Loretta and I were quite silent as we looked at each other across a graveyard of buried memories, and for a moment I felt as if we were separated from the other occupants of the room by a wall of glass.

At last she said: "It's okay," and I realised with an overpowering relief that I was safe. "I mean," she added in case anyone was eavesdropping, "it's okay to come out with all the usual clichés such as 'where are you living now' and 'what are you doing at the moment.' I shan't be bored, I promise you."

Finally daring to share her ironical amusement I said: "Tell me everything."

3

I HAVE no intention of describing here exactly what took place when I met Loretta in 1937. It is sufficient to underline the fact that the meeting occurred at the time of my spiritual breakdown when I found myself temporarily unable to behave as a clergyman should. I hardly think it necessary to add that once I had fully recovered and embarked on my second marriage, I never looked at any woman but Lyle.

Loretta had already been a professor when I first met her, and although in the United States this title is more widely available than it is in England, she had consolidated her early success to the point where even a former Cambridge professor was obliged to regard her achievements with respect. She was an authority on seventeenth-century English literature and had published three books on the subject; since her retirement she had been working on a definitive study of John Wilmot, Earl of Rochester. When I enquired about her home I was told that she shared a New York apartment with several thousand books and a very large plant which had survived infancy by thriving on coffee-dregs. The plant had become so large, in fact, that she was beginning to feel intimidated by it. Had I ever read John Wyndham's *The Day of the Triffids*? She was sure she already had too much in common with the beleaguered heroine of a science-fiction novel.

I listened and nodded and laughed as I tried to absorb this information which told me so much and yet so little, but all the time I was concentrating on our dialogue I was carrying on a silent conversation with myself. I was trying to remember how old she was. Was she two years my senior or four? She looked about ten years my junior, although I could see now I had been mistaken in thinking she could pass for fifty. But what a superb triumph she had achieved over the ravages of time! I concluded that American women had much to teach the women of England on the subject of growing old with glamour.

Loretta began to ask me about my post-war career at Cambridge.

The hour-glass figure which had so attracted me at the age of thirty-seven was now a mere potent memory, but the cunningly cut pink trouser-suit played down the vanished waist while the frilly white blouse emphasized that her bosom was still resplendent. The trouser-suit was really most remarkable. I dislike trousers on a woman, but this trouser-suit was designed in such a way that its wearer's femininity was not destroyed but enhanced; in fact the more I looked at that suit the more erotic it seemed. I had never before seen such an outfit. I was entranced. America is without doubt the most astonishing country and despite its shortcomings I cannot help but admire the innovative—one might almost say courageous—vitality of its inhabitants. I was quite sure no English woman would have dared to wear a pink trouser-suit to a clerical dinner-party. I wondered what Lady Markhampton privately thought of her friend's nerve. I wondered what Dido thought. I wondered what Lyle would have thought. I supposed the traditional British reaction would have been to say that allowances had to be made for foreigners.

Having reached that conclusion it occurred to me that I should turn my attention to my other neighbour at the table before everyone noticed how well Loretta and I were getting on, so I had a word with Lady Flaxton. However, as her main interest in life was gardening, a subject about which I knew little, our conversation was necessarily brief. I then exchanged a few sentences with Christian's friend Perry Palmer, who was sitting opposite me. He was one of those well-mannered young bachelors who lead quiet, conventional, law-abiding lives in which little of interest ever happens. Not for the first time I thought how typical it was of Christian to choose such a bland foil for his brilliant intellect and exceptional good looks.

By this time the curious soup had disappeared and we were consuming some excellent roast lamb accompanied by leeks in a first-class cream sauce. Unfortunately the potatoes were undercooked, but since I had now switched from the hock to the claret, which was magnificent, I felt more inclined to be charitable about the erratic nature of the cook's achievements.

Having paid the obligatory amount of attention to Lady Flaxton and young Palmer I turned back to Loretta.

"I've visited New York several times," I said. "I've given guest-lectures there and preached at St. Thomas's on Fifth Avenue. Whereabouts is your apartment?"

"Not far from St. Thomas's. In fact that's my local Episcopal church."

"That sounds as if you actually go there."

"Sure I go there! Why shouldn't I?"

"But in 1937 you were just a vague theist!"

"I got wiser with age. Or maybe I should say that I became a Christian as the result of an encounter with a priest. I felt I needed to understand him and his God."

"An Anglican priest?"

"Yes, but he wasn't an American Episcopalian. He was a clergyman of the Church of England."

"Am I allowed to ask his name?"

"Why not? It was Charles Ashworth," she said amused, and turned away from me to respond to an overture from her other neighbour, Lord Flaxton, who also appeared to be fascinated by the pink trouser-suit.

I was so astounded by her disclosure that my knife slipped in my hand and one of the undercooked boiled potatoes shot off the plate to torpedo my glass of claret.

"Bull's eye!" cried Christian with an inebriated wit. "Well played, my lord!"

"Don't worry, Charles!" shouted Dido before I could draw breath to apologise. "This table-cloth adores claret—soaks it up all the time!"

"Have another glass," said Mine Host the Dean, appearing speedily at my elbow with the decanter.

". . . and I must say, I very much admire America for not succumbing to the demon socialism," Lord Flaxton was confiding to Loretta, and added to me: "Don't you agree, Bishop?"

I did agree but this was a mistake because I then got embroiled in one of those futile conversations about politics in which everyone who opposes socialism and espouses the conservative cause is written off as a tiresome old reactionary. I happen to oppose socialism because I am a realist; in my opinion socialism is fatally flawed because it has far too high an opinion of human nature.

"St. Augustine—" I began but was interrupted. The dinner-party was hotting up as the last of the lamb vanished and everyone abandoned the potatoes. The claret decanter appeared to have acquired a life and will of its own.

"No conservative theologian has ever been able to grasp the essence of social problems!" declared Lord Flaxton, the agnostic who always voted with the Liberals in the House of Lords.

"Nonsense!" I said. "What about Reinhold Niebuhr?"

"Moral Man and Immoral Society," said Primrose, quoting the title of Niebuhr's most famous book as Lord Flaxton looked flummoxed. "Our problem is an immoral society which the conservatives are unwilling to change. Women—"

"We should all go forward with the Liberals!" proclaimed Lord Flaxton. "We should all adapt to modern times!"

"But my dear, you haven't adapted at all!" said his wife with bewitching mildness. "You live exactly as you did before the war!"

"The Liberal party was destroyed by the war," said Lady Markhampton. "The First War, I mean."

"Everything was destroyed by the First War," said Primrose. "Philosophies, social systems, antediluvian attitudes to women—"

" 'The old order changeth, yielding place to new,' " declaimed little Miss Elizabeth with a fetching dramatic flourish.

"Dear Lord Tennyson," said Dido. "Always so apt. Christian, why are you hogging the decanter? Give everyone a refill!"

" 'Eat, drink and be merry,' " said Christian, swaying as he rose to his feet.

" 'For tomorrow we die,' " said his friend Palmer with a singular lack of originality.

"Sit down, Christian," commanded Primrose. "I'll play Ganymede."

"A woman can't play Ganymede unless she changes sex," objected Lord Flaxton.

"People change sex all the time nowadays," said Dido. "There was the most extraordinary article in one of the papers last Sunday—"

"Feminists have a hidden urge to change sex," said Lord Flaxton. " 'O tempora! O mores!' What decadent times we live in!"

"I thought you were urging us all to adapt to them," said Aysgarth, the killer in debate.

"There's no reason why one can't heave a nostalgic sigh for the old order," retorted Lord Flaxton, "even while one accepts the inevitability of change and the duty to adapt to it."

"But not all change is inevitable," I said. "History does in fact prove that some things never change at all."

"In my opinion," said Aysgarth, having knocked back the last of the claret, "history proves that all things change all the time."

"Who said 'History is bunk'?" asked Dido of no one in particular.

" 'Those who cannot remember the past,' " quoted Loretta, " 'are doomed to repeat it.' "

"Who said that?" demanded several voices simultaneously, and I said before Loretta could reply: "George Santayana."

"I do so adore intellectual dinner-parties!" exclaimed Dido. "Isn't this one absolutely heavenly?"

Repressing the urge to get drunk I left my new glass of claret untouched and asked Palmer to pass me the jug of water.

4

I SUCCEEDED in restricting myself to one glass of port after the ladies had withdrawn, but this feat was easily accomplished since Dido was opposed to the gentlemen segregating themselves for longer than ten minutes.

"This is the 1960s, not the 1930s!" she reminded us as she led the ladies from the room, and after the door had closed Aysgarth said to me: "Dido's unwittingly given me her support—think how things have changed in Starbridge since the 1930s, Charles! Doesn't that bear out my view of history?"

"Christ is still being worshipped in Starbridge Cathedral. Doesn't that bear out mine?"

"Talking of the 1930s," said Christian as the port began to circulate, "what do you think your predecessor Alex Jardine would have made of this present decade, Bishop?"

"I've no idea. But I'd have been interested to hear his views on the permissive society."

"I liked Jardine!" declared Lord Flaxton with enthusiasm. "A great man!"

"The best Bishop on the bench!" agreed Aysgarth, and when he looked to me for a comment I said: "He was certainly the most original."

"Of course your wife knew him well, didn't she, Bishop?" said Lord Flaxton, unburdened by any middle-class reticence on the subject of death and referring to Lyle with an ease which I found refreshing. "She was almost like a daughter, I believe, to Jardine and his wife."

"Almost."

Sir Miles Calthrop-Ponsonby suddenly roused himself from a morose meditation to demand: "Who's that 'strordinary woman in pink trousers?" and the conversation turned to Loretta's attire.

"Venetia likes to wear trousers," said Lord Flaxton, remembering his daughter. "I disapprove but I have to admit they suit her."

"How is Venetia?" I said, reminded painfully of Lyle's journal.

"Oh, rattling around. Haven't seen much of her lately."

Aysgarth, who had been listening in silence while fidgeting with his glass, now turned the conversation abruptly away from Venetia by remarking: "Funny to think Loretta knew Alex. He never mentioned her."

"Damned handsome woman," said Sir Miles, "even in pink trousers."

This seemed to be a fair summing-up of the general consensus of opinion.

After the allotted ten minutes had expired Aysgarth led us back to the drawing-room where Loretta was examining the contents of a tall bookcase.

"Are you staying in Starbridge long?" I said idly, joining her after refusing Dido's offer of coffee.

"No, I'm at the end of my visit and leave tomorrow."

"Heading for the airport?"

"Not just yet. My next stop is Brown's Hotel in London." She opened the door of the bookcase and pulled out a battered volume for a closer inspection. "I want to see some plays before I go home."

Moving nearer I saw that the book in her hands was one of the novels of E. F. Benson. "I'm sure you know that Benson's father was Archbishop of Canterbury," I said, "but did you know Benson's mother had an affair with the daughter of Archbishop Tait and that the Benson children were all homosexual and/or mad?"

"Proving that truth was far stranger than Trollope's fiction? Or that the office of Archbishop of Canterbury is death to a normal family life?"

We laughed, but this light, brittle conversation, which kept my mind well away from any thoughts about Loretta's approaching sojourn at Brown's Hotel, was at that point interrupted by our hostess. "Charles my dear, don't think for one moment that I've forgotten you—"

I resigned myself to a further round of social mauling.

5

"IT WAS a delightful surprise to meet you again!" I said to Loretta in front of our host and hostess as I eventually embarked on my farewells. "Good luck with the book on Rochester!"

"Good luck with the book on Hippolytus and Callistus!" she said smiling at me, and held out her hand.

Our fingers clasped briefly but we said no more, and having stepped past her to say goodbye to Lady Markhampton I took care to leave the room without looking back.

6

IT WAS raining as I walked back to the South Canonry, but I barely noticed because I was so absorbed with thoughts about Loretta. I was still digesting the astonishing information that I had been responsible for bringing her to Christianity at a time when I had been a deeply confused priest, spiritually adrift, who had behaved towards a woman in a manner which I still could not recall without shame. I knew, of course, that I wanted to meet her again and hear more about this most unlikely conversion, but I knew too that a further meeting would be most unwise. Even though there was no danger that I would do anything unforgivably stupid—how could there be, since I wanted no one but Lyle?—a rendezvous with an attractive woman would only emphasise all I had so recently lost and ensure that I became even more disturbed than I was already.

Hurrying the last few yards through the rain I fitted my key in the lock and opened the front door.

Charley sped from the drawing-room to minister to me. "How did it go?"

"Aysgarth was at his best and Dido was at her despotic worst."

"Poor old Dad! Shall I make you some tea?"

Anxious to give him something to do I consented to this suggestion and wandered into my study to select a book for my bedtime reading. Thanks to my long afternoon rest I was still feeling alert, and I thought a quick skim through one of my old favourites would stop me replaying again and again in my mind my meetings with Loretta in 1937.

I was just turning away from the bookcase with Austin Farrer's *Said or Sung* in my hands, when I saw that my letter to Michael was missing from the out-tray.

For one long moment I was motionless, paralysed with disbelief. Then setting aside the book I strode to the door and shouted: "Charley!" in a voice loud enough to travel from the hall to the attic.

He pattered rapidly out of the kitchen. "Yes?"

"Come in here, please."

He followed me into my study and we faced each other across my desk. "There was a letter in the out-tray," I said. "What have you done with it?"

"Me?" said Charley. "Nothing! Obviously Miss Peabody must have cleared the tray—she left late tonight."

"Miss Peabody never clears this tray. If I have any letters to add to the official post I take them to her myself, but this particular letter I intended to take to the main post office tomorrow morning in order to send it to London by the express rate. Now stop lying and tell me the truth. What have you done with it?"

Charley was by this time very pale. Fumbling in the inside pocket of his jacket he produced the letter and handed it over without a word. Immediately I turned over the envelope to examine the flap.

"I didn't open it," said Charley in a rush. "I admit I took it with the idea of steaming it open, but then I found I couldn't—I mean, I realized clergymen just can't go around doing that kind of thing. So I put the letter back in the tray—but then I saw I couldn't do that either because you'd be expecting the tray to be cleared by Miss Peabody (or so I thought) and by that time Miss Peabody had left. I took it before she left, you see, although I didn't boil the kettle to steam open the envelope until—"

I held up my hand. He stopped. Carefully I replaced the letter in the out-tray. Then I said: "Sit down, Charley."

We both sat down. After allowing a pause for us to compose ourselves I said: "Please explain to me why you felt driven to behave like this."

"I suppose I finally went mad. I've felt increasingly desperate ever since Mum died—I couldn't tell what you were thinking, and I thought the letter might give me some kind of clue."

When I was sure I could speak in a neutral voice I said: "I was worried because I've been unable to speak to Michael on the phone. The letter is an attempt to make contact. I'm sorry you've been finding me so withdrawn."

"Well, of course it's the bereavement, isn't it, and I know I have to make allowances for you . . . But when you seemed so completely unfathomable I kept remembering that Mum was the main reason—the only reason—why you adopted me, and I suddenly saw that her death might trigger some sort of crisis in your attitude towards me, I suddenly saw that you might start to feel quite differently, I suddenly saw—"

"You suddenly saw an astonishing amount of nonsense! Charley, you can't seriously think I intend to behave like a paterfamilias in a Victorian melodrama and tell you never to darken my door again!"

"Okay, I know it sounds ridiculous when you put it like that, but I've been feeling so worried and baffled and nervous—"

"But you know perfectly well how proud I am of you and how much you mean to me and how pleased I am that you've gone into the Church!"

"I'm worried about all that too."

My scalp prickled with fright. I leant forward to sit on the edge of my chair. "What do you mean?"

"I don't think I'm really your kind of clergyman. I just can't connect with all that Catholic spirituality which you find so attractive."

"But you told me the other day at Fortnum's that you wanted to be a monk!"

"I know, but I didn't mean it. I was only taking that line to try to get across to you how worried I am about girls."

"My dear Charley—"

"I know you'll be expecting me to marry as soon as I've got my own parish, but I'm just so frightened of letting you down and picking the wrong woman and winding up like—"

"For heaven's sake! How many more times do I have to tell you that since I've brought you up and you've modelled yourself on me you're going to be fine?"

Charley whispered: "I'm sorry," and looked wretched.

Immediately I knew I had said the wrong thing but I knew too that I had no idea what else I could have said. In despair, groping for understanding but receiving no enlightenment, I covered my face with my hands.

"Oh Dad, please don't get so upset, *please—*"

"I'm not upset," I said, letting my hands fall. "I'm fine." But I scarcely knew what I was saying. I had at last realised I was being reminded of a section of Lyle's journal which I had been wholly unable to accept: "The truth is that Charley only gets upset because he senses Charles gets upset . . ." I could see Lyle's handwriting clearly in my mind's eye, but even as I saw it I was struggling to blot those words from my memory. "You're the one who's upset," I said, "not me. The truth—the absolute truth—is that as far as I'm concerned you're my son, no one else's, and Lyle's death makes no difference to my feelings for you. So put all those distorted fantasies out of your mind, please, and stop worrying about them."

There was another pause. Then Charley thanked me, said he felt much better and asked if I still wanted tea; he was so sorry to have troubled me and would quite understand if I now preferred to go straight to bed.

Seconds later I was once more escaping upstairs to my room.

7

ANOTHER LONG night passed.

I dreamed that although I had disembowelled Samson he had risen from the dead and was trying to castrate me with a butcher's knife. As soon as I awoke I was tormented by memories of butchery in the concentration camp, and at once I turned to embrace Lyle, who was always able to smooth those memories away, but her side of the bed was ice-cold, and the next moment I felt as if a glacier were grinding into the very core of my consciousness.

After a while I realised the pain of loneliness was so unendurable that there were only two ways of easing it: I could either drink myself into a stupor again or else I could seek a physical release—and an emotional anaesthesia—in the most obvious and pathetic of ways. The first option I discarded; I was too afraid that Charley might see me suffering from a hang-over. That left the second option, the resort (as Bishop Ashworth had declared with such certainty in the past) of the inadequate, the disordered or the grossly immature. I did pray for the strength to avoid both options and merely endure the pain, but in the end I decided my first duty to God was not to avoid humiliation but to keep sane.

Ashamed of my weakness, ashamed of my disorder, ashamed that I was so utterly unable to reason myself onto an even keel, I felt as if I had been battered, bloodied and beaten to my knees.

I finally fell asleep at three o'clock in the morning.

8

I HAD set my alarm to ensure I awoke at the right time; I could not have allowed Charley to find out that I had abandoned my old morning routine, and when I arrived downstairs I realised I also could not allow him to find out that I had no appetite. Carefully I thanked him when he brought me a cup of the coffee he had already brewed; carefully I thanked him when he made me toast and boiled me an egg; carefully I thanked him for being so kind and thoughtful; carefully I thanked him when he offered to take me for a drive or play golf with me or do any shopping I might need. Then having exhausted myself by this immaculate behaviour I proceeded to make a very big mistake. I said: "Much as I'd like to spend time with you this morning, I have to go to Starrington to see Jon."

Charley flinched as if I had struck him across the face.

"I'm very sorry," I said, panicking as I saw the size of my error, "I know that sounds like the rudest of rebuffs, but—"

"Yes, it does," Charley's voice shook. He was pale with emotion. "I make this very special effort to come down here to look after you, and all you can do is make excuses to escape from my company!"

"I assure you I—"

"If I were Michael you'd never dream of going to see Father Darrow!" shouted Charley, and rushed out, banging the door.

9

WHAT WAS I to do? I knew I was being subjected to emotional blackmail but I knew too that I was powerless to do other than give in to him. I could not allow Charley to be so deeply upset. I could not allow Charley to be rejected. I could not allow Charley to be neurotic and tormented. Charley had to be bright, happy and successful in order to redeem the past and provide me with my reward.

Another unacceptable section of the journal seared my memory but again I wiped the words from my mind. I could not cope with Lyle questioning my behaviour towards Charley. All I knew at that moment was that Charley had to be handled with kid gloves; Charley had to be appeased and propitiated; Charley had to have his misery removed so that he could be bright and happy again.

Having caught up with him in the hall I said rapidly: "I won't go to Starrington. I wasn't thinking too clearly. There's no need for me to see Jon today."

I saw Charley's expression of relief, but before either of us could say another agonising word the telephone started to ring.

10

I WAS so afraid Michael was phoning—an event which would inevitably have driven Charley to new heights of neurotic behaviour—that I took the call in my study, but the caller proved to be Paul Dalton, the Cathedral Canon with whom I felt most at ease. He asked if he could come and see me for a few minutes. Disappointed not to hear from Michael but guiltily grateful to have another respite from Charley, I told Paul to come over straight away.

Returning to Charley I said to assuage my guilt: "I've got to see Paul Dalton for a few minutes but as soon as he's gone we'll go up to the golf club and play a few holes." At least if I were playing golf the need to concentrate would reduce the dialogue to a minimum.

I saw Charley relax. "How is Canon Dalton?" he asked, making a big effort to sustain a normal conversation. "Is he still hellbent on remarriage?"

"Very much so, yes. He currently has hopes of a young lady who works for the Red Cross."

"I can't think why he wants to bother at his age! Why doesn't he just employ a woman who'll clean the house and cook for him?"

"Evidently he feels he needs more than a clean house and full stomach."

"That's amazing!" said Charley sincerely. "Surely he must be over sixty?"

I somehow managed to stop myself making a very irritable response and reflect instead how odd it was that Charley should still be so prone to tactlessness even though I had laboured so hard to bring him up to be as diplomatic as I was. Then I saw that this was quite definitely not a line of thought I wished to pursue. I wiped it from my mind, but unfortunately my powers of censorship seemed to be weakening, and when I remembered later that the Halls were due to dine that night at the South Canonry, I could not stop myself heaving a sigh of relief that I was to be spared an evening alone with Charley.

I began to feel more guilty than ever.

11

WHEN PAUL arrived I discovered he had come primarily not to discuss the Cathedral's affairs, but to moan about his love-life. It turned out that his latest potential wife, the young woman who worked for the Red Cross, had rejected him on the grounds of age. I found it perversely comforting to know that I was not the only man in the Close who was enduring a hellish morning.

"I'm very sorry, Paul," I said, "but I thought she always told you the age-gap didn't matter? What happened to change her mind?"

"No idea." Paul was sunk in gloom. "I must have gone wrong somewhere and now she's using the age-gap as an excuse to ditch me. I'm sorry, Charles, I know I shouldn't be burdening you with my pathetic minor problems when you're grappling with a major tragedy—"

"Not at all, gives me something new to think about."

"Honestly? Because if you feel you can't cope, for heaven's sake tell me to buzz off—although I must say, I hope you don't because I feel you're the one man I can really talk to about this disaster. (Can't talk to anyone at the Cathedral, of course.) If only I could convince myself that I'd had a lucky escape, but I can't. All right, I know thirty-five *was* a bit young and I might have gone through hell when I was in my seventies, but when one's past sixty one just wants to make hay while the sun's shining and, who knows, one may never reach seventy anyway. Am I being perverted and unreasonable?"

"No. But since you do concede that the lady was a little young—"

"Oh, I'd be quite happy to settle for something fifty-ish who dressed well and didn't mind my passion for cricket and knew exactly how to be the ideal clerical wife, but what worries me, Charles, is that according to my sister most women at that age are dead keen to give up sex, and I don't want to wind up in bed with someone who just lies back and thinks of England. Am I being gross and self-centred?"

"No. But I think your sister's exaggerating the risk. I'm sure there must be plenty of fifty-year-olds willing to forget entirely about England in those circumstances."

"But how can one find out beforehand how willing a woman is to succumb to patriotic amnesia? I mean, one can't just ask, can one? Or maybe, in 1965, one can. Lord, Charles, isn't it odd how nowadays everyone talks about sex! I met an old buffer at a dinner-party the other day—a really old buffer, much older than us—who reminded me that before the war nobody even thought about sex, let alone talked about it."

"Well, I certainly thought about it!"

"So did I, but the old buffer said: 'Consider Archbishop Lang—he never thought about sex and he lived a celibate life with no trouble whatsoever!' And somehow, Charles, when he said that, I felt in such despair that I hardly knew how to stand it. Am I being weak and neurotic?"

"No. You just need to be more sceptical about the pronouncements of know-it-all old buffers. The truth is that even Lang must have thought of sex at some stage because he always said he made a conscious decision not to marry."

"Yes, but if he wasn't a repressed homosexual—and even if he was—how did he make such a success of the celibate life? All right, I know one can say he did it by the grace of God, but nevertheless he must have organised himself into a state where the grace could be received, and how did he do *that?* I started to miss sex almost as soon as I became a widower. I know one's not supposed to—one's supposed to be so knocked out by grief that one feels no desire at all for at least six months, but the fact that I was knocked out by grief just made matters worse because I couldn't stand the loneliness, and now I feel that if I don't get myself organised soon I'll go round the bend—or have I gone round the bend already?"

"No. But are you signalling that you feel you've reached the point where you might do something frightful?"

"Like what?"

"You tell me."

"Oh, don't worry, I'm not about to go on a drunken binge like some pathetic old clergyman who's lost all his self-discipline! And there's no question of me sidling off to a red-light district like a clergyman who's completely broken down. I think what I'm really afraid of is that I'll throw good judgement to the winds out of sheer frustration and marry a monster, just as Stephen did when he married Dido. Ye gods, that woman! How does he stand her?"

"No idea. Incidentally, talking of Stephen—"

"Oh my stars, yes, the Christie's débâcle—that was the other thing I wanted to speak to you about! I assume Malcolm did tell you that we Canons knew nothing about Stephen's machinations?"

"Yes, but I'm afraid I barely took it in. Lyle's death—"

"It was the day after Lyle died that Malcolm descended on us like the wrath of God and demanded to know how we could have sanctioned the Christie's plot, but luckily our horror was so obvious that he instantly realised Stephen had been playing a lone hand."

"Stephen himself told me that the flaunting of the St. Anselm manuscript was just a publicity stunt, but I was disturbed to discover he's genuinely keen to sell some of the minor books."

"Is he? Well, of course we'd be the last to know, but don't worry, Charles, he can't do that without the consent of Chapter and we'll veto it. As far as the library's concerned our powers are clearly spelt out in the Cathedral statutes."

I felt greatly relieved to receive this assurance. "Well, if I can rely on you to stand up to Stephen there—"

"It's easier to stand up to Stephen when we have the statutes on our side. The real difficulty comes when we hit the whole murky area of twentieth-century fund-raising and encounter situations which the medieval lawyers who drafted the statutes never imagined. That's when Stephen starts to write his own rules and we Canons get left in the dark . . . Honestly, Charles, what with Stephen trampling all over us on the one hand and Malcolm breathing fire all over us on the other—"

"Why do you suppose Stephen feels so driven to go to such outrageous lengths to raise money?"

"That was exactly the question I wanted to ask you. We're all puzzled. Tommy says that since Stephen's not a gentleman he simply has no idea where to draw the line, but can we really write this off as just an off-key breach of fund-raising etiquette?"

"The Appeal's not in any kind of difficulty?"

"Stephen always insists that it's going wonderfully well."

"But you've seen the accounts which confirm that?"

"We saw the accounts for the financial year of '63–'64, and they were first-class."

"That must have been some time ago. What's been happening since then?"

"That's the big question. Since then we haven't seen any accounts."

"But doesn't Gerry, as Cathedral treasurer, get some sort of regular report from Bob Carey?"

"Oh, didn't Stephen tell you? He decided ages ago that old Bob couldn't cope with the Appeal accounts in addition to the ordinary Cathedral accounts, so he took the Appeal accounts away from Bob and gave them to a firm in London—and they report only to Stephen."

"Which firm?"

"I don't know, but they must be all right because Stephen used them when he was a canon of Westminster after the war and doing all that fund-raising for the Germans."

"But surely you know the name of the firm!"

"Stephen did mention it, but I can't quite—"

"But there must have been letters, reports, bank statements—"

"They'd all go straight to Stephen at the Deanery."

"Are you trying to tell me the Chapter never now see any papers relating to the Appeal?"

"All right, all right, I know how slipshod it sounds, but . . . Look, we didn't deliberately set out to create this situation, it just sort of crept up on us. To begin with, there was no treasurer in place when the Appeal was launched because Eddie Hoffenberg had gone to London and Gerry hadn't been appointed. That meant Stephen was doubling as treasurer, in charge of all the finances, and even after Gerry arrived Stephen thought he was too inexperienced to cope with the Appeal as well as with the Cathedral itself."

"But surely you and Tommy—"

"Tommy and I aren't too hot on fund-raising, Charles. That's the honest-to-God truth of it. So it seemed best to ask Stephen to carry on managing the Appeal single-handed. I know that sounds questionable in retrospect, but Stephen's such a gifted fund-raiser, so experienced, that we had complete confidence that he knew what he was doing. In fact I'm still sure there's nothing wrong with the Appeal. There couldn't be. It's not possible."

After a pause I said: "But surely you've now queried the status of the Appeal? When was the last meeting of Chapter?"

"Last week. But we couldn't agree on who was to tackle Stephen so nothing was actually said."

"But my dear Paul—"

"I know, I know, we've got to do something—and we will, I promise, but the trouble is that Gerry's too young and Tommy's too old to take on a despotic dean, and I'm currently in such a state about my private life that I can't summon the nerve to play the hero by offering myself to Stephen to be mauled, minced and mashed into dust. If I could only find the ideal clerical wife . . ." And he began to drone on again about his pipe-dream.

I waited with superhuman patience until he had departed. Then I immediately telephoned Malcolm at his vicarage by St. Martin's-in-Cripplegate.

12

AS IT was a Saturday Malcolm and Nigel were not due to appear in the office; Nigel was preoccupied in catching up with his own work in

Starmouth while Malcolm was busy with parish matters. When I telephoned he was preparing for a wedding at eleven.

"Obviously we're on the brink of scandal," he said when I had passed on Paul's information that Aysgarth had by-passed Bob Carey, outflanked the Chapter and managed the Appeal single-handed for some months without producing even a bank statement for his colleagues' inspection. "Why would he hijack the Appeal like that unless something shifty was going on?"

"What I'd like to know is why Bob Carey didn't tip you off that he'd been removed as the Appeal accountant."

"Too terrified that Aysgarth might sack him altogether if he started complaining to the diocesan office. Did Paul really have no idea what these new accountants are called?"

"None. But since Aysgarth used them when he was a canon of Westminster the implication is that they must be completely above board."

"Well, that may be the implication but we don't have to be stuck with it!"

"Malcolm—"

"Hang on, I'll come over for a quick word. We shouldn't be discussing this on the phone."

"What about the wedding?"

"I can still fit in a ten-minute conference."

The line went dead. Emerging from my study I found Charley and reluctantly explained that I now had to see Malcolm, but Charley went to elaborate lengths to tell me he was quite happy to wait a little longer before adjourning to the golf course. Reflecting that even an invasion by my archdeacon would be less stressful than this exquisitely polite dialogue with my son, I withdrew again to my study.

"I think we should have a conference with Sir Reginald," announced Malcolm on his arrival ten minutes later. Sir Reginald Barrington-Frazer, the diocesan Chancellor, was our chief legal officer. "I think—"

"Wait a moment, Malcolm," I said, realising that I had to take control of the scene before I was left looking fatally ineffectual. "I've now had the chance to reflect on the conversation with Paul and I believe we have to be very careful here not to jump to all the wrong conclusions. First of all answer me this: do you seriously believe—*seriously* believe—that the Dean of a great cathedral would stoop to criminal behaviour?"

"My dear Charles, that man's capable of anything, *as we all know.* Think of 1963. Any dean who commissions pornographic sculpture for his churchyard must be completely cut off from God."

"He didn't see it as pornographic."

"Well, there you are!"

"Yes, but . . ." I broke off, took a deep breath and tried again. I was as worried as he was but I felt I had to make at least some attempt to reason our way out of our fears. "Just let's consider this calmly for a moment," I said. "What do we actually know? Only that Aysgarth has (a) taken complete control of the Appeal Fund, (b) engaged new accountants for it and (c) behaved abominably with Christie's. The abominable behaviour is certainly embarrassing but I'd be very surprised if Sir Reginald judges it to be criminal. Similarly, it's not a crime to hire new accountants, particularly if Aysgarth felt Bob Carey hadn't the time to do the extra work properly. And finally although I agree that the Canons' ignorance is a most undesirable state of affairs, they've only themselves to blame—it seems they were all too willing to let Aysgarth play a lone hand."

"But why should he want to play a lone hand?" demanded Malcolm. "Surely he must have had some shady purpose in mind!"

"No, that doesn't necessarily follow at all. Just think: if you were Aysgarth, a gifted fund-raiser, wouldn't you seize every chance you had to circumvent the sluggish fusspots in Chapter and embark on a brilliant solo? I agree it's easy to give the current state of affairs a sinister interpretation, but don't let's forget that Aysgarth's behaviour could be entirely non-criminal."

"All right," said Malcolm, calming down and in consequence arguing more effectively, "all right, I agree that the flirtation with Christie's, the power-grabbing and the accountant-switching are all capable of an innocent explanation when considered separately, but together they add up to the biggest rat I've smelt during all my years as an archdeacon. For heaven's sake, Charles, make a visitation before the lid blows off that Cathedral and showers scandal all over the Church of England!"

I knew it was time to exert my authority again but I was so debilitated by Charley's emotional blackmail, Paul's agonised meditations on sex and my renewed anxiety about Aysgarth that once again I wound up saying the wrong thing. It was: "I'll have to discuss this with Nigel on Monday."

"With all due respect, Charles," said Malcolm, using the phrase which in my experience invariably means that some gross impertinence is about to be uttered, "I really can't see what Nigel's got to do with this matter. I know you've been relying on him more than usual during this difficult time, but the fact is that his presence here is a temporary arrangement, and *I'm* the one who's best qualified to advise you about the Cathedral."

Trying to assume a voice of steel I said: "Am I not allowed to consult my suffragan about a matter which could ultimately affect the whole diocese?"

"Oh, I quite understand that he must be kept informed! All I'm saying is that as he knows nothing about my archdeaconry he's ill-equipped to advise on its problems—oh, and talking of problems, I must just mention Langley Bottom before I run off to that wedding. Desmond's due back on Monday from his little holiday in Devon, but since it's most unlikely that he'll be capable of returning to work straight away there'll be no need to suspend him prior to the sacking. Heavens above, look at the time, I must fly—" And he raced away to the wedding at St. Martin's.

I was still taking deep breaths in an attempt to calm myself when Charley arrived, over-attentive, with a cup of coffee for me.

I felt more in need of a double-brandy.

XII

"Bad things don't reveal a cruel God; they hide from us the God of love."

AUSTIN FARRER
Warden of Keble College, Oxford, 1960–1968
A CELEBRATION OF FAITH

I

"HOW OLD is this child who's coming here tonight?" enquired Charley later.

"Seventeen."

"What a pity—a very boring age! I suppose she'll only be capable of simpering about the Beatles."

I made no comment. I was trying to work out how to survive the remainder of the morning, but it passed more easily than I had dared hope as Charley himself suggested postponing our outing to the golf course. He had decided to do some shopping for the dinner-party; he had noticed there was very little gin, no Schweppes tonic and no lemon. During his absence I tried to answer some sympathy letters, but when I opened the file I could do no more than reread the letter from Sheila Preston, the wife of the late Bishop of Radbury, and reflect how odd it was that she had wound up living in Pimlico, that shabby hinterland south of Belgravia, in a street which shared the same name as one of the Channel Islands. Lyle and I had spent a holiday with the boys on that particular island not long after the war. Michael had learnt to swim there. I could clearly see him, aged eight, small, sturdy, tanned, smiling—and a second later I was remembering the letter which was still lying in my out-tray. Passing Charley in the hall as he returned from his shopping expedition, I drove to the post office and sent the letter by the express service to London.

By the time I arrived home Charley had selected some food from the deep-freeze and was organising lunch.

"I expect you want to rest this afternoon," he said neutrally as we finished eating, but I knew I had reached the point where I had to pay him attention. We set off for the golf course with a five-iron and a putter apiece and played a few holes, but a driving sleet put an end to this unpleasant exercise and we retired, damp and chilled, to the South Canonry. I then declared I needed a hot bath, and I managed to make this luxury last for a very considerable time.

When I had summoned the strength to venture downstairs I found that Charley had changed into a clerical suit for the dinner-party, and this pleased me; I disapproved of young clergymen who felt so coy about their uniform that they refused to wear it unless they had to. I myself was wearing a clerical suit with a purple stock. At an informal dinner-party in my own home I felt the traditional episcopal uniform would have been too showy.

"Maybe Hall will wear a biretta," said Charley frivolously, having gossiped with the chaplains that morning and learnt of Hall's brand of churchmanship.

But Hall had dressed with scrupulous care in the height of convention in order to make amends for his wild appearance at our previous meeting. He was attired, just as he had been when I had first seen him in the Cathedral, in a well-cut clerical suit, a black stock and only the smallest of pectoral crosses. His shoes were so highly polished that they gleamed like metal. His hair had been trimmed. The sideboards had been eliminated. Undoubtedly he was now shaved, groomed and buffed to a high lustre, but by some bizarre feat he managed to look far more arresting and sinister than he had appeared in his casual clothes. I had forgotten how every head in the chapel had turned to look at him when he had attended the Cathedral's early services.

So struck was I by the fact that Hall's heroic attempt to look wholesome had met with such singular lack of success that I did not at first see the girl who was lingering behind him, but as Hall stepped forward to shake my hand the light from the porch shone upon her and I saw that she was not merely pretty, like Elizabeth Aysgarth, but beautiful. The beauty was not classical, but in its modern originality it was very striking. She had long straight dark hair and a pale skin and such a slim neat figure that she looked like a little china-doll in her plain straight plum-red frock. She appeared to be wearing no make-up except around the eyes, which were dark, glowing and enormous. Her strong, sculpted jaw formed a fascinating contrast to her full-lipped, very feminine mouth, but although I was conscious of her sexuality I was conscious too of her innocence;

she seemed so young, so fresh, so unmarred by the sheer nastiness of so much of modern life. My heart turned over. I forgot little Miss Elizabeth and her knowing, winning ways. I found myself wholly enchanted by little Miss Rachel, and for a painful moment Lyle returned to me as we grieved again for the daughter we had never had.

Introductions were made. The girl was very shy, but Charley concealed his inferiority complex by assuming a bossy manner which she seemed to find reassuring. Hall, of course, was on his best behaviour. No ambassador to the Court of St. James's could have been more courteous.

"What will you drink?" I said to him in the drawing-room, and as his sharp glance flicked over the collection of bottles on the sideboard I knew he was calculating which drink I felt was most appropriate. With a canniness which bordered on the telepathic he asked for a Tio Pepe.

"Would you prefer a gin-and-tonic, Rachel?" said Charley. "I hated sherry when I was your age—in fact when I was very young I hated gin too. Would you rather have the tonic on its own?"

Rachel said she would. Fortunately she did not seem in the least affronted by these questions which implied she was barely out of the nursery, but although she continued to gaze at him with her glowing dark eyes, Charley was far too busy opening a bottle of tonic to notice.

I found myself remembering the famous acid comment that youth was wasted on the young.

2

AT THE dining-table the girl overcame her shyness and revealed an intelligence and spontaneity which I found charming. Living with her mother in London she had reached the top form of St. Paul's Girls School and was studying English literature, French and German. She played the piano "but not very well." Her mother wanted her to be a debutante but Rachel "wasn't too keen" because even though the formal presentation had been abolished, the frenetic social life of the Season seemed "all rather shallow." Mrs. Hall, it transpired, lived in a small house in Belgravia and did her shopping at Harrods. Unable to imagine Hall being married to this sort of woman I found myself experiencing a renewed curiosity about his background.

"Whereabouts do you come from?" I demanded.

"Sussex," he answered, but said no more.

"Daddy was brought up by an uncle and aunt," said little Miss Rachel, unable to bear this reticence. "They had a super house near Chichester which is now owned by the National Trust."

"As you can imagine," said Hall to me, "all that has no bearing on my present life." But obviously it was this monied background which gave him the freedom to work for the Church without taking a salary.

"Were your family Anglo-Catholic, Father Hall?" Charley was enquiring.

"I'm sorry to say my uncle and aunt had no interest in religion whatsoever, but my great-uncle ensured that I was educated at Starwater Abbey."

Rachel said: "Daddy's great-uncle was—"

"—the family eccentric," interrupted Hall. "I always find him much too exhausting to discuss." I deduced that this great-uncle represented the family connection with the Fordite monks, the connection which the Abbot-General had mentioned in his reference, but before I could speculate further Hall remarked to me: "I wish all those people today who dismiss Anglo-Catholicism as effete could have experienced the Fordite ethos at Starwater in the 1930s. Cyril Watson ran the school like a military academy."

"I knew Father Watson," I said, wondering if this was the great-uncle, "but not well. I knew Father Ingram better."

"So did I," said Hall, and at once I was sure I had solved the mystery. Francis Ingram, the present Abbot-General's predecessor, had come from a monied, aristocratic background. "Francis was assigned to take me for walks in the park," Hall was saying, "when I spent my school holidays at the Fordites' London house."

"Like a little dog!" said Charley amused.

"Jon Darrow often mentions Father Ingram," I said. "They were good friends."

Hall said: "Is it true that Father Darrow's a recluse nowadays and sees no one? I was hoping our paths would finally cross."

"You might try writing to him. I'm sure he'd be intrigued to hear from anyone who was a protégé of his mentor Father Darcy."

"He loves to talk about Darcy!" said Charley. "He wallows in blissful nostalgia as soon as the name's mentioned!"

"In that case I accept I'm not meant to meet him," said Hall dryly. "My idea of fun quite definitely doesn't include looking back at Darcy through rose-tinted spectacles. But tell me more about Father Darrow, Bishop! He must be very old—is he still in good health?"

As I began to talk of Jon's eremitical way of life Charley decided to hold forth to Rachel about music. I longed to tell him to be less dogmatic, but the girl, listening wide-eyed, still seemed fascinated by his masterful manner. Halfway through the meal I heard her exclaim: "It's so nice to find someone who can express his opinions clearly!" and I had a sudden vision of her usually surrounded by callow youths who could only communicate in the monosyllabic fashion which was so widespread among the younger generation. No doubt Charley, now nearer thirty than twenty, seemed thrillingly sophisticated to her.

Meanwhile my housekeeper had been excelling herself in the kitchen. We enjoyed celery soup (a triumpant contrast to the pale liquid I had encountered at the Aysgarths' table), a fish pie in which cod, glorified by shrimps in a cream sauce, luxuriated beneath a crisp thatch of mashed potato, and finally apple crumble, hot, crunchy and accompanied by the smoothest of custards. Making a fresh resolution to eat properly I was tempted to attribute a large part of my recent debility to inadequate nutrition.

After the housekeeper had brought coffee to the drawing-room I said to Charley: "Why don't you play Rachel some records?" This prearranged suggestion was made to enable me to talk to Hall about the future.

"What a good idea!" said Charley brightly, and commanded Rachel to accompany him as if she were a small child in danger of getting lost. They departed with their coffee. As the door closed I offered Hall a glass of port, which he declined, and a cigarette which he eyed with longing before saying: "Thanks, but not when I'm in uniform."

I deduced that someone had tipped him off about my old-fashioned views on the subject. Giving him no chance to mourn his decision I closed the cigarette-box and said abruptly: "Very well. This is your golden opportunity—make the most of it. How would you use that dying church?"

3

HALL BEGAN by giving his views on the ministry of healing. He insisted that the healer should be a mere channel for the Holy Spirit; he denounced all healing ministries in which the healer allowed the cult of the personality to flourish; he condemned the healers who ignored the fact that humility and a devout life were essential if they were to avoid corruption; he rejected the idea of a ministry which involved regular, large, emotional services of healing; he insisted that although healing centres might accept donations for the furtherance of their work, the people who worked there should never charge the sick for their ministrations, and he recoiled from the notion that his own services should ever be marketed in a commercial manner.

Then having erected this strictly orthodox framework for my approval he became more original. Highly sceptical of instant wonder-cures, he thought healing took place best over a period of time within the quiet, undramatic context of a prayerful community.

"In the mental hospital where I worked," he said, "we had a small core of praying people—both staff and patients—and the daily mass. I did practise the laying-on of hands, and also anointing where appropriate, but it was all done in an atmosphere devoid of melodrama. The aim was to make each patient feel cherished and cared for, and the aim was expressed through counselling and befriending. I also introduced music therapy, because music often speaks to people who can't be reached by words. I wanted to introduce painting as well, but the occupational therapists decided I was trespassing on their territory and they made a fuss."

"Was that when you decided you'd be better off in a less narrow environment?"

He said it was. "And as soon as I tried to visualize the ministry outside the hospital," he added, "I saw myself in an Anglo-Catholic parish setting with a daily celebration of the mass and a congregation who would pray for the sick. I would still be healing in small groups but there would be more opportunity to be innovative—and certainly more opportunity to help a wider range of people. I thought how I could train volunteers to share the task of listening and befriending—that was an idea I got from Chad Varah's Samaritans, of course . . ."

He went on to draw the vital distinction between a cure and a healing; a cure signified the banishment of physical illness but a healing could mean not just a physical cure but the repairing and strengthening of the mind and spirit to improve the quality of life even when no physical cure was possible. ". . . so the role of befriender, providing strength through the alleviation of loneliness and fear, can be in its own way as vital as the role of the doctor—although I would hope to have doctors too at my healing centre eventually, because orthodox medicine and spiritual healing should be complementary and not opposed to each other . . ."

He began to describe the place of his dreams. A diagram of the crypt of St. Paul's appeared in my hands. I was shown how the area could be divided into consulting rooms, a music room, an art studio, a reception area, administrative offices, a cafeteria, kitchen, lavatories . . . He had thought of everything.

"This is all very well," I said, deciding it was time to prove he had not succeeded in hypnotising me into a state of mindless acquiescence, "but is Starbridge the best place for this?"

"If I specialise in clergy breakdown, men would come from all over the country and it wouldn't matter where the ministry is based."

"Yes, but presumably—in the beginning at least—your ministry will be more broadly based, and I can't see it attracting much interest in comfortable, conservative Starbridge. Wouldn't you be better off in London?"

"If I were founding a shady cult which depended for its success on the power of my personality," said Hall, "I'd say yes, you're right, I'd be better off in London alongside all the charlatans who feed off dying people by selling them overpriced cures that don't work. But *my* ministry will be built by the grace of Our Lord Jesus Christ on the power of the Spirit, and you can't confine *that* to London. Give me your comfortable Starbridge conservatives! A fat bank balance and a nice home can't protect anyone from random tragedy—in fact such disasters can strike all the harder when one's previously had the means to keep all thought of such unpleasantness at bay."

I felt I had no alternative but to say, "That's true," and it was with regret that I added: "But nevertheless I'm afraid your scheme will cause considerable opposition in some quarters."

"Of course. The New Testament spells out all too clearly how threatening some people find a ministry of healing."

"And its companion, the ministry of deliverance. You've kept very quiet about that so far."

"Only because the vocabulary relating to it is so archaic and debased that one ends up sounding like either a fundamentalist or a lunatic."

"Then let's accept the language as an awkward collection of metaphors and symbols and try to do our best with it. How do you see deliverance from your standpoint within the healing ministry?"

I had apparently reassured him that I was willing to be fair-minded about this, the wildest and woolliest corner of clerical activity within the Church. At once he said: "My job is to help people. This is a very normal activity, but occasionally it will shade into the paranormal—occasionally people will be harassed and tormented by events which fall beyond the scope of those explanations normally defined as 'rational.' In that case my job is to end the torment not only by prayer but by the use of various rituals which are known to be effective—but let me stress that I'd never attempt to exorcise a person without the aid of a psychiatrist, the support of other priests and your express permission. The deliverance ministry seldom deals with the exorcism of people anyway. The exorcism of places is by far the most frequent item on the agenda, and that's usually very straightforward."

I tried to muzzle my curiosity but failed. "What sort of results have you had with the exorcism of people?"

"Mixed."

"I'm surprised the psychiatrists sanctioned it!"

"What did they have to lose? They weren't getting anywhere. One of them was actually a Christian and keen to give it a go."

"And you succeeded in curing people?"

"We had two complete cures where the patients were able to leave the hospital—although of course the appropriate after-care was arranged. Then we had two semi-cures where the patients remained mildly schizoid but were no longer troubled by demonic invasion. And finally we had a complete failure—the patient tried to kill me, but I think now that he was merely deranged and not possessed. It's not always easy to make a diagnosis, and if the diagnosis is wrong an exorcism's worse than useless."

"A demanding ministry," I said dryly.

"It's a very small segment of my work—"

"—but the one most likely to be reported in the *News of the World* if anything goes wrong. And while we're on the subject of scandal, how do you protect yourself from neurotic females in a ministry which involves the laying-on of hands?"

This, in cricketing terms, was really bowling him a yorker, but he kept calm and presented the straightest of bats. "I never touch patients unless other people are present," he said, "and anyway if touching is required it would involve no more than applying pressure to the head. But most of the time it's not required. One merely holds one's hands over the affected part of the body. The clothed body," he added neutrally as an afterthought.

I sharpened my interrogation still further. "Have you ever felt attracted to a patient?"

"Yes, but there's never any risk because if that happens I can't treat her. The ambiguous feelings get in the way and then my powers don't work—or to be correct I should say that the Holy Spirit can't use me as a channel of healing because the channel's clogged up."

I found I could believe this. Jon, who had once engaged in a brief ministry of healing, had reminisced to me in similar terms. But I decided I had a duty to probe further still.

"How do you get on with celibacy?" I said, bowling him not a mere yorker but a bouncer. "I can well understand that a healing ministry takes so much energy that you feel unable to sustain a family life, but presumably there must still be times when you feel married life has certain advantages."

Hall at once said: "Naturally I sometimes feel I'd like to be married. And when I was married I often felt I'd like to be single. There are always times when the grass seems greener over the hill, but I know myself, Bishop, I know which side of the hill I have to be on, I know the life I've been called to lead and I know what sacrifices I have to make in order to lead it. And besides . . . can a married priest really be guaranteed to have fewer problems than a well-integrated celibate? I wonder! When I was married I used to think marriage created more problems than it solved . . . But of course I wasn't designed for married life."

This struck me as being not only an honest reply but the reply of a man who was clear-eyed about life and spiritually mature. In a moment of restlessness which reflected some deep shift in my attitude to him I stood up and moved to the fireplace. I was thinking that when the subject of that church in Langley Bottom was under discussion, it was not my down-to-earth archdeacon who was in touch with reality but this eccentric divorced priest whom Malcolm and I had wanted to dismiss as unemployable. I saw too, as I looked back, that not only had I been led, very much against my will and conventional judgement, to see this man again and again, but that no matter how hard I tried to take a sceptical view of his vision, this view was always systematically demolished.

Standing by the fireplace I felt this conclusion pressing on my mind and I felt I knew too the source of the power which was driving that conclusion home, but still I felt obliged to say to myself: I'm debilitated; my judgement could be flawed; I may have fallen victim to the power of Hall's personality. I told myself I needed a further sign, a further increase in that unmistakable pressure on my mind, the pressure capable in the end of blasting aside all doubt so that no other course remained to be taken.

Aloud I said warily: "There are certain problems attached to St. Paul's. Whether Father Wilton will be well enough to continue there is far from certain, and—"

"But I was counting on his support!"

I stared at him. *"Counting* on it?"

"Oh, absolutely! When I visited him in hospital," said Hall with enthusiasm, "I realised he could provide just the kind of gentle, devout—even, I'd go so far as to say, holy—atmosphere which I need at the heart of the parish. I could support him by helping out with the services and he could support me by prayer. We'd complement each other. It would be the ideal arrangement."

I was dumbfounded.

"Well, never mind Father Wilton for the moment," said Hall hurriedly, interpreting my profound silence as an indication of episcopal disapproval. "I wouldn't of course presume to dictate to you about how you should deploy your priests—and talking of priests, what an original young man your son is! You must be very proud of him."

I recovered myself sufficiently to say: "No more proud, I'm sure, than you must be of your attractive daughter." I still felt quite extraordinarily confused.

"The trouble with having an attractive daughter," said Hall, "is that one spends such an enormous amount of time worrying about what she's getting up to . . . which reminds me: where is she?"

To allay his anxiety I took him upstairs to the games-room.

4

WHEN WE had moved to the South Canonry eight years before, the boys had been adolescent and in order to preserve our sanity Lyle and I had decided to assign them a remote corner of the house where they could make as much noise as they liked. The attic had originally been partitioned in order to provide accommodation for servants, but it was easily converted back into one large area where the boys could play table-tennis or darts or gyrate to the racket issuing from the gramophone.

As I led Hall up the attic stairs, the music drifted to meet us. One of the hoard of old records was being played, but although I recognised the waltz I was at first unable to recall its title. Opening the door I paused on the threshold and was immediately besieged by all manner of complex emotions at the sight which met my eyes.

Charley and Rachel were dancing, very sedately and with absolute propriety, to the slow waltz which was so well known. Although he had never excelled at games during his years at school, Charley could move gracefully and he danced particularly well, far better than Michael, the star of the school playing-fields. When one watched Charley dance one forgot his lack of inches and noticed only how lithe and well proportioned he was and how elegantly he responded to the music. At that moment his pale brown eyes were golden with delight. I realised he was enjoying himself immensely.

The memory of Samson flicked across my mind but made little impression. It was the next memory which devastated me, the memory of myself as a young man moving through a world which was now lost, and as I looked at Charley I felt old, spent and finished, stripped as I was of the loving wife who had kept the dark side of old age at bay.

Appalled by this glimpse of a finished life and a solitary wait for death, I found myself so mesmerised by Charley that I was unable to look away. He seemed so new, so shining, so full of vitality as his future stretched bewitchingly ahead of him, and when I remembered how it felt to be under thirty with the best years of life still to come, I could only feel numb with envy as I saw him dance with that beautiful girl.

I stared at Rachel, but now I no longer saw her as Hall's daughter. I saw her as the personification of youthful beauty, as an example of a life still unmarred by sorrow and suffering, as an inhabitant of that fresh, new-minted, dazzling world which I myself would never know again. I was painfully conscious not only of her beauty but of her sensuality, and as this awareness made its imprint on my mind I felt as if I had been struck across the face with an iron bar. Shattered by the terrible reality that I would never again experience either the beauty or the sensuality of the woman I had loved so much for so long, I could see for myself only a sterile, dwindling existence in a world which now derided all the values to which I had dedicated my life. Honour, decency, modesty, unselfishness—order, stability, tradition—goodness, truth and beauty—faith, hope and love—all those ideals, all those luminous values seemed to be crumbling in a new era where nothing was sacred, everything was trivialised and all the precious wisdom which gave life meaning was being hurled into the raging furnace of change.

Then I hated the 1960s, *hated* them, hated that decade more than I had realised it was possible to hate one arbitrary segment of time, and as I was again racked by the longing to be young, I saw clearly that it was not Charley I truly envied but Michael, who was so busy grasping the modern freedom to savour all the joy and pleasure I was now denied.

I remembered Lyle writing in her journal about my jealousy of Michael, and I remembered too how I had automatically rejected this diagnosis, even felt affronted by it. Now I saw it was true. So long as my sexual needs had been satisfied I had been able to clamp down on the jealousy, but now I was on my own it was no longer possible to draw a veil over the dark corners of my mind where unmentionable emotions festered. Lyle's death had slashed the veil to ribbons. I looked upon the truth at last and the truth was terrible to me.

It then occurred to me that if this unwelcome allegation in the journal was true, other equally unwelcome assertions might also have hit the mark, but this possibility was so horrific that I could only push it aside. I had reached the point where reality was proving too harsh to endure. Within seconds I had been confronted by my lost youth, my unpromising future, the sexual deprivation implicit in my bereavement and a brilliantly lit view into the dark corners of my psyche. The shock disorientated me to such an extent that I even looked around for Lyle because I knew she would take me in her arms and put everything right. But of course Lyle was no longer there.

Instead it was Rachel whom I saw. She had parted from Charley and was moving towards me with her hands outstretched. In the brightness of the lights her hair gleamed, streaming across her slim shoulders to brush the curve of her breasts, and her dark eyes were radiant. Here indeed was the acceptable face of modern youth, but my grief was such that I could hardly bear to look upon it. How can the old order look upon the new without feeling bereaved beyond measure for the world which has slipped away? What has the old order to say to the new, and what use has the new for the old? I felt as if I were facing Rachel across an abyss which no gesture could bridge, and yet there Rachel was, holding out her hands to me as if the abyss did not exist and behaving as if she even had something important to say to an elderly man devastated by despair.

"Do dance with me, Bishop!" she begged, quite forgetting her shyness in her exhilaration. "You mustn't feel left out! Please dance—it's such fun!"

And in a moment of revelation I saw then the other side of the 1960s: I saw the exuberance and the vitality and the generosity which existed among the young, and I realised I had to respond not only with warmth but with an equal generosity of spirit. It was no use cocooning myself in misery so that I was cut off from the new order. I had to reach out and clasp hands with its ambassadors. I had to summon all my strength to wish them well.

I took Rachel's hands in mine.

"I've told her how well you dance!" Charley called as he prepared to replay the record on the turntable.

I moved with Rachel to the centre of the floor, and as the record began to play I finally remembered the name of the tune. It was "The Tennessee Waltz." I could remember hearing it at the last ball which Lyle and I had attended in Cambridge. I could remember what Lyle had worn, a pale green gown, very simple, the skirt long and straight. The memory was so vivid that I fancied I could even smell the scent she had used.

The agony of bereavement assaulted me again, but I fought back and conquered it. The old order might be changing, yielding its place so painfully to the new, but at least it could yield with courage, with dignity and with style.

I danced and I danced and I danced.

"Bravo!" shouted Charley as the record ended.

"Congratulations, Bishop!" called Hall, laughing as he clapped his hands, and Rachel, naively delighted, breathed: "Super!"

"It takes two to dance well," I said smiling at her. "Thank you, Rachel." But having completed my task I felt as if my heart were disintegrating beneath the weight of my grief. I looked around again for Lyle, but she seemed to have disappeared somewhere. Perhaps she had slipped down to the kitchen to make some more coffee. Lyle was always mindful of the needs of our guests.

Knowing I had to find her without delay I murmured: "Will you all excuse me for a moment?" and hurried away down the attic stairs.

On the landing I opened my mouth to shout: "Darling!" just as I always did when I returned home at the end of an arduous day, but as soon as I drew breath to speak I knew she would never reply. For a moment I shuddered, horrified that grief should have so twisted my mind. Then I blindly wiped the sweat from my forehead, blundered into our room and collapsed in the dark on the edge of the bed we had shared.

Tears began to stream down my face, but they were triggered not by the huge emotions generated by Rachel. They were triggered by my memory of that trivial little routine—the memory of all those evenings when I had shouted: "Darling!" on my return from work and received the answering call which represented love and security. I thought what a comfort it had been to discuss the day's events, no matter how dreary, with someone who always gave me unfailing support. I thought of that small recurring pattern which had been utterly wiped out. I did not think: I have been wholly deprived of Lyle—for I still felt I could always retreat to her sitting-room and recapture her in my imagination. But what I did think was: I can never call out to her like that again.

At last I groped my way to the basin in the corner of the room and dowsed my face in cold water. I did not dare turn on the light for fear of glimpsing my shameful reflection in the glass, but as I dried my face I realised I had to see how far my appearance betrayed me. How could I face my guests with bloodshot eyes? In panic I tried to pray for composure but I was in such a state that I could only whisper over and over again: "Help me. Do something. Help me." Naturally nothing appeared to happen; the black cloud of that terrible reality which I was enduring not only smothered my words as I uttered them but blocked from my mind all concept of a loving God, and at last, acting on the cynical old maxim "God helps those who help themselves," I decided I could only survive the evening with the aid of the brandy decanter.

Lurching to the door I blundered out onto the landing—and stopped dead.

Lewis Hall was leaning over the bannisters and gazing meditatively at the elegant curve of the stairs.

XIII

"The sufferer finds his action, in the ordinary sense, cramped or enfeebled. The mere supporting of his trouble uses up such energy as he has."

AUSTIN FARRER
Warden of Keble College, Oxford, 1960–1968
LOVE ALMIGHTY AND ILLS UNLIMITED

I

"WE MUSTN'T outstay our welcome," said Hall, straightening his back. "I've told Rachel we must leave in ten minutes." He did not look at me. He was apparently still fascinated by the staircase.

"No need to rush." Having delivered this response firmly in the most normal of voices I realised in panic that I had exhausted my strength. The performance of normality was one which I was unable to sustain. "Excuse me," I said rapidly, "shan't be a moment, I've just got to . . ." I ceased speaking, bolted back into the bedroom and remembered to switch on the light. Obviously I could not continue to cower in the dark, but now at last I was unable to avoid glimpsing my reflection in the mirror and instantly my despair doubled as I saw my haggard face. I decided I was unfit to be seen by anyone, least of all by one of my clergy.

At that point I slumped down on the bed again and covered my face with my hands because I could see no solution to my predicament. My mind was quite blank. I felt annihilated.

The next moment I heard a small stealthy click as Hall opened the door.

I froze, immobilised with rage, and prayed violently to be spared this final humiliation.

But it seemed I was not to be spared. I heard the faint squeak of the hinge which had remained unoiled since Lyle's death and then another click as the door was closed again. The thick carpet muffled his footsteps but I knew he was crossing the room. Leaning forward with my elbows on my knees I kept my face covered, squeezed my eyes shut and waited for him to do what any normal clergyman would do to preserve his bishop's dignity: I waited for him to leave as unobtrusively as he had arrived so that afterwards we could pretend he had never entered the room at all.

But of course Hall was no ordinary clergyman.

Dumping himself on the bed beside me he said in the laconic voice he had used earlier while discussing his exorcisms: "Don't worry about Desmond. I'll look after him."

These eight words, selected with such apparent ease, had the most electrifying effect. I was so startled that I opened my eyes, let my hands fall from my face and swivelled to face him. Diverted from my agony I found myself mesmerised by all those two sentences implied: the knowledge that Desmond was an episcopal problem, the understanding that he required special care—and above all the realisation that I could best be jolted out of my self-centred misery by having my thoughts bent outwards to focus on someone who was worse off than I was.

Slowly, unsteadily, still grappling with my astonishment, I said: "You know about Desmond?"

"Uh-huh." Hall suddenly became off-beat, informal, daring. I had a vivid impression of him as a priest who because of the strict orthodoxy of his religious life knew instinctively when it was safe to step with confidence outside the ecclesiastical rules and apply unconventional pastoral care. Ignoring my rank, ignoring everything except that I was a distressed man who could only be reached by the boldest of moves, he said: "Remember I mentioned that I'd visited Desmond in hospital? Well, I called every day and it was lucky I did. He needed someone to talk to so I got him moved into a side-ward for an hour, and as soon as he had some privacy he spewed everything out."

"Everything?"

"Everything. He was very upset after the Archdeacon had beaten him up."

"Beaten him up?"

"Metaphorically speaking. Imagine telling a sick old priest that the Bishop's seen his porn collection! Doesn't Lindsay have anything that remotely resembles sensitivity? Of course Desmond felt like committing suicide."

"Suicide?" By this time I was beyond any response except a parrot-like repetition.

"Don't worry, it's okay, I fixed everything, hauled him back from the brink, gave him hope. I said: 'Forget that queer-bashing martinet of an archdeacon, remember your bishop, remember Ashworth's known to be sympathetic to priests who are on the ropes. I wouldn't be here now,' I said, 'if I hadn't heard about Ashworth's interest in that area. Ashworth knows about suffering,' I said, 'knows about hell, he's been in the war, he's seen it all, he's not one of those lily-livered sentimentalists who talk of a heaven for little children above the bright blue sky, he knows just what hell everything can be down here on earth and how vulnerable we all are and how we all need love and compassion and forgiveness if we're not to kick the bucket or go round the bend out of sheer despair. Have faith in your bishop!' I said to Desmond. 'And pray for him!' Desmond likes praying, he's good at it, I could tell that at once. *'Pray for him!'* I ordered after your wife's death, and he did, it perked him up no end, gave him something positive to do, and after I'd heard his formal confession and given him absolution he trotted off to Devon to recuperate in a very positive frame of mind. I've been sending him a postcard every day to keep him topped up and he's written back to say the natives are friendly, the library at Allington Court is excellent and he can't remember when he last had such a good time. He said he realised now that if only he'd had a holiday earlier he wouldn't have got overstrained and started messing around with the porn."

I managed to say faintly: "But why didn't he take a holiday earlier? I always encourage my clergy to take holidays!"

"Couldn't afford it. Supports his widowed mother in a private nursing home in Starmouth. She's ninety-two."

"But something could have been arranged! If I'd only known—"

"Evidently the Archdeacon Rampant never thought that piece of information was worth passing on, but don't worry about Lindsay, I can deal with him, I know that type. The important thing is to get him to stop persecuting Desmond so that Desmond can realise his full potential. I feel very strongly that with his gift for prayer he can be a real source of spiritual power in that parish . . . By the way, what's Lindsay going to do with the porn? Desmond says he'd like to burn it himself, and I think that's good—a burning would be helpful, cathartic. We could have a bonfire in the backyard. I like bonfires, don't you?"

"I—"

"Never mind, we can talk more about that later. How are you feeling now?"

"Fine."

"You don't look fine, you look as if you're on your last legs. Why don't you drop that stiff upper lip and smash something?"

"I hardly think that would be appropriate behaviour for a bishop!"

"Ah well, if we're talking about what's appropriate, let me take you downstairs and give you a stiff brandy! Then you might feel strong enough to ditch that stiff upper lip, get human, roar with rage, scream with pain, shed enough tears to fill a bucket—well, why shouldn't you, you're bereaved, it's your right to grieve—and don't think I'd mind because I wouldn't, it's all the same to me, wouldn't bother me at all, in fact I'd admire you, think you were being constructive."

"Constructive? But how could it ever be constructive for a bishop to behave in such a disgusting fashion?"

"Oh, forget all that bishop business for five minutes," said Hall crossly. "Ditch it along with the stiff upper lip, why not, and stop worrying about what I'd think of you because just at this moment I don't care who you are, I wouldn't even care if you were the Pope or Marilyn Monroe, all I care about is helping you bash your way out of this bugger-awful corner you're in."

"That's all very well, but if I go to pieces—"

"I'm not talking about going to pieces, I'm talking about facing the pain. Did you ever meet Aidan Lucas, the Fordite abbot up at Ruydale? He used to say: 'It's a question of facing the pain.' He got that from Father Darcy, of course. Everyone got everything from Darcy. If Darcy were here now he'd say: 'Come along, Charles, have a stiff brandy and stop beating about the bush! You're saying the words you want me to hear, but I hear the words you can't bring yourself to say!' "

Utterly dazed I said doubtfully: "I can't imagine that most illustrious Abbot-General ever advocating a stiff drink," but this objection was instantly swept aside.

"Advocating it?" exclaimed Hall. "He'd have insisted on it! Darrow was the one who always looked down his nose at alcohol, but Darcy couldn't stand Darrow's asceticism, he thought it was all moral pirouetting, a show-off exercise of Darrow's strong will—and here you are, trying to ape your spiritual director, but all I can say is forget the pirouettes and hang up your ballet-shoes. We're off to hit the brandy."

The next moment I found myself being deftly piloted out of the bedroom and steered downstairs. Once or twice I did think I should protest, but I never got around to opening my mouth. It seemed so much simpler just to keep quiet and do as I was told.

"Let's smoke," said Hall, having installed me in an armchair in the drawing-room. "You've got a fixation, haven't you, about not smoking in your clerical collar, but don't worry, I'll whip it off for you."

"I think I can just about manage to whip off my own collar," I said in the manner of an invalid who was now well enough to be querulous. "And it's not a fixation, it's a discipline."

"Great. I'm keen on discipline, trains one up, stops one going down the drain, kicks the Devil in the teeth. I'll take off my collar too."

We took off our collars and lit cigarettes. Two brandy-and-sodas were mixed. A glass was thrust into my hands and a chair was pulled up so that he could sit close to me. Even before I had taken a sip of my drink I realised I was calmer. I felt as if I had been grabbed from some sordid gutter where I had been bleeding to death, and was now being bandaged from head to toe. All my ragged edges had been smoothed. The blood had been staunched. The pain had been dulled. Ruthlessly enfolded by this intensive unorthodox care I was able to sit quietly, smoke my cigarette and take small sips from my glass.

"Bit like the war, isn't it?" said Hall after a while. "Life hell, barriers down, everyone sticking together, living from day to day."

"Sounds familiar."

"You should dig a trench and hole up for a while. If you go on playing the hero you'll wind up liquidated. Errol Flynn might have been able to win wars single-handed in the gospel according to Hollywood, but the rest of us need help."

"True."

"Is old Darrow still *compos mentis?"*

"Completely."

"Then why hasn't he kidnapped you for a couple of weeks?"

"He tried."

"So what happened?"

"I thought I needed to stay on here and say goodbye to my wife properly. But then I got bogged down in diocesan problems—"

"For heaven's sake! Leave them all to the Archdeacon Rampant!"

"—and then there's a problem with the Cathedral—"

"Set it aside. I've got your wife's prayer-group praying for the Cathedral."

Once more I was astounded. "How on earth did you find out about the prayer-group?"

"I had a little chat with Mrs. Lindsay during one of my visits to her vicarage to keep the Archdeacon well buttered."

"But who told you the Cathedral needs to be prayed for?"

"No one. But I only had to cross the threshold to realise that the whole place was steeped in bad vibes . . . Ah, I hear the younger generation approaching, but don't worry, the young are always so absorbed in themselves that they seldom notice if anyone over thirty looks more beaten up by life than usual. We'll start talking about nothing. Did you ever hear the story of the Fordites' cat who was raised from the dead?"

"I don't think so," I said, clutching my glass and wondering what Charley would think when he saw me. Despite Hall's remarks about the younger generation's poor powers of observation I thought Charley could hardly fail to notice that I had taken off my collar to smoke and had resorted to drinking spirits. I never normally did either at dinner-parties.

Meanwhile Hall had embarked on his story and adopted the cosy tone of the raconteur. ". . . and I never did succeed in discovering the name of the monk who played the charismatic crook," I heard him conclude regretfully. "The whole story was one of the Fordites' state secrets, and if Francis Ingram hadn't become garrulous one night after an extra glass of claret—ah, there you are, Rachel! Danced yourself to a standstill?"

"We're panting with thirst," announced Charley before Rachel could reply, "and we've arrived for a drink. Heavens above, Dad, what's this? Smoking a cigarette—drinking spirits—aren't you rather letting your hair down?"

"Isn't it splendid?" said Hall at once. "The human face of the episcopacy!" And to his daughter he added: "Drink up, my love, and then we must go."

When I was standing by the open front door five minutes later I said to him: "I'll be in touch with you about St. Paul's."

I saw him hesitate, glancing past me to Charley and Rachel who were already standing in the drive beside his Volkswagen. Satisfied that they were too busy talking to listen to another conversation he thanked me and added: "You'll go back to Father Darrow as soon as possible?"

"Of course. I'm not a complete fool."

"Forgive me, I—"

"There's no need to apologise."

We parted. The red tail-lights of the Volkswagen vanished beyond the gateposts. Moving abruptly away from the threshold I returned to the drawing-room, and in order to face my final bout of pastoral care from Charley that day I mixed myself a second brandy-and-soda.

2

AS SOON as Charley joined me he said concerned: "Are you all right?"

"No, but it doesn't matter," I said, trying to imply as tactfully as possible that I was not in the mood to be cross-questioned, and added in an attempt to change the subject: "What did you think of that girl?"

Charley's expression of concern at once changed to one of lofty indifference. "Very young and unformed!" he said grandly. "A nice child who would have been more at ease in a gym-slip."

"She seemed to like you."

"Oh, I hardly think so!" exclaimed Charley, much alarmed by the possibility that an obtainable girl might find him attractive.

I find it hard to describe what happened next. I can only say that I felt as if a part of my mind had snapped under pressure, and it was the part of my mind which controlled my behaviour towards Charley. I had never before realised this part existed. I only became aware of the separate control-system when it finally ceased to function.

Having drained my glass of brandy-and-soda I swung round so suddenly on Charley that he jumped.

"You fool!" I shouted with a passion which shocked me just as much as it shocked him. "You're wasting your youth—*wasting* it—because you've got it into your head that being priggish makes you a good Christian! How are you ever going to be a mature priest unless you know what love is all about? How *can* you be a mature priest when you persist in treating women as a source of danger and contamination? God knows, I had to be chaste too when I was your age, but at least I knew what I was missing and at least I was moving heaven and earth to find a girl to marry! You're not moving heaven and earth to get anything except a prize for arrested development!"

Charley looked both stunned and appalled. I saw the colour drain from his face.

"For God's sake," I said, "go out into the world and *live*—and when I say live I mean *love,* because it's love that matters, it's love that's at the heart of Christianity, it's love that's the absolute truth of all absolute truths, not fear, repression and self-hatred!"

Charley was more appalled than ever. "But Dad, you're talking like Bishop Robinson—you're regurgitating all that rubbish he wrote in *Honest to God*—you're talking like all those liberal-radicals you despise!"

"Well, why not? Aren't we all groping after truth, all of us in our different ways? And if we all begin to sound alike, doesn't that mean the truth is getting closer and all its facets are finally becoming one?"

"But what about morality? What about all the dangers of fornication and adultery? What about all the rules one has to follow in order to live decently?"

"Slavishly sticking to the letter of the law can result in a distortion of justice. 'The letter killeth,' " I said, " 'but the Spirit giveth life.' "

"But we've got to have moral laws!"

"I'm not saying that we shouldn't. I'm merely pointing out that if you get too obsessed by the laws you wind up worshipping them—and that's not only idolatry but the destruction of the very things that the laws are trying to preserve!"

"But Dad, what does all this mean in practice? Are you saying I should run out and jump into bed with someone? Are you saying that *Michael's got it right after all?"*

"No, Charley," I said, removing the stopper from the decanter and pouring myself a measure of neat brandy, "I'm not saying Michael's got it right after all."

"Thank goodness for that! You had me worried for a moment, but obviously you're all churned up and unable to express yourself clearly. By the way, talking of Michael—"

"I don't want to talk of Michael."

"But I really ought to tell you that I'm seriously concerned about him. I've been waiting for the right moment to say this, and now that the subject of fornication's come up—"

I took a large mouthful of brandy.

"—this is obviously the time to inform you that Michael's carrying on with two women at once again—which wouldn't matter so much if they were just tarts like Dinkie, but Holly's a nice girl, even though she shares a flat with that frightful Marina Markhampton, and I just think it's the height of immorality to show the keenest interest in a nice girl while simultaneously messing around with yet another slut—who's called Nadia, I heard about her the other day from—"

I heard myself say in a polite voice: "Be quiet." I was keeping my gaze fixed on the silver salver which stood on the sideboard. I was particularly fond of that salver. I had won it long ago in a golf tournament despite intense competition.

"Okay, I won't say any more now when you're all churned up, but I do think Michael's behaviour is very, very sordid."

"Not half so sordid as your disgusting compulsion to play the sneak!"

"But Dad—"

"Shut up!" I shouted, finally losing all control over myself. "Shut up, you bloody little bastard, *shut up!"* And I slammed my empty glass down upon the salver.

There followed a long silence during which I leaned against the sideboard and squeezed my eyes shut as I struggled to regain my self-control. When I finally looked around I saw Charley had gone. So silently had he crept away that I was almost tempted to think the entire disastrous scene had been a hallucination, but I knew he had been there.

Horror hit me. Sanity slunk back, cringing like a loyal servant who had turned traitor and lived to regret it. I rushed into the hall.

"Charley!" I yelled, demented with remorse, and although there was no reply I saw the light was on in the kitchen.

I found him seated, crying quietly, at the table. Blundering against it in my haste to reach him, I sank down in the chair by his side.

"I didn't mean that," said my voice. "I swear I didn't mean what I said, didn't mean it—" But he barely heard me.

"If you don't like the way I am," he said, tears still streaming down his face, "you've only yourself to blame. After all, I've always tried to be just like you."

Then indeed I was utterly silenced, shocked beyond measure, for now I saw not Charley, not even Samson, but myself, in the cold hard glare of truth.

3

I SAID: "I've gone very wrong somewhere." But I found I was unable to explore this statement. I could only say helplessly: "Forgive me," and as I spoke I remembered how Jon had said "Forgive" on the night of Lyle's death. I remembered too how I had thought this response was typical of a hermit who lived apart from the world and did not have to battle away against sinners as I did. Yet now I was the one in need of forgiveness.

"It wasn't your fault," said Charley. Finding a handkerchief at last he blew his nose and wiped his eyes. "It was my fault for making you so angry. I'm sorry I'm a disappointment to you. I worry so much about letting you down and not being the kind of reward a hero like you deserves."

Utter horror enveloped me but I fought it off. Being horrified was an unpardonable self-indulgence in such circumstances and no use to Charley at all. Summoning every ounce of my strength I said very firmly in the clearest possible voice: "Charley, your mission in life is not to be a cardboard figure labelled CHARLES ASHWORTH'S REWARD. Your mission in life is to serve God by becoming the man he designed you to be."

There was a silence. I allowed it to lengthen but Charley, staring down at the table, did not reply.

At last I said: "And you're not a disappointment to me. I'm convinced you have the potential to be a first-class priest and I'm very proud of you."

Another baffling silence ensued.

"Charley?"

He roused himself. "Yes?"

"Do you hear what I'm saying?"

"Yes, but we won't talk about it any more, it makes you too upset. Let's draw a veil over this entire conversation and pretend it never happened."

Now I was the one who was unable to speak. I was appalled by my complete failure to communicate with him.

"I feel so guilty that I made you so upset," he was saying in a rush, "and now I just want to do all I can to make it up to you. Look, why don't you come to London with me tomorrow—why don't you take a day off and get right away from the diocese? I promise I'll give you the most wonderful time!"

"How very kind." I was still so shattered that I hardly knew what I was saying.

"Oh Dad, don't say no! You'd really enjoy the sermon I'm going to give at Matins—it's modelled on one of your Bampton lectures, the one about Athanasius. I talk about the importance of standing up for one's beliefs even if they happen to be deeply unfashionable—and then I tie this theme in with the 1930s and the task of opposing Hitler—and then I go on to the 1960s . . ."

I ceased to listen. I was seeing more clearly than ever that although he had heard my words earlier they had held no meaning for him. He was still trying to cast himself in my image, still trying to be Charles Ashworth's reward, as if there was no other course he dared to take.

". . . and then afterwards I can give you lunch at the flat, and then after that—"

"Charley, I'd love to come, of course I would, but—"

"I know you want to see Father Darrow, but surely he can wait till Monday! If you could only hear my sermon, you'd feel so pleased and proud—"

I gave in. Of course I gave in. I felt too guilty about my loss of control, too driven by the compulsion to make him happy, to do anything else. I consoled myself by thinking that since I had waited so long to see Jon, waiting another day would hardly make any difference to my spiritual health.

But I was wrong.

4

CHARLEY HAD come down to Starbridge by train, but he decided I might enjoy the drive up to town so we departed the next morning in my car. Unfortunately I was a nervous passenger when either of my sons was driving, but although I offered to take the wheel Charley insisted on acting as my chauffeur. I felt relieved that as it was early on a Sunday morning, the traffic was light and the strain on my nerves was minimal.

Since I was having a day off, far from the diocese, I had abandoned my uniform and was wearing a dark suit with a white shirt and a Carlton Club tie. This sartorial retreat into anonymity proved soothing, and as we approached the suburbs of London I thought how pleasant it would be to walk down a street without attracting the stares of the passers-by. I had even left my pectoral cross behind in my bedroom. Jon would no doubt have recommended that a smaller cross should be worn beneath my shirt, but I belonged to a generation which regarded the wearing of a cross as Romish and even now I tended to think of it as merely part of my uniform. I knew Jon insisted that a cross repelled demons, but that was just his old-fashioned way of saying that by reminding its wearer of Christ a pectoral cross was an aid in promoting Christian behaviour. To invest a piece of metal with miraculous powers is to flirt with superstition—and with the error of mistaking a symbol for the reality to which it points. Besides, a bishop hardly needs to adorn himself with a cross in order to remember his obligation to behave properly.

I was just indulging in these brisk, sensible thoughts and reflecting that several hours of deep sleep had wrought a miraculous improvement in my health when Charley yelped: "Jumping Jehoshaphat!" and nearly drove through a red light.

"What on earth's the matter?"

"I've just remembered I'm supposed to be having lunch with the Welbecks and I can't possibly cancel it—they've recently given two thousand pounds to the Church Roof Fund! I'm so sorry, Dad—I was really looking forward to our lunch at the flat—"

"Never mind," I said, taking care to look acutely disappointed. "I'll get a sandwich somewhere, take a walk in the park and return to your flat for tea." And when I saw that the promise of tea cheered him up, I tried to cheer him still further by adding: "You did quite right to persuade me to have a day out! I'm already feeling much better and I can't wait to hear this sermon of yours."

The sermon was indeed excellent and reminded me of my Bampton lectures which I had so greatly enjoyed composing. This memory in turn made me think of my unfinished book. If I could only take a month off to do some writing . . . I began to dream of a miniature sabbatical which would miraculously restore me to an even keel.

There was a Communion service directly after Matins, but I decided not to attend it; I wanted to make my confession to Jon before I took the sacrament again, so after repeating my promise to Charley that I would return to his flat for tea, I left the church, ignored my parked car and began to stroll downhill through Mayfair. The sun was shining and I knew the exercise would do me no harm.

I had just reached the Connaught Hotel in Carlos Place and was trying to remember how long it had been since I had lunched there when I remembered that other, very exclusive, very English hotel in Albemarle Street, now only a stone's throw away. Or perhaps I should say that I allowed myself to remember it. Of course I could not have forgotten entirely that Loretta was staying there, but since I had made up my mind not to see her again I had until that moment suppressed all thought of her hotel.

I skirted Berkeley Square and decided not to go down Albermarle Street but to take the parallel Dover Street instead. I supposed I had forgotten—or had I?—that Brown's had a Dover Street entrance. The next moment I had halted outside it.

I glanced at my watch. It was only quarter past twelve but I was sure that Loretta, having inevitably been invited somewhere for Sunday lunch, would have already left the hotel. Still loitering on the pavement I toyed with the idea of leaving her a note to say how much I had enjoyed meeting her and how I hoped one day to hear more about her journey towards Christianity. This plan struck me as being perfectly safe and well within the bounds of propriety. I entered Brown's.

The porter directed me to a desk where I could write the note, and after I had given him the sealed envelope I prepared to leave by the Albemarle Street entrance. Then it occurred to me that there would really be nothing improper and very little that was unsafe in drinking a quick Tio Pepe with Loretta. In my acute anxiety to do nothing foolish I was being over-cautious and even, possibly, neurotic.

I returned to the porter. "I'm almost sure Professor Staviski's out," I said, "but could you try her room for me?"

The porter said encouragingly that she had not turned in her key, but when he telephoned the room there was no reply.

I decided that she was out, that this was all for the best and that I could be quite happy drinking Tio Pepe on my own.

I did take a look at the dining-room as I moved past the open door, but it was too early for anyone to be lunching. Drifting on through the quiet, old-fashioned, sparsely populated reception rooms I finally reached the bar.

The first person I saw as I crossed the threshold was Loretta.

She was drinking a very sparkling, very stylish champagne cocktail.

5

AFTER WE had recovered from the shock of seeing each other I realised with relief that there was a large, loquacious group of some six people in another corner of the room and that their noise would guarantee us a certain degree of privacy. Having grasped this important detail I then had the chance to note that Loretta herself, no doubt in deference to a London Sunday, had left the pink trouser-suit in her wardrobe and was wearing a jacket and skirt, both cherry-red, with a frilly black blouse. When she stood up to greet me I was interested to see that the skirt barely covered her knees, and when she sat down again, crossing her legs, the hem of her skirt rose to daring heights. She wore black stockings, a fashion which seemed to have returned after a long absence, and very high-heeled black shoes which drew attention to her excellent ankles. Lyle would have approved. She had always hated what she called "old ladies' footwear" and had worn youthful shoes until the bones of her feet had finally rebelled six months ago. I wondered how Loretta's bones were faring, but it was hard to remember that she was older than Lyle. Immaculately groomed and effortlessly smart she appeared, in our dim, secluded corner of the bar, to be no older than forty-nine.

"You look quite wonderful," I said. "Do you dress up like this every day?"

"I could hardly go moseying around London in my muu-muu!"

"What's a muu-muu?"

She laughed. A waiter arrived to ask what I wanted to drink, and suddenly a Tio Pepe seemed a symbol of everything I had temporarily escaped: the agonies of the bishopric, the agonies of parenthood, the agonies of life at the South Canonry without Lyle.

Turning to the waiter I said impulsively: "Bring me a champagne cocktail."

6

LORETTA SAID: "I thought you'd be pussy-footing around in purple this morning!"

"I'm still officially incapacitated." I explained my presence in Mayfair before demanding: "Why aren't you visiting friends for Sunday lunch?"

"What friends? Apart from Enid Markhampton in Starbridge my friends from before the war are either dead, like Evelyn, or senile, like poor Sybil Welbeck. Incidentally, talking of Enid and my visit with her, what did you make of that Bacchanalian orgy at the Deanery?"

"I was in such a state of shock that I barely remember it."

We both laughed before she exclaimed: "You were wonderful, Charles—so debonair!"

"I only hope that dreadful Dido didn't suspect anything!"

"Oh, don't you like her? I thought she was adorable, a real British eccentric! And *he* was adorable too, so cute and cuddly—"

"I'll never understand what women see in that man."

"You think all men have to look as gorgeous as you before they qualify for a sex-appeal rating?"

"I'm sure that at present I look about as gorgeous as Methuselah on the day he finally died! I feel like knocking on the door of the nearest old people's home and begging for admittance."

"Well, don't be surprised if all the old gals fight to push your wheelchair."

The waiter arrived with my champagne cocktail.

"Put that on my check," said Loretta to him.

"No, no, I can't have that!" I exclaimed scandalised. "I couldn't possibly let a lady pay for my drink!"

"Oh Charles, Charles, surely you haven't turned into one of those hidebound old-timers who think all women should be kept in the kitchen along with the stove, the ironing board and the washing machine—"

"I'm not laying down the law about how a lady should be treated at home! All I'm saying is that when a lady's in the bar of Brown's in the company of an English gentleman, it's unthinkable that she should pay for his drink!"

"Then maybe it's time you had fun thinking the unthinkable," said Loretta amused, and added kindly: "Relax—lie back and comb your mane, Mr. English Lion! Miss American Eagle's winged in to take care of you . . ."

7

"I ALMOST visited St. Mary's myself this morning," said Loretta later, "but then I decided I could do without that particular trip down memory lane, so I looked in on the Grosvenor Chapel instead to salute the shade of Rose Macaulay . . . And talking of memory lane, do we refer to 1937? Or do we just preserve a discreet silence?"

"Wouldn't that be taking discretion to unnecessarily heroic lengths?"

"I'm used to being heroically discreet where you're concerned. The only person I ever told about our meeting was my analyst and he's dead now."

"I only told my spiritual director."

"What about Lyle?"

"Lyle . . ." I hesitated as I recalled the events of 1937. Then I said simply: "Yes, she knew."

"What a pity! If I'd been in your shoes I wouldn't have told her—I'm always suspicious of married couples who tell each other everything, but no doubt that's because my sadist of a husband made a habit of telling me every detail of his homosexual affairs."

"You never remarried?"

"Never. Once was more than enough, as I'm sure I told you."

"But you were never tempted to change your mind?"

"Oh, I did toy with the idea of remarrying, yes, I did, but I had my career, and marriage is really a very dispensable institution when one's middle-aged and professionally successful."

"I never found it dispensable!"

"Of course not, you're a man. I'm talking about women, and middle age is the time when most women finally have the opportunity not only to find out who they are but to do something about it."

"I don't remember you being such a feminist!"

"What do you mean—'such a feminist'! I'm just interested in women having the chance to develop spiritually by getting to know themselves as people other than wives, mothers and daughters. You're a priest—aren't you interested in the spiritual development of half the human race?"

"Of course, but—"

"And I'm interested in justice too. How would you like to be treated as second-rate just because you'd latched on to the wrong bundle of ingredients at your conception?"

"Surely a feminist should insist that it was the right bundle!"

"Oh, I don't want to convert you to feminism too quickly—you might panic and make a new attempt to pay the bill! But forget feminism for the moment and answer me this: am I allowed to ask what happened at the end, back in 1937? You never told me, did you? You promised to write, but you never did."

"I'm sorry. I felt—"

"—that some angles of the story just couldn't be committed to paper?"

"I'm afraid so. And perhaps too I thought that my silence would say all there was to say . . . Is it too late to thank you for having the strength of mind not to get in touch with me to satisfy your curiosity?"

"That was no strength of mind, that was just sheer mixed-up emotions and general cowardice. As soon as Evelyn wrote and told me you were married, I knew I couldn't handle seeing you again, Charles. You'd made too big an impact on me."

"I'm sorry—I think I knew even at the time that our meeting was a disaster for you—"

"No, it wasn't."

"—and bearing that in mind, I can't begin to understand how I helped you find a Christian faith! How could I possibly have achieved such a feat by behaving like a clergyman who deserved to be defrocked?"

"Let's make a deal," she said amused. "You tell me what finally happened in Starbridge in 1937, and I'll tell you how a roll in the hay—or in this case the heather—resulted in my conversion."

"Surely it was bracken? I seem to remember—"

"Whatever it was, it wasn't half as comfortable as D. H. Lawrence would have us all believe. How about another round of champagne cocktails?"

Without hesitation I raised my hand to attract the waiter.

8

I DID not tell her everything. I never disclosed that Charley was not my biological son. But I did tell her how I had come to marry Lyle and what had happened to the people who had been involved with us in 1937. By the time I had finished, Loretta and I were sitting in the dining-room, lunch had been ordered and I had made it clear who was paying the bill. It never occurred to me not to suggest that we lunch together. The time was past one, I was hungry and I had yet to hear the story of her conversion.

". . . and there you were," Loretta was saying, having embarked on her narrative, "wholly committed to this religion which I'd long since dismissed as a bunch of unsatisfactory myths for misfits, morons and menopausal women—"

I said horrified: "But you never told me you regarded Christianity in that light!"

"Well, I wouldn't, would I? Give me credit for a little tact!"

"So you were really an atheist and not just a vague theist?"

"More or less, yes. Anyhow, there you were—"

"There I was, a priest, rolling around in the bracken—"

"Heather."

"—and behaving like a participant in some pagan fertility rite—surely you must have felt more contemptuous of Christianity than ever?"

"Well, of course I realised that you didn't normally make a habit of seducing casual acquaintances! It was obvious to me too in retrospect that you were all mixed up and barely responsible for your actions."

"But even so—"

"There were two facts which fascinated me. First, you were sexually normal; that meant I couldn't write you off as someone who was using religion to compensate for an abnormal sexuality. And second, you were a clever man who found Christianity intellectually satisfying, and that meant I couldn't write you off as someone whose belief involved putting his intellect on ice while he satisfied some emotional need. Now—as I told you in 1937—you weren't the first priest I'd met who was sexually normal and intellectually smart. I'd put that other priest out of my mind and rejected his God, but when I met a second priest who was like that—"

"You began to wonder if God was trying to tell you something."

"I certainly began to wonder if there was something about Christianity I'd missed. So I took a look at it again—and when I tried to be as detached and scholarly as possible, I was astonished that earlier I'd dismissed two thousand years of accumulated wisdom about the most vital issues of life without bothering to study even one aspect of that wisdom properly."

"It's a very common syndrome. Far too many people ignore the intellectual side of Christianity."

"Yet there's no need to have a high IQ to be converted, is there? I certainly preferred to take an intellectual approach because I'm the way I am, but there are other approaches and I could have been converted even if I'd been a peroxide blonde with the brains of a louse. I saw eventually that a good religion resembles a language—it can be spoken by adults and children alike, by the uneducated and the educated, the geniuses and the morons, and like all languages it's powered by metaphor, symbol and analogy . . . Do you remember spinning me that analogy about how plants respond to sunlight?"

"No."

"I must say, Charles, I don't think your memory's nearly so good as mine!"

"But what did I say?"

"Never mind. The point was that I thought: how powerful an analogy can be! And once I'd started thinking of religion as a language which expresses truths so complex and profound that they lie beyond the boundaries drawn by the logical positivists, I was hooked. I started reading in order to acquire the basic skills in this new language, and eventually I found that in order to gain fluency I needed to go to a place where the language was regularly spoken."

"And church-going's made you fluent?"

"I'm still working on it. Parts of my grammar are still pretty unorthodox."

"Which parts?"

"Oh, the sex-parts, of course . . . My, look at this smoked salmon! Doesn't that look delicious?"

I agreed that it did. After the waiter had performed the ritual with the pepper-pot I said: "Are you sure I can't offer you more to drink?"

"Not if you want me to discuss sex intelligently. Didn't we eat smoked salmon at that lunch in 1937?"

"Yes, we did. And I remember ordering a very good white Burgundy—"

"Pouilly-Fuissé, wasn't it?"

"Chablis."

"Are you sure?"

"No. Tell me more about your unorthodox grammar."

"Well, I hesitate to say this to a bishop whose sobriquet is 'Anti-Sex Ashworth,' but I think there are worse sins than fornication. Cruelty, for example."

"Fornication often coexists with cruelty—or leads to it."

"And when it doesn't?"

"Then we start to talk about the exploitation of others and the devaluation of the self—which is in fact just a more subtle form of cruelty. It results in the maiming of people psychologically, making it harder, if not impossible, for them to reach their potential and find fulfilment."

"I agree that promiscuity can only be ultimately demeaning, particularly for women," said Loretta. "I'm sure any mature human being would say that. But if you have a loving relationship which involves mutual respect—"

"Why not make the commitment of marriage? Oh, of course marriage can be perverted and debased, just like any other institution, but at least when it's undertaken in the right spirit it's rooted in reality, and at least it represents an ideal of commitment. Liaisons are usually rooted in self-deception and seldom represent anything but an all-consuming self-centredness."

"Okay, I concede we all need ideals to aspire to, and okay, I concede liaisons can mask countless unpalatable realities, but what about those times when the liaisons are reflecting a reality that's very palatable indeed? Take you and me, for instance. We're instantly compatible. That was obvious in 1937, and it's just as obvious now as it was then. That's not only something real; it's something good. So when we made love, the sex wasn't just a casual exploitation but an expression of genuine feeling."

"Rubbish."

"Charles!"

"I'm sorry, but it's not true! You're looking back through rose-tinted spectacles—and perhaps that's necessary for you, perhaps that's your way of coming to terms with a painful experience, perhaps I should say no more."

"But Charles, there was this tremendous chemistry between us and we both benefited from it!"

"In what way? The truth is that I used you, very selfishly, to keep my problems at bay."

"Okay, you used me. But I loved it! I was lonely and wanted someone—"

"Exactly. I used you and you used me too—it was a mutual exploitation which proved harmful to both of us. It was harmful to me because I betrayed the vows I'd made at my ordination and increased the self-disgust which led to my complete spiritual breakdown. And it was harmful to you—as I sensed when I walked away—because I only increased your loneliness and reinforced the dread, which your husband had fostered, that men always let you down and didn't deserve any long-term commitment. Isn't that dread the real reason why you've never remarried?"

"Okay," she said, "you win. But only up to a point. There was exploitation on both sides, but there was also something else going on—and if that something else hadn't been going on we wouldn't be sitting here now, enjoying each other's company and effortlessly picking up the threads of our acquaintance after a twenty-eight-year interval. I agree I may be looking back through rose-tinted spectacles at our roll in the heather—"

"Bracken."

"—but the fact remains that it was a turning-point in my life and much good came out of it . . . By the way, I think you were right about the wine back in 1937. It *was* a Chablis."

"Of course it was! The perfect accompaniment for our grilled trout!"

"Grilled trout? But it was grilled sole!"

We began to laugh. We laughed so much that in the end Loretta got hiccoughs and I had to order half a bottle of Chablis to aid our digestions.

I was unable to remember when I had last enjoyed myself so much.

9

BY THE time we had reviewed our lives since 1937, reminisced about all the major events from Munich to the Kennedy assassination and exchanged fascinating information about the books we had written, the dregs were cold in our coffee-cups, and around us in the largest of the panelled reception rooms the waiters were beginning to serve tea.

"If I eat any more before nine o'clock tomorrow morning," said Loretta when I drew her attention to the availability of another meal, "I shall be unable to wear anything but my muu-muu."

"I'm becoming increasingly intrigued by this mysterious garment!"

"And I'm becoming increasingly keen to show it to you! Come upstairs and have a scotch—I've got a bottle of Chivas Regal stashed in my wardrobe alongside the muu-muu."

At once I knew any hesitation would be disastrous so I said lightly: "How very stylish! But I must keep a clear head for the journey home." As I spoke I was glancing around at the waiters, flitting from armchair to armchair with their cakestands and trays, and suddenly the softly lit room seemed so warm, so comfortable, so luxurious that I shuddered at the thought of the long journey through the dark to my deserted house.

Beside me Loretta murmured: "It's okay. No one's recognised you."

"I'm afraid I have to behave as a bishop whether anyone recognises me or not," I said automatically, but I continued to recoil from the prospect of returning home.

There was a pause while Loretta stubbed out her cigarette but finally she said: "I'm sorry. I should have realised you'd still be much too bound up with Lyle to be in the mood for anything but a light-hearted lunch, but I know from past experience that sometimes when one's feeling very lonely, the company of an old friend—"

I knew I had to interrupt her. "It's got nothing to do with Lyle," I said abruptly, but this sounded unnatural, even callous, as if I had already thrust Lyle entirely from my mind. Struggling to express myself better I added: "Lyle's sealed off, rather as she was when I met you in 1937. It's not that she's unimportant. It's just that she's unobtainable."

"Well, if we're rerunning 1937—"

"We can't. But that's not because of Lyle. It's because of you."

"I guess you're trying to say as tactfully as possible that you don't fancy mutton dressed up as lamb."

"You couldn't be more wrong. I'm trying to say that although I used you in 1937, I can't use you like that again. Do you really want me to prove myself a complete and utter hypocrite?"

"Okay, let's call it a day."

"The truth is that after speaking so strongly against the abuse of sex—and the abuse of women—"

"I know. Don't worry. I understand."

"—I can't act in any other way, I've got no choice, I'm not a mixed-up young priest any more, I'm a bishop—a *bishop*—and there'd be no excuse for such abject clerical failure this time, it wouldn't just be disgraceful, it would be absolutely unforgivable—"

"Charles." She leaned forward and briefly put her hand over mine. "It's okay," she said in the gentlest of voices. "I accept your decision and respect you for it. It's okay."

Pulling myself together I said: "I'm sorry."

"And there's no need to apologise either." Rising to her feet she added lightly: "Why do the British say 'sorry' so often?"

"Tradition." I tried to speak equally lightly and failed.

"And why do the British always use 'tradition' to excuse their more irrational activities? No, don't answer that, I'm in no mood for a debate about culture . . . Thanks for the lunch, Charles."

"Thanks for the champagne cocktails." We were leaving the drawing-room now, leaving the warmth and the soft lights and the waiters with the silver cakestands, and as we stepped into the hall I could see beyond the main entrance the grey light of that dying afternoon.

". . . and let me wish you luck again with your book," Loretta was saying. "Will you send me a British copy so that I can meet the sexually lax Bishop Callistus before he appears in print in New York?" And as she smiled she passed me one of those calling-cards which have never gone out of fashion in America.

I stared down at the card but was too distracted to read the address. I could only say: "Will you send me your book on Rochester?"

"The sexually lax John Wilmot? Of course!"

She was still smiling at me but I knew I could risk no kiss; I did not even dare to risk clasping her hand. Slipping her card into the inside pocket of my jacket I said rapidly: "I'm glad we met again. Look after yourself." And then leaving the hotel I proceeded to walk at high speed into the deepest possible trouble.

XIV

". . . the will is pushed around by passion and instinct, and where it lands us is too obvious for me to need to mention."

AUSTIN FARRER
Warden of Keble College, Oxford, 1960–1968
SAID OR SUNG

I

I WAS so disturbed that I forgot I had promised Charley to return to his flat. I moved down Albemarle Street to Piccadilly, and it was only when I looked at the clock above the entrance to Fortnum's that I remembered him. But I did not turn back. I was afraid to retrace my steps through Mayfair in case my resolve weakened and I returned to the hotel. Heading west along Piccadilly to the underground station at Green Park I found a telephone kiosk, shut myself inside and dialled Charley's number.

"Look, don't wait around for me," I said. "I've got delayed and I'm not sure when I'll be back to pick up my car."

"What's happened?"

"I met an old friend for a long lunch and now I need some exercise in the park."

"Are you just making an excuse because you want to see Michael?"

"No." I hung up, unable to face further questions in this vein, and reflected how utterly I had failed to solve Charley's problems.

The twilight was deepening as I stepped back into the street but I now felt it was essential to go for a brisk walk to clear my head before I embarked on the journey home, and I calculated that I could walk across Green Park to Buckingham Palace and back before the light had entirely faded. Turning my back on the noisy streams of traffic I plunged into the oasis of trees and grass between Piccadilly and Constitution Hill.

In the grand buildings south of the Ritz some of the windows were already lighted squares, but in the park the Victorian lamps were not yet glowing. Walking beneath the bare trees I heard the noise of the traffic fade to a muffled roar and I became aware of the stillness, the bleakness, the chill of that winter afternoon. There were few people about. I walked at a fast pace, partly because I needed to keep warm and partly because I was anxious to expend energy to ease my tension, but once I had adjusted to the coldness of the air I found myself moving more slowly. Simultaneously my thoughts, as if thawing from some frozen state, began to quicken. I was thinking of the final moments of my conversation with Loretta when I had referred to Lyle being "sealed off." What had I meant? I had spoken as if Lyle could at some future moment be "unsealed"—recovered, reclaimed, rejoined. I had certainly "unsealed" her in 1937. But this was 1965, and no matter how often and how obstinately I sat in her sitting-room at the South Canonry and recalled her in my imagination in order to ward off the reality of her death, the fact remained that I would never recover or reclaim or rejoin her in this world again.

By the time I reached the other side of the Park and saw the bulk of the palace beyond the trees, I felt so upset that I did not turn to begin the journey back to my car but walked on, crossing the bottom of Constitution Hill, skirting the palace railings and heading, like a rudderless ship, towards Victoria. I had realised that the disturbing end to my meeting with Loretta had exposed to me how futile it was to continue the fight against acknowledging Lyle's permanent absence. What I had wanted, at Brown's Hotel, with Loretta, Lyle could no longer give me. She was not merely "sealed off," that convenient fiction which enabled me to survive the full blast of bereavement. She was dead. She was gone. She was lost beyond recall.

I rubbed my eyes as I struggled to endure the pain of this reality, and when I opened them again I saw I was standing on the corner of Grosvenor Gardens while away to my left, ablaze with lights and encircled by streams of roaring traffic, stood the massive facade of Victoria station.

I wandered over, acting as instinctively as a moth drawn to a flame. I felt I was beyond everything now except grief. I kept saying: "Lyle, Lyle, Lyle . . . ," and as I stared around at last some unknown time later I realised that I was not only mentally and spiritually lost but physically lost as well. What had happened to the station? It seemed to have dissolved into a network of shabby streets. Profoundly confused I moved on into unknown territory.

A minute later I found myself in a red-light district crammed with seedy hotels. Unsavoury people loitered, and as I paused to make a fresh attempt to get my bearings I was accosted by a prostitute. I moved on, but almost at once stopped dead with horror. It had dawned on me that a prostitute was in fact exactly what I wanted at that moment: complete anonymity, a temporary escape from unbearable pain and no possibility of apocalyptic consequences.

I was so appalled by this insight that I nearly walked under the wheels of a car. A blaring horn, the screech of brakes and a string of bawled obscenities shocked me into redoubling my efforts to escape from this labyrinth. This was quite definitely not an area where a bishop could afford to be run over. For a quick, queasy second I thought of the man who might have been Desmond Wilton, glimpsed at Piccadilly Circus on a Saturday night. Then I pushed that chilling image aside and applied myself single-mindedly to the task of survival.

I was standing at a minor junction, and when I peered up at the street signs I saw that Wilton Road—a malign coincidence, reminding me again of spiritually debilitated priests—was intersecting with Warwick Way. Surely Warwick Way was one of the main thoroughfares of Pimlico? It was unfortunate that my knowledge of Pimlico was so skimpy. I looked around for an underground station but saw none. There was no sign of a taxi either, and although a bus passed, its number was unfamiliar. Another prostitute accosted me. I moved on at once, stumbling to the right into Warwick Way, but the whole street seemed to be crawling with seaminess and in haste I took a left turn into the Pimlico grid.

The grid was a network of streets designed by Thomas Cubitt over a hundred years before when London was expanding beyond the marshes of Westminster. In abrupt contrast to the sleazy life of Warwick Way, this area was quiet, semi-dead, bowed down with the effort of preserving its decayed respectability, and within two minutes I found myself in a not unpleasant environment where rows of stucco-fronted houses, some smartly painted and even dignified, bordered a long, straight, empty street. Again I wondered where I was, and at the next intersection I found out. The sign on the corner read GUERNSEY STREET, and at once a memory stirred in my mind. I knew that recently I had been introduced on paper to that Pimlico road which bore the same name as one of the Channel Islands, and the next moment I was recalling the letter from Sheila Preston, the widow of the late Bishop of Radbury.

With enormous relief I realised I was near a safe haven. I could have a cup of tea with a good, decent woman, we could talk about such easy subjects as the Old Days and Mutual Friends, and for a precious hour sexual intercourse would be no more than an esoteric activity performed by savages in a distant corner of the globe—or in other words, I would have the chance to regain, in soothing, asexual surroundings, my shattered equilibrium.

My one remaining problem, I realised as I embraced this vision with the enthusiasm of a drowning man clasping a life-belt, was that I could not quite remember the full address and Guernsey Street was very long. Leaning against the railings of the nearest house I made a mighty effort and flexed my memory, not as remarkable now as it had been in my youth but still capable in an emergency of a photographic recall. This was without doubt an emergency. Fiercely I concentrated on visualising the address, printed on the top right-hand corner of Sheila's writing-paper. But the number of the house remained indecipherable.

Walking down the street I eyed the number of each house to see if my memory would twitch at the sight of the number I was trying to recall, and when I reached thirty-seven I halted. I had been thirty-seven when I had married Lyle, twenty-seven when I had married Jane—and twenty-seven was the right number; I knew that now, just as I knew that thirty-seven was the wrong one. Backtracking rapidly I reached an identical house, large and well-kept, which had been divided into flats. By the flame of my cigarette-lighter I examined the list of names by the doorbells in the porch, but there was no card marked PRESTON. Then I realised that there was a basement flat, approachable from the outside by steps. Leaving the porch I opened the gate set in the railings and descended to the front door. The name by the bell was Preston. Even more welcome was the evidence that someone was at home. Although the curtains were drawn across the window which faced the basement steps, I could hear the strains of music in the room beyond. Weak with relief I rang the bell and waited to be rescued.

The outside light was switched on. The door opened with caution but swung wide as I was recognised.

"Charles!" said Sheila amazed. "But how extraordinary—come in!"

I crossed the threshold into my sanctuary.

2

SHEILA WAS one of those women who always look exactly right for every social occasion and always look exactly right in the most tastefully unobtrusive way. She was of average height and still managing, I noted, to repel the advances of the dreaded "middle-aged spread." Indeed she looked thinner than when I had last seen her at her husband's funeral eighteen months ago. I was unsure how old she was, but I had been some years Derek's senior and I thought it probable that his wife had been some years his junior. That made her about fifty. She had dark hair flecked with silver, dark eyes and a good skin, pale and smooth. Although not pretty she was undeniably pleasant to look at because nothing was permitted to jar the eye. She was wearing a dark skirt with a beige twinset. Her nylons were just the right shade of brown. The heels of her shoes were neither too low nor too high. She wore no jewellery, only her wedding ring. Even though she had not been expecting a visitor she still contrived to be faultlessly presentable.

Meanwhile as I absorbed all these soothing details I was making a series of somewhat disconnected comments to explain my arrival on the scene and she was murmuring exactly the right courteous phrases in reply.

". . . up in London unexpectedly . . . lunch with an old friend . . . fancied a walk afterwards before driving home . . . do forgive me for not telephoning first . . . if this is in any way inconvenient—"

"No, not at all. What a pleasant surprise!" said Sheila agreeably, leading us out of the cramped hall into a room arranged with such care that the furniture seemed to occupy the floor-space in a pattern geometric in its precision. Yet the effect was not unpleasing. The atmosphere of rigorous order, tempered by the soft colours of the upholstery and curtains and by the polished wood of the antique bookcases, was both restful and satisfying. On the far side of the room at the back of the house French windows opened onto a small courtyard where ivy rambled over white walls and plants in tubs awaited the arrival of summer. There was a light on outside to illuminate this attractive sight, but as we entered the room Sheila flicked off the switch and pulled the curtains. The wireless, which I had heard on my arrival, had already been silenced.

"What a charming room!" I said, feeling the need to break the brief pause and glad that I could be sincere.

"Thank you—yes, I'm fond of it. Pimlico's a patchy area, but there are some pleasant nooks and crannies . . . Do sit down, Charles. Would you like some tea?"

I said I would.

"And do go ahead and smoke," said Sheila, noting the absence of my uniform. "I see you won't have to remove your clerical collar! I'll just get an ashtray."

I was impressed that she had remembered this foible, but the ideal episcopal wife remembers every eccentricity about the people whom she may one day be obliged to entertain. An ashtray arrived. So, eventually, did tea, complete with some neat little strawberry-jam sandwiches, shorn of their crusts and arranged daintily on a Wedgwood plate. Sitting by the electric fire in a well-sprung armchair as I was waited on hand and foot, I began to feel I had miraculously recaptured the warmth and comfort of that old-fashioned drawing-room at Brown's.

"Thank you very much for your kind letter about Lyle," I said as she poured the tea. "I would have written, of course, but when I found myself in London today it seemed a good opportunity to call and thank you in person."

"I'm glad you felt you could drop in unannounced. I regard that as a compliment."

Even Lyle would have been proud to utter this effortlessly diplomatic reply. Lyle had never been particularly friendly with Sheila but she had respected her ability to be a first-class wife for a senior churchman. "Very competent," had been Lyle's judgement. "Not frumpish, not gushing and no more churchy than is strictly necessary." This had been high praise from someone whose opinion of her own sex had tended to be low. "Not my sort of person, of course," Lyle had added, unable to resist setting her praise within certain limits. "She'd never wear black underwear. But at least she doesn't drone on and on about her offspring."

Since Derek and Sheila had had the misfortune to be childless, however, this lack of droning could hardly be cited as an example of admirable self-restraint.

". . . and how are you getting on, Charles?" Sheila was asking as I sat sipping Earl Grey tea and thinking how wonderfully better I felt, secure in my unexpected sanctuary and pampered by the ideal episcopal wife. "It must have been the most terrible shock."

"Yes, but . . ." I began to make the conventional remarks about how kind everyone had been, how sympathetic, how understanding. Sheila listened and nodded and occasionally made exactly the right comment, saying neither too much nor too little.

"And how are the boys?"

"Well, I haven't seen much of Michael—the BBC keeps him so busy—but Charley's been a great support, and . . ." I talked on with increasing ease. I suppose I was dimly aware that what I said bore little relation to reality, but after my dangerous exchanges with Loretta I found it such a relief to conduct a conversation which was not only conventional but banal.

". . . and of course I must get back to full-time work soon," I said when I had finished my third cup of tea. "I feel guilty that I've cancelled so many engagements, and now that Easter's on the horizon I feel I must take up the reins again without delay."

"But surely it would be a mistake to return to full-time work too soon! Are you worried about how your suffragan's coping?"

"No, Nigel's managing well," I said, thinking how pleasant it was to talk to a woman who knew exactly what being a bishop involved. "But one of my archdeacons is becoming a trifle magisterial."

"Archdeacons can be such a problem! We had an excellent one at Radbury in the end, but when we first went to the diocese Derek found he had inherited an archdeacon who . . ."

A horrific archidiaconal anecdote unfolded. I listened and shuddered and enjoyed it greatly.

". . . and of course all the Anglo-Catholics were up in arms—the rows over Reservation were quite dreadful," concluded Sheila serenely, and added before I could draw breath to comment: "Charles, would you like a drink?"

To my amazement I realised it was after six o'clock. "How very kind," I said, "but I think perhaps I should be on my way."

"You wouldn't like just one whisky to fortify you for your journey?"

I had a whisky. I also managed to stop being so self-centred and ask her about herself, but her life was apparently pleasant and untroubled. She had various friends in London; she attended evening classes in Italian; she dabbled with various kinds of voluntary work; she was saving up to go on a Hellenic cruise.

"I've been a guest-lecturer twice on the Hellenic cruises," I said. "I gave talks on St. Paul's journeys. Lyle and I . . ." I embarked on a series of reminiscences, but eventually I happened to glance at the clock on the chimney-piece. "Good heavens, look at the time!" I exclaimed. "I must go."

"You wouldn't like to stay to supper? I've plenty of eggs and also some fresh mushrooms—I'm sure we could have a very passable omelette."

"What a splendid idea!" I said, mellow after my whisky and all too willing to seize yet another chance to postpone my return to that empty house. "If it's not too much trouble . . ."

She assured me it was no trouble at all, offered me another whisky, which by a supreme effort of will I declined, and showed me the way to the cloakroom before withdrawing to the kitchen.

On my return from the lavatory it dawned on me that even one whisky had been unwise. So far had I relaxed that the comfortable room now seemed to enfold me in an irresistible cocoon and the whisky only increased my resulting languor. I began to feel somnolent.

I eyed the sofa. The next moment I was slipping off my shoes, loosening my tie and saying sternly to myself: five minutes. Then I adopted a horizontal position on the sofa and sank instantly into unconsciousness.

When I awoke I at first had no idea where I was. The room was in darkness but a light had been left on in the hall so that I was able to see the dim shapes of the furniture. I sat up. That was when I realised that a blanket had been tucked around me. Fighting myself free I leapt to my feet and blundered towards the door in search of a light-switch. On the way I banged into a side-table which instantly crashed to the floor, but although I winced I did not stop. The switch clicked beneath my fingers. I stared at my watch in disbelief.

The time was seven minutes past one in the morning.

3

"MY GOD!" I said aloud before my brain could substitute a more fitting exclamation. Backing away from the door I almost tripped over the fallen table. I picked it up, retrieved the objects which lived on it—a glass bowl, miraculously intact, and a silver snuff-box—and sat down in the armchair in order to tug on the shoes I had discarded. In less fraught circumstances I might have viewed the situation with a touch of black humour, but at that moment I was entirely preoccupied with framing a suitable apology to offer Sheila who, having heard the crash of the table, soon entered the room. She was wearing a long, caramel-coloured dressing-gown which concealed all but the collar of her nightdress.

"Sheila! My dear, what can I say—"

"Please don't worry—I could see you were very tired."

"But what appalling manners I've displayed! I descend on you without warning, talk almost entirely about myself and finally encourage you to make an omelette only to pass out before I can eat it! What on earth can you possibly be thinking of me?"

"I assure you it doesn't matter in the least—"

"It matters to me. I'll leave at once. My car's in Mayfair, but I'm sure I'll find an all-night taxi—"

"Oh, don't be so silly, Charles! You can't struggle over to Mayfair at this time of night and then drive all the way back to Starbridge! Look, the sofa opens out into a bed. Let me make it up so that you can spend the rest of the night in comfort. Would you like a bath? Or tea?"

"Yes."

"Which?"

"I don't know. Sheila, it's most kind of you, but—"

"Don't worry, I'm not about to have hysterics just because I'm alone with a stranded bishop at a scandalous hour! You go and have a bath while I make the tea."

"I just don't know what to say—"

" 'Very well' is the answer you require."

Finally reduced to acquiescence I allowed myself to be steered to the bathroom where I was abandoned with a large white towel. I turned on the taps of the bath. Water appeared. After staring at it for some seconds I realised I was thirsty so I filled a toothmug with cold water from the basin, but before I could drink I saw that I had forgotten to put the plug in the bath. Evidently I was still in a state of great confusion.

Making a new effort to concentrate, I put in the plug, drank the water, bolted the door, shed my clothes and embarked on the demanding task of regulating the temperature of the bath. By the time I was soaking myself I felt more alert. I noted that the room was immensely clean and that on a glass shelf there was a jar of bath-salts which reminded me of Lyle. Yet the reminder was not painful. On the contrary, I found this symbol of a feminine presence comforting.

Having hauled myself out of the water I wondered how many of my clothes I should put on. I could hardly emerge wearing nothing but a towel tucked around my waist, but on the other hand it would be stupid to dress as if I were about to step into the street. This unusual problem of etiquette intrigued me for well over a minute but at last I put on my shirt and trousers and emerged barefoot into the hall. In the drawing-room the sofa had been transformed into a bed. I had just placed my discarded clothes on one of the dining-chairs when Sheila returned with a little dish of digestive biscuits and another pot of tea.

"Are you starving, Charles? If you'd like some scrambled eggs—"

"I wouldn't dream of asking you to cook at this hour," I said, "and after all the fuss I've caused I don't even deserve tea and biscuits." It suddenly dawned on me that not only was her hair immaculately arranged but that she was still wearing make-up. In distress I demanded: "Have you been staying up, waiting for me to surface?"

"I often go to bed late," she answered obliquely, a model of tact.

"You're letting me escape much too lightly!"

"Well, why not?" she said with a brief smile. "It makes a welcome departure from my routine."

We began to drink our tea, I sitting on the edge of the bed, she sitting in the smaller of the two armchairs, and a silence began which contained a quality which I could not quite identify. It was not an embarrassing silence yet it was not a restful silence either; there was a subtle air of expectancy, reminiscent of the atmosphere in a theatre when a new act is about to begin, and suddenly as the curtain began to rise on a very different scene I could look back and see our earlier conversation for what it was: an exchange of empty remarks in which neither of us had given anything away.

Abruptly I said: "What's really going on in your life at the moment?" and she said without a second's hesitation: "Damn all."

We stared at each other. Then she looked away in confusion and added: "Sorry, I shouldn't have said that."

"Why not? Having kept you up until the early hours of the morning I think the very least you're entitled to is the chance to say exactly what you like! Aren't you enjoying the evening classes and the voluntary work?"

"Oh, they're just widows' activities, the things women are supposed to do after they've been tidied away by society."

"Tidied away? I realise, of course, that the more insensitive sections of secular society find an unattached woman *persona non grata,* but surely your local church—"

"I don't go to church now. Oh God, I shouldn't have disclosed that—"

"On the contrary, shout it out with all your strength! Why did you stop going?"

"I couldn't get used to anywhere. Pimlico and Westminster are High Church strongholds. I went to Westminster Abbey once but that just reminded me of all I lost when Derek died and I was deprived of my home, my job and everything that made life worthwhile. Believe me, Charles, the Church is far worse than those 'insensitive sections of secular society' you mentioned a moment ago. To the Church a clerical widow isn't even *persona non grata*—she's simply a non-person."

"But you had so many friends!"

"Most of them just saw me as Derek's wife—which meant that after Derek died they didn't see me at all. The others have stayed in touch, but since I'm in London I seldom see them."

"I suppose if you'd stayed at Radbury—"

"I couldn't," she said fiercely, "I *couldn't.* I'd been deprived of my beautiful home and my cherished way of life—I couldn't bear to stay on and watch some other woman enjoy herself living the life I'd lost."

"But why choose to settle in London?"

"I thought there'd be more scope here to make a new life for myself, but I can't get a decent job because I've no proper qualifications, and although I do the voluntary work I find it so boring after the stimulating life I led at Radbury. I know I should get involved with a local church, I know I should, but I suspect the truth is—"

"You're too angry."

"Yes, I feel the Church has humiliated me, turning me out of my home, hustling me off the stage, sweeping me under the rug like a piece of unwanted debris—oh, how I hated all that smarmy Christian sympathy which oozed from those executive churchmen after Derek died! The sheer boneheaded male insensitivity was beyond belief." Taking a deep breath she struggled for composure. "I'm sorry," she said again, "I shouldn't have said all that. Let's talk of something else."

"Certainly not, this is the sort of story I ought to hear. Sheila, if only I'd known—if only you'd contacted me—"

"No, Charles. *You* were the one who should have contacted *me.* But you thought, didn't you, along with all the other unthinking churchmen: poor Sheila, very sad, but she'll be all right, she'll have the support of the Christian community and eventually she'll make a new life for herself, she'll attend evening classes and do voluntary work and be just as successful as a bishop's widow as she was as a bishop's wife—"

"Yes, I did think that. That's exactly what I thought," I said, "and of course I can see now how unforgivably complacent and unimaginative that was, but why didn't Lyle set me straight? Surely she must have seen your position through feminine eyes and imagined what you were going through!"

"Oh, I'm sure she imagined all too clearly, and that was why it was easier for her to let me slip out of your lives! I was a horrible reminder to her of how her own life might go vilely wrong."

"Even so—"

"Actually I was never sure how well Lyle liked me."

"I know she respected you," I said at once, "but she didn't find it easy to get on with her own sex."

"Yes, I realised that . . . Poor Charles, you must be missing her so dreadfully and yet here I am, whining away about my very unimportant problems—"

"I think they're very important indeed. Any seriously diminished life should be of importance to a clergyman."

"Yes, but—"

"Come down to Starbridge for a few days and visit me."

"How very kind!" she said, startled and, it seemed, genuinely moved. "But no, I couldn't, Charles—I couldn't bear to see that Cathedral and be reminded of all I'd lost at Radbury."

Setting aside my cup I rose to my feet. Immediately she too stood up, but I felt sure this was a mere automatic response because she looked bewildered, as if the late-night tea-party had deviated so sharply from its script that all her lines had become irrelevant.

I said: "I can't believe there's nothing I can do to help. Please—won't you at least take time to consider the invitation? I'm so very sorry I've been no better than all the other insensitive churchmen you've dealt with since Derek died." And as I spoke this last sentence I embarked on what I intended to be a brief symbolic gesture of reconciliation and held out my arms to her.

For a moment she was motionless, paralysed by surprise. Then she said in a faltering voice: "Why should such genuine kindness be so very hard to bear?" and she moved forward, slipping her arms around my neck and pressing her face against my chest to hide her tears.

Automatically I tightened my clasp, but as I at last held a woman in my arms again my control over the scene vanished, my body acted independently of my will and I found myself giving the one response which I knew I could never afford.

At once she was perfectly still. I tried to speak, thought better of it, released her, stepped back—all within the space of three seconds—but to my surprise she grabbed my hand and said very clearly in an abrupt, matter-of-fact voice: "It's all right. You're quite safe. I know how it is. A bishop needs to feel there's always one person with whom he can be wholly human and vulnerable."

It was a speech Lyle could have made.

In fact I felt she had come back to me after all. It was a very potent illusion.

I bent my head. The woman—Sheila, Lyle, whoever she was—raised her face for the kiss, and so it came to pass that after my long journey through the arctic wastes of bereavement, I finally managed to crawl out of the cold.

PART THREE

PARADOX AND AMBIGUITY

"We learn by the bitter experience of temptation that the spiritual life is not a matter of devout feeling or mere desire to be good. It is through temptation that most of us comprehend how serious a matter it is—a very matter of life and death, involving struggles for survival which are fierce and primitive."

REGINALD SOMERSET WARD
(1881–1962)
Anglican Priest and Spiritual Director
THE WAY

XV

"Temptation is what distracts us, beguiles us or bullies us off the path. Temptation is what makes real life different from the world of our dreams. We dream a world which is wax under the moulding of our ambitions or of our aspirations; we meet a world which faces us with trials we have not the character to surmount, and with seductions we have not the virtue to resist."

AUSTIN FARRER
Warden of Keble College, Oxford, 1960–1968
A CELEBRATION OF FAITH

I

ONE OF the Desert Fathers, living his ascetic life many centuries ago, said that if one thinks of fornication one can avoid committing it, whereas if one fails to give it sufficient consideration one inevitably winds up in the wrong bed. Abba Cyrus of Alexandria was no stranger, it seems, to the dangers of allowing powerful drives to remain hidden in the unconscious mind.

I had stopped consciously thinking about fornication the moment I had entered Sheila's flat. It had never occurred to me that fornication would be possible with a bishop's widow who was the soul of propriety, and when the opportunity to err presented itself with such peculiar suddenness, I certainly did not observe to myself: I am about to commit fornication. This is a sin. I must desist at once. Indeed I cannot remember conducting any interior dialogue with myself at all. The sexual drive, which I had been suppressing so hard, merely rose to the surface of my mind and wiped out all the thoughts I should have had—the rational thoughts, the moral thoughts, the thoughts of a bishop, a theologian and a man not inexperienced in the ways of the world. In the resulting amnesia I only knew that my battered self, tormented beyond endurance, had at last been reprieved from pain.

Sheila's nightdress was a very pallid shade of yellow. I remember feeling surprised that Lyle should have chosen to come back to me in such an anaemic colour, and this surprise indicates how far I was beyond the processes of rational thought. Certainly I was far beyond remembering Abba Cyrus of Alexandria making pithy comments about the psychology of fornication.

There followed, as I can see now, a very typical episode of casual sex, and I cannot, in all honesty, dress it up by saying I "made love" to Sheila. This is because the episode had nothing to do with love and almost nothing to do with Sheila; any woman exuding a passionate sympathy would have sufficed, although I concede my initial reaction was to feel more comfortable with a woman who I had every reason to believe was discreet. Nor can I dress up the act by saying (in the manner which was so fashionable in the 1960s) that I was being "healthy" and "natural" in behaving in this way. I was not in the least "healthy"; I was maimed by bereavement and utterly destabilised by a series of events over which I had lost control. And it was certainly not "natural" either for me to use a woman as a painkiller of only slightly more significance than a couple of aspirins. I liked women; for me to treat a woman as a mere convenient object was contrary not only to my religious beliefs but to my nature. The truth is that even normal sex, when it takes place in depersonalising circumstances, can be very unnatural indeed.

But these were all thoughts which came later. At the time I was entirely preoccupied with physical matters, but I think some memory of my normal self must have stirred in my anaesthetised brain because afterwards I automatically tried to personalise the impersonal. I gripped her hand, kissed her cheek, held her tightly for another moment. Eventually I asked if she was all right. She said she was. She sounded mildly surprised, as if we had met on a cloudless afternoon at a church fete and I had asked about the likelihood of rain. After that there seemed nothing more to say so she went to the bathroom and I retrieved my cigarettes from my jacket. Neither of us turned on the light. When she returned I offered her a cigarette before I remembered she was a non-smoker. The prospect of smoking alone after intercourse seemed odd. But this was hardly the moment to think of Lyle because if I did I would have to face my fanciful belief (which I now knew to have been insane) that she had come back to me through Sheila.

I decided to go to the lavatory instead, and when I returned I found I did not want a cigarette after all; to smoke without Lyle in such circumstances was too difficult. Eventually Sheila, tactful as ever, asked: "Do you want to be alone now?" but at least I had the humanity to say "no" without a second's hesitation.

She pressed close to me in gratitude. It was strange how large she seemed, but I realised that she only seemed large because Lyle had been so small. But I had already decided to save all thought of Lyle for later. I now decided to save all thought of everything for later. A queasiness in the pit of my stomach indicated all too clearly that thought in these circumstances was a luxury I could no longer afford.

Having given Sheila one last kiss I turned away from her and closed my eyes in exhaustion.

2

WHEN I awoke I found myself alone. Faint sounds of activity came from the kitchen across the hall. The time was twenty minutes to eight.

Memory blasted me to an upright position on the edge of the bed, and then the implications of all that I remembered began to spread smoothly, stickily, slimily across my mind like mud poured from a bucket over an uncarpeted floor. Rigid with horror I sat on the edge of the bed for some time.

However at last my instinct for survival stirred and I stopped harbouring such demented thoughts as: it never happened—I shall wake up in a minute. And: if I don't think about it, it'll go away. Picking up my clothes I dragged myself to the bathroom and found that a woman's razor had been placed by the basin alongside a note which stated: "The water's hot if you want a bath." I did take a bath, a rapid one to sluice away all the physical traces of what had happened, but I ignored the little razor; I was unable to face looking at myself in the glass. As I dried myself clumsily I became aware of my overpowering desire to escape, but I knew I had to restrain the impulse to blunder immediately from the flat. My entire future could depend on what I did next. Pulling on my clothes I began to focus my mind, sharpened now by fear and dread, on the task of severing myself from this woman whom I knew so imperfectly yet so very much too well.

On my return to the drawing-room I found that the bed had been reduced to a sofa and all the curtains had been drawn back. A shaft of sunlight was filtering into the courtyard beyond the French windows. Slowly I moved to the kitchen. Sheila was drinking coffee and reading the *Daily Telegraph* at the small table in the centre of the room. After I had forced myself to kiss her she said: "Do you want a cooked breakfast?" and I contrived to answer in a casual voice: "Not this morning, I think." We might have been married for years.

"I'll make some toast." She was pouring out a cup of coffee for me as she spoke. "Do look at the paper—I can always finish it later."

I hid behind the *Telegraph* for a couple of minutes but read nothing.

When the toast had been placed in front of me she enquired tranquilly: "Was my razor no use?"

"It looked so dainty that I was afraid of breaking it."

She smiled, and it occurred to me that she was looking not only happier but smarter. She was wearing a straight dark skirt and a green jumper with a row of pearls. Her hair waved smoothly in all the right directions. She was immaculately made up. She might have been the hostess of a large country house, a chatelaine well accustomed to providing for unexpected guests.

"But that's exactly what I was!" she exclaimed when I had voiced this opinion. "People were always descending in droves on the palace at Radbury—Derek used to leave me notes saying: 'There'll be thirty for dinner tomorrow.' "

"I'd say that was grounds for divorce!"

"Oh, Derek knew I enjoyed the challenge!"

"Lucky old Derek." I drank some coffee and resumed staring at the front page of the *Telegraph,* but I was unable to read beyond the headlines.

"Don't you want the toast, Charles?"

With dread I realised I could no longer go on hiding behind the *Telegraph* and producing the occasional remark. Setting the paper aside I began to butter my toast as I tried to work out how to speak the unspeakable, but in the end it was she who made the first move. She said suddenly: "Don't worry. It's all right."

This attempt to be direct was admirable but I was at a loss to know how to reply. Obviously I could not say: "No, it's not all right and I'm worried to death." At all costs I had to avoid any comment which she might feel was unchivalrous. I looked down at the butter, now melting on the toast, but as the silence began to lengthen I set down my knife, removed my reading-glasses and looked her straight in the eyes.

"I'm very grateful," I said, "that you're being so understanding." One can never go too far wrong by expressing gratitude.

"Sudden bereavement's such a shock. It's enough to make anyone act out of character, so please—don't feel embarrassed by last night! I'd so like us to be friends!"

Here at last was the sentence which chilled me to the bone and opened up an appalling vista into the future. Looking down at my toast I saw the butter had congealed and I knew the thought of eating now revolted me. Finally I managed to say: "Of course we can be friends, although you must forgive me if I'm not at present the best of correspondents."

"I do realise you'll have to be very discreet. Clergymen are allowed a 'lapse,' aren't they, but not a regular mistress . . . You see? I know the rules of the game."

Too devastated to reply I finished my coffee and rose to my feet. "I'd better rescue my car before it falls foul of the parking regulations." I was amazed by how casual my voice sounded. No claustrophobic locked in a cupboard could have experienced a stronger desire to escape than I experienced that moment in that kitchen.

". . . lovely to see you again . . ."

". . . many thanks . . . wonderfully kind and sympathetic . . . most grateful for all your understanding . . ."

The hideous dialogue seemed incapable of termination but at last the front door was opening and I was steeling myself for the final kiss. She was wearing scent, I noticed, the kind of tasteful, lilies-of-the-valley fragrance sold for middle-aged women at Boots. Lyle had scrimped and saved and bought expensive scent at Harrods. Once I had bought her scent for her birthday, but this had been considered a deprivation of her pleasure. She had enjoyed the scrimping and the saving. It had made the extravagance more fun.

"Charles?"

"Sorry. Just trying to work out the best way back to Mayfair." I said a final goodbye, and having forced myself to ascend the basement steps at a leisurely pace, I hurtled back in panic into the Pimlico grid.

3

MY CAR was still standing a few yards from St. Mary's church and I realised I would have to do some careful explaining to Charley later, but now all I cared about was escaping from London. Having paid off the taxi-driver who had rescued me from Pimlico I drove rapidly through Knightsbridge towards the western suburbs.

Mile after mile slipped by. It was another grey day, not cold, but I felt increasingly as if I were encased in ice. After an hour and a half I felt I could drive no more. My neck and shoulders ached with tension. I was struggling against a humiliating urge to cry.

I had been driving along the road which looped through the hills towards Starbridge, the road I could remember so well from my journeys to Starbridge in 1937, and I halted the car in a new parking area created at the point where the road completed its final bend and the city lay below in the valley like a jewel embedded in a sumptuous case. It was the sight of the Cathedral, towering on its mound in the heart of the city, which finally made me realise I was unable to go on. The sight underlined how profoundly I had betrayed my calling to serve God and follow Christ. I thought of the trespass: the seamy, selfish intrusion, without love, into the most private and sensitive areas of Sheila's body and personality. I thought of the exploitation: the influencing of a lonely, vulnerable woman by a priest whose position demanded that there should be no breach of her trust. I thought of the shoddy evasions of the morning after: the shifty sentences, the rank hypocrisy, the perversion of truth. I thought, in short, not only of the act of intercourse but of the spiritual degeneration it symbolised, and the next moment I was remembering how I had condemned from pulpit after pulpit the immoral life which I had always prided myself I had been far too virtuous to lead.

At last I summoned the strength to light a cigarette. That made me avert my gaze from the Cathedral, but as the flame died all the colour seemed to fade from the landscape. I was remembering Sheila's words: "I'd so like us to be friends," and as I faced the fact that this was the last thing I wanted I heard again that other terrible sentence: "I know the rules of the game."

I considered those rules. As Sheila had pointed out, a clergyman was "allowed" a lapse though not a regular mistress, but this summary omitted a dimension which Sheila, ever tactful, had left unspoken. A lapse—an isolated incident which could be confessed, regretted and forgiven without necessarily incurring disastrous consequences—was supposed to take place only with the sort of woman whom no clergyman could be expected to marry. In contrast, an act of fornication with a respectable widow could only be considered, according to the rules of the game, as premarital intercourse. How else could one justify the unjustifiable?

I smoked the cigarette down to the butt and tried to convince myself that Sheila would be uninterested in marrying me, but it was obvious she longed to regain that rewarding life of which she had been so brutally deprived. If she had the chance to marry another bishop she was hardly going to ignore it. No wonder she had been so smartly dressed and cheerful that morning.

I tried to muzzle my panic by telling myself she was a decent, reasonable woman who would never behave like an adventuress, but unfortunately this assumption was difficult to support with hard facts. All I really knew about Sheila was that she had been an effective wife for a bishop. This implied a range of executive skills but told me little about her basic nature. Moreover, even if her nature was fundamentally kind and sympathetic, it could well have been seriously soured by bitterness, frustration and the desire to hit back at the Church which she felt had treated her so shabbily.

By this time, halfway through my second cigarette, I was coming to the conclusion that even if I had not laid myself open to blackmail, I had almost certainly raised the curtain on a most unpleasant series of scenes in my private life. Or in other words, I could not quite imagine any woman so thoroughly middle-class and respectable as Sheila saying: "Marry me or I'll tell our story to the *News of the World,*" but I could all too easily visualise a future in which she behaved as if she had a right to a wedding ring.

I lit a third cigarette from the glowing tip of the second. Chain-smoking, unshaven, dressed in yesterday's clothes—all I needed now, it seemed, was an empty bottle of whisky to complete the picture of the roué crawling home after a lost weekend, but I was so paralysed by my predicament that I could not even shudder and the next moment an even darker view of yesterday's catastrophic sequence of events was inching with loathsome plausibility into my mind. I had finally remembered Abba Cyrus's acid comments about the psychology which led to fornication.

I thought of all the self-knowledge I had repressed. Jon in his letter had urged me to be on my guard against my weaknesses—surely when I had read his words I had automatically recalled the errors I had made with women in the past? Of course I had, but I had immediately erased them from my memory. I then saw, with revulsion, that although I had told myself I was going to London merely to appease Charley, I had also been motivated by the desire to escape from my troubles by flirting with disaster. Why else should I have wound up loitering outside Brown's Hotel when I could have had a quick lunch elsewhere? And after leading Loretta on only to reject her—another disgusting piece of behaviour—why had I wound up in a red-light district on the wrong side of Victoria instead of outside Charley's flat in Mayfair? The truth was I had failed to be honest with myself, failed to face my weaknesses in order to survive them, failed to behave as a priest should—and now because of those multiple failures I was trapped in a mess which had the potential to destroy me.

I crushed out my cigarette. Fortunately no divine revelation was required to tell me what I had to do next. I needed help, and in such a desperate crisis there was only one man to whom I could turn.

I paused at the South Canonry only to shave, change and drink some milk. Then having retrieved Lyle's journal from my study I hurried away at last on my long-delayed journey to Starrington.

4

THE DOOR in the wall surrounding the grounds of the Manor was locked. At once I wondered if Jon was ill, for usually he unlocked the door himself every morning, and when I noticed seconds later that a smart car was parked off the road beneath the trees I wondered if it belonged to some unusually affluent local doctor.

Driving back to the front entrance of the Manor, I parked outside the gates in the hope of avoiding the residents and made a series of rapid manoeuvres which took me around the edge of a lawn to a path which led into the woods.

I walked for some minutes. It had been raining earlier and the woods were still dank. Eventually the path brought me to the brink of the dell, and looking down I saw to my relief that smoke was rising from the chimney of the cottage. At least if Jon was ill he was not in hospital. Quickening my pace as the path zig-zagged downhill I reached the floor of the dell and hurried over the grassy sward to the cottage door.

At first no one responded to my knock, but just as I was deducing with relief that Jon was not only well but praying in the chapel nearby, the door was flung open and I knew this optimistic conclusion was wrong.

I found myself facing Martin Darrow, Jon's son by his first marriage. Although he was an actor who preferred the theatre, Martin had become nationally famous in the 1960s as the result of his television series "Down at the Surgery," a curious exercise in comedy in which Whitehall farce met "Emergency Ward Ten" with beguiling results. He was only five years my junior but looked considerably younger. In fact I often wondered if he had had a face-lift. At least he did not dye his hair, which was a distinguished shade of grey. (Or did he dye it? Was it possible that nature alone could have achieved such a supremely distinguished shade?) His choice of expensive clothes made him look like a model in an advertisement: very well turned out, but not quite a gentleman. He was exceedingly good-looking, much better-looking than his father; he also had a fine resonant voice, various stagey mannerisms and a facile charm which made him seem as if he were perpetually acting in a comedy by Noel Coward. What he was really like, I had no idea. Nor, I confess, had I ever made any effort to find out. I admired him for triumphing over his alcoholism; I thought he was an excellent actor; but we inhabited such different worlds that I could not imagine having a conversation with him that lasted longer than five minutes.

"Good God!" he exclaimed when he saw me. "Come in." And turning aside he called: "Dad, it's your pal, the Bishop!" before he added to me: "He's in the lavatory."

No sooner had I crossed the threshold than I saw Jon's son by his second marriage, Nicholas, twenty-two years old and supposed to be doing voluntary work in Africa. He was sitting cross-legged on the rug in front of the fire and holding Jon's tabby-cat in his arms. He looked over his shoulder at me but did not speak. A second later he gave a convulsive shudder. He was ash-white and looked ill.

Martin said to me airily: "Nicholas has been flown home unexpectedly—I took Dad to Heathrow this morning to meet him and we've only just got back."

"What happened?"

"Oh, just a little disagreement with one of the local yokels. You'll be all right now you're home, won't you, Nicholas?"

The boy shuddered and went on clutching the cat. Apparently he was beyond normal social intercourse. Thin, bony and with his father's unusual pallor, he wore glasses which gave him a serious, scholarly look. Jon too had been obliged to wear glasses in his youth. The boy greatly resembled him.

I was just thinking that I should make some elementary pastoral gesture when Jon emerged from the bathroom. He looked both flustered and upset. In fact the contrast between his usual serene manner and this distressed appearance was so great that I knew at once I had chosen quite the wrong moment to call.

"I'll come back some other time," I said at once. "Obviously Nicholas needs your undivided attention."

"But I want to talk to you!" Torn between his inclinations as a priest and his obligations as a parent, Jon now became almost frantic. "I've been praying for days that you'd visit me!"

"I'll stay with Nicholas," said Martin soothingly. "You and Charles go and talk in the chapel."

But Nicholas at once began to shudder continuously and Jon, hurrying over to him, made no attempt to reply. As Martin glanced upwards in an eloquent gesture of exasperation, the boy, still seated on the floor, grabbed Jon's leg as if to anchor him to the room and I made the decision to introduce a note of reality into this increasingly bizarre scene. Crisply I said to Jon: "Have you called a doctor?"

"He's not ill, just frightened. It's a question of demonic infiltration."

"Oh my God!" muttered Martin under his breath as if about to expire with embarrassment.

Jon managed to say in a neutral voice: "Martin, take Charles up to the house and give him some lunch."

"What a splendid idea!" said Martin brightly. "Come along, Charles!"

I said to Jon: "If there's anything I can do—"

"No. Forgive me, Charles, I know I'm letting you down—"

"Obviously Nicholas must be your first priority. But I wonder if I could leave this packet with you?" I held up the journal which I had placed in an envelope. "Perhaps later when things are less fraught—"

"I'll look at it. Yes, of course." He was already turning away. Placing the envelope on the mantelshelf I glanced back at him and saw he was kneeling beside the boy who was still shuddering with his mysterious emotion. The cat, watching me with sleepy subhuman eyes, somehow heightened the atmosphere of eerie abnormality and made me glad to escape from the room.

Feeling considerably shaken I said to Martin as soon as the front door closed behind us: "What on earth's been going on?"

"The silly little muggins tried to exorcise a witch-doctor." Martin sounded both glum and disgusted. "Trust that child to make a complete psychic balls-up and create havoc! Typical."

This extraordinary information at least diverted me from the fact that Jon was temporarily unavailable. "But what was he doing trying to exorcise a witch-doctor? I've heard the majority of witch-doctors nowadays do a lot of good and are pillars of their communities!"

"Well, either the witch-doctor wasn't one of the majority or else—and this is far more likely—Nicholas pranced around being such a psychic menace that the witch-doctor lost patience and decided to give him a good fright—no, don't go that way, Charles, we can drive back to the house—I've got my car parked outside the door in the wall and there are six bottles of ginger ale in the boot. I always travel fortified for emergencies, particularly when I'm dealing with those two loonies we've just left."

I was determined not to stay for lunch but I was ready enough to accept a lift back to the gates of the Manor. Falling into step beside him I began to walk down the track to the wall.

"Christ, what a morning!" Martin was exclaiming, sounding glummer than ever. "Sorry, wrong expletive, no offence meant, but really—*really!* I feel like roaring around like King Lear. What have I done to be saddled with such a family, I ask myself, *what have I done?* I feel like going to Banbury before I can throw sanity to the winds and hit the bottle in the biggest possible way."

"Why Banbury?"

"Oh God, haven't you heard what goes on at Banbury? There's a marvellous nursing-home there where they dry out the loathsome rich and the even more loathsome show-biz types who have been trying to destroy themselves. In fact I've only just emerged from the place after going on a bender, and—Christ, listen to me, why am I letting my hair down like this? One glimpse of a purple stock and I'm babbling my confession at top speed! Sorry, Charles, I really must stop saying 'Christ' like that, I know priests find it offensive, and anyway I find it offensive myself these days—did Dad tell you I've started going to church again?"

"As a matter of fact he did mention—"

"To be strictly accurate, I haven't been to church lately. I'm in a spiritual limbo after being clobbered by a disaster—no, not Little Muggins and his witch-doctor, but a sex-disaster of indescribably awful dimensions—and now I'm cut off from God again, I'm up shit-creek without a paddle, and I can only suppose I'm being punished—do you see God as vengeful, Charles?"

"No."

"How interesting! I thought you'd say yes."

With a sinking heart I was realising that some sort of pastoral response was being required of me. I wondered if I had ever since my consecration felt less like being a bishop. I even wondered if I had ever since my ordination felt less like being a priest. Making a huge effort I said tentatively: "Was the sex-disaster the result of your lapse with the bottle?"

"No, the lapse was the result of the disaster."

In a last-ditch effort to turn the conversation into another channel I murmured: "I'm sorry, I don't mean to pry."

"My dear Charles, I'm in such a state at the moment that I wouldn't even care if you'd been ordered to interrogate me on behalf of the KGB! What I'd like to do is go back to my church in London and make my confession but I'm afraid of the priest telling me I'm a disgrace—with the result that I'd run out and hit the bottle all over again. However, if you don't see God as vengeful—"

"I'd rather emphasise God's mercy."

"How extraordinary! I'd have thought that you, of all bishops—"

"Anyone can suffer a sex-disaster." I paused. I think I was waiting for Bishop Ashworth, that moral paragon, to take control of the scene with a suitably smooth-tongued pastoral performance—the kind of performance I had staged for Desmond in hospital—but nothing happened. It seemed the Bishop had gone away. Instead someone else—the "I" who was quite other than this glittering image—said: "Anyone can repent too, and be forgiven. Where do you go to church?"

"St. Mary's Bourne Street."

"But surely they'd be sympathetic there!"

"They've certainly been sympathetic in the past, but that was when I was a communicant, living a celibate life and being good as gold. I feel I simply can't go back there now and say—"

"All right, tell me instead."

"Oh, I couldn't possibly! You'd be revolted."

"What's so revolting about being human?"

"What's so revolting about . . . My God! Charles, I never knew you could be like this, it's extraordinary, I'm *stunned.* But can one really make a confession to a priest while ambling through a wood?"

"I've heard confessions while ambling through a concentration camp. But I agree that ideally a confession should be heard in a church. Why not regard this as a rehearsal for your priest at St. Mary's?"

"I quite like the idea of a rehearsal," said the actor, gaining confidence. "But I need to be fed an opening line."

At once I said: "What sort of a man was he?"

"After the way he treated me I refuse to do him the honour of calling him a man."

"Then what kind of a creature was he?"

"Tall, dark, handsome, brilliant, charming and young enough to be my son."

"Hardly the sort of creature one runs across every day."

"Exactly—that was why I fell so hard! But I did try not to. First of all I thought: I can't. Then I thought: I shouldn't. And finally I thought: well, I might if he were to show interest. But he didn't show interest, month after month passed and he showed no interest, and then just as I thought I was finally recovering from my infatuation—*wham!* He did show interest and I was led as a lamb to the slaughter. It didn't last long. He demolished me and walked out. That was when I hit the bottle and wound up at Banbury, but I recovered, I crawled back to sanity and I was all set to begin enjoying life again, or trying to, when—*wham!* Little Muggins gets sent home and I have to survive a family crisis—no wonder I feel as if God's clobbering me, but that's an illusion, isn't it, I can see that now because he's sent you along to proclaim that I'm still forgivable—bloody hell, here we are at the door in the wall and I've just seen that key, tucked in the lock. How do I lock the door after us and leave the key on this side of the wall?"

"Push it under the door."

"God, that's wonderful, the voice of sanity, just what I need. Thank the Lord you turned up, Charles! I can't wait to reward you with some absolutely delicious bread and cheese." And when he smiled at me I could no longer find the words which would have enabled me to avoid lunch and escape from him. Indeed it occurred to me that although I was in a grossly debilitated state I had a duty to stay so long as I could be of use; I might have been a complete clerical failure in London, but it seemed I was still not quite a write-off in my own diocese.

I began to feel fractionally less contemptible.

5

MARTIN'S CAR, which I had noticed earlier, was a white Jaguar. All my life I have fancied fast exciting cars and all my life since my ordination I have been obliged to accept the sad truth that fast exciting cars are quite inappropriate for a clergyman.

"I envy you the Jaguar," I heard myself confess as we completed the short but perfect journey around the boundary wall to the front entrance of the Manor.

"Yes, I thought you were looking a trifle pea-green. Personally I think all bishops should have Jaguars—it would boost their image no end." Having parked in front of the house, he removed from the boot his six little bottles of ginger ale, all packed in a cardboard frame, and commented apologetically: "If you want real booze, Charles, I'm sorry to say the Community only keep medicinal brandy and Communion wine."

"Luckily I'm in an abstemious mood."

"God, how marvellous, sincere congratulations. Look, why don't you sit down in the library, which is the one ground-floor room the cranks don't use, and I'll go scavenging in the kitchen . . ."

The front door was on the latch. In the hall Martin passed me the ginger ale and we parted, he heading towards the green baize door and I wandering into the library where a hoard of antiquarian books had stood unread for decades. Volumes of Victorian sermons jostled with tomes on field sports to bear witness to the interests of the nineteenth-century owners of the Manor. Stuffed fish of immense size were displayed in glass cases adorned with brass plates which recorded the fish's weight, place of death and the name of their murderer, Algernon Barton-Woods. Jon's second wife, whose family had owned the Manor for many generations, had preserved the library as a tribute to a vanished past, and Jon had changed nothing since her death.

Sitting down in one of the leather armchairs I attempted to gather my wits and decide what I should do with myself while Jon was inaccessible, but no solution sprang conveniently to mind. Being a member of the Church of England, not the Church of Rome, I was under no obligation to make a formal confession to a priest; provided I confessed my sins to God, prayed for forgiveness and asked for the grace to lead a better life, I was not barred from attending church and receiving the sacraments. Yet for years I had known I was a man who needed the spiritual discipline of a confession to a priest, and I was very reluctant, particularly when I was in such a spiritually disabled condition, to dispense with this aid to putting myself right with God. It also seemed to me indisputable that I needed immediate help from a sympathetic priest whom I could wholly trust. If necessary I could wait to make that formal confession to Jon. But what I absolutely could not afford to do, I now saw clearly, was to go soldiering on alone until Jon became available.

I began to review the people who could fill the role of temporary help-mate, but almost at once I became uneasy. I had no intention of telling anyone but Jon about the fornication, but was it wise even to admit to drinking too much and being so sunk in depression that I was currently the most inert and inept bishop on the bench? After all, I had a duty to the Church to keep up appearances. A bishop who ran around whining that life was intolerably tough would be a most unedifying spectacle even to the most loyal of his ordained friends. In fact I could almost see the Abbot-General of the Fordite monks pursing his lips as he thought: poor Ashworth, very sad, but he's letting the side down, not playing the game. The Abbot-General and I had been to the same public school. I knew exactly how he would react. Perhaps soldiering on and keeping my mouth shut for the time being was simply a cross I was being called to bear . . . Or was this a gigantic delusion fuelled by a spiritual pride which made the confession of inadequacy intolerable? I tried to think clearly but I knew I was getting in a muddle. Whom could I talk to and what could I say? I stared at the nearest stuffed fish as if I expected him to reply to these baffling questions, and I was still staring when Martin returned to the room.

"I didn't tell the gang that the Bishop was here," he said, setting down a tray of bread, cheese and apples. "I just said you were a friend of mine. I thought you mightn't be in the mood to see them all genuflecting at the sight of your pectoral cross."

"How very understanding." Making an effort I began to concentrate on the task of sustaining a conversation.

"Ah well, there's an actor for you—always trying to imagine what it's like to be someone else! Here, take the glasses and pour out the ginger ale while I slice the bread. God knows what this cheese is but I think it might be a variety of Double Gloucester. The green flecks are chives, not mould." And when the picnic had been prepared he added unexpectedly: "Say grace, would you? I'd like that," so I produced a suitable sentence for the occasion.

"I'm feeling slightly more normal," he remarked afterwards. "Sorry I was so demented earlier—and while we're on the subject of apologies,

I'm sorry I didn't write to you about your wife. I should have written even though we've never been more than mere acquaintances."

"No doubt if I'd been friendlier to you in the past you'd have responded differently."

"Well, I wasn't exactly friendly myself, was I? Dad screwed everything up, of course, by falling in love with you back in 1937."

"Falling in love? My dear Martin!"

"Oh, I don't mean sexually! But it was a very intense father-son relationship, wasn't it?"

"Nonsense! Jon's always been the detached spiritual director!"

"It didn't look that way to me, old chap. In fact every time he spoke of you dotingly I wanted to run screaming in the opposite direction—but no, don't get upset! I did recover from my sordid jealousy! Dad and I straightened out our relationship during the war, but even so I still felt, whenever I saw you, that I was hopelessly inadequate—no, forget that, don't take me seriously, I'm just hamming it up, but I'm only hamming it up to let off steam and avoid exploding with rage. How could Dad be so bloody stupid about silly Little Muggins! Why doesn't he just give him a good slap instead of laying on the white magic with a shovel? Charles, tell me frankly: do you think my father's round the bend?"

"On the contrary, Jon always strikes me as being the sanest, most balanced man I know."

"It really is extraordinary how he manages to give that impression to so many people."

"Of course I'm not saying he doesn't make mistakes—"

"Mistakes! Where family life's concerned it's just one long balls-up! The only thing Dad's ever been able to bring up successfully is a cat—in fact sometimes I think Nicholas is just like a mixed-up kitten and I half-expect him to screech 'Miaow!' whenever he sees me. If Anne hadn't died it would be different, but ever since those two loonies have been left stranded without her, they've become increasingly peculiar and now they're cocooned in this bizarre psychic cosiness which I think is extremely unhealthy."

I could not help but admit: "I've been worried myself about Nicholas since Anne died."

"Thank God—an ally! I wish now I'd played a bigger part in Nicholas's upbringing, but I didn't, I opted out, and now Nicholas resents me, sharpens his claws and gives me steely looks whenever I appear on the scene. I don't *think* homophobia's at the bottom of the aversion, but of course it doesn't help that I'm a homosexual—and in fact that was the main reason why I opted out; homosexuals aren't supposed to hang around adolescent boys and Dad would hardly have thought I was a suitable role-model, but actually I could have given Nicholas a whiff of normality. I could certainly have given him a sense of proportion about the psychic rubbish, but now—just because I chose to do damn all—Nicholas winds up in a catatonic state after trying to exorcise a witch-doctor and Dad's in such a flat spin he could wind up having a stroke! Oh, the whole situation's a catastrophe—and there's Dad, supposed to be a brilliant spiritual director! God! I hardly know whether to laugh or cry."

Recognising his feelings of guilt I said: "Don't be too tough on yourself. I've made several moves over the years to provide Nicholas with a whiff of normality, but Jon was never able to relax his grip. I think he knows in theory that it's got to be done but for some reason he finds it impossible in practice."

"Dad finds all family life impossible in practice. I really can't think why he ever married, particularly since he seems to have the kind of sex-drive that can be turned on and off like a tap—"

"Talking of sex," I said, carving myself some more cheese. "Tell me more about Attila the Hun, the destroyer who laid waste your life."

"Ah, the creature! Well, I certainly didn't intend to inflict all the gory details on you, but since you're being so extraordinarily sympathetic . . ." He embarked on a description of the affair.

By the time I had finished my second bottle of ginger ale it had occurred to me that although I had suffered a great deal in recent weeks, I had not suffered the experience of being mocked and ridiculed by someone I loved. Nor had I had to suffer the frustration of an intense love which was not reciprocated. Nor had I had to endure the voluntary departure of the one I loved. Nor had I had to suffer the loss alone, deprived of the support of a community which cared about me. Nor was I without children who had the special power to keep precious memories alive. In short, it had occurred to me for the first time that although my bereavement had been and continued to be terrible, there were other bereavements which could be worse.

". . . and of course he was bisexual, neither one thing nor the other, someone who had never made a real commitment to either sex," Martin was saying, concluding the description of the Oxford academic who had done so much damage, but I heard myself comment: "I wonder. He sounds more like a heterosexual who was very emotionally disturbed, possibly even on the brink of breakdown." Quickly I added: "I'm not saying a man has to be on the verge of breakdown to have a homosexual affair. I'm just saying that this particular man doesn't strike me as being a typical bisexual—unless he was lying to you when he said there'd been no homosexual episodes in his past."

"He could have been lying. I'll never know. And I suppose it doesn't matter now anyway what he was."

"Doesn't it? But surely if he was very emotionally disturbed—profoundly unhappy—doesn't that make it easier to forgive him?"

There was a pause while Martin worked out the implications of this question. Finally he said: "I do see I've got to forgive him in order to be free, but the truth is that the person I find hardest to forgive is myself. Imagine going off the rails like that at my age! When I think how I hit the vodka—"

"After Lyle died I hit the scotch."

"Did you, Charles? Did you really? But how hard did you hit it?"

"Hard enough to be hung-over."

"How wonderfully reassuring! But of course you then pulled yourself together and behaved like a paragon."

"Not quite."

"Honestly? In that case perhaps I can feel a little less disgusted with myself. I didn't behave like a paragon at all when I finally emerged from Banbury."

"Difficult to get back to normal?"

"Crucifying. I was so bloody lonely that I was even tempted to head for a red-light district. I'm sorry, I know how sordid that sounds—"

"No need to apologise."

"Anyway, in the end I resisted the red lights and jumped into bed with an old friend instead. I'm sure you must find it quite incomprehensible that I should have done such a thing—"

"Not at all."

"—and I wish to hell now that I'd abstained, because it turned out to be a damn fool thing to do and there's bound to be an unpleasant scene waiting for me later. God, isn't life bloody sometimes!"

"Yes."

"Are you just saying that to be nice to me?"

"No."

"Thank God. Lord, this is a damned odd conversation to be having with a bishop! Excuse me while I just pinch myself to make sure I'm not dreaming—"

"It's no dream. Good to meet someone else who's gone through hell lately."

"Isn't it wonderful? It makes all the difference to know there's someone else screaming alongside you—and that's the point of the Incarnation, I can see that so clearly now. God came into the world and screamed alongside us. Interesting idea, that. I had a big row once with a Buddhist who played down the hellishness of suffering by . . . but no, forget the

Buddhist, and forget me too. Let's hear about *you,* Charles. Let's hear about *your* pain."

I thought: I can't possibly unburden myself further to a homosexual actor with whom I have nothing in common.

But then it seemed to me that we had a great deal in common at that moment and that with his actor's ability to empathise he would give me the support I needed as I struggled to survive my ordeal.

"I bet you're asking yourself how the hell you're going to endure the unendurable," said Martin suddenly, and when I said: "Yes, I am," I saw at last that in my darkest hours since Lyle's death I was to be helped not by a priest at all, nor indeed by any of my familiar Christian friends, but by a stranger who stood on the margins of conventional society, by one of the outcasts and sinners to whom Christ had long ago stretched out his hand.

6

"THE TROUBLE with bereavement at our time of life," said Martin, "is that it raises the curtain on death. At least when one's young one can think: this is hell but I'll live to fight another day. But at our age you think: this is hell and all I've got to look forward to is the grave."

Reaching for each word with difficulty I said: "Last Saturday night I felt like a dinosaur which had been heaved into a rubbish-pit for burial."

"How perfectly frightful. Tell me more."

"The bereavement evoked exactly the thoughts you've just described and I suddenly felt I couldn't stand the hell of the 1960s a moment longer."

"Isn't it torture? So trivial! So vulgar! So *noisy*—my dear, the music!"

"I know it's foolish to look back at the past through rose-tinted spectacles, but—"

"If the younger generation weren't wallowing in rubbish we wouldn't be driven to reach for the rose-tints."

"And talking of the younger generation," I said, painfully recalling past quarrels with Michael, "I resent being despised just because I represent certain values which are now labelled 'irrelevant.' "

"So do I! 'Martin Darrow,' the young actors sneer, 'that dead relic of drawing-room comedy!' "

The thought of the performing arts jolted my memory and I recalled a film which Lyle and I had seen earlier in the decade during a visit to London. Impulsively I asked: "Did you ever see *The Leopard?"*

"The Visconti masterpiece? Three times, yes—oh, I know what you're thinking! You're remembering Burt Lancaster, the relic who was living out those spine-chilling lines of Tennyson: 'The old order changeth—' "

"I was very moved by that film."

"Moved! I wept shamelessly. That moment when Burt Lancaster danced with Claudia Cardinale—"

"That was the young girl, wasn't it? He danced with the young girl who represented the new order, and although her beauty touched his heart he was silently grieving for everything that was lost or passing away—"

"That scene where he looked in the mirror—"

"I could hardly bear to watch."

We went on discussing the film. The last of the ginger ale disappeared. Only the crumbs remained from our lunch.

"But surely the point to remember," said Martin at last, "when the old order changes so catastrophically that you want to vomit, is that our whole demarcation of time—all this business of eras and decades—is actually a grand illusion. The 1960s belong just as much to us as they do to your sons and Little Muggins. We're all in the same kitchen, all still cooking the future—which means the future's not fixed. Anything could happen. You may be on the ropes now, but you could still have a destiny beyond your wildest dreams, even though the younger generation are currently calling you a has-been. Look at me, for instance."

"You?"

"Yes, look at my career. In the 1950s I went through a rocky patch when the angry-young-man and kitchen-sink dramas came into fashion. By the time the 1960s arrived I'd concluded I was washed up. And then what happened? Television comedy! And now I'm a household name and adored by hordes of middle-aged women and I drive that heavenly chariot and my bank manager thinks I'm no end of a swell—and the oddest part of this whole resurrection is that it's happening in an era I detest! So to my fury I have to thank God for the 1960s because they've given me a whole new life—in fact I've come to see that the era actually requires old-timers like us in order to balance the present with the past and produce a future which isn't a complete nightmare. So never think the future's just a black void. My career changed radically when I was middle-aged; maybe it'll change radically again when I'm very old. Actors' lives are full of endings and new beginnings, so the important thing is always to live in hope of a resurrection even when to hope seems the most insane thing you can possibly do."

"Never despair?"

"*Never* despair!"

There was a pause. I found I was staring again at the fish in his glass case, and suddenly it seemed to me that I too had been living under glass, distanced from the underlying reality of the 1960s not only by the isolating side-effects of my career but by Lyle's unflagging efforts to ensure my life ran smoothly. Yet now the glass had been smashed, and unlike the fish I did not have to remain a mere memento of a dead past. Exposed at last to the icy draught of reality, I could draw a deep breath and begin again.

Abruptly I demanded: "What are your plans, Martin? Are you staying here?"

"With the Community? No fear! I'll hole up in Starbridge while the crisis lasts."

"Come and stay at the South Canonry."

"Seriously?"

"Very seriously. You'd stop me giving the whisky another wallop."

"Ah well, if I can be of some modest use . . . Thanks very much, Bishop's Guardian sounds a most intriguing new role, but I'd better get back to the cottage now and see how the loonies are getting on. Shall I ring you later to let you know my arrival time?"

When we had arranged that he would be at the South Canonry by seven unless he telephoned with a change of plan, we left the house and he wandered down the drive with me to my car.

"Jon was lucky that you were able to drop everything and take him to the airport," I said as we paused to say goodbye.

"Little Muggins picked the right time to stage a crisis. I'm back in the studios next week for another bout of comedy . . . Do you think I'll ever get to play King Lear?"

"*Never* despair!"

We laughed and shook hands. Then I set off on the next stage of my journey through territory which before Lyle's death I would have been unable to imagine.

7

ON THE drive home I started worrying about Sheila again, but I soon realised it was more important to worry about how I was going to survive until Jon was ready to see me. Enlisting Martin as a companion had without doubt been a sensible move, but Martin's arrival at the South Canonry was still some hours away and as I approached Starbridge I knew how unnerved I was by the thought of that empty house. Monday was my official day off; no one would be there; guilt and shame would soon make solitude intolerable—and dangerous. I seriously began to consider whether I should pour my entire stock of wines and spirits down the drain.

It was at that moment that I saw the sign to Langley Bottom and remembered that Martin had not been the first outcast from the margins who had given me a helping hand as I flailed around at the bottom of my personal pit. At once the steering-wheel moved beneath my fingers and the car turned aside from the main road. I had realised that the only man in my diocese whom I now felt inclined to see was that divorced priest whom only recently I had been far too arrogant to want to know.

8

ONCE AGAIN he was looking extraordinary. He wore an unbuttoned shirt which gaped to reveal a string-vest, one of those appalling items of underwear which I believe became fashionable earlier in the decade. Below the waist he wore dirty trousers, flecked with paint, and his sandals.

"I seem to remember we've played this scene before," he said as I boggled at him. "Bishop, I do apologise for my appearance, but—"

"It couldn't matter less. Can I come in?"

Now it was his turn to boggle. Holding the door open for me he managed to say as I entered the hall: "I've just been redecorating Desmond's bedroom. I completed his study at the weekend."

I paused abruptly as I remembered Malcolm's information that Desmond was due to return home that day after his convalescent holiday in Devon. "When does his train arrive?"

"It's been and gone. He's here," said Hall, and as he spoke the door of the study slowly opened to reveal Desmond himself. His face still showed signs of damage but he was a healthy colour and—most unexpectedly—he looked smart. He was wearing his cassock, which had clearly been on a visit to the cleaner's, and a new pair of shoes, unscuffed and highly polished. Normally Desmond was blind to dirt and wore his shoes until they became disreputable. I deduced that Hall's idea of a welcome home extended to more than the redecoration of the study and bedroom.

This transformed appearance made the fear in Desmond's eyes all the more pitiable. With extreme reluctance he edged into the hall, but before I could speak Hall declared in the manner of a boxing manager resolutely introducing an unpromising protégé to a cynical audience: "As you can see, he's fighting fit now and ready for anything!"

Desmond immediately wilted. No longer able to look at me he stared down at his unfamiliar shoes with all the despair of a convicted murderer awaiting his sentence to the gallows.

But I found I was unable to play the black-capped judge. Indeed I found I was unable to play a judge of any kind because I was remembering my own excursion through the darker streets of London. I saw myself as no better than Desmond, and I found I had nothing to say.

Then suddenly that black moment of self-knowledge was infused with light. I felt as if someone had walked through the nearest door and switched on a mighty torch which destroyed every shadow in the hall. I could not see this great surge of light, but as it streamed into the deepest reaches of my mind I realised what was happening. In the face of such appalling self-knowledge, stripped of all illusions, one can only repent, and in the face of such repentance one can only be forgiven, and in the face of such forgiveness one can only receive healing and bestow it. I was witnessing the process of salvation. I was witnessing redemption. I was witnessing an absolute truth which in my past rush to pass judgement I had been so willing to overlook for so long.

For one timeless moment all self-centred preoccupation with my own suffering was eclipsed. The darkness had disappeared, and by the brilliant light which remained I saw clearly—so clearly that I was almost blinded—what I was now being called to do.

"My dear Desmond," I said, uttering the words I had always thought I would never say, "how very glad I am to have you back in the diocese. Welcome home."

And moving forward I held out my hand.

XVI

"What it amounts to is this. Christians do not need to be perfect, before they can find in one another an acceptance and an approval which is that of the truth itself; or rather, let us say, the truth himself, Jesus Christ."

AUSTIN FARRER
Warden of Keble College, Oxford, 1960–1968
A CELEBRATION OF FAITH

I

DESMOND'S SOFT, moist hand trembled in mine.

Somewhere nearby Hall murmured: "Well, if you'll both excuse me . . ." I was aware of him moving rapidly upstairs as I said to Desmond: "Perhaps we can have a brief word in your study."

He led the way into that crowded room which I could remember so clearly from the day I had searched it, but now I found it had changed. The smell of mice and musty paper had disappeared. The desk had been tidied, the books dusted, the windows washed. The curtains were several shades lighter.

As I sat down I said: "I'm glad to see you're looking better, but you shouldn't try to force the pace of your recovery. Even if the doctor judges that you're now fit for work, you must take things easy for a while." But Desmond, still hardly able to believe in this future which he had thought utterly lost, proved quite unable to reply.

"Once you've settled down again," I continued hastily, anxious to break this pause before it became too emotional, "I'd like you to come and see me so that we can discuss how I can best help you with your ministry here. I'm conscious that I've been at fault for not giving you more support in the past, and I want to avoid that mistake in the future. We must also discuss Father Hall; you mustn't think I intend to impose any changes in the parish without consulting you."

With relief I realised that Desmond was now capable of speech. Indeed he became voluble. "He's the most wonderful priest, Bishop—so gifted, so devout, so imaginative in his care for others! I consider it a true miracle that he should wish to remain here!"

I was not unpleased by this comment but felt his euphoria should be tempered by realism. "Miracle or not," I said dryly, "he's a strong character and if he's to stay we need to work out very carefully how the two of you are going to coexist. But all that can wait till later. Now, Desmond . . ." Moving to the window I fixed my gaze on my car, parked in the forecourt, and forced myself to say: "I can't let this conversation end without apologising to you for removing that box from your bedroom. I did it because I feared you'd been involved in illegal activity which would justify the police in making a search of the vicarage, but no matter how benign my motives it was certainly a questionable way to behave. The box will be returned to you and I know you'll deal with the contents as I would wish." I finally managed to wrest my gaze from the car and face him. It would have been hard to judge which of us was the more disabled by our embarrassment at that point, but fortunately the realisation that Desmond was moist-eyed galvanised me into concluding the interview as rapidly as possible. "I must now have a word with Hall—I'll telephone you later to arrange a time when you can come to see me," I said, speaking so fast that I almost ran out of breath before reaching the final syllable, and hurried out of the study without waiting for a reply.

Upstairs Hall was whistling "The Tennessee Waltz."

I decided it was time to inspect the redecoration of Desmond's bedroom.

2

THE FORMERLY dingy walls of the room were now a very bright white. The curtains, so dirty that their true colour was impossible to discern, lay piled in the middle of the threadbare carpet which I remembered as mud-coloured but was now a pale beige. Hall was washing his paintbrush in the corner basin. He had buttoned his shirt and the sandals had been replaced by shoes. He jumped when I entered the room.

"I was about to come downstairs," he said. "Would you like some tea?"

I shook my head and moved to the window which faced not only the Gothic architecture of the church but the new Starbridge by-pass, a monstrous ribbon on stilts. The slate roofs and blackened chimney-pots of Langley Bottom were jumbled together between the church and the by-pass like debris on a slag-heap.

" 'The old order changeth,' " I said. "And so it should. Without change there'd be no renewal." I turned back to look again at the bright white walls and the rotting cloth piled in the centre of the room. Then I said: "Thank you for coming to my diocese. I'm glad you're here. I want to make it possible for you to stay."

Hall sat down heavily on the edge of the bed as if all the strength had drained out of him.

"You'll notice that I make no promise about St. Paul's," I said. "There may well be insuperable difficulties which prevent it being used in the way you wish. But if we can't have the healing centre here then I shall find a place for it somewhere else."

Hall managed to thank me. I was surprised how overcome he was by my decision. "Didn't you realise last Saturday," I said, "that you'd won me over?"

"I thought I'd wrecked everything by crashing in on you when you were upset and ignoring your rank while I applied first aid."

"Ah." I paused to reflect on this memory, but as I had now acquired memories which were infinitely worse, I found I could recall the first aid without embarrassment. "It was an interesting intervention of yours," I said vaguely. "A brilliant but high-risk pastoral move—the sort of thing, perhaps, that Jon Darrow might have attempted when he was your age. Or his hero, Father Darcy."

Hall moved back to the basin again without a word; presumably he was too relieved by my benign comments even to thank me for them, and it was only when he picked up the pumice-stone to scrub the paint from his hands that he asked: "Did you manage to see Father Darrow?"

"Yes, but only for a couple of minutes. He has domestic problems."

"I thought the whole point of being a hermit was that one escaped domestic problems! How long is he likely to be out of action?"

"I'm not sure."

"Maybe I should chloroform you and bear you off to Starwater Abbey in my Volkswagen."

"That would certainly be a high-risk pastoral move!"

"I'm serious, Bishop. You need peace, quiet, light, space and rest. You need to be looked after. You need to have your psyche stroked. You need, in other words, all the things that you're not going to get at the South Canonry within spitting distance of that sick Cathedral."

This was obviously my day for hearing bizarre remarks from psychics, but before he could start talking again about the Cathedral's "bad vibes" I decided I must make some attempt, no matter how painful, to ground our talk in reality. "I'm sorry," I said with difficulty, "that you should be seeing me at my weakest."

Hall abandoned the pumice-stone and turned to stare at me. "You may be emotionally beaten up and physically exhausted," he said, "but I see no sign of spiritual weakness."

"Obviously I'd like to believe that. However—"

"*This* is spiritual weakness? Forgiving Desmond and welcoming him back into the diocese? Forgiving me for bulldozing my way around the South Canonry last Saturday? Inviting me to stay in the diocese even though you know a lot of people are going to disapprove because of my divorce? Having the courage not only to recognise the need for my controversial ministry but to give it the green light? A spiritually weak bishop," said Hall, "would have booted me out and washed his hands of Desmond—and he would have acted in the belief that he was being spiritually strong."

I moved back to the window and stared again at the muddled urban view where the new intermingled with the old. At last I heard myself say: "The paradox is that I'm sure I shall always be a conservative bishop no matter how many liberal decisions I make."

"In the end words like 'conservative' and 'liberal' don't matter—they're just ways of describing reactions to current situations, just code-language for attitudes which will date. But a truly Christian bishop, Dr. Ashworth, doesn't date; he'll never go out of fashion, even in the 1960s, because Christianity mirrors the values which are eternal." Having dried his hands he hung up the towel and led the way to the door. All he said as we went downstairs together was: "Phone me any time of the day or night if you need company at the South Canonry."

I nodded. I found I was feeling better, safer, more ready to face the ordeal of returning to the empty house and waiting for Martin to arrive. I had, of course, no intention of summoning Hall to the South Canonry in a fit of panic, but it was reassuring to know that if I did finally fall apart he would promptly rush forward to stitch me together again.

Leaving the vicarage I drove back at last into the shadow of the shining Cathedral.

3

AS I stepped into the hall of the South Canonry I heard the phone ringing and felt sure that my letter to Michael had produced the desired effect. Hurrying to my study I grabbed the receiver.

"Where have you been?" demanded Charley instantly. "What on earth happened to you? And why didn't you phone again to let me know there was no need to wait up for you?"

My acute disappointment was promptly replaced by an equally acute guilt. I said: "I really am very sorry. After we spoke I got mixed up with yet another old friend, and by the time I detached myself it was too late to phone you again."

"But why didn't you spend the night at my flat? When I got up this morning and saw your car was still parked by the church, I was so worried that I nearly called the police! And after you finally returned to collect the car, why didn't you drop in to see me? I suppose the truth is you went to see Michael and spent the night at his flat, and now you're trying to cover up the fact that you ditched me in favour of him!"

"I haven't set eyes on Michael. Charley, all I can do is apologise again and say that I got in a complete and utter muddle."

"I wish to God Mum was here to sort you out. I miss her dreadfully. I know she and I didn't always get on but at least I knew where I was with her and I just can't work out where I am with you at all—okay, okay, I know I have to make allowances for you at the moment, but frankly I'm fed up with making allowances! What about me? It's my bereavement too, yet you never once ask how I'm coping—you're utterly self-absorbed! At least I've been making some sort of Christian effort to think of someone other than myself—at least I trekked down to Starbridge to look after you—"

"And I'm very glad you did."

"I don't think that's true. In fact I think that's a complete lie. What's the matter with you, for God's sake? *What's going on?*"

"Charley, I do understand that you're upset, but I really think this melodramatic shouting does neither of us any favours—"

"Well, how else am I supposed to get through to you and hammer home how bloody desperate I feel?" yelled Charley, and slammed down the receiver before I could attempt a reply.

I hung up and waited for him to call back to apologise for his loss of temper, but the silence only lengthened. After three minutes I rang his flat and when there was no reply I could only assume he had rushed out in a frenzy of fury and frustration. The level of my distress became unbearable. Unlocking the drawer of my desk I reached inside for the journal in the hope that Lyle's words would point the way out of the emotional maze in which I was now lost, but of course the journal was no longer there; I had left it on Jon's mantelshelf.

At that point the telephone did ring, but I now felt too debilitated to cope with Charley. Then I remembered that I was still hoping to hear from Michael, and at once I grabbed the receiver. "South Canonry."

"It's Martin, Charles. This is just to report that Little Muggins is still quivering on the hearth but Dad said I could retire from the fray until tomorrow. Can I come straight to the South Canonry?"

"Please do." I made no effort to conceal my relief.

He arrived half an hour later. When the doorbell rang I could only mutter: "Thank God," and hurry to meet him.

"Tea?" I offered, having ushered him over the threshold, and Martin said promptly: "Lovely! Do you have a few little leaves of Earl Grey?"

We retired to the kitchen where I inspected the tea supplies and Martin filled the kettle. "There's a cake in the larder," I said as an afterthought. "One of my Cathedral ladies brought it last Saturday and the chaplains haven't yet had time to eat it."

"I'd adore a Cathedral lady," said Martin. "Do let me know if ever you have one to spare. Incidentally, talking of the Cathedral, I'm seized by a wild urge to attend Evensong tonight. Are you going?"

"Well—"

"Sorry, silly question, of course you're going, someone like you goes to church every day, but do you mind if I trot along with you? After such a hard day I can hardly wait to sink into a pew and tune in to some celestial music."

I did, of course, remember Hall's negative comments about the Cathedral, just as I remembered Lyle's feelings of revulsion. I also remembered that Jon had told me firmly not to go there. But I thought there were rational explanations for their reactions and that the Cathedral itself remained a hallowed place which could not harm me. Jon had been primarily worrying that I would find playing the role of bishop too much of a strain; Lyle had merely been projecting her deepest fears on to the building, and Hall, by casting the Cathedral as the villain of the piece, had been tactfully referring to the bad feeling which existed among the senior churchmen in charge of it. (By this time, of course, he would have heard all the gossip.) I myself was certainly not keen to see Aysgarth, but there was always the chance that he had decided to miss Evensong; contrary to what Martin fondly supposed, not all eminent clergymen went to church every day. I was certainly not keen to play the bishop either, but at this particular service I would be required to do no more than kneel, sit or stand at the appropriate moments, and besides, there was a strong chance that a well-rendered, numinous choral Evensong might provide some of the peace, light, space and rest which Hall had advocated earlier.

I made up my mind to go.

But it was strange how difficult it was to rid myself of the irrational notion that by entering the Cathedral I was stirring up malign forces which remained beyond my power to control.

4

THE CATHEDRAL was lying limply amidst the lawn of the churchyard like a shark dozing in a green lagoon. The spire, razor-sharp despite the fading light, seemed to be swaying faintly, an optical illusion caused by the fast-moving bank of cloud behind it. Above the hard angles of the octagonal chapter house, the tower eyed our approach with black, blank, oblong windows.

"Stunning, isn't it?" Martin remarked as we began to cross the Choir School's playing-field.

"Unique." I was reminding myself that although a building could be hallowed by prayer, it was not alive. To treat it as a living entity—as if the stones had beating hearts—was to be guilty of animism.

"Funny what strong personalities the old cathedrals have," said Martin. "Just like people. It's as if they have memories which exude all kinds of odd emanations. I remember visiting Canterbury once and getting the most extraordinary frisson on the spot where Becket was killed."

I said abruptly: "Memories projected on to a building can create a powerful atmosphere, I'll concede that, but the memories belong to the visitors, not to the buildings." Fearing I had been brusque to the point of discourtesy I then added hastily: "I'm not denying the reality of your frisson. All I'm saying is—"

"My dear Charles, I understand perfectly, and after a day spent largely in the company of two psychic loonies, I can't tell you how refreshing it is to hear a bishop being robust about the paranormal!"

I murmured: "One really does have a duty to avoid superstition," but I found I could not continue to look at the Cathedral. The blank black windows of the tower had begun to glitter as the sun sank to a new angle, and enhanced the absurd illusion that the building was alive.

Minutes later we reached the north porch, and after instructing the verger to find Martin a good seat in the choir I made my way to the vestry. Here I encountered sixteen choirboys, twelve vicars-choral, the choirmaster, one minor Canon, two of the residentiary Canons and—my heart sank—the Dean. Everyone looked startled to see me. The little boys became hushed; the vicars-choral assumed serious expressions; Tommy Fitzgerald, the Canon in residence, asked me in a reverent voice if I wished to read one of the lessons but I declined, saying I was happy to take a back seat. At that point Aysgarth, whose presence was spiced with a faint aroma of claret, remarked that he had never heard an episcopal throne described as a back seat before.

We all laughed dutifully.

"How are you, Charles?" enquired Paul Dalton, and everyone looked at him as if he had said something immensely daring.

I told him I was better, but wondered what would have happened if I had said: "Well, actually I'm just recovering from a bout of fornication." I had a fleeting vision of shocked faces as everyone decided I was in the middle of a breakdown and fantasising uncontrollably.

It was only when I had to struggle to beat back the desire to laugh that I realised I could be nearer that breakdown than I had dared imagine, and as soon as this fearful truth dawned on me I found myself becoming disorientated. What was I doing in church? I wondered how I could have summoned the nerve to cross the threshold. The betrayal of my consecration and ordination vows now seemed the grossest of crimes.

"Are you sure you're all right, Charles?" said Paul, speaking in a low voice as he moved closer to me, but I insisted that I was well. By this time one of the vergers had arrived and everyone was filtering out of the vestry to form the procession. Grabbing my pectoral cross I tried to re-establish my mental balance by focusing on the memory of Lewis Hall telling me that I was spiritually strong. I also reminded myself that since I so profoundly regretted my disastrous behaviour and wanted so much to be forgiven, there was no reason why I should not seek God in church to tell him so. Sanity edged back; confidence returned; the hideous moment passed. As the head verger led me into the Cathedral I summoned my remaining strength to concentrate on the service.

I had another bad moment when I reached the episcopal throne which I was currently so unfit to occupy, but I recovered by opening my prayer-book and staring at the first psalm I saw. I was beginning to feel as if I were being subjected to repeated demonic attacks, but of course this was nonsense. What was really happening was that the Cathedral was arousing in me intense feelings of guilt. Achingly beautiful, overpoweringly holy, radiantly numinous, it was oppressing me to such an extent that I hardly knew how to withstand the knowledge of all my recent errors.

It seemed that I had a psychological need to make that formal confession to Jon before I could feel truly forgiven. Or was there perhaps some other guilt which was causing the trouble, some guilt buried so deep in my mind that normally, when my mind was not rubbed raw by stress, I was able to ignore all the symptoms? But now was hardly the time for that sort of dangerous soul-searching; now all that mattered was to get through the service without making some elementary blunder which would betray how disturbed I was. Wishing—too late—that I had avoided the Cathedral entirely that evening, I sank to my knees for the recitation of the General Confession.

5

GRADUALLY I made a full recovery. Less concentration became required, and by the time the anthem started I had the courage to take my nose out of my prayer-book and dart a glance at my fellow-worshippers. At the other end of the choir Tommy and Paul sat in their Canons' stalls, and nearby them was the minor Canon who had been on duty in the Cathedral that afternoon. Aysgarth was sitting across the aisle. Close at hand the choirboys and the vicars-choral were tackling an anthem by Elgar with mixed results, and above and on either side of the Choir sat the congregation, a mixed bunch who on weekdays numbered about thirty. I soon noticed Martin, occupying one of the back stalls, and a second later I saw to my astonishment that he was sitting next to a certain Mrs. Harriet March, a woman whom I had no wish to meet again.

Mrs. March was a sculptress. Her husband, a famous mountaineer, had died on Mount Everest some years ago, and after his death she had retreated from London to a house in my diocese; she lived three miles from the city in a village called Upper Starwood. In 1963 Aysgarth had commissioned her to produce the now notorious sculpture which I had succeeded in banning from the Cathedral churchyard. I trust I am not betraying an unreasonable prejudice against modern art when I write that some wilful urge had prompted Mrs. March to create a work that was ugly as well as obscene.

In my fight to thwart Aysgarth's plan to litter the churchyard with an object which resembled a gigantic box of used condoms, I had assumed I had irrevocably alienated Mrs. March, whom I had met when I had been obliged to visit her studio to confirm that the work in progress was as pornographic as the photographs which she had sent to the Dean and Chapter. She was a slim, willowy woman in her late thirties, with long dark wavy hair which cascaded over her shoulders and foamed down her back. In my opinion all women over thirty should either wear their hair up or have it cut short. Cultivating a pre-Raphaelite look at that age can only convey the impression of an unedifying private life.

As I observed the presence of Mrs. March with antipathy and wondered what could have induced her to enter a church on a weekday—or indeed on any day—the anthem ended and Tommy prepared to lead the final prayers. I did my best to concentrate on them but I was soon wondering if the whiff of claret which had emanated from Aysgarth indicated the occurrence of a lavish lunch to which Mrs. March had been invited. It was the only theory I could devise which explained her attendance at the service. In 1963 at the time of the sculpture scandal, a rumour had circulated that he had known Mrs. March rather better than he should have done, but if a dean commissions a work which resembles contraceptives from a young woman with pre-Raphaelite hair, being flagellated by a malign rumour is the least he deserves for his foolishness. Perhaps in fairness I should make it clear that the seven objects in the box were not intended to be identified as used condoms. They were supposed to represent the seven deadly sins, and above them a skeletal man, ascending a climbing frame, symbolised humanity's efforts to rise above an animal existence towards God. The predominant colours were red, white and blue but I shall say no more. Merely to describe the work is to damn it.

After we had all retired to the vestry sheer relief that I had survived the service made me light-headed enough to embark on a conversation with Aysgarth. "I see Mrs. March was in the congregation," I remarked blandly.

"Yes, Dido had a meeting of her Arts Group today—Harriet gave a talk and stayed on for tea."

"Is she still sculpting French-letters?" enquired Tommy Fitzgerald, unable to resist the opportunity to needle the Dean about the fiasco of 1963. By that time the choirboys had been marched away through the cloisters, the vicars-choral were heading for the pubs and the minor Canon had gone home to watch the tail-end of the six o'clock news. I was alone with the Dean and the two residentiary Canons as the vergers toured the Cathedral before locking up for the night. We had all disrobed. Tommy was struggling into his overcoat, Paul was retying a shoelace and Aysgarth was moving towards the vestry door.

"As a matter of fact," he announced, pausing to reply to Tommy's gibe, "Harriet's been sculpting *me.*" And having stunned us all by this disclosure he sailed out of the vestry on a tide of satisfaction.

"Ye gods!" muttered Tommy. "What on earth will that woman sculpt next?"

I offered the pacific comment: "Sculpting Stephen must surely be an improvement on sculpting French-letters."

"Not necessarily," said Paul. "Supposing she's doing him in the nude?"

We all blanched.

"Impossible!" I said hastily, dismissing the idea as a joke, and escaped from the vestry into the side-aisle.

The first person I saw was Martin, waiting for me, and the second person I saw was Harriet March. She was standing beside him, and it occurred to me then that it was not unlikely that they should know each other. Mrs. March exhibited in London and was well known in her branch of the arts; Martin lived in London and was well known in his; I could imagine them meeting in various Bohemian drawing-rooms.

"Ah, there you are, Charles!" Martin was exclaiming. "You remember Harriet, don't you?"

"How could he ever forget?" said Mrs. March dryly, but she smiled, showing no trace of hostility. To Martin she added: "I showed him my studio in 1963."

"Well, so long as that was all you showed him, darling—"

"Oh Martin, do ease up on the brittle one-liners! I'm so exhausted by my five-hour sojourn at the Deanery that I don't have the strength to stand them!"

"I intercepted her as she reeled into the Cathedral," explained Martin to me, "and virtually had to carry her to her stall."

"I didn't realise you two knew each other," I said, feeling it was time I contributed to the conversation.

"We met at Perry Palmer's flat in Albany," said Mrs. March in her low, hypnotic monotone. "I met Perry through Christian Aysgarth, and I met Christian through his father—whom I met at one of Dido's art evenings soon after I moved to Upper Starwood. That was when the Dean gave me his celebrated commission," she added to Martin, "and I started work on what the Bishop later judged to be hard-core porn."

"Soft-core, surely!" said Martin gallantly.

"It looked pretty hard to the Bishop," said Mrs. March poker-faced, "in more ways than one."

Taking care not to bat an eyelid at this most questionable remark I said courteously: "Am I permitted to offer you the olive branch of peace, Mrs. March, and invite you to join us for a drink at the South Canonry?" I could not imagine at the time why I felt driven to make this offer, but I can now see it stemmed from my annoyance that she should have implied, no matter how obliquely, that I was a pathological old prude who could not tolerate sexual behaviour of any kind. I can forgive young people who nickname me "Anti-Sex Ashworth"; they at least have the excuse that they are too immature to know the difference between sex (which I was for) and the abuse of sex (which I was against). But when a member of the liberal intelligentsia starts smirking at me on account of views which I have never held, I confess I become very irritated indeed. I felt extremely irritated at that moment by Mrs. March. Her pre-Raphaelite hair irritated me, her low hypnotic monotone irritated me, her dry deadpan humour (bizarrely like Lyle's) irritated me and her attitude to conservative bishops irritated me. Adopting my most charming manner and inviting her home for a drink was my way of saying that even though I was a bishop I was no mean-spirited puritan but a sophisticated man of the world.

Few things could have indicated more clearly than this almost adolescent reaction, preoccupied entirely with my self-image, that I was still in a very disturbed state of mind.

"What a splendid idea!" Martin was exclaiming, delighted by my invitation. "Do say yes, Harriet!"

"If I hesitate, it's only because I'm dazed by the thought of being entertained by a dean and a bishop in rapid succession."

"But I'm quite different from the Dean," I said rashly before I could censor myself, "and isn't variety supposed to be the spice of life?"

"My dears!" said Martin aside to an imaginary audience. "The Bishop's moving downstage coruscating like a Christmas tree!"

"More like a diamond," said Mrs. March, languidly flicking back her long hair as she allowed her glance to travel over me. "The smooth, highly polished, enormously expensive kind."

"And diamonds, as we all know," said Martin inevitably, "are a girl's best friend."

Even before Mrs. March gave a throaty laugh I was asking myself if I had bitten off rather more than I could chew.

6

BY THE time we left the Cathedral I had quelled my misgivings by reflecting that this was clearly a time when I was destined to rub shoulders with the most unexpected people. But it then occurred to me that the words "rub shoulders" hardly formed the most appropriate phrase for a bishop to use in connection with Mrs. March.

While I fought my way through these thoughts, my companions were discussing the service. Both of them had enjoyed the anthem; there was a disagreement about which of the choirboys had looked the most angelic; Mrs. March confessed her admiration for the vicar-choral who sported a black beard. Trying not to feel depressed that both she and Martin had treated the service as little more than a free concert, I kept quiet and wished fiercely that Lyle were waiting at the South Canonry to rescue me.

"You're very silent, Bishop," said Mrs. March as we approached the front door.

"I'm merely overwhelmed by the calibre of your conversation."

"Ouch!" said Martin.

"Tell me," ordered Mrs. March, egged on to match my barbed remark with an equally barbed reply, "why did you do nothing at that service except move in and out with that long stick?"

"Crozier, darling!" exclaimed Martin with a light little laugh, and gave me an anxious look.

"And why did you do nothing, Mrs. March, except lie back and think of black beards?"

"Not all women get a kick out of lying back and thinking of England," said Mrs. March.

"Help!" said Martin.

"Obviously you want me to think you have hidden depths, Mrs. March," I said, "but you must forgive me if I treat them as unavailable for plumbing."

"Gosh!" said Martin.

"I'm beginning to like this man!" purred Mrs. March.

In panic I thought: what on earth am I doing with such frightful people?

But then I realised with horror that I was enjoying myself.

7

FORTUNATELY SOME part of my brain remained intact despite my witless compulsion to make suggestive remarks, and by the time I was mixing the drinks I had worked out what had happened. I was not merely celebrating my survival of Evensong; I was escaping from the unrelieved stress of the entire day. Such behaviour may well be excusable when displayed by a soldier home on leave from some grim battle zone, but any clergyman who embraces this form of retreat from reality should remind himself that he plays Russian roulette with his reputation.

Since I was still sane enough to realise what was happening to me I was also still sane enough to calm myself by reasoning that I did not have to deny myself all amusement to ensure my safety; I just had to avoid combining that amusement with an idiotic degree of risk. But having asked myself when idiocy began I knew the answer was: almost straight away. I knew exactly how far I could go with women without giving them all the wrong ideas. Any friendliness had to be mixed with an emotional neutrality, and emotional neutrality certainly did not include indulging in dialogue which produced sensual smiles and intimate looks. If I had been bald, bespectacled and bloated no doubt I could have allowed myself more leeway, but none of these distressing adjectives could be applied to me. How tiresome it is that sexual attraction can be conveyed merely by one stray look or a single unguarded inflection! I did not like Mrs. March and I had absolutely made up my mind to regard her looks with distaste, but the more interest she took in me the more conscious I became of her appeal.

"How did you manage to wind up at the Deanery for five hours?" I said as I handed her a gin-and-tonic. I was just congratulating myself on uttering a blameless question in an exemplary manner when I heard myself add frivolously: "That seems a little punishing for someone who doesn't usually move in clerical circles!"

"Dido invited me to lunch before I addressed her Arts Group," said Mrs. March, giving me a look which seemed to suggest there were circumstances in which she might find punishment attractive, "and somehow everything seemed to slide right out of my control before we even sat down to eat. She served dry martinis."

"I adore Dido," said Martin. "Can I have a plain tonic, Charles, if you've no ginger ale?"

As I poured out the tonic for him I said to Mrs. March: "But how did the Dean seduce you into staying on for Evensong?"

"I'm always ready to be seduced by a good offer."

"Do be serious for a moment, darling!" said Martin, becoming uncomfortable again.

"I don't think the Bishop wants me to be serious at all," said Mrs. March, "but let that pass. What happened was that by three-thirty everyone had either passed out or dropped out and only Stephen and I were left. He then suggested tea and I hadn't the strength to resist."

"Where was Dido?" demanded Martin.

"She'd taken a poet called Toby to the greenhouse so that he could recite to the plants. Apparently she recites Browning to them every day."

"I'm surprised they don't wilt and die," I said.

"Plants worship being talked to," said Martin. "I talk to my window-box all the time. Go on, Harriet. There you were, drinking à deux with the Dean—"

"There I was, drinking gallons of strong tea while Stephen told me how awful everything was—"

"How interesting!" I exclaimed, genuinely intrigued. "Whenever I get together with Stephen he does nothing but tell me how wonderful everything is. How do I get him to change the record?"

"Try growing your hair and wearing a short skirt."

"Don't get side-tracked, darling," said Martin. "We're simply yearning to know how the Dean lured you to the Cathedral."

"He said: 'This is your lucky day! The Evensong anthem's that marvellous piece by Elgar—do come and hear it!' and I was so exhausted by that time that all I could do was whisper: 'How lovely! I can't wait!' So after we'd had a little tot of claret to pep us up for the service—"

"I'm not sure Charles wants to hear about little tots of claret before Evensong," said Martin.

"On the contrary," I said, magnificently urbane, "I'm delighted to hear you enjoy wine, Mrs. March! Perhaps I should have offered you a glass of claret instead of a gin-and-tonic."

"If I see another glass of claret today I'll scream—the whole table was awash with it at lunch. And do please call me Harriet. Don't worry, I shan't attempt to call you Charles. I know men like you find it offensive when people take liberties with Christian names."

"Where clergymen are concerned," said Martin warningly, "people shouldn't take liberties with anything."

"Phooey! What do you know about clergymen?"

"More than you do, my sweet! I may be just an actor, but my father's a priest!"

"Priests can be actors," I said in between gulps of sherry, "in their way."

"Bishops certainly need a flair for stagecraft," remarked Martin. "And those robes! My dear, such style!"

"This particular bishop would look good on the stage," mused Harriet. "In fact in his younger days I daresay he would have qualified as a matinée idol. I'd have been tempted to sculpt him."

"I'm sorry you should consign my allure entirely to the past," I said, "but I hear it's not only matinée idols whom you sculpt. In fact there's a rumour going around the Close that you're sculpting Stephen Aysgarth in the nude. Do please assure me that this is just a figment of someone's imagination."

"Good God!" exclaimed Martin, transfixed in the act of lighting a cigarette.

Harriet gave a small, secretive smile, caressed the curtain of hair on one side of her face and looked up at me with a limpid expression in her eyes. "I'm certainly dealing with uncovered flesh," she said, "but it's only a part of him."

"Which part?" demanded Martin promptly and they both laughed, but Harriet made no reply.

"We're shocking our host!" said Martin becoming nervous again as I too remained silent, but Harriet said: "I think not." And gazing into the depths of her glass she added: "How ironic it is that Stephen Aysgarth, who's supposed to be so worldly, particularly about women, is actually idealistic to the point of naivety, whereas the Bishop here, a man who's supposed to be puritanical to the point of ingenuousness, is obviously very sophisticated about the opposite sex."

"Crikey!" said Martin. "How do you field that one, Charles?"

"I'm not fielding anything. I'm too busy wondering what Harriet's going to do with Stephen's nude part."

Martin started to laugh.

"I mean," I said, "the sculpture of Stephen's nude part. I mean . . . well, what I'm trying to say is, why bother with any nude part of Stephen at all?"

By this time none of us could keep a straight face.

Seconds later I found myself inviting Harriet to join us for dinner.

8

AS I tried to justify the unjustifiable I told myself that since I had Martin for a chaperon nothing could possibly go wrong. I even told myself I was being neurotic, doubting the wisdom of enjoying myself with these particular people at this particular time. It never ceases to amaze me that excuses drummed up to permit reckless behaviour so often sound like the last word in common sense.

After I had distributed another round of drinks we retired to the kitchen where I removed from the deep-freeze some portions of duckling à l'orange, and Harriet and Martin volunteered to cook the vegetables. They then instructed me to sit at the kitchen table and keep an eye on the oven, a task which they realised was compatible with my limited ability to cook, but barely had the oven door closed on the duckling than I became aware of my longing for a cigarette. I began to remove my collar.

Harriet said to Martin: "The Bishop's taking off his clothes."

"Hush, dear girl, pretend not to notice."

"Since you're so enthralled," I said, "I won't stop at the collar. I'll pay tribute to the informality of the occasion and take off my stock as well."

"What a pity there's no music!" exclaimed Martin. "David Rose and his orchestra should be blasting out 'The Stripper' . . . Out of my way, Harriet darling, I want another potato from the vegetable rack."

Having removed my stock I folded it neatly and put it on top of the refrigerator alongside my clerical collar. Then I opened my shirt at the neck, replaced my jacket and readjusted my pectoral cross before finally producing my cigarettes.

"I can't possibly continue to call you 'Bishop' after that erotic performance," said Harriet. "I'm going to call you Charles, and if that's taking a liberty, what the hell, I'm grabbing it with both hands."

"No lust here, dear, it's taboo," said Martin, "and for God's sake stop fondling those peas. Charles, pass me one of your ciggies, there's a good chap—I've left mine in the other room."

"Could I have another drink?" said Harriet.

"You've already had two!" objected Martin before I could reply.

"Yes, but didn't you notice the way he mixes gin-and-tonic? He simply shows the glass to the gin bottle!"

"That was the second time around!" I retorted. "The first gin-and-tonic is always a standard measure, but the ladies of my acquaintance prefer the next one to be milder."

"Isn't it obvious I'm no lady?"

"Surely you're sick of alcohol by this time!" said Martin severely. "What about all that claret the Dean poured down your throat?"

"It mostly went down his. Good God, after five hours at the Deanery, a visit to church and an episcopal striptease, aren't I at least allowed to down a couple of stiff gins?"

I retrieved the bottles from the drawing-room and Harriet showed me how to mix what she called a "proper" gin-and-tonic.

"It looks very improper to me," I said.

"Want one?"

"No thanks."

"Oh, go on—you're aching for it!"

"That's a Noel Coward line," said Martin. "When I played the juvenile lead in *Hay Fever* back in the thirties—"

"Where are we going to eat?" demanded Harriet, ruthlessly cutting short the theatrical reminiscences.

"Maybe we should eat here in the kitchen," said Martin, cross at being interrupted, "and pretend we're in some play by Wesker."

"I refuse to be in a play by Wesker!" I declared. "We'll eat by candlelight in the dining-room!"

"Yippee!" yodelled Martin, his good humour instantly restored. "We can pretend we're in a play by Oscar Wilde!"

"What a pity we're not all wearing evening dress," said Harriet. "I see myself sheathed in a midnight-blue gown, very décolleté, with trailing skirts which whisper over the carpet as I walk."

"Like Mrs. Erlynne," I said, "in *Lady Windermere's Fan.*"

"Who was she?"

"The fallen woman."

"Steady, Charles," said Martin. "Keep your eyes on the oven."

"The oven can look after itself while I raid the cellar. Would you really scream at the sight of another glass of claret, Harriet?"

"Yes—with ecstasy."

I retired to inspect my wine collection.

9

I SELECTED a Médoc, and by the time the wine had been allowed to breathe, the duckling was ready, Martin was dishing up the vegetables and Harriet was lighting the candles on the dining-room table. When Martin asked me to say grace Harriet objected: "But he's off-duty!" and I had to point out that I was still wearing my pectoral cross. It seemed wise to underline to myself that even an off-duty bishop has certain standards to maintain, but the further the meal progressed the harder it became not to relax as fully as I would have done with my old friend Jack Ryder. After the duckling had disappeared and the bottle of claret was empty, Harriet helped herself to some ice cream from the deep-freeze and Martin and I decided to sample the remains of a tub of Stilton. Harriet had already returned to the dining-room when in the larder I came across a bottle of vintage port which for some reason had failed to find its way down to the cellar.

"I must have port with my Stilton," I declared at once.

"I bet Harriet'll say she has to have port with her ice cream."

"That girl drinks like a fish."

"You're flexing your gills pretty energetically yourself, old chap! Would you like me to tell you when you're tight?"

It finally occurred to me how thoughtless I was being. "I'm sorry," I said upset. "Are you finding it difficult to abstain? Because if you are—"

"Charles, I'm enjoying myself so much that I wouldn't be tempted by a bottle of vodka even if it grew legs and danced on the table."

We returned to the dining-room.

"You'll be relieved to hear I loathe port," said Harriet as I revealed the bottle. "Should I now retire to leave you two gentlemen on your own? I can't quite remember which decade I'm supposed to be in."

"Stay and enhance the pleasure of our Stilton, darling," said Martin, who although sober was talking as if he had consumed a bottle of champagne. "And with that glorious hair of yours and that heavenly Mary Quant dress you couldn't be in any decade but the sexy sixties. Isn't she gorgeous, Charles?"

"Gorgeous," I said, pouring out the port.

"Lucky old Stephen Aysgarth," added Martin, "having such a breath-taking creature to sculpt his private parts!"

"Silence!" I thundered, equally frivolous. "I must defend my dean from all charges of indecent exposure!"

"Well, you can try," said Harriet, "but as his enemies would say: 'Will you succeed?' "

"Excuse me while I just ring up the *News of the World,"* said Martin. "Keep talking, darling."

"The *News of the World* would find Stephen a great disappointment," I said. "He merely enjoys talking to attractive young women. It's his hobby."

"Today that's not a hobby, that's a hang-up," said Harriet.

"That's not a hang-up, that's down-to-earth, common-sense morality," I retorted, deciding I had a duty to the Church to leave them in no doubt about the propriety of Aysgarth's private life. "Stephen's a married man and a distinguished clergyman. Of course he's going to be all talk and no action with his ladyfriends. What other option does he have?"

"But is there really no action?" persisted Martin mystified. "Absolutely, utterly *none?"*

"Surely there's always an option," said Harriet to me, "but I agree with you that Stephen would never take it. He's much too devoted to his wife."

"That's so unlikely that I suppose it just has to be true," said Martin, "but Harriet darling, you seem to know our friend the Dean quite amazingly well! Are you sure he's never even held your hand?"

"Well, of course he's held my hand—don't be idiotic! He likes me. But if you think he's ever done more than that you couldn't be further from the truth—and by the way, I don't like you treating him as a figure of fun. He may not be a smartly dressed glamour-boy like you but he's bright and brave and kind, he's passionate about art, he's devoted to his family, he's a very amusing friend and I'll defend him to the last ditch."

We stared at her. She stared back defiantly. Finally Martin murmured: "Fancy!" and looked astonished.

"In other words," I said, "you see him as a hero."

"Of course I do! Only a hero could be married to Dido for twenty years and still be dedicated to her welfare at the end of it."

"I thought you liked Dido," Martin said at once.

"I do. But if she was my wife I'd murder her."

Martin turned to me. "What do you think, Charles? Do you see the Dean being every bit as devoted to Dido as she obviously is to him?"

After a pause I said: "I've never pretended to understand that marriage, but Lyle always thought there was far more to it than ever met the eye."

There was another silence as the mention of Lyle reminded us of my bereavement, and suddenly I felt as if my profound unhappiness, penned up behind the dam created by the frivolous dinner-party, was about to burst free. When Martin enquired at last: "Coffee, anyone?" I could only shake my head, and Harriet too declined.

"I must be going," she said. "What time does the constable lock the gates of the Close?"

I roused myself sufficiently to glance at my watch. "You've got fifteen minutes."

"Harriet angel," said Martin, attempting to dispel the shadow which had fallen over the party, "when do I see you again? Do we really have to wait for another brief encounter at Perry Palmer's?"

"Well, I'm open to offers. Make one."

"How about a delicious lunch somewhere wildly fashionable when you're next up in town?"

They produced diaries and fruitlessly compared vacant spaces. "Can I phone you?" said Harriet at last. "It's all so confusing."

"The familiar line!" sighed Martin. " 'Don't call us, we'll call you!' "

"I really will call, I promise—"

"Lovely, darling. I look forward to my long vigil by the phone."

"So glad I've made you happy. Goodbye, Charles—thanks for a memorable evening. Next time I see you being puritanical on television I'll think of you doing that strip-tease."

"I'll see you out to your car," said Martin, as we all moved into the hall.

"My car! God, I'd quite forgotten—it's still parked by the Deanery!"

"In that case let me give you a ride up the road in my chariot. Leave the door on the latch for me, Charles . . ."

I waved them goodbye from the doorstep.

Returning to the kitchen I sat down at the table and thought how odd the dinner-party had been, how far removed from any formal clerical dinner-party which Lyle and I had given in the past. Yet I did not think Lyle would have found the impromptu meal with Martin and Harriet unamusing. Perhaps she had secretly wished our evenings could have been more adventurous but for my sake had kept quiet about her own preferences.

Thinking of Lyle's secret wishes reminded me of the journal but although I tried hard at once to turn my thoughts to a less difficult subject, all that happened was that I wound up picturing myself in bed with Harriet.

Then I did despair, not because I was thinking an unnatural thought—what could be more natural than thinking about sex after dining with a *femme fatale?*—but because I saw clearly that despite the catastrophic incident with Sheila I was still in a frame of mind which could result in yet another disastrous mistake. Or in other words, I was still not in control of my impulses but at the mercy of them. And what did "impulses" really mean in this context anyway? Dimly I began to grasp that I was dealing not merely with the sexual instinct but with the drives of the unconscious mind; I began to perceive that I was in the grip of a malign psychological force which was fuelling a desire for self-destructive behaviour, but as I remained unable to identify this force I knew the likelihood that I could master it was minimal.

Reluctance to accept this sinister theory made me try to explain my behaviour in more facile ways, but no explanation convinced me. It was useless, after my night with Sheila, to claim I was sexually frustrated. It was equally useless to tell myself I was falling irrationally in love with Harriet; I knew very well I would be happy never to see her again. And it was useless to tell myself that drink had loosened my inhibitions. This was certainly true, but I was not drunk to the point of insanity. Indeed I was not drunk at all; I had had a couple of small sherries, two glasses of claret and a single glass of port, and normally I was quite capable of consuming this modest amount of alcohol without feeling driven to bound around like a satyr. Moreover, I was no longer alone at the South Canonry and isolated by my grief; I had taken the trouble to acquire a sympathetic companion who I knew would listen with understanding if I needed to confide in someone. I had been sensible in recruiting Martin, careful in my consumption of alcohol and rational in working out how I could best protect myself while I waited to see Jon. So why was I still suffering from the urge to behave like a lunatic?

I was still immersed in this bout of unsuccessful self-analysis when Martin returned from his brief excursion up Canonry Drive.

"A marvellous woman, isn't she?" he exclaimed as I moved into the hall to meet him. "I'm mad about her."

I said in my most casual voice: "She's certainly attractive. Why hasn't she remarried?"

"Wedded to the memory of her husband the mountaineer—or so the story goes, but I hear she gets around quite a bit. Funny about her friendship with the Dean, isn't it? I think she's genuinely fond of him."

"Did she tell you which part of him she's been sculpting?"

"No. Which do you think it was?"

"His head. Do have a bath if you want one, Martin—no, don't worry about clearing everything up. I'll send an SOS to my housekeeper tomorrow."

"Wonderful—but where do I go to collapse in a non-alcoholic stupor? You haven't assigned me a bedroom yet."

I escorted him to the smaller and warmer of the two spare-rooms. The bed was unmade but at his insistence I abandoned him with the necessary linen while I went downstairs to lock up.

I switched off the porch light, attended to the front door and retired to my study to select some tranquillising bedtime reading, some novel which would transfer me to a masculine world of long ago where women were kept firmly on the sidelines and nobody ever thought about sexual intercourse. Sapper's *Bull-dog Drummond* caught my eye. Pulling the battered old copy from its shelf I wandered back into the hall.

The doorbell rang.

I gave a violent start but was at once convinced that Michael had finally arrived. Switching on the porch light again I drew back the bolts and flung wide the door.

Outside stood Harriet March.

XVII

". . . the process of artistic invention probably casts as much light as anything human on God's devising of the world."

AUSTIN FARRER
Warden of Keble College, Oxford 1960–1968
LOVE ALMIGHTY AND ILLS UNLIMITED

I

"CHARLES, I'M terribly sorry," she said, "but my car's expired at the top of Canonry Drive, the gates of the Close are locked and I'm marooned. What's the best thing to do?"

After a fractional pause I said: "I've got a key for the gates. I'll drive you home."

"If there's a taxi-service I can call—"

"No, the last taxi will have left the station by now, and you won't get anyone turning out at this hour. Just let me tell Martin what's happening."

I retreated upstairs knowing I should ask Martin to rescue me but he was in the bath. Moreover his reaction when I called out the news was: "What a lovely treat for you, old chap, but do be careful if she invites you to see her etchings," and after this breezy display of sanity I felt that any show of reluctance on my part could only seem neurotic.

I tried to pull myself together. I told myself that I was not going to bed with Harriet March, that there was no question that I would go to bed with Harriet March, that it was utterly beyond the realms of possibility that I would go to bed with Harriet March—but immediately I was haunted by those famous words of St. Paul: "For the good that I would, I do not: but the evil which I would not, that I do." There indeed was a desperate and chilling glimpse into the darkest corners of the human psyche.

Still inwardly shuddering I retrieved the appropriate key from my study and rejoined Harriet in the hall.

"This is very good of you, Charles," she said, and as I realised she was genuinely grateful I saw her not as a siren but as a woman now merely anxious to return home after an arduous round of socialising. My uneasiness ebbed—until I remembered Abba Cyrus of Alexandria saying that one had to think of fornication in order to avoid it. Perhaps I needed to remain uneasy. Perhaps uneasiness was not, after all, a neurotic symptom but a manifestation of sanity, a hint that my instinct for self-preservation was still alive.

Feeling almost as if I were taking my life in my hands I led the way outside to my car.

2

ONCE I had relocked the gate of the Close behind us we said little. Starbridge was at that hour deserted, its lighted streets casting long shadows down the ancient alleys which honeycombed the centre of the city. After following the boundary wall of the Close past St. Anne's Gate I drove under the new by-pass and headed south on a minor road which led to Upper Starwood, three miles away.

Beside me Harriet was very still, her long mane of hair falling forward and shielding her face. Her coat was unbuttoned; the short skirt of her dress rose above her knees; I could see the curve of her legs in the glow from the dashboard.

"You'll have to direct me," I said abruptly as we entered the village. "I'm not sure I can remember where your house is." It seemed a long time since my visit to her studio at the height of the pornographic sculpture scandal.

We turned down a lane by the church, and soon afterwards forked left towards open fields. Seconds later Harriet's cottage appeared on the right and I recognised the outline of the barn which she had converted into a studio.

"Come in for a moment," she said. "There's something I want to show you." And as I hesitated, immobilised by all my uncertainties, she added dryly: "It's okay—I shan't tear all my clothes off once the door's closed."

"To what do I owe this disappointing departure from routine?"

She laughed and suddenly, to my astonishment, I found I could relax. It was as if we had succeeded in domesticating the undercurrent of sexual attraction by acknowledging its presence and treating it as mundane. "I'll give you some coffee," she said. "It's the least you deserve for your chivalry in bringing me home. And we'll drink it in the studio. You'll feel quite safe there."

"Will I?"

"Oh yes. In the studio I never waste time on mere trivialities like sexual intercourse."

"You see sex as trivial?"

She shrugged her shoulders. "It's all right if you've got nothing better to do." As I halted the car she added: "When I'm working sex just seems an inexcusable waste of time and energy."

I then had the most unexpected thought; perhaps the realisation that she was obviously speaking the truth set me free to relax and view the situation more imaginatively. I saw that she too, like Hall and Martin, was someone whom before Lyle's death I would have dismissed without a second thought. And I saw that perhaps she too, like Hall and Martin, might have some message which could help me as I struggled to survive my bereavement. The possibility seemed fantastic, but I felt that if I could stop thinking about Harriet's sex-appeal and start listening to her views I might not only survive the night without making a disastrous mistake but even survive the next few days without having a breakdown.

"Can you see anything?" enquired Harriet. By this time we were moving down the path to the barn. "You'd better hang on to the back of my coat."

"I can't see the back of your coat."

"Never mind, we're almost there."

A moment later she was turning the key in the lock, crossing the threshold and switching on all the powerful lights.

Following her I found myself in the long rectangular room which I had seen two years ago. At first sight it seemed chaotic, crammed with alien paraphernalia, but gradually it became clear that the chaos was an illusion and that all the tools and materials, all the work finished and unfinished, were arranged with an intricate order. I was reminded of the appearance of my study when I was working under pressure but still well in control of all the mounds of paper on my desk.

"Have a seat," said Harriet, plugging in the heater which stood by the small iron table, but I ignored this invitation and stood gazing at my surroundings. Unlike Elisabeth Frink, Harriet did not work in quick-drying plaster which was then chiselled into its final shape. I noted a large clay-bin and a block and plenty of wire, and a couple of finished pieces, heads cast in bronze, not large, which were labelled as if about to depart on a journey to some exhibition. Various tools were lined up on a bench which ran along one wall, and beyond this a small shape, shrouded in white cloth, rested on a plinth.

" 'Clothed in white samite,' " I quoted, " 'mystic, wonderful.' "

"That's what I wanted to show you." Harriet switched on the electric kettle and joined me. "Come and look."

I followed her over to the plinth, and when she pulled away the cloth I found myself staring at a pair of ugly hands which had been modelled with such skill that the result was a work which manifested both extreme delicacy and extreme power. In fact so struck was I by the innate ugliness of the object and its transformation into a creation which radiated both beauty and truth, that I could only gaze at the hands in silence.

"Recognise them?" said Harriet at last.

"No." Then light dawned. "Good heavens!" I exclaimed stupefied. "Aysgarth!"

"Yes." She touched the clay with a sensuous gesture which implied a satisfaction physical in its intensity, and not for the first time I thought how strange artists were. With their capacity to seal themselves away in a private world and retreat deep into a forest of mental forms which no ordinary person could penetrate, they seemed almost inhuman as they slaved constantly to explore humanity. Harriet caressed her work like a mother; I suspected it would always mean more to her than any infant of flesh and blood, and that it was probably no accident that she was childless. Yet I felt that she must know more about the deepest emotions of maternity than some mothers, and I saw then that although she was obviously capable of profound passion, every ounce of it was poured into her work. I saw too why she was so fond of Aysgarth. Any affectionate, amusing, intelligent male who made no time-wasting demands would be a highly prized acquaintance.

"It must be very good," I said as I continued to gaze at Aysgarth's broad, gnarled hands clasped in prayer, "because I find it disturbing as well as moving."

This was evidently the right thing to say. She decided to confide in me. "I always wanted to do those hands of his," she said, "but I could never see the right way to present them. Then about a year ago they began to haunt me. I dreamed about them, thought of them night and day—until finally I saw how they had to be done."

"And after that did everything go smoothly?"

"Good God, no! Quite the reverse." She sighed before adding: "Creation has to be the greatest pleasure in the universe, but it can be pretty damned harrowing when the work's in process."

I gestured towards the hands. "You never thought of giving up?"

"Don't be ridiculous! When things go wrong I don't chuck in the towel," she said, caressing the hands again with her forefinger. "I just slave harder than ever to make everything come right." She ran her forefinger down the back of the left hand and around into the hidden area at the base of the palm. "Making everything come right," she said. "That's what it's all about. No matter how many disasters happen, no matter how many difficulties I encounter, I can't rest until I've brought order out of chaos and made everything come right." She moved dreamily around the plinth. The caressing hand seemed almost to impart life. I half-expected the sculpted hands to unclasp themselves in response to her touch.

"Of course I made a lot of mistakes," she was saying. "I turned down various blind alleys and had to rework everything to get back on course. But that's normal. You can't create without waste and mess and sheer undiluted slog—you can't create without pain. It's all part of the process. It's in the nature of things."

On the counter behind us the electric kettle was coming to the boil but she was oblivious of it. She was almost oblivious of me. At that moment she had eyes only for those ugly hands which were so beautiful. "And don't throw Mozart at me," she added as an afterthought. "I know he claimed his creative process was no more than a form of automatic writing, but the truth was he sweated and slaved and died young giving birth to all that music. He poured himself out and he suffered. That's the way it is. That's creation."

Suddenly she swivelled to face me. "You theologians talk a lot about creation," she said, "but as far as I can see none of you know the first damn thing about it. God didn't create the world in seven days and then sit back and say: 'Gee-whiz, that's great!' He created the first outlines of his project to end all projects and he said: 'Yes, that's got a lot of potential but how the hell do I realise it without making a first-class balls-up?' And then the real hard work began."

"And still continues. Theologians don't believe God withdrew from the world after the first creative blast and forgot about it."

"Of course he couldn't forget! No creator can forget! If the blast-off's successful you're hooked, and once you're hooked you're inside the work as well as outside it, it's part of you, you're welded to it, you're enslaved, and that's why it's such bloody hell when things go adrift. But no matter how much the mess and distortion make you want to despair, you can't abandon the work because you're *chained* to the bloody thing, it's absolutely woven into your soul and you know you can never rest until you've brought truth out of all the distortion and beauty out of all the mess—but it's agony, agony, *agony*—while simultaneously being the most wonderful and rewarding experience in the world—and *that's* the creative process which so few people understand. It involves an indestructible sort of fidelity, an insane sort of hope, an indescribable sort of . . . well, it's love, isn't it? There's no other word for it. You love the work and you suffer with it and always—*always*—you're slaving away against all the odds to make everything come right."

She turned away but I went on staring at Aysgarth's hands as she made the coffee. Eventually I heard her say: "There's no milk."

"It doesn't matter." I moved to the counter to join her. "And when the work's finally finished," I said, "does every step of the creation make sense? All the pain and slog and waste and mess—how do you reconcile yourself to that? Is every disaster finally justified?"

"Every step I take—every bit of clay I ever touch—they're all there in the final work. If they hadn't happened, then this"—she gestured to the sculpture—"wouldn't exist. In fact they *had* to happen for the work to emerge as it is. So in the end every major disaster, every tiny error, every wrong turning, every fragment of discarded clay, all the blood, sweat and tears—*everything* has meaning. I give it meaning. I reuse, reshape, recast all that goes wrong so that in the end nothing is wasted and nothing is without significance and nothing ceases to be precious to me."

"So you're saying that the creative process includes a very strong doctrine of redemption."

Again she turned away abruptly. "I don't trust those theological words."

"But why? Surely—"

"I don't rate that God of yours very highly. Speaking as a creator I'd say he makes too damn many mistakes."

"But if, as you've just said, all things work together for good by a creative process of redemption—"

"I deal in inert materials. God deals in living creatures. If I were one of God's creative mistakes—a child dying of congenital disease, perhaps—I'd want to kick God in the teeth."

"So would I, but if God never wills the suffering and works always to redeem it—if he's driven on by hope, faith and love to make everything come right—if he's inside the work as well as outside, sharing the pain and suffering alongside his creation—"

"I'd still want to kick him in the teeth and scream at him for making such a mess."

"Now you're talking as one of the created. But when you were talking as a creator a moment ago you said very firmly that mess was inevitable, an unavoidable part of the creative process. You said—"

"Oh shut up, Charles, for God's sake, before I kick *you* in the teeth for turning this into a bloody theological debate! To be frank, I'm not interested in any creation but my own, and anyway I don't believe our world was created—and is still being created—by a god. I believe it's always been created solely by chance and necessity."

"That's the equivalent of saying you believe that sculpture over there was created solely by your tools and not by you."

"Christ!"

"Sorry. I'll stop." Carrying my cup of coffee to the iron table I sat down on one of the canvas chairs and said mildly: "What does Stephen think of the work? I hope he's pleased."

She was clearly relieved by my attempt to change the conversation. "Yes, he is," she said. "He's got a good eye for art—in fact he's one of the few laymen I know who can discuss it intelligently."

It seemed odd to hear the word "laymen" used in a context which had no clerical connection, but I saw now that her art was her religion and she felt no need of another. I then found myself wondering how far she could ultimately journey in her art if she remained self-centred and not God-centred. To be centred entirely on the self is inevitably to be limited in one's range; to be centred on God, aligning one's own puny self with the power of the Creator, is to be open to the spiritual range of all humanity, to be in touch with the eternal, not merely the ephemeral. Harriet was a fine artist, but with her narrowed vision she risked failing to reach her full potential—or was she, in her preoccupation with beauty and truth, not so far from being God-centred as I in my arrogance supposed? Certainly one could argue that God was using her talent to express beauty and truth—with the result that in her Godlessness God was still revealed.

I was still meditating on this paradox when I heard Harriet say the words "west front." My theological speculations were abruptly terminated as the thought of the Cathedral leapt back into my mind.

"Sorry," I said, "I wasn't listening. Could you—"

"I said that once the hands are cast in bronze they'll be sold to raise money for the West Front Appeal."

"But that's wonderful!" I exclaimed at once. I was indeed impressed by the generosity of the gift.

"Oh, I'm not the only artist who'll be contributing to the Cathedral! There's a gang of us—Stephen's going to have an auction of our work later this year, and of course that was why he was hobnobbing with Christie's. It was to be the first stage of a publicity campaign to generate interest in our auction." She paused, idly examining her thumbnail. Then she flicked back her curtain of hair, gave me another of her long limpid looks and asked innocently: "Charles, can I have a quick word with you about Stephen?"

And that was the moment when I realised I had not been invited to the studio merely to view the sculpture of Aysgarth's hands.

3

AT THAT point I should have left. I had received my unexpected enlightenment, the theological insight from an atheist; the murky sexual resonances which had been echoing between us earlier had faded, and all our past dislike had been overcome. If I had left then we would have parted on agreeable terms and I would have stored up no trouble for myself in the future. But I did not leave. The mention of the West Front Appeal had the effect of riveting me to my chair, and with the introduction of Aysgarth's name all the negative emotions he aroused in my mind streamed forth to pollute the conversation.

"I was wondering," said Harriet, "if you realise just how lucky you are to have such a gifted fund-raiser working for that Cathedral."

I took care to exude friendliness. "I assure you," I said very pleasantly, "I take the greatest possible interest in Stephen's fund-raising activities."

She gave a short laugh. "My God, you're smooth!"

"Is that a compliment?"

"No. You don't like him, do you? There's this wonderful man, slogging his guts out for you, and yet all you can do is give him a hard time!"

"What nonsense!"

"Is it? It doesn't look like nonsense to me! Obviously you see yourself as the virtuous Bishop, pure as driven snow, and Stephen as the hard-drinking, shady Dean who's a terrible cross for you to bear, but let me ask you this: has it ever occurred to you that you might have got everything wrong?"

"What do you mean?"

"Well, supposing it's you, not Stephen, who's actually the villain of this story. And supposing it's Stephen, not you, who's the true Christian hero."

"I admire your creative attempt to convert fact to fiction, but I'm at a loss to know how to respond. Am I supposed to laugh? Or am I supposed to stamp my foot and throw a tantrum?"

"Neither. Just pin back your ears and listen to this: Stephen's the only clergyman I've ever met who reminds me of Jesus Christ. He's tough and magnetic but patient and long-suffering. He's not afraid to mingle with the modern equivalent of 'publicans and sinners.' He's got the guts to lash out against ecclesiastical claptrap. He doesn't live intellectually in a religious ghetto and look down his nose at the outsiders. He likes food and wine and women, and he preaches the primacy of love. He's the kind of Christian whom outsiders like me can really relate to—and how many other senior churchmen could you say that about, I'd like to know? Damn few! So give him a break. Leave him alone for once. Don't beat him up as you did back in 1963."

"My dear," I said, "you should beware of the eloquence which stems from a surfeit of alcohol. You'll regret this conversation when you wake up tomorrow morning."

"Why, you absolute monster! How dare you put me down in such a revoltingly superior fashion? You're just jealous because I think Stephen's more heroic than you are!"

"Did Stephen tell you to approach me like this?"

"No, of course not! He just told me you were giving him hell over the Christie's business and I thought it was time someone crusaded on his behalf."

"Dido's constantly crusading on his behalf. Incidentally, what does Dido think of your passionate admiration of her husband?"

"Loves it. Gives us something in common."

"She doesn't mind when he flirts with you?"

"I thought you said at dinner that the only thing Stephen did with his ladyfriends was talk to them!"

"It sounds as if you're the exception that proves the rule!"

"I denied that earlier and I'll deny it again now. Stephen's entirely devoted to Dido—in fact he still sleeps with her."

"How do you know?"

"He told me. Stephen tells me everything."

"Whenever a woman makes a remark like that I'm always sure the man's told her nothing."

"You *are* jealous, aren't you? You're jealous as hell and don't think I can't work out why!"

With horror I woke up to the fact that the conversation had spiralled into an abyss where any monstrous accusation was utterable. "You yourself may choose to indulge in fantasy," I said, "but I don't have to connive at it."

"Don't make me laugh, you've been conniving from the start! And it's not fantasy—it's reality, but you're so wrapped up in your convoluted prurience that you can't call a spade a spade!"

To rebut the charge I immediately moved away from her, gestured to the sculpture and said: *"That's* reality. And so was your talk of creation, but ever since you switched the subject to Stephen you've talked romantic drivel. Obviously you're obsessed with him."

"I'm obsessed with his hands. They fascinate me because they illustrate the dichotomy within his personality. Just look at them! They're brutal—

and so is his mouth in repose—yet to me he's always been the kindest, gentlest person, and when those hands are clasped in prayer there's such strength there, such idealism, such nobility—" She broke off before concluding abruptly: "I must stop or you'll accuse me again of talking romantic drivel. How inadequate words are sometimes!"

"But I think I now understand why I found the sculpture disturbing," I said, diverted in spite of myself. "The brutality of the hands contrasts so sharply with the grace of the spiritual pose." And on an impulse I added: "Don't you think the sculpture's making a profoundly religious statement? You're saying human beings can transcend their baser natures by turning to God."

"No, that's what you're saying—and that's fine, you can read into it what you like. But all I'm trying to do is say something truthful about Stephen . . . More coffee?"

"No thanks. I've got to go," I said, staying exactly where I was.

"You can say 'yes' if you like," she said agreeably. "I'm not cross with you any more. You've redeemed your detestably smarmy rudeness by making intelligent remarks about my work."

"You were pretty rude to me," I retorted, "and you didn't even take the trouble to be smarmy about it."

She was amused. "I rather enjoyed stirring you up," she said, "and unless I'm much mistaken you rather enjoyed it too."

At once I embarked on my journey to the door but I was only halfway across the room when she murmured behind me: "The dinner tonight was fun, but it would have been even more fun, wouldn't it, if Martin hadn't been there."

"You think so?" Greatly against my better judgement I stopped. We were now six paces apart. She was examining her thumbnail again. Her long, wavy hair, framing her thin, white, pointed, predatory face, was sliding around her shoulders and bosom in a cascade which reflected the studio's harsh artificial light. I was aware of her long fingers and her thin wrists and the heavy black make-up on her downcast eyes. "Personally," I heard myself say, "I enjoyed Martin's company."

"I thought he was a bore. I've no time for elderly queers."

The spell was abruptly broken.

I can remember the exact emotions which set me free: disgust for the two-faced behaviour which had led Martin to assume he was her friend; repulsion for the casual cruelty for which she evidently felt no shame; dismay that someone who could produce such a sensitive work of art should exhibit such a complete lack of feeling. But even as I reacted so adversely I found time to wonder if artists needed the flaws in their personalities to stoke up the tension which fed the creative impulse, and

I thought again how mysterious creation was, with its veiled enigmatic dynamics, its obsessive commitment, its costly toiling to express slivers of truth in symbols.

"What's the matter?" Harriet was demanding sharply. "Why should you look so shocked? Your Church has no time for queers, does it, and no time either for women like me who don't fulfil your masculine ideas about how women should behave!"

"As far as I can see you're hellbent on fulfilling one very conventional masculine idea about how certain women behave! No doubt at my age I should be flattered, but to be quite honest—"

"The last thing you evidently intend to be is quite honest! Of course you're flattered! I'm young enough to be your daughter, I'm rich, talented and famous and I still look pretty damned good. Most men of your age would give their back teeth—if they had any left—for me to bat my eyelashes at them, and why shouldn't they? And why shouldn't I do a bit of batting if I fancy it? I rather like older men actually, provided they're in good shape, have sex-appeal and don't smell—"

"So the rumour that you're wedded to Captain March's memory is no more than a charming fable!"

"Of course I'm wedded to Donald's memory, just as I'm sure you're wedded to your wife's, but what's that got to do with the present situation?"

"Just about everything, I'd say, but of course I'm incurably old-fashioned." I finally managed to reach the door.

"My God, I think I've finally dented that glass-smooth surface!" exclaimed Harriet. "Was it the mention of your wife? I'm sorry, that sudden death must have been terrible, don't think I can't understand—"

"You couldn't begin to understand." I tried to open the door but it had stuck. I began to shake the handle impotently.

"Here, I'll do that—" She was suddenly much too close to me. "You have to lift the latch as well as turn the handle—" The door swung open. I blundered outside. "No, wait, Charles, let me get a torch!"

"Don't need one." But the night seemed so dark, after the brightly lit studio, that I felt as if I had plunged down a mine-shaft.

"Don't be a bloody fool!" shouted Harriet as I floundered down the flagstone path. "Supposing you fell and broke a hip?"

"I don't do that sort of thing!" I shouted back, but I did stop. I was imagining my lay-chaplain trying to explain to the press why I should have been visiting Mrs. March's studio at such a very inappropriate hour of the night.

When Harriet reached me with the torch she said: "I'm sorry I mentioned your wife."

"Never mind."

"And I'm sorry I went on and on about Stephen."

"Doesn't matter."

"I'm sort of worried about him at the moment, that's all. He's under a lot of pressure."

"He'll survive." I said nothing more until I reached the car. Then as I slumped into the driving-seat I remarked: "You really care about that man, don't you?"

"Is that a sin?"

"Not if Stephen's in his right mind."

"Actually I wouldn't sleep with Stephen even if he asked me."

"Stingy of you."

"Well, he's not my type physically. Unlike you. Let me know, won't you, if ever you get just the teensiest bit bored with being in your right mind."

"What a relief to know you think I'm in good shape, have sex-appeal and don't smell! But my dear Harriet," I said, finally making a very big mistake as I dared to believe I was going to avoid making the biggest mistake of all, "nymphomaniacs who seek a cure for their frigidity should look to a psychiatrist, not a bishop." And slamming the door, I drove away much too fast into the night.

4

THERE WAS no sound from Martin's room when I arrived home and this was a relief to me for I was too exhausted for further conversation. Stripping off my clothes I fell into bed and slept.

I awoke at three with indigestion. I immediately blamed the coffee which I had been too preoccupied to refuse, but it also occurred to me that indulging in port and Stilton after duck and claret is not the wisest behaviour for a man of my age whose stomach has never quite recovered from the deprivations of war. I trekked to the bathroom for the necessary tablets, but by the time I returned I was wide awake. I was wishing I had never uttered that last sentence to Harriet, a remark guaranteed to rouse her to fury. Then I started wishing I had never entered her studio, but no, I could not wish that; she had given me too many illuminating insights to make me regret my visit, and in fact I wanted to review those insights and meditate upon them but I now had to quieten my brain, not stimulate it, so all meditation had to be saved for later.

However, no sooner had I made this sensible decision than I found I was meditating about Lyle; I was finally trying to work out what she would have thought of my new career as a satyr, and my conclusions were most unpalatable. I was sure she would have understood that I had only fallen into bed with Sheila because I had felt so bereaved, but I was sure too that she would have garnished her forgiveness with some very caustic comments about women who wore beige and eschewed black underwear; such a female would have been judged quite unsuitable for my private life no matter how able she was at running an episcopal household. As for Harriet . . . I could only wince. "Messing around with someone young enough to be your daughter," Lyle would have said severely, "is carrying your sentimentality towards young women to an absolutely lethal conclusion." After that I hardly dared consider what Lyle would have thought of my interlude with Loretta but I pictured her looking feline as she composed a remark about old age pensioners who jangled around in short skirts when they should have been sipping tea with dignity in front of their television sets.

I did sleep again after this meditation; in fact I slept twice but each time I awoke after a nightmare which I was unable to recall. Much depressed by this disjointed and unpleasant night I finally dragged myself downstairs, but here I was greatly cheered by Martin, who was in excellent spirits. He was sitting at the kitchen table with a boiled egg and *The Times.* All the dinner-party debris had been cleared away, the kitchen was spotless and freshly brewed coffee was waiting for me on the counter. "Nothing's more dreary than dirty dishes on the morning after the night before," he said when I thanked him for the transformation, "and I decided they couldn't wait for your housekeeper." He even volunteered to cook me breakfast. I did try to say that toast would be sufficient, but I was told I had to have plenty of protein in order to survive "the slings and arrows of outrageous fortune."

"Possibly you also need plenty of protein to revive you after chauffeuring the lovely Harriet," he added, extracting two eggs from the larder, "but of course I'm much too discreet to ask questions."

"She showed me the nude part."

"Was it the head?"

"No, the hands."

"But the Dean's hands are nothing special, are they?"

"They are now."

"A masterpiece?"

"I thought so."

"What a privilege to be given a private viewing! But I could see she fancied you."

"As I'd banned her sculpture in 1963 she was probably just suffering from a compulsion to win me over . . . When are you off to Starrington?"

"When you've consumed your protein. Shall I phone and report on the state of play?"

"Please—but do make it clear to Jon that he doesn't have to see me until Nicholas is better."

"Silly Little Muggins," muttered Martin. Easing the eggs into a saucepan he added: "How long do you want these tortured for?"

"Four minutes." By this time I was feeling so much better that I was ready to make plans to spend the morning constructively. It occurred to me that after my turbulent night my most sensible course of action was to soothe myself by playing a few more holes with a five-iron, and I was just picturing an idyllic walk along the fairways of the golf course when my chaplains arrived with Miss Peabody. All were enchanted to discover Martin, star of "Down at the Surgery," and Martin was equally enchanted to find himself with a small but admiring audience. Having informed them of the previous evening's dinner-party ("We all pretended we were in a play by Wilde, my dears, even the Bishop!") he embarked single-handed on the best scenes in *The Importance of Being Earnest.*

The water in the saucepan almost boiled dry but the eggs were rescued before they could be roasted, and I ate them with bread and butter. (The toast had burnt.) By this time Martin was playing Lady Bracknell, the chaplains were cheering every reference to the handbag and Miss Peabody could even have been found guilty of giggling. I was just drawing breath to bellow "Encore!" at the top of my voice when this lax scene, quite unsuitable for an episcopal residence, was unfortunately interrupted by the arrival of my archdeacon who swept into the kitchen in a fine flurry of righteousness and demanded: "What's this—a circus?" He then saw to his astonishment that the Bishop was present and actually appeared to be enjoying the uproar. I could see this worried Malcolm very much. I was not normally the kind of bishop who breakfasted in the kitchen with my subordinates in the presence of a television star.

"Are you all right, Charles?" he said concerned after being formidably diplomatic to Martin.

I said I was. By this time the party was breaking up. The chaplains melted away to the office. Miss Peabody swept off with a steaming coffee-mug. Martin said with a sigh: " 'Once more unto the breach, dear friends!' " and departed for Starrington. Having finished my second egg I was just about to announce my decision to take an idyllic walk along the fairways when Malcolm said: "How charitable of you to offer Martin Darrow hospitality, Charles! Hardly your sort of person, is he?"

After a pause I said: "Martin is a regular worshipper at St. Mary's Bourne Street."

"Oh, splendid! That must be a great consolation to Father Darrow.

Now, Charles, I do hope you intend to take it easy—I know you want to get back to work but I really feel it would be a big mistake to pick up the reins again before you were fully fit. There's nothing for you to do today anyway. Nigel and I are just going to have a little conference."

Filled with foreboding I said: "What's the main item on the agenda?"

"Langley Bottom. We're going to hammer out the details of how we can pension off Desmond, evict that shady adventurer Hall and close down St. Paul's."

I silently bid farewell to my idyllic walk on the fairways.

5

"I HAVEN'T forgotten the problems involved in closing the church," added Malcolm when I failed to demonstrate enthusiasm for his agenda. "But I think now that Desmond's home again we really have to get down to brass tacks and map out a plan of action."

Another pause followed.

"Charles, are you quite sure you're all right?"

"Recovering fast, Malcolm."

"Listen, if you'd rather I put St. Paul's on ice until you're feeling more rested, I'll place the Cathedral at the top of the agenda instead and Nigel and I can begin planning the visitation."

I opened my mouth, drew in some air to ensure I remained conscious and contrived to say in my most colourless voice: "I think if you examine your memory carefully, Malcolm, you'll find that I've never agreed to a visitation."

"Yes, but since that's the only course you can now take to bring Aysgarth to heel—"

"Aysgarth's not a dog. He's our brother-in-Christ."

"Yes, yes, yes—of course he is, but I really do feel that unless you step in soon and take the hardest of hard lines—"

"Could you let me know, please, when Nigel arrives? I'd like to attend this meeting."

"Oh but Charles, there's no need—we'll only be doing the basic spadework this morning!"

"Good," I said. "I feel in the mood for some basic spadework. I'm sure I shall find it most stimulating."

Malcolm gave a guarded little smile. So might a nurse have smiled at the bedside of a feverish patient who had announced his intention to get dressed and go home. Such madness had to be handled with care.

Retiring to my study I slumped behind my desk, put my head in my hands and wished futilely that I was far away in Cambridge. It was without doubt one of those moments when I hated being a bishop—but of course bishops weren't allowed to hate being bishops.

That wasn't the done thing at all.

XVIII

"The universal misuse of human power has the sad effect that power, however lovingly used, is hated."

AUSTIN FARRER
Warden of Keble College, Oxford, 1960–1968
SAID OR SUNG

I

TIME PASSED while I waited for Nigel to arrive from Starmouth. I knew I should be praying for the strength and skill to manage the difficult scene which lay ahead of me, but I was soon in such a state of tension that I could recall only the worst memories of my bishopric: the interviews with the occasional clerical failure, the rows with Aysgarth, the appearances on television when I had debated the permissive society with atheists. In truth hating my job was not as novel an experience for me as it should have been.

I tried to cheer myself with the thought that at least on this occasion I did not have to face the television cameras, but this did not alter the fact that I still had to solve a severe management problem. This is an aspect of my job which few people are willing to believe can exist. The popular vision of a bishop's life is that it must be all God-given glory and spiritual fulfilment and silver-tongued oratory in the House of Lords. A bishop is supposed to be far removed from the harassed executive driven to execute a series of Machiavellian manoeuvres in order to control his power-mad subordinates. This dark underside of ecclesiastical life forms the paradox of all Christian organisations: the kingdom of Christ is not of this world, but this world is the place where those who preach that kingdom have to live. And men who are valued for their spiritual gifts—who indeed come to prominence as the result of their spiritual calling—find themselves expected to do worldly work for which they have neither the training nor the inclination.

The sound of a car interrupted my train of thought. Moving to the window I saw Nigel halting his Humber in the drive.

I tried to estimate how far I could rely on his support. I knew he would welcome any attempt I made to re-introduce Malcolm to the limits of archidiaconal power, but I was unsure how far he would back me up if I tried to make a decision which he might well judge unsound. In fact if the scene were to go very wrong I might even end up achieving the impossible: an alliance between the suffragan and the Archdeacon, hitherto at loggerheads, against the Bishop whom they decided had finally succumbed to a nervous breakdown.

Making a big effort I made a new attempt to gather my wits and think like a layman. What I had to do was to play my cards so that Nigel would support me against Malcolm no matter how much he disagreed with my proposals about Langley Bottom, but how was I to achieve such rigorous loyalty? I toyed with various manoeuvres. I could increase the diocesan grant to Starmouth, but no, that would be too tricky because the diocesan board of finance was currently in a sullen mood and might suggest I cut back on education—which would affect the Theological College, my pride and joy. I could pull strings in the House of Lords in an attempt to get government funding to boost Nigel's pet housing project in the Starmouth slums, but because there was a Labour government in power my strings were not as strong as they might have been. Nevertheless the government would inevitably have a soft spot for the slums—and possibly also for Nigel who made no secret of his commitment to Christian socialism and was well versed in sociology, that tiresome subject which the secular masses now seemed to be regarding as a new religion. I had indeed hesitated before appointing a suffragan who had socialist interests, but in the end I had put the welfare of the diocese first; I had needed someone like Nigel to manage those Starmouth slums, and besides, I had never been opposed to a decent Christian socialism, only to socialism as a secular ideology which created economic havoc and called it progress.

"Nigel's here, Charles," said Malcolm, putting his head around the door.

"Splendid!" I exclaimed, effortlessly concealing my dread, and moved at once into the hall to meet him.

2

"I'M GOING to chair this meeting this morning," I said briskly to Nigel. "I'm feeling much better."

"Ah," said Nigel, taking care to assume a delighted expression, but I knew then that during the cat's absence Malcolm had not been the only mouse enjoying a happy play-time.

I led the way back to my study where we all sat down and indulged in small-talk until Miss Peabody had brought us coffee.

"How's the Lower Quay housing project?" I said to Nigel as soon as she had withdrawn. "Have you had that report yet from the social workers about the West Indians?"

"Not yet, no. As a matter of fact I'm getting rather worried about the funding," said Nigel, unwittingly playing into my hands. "The conversion of the warehouse is going to work out at considerably more than the legacy because the lifts will be so expensive."

"If I'd been in your shoes," said Malcolm, unable to resist meddling in the conversation, "I'd have demolished that warehouse and built low-rise housing which wouldn't require lifts at all."

"The trend now is entirely to high-rise," said Nigel, unable to resist the urge to slap down this impertinent comment, "and you're quite forgetting that the cost of demolition would have been very considerable."

"Talking of cost," I said as I began to manipulate the conversation, "I've been thinking that I ought to try and do more to help you on that project—in fact I believe the time could now be ripe for me to try pulling a string or two at Westminster to get some extra money."

Nigel immediately became both excited and grateful. "That would be wonderful, Charles! Now, make sure you stress to those politicians how important this project is from a sociological point of view—we're not just building a ghetto for coloured immigrants. This is true integrated housing, part of a vision which will ultimately transform our slums into soaring multi-racial towers—villages in the sky—"

"I wouldn't want to live in a village in the sky," said Malcolm. "I'd want a nice home down on earth with no more than a staircase between me and the ground, and when we demolish St. Paul's I think we should insist on low-rise housing and tell the sociologists to get lost."

"This seems an appropriate moment to start talking about Langley Bottom," I said swiftly before Nigel could make some furious riposte. "But before I begin I'd like to thank you both for all your hard work and unstinting support during these past days. I consider myself extremely fortunate that at such a difficult time I was able to delegate my work to you with complete confidence." And having buttered both of them up so lavishly, I added in my most austere voice: "Now . . . shall we take a moment to pray?"

Here I have the advantage over a layman in a similar managerial position who cannot begin a meeting by reminding his subordinates of their ideals, their beliefs and their Maker. I framed a short, crisp prayer, asking God to grant us patience, respect for each other's views and discernment, and at the end we all said a firm "Amen." So far so good. I then prepared to venture into the ecclesiastical jungle.

"It seems to me that Langley Bottom presents three questions," I said. "One, what happens to Desmond; two, what happens to Hall; and three, what happens to St. Paul's. Let's take the last question first. Nigel, I'd be glad to have your views, please, on closure."

"As I've already said, Charles," said Malcolm before Nigel could open his mouth, "it's impossible for Nigel to have an *in depth* view on this particular subject as he doesn't know the background. On the other hand, I, as the Archdeacon—"

"Of course no one could know the situation in your archdeaconry better than you do," interrupted Nigel with the most formidable smoothness, "but no doubt Charles will take that into account when I offer him my opinion, which is this: St. Paul's offers a form of worship which is simply not available elsewhere in this area, and if it closes, the congregation will be caused a substantial amount of distress which will be bad for their spiritual welfare. Surely the best solution is to keep the church open but bring in a dynamic priest—preferably someone not long out of St. Stephen's House or Mirfield—to beef up the numbers so that the place becomes less of a financial drain on the diocese."

"That's no solution!" exclaimed Malcolm. "That's a pipe-dream! And anyway, how can you justify spending money and manpower on keeping alive such a fatally old-fashioned ritualism?"

"Well, of course I know it's hard for an Evangelical like you to identify in a positive way with any form of Anglo-Catholicism, but—"

"May I," I interposed, "as a representative of the Church's Middle Way, call you both to order? We're not here to stage a boxing match between the Evangelical and Catholic wings. Nigel, thank you for your views. Malcolm, I shan't ask you to repeat your opinion on closure, since you've already made your position very clear, but let me support you in your desire to face the facts realistically." As Malcolm looked triumphant I immediately added to Nigel: "And let me also support you in your belief that this particular church should stay open—let me attempt, in other words, some sort of synthesis here. One of the facts we must face is that there's a shortage of clergy today, and that means we're most unlikely to get a dynamic young Anglo-Catholic priest who wants to fulfil a mission to the poor by working in Starbridge; that kind of priest heads nowadays for the big cities and large-scale deprivation. So having faced that fact, let's by all means be realistic and consider the one dynamic Anglo-Catholic priest we do have on offer—the one who against all the odds has appeared out of the blue with the claim that he's called to work in Starbridge. If the church stays open, I think there's a case for keeping Lewis Hall."

"Not as far as I'm concerned," said Malcolm. "I like Hall but let's face it, employing him involves too many risks. He's got all the women in Langley Bottom in a tizzy—all right, I know it's not the poor chap's fault that he has that peculiar effect, but you can't convince me he's ever going to make a success of living a celibate life, and anyway ordinary church people don't like divorced priests in parish work—in fact some of those really Romish ritualists don't even like married men in parish work—"

"Ah, but this is different!" I said quickly. "This is a unique situation which enables us to use Hall without actually employing him as the parish priest. If he runs the healing centre he won't be the incumbent—yet at the same time he'll be there to support the incumbent and provide a dynamic influence on the parish."

"I utterly oppose a healing centre!" said Malcolm strongly. "Charismatic quackery, Mumbo-Jumbo, undesirable publicity, hysteria, scandal, the laying-on of hands in all the wrong places—"

"I can't say I share Malcolm's colourful view of the ministry of healing," said Nigel, "but I do think it would be an unusually controversial and risky venture."

"I believe we need unusually controversial and risky ventures sometimes," I said. "We can't always be playing safe. After all, what about your admirable project at Lower Quay?"

"Ah well," said Nigel, suddenly very thoughtful, "yes, I see what you mean."

"Now look here!" exploded Malcolm outraged. "If you two want to float a high-risk project in Starmouth, that's fine, nothing to do with me, good luck to you, but I'm not having an exorcist running wild in my archdeaconry and seducing women in some grotto which he chooses to pass off as a healing centre!"

"You'd still have the problem of finding a new incumbent, Charles," mused Nigel exactly as if Malcolm had never spoken.

"With Hall around to give the necessary spiritual support, I think there's a case for keeping Desmond."

"What!" shouted Malcolm.

"Less risky to pension him off, surely," said Nigel, "but of course I do see your point of view."

"Wait a minute," said Malcolm. "Wait a minute. I just want to make sure I've got this absolutely straight. Are you saying, Charles, that you (a) want to keep St. Paul's open even though it's a financial millstone round our necks, (b) want to keep Desmond on even though he nearly put us all in the soup with his ghastly homosexual pornography, (c) want to retain a divorced man permanently in a parish situation even though he's bound to get into a sex-mess of indescribably awful dimensions, and (d) want this divorced man to found a healing centre for which there's not one single penny available—"

"He'll raise the money."

"—and which will give him the opportunity to get into not just a sex-mess but also a charismatic-mess—which in turn will ensure that my archdeaconry *(my archdeaconry!)* hits the headlines in the *News of the World?"*

"I want him to start a privately funded healing centre at St. Paul's. I don't subscribe to your apocalyptic view of his future."

"But my dear Charles . . . I'm sorry, but I just don't understand. Nigel, surely you're as amazed by all this as I am?"

"I confess I *am* a trifle surprised," said Nigel, "but every now and then a radical vision really is called for. As it was for my Lower Quay project in Starmouth."

"Exactly," I said. "But I quite understand that you may need a little time to think about this, Malcolm. And to pray." I was gradually bringing out all the weapons in my episcopal armoury. No secular executive can give the sinister hint to his subordinate that he should spend a little more time thinking about God and a little less time thinking about himself.

"I think we should all pray about this!" said Malcolm at once, losing sight in his agitation of the crucial fact that although I wanted his consent in order to prevent the matter blighting our working relationship, I did not ultimately require his seal of approval. "What baffles me, Charles, is that this is so completely contrary to your traditional thinking! All right, I know you've always had a keen interest in the ministry of healing, but it's one thing to have a keen interest and quite another to set up an over-sexed divorced priest in a diocesan white elephant! Surely you can see a scandal's inevitable? And who'll have to clear up that scandal when it happens? *Me!* And talking of scandal, how can you be so soft on Desmond—you, who have always been so tough on sexual transgression? I'm sorry, forgive me for being so shocked and horrified, but I feel I must ask for some explanation of why you've suddenly decided to act so completely out of character."

I pulled out the heaviest weapon in my armoury, the one a bishop should never use unless it is absolutely necessary—and even then the Bishop should hesitate before he drops this ecclesiastical atomic bomb. I examined my thumbnail with care. Then I looked meditatively out of the window and said in a voice devoid of emotion: "I feel it's the will of God." The only way I can defend this naked exercise in power is to say that at least the statement was true.

There was a deep, deep silence. When I looked at both men again I saw that Nigel now appeared almost as perturbed as Malcolm, and I realised I had to back-pedal in order to emphasise my episcopal stability.

"I assure you I've prayed a good deal about this," I said in my most businesslike voice. "I've also talked extensively to Hall, seen Desmond and tried to approach the scheme with the necessary hardheaded common sense. When I said: 'I feel it's the will of God,' I wasn't just making an off-the-cuff remark. I spoke out of a sincere and earnest conviction that over the past few days God has made his will very clear to me."

"Yes, of course, Charles," said Nigel. "Of course we recognise your earnestness and your sincerity and of course we wouldn't dream of disputing your conviction; if you feel it's God's will that there should be a healing centre in the diocese, that's fine. But it may just possibly be the case that St. Paul's isn't the best place for it—and indeed that Lewis Hall would be less riskily employed in some job where he wouldn't be constantly dealing with vulnerable women. Perhaps a chaplaincy in a prison—or in a public school—"

"Not in *my* archdeaconry!" declared Malcolm with the air of a man prepared to fight to the last ditch. "Charles, I feel bound to say—and you'll realise that I speak as one of your most loyal and devoted friends—"

"Malcolm," said Nigel, "this may not be quite the moment to take the matter further." But unfortunately Malcolm was too outraged to listen.

"I feel bound to say," he repeated, furious at being interrupted and now quite carried away by his emotion, "that in my opinion, Charles, you're still suffering from the effects of your bereavement and it's clear you need to get right away from the diocese in order to recuperate. Of course I accept that you feel you're responding to the will of God, but—"

"Then accept it," I said, "Mr. Archdeacon."

3

I WAS reminded of the *Titanic* at the moment when it hit the iceberg. I never raised my voice; I merely drained it of warmth as I underlined his subordinate rank, and the next moment Malcolm was very pale and still, no longer calling to mind images of an over-confident liner or even of a militant despot, but of a little boy who had just been caned by a favourite teacher. He managed to say stiff-lipped: "Yes, Bishop," and out of his sight behind my desk I wiped my sweating palms upon my trousers.

Another deep silence ensued.

"Well!" said Nigel brightly at last in the manner of a hostess at a vicarage tea-party where two guests had been so ill-bred as to quarrel over the last cucumber sandwich. "Now that we've established the line we're taking on St. Paul's, should we go on to discuss the Cathedral?"

I longed to postpone the discussion but I knew I had to use the advantage I possessed now that Malcolm had been reduced to submission. Loathing my job more than ever, I leant forward in my chair and said with the calm authority of the chairman who was finally in control of his board: "Yes, let's go on."

4

"THE QUESTION is whether I should make a visitation," I said. "I'm still not convinced this is the best way forward, but I'm open to persuasion. Nigel, let's hear from you again."

"I think there's an increasingly strong case for a visitation," said Nigel. "Malcolm rang me on Saturday, Charles, to tell me about your interview with Paul Dalton and his disclosure that Aysgarth has well and truly hijacked the Appeal. I was appalled—and certainly I believe it's quite wrong in principle that the Dean should be in sole control of the Appeal fund while those Canons abdicate their responsibilities out of sheer spinelessness. If you make a visitation you'll at least be able to recommend that in future all major appeals are run in a professional manner by a team of qualified laymen. Also, Aysgarth's shady flirtation with Christie's really was beyond the limit of behaviour acceptable for a senior churchman, and in your visitation report you'd have the chance to deliver a reprimand which would make it very clear to the public that the Church doesn't condone such antics. I do think it's unlikely that Aysgarth's in a financial mess and I can't believe he's done anything criminal, but he definitely deserves to have the Riot Act read to him."

I turned to my chastened archdeacon. "Malcolm, would you please be good enough to state the case as you see it?"

Malcolm gave a small cough and said with care: "I wouldn't disagree with anything Nigel's said except for that last sentence about the likelihood of a financial mess. The truth is we can't turn a blind eye to the possibility that something's gone very wrong with the Appeal. Aysgarth may be the most gifted fund-raiser in the Church of England, but that doesn't mean he's incapable of making a mistake."

"I'm afraid that's true," said Nigel with reluctance. "He could easily have got over-confident, made a bad error, tried to redeem it and ended up making the mess worse."

"I agree it's hard to believe he'd embark on any criminal activity," said Malcolm, becoming more confident, "but law-abiding people do get sucked into the downward spiral of embezzlement if they make one crucial financial mistake: it's not unknown. And think of Aysgarth's character. He's a clever man, he's an able man, but he does have a habit of taking dangerous risks when he's under pressure, and I don't think we can ignore this trait when assessing the present situation. We need a visitation not just to recommend rules about future fund-raising and deliver a reprimand about the Christie's flirtation but to expose the truth about what's going on in the accounts."

"But if there really is a financial disaster being concealed," objected Nigel, "surely it would be better for the Church if we mopped up the mess as discreetly as possible?"

"We've now reached the point where we should consider the arguments against a visitation," I said. "Nigel's just outlined one of them: the worse the mess, the less appropriate a visitation becomes. We also can't avoid the unfortunate fact that Aysgarth and I have a difficult relationship, and a visitation would make that embarrassingly public. Maybe I'm being too influenced by my guilt about this state of affairs, but I think there's a serious risk we could make a visitation for the best of motives and yet achieve nothing but the washing of a lot of dirty Church linen in public."

"What we need," said Nigel after we had all paused to view the horns of the dilemma on which we were impaled, "is hard evidence of financial mismanagement. Our difficulties arise because of insufficient information."

Malcolm said reasonably enough: "But how can we get hard evidence without making a visitation?"

This indeed was the problem. None of us could imagine Aysgarth showing us the accounts in a burst of friendly generosity.

"Eureka!" exclaimed Nigel suddenly. "I've got it—the truth is we can make all the deductions we need just by putting Aysgarth under pressure and seeing how he reacts."

"Wonderful!" said Malcolm, now displaying marked signs of a full recovery. "Can you recommend a shop which would supply us with a thumbscrew and a rack?"

"Never mind the thumbscrew and the rack!" declared Nigel, so aglow with triumph that he was prepared to meet Malcolm's sarcasm with good humour. "All we need is our bishop!"

I said with increasing foreboding: "I confess I've never quite seen myself as an instrument of torture."

"No, listen, Charles, it's all very simple. You ask Aysgarth if you can take a quick look at the accounts in order to quash a rumour about the Appeal which has been circulating at the diocesan office since the Christie's fiasco. If he's innocent, there's no reason why he shouldn't let you have a look—he'll be keen to quash the rumour. But if he's guilty, he'll either refuse or procrastinate, and then we'll know where we stand."

I was too appalled by the thought of such a scene to reply, and it was left to Malcolm to make the obvious response.

"It won't work, Nigel," he said. "You don't know our Mr. Dean as we do. He's quite capable of refusing to show us the accounts even if he's innocent—he'd see it as a chance to underline his autonomy at the Cathedral."

"Yes, but supposing Charles threatens him with a visitation. If Aysgarth's innocent I bet he'd then backtrack quickly and cough up the accounts—he wouldn't go on being bolshie once he'd realised that bolshiness was provoking the one procedure which strips away that cherished autonomy of his. But if he's guilty he'll play for time and try any desperate manoeuvre to put off the evil day when the accounts have to be disclosed. He might even call Charles's bluff and invite a visitation in the knowledge that a visitation takes some time to set up."

I found myself at a loss for words.

"You could be right," said Malcolm slowly to Nigel. "In fact that's a line of thinking which seems to crack the entire problem."

My feelings of foreboding immediately quadrupled.

"One big advantage of the scheme," added Malcolm with increasing enthusiasm, "is that it would be certain to increase our knowledge in some way or another. We're still unlikely to get concrete proof of financial misconduct, but if Charles conducts the interview on the lines you suggest, I do agree that he's most unlikely to emerge none the wiser."

"And that in turn will help us make the correct decision about a visitation and move out of our current impasse."

"Exactly!"

They turned to me to present the spectacle I had dreaded most: a united front.

Privately cursing myself for the lack of incisiveness which had fostered it, I said in despair: "I just have this terrible feeling that we're barking up the wrong tree. After all, if it hadn't been for the Christie's fiasco we wouldn't have thought of questioning the state of the Appeal, and the fact is that the Christie's episode could be exactly what Aysgarth says it was: not evidence of financial mismanagement but of a publicity spree which misfired. I discovered last night that he's arranging an auction of work donated by leading artists. Bearing that in mind, doesn't it seem entirely plausible that he was using the St. Anselm manuscript to grab the headlines so that he could gain maximum press coverage later for the art auction? In short, what we're witnessing could be none other than the triumphant conclusion of a brilliantly successful fund-raising campaign."

"Fine," said Nigel. "In that case he'll be delighted to show you the accounts and we can all relax."

I saw that defeat was staring me in the face. I also saw that a horrific scene with Aysgarth was to be the price I had to pay for getting my own way on Langley Bottom—if I were sensible. I fear one of the hallmarks of a successful corporate manager is knowing exactly when and how to appease his subordinates after an unappetising display of power.

"So be it," I said. "I'll see Aysgarth."

"I'm sure that's the right decision, Charles," said Nigel, realising I needed strong support.

"I agree," said Malcolm firmly, but added with uncharacteristic meekness: "Charles, please could you explain why you're now so reluctant to tackle Aysgarth? At the time we uncovered the Christie's fiasco you were screaming for his head on a platter."

"It's one thing to scream for a head," said Nigel dryly, "but quite another to hack it off. No bishop in his right mind would welcome a bloodthirsty scene with that particular Dean."

"If only he'd retire! Incidentally, I've heard yet another report that he's become very cosy with Harriet March. Tommy Fitzgerald says she went to lunch at the Deanery yesterday, stayed to tea and arrived with the Dean for Evensong. Tommy says Aysgarth reeked of claret."

"I must say," I commented with a strength which surprised me, "I'm getting very, very tired of Tommy Fitzgerald telling tales to the Archdeacon whenever he sees Aysgarth enjoying the company of an attractive woman."

"But Charles, surely Tommy has reason to be alarmed when he sees Aysgarth cavorting with La March? Tommy says that according to the newspapers she sleeps with everything in sight."

"In that case Aysgarth must be a welcome holiday for her."

"I'd love to know which newspapers Tommy reads," murmured Nigel. "I can't wait to switch from *The Times.*"

"If there was anything improper going on between Aysgarth and Mrs. March," I said to Malcolm, "Dido wouldn't have allowed the two of them to drink tea privately together yesterday—as I'm told they did. And Aysgarth didn't reek of claret. There was just the faintest of aromas."

"There you go, taking a soft line again!" said Malcolm baffled.

"I think it's called Christian charity, Malcolm," said Nigel, closing the discussion on a truly ferocious note.

"Is there any other urgent matter," I said rapidly, "which we should discuss before we end this meeting?"

Nigel said he thought not. "But if you're really determined to pick up the reins again without taking further time off," he added, "perhaps you'd like me to look out the most important of the current files and dictate some explanatory notes on them to Miss Peabody."

I thanked him and said that would be very helpful. The meeting then broke up, but although Nigel departed to the office Malcolm appeared to be glued to the seat of his chair. He had also become very pink and had embarked on a series of nervous little coughs. With a sinking heart I realised that my ordeal at the hands of my colleagues was not yet over.

I steeled myself for a tidal wave of archidiaconal remorse.

5

"CHARLES, I hardly know how to find the words—"

"It's all right, Malcolm."

"No, it's not all right." Malcolm became pinker than ever. "I've got to say how sorry I am that I gave you such offence. I admire you more than any other clergyman I know, and—" He became stuck.

By this time I was almost as agonised as he was. Not having his fair complexion I was incapable of matching his blush but I was certainly very hot beneath my clerical collar. I said: "No need to say any more."

"But there is! You see, I've modelled myself on you for a long time now, and if I've wound up making you upset I want to understand where I've gone wrong so that I can—"

I held up my hand. He stopped, and in the fraught silence which followed I remembered Charley, yet another priest who had cast himself in my image with such unsatisfactory results. I felt as if I had been dumped in front of a looking-glass and forced to look at a reflection I had no desire to own.

At last I managed to say: "The Archdeacon reflects the Bishop who chose him. If I was angry with you, I should really have been angry with myself. In fact I can see now I've got a lot of things wrong."

Malcolm was astounded. "What sort of things?"

"I've taken too hard a line too often."

"But that's what we've all admired so much! If ever we need a strong traditionalist bishop we need one now!"

"Even a strong traditionalist bishop—perhaps especially a strong traditionalist bishop—needs to be able to say now and then: 'I was wrong.' Without humility strength can only be weakness, and without compassion traditionalism parts company with tradition."

"I still don't understand. Are you saying—"

"There were two aspects to Christ's ministry, weren't there? The prophetic and the pastoral: he spoke out against sin but at the same time he behaved with compassion towards sinners. And he held those two aspects of his ministry in perfect balance. But I haven't. I've emphasized the prophetic at the expense of the pastoral."

"So what you're saying is . . . in relation to Langley Bottom . . ." But he could not quite work it out.

"I was wrong in putting all the blame on Desmond," I said. "The truth is he was our pastoral failure: he got overstrained and couldn't cope and he felt he couldn't ask either of us for help. But we're not going to fail him in future. We're going to see that he's given proper support and that his special gift for prayer is drawn out and fully used."

"By Hall?"

"By Hall." I paused to choose my words with care. "I talked to the Bishop of Radbury about him," I said at last. "He did make the cynical remark that Hall was the kind of priest who might occasionally commit the sin of fornication but would never commit the sin of being found out, but it's easy to be cynical, isn't it? You and I have been cynical too, but the fact remains that throughout Hall's ministry as a celibate priest there's no record of him getting into trouble. Doesn't that suggest that in our cynicism we're doing him an injustice and that he deserves our trust instead of our doubt?"

Malcolm said cautiously: "I suppose the Abbot-General was trying to signal as much when he wrote that glowing reference." With a sigh he added: "I foresee plenty of problems with that healing centre. I'm not saying it won't eventually be an asset to the diocese, but it's bound to be a strain on my nerves."

"Let me know if you feel an ungovernable urge to dress up in black leather and head for Piccadilly Circus."

At that point the intercom buzzed and Miss Peabody informed me that Martin was telephoning from Starrington.

6

"LITTLE MUGGINS is on the mend," Martin informed me. "He's sitting on the hearth with the cat again, but he managed to stagger to the chapel for mass and just now he even returned to normal by asking me hopefully if I intended to leave soon."

"Did Jon mention—"

"Yes, he's dead keen to see you, but he had to admit you'd get more mileage out of him if you postponed your visit till tomorrow. He's exhausted."

"I understand." In an effort to conceal my disappointment I said quickly: "Will you be staying on for another night at the South Canonry?"

"No, Dad assures me I'm free now to head back to London—but thanks for all your hospitality, Charles, and let me take you to dine at the Garrick when you're next up in town."

I said that would make a most interesting change from dining at the Athenaeum. Then after concluding the call I felt I had no choice but to begin plotting my next searing session with Aysgarth.

7

SHEER COWARDICE made me toy with the notion of postponing the interview until I had talked to Jon, but I suspected that the longer I postponed my ordeal the more upsetting it would become, and I recoiled from the prospect of the sleepless night which would be my inevitable reward for procrastination. It did of course occur to me that Jon could have offered some practical spiritual advice about how to have a Christian dialogue with Aysgarth instead of a secular free-for-all, but this seemed to me to be a situation where a bishop accustomed to dealing with tough ecclesiastical problems was more likely than a hermit to spot the most suitable spiritual path through the worldly jungle—or so I thought. I should have realised that after a particularly arduous morning I was ripe to make a fatally bad decision.

I pictured my suitable spiritual path. It was clear that I was obliged to treat Aysgarth with courtesy, patience, kindness and as much Christian charity as I could muster, and that I was on no account to display that deadly sin, anger. I liked this spiritual path very much. I surveyed it for some time and soothed myself with edifying Christian thoughts about turning the other cheek and loving one's neighbour as oneself.

However, I then had to decide how this truly admirable behaviour could be achieved in what I was sure would be very inflammatory circumstances. Naturally I had to pray for help and trust in God's grace. Naturally. But it seemed to me it was also my absolute moral duty to use my worldly savoir-faire in order to ensure my spiritual path was not promptly eliminated. Even the most beautiful path through a jungle stands no chance of surviving for long unless the undergrowth is controlled by a machete.

Accordingly I activated my worldly savoir-faire and spent ten minutes in concentrated thought which produced some very unattractive conclusions. (But unfortunately no machete is likely to be described as attractive.) The first conclusion was that since Aysgarth was a killer in debate, I had to take great care not to wind up as a corpse. Or in other words, debate had to be wholly avoided. The tone of the interview had to be casual, even cosy, and in order to achieve this remarkable atmosphere I had to go to great lengths to appear unintimidating. This was most definitely not the occasion to don full episcopal uniform and summon the Dean to the South Canonry; nor was it the occasion to wear one of my Savile Row suits which would inevitably inflame the chip on Aysgarth's shoulder and remind him that my upbringing had been socially superior to his. I had to be casually dressed—but not in that gentlemanly style which makes even shabby informality look elegant.

I trailed upstairs to my dressing-room.

Here I selected an elderly sports-shirt and a pair of slacks which I had bought off-the-peg a couple of years before during a business trip to Canterbury when I had received an unexpected invitation to play golf. I also remembered a brown pullover which I had bought as a charitable gesture in a local jumble sale. My oldest raincoat would complete this unfortunate ensemble and render me fit for the battlefield.

My next unedifying conclusion was that in order to make this informality credible I had to drop in without warning at the Deanery. If I made an appointment yet arrived looking like some grammar-school *arriviste,* Aysgarth would at once see through my ruse and deduce I was playing power-games (which I was). This in turn would mean I had lost not only the first round of the battle but any chance of establishing the cosy atmosphere necessary to avoid a blood-bath.

My final unedifying conclusion was that if I dropped in unannounced and found he was out, I would have to forfeit the chance to look excessively informal when we met. To drop in once in appalling clothes was just about acceptable, provided I claimed I was on my way to the water-meadows for a walk, but to drop in twice in appalling clothes would be to push the bounds of eccentricity beyond plausible limits. I had to hit the jackpot on my first call, but how could I find out if Aysgarth was at home? Fortunately I then remembered that through sheer mental stress I had forgotten to write a note to my hostess to thank her for Friday's dinner-party.

I dialled the number of the Deanery.

"Charles my dear!" said Dido almost before I could complete my routine greeting. "What a relief to hear your voice, I'm told you were kidnapped after Evensong last night by Harriet March and Martin Darrow and I was afraid their conversation might have shocked you to death, although personally I like Harriet because she reminds me of my unconventional past before I settled down with darling Stephen and lived happily ever after, and of course I adore dearest Martin, *so* charming, how wonderful that he survived that peculiar old father of his, but you're devoted to Jon Darrow, aren't you, so I must watch what I say, but frankly, my dear, I don't think anyone should live as a hermit in a wood, it's so dreadfully showy and self-centred. Do you want to speak to Stephen?"

"Well—"

"He's not here at the moment, but he'll be back by half-past three. Can I give him a message?"

"As a matter of fact, Dido," I was at last allowed to say, "you were the one I wanted to speak to. I'm phoning to apologise for not writing to thank you for that splendid dinner last Friday. I—"

"Oh, of course I realised you were much too devastated by grief to lift a pen! But how nice of you to phone. We were delighted to see you, and after you'd gone all the ladies agreed that being haggard suited you—in fact Harriet said on the phone this morning how handsome you still were"—she paused for breath; I winced in anticipation—"even in old age, and I'm bound to say I agree with her. Well, my dear—" And she talked briskly for a further twenty seconds before replacing the receiver.

I did wonder why Harriet had telephoned the Deanery, but soon remembered that she herself had just enjoyed the Aysgarths' hospitality and would have been under a similar obligation to thank her hostess. I then had to decide how I could pass the time until Aysgarth returned home, but the mere thought of the approaching interview was sufficient to immobilise me. I supposed I should telephone Charley to see if he had recovered his equilibrium, but I felt unable to face another melodramatic exchange with him. I wanted to telephone Michael but dared not for fear any further rebuff would induce a profound depression. I knew I should start answering the sympathy letters, but the moment I opened the file and saw Sheila's letter I felt physically sick. Finally I took a look at *The*

Times, but flung it aside when I read that Sunbeam had given an interview on the wireless about the religious significance of the Beatles. I decided to have lunch but all I could eat was a water-biscuit.

Time crawled by. Nigel appeared with some selected files and said Miss Peabody was engaged in typing the appropriate notes to accompany them. Malcolm was not mentioned. I suspected that Nigel longed to discuss the archidiaconal subjugation but had decided that any expression of approval, no matter how muted, could only be interpreted as a most unchristian demonstration of glee. I told him about my approaching journey to the Deanery and before retiring to Starmouth he very sincerely wished me luck.

Left on my own once more I ate another water-biscuit and began to do the crossword in *The Times.*

Finally at half-past three I went upstairs to dress as a grammar-school *arriviste.* At quarter to four I went to the lavatory. At ten to four I was leaving the house and at five to four I was ringing the doorbell of the Deanery.

By that time I would have preferred to confront a starving lion at the Colosseum.

8

THE DOOR was opened by Dido's companion, Miss Carp, but almost before she could draw breath to greet me, Aysgarth himself came out of his study.

"Charles—I saw you coming up the front path!" he exclaimed genially. "Why are you dressed as a private detective?"

"Am I?"

"Well, aren't you? Nondescript raincoat, plain hat pulled down low—you look distinctly shady! Come into the study and tell me what you're up to!"

This was hardly a promising start to the interview but I kept calm and stuck to my script. "I was actually on my way for a walk along by the river," I said, "but as I passed the Deanery it suddenly occurred to me that this might be a convenient moment to drop in for the briefest of words—"

"Of course! Have some tea! I'm halfway through my first cup."

Uneasily I followed him into his study, a large well-proportioned room where bookcases stretched from the floor to the ceiling and the mantelshelf was covered with photographs of his numerous remarkable children. Beyond his desk, beyond the diamond-shaped panes of the old windows, beyond the gates of the Deanery's front garden, the Cathedral glowered brutishly beneath a bright white sky.

"Have a seat," said Aysgarth, removing three books from the visitor's chair in front of his desk.

But I remained standing. "Why do you have your desk placed so that you sit with your back to the Cathedral?"

Aysgarth looked startled, as if the eccentric question, combined with my eccentric choice of clothes, had led him to wonder if I were unhinged. However, he remained scrupulously affable. "I can't stand looking at all the scaffolding on the west front," he said. "I'll turn the desk back to face the Cathedral when the repairs are finished."

Miss Carp chose that moment to appear with an extra cup and saucer for me. As she withdrew, Aysgarth began to pour the tea and I began to work out how I could best convey an impression of mental stability. Obviously the first step was to ask no more idiotic questions about the positioning of the furniture.

"Harriet tells me she showed you my hands last night," said Aysgarth unexpectedly, handing me my tea and gesturing that I should help myself to milk from the tray. "Good, aren't they?"

"Outstanding." As I sank slowly down upon the chair he had cleared for me, I realised I was far from happy that he should know about my nocturnal visit to Harriet's studio. "No doubt she told you that her car had broken down and I'd given her a lift home," I said, compelled to make sure he understood the innocent sequence of events. "I suspect that showing me the sculpture was her way of saying thanks."

"Obviously she felt very benign towards you," said Aysgarth, eyes watching his cup as he refilled it, and before I could offer a further comment he added abruptly: "Did she tell you about the art auction I'm planning?"

"She did, yes. A brilliant idea. Congratulations."

"I'm delighted you're so enthusiastic. Perhaps now you'll stop worrying about the state of the Appeal."

I was well aware by this time that I was allowing him to dictate the direction of the interview and I decided I had reached the point where I had to take control. Unable to drink my tea I leaned forward in my chair and said in what I hoped was a friendly voice: "In retrospect I can see the full publicity value of the Christie's incident, but unfortunately the gossip generated by it shows no signs of dying down and there's still considerable speculation about the Appeal's finances. That was why I thought I'd just drop in for a quick word—I felt you should know that the rumour of financial trouble's still going strong, and I think the time has come when I have to deliver a very firm rebuttal."

"Good idea!" said Aysgarth, radiating approval. "Nasty things, rumours."

"Quite. Well . . ." It occurred to me that I must be looking much too tense, sitting as I was on the edge of my chair, so I forced myself to lean back and fold my hands loosely in my lap. "The truth is," I said, "that I need a little help from you in order to kill this particular nasty rumour stone dead."

"Delighted to assist you in any way I can. But surely all you have to do is tell those scandalmongers at the diocesan office that everything's fine?"

"Nothing would give me greater pleasure, but unfortunately I feel this rumour can't now be killed without the aid of concrete proof. Of course I perfectly understand that you're under no obligation to provide such proof, but I was hoping you might see your way to providing it as a friendly gesture."

"What sort of proof do you have in mind?"

"Well, if you were to show me some interim accounts for the current financial year—"

"I see." Aysgarth leaned forward on his desk, clasped his powerful hands and looked straight at me. It was a very intimidating sequence of movements. "Stripped of your elaborate courtesy," he said, "this is a hostile demand. And I'm supposed to respond with a 'friendly gesture.' "

I willed myself to sustain a tranquil appearance. "There's no question of hostility, Stephen. I'm on your side in my desire to end the rumours, and one glance at the accounts would, I'm sure, enable me to exonerate you completely."

"What you're really saying, of course, by demanding to see some accounts, is that you can't accept my word that all's well."

"I—"

"If I'd attended your public school you'd never dream of questioning my word! But just because in your eyes I'm not a gentleman—"

"Stephen, let's not demean ourselves by sinking into some futile discussion of the class system when all that matters is that we should be working together for the good of the Church. Surely you can see that I'm in an awkward position? If the rumours at the diocesan office get picked up by the press—"

"If that Archdeacon of yours has been screaming that I'm an embezzler it's your job to muzzle him, not mine!"

"I assure you that no one's been making slanderous accusations—"

"Rubbish, you've obviously been inundated with them! What else can these so-called 'rumours' be? And if you didn't suspect me of financial mismanagement you wouldn't be making this request which is nothing less than a slur on my integrity—and which in my opinion ill becomes a bishop who's supposed to regard his flock with charity!"

I was aware that a metaphorical dagger was being brandished. My worst fears had been realised, the benign tone of the conversation had been murdered, and once more the killer in debate was on the loose.

"I'm sorry you should take such exception to my effort to solve this problem," I said, trying to defuse the mounting tension by keeping my voice flawlessly polite. "Perhaps you're unaware that the rumours weren't generated just by your manoeuvres at Christie's. They also stem from the fact that you're running the Appeal in a highly unconventional manner. The Chapter—"

"The Chapter are useless in the matter of fund-raising. The only thing Tommy can raise is a fuss. Paul's no good at concentrating on anything except where his next wife's coming from, and Gerry's idea of raising money is to stand on street corners rattling a box! And what's more, they know they're useless here, they admitted as much when they begged me—yes, *begged* me—to manage the Appeal on my own. Yet now, it seems, I'm being accused of gross mismanagement just because I've gone along with the wishes of the Chapter and slaved my guts out to save the Cathedral single-handed for posterity! I must say I deeply resent the implication that I'm a dictator riding roughshod over my colleagues instead of a dean working as *primus inter pares* with his canons in accordance with the Cathedral statutes!"

"Of course you resent it," I said, doing my best to wrest the metaphorical dagger from him before I was disembowelled, "but there's a very simple way to silence all these unjust criticisms. If you were to produce some accounts—"

"Why should I?" demanded Aysgarth, whipping the dagger out of my reach. "Why should I submit to the bullying of the diocesan office? Why should I open up private files so that you can appease your obstreperous archdeacon who's currently browbeating you into taking up this most undignified and unedifying stance? If I were to give in to this request I'd be setting the most dangerous precedent, and I assure you that the Canons will back me to the hilt in asserting the Dean and Chapter's right to withstand any interference from the Archdeacon in the ordering of the Cathedral's affairs!"

I waited a moment before saying: "I understand your anger. I see your point of view. But Stephen, I do beg you to listen most carefully to what I'm about to say: I myself don't suspect you of any deliberate wrong-doing, but it's a fact that anyone, even someone as financially adroit as you, can make a mistake which proves expensive. If there has indeed been a mistake made somewhere along the line, please tell me now so that I can give you my full support in sorting out the consequences. I quite see that there might be circumstances which you wouldn't want to discuss with the Canons, but I'd be failing you as your bishop if I didn't at least give you the chance to confide in me."

"How extremely kind of you," said Aysgarth, "but I'm in no need of a confessor." And by swivelling his chair he turned his back on me to stare out of the window at the scarred west front.

My fists clenched but I still managed to keep my voice level. "I feel I must warn you," I said, "that if you persist in your refusal to cooperate with me I shall be obliged to make a visitation."

"Then make it!" said Aysgarth, swivelling back to face me. "And I hope you enjoy the moment when I present you with immaculate accounts!"

"That's a very irresponsible attitude for a senior churchman to adopt!" I exclaimed as anger finally loosened my grip on my self-control. "Shouldn't you be thinking of doing your best to avoid unfortunate publicity for the Church?"

"Shouldn't you? Isn't this lust to play the Grand Inquisitor in the chapter house more than a little distasteful? You're supposed to be running around being everyone's father-in-God, not prying into the Cathedral's affairs like a fraud squad detective! Let me repeat: everything's fine; I'm in control of the situation; the Appeal's on course. Now, why don't you get on with the job of playing the good Bishop and leave me in peace to play the good Dean?"

"Because I know from past experience," I said, suddenly finding the metaphorical dagger planted snugly in my hand, "that the role of the good Dean is one which you sometimes have great trouble sustaining."

I heard his sharp intake of breath. I saw the muscles tighten around his mouth. "How dare you," he said, and his voice was shaking with rage, "how *dare* you—"

"Since you insist on calling a spade a spade, I hardly think you're in a position to complain when I follow your example. Now, Stephen, let's get a grip on ourselves and try to discuss this in a calm, civilised and—dare I say it?—Christian manner. I'll start by offering you some information which is true and which I hope you'll accept as a peace-offering, signifying my good intentions. It's this: I don't want to make a visitation. I think it would be infinitely better for the Church if—"

"That's a lie!" By this time Aysgarth was beside himself with fury. "You've been longing for years to make a visitation in order to rub my nose in the mud, and don't think I can't guess why! You've never forgiven me, have you?"

With horror I realised that not only was the dagger back in his hand but that disembowelment was about to begin. "Stephen—"

"You can never forget that I once made a pass at your wife and that your wife was very far from being as upset as she should have been!"

Silence fell at last, but beyond the jagged panes of the window the Cathedral seemed to crackle with a force no eye could see and no scientist could measure. No longer was it a mere sullen lump glowering beneath the dull white sky. It was radiating malignancy, the scaffolding on the blighted west front as monstrous as a magnified scab, the spire resembling an open sore which had begun to fester. The entire building seemed deformed and rank.

Someone was saying: "You bloody liar!" But of course the man speaking was not me. It could not have been me because I never spoke in that tone of voice and I never used that kind of language. Bishops never did. No decent clergyman ever did. Such behaviour was unthinkable. "You bloody liar, she didn't want you, she fought you off—" The Cathedral had begun to writhe like a stone serpent. I was clearly aware of it writhing on some other plane of reality in a dimension which existed just beyond the corner of my eye. "—I know she fought you off, I know she did—"

"She didn't fight very hard! In fact for a long time she didn't fight at all. If I hadn't had too much to drink—"

"You always have too much to drink! The only reason why you don't spend your whole damned time committing adultery is because you're always too bloody sodden to achieve it!"

"Why, you self-righteous, hypocritical—"

"What's so self-righteous and hypocritical about speaking the truth?" I shouted, and at once Aysgarth shouted back: "It's not the truth! *I'm* the one who's speaking the truth when I call you self-righteous and hypocritical—how the bloody hell do you have the nerve to accuse me of immorality when it was you, not me, who went to bed with Harriet March last night?"

"Went to—"

"No, don't pretend you don't know what I'm talking about, and don't think I'll necessarily keep quiet for the good of the Church! In fact if you go ahead with that bloody visitation, I'll make sure Harriet tells her smart friends in London about your affair with her—and then the *News of the World* will be on your doorstep before you can even draw breath to lie about your innocence!"

I stared at him. I could not believe my ears, and automatically, still too stunned to understand what was happening, I said: "But there's no affair."

"According to Harriet there is!"

"But she's lying."

"I don't believe you! And neither will the *News of the World!*"

I finally realised what was happening. I was being blackmailed. I was almost too shocked to speak but at last I managed to say: "You've just convinced me beyond any shadow of doubt that you're utterly unfit to be the Dean of a great cathedral. I'm going to force you out of Starbridge even if it's the very last thing I ever do."

PART FOUR

REDEMPTION

"You have here a parable, the subject of which might be called The Persistence of Truth . . . Whatever fears, adversities, or doubts assail you, go forward calmly in the knowledge that the truth persists, and will prove itself in persisting. Though prayer be hard, though your soul walk in darkness, though your spiritual memories be shadowed by many a doubt, go forward secure in the knowledge that the truth of God endureth to all generations, and by its endurance will prove itself the very truth."

REGINALD SOMERSET WARD
(1881–1962)
Anglican Priest and Spiritual Director
THE WAY

XIX

"The evils of our life have an alarming tendency to spread, and breed other evils. Every extension of the trouble is a possible occasion of good, through the challenge it throws down to character, or the appeal it makes to kindness. But how far the evil may have run and multiplied before the appeal is heard, or the challenge taken up!"

AUSTIN FARRER
Warden of Keble College, Oxford, 1960–1968
LOVE ALMIGHTY AND ILLS UNLIMITED

I

I ERUPTED from the Deanery.

I never looked at the Cathedral, but I felt as if its shadow swept across the sward to pursue me as I stumbled down Canonry Drive in the bright white light of day.

As soon as I reached home I poured myself a brandy and took the glass upstairs to my bedroom where I knew no member of my staff would interrupt me. I glanced at my watch. The time was still only half-past four. I wanted to leave immediately for Starrington but I knew it would be suicidal to drive a car until I was calmer.

Curiously enough I could not think of Harriet's monstrous behaviour. I could only think of Lyle and Aysgarth embracing. Of course Aysgarth could have been lying. But now Lyle was dead how could I ever find out? Sitting on the edge of the bed I shuddered with misery, jealousy, rage and despair.

But shuddering in this self-indulgent fashion could hardly be rated a profitable occupation in such circumstances and indeed could even be judged an escape from this new reality—which was that I was in the biggest mess of my episcopal life and that my diocese was now facing the seamiest of ecclesiastical scandals.

Setting aside my empty glass of brandy I finally nerved myself to drive to Starrington.

2

FEARING THE door in the wall might be locked, I made no attempt to take the shortest route to Jon's cottage but parked again outside the main gates of the Manor. It was still light but I took a torch from the glove compartment for the return journey.

I had not forgotten Martin's advice to postpone my visit until the next day, but I knew Jon would never turn me away when I was in such a truly desperate situation. I wondered if Nicholas was still at the cottage. What would he think when I arrived looking distraught? Young people were not supposed to see bishops looking distraught. In fact no one was supposed to see bishops looking distraught . . . My anxious thoughts, banal yet tormenting, scampered round and round in my brain like a bunch of greyhounds at a race-track, and were only stilled when I reached the edge of the dell and could look down on the chapel, pale amidst the dark trees. The lights were already glowing beyond the windows of Jon's cottage.

The cat was washing his paws on the cottage's doorstep. As he saw me he hesitated, one paw still upraised, but before he could decide what to do the door opened abruptly and Jon ordered him inside. Then Jon caught sight of me. He paused, a gaunt figure in the doorway, and I broke into a run to cover the last yards which separated us.

"Charles! Why are you dressed as a commercial traveller?"

"I—"

"Never mind, I'm extremely glad to see you."

Encouraged by this unmistakably genuine welcome, I then noticed that far from looking worn out he appeared to be stimulated and alert. The frantic father, grappling with debilitating parental problems, had vanished. The subtle spiritual director, compassionate but essentially detached, had returned. I felt as if having seen a man stumbling around in clogs I had returned to find him dancing in handmade shoes.

Tentatively I said: "Is Nicholas here?" but Jon replied firmly: "Nicholas is much better and I've sent him to meditate in the chapel." That disposed of Nicholas. So might Jon, in his former role as Abbot of Grantchester, have talked of a troubled novice who had been collared, counselled and cast back into the scriptorium. Could one, in the middle of the twentieth century, treat one's son as an abbot would treat a novice? Apparently one could, but I wondered what Nicholas thought of being packed off to meditate in a darkening chapel when he was probably still shaken from his sinister experiences.

"He'll be all right," said Jon as if sensing my doubts, "because he knows he'll be all right. He's lit a candle and he's in the presence of the Blessed Sacrament. No demon can withstand the power of Christ." These statements were made in a very casual manner as if he were discussing some obvious stage in the housetraining of a cat. Against my will I remembered Martin describing Nicholas as a mixed-up kitten.

"Come along in, Charles," Jon was adding, ushering me across the threshold. "I must say, you've chosen the most interesting moment to call."

Pleased but puzzled I walked into the room—and immediately recoiled in horror.

Aysgarth was sitting at the table by the window.

3

IT WOULD have been hard to judge who was the most flabbergasted by the situation in which we now found ourselves. Paralysed by the reluctance to believe we could both be present at the cottage, Aysgarth and I stared at each other aghast while Jon, well pleased to have escaped from the rigorous demands of parenthood, was prowling around purposefully, closing the door, extricating a folding chair from a cupboard and saying: "Sit down opposite Neville at the table, Charles."

I had never before heard Jon call Aysgarth by his Christian name, and I realised that Jon was speaking not merely as a priest but as the spiritual director who had helped Aysgarth in the past and had now been asked to help him again. I was additionally startled to hear Aysgarth being addressed not as Stephen, the name Dido had given him, but as Neville, the name he had been using long ago at our first meeting in 1940 when his first wife had been still alive. In my shock my mind attempted to calm itself by fastening on this trivial detail. Absurdly I said to Aysgarth: "I didn't think anyone called you Neville nowadays."

"This is a new Neville," said Jon before Aysgarth could reply. "This Neville incorporates not only the previous Nevilles but also Stephen. He's been in place since the end of 1963."

After a pause I said: "I'm not sure I understand."

"No? Have you never had to strip aside various versions of Charles Ashworth in order to uncover your true self?"

At this point Aysgarth rose to his feet, cleared his throat and said politely: "I'll wait outside until Charles has finished."

"Sit down," said Jon.

"But surely—"

"Sit down."

Aysgarth sank reluctantly back into his chair.

"In that case I must be the one who waits outside," I said. "Obviously you can't talk to both of us at the same time."

"Why not?"

"Well . . ."

"In fact it's not I who have to talk to both of you; it's both of you who have to talk to each other. Take a seat, please."

Reluctantly I did as I was told. Aysgarth and I were now facing each other. Jon, who had by this time set up the folding chair for himself, drew it to the table and sat down between us.

There followed a long silence which finally became so unendurable that I felt it was worth uttering any idiocy to break it. To Aysgarth I said: "I didn't see your car."

"It's parked outside the door in the wall."

"Ah. I thought that might be locked. I parked at the gates."

"Splendid!" said Jon. "A very civil little exchange! Perhaps I may even dare to hope that you can stay in the same room for a few minutes without generating another unspeakable scene. I say 'another' because I assume that only an unspeakable scene could have driven you both to take refuge here at more or less the same moment."

I turned to Aysgarth. "Haven't you told him anything?"

"I've only just arrived."

"His words on arrival," said Jon, "were: 'All hell's broken loose and you've got to do something'—which is perhaps what you would have said, Charles, once you'd established that Nicholas was safely out of the way."

I had to concede that I might well have made a similar remark.

"So you're in agreement, at least, about the appalling nature of your situation. Very well, I suggest you take it in turns to tell me your stories, and I also suggest you toss a coin to decide who goes first. That'll eliminate any unedifying squabble about precedence."

Aysgarth said cautiously: "I quite like the idea of a coin," and I said: "Very appropriate. Conjures up images of cricket and civilised behaviour."

"More agreement!" said Jon. "We're getting on nicely!"

"You dreadful old pirate," said Aysgarth in disgust, "you disgraceful old ecclesiastical buccaneer, I can't stand to see how much you're enjoying this!" He turned to me. "Remember when we had that row back in 1946 and you smashed the glass in the grate of his dining-room? The old pirate enjoyed every minute of that too—what a way to get vicarious thrills!"

I found this speech extraordinarily offensive, but before I could make some outraged riposte on Jon's behalf Jon himself said in his most placid voice: "Toss the coin, would you, Charles?" and I realised I was being advised to keep my temper.

Searching my pockets I finally remembered that I had no change; I had not foreseen I would remain dressed up as a grammar-school *arriviste* in circumstances which required me to produce coins. In the end Aysgarth had to come to my rescue.

"Heads!" he called confidently as I spun his half-crown in the air.

My heart sank as I saw the image of the Queen. "Trust you," I could not help but say, "to take a risk and win."

Aysgarth, looking pleased with himself, proceeded to make the inevitable decision. "I'll put you in to bat."

Panic led me to appeal to the umpire. "Jon, wouldn't it be better if we took turns to brief you in private?"

"No," said Jon.

"But I can't help thinking it would be so much easier if—"

"What's easiest isn't necessarily what's best. Remember that after bracing exercise the body invariably feels much healthier."

"After bracing exercise my body invariably feels as if it wants to drop dead," said Aysgarth. "I'm sorry, but I honestly can't see why you're so against private briefings."

"They'd enable you both to preserve your pride by hiding your weaknesses from each other. No, much better to have everything out in the open! No more running away and taking comfort in illusion—no more hiding behind glittering images! Let's look upon the truth at last before you're both destroyed by your efforts to escape from it!"

At that point I realised I could hardly argue in favour of side-stepping the truth, and feeling increasingly queasy I forced myself to embark on my narrative.

4

"*I DROPPED* in at the Deanery," I said. "My sole desire was to make a polite request to see some interim accounts for the West Front Appeal. Malcolm and Nigel had convinced me that this was the best way forward in our attempt to quash the rumours which are currently circulating, and I'd planned to be non-abrasive, non-intimidating and thoroughly friendly in every way."

Aysgarth tried to speak but Jon raised a hand to forestall him. "Your turn will come later. Go on, Charles."

"Almost from the start," I said, "he adopted a bellicose position quite inappropriate for a senior cleric, and eventually his refusal to cooperate forced me to admit my fear that something was financially amiss. However, in an attempt to ease the situation—which he had made extremely fraught—I offered, just as a bishop should, to give him any help that might be necessary if he were in trouble. He rejected this suggestion very offensively and from that point the interview became not merely unpleasant but disastrous."

Aysgarth again tried to speak and was again cut off. "Be quiet," said Jon, and although I expected Aysgarth to rebel against this toughness I saw to my surprise that he respected it. Obediently he clamped his mouth shut and waited.

"I happened to point out then in my distress," I said, trying not to sound too glib, "that he had had problems as a dean in the past and that I therefore couldn't be blamed for wondering if he was having problems again. But unfortunately this oblique reminder of the events of 1963 angered him so much that he made a series of remarks which I can't possibly repeat."

"Why not?"

"Well . . ." I took a deep breath, thought furiously and produced the dignified reply: "I feel it would be lacking in charity to repeat them."

"Let's not argue about charity for the moment; let's just concentrate on giving birth to the truth. Charles, what on earth's the point of coming here to confide in me and then offering only a censored version of the facts?"

"I want to spare him the embarrassment of hearing his appalling behaviour described."

"You mean your own behaviour was irreproachable?"

"All right," I said, now very hot under the collar of my cheap shirt. *"All right.* The rock-bottom truth is that we both lost our tempers, and it's hard for me to talk of what happened because it's so shameful."

"That's better. Very well, let's hear the worst."

"He dragged up that scene which took place between him and Lyle after Alex Jardine's funeral. He made some disgusting allegations which I know—*I know*—were false. Then having told me—with liberal use of blasphemous language—that I was self-righteous and hypocritical, he proceeded to threaten me in the manner of an East End gangster: he said that if I made a visitation he'd see the *News of the World* heard that I'd been to bed with Harriet March. (Of course I don't have to tell you that this statement about Mrs. March was a complete and utter lie.) At that point I informed him that he was unfit to be the Dean of a cathedral and that I'd do my best to get him removed. End of conversation. End of scene. Now I'm sure you can understand why I'm so upset. Having been verbally beaten up, slandered and blackmailed—"

"I can contain myself no longer," said Aysgarth. "Jon, if you don't allow me to speak immediately, I shall burst a blood-vessel."

"Pray save us all from such a tiresome inconvenience," said Jon dryly, and Aysgarth, forearms on the table, ugly hands interlocked, at once embarked on a passionate speech in his own defence.

5

"HE DESCENDS on me out of the blue," said Aysgarth, "without even being courteous enough to phone to ask if his visit would be convenient. Who does he think he is? Napoleon? Frederick the Great? The Emperor Constantine? I thought a public-school education was supposed to teach a man how to behave in a civilised manner, but no—all it teaches him is how to behave like an upper-class thug! And to think Charles looks down on me just because I didn't go to that expensive dump where he idled away his time in ridiculous rituals! I can't stand this appallingly arrogant snobbishness of his, *can't stand it.* To me it symbolises all that's wrong with England—and with the Church—but thank God the 1960s are finally sweeping away all those old-fashioned attitudes, thank God the 1960s are raising the curtain on a different world, thank God the 1960s are—"

I said to Jon: "Do we really have to listen to this tasteless exercise in rhetoric?"

"Neville merely wishes to stress how angry he was that you should have descended on him in the manner of a secular tyrant, but I agree he's made his point. Go on, Neville, please. Charles, you said, descended on you out of the blue—"

"He sweeps into my house," said Aysgarth, "and I note at once that to disguise the fact that he's on the warpath he's dressed in his shabbiest clothes. I know the way his mind works! He's as addicted to power-manoeuvring as a boardroom tycoon, and if he'd been wearing his pectoral cross he would have chosen exactly the right psychological moment to stroke it. He always does that whenever he wants to put me in my place by reminding me that he's reached the bishops' bench in the House of Lords and I haven't—"

"But that's nonsense—it's never occurred to me to fidget with my cross for that reason!" I exclaimed. I was genuinely distressed to think that this trivial nervous habit of mine should have been given such a revolting interpretation.

"Can we forget about class for the moment, Neville?" said Jon. "Can we try and keep this a straightforward narrative? Charles arrived at the Deanery, you said—"

"—and within five minutes of being ushered into my study he's demanding to see the Appeal accounts and implying I'm a criminal. Of course he then realises he's gone too far and tries to backtrack; playing the father-in-God, he starts to ooze unctuously about how happy he would be if I confided in him. What a nerve! He crashes around like some tinpot dictator and then suggests that *I'm* the one in need of spiritual help! Naturally I'm driven to point out that he has no business behaving as if he's a detective from the fraud squad, and naturally I assure him—and wouldn't you think the word of a priest would be sufficient?—that I'm well in control of the Appeal, but is he satisfied? Of course not! He's quite unable to resist the temptation to play the proud prelate and tell me I've been a failure as a dean. All right, I admit I got in a dreadful mess in 1963, but we all make mistakes and I've repented, I've reformed and I've put that part of my past resolutely behind me in order to serve God as well as I possibly can. So how dare Charles be so unchristian as to fling the past in my face like that? Has he really no idea how a bishop's supposed to behave towards a sheep that's returned to the fold?"

"This is sheer demagoguery," I said. "This is—"

"This is how the scene seemed to Neville," said Jon, "and I think that if you wish to rebut his accusation of dictatorial behavior, you'd be wise to allow him freedom of speech."

"Well, after he'd rubbed my nose in the mud and kicked me in the teeth," said Aysgarth, "I couldn't restrain myself, I'm sorry but I just couldn't. I felt I had to hit back at him with the truth—which is, of course, that he's had his knife into me ever since he found out about that idiotic scene after Alex Jardine's funeral. Then *he* was the one who descended into blasphemous language—how typically hypocritical that he should accuse me of the sin he himself had committed before I did!—and he implied I'd tried to force myself on his wife when she was unwilling. Well, that's an allegation of attempted rape, isn't it? He was accusing me, a devout Christian, a clergyman, an archdeacon (as I was then) of a most repulsive criminal offence! I tell you, Jon, that was the last straw. I said . . . well, no, on second thoughts never mind exactly what I said—"

"But I do mind," said Jon. "And are you really going to get cold feet now that you're basking in the luxury of freedom of speech?"

"All right, you wily old conjuror, you cunning old pirate, I implied that Lyle found me very far from unattractive and said that I could have had her if I hadn't been so plastered—and the next moment Charles was accusing me of being a permanently impotent drunk. Well, what was I supposed to do next? Receive this gross slander with a smile? I know I've had periods of heavy drinking in the past, but I've got all that under control now, and as for the suggestion that I'm always too sodden to—"

"I hardly think the question of your sexual potency need detain us here. Continue, please. Charles, you said, accused you of being a permanently impotent drunk—"

"—and at that point I unleashed the weapon which I'd hoped I wouldn't be driven to use. Harriet March rang me this morning to say that Charles had given her a lift home last night after a dinner-party at the South Canonry, and she'd seduced him."

"But that's a lie!" I shouted. "It's preposterous! It's utterly beyond the realms of possibility!"

"I still don't believe you," said Aysgarth.

"Why, you absolute—"

"No, don't you dare call me a bastard! Go and talk to the mirror if you want to spew out that kind of language!"

We both sprang to our feet in rage, but Jon rose too, and Jon, drawing himself up majestically to his full height, was taller than either of us. For a moment after that no one moved. Then Jon made a sharp gesture in the direction of our chairs. We sank down again but Jon remained standing, towering above us both and looking at us with his most inscrutable expression.

At last when we were both utterly silent and utterly still he said: "I have but one comment to make on your behaviour and that's this: it all seems a very long way from Jesus of Nazareth." And turning his back on us abruptly, he stalked away into his kitchen.

6

WE STARED after him. Then we stared at each other. Aysgarth looked appalled but I doubt if he looked more appalled than I did. He was the one who first recovered his power of speech. He bawled: "Jon, come back here this instant!" but Jon shouted from the kitchen: "Not while you're behaving like a couple of infantile pagans!" and we remained on our own. He was still near us; the kitchen was a mere galley tucked behind the main room. I pictured him standing by the sink with his arms folded across his chest while he waited to hear how we would respond to his challenge.

Aysgarth said urgently to me: "*You* try," and I called in my mildest voice: "Jon, if you'd be good enough to return—we both realise we can't go on without your help—"

"I don't spoonfeed. Be your age, remember your calling and get out of this disgraceful impasse by yourselves."

To Aysgarth I said: "There's no shifting him."

"Then what on earth are we supposed to do?"

"Let's be quiet for a moment. At least if we're silent we can't quarrel."

"I don't want to quarrel."

"Neither do I."

"Then why are we beating each other up like this?"

"I don't know."

We stared at each other again. Eventually Aysgarth said with fury: "This is entirely his fault! If he hadn't insisted on this mad three-cornered conference—"

"But weren't we beating each other up long before we got here? And talking of that scene at the Deanery, how can you possibly have believed that rubbish from Harriet March?"

"She made it sound like gospel truth."

"Obviously she's certifiable."

"You mean it really isn't true?"

"Of course it isn't true! If it were true, *I'd* be certifiable!"

"But you did go to her studio."

"Certainly I did—as I've already told you, I saw the sculpture of your hands. But I give you my word of honour as a priest—I'll even swear on the Bible—that I never touched her."

Aysgarth at last showed no sign that he disbelieved me. Baffled he demanded: "But why should she lie to me like that?"

"She thinks I'm persecuting you. Obviously she wanted to offer a lethal weapon for your defence."

"But why on earth should she go to such extraordinary lengths on my behalf?"

"She appears to be rather fond of you."

"Do you think so?" said Aysgarth, much surprised. "How interesting! I'm fond of her, I admit, but I thought she just regarded me as an amusing old buffer." Astonishment was eased aside by gratification. "Well!" he exclaimed, becoming cheery. "Fancy that!" However, remembering the horrific consequences of Harriet's affection, he quickly added: "But it was quite scandalous that she should lie to me like that, and I'm extremely sorry, Charles, that I was fool enough to believe her. Of course I can see now that the very idea that you might behave in such a way is ridiculous. You of all men would never go to bed with a woman within days of your wife's funeral."

In the terrible pause that followed this revelation of my self-righteousness and hypocrisy, I examined my episcopal ring as if I had never seen it before and Jon finally emerged expressionless from the kitchen with his tabby-cat padding at his heels.

7

"SO THERE you are!" exclaimed Aysgarth to him irritably. "About time! What a histrionic way to behave!"

I was becoming increasingly annoyed by his rudeness to my distinguished spiritual director, but Jon, still unflurried, even smiled at him before saying equably: "I came back to tell you how well you're doing, Neville."

"I can't imagine how you reached that conclusion," said Aysgarth, sounding more irritated than ever.

"How do you think I reached that conclusion, Charles?"

"No idea." I was still struggling to regain my equilibrium after the devastating insight I had just received.

"No idea at all?"

Pulling myself together I made a big effort. "Stephen," I said, "admitted he got it wrong about Mrs. March."

"Not only that. Before I left the kitchen I heard him utter the words 'I'm extremely sorry.' "

Quickly I replied: "Yes, that was admirable." It would never do to sulk just because Aysgarth had put himself in Jon's good books.

Meanwhile Aysgarth himself was blossoming as the result of Jon's approval and was now positively wallowing in the waters of repentance. "I'm extremely sorry for that whole quarrel at the Deanery, Charles," he was saying. "I know you had the Cathedral's best interests at heart. I withdraw my suggestion that your demand to see some accounts was all part of a long-standing vendetta arising from that scene with Lyle."

I found myself unable to reply.

"And while on the subject of Lyle," said Aysgarth, speaking much faster, "I'd just like to say that I grossly exaggerated that scene in order to hit back at you. I did manage to swipe a kiss but only because she'd hit the gin so hard that it took her a moment to realise what was happening. As soon as she realised, she fought me off and was utterly loyal to you."

"Quite." A vast relief made it difficult for me to say more, but after a moment I managed to produce the sentence: "I apologise too for that scene at the Deanery." I even willed myself to add: "I should never have referred to your troubles in 1963."

But Aysgarth was still deep in his memories of 1945. "If you only knew how much I regretted that incident with Lyle—"

"No need to say any more."

"—especially when it really did seem as if you'd never forgiven me—"

"All an illusion, I assure you."

"—and I couldn't stop thinking how stupid it was that I should have got into such a mess when Lyle and I didn't even like each other—"

"There's really no need for you to continue to speak of this incident, Stephen, although of course I greatly admire the way you've now been so scrupulously honest about it."

"This is such an edifying dialogue that I hesitate to interrupt," said Jon, not unkindly, "but I must tell you that in my opinion you're both now playing to the gallery. What I suggest is that you stop trying to impress me with all this fancy spiritual footwork and focus instead not on a past nightmare but on a present one. How are you going to resolve your conflict over the West Front Appeal?"

Silence again fell on the room.

8

"YOU GO first," said Aysgarth to me at last.

"No, no—after you."

"But you're the Bishop—it's your privilege."

"But I went first last time—it's your turn."

Jon said briskly: "Instead of behaving like a couple of cowards, why doesn't one of you do the brave thing and volunteer?"

"Very well," I said at once. "My position's very simple: all I'm asking for is some sort of evidence that the Appeal's on course."

"I give you my word that it's on course, and if I'd been educated at your public school you'd accept my word without hesitation and take the matter no further!"

I said to Jon: "Here we go round the mulberry bush again."

"But I resent the fact that you won't take my word! You're being deeply unfair!"

"Well, that's certainly an accusation spoken from the heart," said Jon, "but is it true? Have you in fact interpreted the situation correctly? You're accusing Charles of playing a class game, but now look into your heart, continue to be honest and answer me this: are you sure you're not playing a class game yourself?"

Aysgarth said cagily: "I don't understand."

"It occurs to me that you're actually using Charles's public-school code of honour against him. Is it really fair in these circumstances to try to lever yourself out of this tight corner by saying: 'Trust me, I'm a gentleman'? Of course Charles would like to trust you—what a lot of trouble that would save him!—but he has his suffragan and his archdeacon breathing down his neck and the diocese vibrating with rumour. How would *you* feel if you were the Bishop? Take a moment to use your imagination."

I wanted to stand up and cheer.

Aysgarth, obviously feeling threatened, became mutinous. "Whose side are you on?"

"You'd do better to ask yourself whom I'm trying to represent, but do I really have to invoke Our Lord's name again to pull you to your senses? Now stop talking mindlessly of 'sides' and ask yourself what the appropriate response to Charles should be."

Mysteriously tamed yet again by this aggressive approach which I knew was far from characteristic of Jon, Aysgarth meditated obediently for some seconds before proffering the statement: "I know I have a duty to assist my bishop but I just feel so strongly that I'm being harassed and victimised."

"I realise that. But nevertheless, if you were in Charles's shoes—"

"Very well," said Aysgarth with extreme reluctance, "I'll get hold of some draft accounts. But Charles must in turn guarantee there'll be no visitation."

In despair I said: "I couldn't possibly give such an undertaking! Even if the accounts are satisfactory, there might be pressure to make a visitation in order to lay down rules about future fund-raising, and—"

"But you swore at the Deanery that you didn't want to make a visitation!"

"I don't want to wash a lot of dirty Church linen in public. But if your accounts are clean as a whistle, then there's a case for thinking of the future and—"

"This is pure malice, Charles—the truth is you just can't wait to roast me in the chapter house!"

"That's not the truth at all! I'm simply trying to—"

"May I," said Jon, "intervene? Neville is suffering from a failure of the imagination again, Charles is too flustered to think clearly and both of you are getting bogged down in the visitation issue which, as I see it, is a red herring which should be ignored. The truth is surely this: if the accounts are unsatisfactory, Charles won't want to make a visitation, and if they're satisfactory he won't need to make a visitation. So the matter can be shelved. Of course it might one day be beneficial to you both if a friendly visitation is made in order to clarify the fund-raising rules for the future, but I don't see why either of you should worry about that at the moment. I suggest you focus instead on the draft accounts—when they arrive. Now . . . isn't that the most pragmatic way forward?"

After some cagey rumination we had to agree that it was.

"Excellent!" said Jon swiftly. "Then we can move on."

Aysgarth looked blank. "What is there to move on to?"

"Don't you think it might be a good idea if you both spent a little time working out why you find it so impossible to get on with each other? How can either of you serve God properly when you're expending so much energy either to avoid or survive the sort of scene which took place at the Deanery today?"

"That's between us and God," said Aysgarth, displaying the traditional Protestant suspicion of intermediaries, "although please don't think I'm ungrateful for your help this afternoon." And rising to his feet he added: "I must go."

"What a pity! I was hoping you could begin the discussion by telling Charles why you believe he's sex-obsessed and power-mad."

As Aysgarth slowly sat down again I said: "I don't think I want to hear this."

"Why not?"

"Well, it's such a ludicrous judgement!"

"You've no curiosity to find out why Neville, an extremely able and intelligent man, has formed this most unflattering opinion of you?"

"I'm not interested in his biased fantasies!"

"No? But don't you think your first step in achieving a better *modus vivendi* might be to listen to him?"

"I—"

"Indeed hasn't a bishop an absolute moral duty to listen to a troubled member of his flock?"

I was finally silenced.

9

"NOW, NEVILLE," said Jon briskly, "it's some time since our talks in 1963, so I don't know how far your thoughts have progressed on this subject, but I remember how I urged you to make more effort to understand Charles and how you responded: 'I've got to understand him in order to survive him.' So let's hear, if you please, the results of this meditation, but don't try and score points, don't lapse into what Charles described earlier as 'sheer demagoguery' and don't try and pass yourself off as a persecuted underdog no matter how harassed and victimised you may

currently feel. Just offer your theories as if you were talking to an old friend—by which I mean be frank but not brutal. There's no need to behave as if honesty and kindness are incompatible."

"Bossy old magician," muttered Aysgarth, as if honour-bound to make a negative response, but he was finding the opportunity irresistible. Cautiously he said to me: "I don't want to make it sound as if I'm blaming you entirely for our inability to get on, Charles. I'm quite prepared to admit that mistakes have been made on both sides, but I do think that a large part of the trouble has arisen from the fact that you're much too keen on power. Of course you'll deny you're much too keen on it—you'll probably insist that you're not keen on it at all, but just consider for a moment: can it really be the purest chance that you've got a pushy, authoritarian archdeacon and a smooth, shrewd operator of a suffragan who protect your interests like a brace of tigers? And is it just an unfortunate coincidence that the one man in the diocese over whom you have almost no power—me—you repeatedly regard with suspicion and hostility? I always feel, whenever you and I have dealings, that I'm under threat and obliged to fight to protect myself—and why should I keep picking up that message if there wasn't a grain of truth in it? And having picked it up so consistently, is it really surprising that I've long since begun to wonder what motives lie behind your behaviour?"

He paused as if waiting for me to object, but since it was obvious that any objection would merely confirm his allegation of power-mad hostility, I kept quiet.

"Of course one can explain our failure to get on merely by saying we're incompatible," Aysgarth continued, carefully maintaining a mild tone of voice, "but in fact all the evidence suggests we ought to get on well. Jon said once—how did you put it, Jon?"

"I said you were both well-educated men in the same line of business who liked good food, good wine and attractive women. You may remember that I made a similar remark recently to you, Charles."

"But if we decide the facile explanation of incompatibility won't do," pursued Aysgarth without waiting for me to reply, "we have to dig deeper, and once we take a closer look at what's going on in our professional lives, two very obvious facts emerge. First, I'm not the kind of executive who can be pushed around, and second, you're the kind of executive who takes a very tough line. Laying aside my own shortcomings for a moment, I ask myself what's going on with you. Why are you like this? I can't help but think you've got the Bishop's role seriously out of alignment and that you're obsessed with appearing strong and powerful because you're subconsciously afraid of weakness—your own weakness, which is so threatening to you that you can't acknowledge it. All you can do to reassure yourself is stalk around like a dictator—and of course I, being the kind of man that I am, don't take that lying down. All right, obviously I'm at fault too, but it really does seem to me that the main problem here is this compulsion of yours to take a tough line."

He paused again. This time I did speak. I said to Jon: "I can't believe you approve of this fantastic exercise in character-assassination."

"I approve of Neville's genuine attempt to engage in the quest for truth. How far he succeeds in his quest is open to debate, but I feel the quest itself deserves encouragement."

"Let's leave the question of power," said Aysgarth not unkindly to me, "and put another part of our lives under the microscope. I'll pass over what I call 'the Lyle factor.' You've said this has never been an element in your hostility to me, and although I'd still query that, I won't argue further now. But let's stay with the subject of sex. For some reason (God alone knows why) attractive young women seem to like me, and you can't stand that, can you, Charles, it arouses in you very deep feelings of hostility. All right, I concede that in 1963 I did behave very foolishly, but apart from that one instance involving a lady I never now see, all my friendships with women have been harmless and my wife has been content to let me enjoy them. But you're not content, are you, Charles? And why? I think it's because you yourself are very attracted to young women in a way that's quite inappropriate for an elderly clergyman, and your disapproval of me is your way of disapproving of yourself. Now perhaps you'll understand why I found it all too easy to believe you'd gone to bed with Harriet. I thought that your bereavement had so dislocated you that all the iron control you usually exercise over your behaviour had broken down with the result that your sexual weakness had been allowed free rein."

At once I said to Jon: "Must we really continue to listen to this deeply offensive speculation?" I was twisting my episcopal ring round and round on my finger.

Unexpectedly Jon used his gentlest voice. He said: "The fact that Neville's taken time to work out these unpalatable theories doesn't mean he wants to hurt you. It means he's very troubled by the difficulties you experience with each other, and he's trying hard to see you in the light of truth so that he may understand, forgive and accept you as you are." Setting down the cat who had been slumbering on his lap, he absent-mindedly brushed the animal's hairs from the skirt of his cassock and added: "The real difficulty here, it seems to me—the underlying difficulty which distorts your relationship—is that you don't know the truth about each other. Neville's attempt to sketch what Jung would call the 'shadow' side of Charles is certainly not without interest, but at best it can only be described as a partial portrait. You're strangers to each other, that's the truth of it. It's lack of knowledge that's blighting this landscape."

Aysgarth said shortly: "I feel I know Charles almost as well as I know my own brother," and I said with equal confidence: "After an acquaintance of twenty-five years I hardly feel I suffer from a lack of knowledge where Stephen's concerned."

Jon sighed. Then he remarked: "Sometimes I despair of you both," and rose to his feet. "I must go and prepare Whitby's evening fish."

"Wait!" thundered Aysgarth. "Never mind that tiresome animal—stay exactly where you are!"

"Whitby is not a tiresome animal," said Jon coldly. "He leads a sensible, disciplined life for a member of his species, and is never either pigheaded or proud or wilfully stupid. I can think of at least two human beings who would do well to emulate him."

Aysgarth turned to me. "How do we stop him walking out again?"

"Jon," I said, "please don't think we're not willing to listen to you. If you could allow for the fact that we're under considerable strain—"

"Very well," said Jon, relenting but still sounding chilly. "If you're willing to work hard instead of lazily presenting me with closed minds, Whitby shall wait for his fish. Let us pray."

10

I WAS not in the least anxious to pray and would have much preferred to retrieve our mistake by asking Jon to expound further on the theory which Aysgarth and I had so tactlessly dismissed, but Jon clearly felt we needed the most effective tool available for waging war on our arrogance and prising open our closed minds.

Aysgarth too was slow to move; I suspected he would have been content to remain seated, but Jon had strict ideas about worship and believed that the body had an important part to play in reflecting the motions of the mind. We all knelt by our chairs, and the cat, waving his tail, stalked around observing this phenomenon until Jon was obliged to remove him to the kitchen.

"We'll start with the Lord's Prayer," said Jon once he was kneeling again. "You need something simple to focus your minds. I shall recite the prayer and you will listen, you will pray with it and you will meditate in the silences I'll create, just as two men of your age and experience should. Are you ready?"

We started out. He paused after "Thy will be done" and "Give us this day our daily bread," but the longest silence came after the prayer for forgiveness.

"What would be the best interpretation of 'daily bread' in these circumstances?" Jon said after the "Amen."

"Grace," I said.

"Courage," said Aysgarth.

"Why not the knowledge which generates understanding, the knowledge you seem so determined to underestimate? I suggest we now ask God to lighten the darkness of ignorance in which you both stand in relation to each other—we'll recite the final Evensong Collect. I'll recite it first. Then you, Charles, and then you, Neville. Are we ready? Very well. 'Lighten our darkness, we beseech thee, O Lord . . .' "

I made a vast but unsuccessful effort to concentrate. The thought of darkness reminded me of my night with Sheila, a memory which I found I could no longer contemplate without feeling ill with shame and dread. A dense fog of misery overwhelmed me. I ceased to listen to the prayer and almost missed Jon saying at the end: "Your turn, Charles."

I tried to recall the familiar words but failed. Only the thought of Aysgarth, smirking as he waited for the moment when he would recite the Collect perfectly, drove me to try again and succeed.

". . . Amen," I concluded much too fast.

"Neville?" said Jon.

I waited for the polished recital but nothing happened.

"Charles," said Jon, "would you be good enough, please, to fetch a glass of water from the kitchen?"

Amazed by Aysgarth's failure I lurched to my feet and withdrew to the kitchen where the tiresome cat, no doubt hungry for his fish, started to rub himself trustfully against my ankles. To buy myself some time I poured a dash of milk into his saucer. Immensely gratified by this gift from a stranger, he settled himself down, purring loudly; his small pink tongue began to whip in and out; I could only envy him his innocent happiness.

Feeling marginally calmer after this brief break from my human companions, I returned to the main room with the glass of water and found Aysgarth looking unnaturally pale. "Sorry," he kept saying. "Not myself at all. Sorry, sorry, sorry."

Jon said in the same gentle voice he had used earlier to me: "Life's unusually difficult, perhaps, for you as well as for Charles at present."

"Nonsense. My difficulties aren't in the same league. Charles has the bereavement to cope with."

"True. But just suppose for a moment that Charles wasn't bereaved—"

"Ah well, then there'd be no comparison. Before Lyle's death Charles always had it easy—no wonder he was constantly gliding along and glittering away, wreathed in triumphant self-satisfaction! In fact, he's still glittering, isn't he? Look at the way he recited that Collect just now! That perfect pause for meditation at the beginning, that perfect recital of each clause, that perfect quickening of pace at the end—every syllable he uttered demonstrated how completely relaxed and at ease he was!"

I said: "Of course you're speaking in jest."

"In *jest?* I assure you I'm wholly serious!"

"But my dear Stephen!"

"What's the matter?"

"You can't possibly believe such rubbish!"

"Rubbish?"

"Rubbish! I was in such a state I could hardly get the words out, and in the beginning I couldn't even remember them!"

"You're just saying that to make me feel better."

"I most certainly am not! And while we're on the subject of people gliding along and glittering away, what sort of impression do you think you've been giving, bragging about all your perfect children and basking in your outstanding talent as a fund-raiser and administrator? You've been gliding and glittering around that Cathedral ever since your installation in 1957!"

"Well, I had to keep up with you somehow, didn't I? It was a question of pride." His eyes widened as he realised where the conversation had led him. "Wait a minute," he said furiously, *"wait a minute!* What's happening here? How did we get involved in this revolting emotional strip-tease?"

I said: "Prayer can open up a pathway to one's truest emotions. Jon wanted to—"

"That man's reaching the stage where he ought to be banned by law!"

"My sole aim was to help you catch a glimpse of the truth that you know rather less about each other than you think," said Jon, evidently making the lightning decision that the best way to survive this onslaught was to speak with brisk good humour. "If the two of you can only cast aside those glittering images which have bedevilled your acquaintance for so long, perhaps I'll finally be able to introduce the real Charles Ashworth to the real Neville Aysgarth."

"You appalling old magician!" said Aysgarth, still disgusted but showing signs of being amused in spite of himself. "You monstrous old clerical buccaneer, how dare you bugger around with us like that? If I had a gun I'd shoot you!"

"No, you wouldn't!" I said, amazed to find myself laughing. "You'd be too busy wondering what he was going to say next! Go on, Jon."

"I rather doubt if that's what Neville wants."

Aysgarth made a noise which sounded like "Arrrgh!" and declared truculently: "If Charles is tough enough to endure this scandalous performance of yours, then I'm certainly not going to fall by the wayside. All right, you old conjuror, what are you going to say next?"

"Nothing," said Jon, outflanking him.

II

"IT'S ENOUGH that I've given you a glimpse of this unknown reality," said Jon, driven to explain himself after Aysgarth had given yet another exclamation of deep disgust. "It's enough if you now accept that although you know each other so well on a facile level, there are vast areas of ignorance on both sides. In fact we've reached a point beyond which I can't go—to do so would betray the confidences which you've both bestowed on me over the years. All I can do now, having pointed you in the right direction, is to leave you to explore this new reality for yourselves."

"I'm not exploring anything," said Aysgarth, very bolshie.

Trying to suppress my irritation I said evenly: "But on reflection, Stephen, would you at least agree that we should both admit to a degree of ignorance about each other? After all, only God can know the whole truth about anyone; our knowledge of others is always going to be imperfect."

"Precisely!" said Jon at once, lured on by Aysgarth's bolshiness to take the centre of the stage once more. "One can never know the whole story about anyone—yet how we all rush to judgement! How we all love to ignore the truth that we know so little about what motivates other people, what shadows from the past distort their psyches, what demons haunt and enslave them. How readily we say with perfect confidence: 'He's despicable!' or: 'He's behaved unforgivably!' or worst of all: *'I'd* never behave like that!' Yet how dare we pass judgement when so much of the evidence is beyond our reach? No wonder Our Lord said so sternly: *'Judge not, that ye be not judged!'* No wonder he said: *'He that is without sin among you, let him cast the first stone!'* Jesus wasn't interested in rushing to judgement. He wasn't interested in 'keeping up a front' or scoring points off those who found him intolerable. *'Love ye your enemies,'* he said, *'Do good to them that hate you.'* And time after time he said: *'Forgive,'* and talked of the truth which sets us free . . . And so we come back again to our own current quest for truth, the truth about one another. As

Charles pointed out just now, we can never see the whole truth; only God can see everything. But we can see so much more of the truth when our eyes are open, viewing people as Christ viewed them, than when they remain resolutely closed."

He stood up, moving slowly to the fireplace, and stared into the flames for a long moment before turning to face us again. "I know so much about you both," he said abruptly. "I know what forces and events have shaped you. I know not only about all your difficulties but about how hard you've worked to overcome them. You look at each other and see only your faults, but I look at you in the light of my special knowledge and find I can overlook those faults because I know your virtues are far more important. How impressed you would be with each other if you knew what I knew! What heroes you would be in each other's eyes! What a lot you have in common and how you would sympathise with each other if ever you began to discuss your past ordeals! Of course you've both made mistakes and got into muddles from time to time, of course you have—you're only human! But unlike so many people you've always repented and struggled to do better—you've always kept trying, no matter how adverse the circumstances, to live your faith with courage and be the best possible versions of the men God created you to be."

He moved back to the table and when he was sitting between us again he said suddenly: "Charles, tell Neville about your call."

"Which call?" I said, but I knew. It was the call to bring up another man's son, but of course I could not talk of that.

"Treat Neville as a priest," said Jon, guessing my thoughts, "and ask him to keep the matter confidential."

That was when I realised my silence arose not from a fear that Aysgarth would betray a confidence but from an inability to talk of Samson.

"I can't," I said confused.

"Neville, perhaps you can tell Charles about your own call."

"Which call?" said Aysgarth, but he knew too; I saw confusion overwhelm him as it had overwhelmed me. "Certainly not!" he said irritably at last. "That's private. But I'll say this: just because I responded to the call doesn't mean I'm a hero, as you seem to be implying. I responded because it was the only thing I could possibly have done—it allowed me to redeem the past."

At once I said startled: "That's the way I felt. And I don't see myself as a hero either. I just did what had to be done."

We gazed at each other with deepening interest.

"But nevertheless one could surely still say," pursued Jon, "that you both in your different ways took part in the redeeming work of the Holy

Spirit: there was a mess which you toiled to put right. Now let's reach a little further back into the past: Charles, tell Neville about your parents."

After a pause I said: "I'd rather not." It was always difficult for me to speak of the harsh treatment which I had received from my strict father and the reasons which lay behind his behaviour.

"Neville, tell Charles about your Uncle Willoughby."

"Over my dead body!" said Aysgarth outraged.

But these refusals had obviously been expected; Jon had asked the questions not to obtain answers but to stimulate our interest in each other. With a smile he stooped to pick up the cat, who had returned to skulk around the hem of his cassock, and announced: "Whitby must now have his fish. I suggest we all keep silence for a while in order to rest." And trying not to look too pleased with himself he stalked away yet again to the kitchen.

12

"I DON'T know how you endure that man on a regular basis," muttered Aysgarth. "I can only tolerate him when I'm desperate."

"He seems to understand you very well."

"That's why I find him intolerable."

"But surely—"

"Oh, don't listen to me, he's got me in such a state that I hardly know what I'm saying! Yes, of course I'm fond of the old boy and of course I'm grateful to him for propping me up occasionally, but I don't like all this spiritual direction stuff, the only person I want understanding me is God and I don't approve of this Catholic fixation with mediators—and yes, I know that's an appallingly bigoted thing to say, but I'm a Protestant by temperament and upbringing, and I get very nervous indeed when some smug, know-it-all of a priest prances around putting me through a series of vile hoops and carrying on as if he were—"

"SILENCE!" shouted Jon from the kitchen.

I laughed. Aysgarth whispered, "I didn't think the old boy's hearing was so keen!" and looked sheepish. An unpleasant smell began to envelop us as Jon boiled a piece of fish for the cat.

"Revolting!" said Aysgarth, driven at last to speak again. "I don't know what he sees in that animal."

"I've often wondered."

"In fact there's something very sinister about Jon's passion for cats. In the old days—"

"Oh, the stake, of course."

Jon reappeared in the doorway. "Getting on nicely?"

"Uniting against you, you old villain!"

Jon looked pleased.

Closing the kitchen door to block out the smell of fish he sat down with us again at the table. "After you'd given your anti-Catholic polemic, Neville," he remarked, "it occurred to me that the three of us form a model—a paradigm, one might say—of the Church. Here we are, all sitting around a table: the Protestant from the Low Church wing, the priest from the Middle Way, the Anglo-Catholic. Or, on another level: the Liberal Modernist, the conservative and the mystic. We clash, interlock, interweave, move apart—and then clash all over again in an unceasing engagement which produces the Church."

"Obviously the only way one can excuse all the fights," said Aysgarth, "is to say that if there were no friction there'd be no change, and if there were no change the Church would be dead."

"Change is all part of the creative process," I said, thinking of Harriet.

"Certainly we're not just required to be," Jon agreed. "We're required to become—and in the process of becoming we're all necessary to each other; we're all interlinked because we all have our part to play in our Creator's grand design. So when the two of you clash you should say to yourselves not: 'How can I get the better of this man?' but: 'What can I learn from him so that I can further my becoming?' For the more we become our true selves, the selves God designed, the better we shall be able to serve God and assist him in—"

"Making everything come right," I said, thinking of Harriet again.

"—in the economy of redemption and salvation," said Jon as if so taken aback by my descent into the simple language of laymen that he felt obliged to produce the appropriate theological phrase himself. "But wait a minute, Neville's looking cross again. What have I said now?"

"I don't like it when you talk like a mystical seer," said Aysgarth baldly, "and I particularly don't like it when you pontificate as if you're infinitely wiser and better than we are."

"But he is!" I said loyally.

Jon laughed. "Ah, how you like to idealise me, Charles!" he said with affection. "But fortunately for my spiritual health, Neville takes a much more robust approach—indeed sometimes I think he's periodically sent to me by God to cut me down to size. No, certainly I mustn't play the mystical seer and pontificate as if I knew all the answers! When I think back over my past—and about all the mistakes and messes *I've* made, most of which you know absolutely nothing about—I can see very clearly that I'm even more in need of forgiveness and redemption than you are."

"The trouble with redemption," said Aysgarth, so pacified by this somewhat excessive exercise in humility that he was tempted to become confidential, "is that it's such a tough road to travel. As far as my own redemptive mission's concerned—my attempt to redeem my extreme past—I keep veering off the road and winding up in a ditch."

"But you always haul yourself out of the ditch, don't you, and stagger on?"

"Well, I'd hardly help Dido, would I, if I just lay down in the ditch and gave up! And if I'm to redeem my past, Dido's always got to come first."

"Put God first and I think you'll find you're better equipped to look after Dido—and better equipped too to haul yourself out of the current ditch."

"Who said there was a current ditch?" said Aysgarth at once. "Not me! And of course I put God first! It's God who requires me to look after Dido."

"I take your point," said Jon in his mildest voice, "but I do wonder if Dido's requirements and God's requirements are always going to be identical." And as Aysgarth gave him a look in which extreme wariness was mingled with a reluctant interest, he turned to me and said: "As you see, Neville's devoted to his wife's welfare, Charles. I'm sure that's something you can understand and admire."

At once Aysgarth said: "You can't equate Dido with Lyle. Dido's not emotionally strong."

"Neither was Lyle when I married her," I said before I could stop myself.

Aysgarth was amazed. "But she was always so tough and capable!"

I could only reply: "You never knew her."

"Evidently not! Even so, I'm sure you didn't feel called by God to put everything right, did you?"

"Well, as a matter of fact," I said, "I rather think I did."

We gazed at each other in fascination.

Finally, still mesmerized by this impression of identical past suffering, I said: "I wish you didn't feel that I was against you. I wish . . ." I hesitated, not wanting to alienate him by referring to a current ditch which he had insisted did not exist, but driven on by my desire to demonstrate that I could be sympathetic. "I do wish you'd let me know," I said, "if you ever have some particularly difficult problem. I'd so like to give whatever help I could." Acutely conscious that he had been infuriated by my offer of help earlier that afternoon I tried hard to speak in a way which he would not interpret as dishonest or patronising. "I expect you're still thinking there's no help I could possibly give you,"

I added, "but I could at least listen and pray and . . ." My voice trailed away as I succumbed to the fear that I was failing to convey my sincerity. At last, resorting in desperation to an unadorned bluntness, I blurted out: "I accept that you think I'm just a persecuting nuisance, but if we really do have more in common than we ever imagined, perhaps I'm capable of being rather more than just a dead loss to you in the future."

I saw Aysgarth hesitate; I knew he had finally recognised that I was speaking from the heart, but unfortunately Jon then chose to make one of his rare wrong moves. It was as if he was prematurely congratulating himself on bringing off a mediating tour de force.

With a satisfaction guaranteed to set our prickly companion's teeth on edge, he said: "Well, here's your chance, Neville—why wait for some future crisis? This is a golden opportunity to have a frank talk with Charles about anything—anything at all, no matter how trivial—which may be troubling you at the present moment."

"Some other time, perhaps," said Aysgarth acidly, and hauled himself to his feet. But all was not quite lost. To me he added pleasantly enough: "Don't take offence, Charles, I'm not doubting your sincerity, but if this bossy old buccaneer thinks he can mesmerise me into some garrulous confession, he'd better think again. I'm glad you and I have made our peace after that quarrel, and I'm glad we've reached agreement on the Cathedral, and I'm glad we seem to have acquired some hope of a more passable relationship, but I see no reason to prolong this discussion further. Jon"—he turned back to our mediator—"forgive me, but I honestly feel I can't stand being spiritually directed a second longer. Can I ask you to pray for me instead?"

Jon, who was by this time trying and failing not to look annoyed, produced a thin smile and said dryly: "I think I may be trusted to pray for you without being asked." With an effort he added: "I can see I've rubbed you up the wrong way, and I apologise."

"No need . . . meant well . . . not ungrateful—" Aysgarth was by this time hurtling towards the door. "—in fact I'm very grateful indeed—I'll be in touch." And grabbing his coat he made a rapid exit into the dusk.

13

AS SOON as the front door had banged shut Jon exclaimed: "How could I have made such an error? I'm ashamed of myself!" And in exasperation he banged his clenched fist upon the table.

To console him I said: "Even if you hadn't started to glow with triumph a shade too soon, Aysgarth might still have engineered an excuse to walk out."

"But he'd already given in to the temptation to confide! He'd revealed to you his call to look after Dido, and if I hadn't said the wrong thing he might well have gone on to reveal something about his current ditch!"

"We agree, I take it, that in spite of his denial a current ditch does exist."

"Of course. The denial was much too emphatic to ring true, but what the ditch is I have no idea."

This surprised me. "But from the way you handled the conversation I assumed you knew much more than I did about what was going on!"

"I knew more but not much more—I knew about the call to look after Dido and no doubt that made me quicker off the mark in responding to his remarks about ditches, but I confess I still found the conversation very enigmatic."

"If there's always a connection between Dido and his ditches—and he certainly implied there was—"

"—then the current ditch will also involve Dido, but how? What on earth can it be?"

I said promptly: "The West Front Appeal. If there's a scandal, Dido would suffer."

But Jon looked doubtful. "That's certainly one possible reading of the situation," he agreed, "but is it the correct one? Personally I have trouble seeing Aysgarth getting into a big financial mess. On the other hand, I can all too easily imagine him getting into difficulties with a woman. Isn't it in fact far more likely that the current ditch is a consequence of his friendship with Harriet March?"

"No, I'm sure that's innocent."

"I wonder. It strikes me as such an odd association that only a sexual attraction could explain it. Just consider, Charles: why should a good-looking successful woman such as Mrs. March, still moderately young, bother to spend her valuable time dancing attendance on an elderly clergyman? I gather she has no interest in either the Church or Christianity, and she must surely have more entertaining gentlemen friends in London."

"She was sculpting his hands. That's why she's had to see him regularly."

"But how did she come to sculpt them? You'd think that after the disaster of 1963, when her sculpture for the churchyard was rejected, she'd have washed her hands of everyone in the Cathedral Close—and in fact I can remember Neville telling me at the end of that year that he hadn't seen her for some time. So what brought them back together again?"

"Apparently the hands had a mesmerising effect on her and she couldn't rest until she'd sculpted them."

"It's a romantic story, certainly. It's probably even partly true. But do we really believe that Mrs. March turned up uninvited at the Deanery one day many months after the disaster of 1963 and announced: 'I'm compelled to sculpt your hands'?"

"She probably met him again by chance through mutual friends and decided to let bygones be bygones for the sake of her art. Believe me, Jon, the association with Harriet March can all be explained away—it's the behaviour over the Appeal which defies an innocent explanation."

"You really think so?"

"I do now. Nigel and Malcolm were both convinced that if Aysgarth were to prevaricate about the accounts, even when threatened with a visitation, we could be justified in thinking the worst, and I have to confess I've come to agree with them. He's behaved like a guilty man in a big mess—and talking of big messes—" I stopped.

Without a word Jon pulled out the drawer of the table and produced Lyle's journal.

For a long moment I was unable to speak but at last I managed to say: "And your verdict?"

"I think this is a very great gift to you," said Jon without hesitation, "and no matter how despairing you may feel at the moment, I believe it offers a profound hope for the future."

Another long moment passed. Then I said painfully: "Before we talk of the future I'm afraid we must talk of the past." And dredging up all my strength I prepared at last to confide in him.

XX

"I go to confession, and it is blindingly clear, as soon as I am dealing direct with Christ in his priest, that his love is very present, but that the perversity of my sin is very great."

AUSTIN FARRER
Warden of Keble College, Oxford, 1960–1968
SAID OR SUNG

I

JON HAD acquired his method of hearing confessions from the Fordite monks; there was an informal discussion at the table followed by a formal act of confession before a cross. Usually he insisted that this formal confession should take place in the chapel, but since the chapel was currently being occupied by Nicholas I knew that on this occasion we would be staying in the cottage.

As I embarked on the narrative which would lead to our informal discussion, the room seemed to become quieter and dimmer. Finally I stopped. I had long since ceased to look at Jon and was examining the surface of the table as I wondered, with a detached professional interest, how he would respond. Since he would know my repentance was genuine, I was sure he would grant me absolution but I wondered if he would drop a hint about taking an early retirement. Certainly he was going to insist on a long retreat during which I could sort out my problems and recover my spiritual health. But perhaps my problems could not be sorted out; perhaps the complete failure of my disciplined life was a symptom of the onset of senility, and I was fit only for the scrap-heap. Of course I was no longer fit to be a bishop, I realised that; but perhaps I was now unfit for clerical duties of any kind.

At that point I was so disabled by sheer misery that I failed to hear the question which Jon was asking and had to request him to repeat it.

"I said: why do you think this incident with Mrs. Preston happened?"

"I was demented."

"Charles, if I were to ask you: 'Why do you have a headache?' would you really answer: 'Because a pain arrived in my head'?"

I apologised and tried again. "I hate to admit it, but Aysgarth's repulsive analysis was right. Obviously I was so dislocated by grief that my normal control over all my weaknesses disintegrated."

"That's certainly a better description of what happened than saying 'I was demented,' but I still don't think it tells us anything important about your motivation. What were you actually trying to do here?"

"Have sex."

"Quite. Charles, you may now think *I'm* demented, but I suspect a desire for sex had very little to do with what was actually going on."

"But I've been bounding around like a satyr—I've felt violently attracted to three women in rapid succession—"

"All that tells us is that you're disturbed and that this disturbance is manifesting itself through your genitals. But what's going on in your brain?"

"I'm slaughtered by bereavement."

"We can certainly assume your behaviour is reflecting an aspect of your bereavement, but what aspect is it reflecting?"

"Sexual deprivation. I'm incapable of leading a celibate life."

"I think you could lead a celibate life for a time if you had to. I'm not saying you'd like it, but you'd manage."

"All right, the other explanation is that I'm not trying to relieve my frustration but to deaden the pain—I'm using sex as an analgesic."

"If all you wanted to do was deaden the pain, why didn't you settle for the far less risky course of getting drunk?"

"Because I like going to bed with women better than getting drunk."

"Very well, but if you'd reached the stage where you merely wanted a woman as a painkiller, why not just pick up a prostitute? After all, there you were, wearing civilian clothes, in a red-light district a long way from your diocese. The risk would have been minimal."

"And I almost took it."

"But you didn't. You could have done, but you didn't. So could we deduce from that, perhaps, that your rejection of the prostitutes means you weren't simply looking for a painkiller? And if you weren't simply looking for a painkiller, what were you looking for?"

"God knows."

"Well, of course God knows! Really, Charles, what a vacuous reply! Now try and think intelligently as I approach the problem from another angle. What have you actually confessed to me? You've said that in a short space of time you've felt powerfully attracted to three women. Very well, answer me this: what do these three women have in common?"

I remained baffled. "Nothing," I said, but realising that this could hardly be the reply I was supposed to make I reconsidered the question by carefully thinking aloud. "Not age," I said. "Harriet's under forty, Sheila's probably in her early fifties and Loretta must be nearer seventy than sixty. And not nationality; Loretta's American. And not class; Loretta's outside the English class system. And not religion; Harriet's a non-believer. And not sexual allure; one couldn't call Sheila a *femme fatale.* And not intellect; Harriet's clearly a clever woman and Sheila's no fool, but Loretta's the only one who could be described as an intellectual." I sighed. "All right, I give up. Tell me what they all have in common."

"Each one represents a certain type of woman. Sheila represents the perfect episcopal wife; Harriet represents the *femme fatale;* Loretta represents the good friend with whom you can feel instantly at ease. Don't you see, Charles? Together they add up to the woman you've lost. What they all have in common is a resemblance to Lyle."

There was a profound silence before Jon said: "We'll pause there for a moment," and when I failed to reply he rose to his feet to put another log on the fire.

2

BY THE time he returned to his chair I was able to say: "That's certainly an insight I can accept, but I don't see how it stops me bounding around like a satyr. Surely so long as I miss Lyle so much I'm going to go on feeling attracted to these women?"

"There's no law which says you mustn't find them attractive, Charles; being attracted to women is a perfectly acceptable masculine occupation. What matters is that you shouldn't continue to use them to work off an aspect of your bereavement which you still haven't grasped."

"You keep talking of an 'aspect' but surely it's the whole bereavement—surely I'm just missing Lyle?"

"The journal suggests that there's something more specific going on. Try this question: if I'm right and these three women do in their different ways represent Lyle to you, what in fact have you been doing by pursuing them?"

I said very slowly: "Pursuing her. Trying to find her. When I finally embraced Sheila I felt as if Lyle had come back to me."

"Now you're getting somewhere."

"I barely know any of these women," I said as the assorted pieces of the puzzle began to fall into place, "but because I was projecting Lyle's image onto them so strongly they seemed so familiar—and so very hard to resist."

"So if you stop projecting Lyle's image—"

"—they'll all become resistible and my career as a satyr will end. But how do I stop projecting Lyle's image?"

"You understand just why you're so desperate to find her. Or in other words, the question you have to answer is this: what aspect of Lyle's loss hit you so hard that on a subconscious level you felt you had to run around trying to find her in every woman you met?"

There was a long, long silence. Then I whispered: "I wanted to tell her I was sorry. I wanted to make love to her and put everything right." And as my fingers closed at last on the journal which lay on the table between us, the tears blurred my eyes until I could no longer see.

3

"I NEEDED her to be there to forgive me," I said after a while. "I felt so ashamed of my blindness and selfishness and stupidity. I felt so guilty that I'd driven her to set out on her great spiritual journey alone."

"Perhaps it was necessary for her to set out alone. Perhaps that was all part of the process of finding out what God required of her."

"But I failed her by being so insensitive and making life so difficult for her!"

"Yet doesn't the journal show that she never stopped loving you despite all your difficulties? And do you think she'd have continued to pray for you with such passion if you hadn't been fully forgiven? She prayed for you every day, indeed it seems she prayed almost without ceasing, she prayed for you right up to the end."

"And what good did it do?" Tears burnt my cheeks as I remembered Lyle dying. "I can't bear being without her," I said, hardly able to speak, "can't *bear* it."

An interval followed during which Jon moved his chair around the table so that he could sit at my side and put his hand comfortingly over mine. It was as if by entering the darkness of my grief he was able to absorb it and lighten the burden. At last I found I could say: "I know her prayers did do good. The journal made clear how greatly her life had changed for the better. But I didn't change, did I?"

"You're changing now."

"But to think she had to die in order to—"

"No, no, you're misinterpreting what happened, implying her death was a punishment for your obtuseness—all that guilt of yours must have produced a theological amnesia! Charles, the death was a random event. God—"

"—never wills suffering, yes, all right, I don't seriously believe he decided to knock some sense into me by killing my wife, I'm not quite ripe to be stripped of my doctorate in divinity—but the fact remains that if she hadn't died I wouldn't have seen the need for change and all her prayers would have been in vain."

"But can't you see? No, obviously not—you've been blinded by grief. Charles, I'm sure you're mistaken—I'm sure everything was set up for a big dénouement, but Lyle's death threw a spanner in the works."

"Obviously you're basing that opinion on the journal, but I can't quite—"

"Lyle was working herself up to confide in you—her prayers had obviously convinced her that this was what had to be done; she didn't pray in vain at all; she prayed for enlightenment and it was granted to her. She refers several times to her desire to talk to you, but she's held back each time because she's sure you'll never believe what she has to say. In other words, she was only silent because the time never seemed right to speak out, but that time would have come, I'm sure of it—and it would have come in the form of a disaster."

"How can you possibly know?"

"Because Lyle knew. The last section of her journal is filled with intimations of an approaching catastrophe."

"I'd assumed that was some sort of eerie foreknowledge of her own death."

"That's not impossible, I agree, but I believe that with the new clarity of vision which prayer had given her, she was looking at her very troubled family and making a deduction which required no psychic foreknowledge whatsoever. Her chief fear seems to have been that you yourself would break down in some way, but it's obvious that she was also extremely worried about Charley and Michael. When a family is as troubled as your family was—and is—all the members become vulnerable and a disaster of some kind is often waiting in the wings."

"So you're saying that if Lyle had lived—"

"If Lyle had lived, she would have at last had the chance to speak out. Disasters have a way of breaking down barriers."

I struggled with this unpalatable vision for some time but finally said: "Could the disaster still happen?"

"Yes, because Lyle's death hasn't solved the fundamental family problems. On the contrary, it will have brought them into sharper focus and exacerbated them, but if Lyle was right, Charles, and the disaster does happen, what will now be utterly changed is your response to it."

"All I want," I said, "is to make everything come right."

"That would be wonderful, but it'll be exceedingly difficult and almost certainly very painful; as Aysgarth reminded us just now, the road to redemption's no primrose path." On an impulse he picked up the journal again and began to flick through the pages. "But don't despair of redemption," he added, having administered this dose of realism. "No matter how impossible it seems, one should never lose hope. I was reminded so strongly of that when I read Lyle's references to her protégée." He found the right page and smoothed it with care. "I met Venetia," he said unexpectedly. "Did I ever tell you?"

"I don't believe you did, no."

"Possibly I felt too guilty—she was one of my failures. Nicholas brought her here in 1963. She was very troubled but I was no use to her. Afterwards I said to God: 'Save her! Put right all that's gone wrong!' and I saw so clearly then how we had *all* failed Venetia, all the churchmen who were involved with her at that time . . . And how do you think my prayer was answered? Nicholas told me before he went to Africa that Venetia's marriage was not a success and that she was leading a more unsatisfactory life than ever. How depressed I was! And how guilty I felt all over again that I'd been unable to help her! In the end I was in such despair that I even asked God for a sign that somehow, against all the odds, the redemptive process was at work, but still nothing happened—until yesterday. Then Lyle's journal was brought to me and I received my sign."

He paused but when I did not speak he said: "I learnt that Lyle had been as frustrated as I was by her inability to help Venetia. I learnt that she too had been driven to prayer—and with the most remarkable results. Her life was changed, the lives of the other people in the prayer-group were changed, and in consequence the lives of those closest to those people will be changed—and all this life-giving work of the Holy Spirit springs from the fact that back in 1963 a muddled unhappy young woman made a series of tragic decisions."

"But what will happen to Venetia?"

"I have faith now that in the end the redemptive process will curve back to encircle her, but of course I shall continue to pray that all will one day be well—indeed we should all pray for Venetia, all of us who failed her in 1963 . . . Even Nicholas is praying for her," he added pleased. "He says he feels specially called to be her spiritual friend."

I made no comment. I thought it unlikely that Venetia felt the need of a "spiritual friend" and more probable that young Nicholas merely had a vague crush on a sophisticated woman some years his senior.

Meanwhile Jon was asking me if I now felt I understood my errors well enough to make my formal confession. With an effort I set all thought of the younger generation aside and said: "You've made sure that I do. But there's still something I want to ask: before you read the journal, did you see as clearly as Lyle did how far adrift I was?"

"No. I think Lyle saw the situation with such agonising clarity because she was the one who was actually living with you—but having said that, I must add at once that I don't want to make excuses for my pastoral inadequacies here. No doubt I should have taken a firmer line—not forcefeeding you truths you couldn't accept, but trying to shine a stronger light into areas where you were self-satisfied and over-confident."

"It's easy to be wise in retrospect."

"And it's generous of you to let me off so lightly. Perhaps the hard truth is that I'm simply too old now and too fond of you to be as useful as I was in 1937."

"Nonsense!"

"Is it? If Father Darcy were here I'm sure he'd judge my attitude to you to be hopelessly sentimental and send you at once to another spiritual director."

"I shouldn't have liked that at all!"

"Father Darcy wouldn't have been in the least interested in whether you liked it or not. He would only have been concerned with the welfare of your soul."

Silently thanking God that I had never been one of Father Darcy's monks, I prepared to make my formal confession.

4

THE PENANCE Jon set me had two parts. First I had to promise to make a retreat under his direction as soon as possible, and second I had to promise to abstain from alcohol until this retreat had been completed. He made no attempt to set a date for the beginning of my retreat; he said he understood how important it was that I should make contact with Michael, but he left me in no doubt that I was to detach myself from the South Canonry as soon as I could.

After I had made my promises he began to advise me on prayer. "Your first task," he said briskly, "is to shore up your spiritual strength when you're in such a debilitated state that your normal rule of life has broken down. A little prayer often is a more realistic aim at this stage than a substantial session in the morning and evening; arrow-prayers will be more suitable than heroic bouts of meditation—in fact, be sure not to set yourself any heroic spiritual tasks because you'll almost certainly be setting them out of a sense of guilt which will double if your efforts end in failure. And don't attempt to read any new books; stick to the old favourites. A sermon a day by Austin Farrer will do you far more good than the latest volume from some learned German theologian. Try to read the office, but don't panic if your concentration is too bad to make the exercise worthwhile; simply look at the appointed daily readings. And don't try to frame elaborate intercessions. Just visualise the people you need to pray for, including yourself, and hold them up to God. Ask for patience and the power of discernment as you try to understand how you can best work with God to redeem your errors."

This last sentence reminded me that so far he had dropped no hint that I should take an early retirement. Reluctantly I said: "Do you think I should resign the bishopric?"

"I don't think that's a profitable question to ask at the moment. It's much more important that you should concentrate on getting yourself fit enough to answer such a question correctly. But I'll say this: I don't think it necessarily follows at all that your recent errors mean you're now incapable of being a good bishop—indeed if all goes well you may become a much better one."

"You seem to be displaying an insane degree of optimism!" I said, but I thought of Hall, talking of spiritual strength, and I began to feel fractionally better.

"All I'm displaying," said Jon, "is a reasonable degree of hope. You're merely too debilitated to know the difference."

"It's just hard for me to have any hope for the future when I remember Sheila. What in heaven's name am I going to do about her? How do I even begin to ease her from my life?"

"You may find you don't wish to ease her from your life. You may eventually find you want to marry her."

"I can't imagine—"

"No, of course you can't. That's the point. All talk of remarriage is futile at the moment because the only woman you really want is Lyle."

"But in the meantime how do I deal with Sheila? Supposing—"

"And it's also futile to worry about disasters which may never happen. Just set Sheila on one side for the moment while you concentrate on recuperating—and set the Cathedral on one side too. You can't do more there anyway until Aysgarth produces draft accounts, and that's not going to happen overnight."

"It may not happen at all. If he's guilty—"

"I'm not nearly as sure of that as you and your colleagues are. It's quite possible that all the prevarication about the accounts can be put down to sheer pigheadedness."

"His pigheadedness, I agree, has to be experienced to be believed," I said with feeling. "And how on earth do you stand his persistent rudeness to you?"

"Because I know why he behaves like that; it's to goad me into taking a tough line. Aysgarth likes people taking tough lines because it enables him to be tough in return, and being tough ensures that all his defences are kept in place. In the past I've attempted more subtle approaches, but it's like trying to catch a tiger with a butterfly net: he chews up the net and bares his teeth at me all over again."

"Obviously he's quite impossible."

"Not impossible. Just difficult. If only Father Darcy were alive to advise me! I'm sure I was right to see you and Aysgarth together, particularly as definite progress was made, but it was a risky manoeuvre and Father Darcy might well have said . . ." And he talked on, deep in memories of his mentor. It was always a surprise to me to remember that I myself had never met Father Darcy. Thanks to Jon's unflagging reminiscences I felt I knew this legendary Victorian eccentric only too well.

Jon was still talking when the front door of the cottage opened and young Nicholas slouched moodily into the room. He wore jeans and a black leather jacket and his hair needed cutting. I reflected in irritation that no future ordinand should wander around looking like a seedy rock-'n'-roll singer, but I supposed there was nothing wrong with the boy that a sound, disciplined theological college would be unable to cure. Or was there? I suffered a pang of anxiety. If Nicholas took to drugs and ruined himself, Jon would never recover.

"I sort of felt you'd finished," he said to his father, but I suspected that what he was really saying was: "I want you to myself now—get rid of him."

I rose to my feet. "I'm glad to see you looking better, Nicholas!" I said with what I hoped was an air of positive approval, but he made no effort to return my smile.

"Yeah," he said, still speaking very sloppily, but the younger generation did speak sloppily; it was the fashion. "I'm okay." But when he made this assertion I heard the note of uncertainty in his voice. He halted by his father, the puppy returning with relief to his master's side, and stood there, waiting for me to go.

Jon immediately became uneasy but struggled to refocus his attention on me. "We should stop at this point anyway," he said. "You're tired and you need time to reflect on what's been said, but do please come back as soon as possible . . . Nicholas, say goodbye civilly to the Bishop, please, and don't attempt to chew gum and talk at the same time. It spoils your ability to enunciate words with clarity."

Young Nicholas stood up straight, held out a cold damp hand and said in a crisp monotone: "Goodbye, Uncle Charles. It was nice to see you. Please give my regards to Charley and Michael." So might a robot have spoken after the correct programming from a scientist. I suffered another pang of anxiety, but now was clearly not the moment to worry about Jon's family problems.

Having taken my leave of them both, I walked back rapidly through the woods to my car.

5

BY THE time I arrived home Miss Peabody had long since departed, but on entering my study I found her typed notes which referred to the files selected by Nigel for my attention. In no mood for studying them, I tossed the notes into the in-tray and moved the files to the edge of my desk as if I hoped they would fall off and vanish. It was not until I had completed this rearrangement that I turned my attention to the message written by Miss Peabody on my memo pad.

Glancing down I read: "Mrs. Preston (wife of the late Bishop of Radbury) telephoned at 5:15 P.M. She is in Starbridge for a little holiday and would like to see you, if convenient. She is staying at the Staro Arms (Tel. no.: 684)."

I was still staring with horror at this appalling information when the telephone began to ring at my side.

6

FOLLOWING MY private interview with Jon I had been feeling calmer, less confused, more ready to believe I was capable of surmounting the difficulties which were besieging me on all sides, but the combined onslaught of Miss Peabody's message and the ringing telephone plunged me once more into a panic-stricken fog. It took me at least ten seconds to remember that I was still hoping to hear from Michael. Finally I managed to pick up the receiver.

"It's me," said my archdeacon. "Any news?"

"News?" I said blankly. "No. Should there be?"

"But I thought you were going to tackle Aysgarth!"

"Ah yes!" I somehow pulled myself together before he could decide I was certifiable. "He's going to produce draft accounts."

"Oh, well done, Charles, *well done!* When?"

"Soon. Look, can I phone you back tomorrow? I've only just got back to the house, and . . ." I got rid of Malcolm and stared again at the memo from Miss Peabody. I was still fighting the desire to head straight for the whisky decanter when the doorbell rang.

Once again my heart almost seemed to stop beating before pounding on at breakneck speed. My first thought was that the caller was Sheila, but common sense soon told me that she would be waiting, discreet as ever, at the hotel. My visitor was almost certainly one of my devoted Cathedral ladies bearing more food for the deep-freeze—or had Michael impulsively driven down from London to see me? Filled with a sudden burst of hope I rushed out into the hall and flung open the front door.

But my visitor was not Michael. It was Harriet March.

7

"I WANT to apologise for my outrageous behaviour," she said before I could display any emotion whatsoever. "Stephen's just ordered me to grovel at your feet. Can I come in for a moment?"

"If you insist."

"I thought clergymen always gave a big welcome to a sinner panting to repent! Don't you want me to bare my soul?"

"Not particularly. Bare it to Stephen."

"It's Stephen I want to talk about."

"All right, come in." By that time it had occurred to me that if I rebuffed her too rudely she might be tempted to make trouble for me all over again.

She was wearing a short, white, belted raincoat, black stockings and black, patent leather, high-heeled shoes. Her long, wavy hair was drawn austerely back behind her ears, secured with a black ribbon and allowed to foam casually down her spine. Her eyes, caked in vulgar make-up, looked very large and very green.

Remembering Jon's insight I realised that Harriet was not much older than Lyle had been in 1937, and I could now clearly see how my memory had been stirred. But I could also now clearly see how far the two women differed. Lyle had been so subtly, so elegantly erotic. In contrast Harriet's eroticism seemed not merely blatant but crude.

"Sherry?" I offered neutrally as we entered the drawing-room.

"How terribly forgiving," she said. "Thanks."

But I did not invite her to sit down. After handing her a Tio Pepe I helped myself to some sodawater and with our glasses in our hands we stood in front of the fireplace like two guests at an unsuccessful cocktail party.

At last she said: "Have you figured out why I did it? All I wanted was to help Stephen by giving him a weapon to use against you."

"You don't seriously expect me to believe that, do you?"

"God, what an ecclesiastical thug you are! I make a meek, mild, little statement reeking of repentance and you take a big swipe at me! All right, you brute, I'll come clean. I could see you found me attractive last night and when you not only turned me down but made that utterly vile remark about nymphomaniacs—"

"I regretted that as soon as I'd said it. I'm sorry, Harriet."

"That's more like it! Okay, I'm sorry too, but you can see why I thought: I'll take that man down a peg or two and at the same time do my heroic Mr. Dean a big favour. I know it was a mad decision but I was mad with rage—and in fact I'm still not entirely sorry I took a swipe at you for your hypocritical behaviour. What a nerve to pretend you're white as driven snow and lay all the blame on me for that sexy undercurrent in the studio! Didn't someone say once in the Bible that when a man looks at a woman and lusts after her he's as good as committing adultery?"

"Yes, it was a gentleman called Jesus of Nazareth. Am I allowed to defend myself against the charge of hypocrisy? It's very easy for people outside the Church to jeer at clergymen, but no matter how often we fall short of our ideals—"

"The important thing is that you have ideals and try to live up to them. You think I don't understand that? Every artist worthy of the name knows about falling short of the ideal but always trying to strive for it . . . You really did like the hands, didn't you?"

"Very much. It was a privilege to be shown them. Thank you."

"All right, Charles, you don't have to grovel on all fours! I was bloody to you and you were bloody to me but now I reckon we can consider ourselves all square."

"I always like happy endings," I murmured, sipping my sodawater and wishing it were whisky.

"Hold on, we haven't quite reached the golden sunset yet. I want to talk about that West Front Appeal."

I nearly dropped my glass on the hearthrug.

"I CAN understand why you're worried," added Harriet, still as nonchalant as if she had just passed some remark about the weather, "but I came here to set your mind at rest. After feeding Stephen such a big lie about you, I feel honour-bound to make amends by feeding you a big slice of truth about him." With astonishment I noted that she appeared perfectly sincere.

"I see," I said, but although I was prepared to believe she wanted to deliver the truth I wondered very much whether she had access to it. Could Aysgarth really have been such a fool as to confide in this unreliable woman? The possibility seemed incredible, but on the other hand Aysgarth was notorious for taking scandalous risks. I decided to keep an open mind. "Is this some plot you and Stephen have cooked up to give him a little breathing-space?" I demanded, seeing no reason to be other than frank.

"No. Look, I'll tell you what happened. He rang me up half an hour ago and stormed at me for telling the fib—except that Stephen doesn't storm, he's too much of a poppet. He was just very depressed and said I'd made everything worse; he said he was sure you suspected him of mismanagement, embezzlement and God knows what else. That was when I decided I had to ride here to his rescue. My darling Mr. Dean! I can't stand by and see him crucified when he's being so wonderfully creative about raising all that ghastly money—"

"Did you say 'creative'?"

"Where fund-raising's concerned he's an artistic genius. All he needs now, I promise you, is a little time to—"

"Make everything come right?"

"Precisely!"

"And if it doesn't?"

"It will."

"But what do you really know about it?"

"Everything. Well, no, perhaps not quite everything. In fact certainly not everything. But what I do know is that he's a hero and I'm going to fight tooth and nail for him."

Carefully setting aside my twinges of envy that Aysgarth should have a sexy woman so devoted to his welfare—and of course I could now recognise and acknowledge every ignominious twinge—I tried to work out how I could persuade her to give me more information. Again I found no reason for being other than completely frank. Perhaps I was afraid that if I tried to execute some smooth diplomatic manoeuvre I would give her another chance to accuse me of hypocrisy.

"Okay," I said, deliberately picking the Americanism to signal that I was willing to be informal and even, in a careful way, cosy. "You may have trouble believing this, but I think we've wound up on the same side. The very last thing I want is for Stephen to be crucified for creative fund-raising."

"Honestly?"

"Honestly. I've got to consider the welfare of the Church, and the thought of a lot of dirty ecclesiastical linen being washed in public is a nightmare." I paused but when I saw she was willing to believe me, I added with more confidence: "Of course there's a limit to what I can do. I can cover up mismanagement which has resulted from bad decisions made in good faith, but what I can't cover up is mismanagement which has spiralled into fraud. So what I've got to do now is to stop him before he crosses that fatal border—or has he already crossed it? Harriet, if you have any information at all about what he's been doing, I do beg you for his sake to—"

"All I really have," she said carefully, "is an unproved theory. I think he was in a mess but now he's almost got himself out of it. That's why I'm convinced that the best thing you can do now is nothing."

"I can't tell you how much I long to do nothing! But what was this mess he got into?"

"I think poor old Dido and all those ghastly offspring bled him white. As I told you yesterday, Charles, Stephen's not the villain of this story. He's the hero."

9

FINISHING HER sherry she set down her glass and began to move restlessly around the room. "Dido has a private income," she said, pausing by the window to stare out into the dark, "but it's all on trust so she can't touch the capital, and Stephen has no money apart from what he earns. That means that although they live comfortably they've nothing to fall back on if disaster strikes."

Wandering on again around the sofa she arrived back at the hearth where I was still standing. "Back in 1963," she said, "Stephen and Dido went through a private crisis. I don't know what it was, but it wasn't connected with the fiasco about my sculpture, couldn't have been, because Dido didn't give a damn whether the sculpture went in the churchyard or not. As the result of this crisis Dido indulged in some huge spending sprees in London—you know how some women plunder shops when they're under emotional stress. Stephen's story was that she was going through a difficult menopause, but I think there must have been more to it than that because whatever the crisis was it happened suddenly and it was devastating. I say that not just because of the effect on Dido but because of the effect on Stephen; one moment he was bouncing along buoyantly, and the next moment he was so ploughed under that he couldn't even get to Venetia Flaxton's wedding. And you know how close he is to Lord Flaxton. They've been friends for nearly twenty years."

She paused but when I remained silent she added: "Anyway Dido ran up some heavy bills and was in such a state she had to see a psychiatrist—I'm sure you know how prone she is to nervous trouble. And when I say 'psychiatrist' I don't mean something available on the National Health. I'm talking about Harley Street and more bills. Then to cap it all, Primrose decided to get married."

"It was certainly a lavish wedding."

"I thought the expenditure was ridiculous—in fact I even asked him if he felt guilty about her in some way, but he just laughed and said how amusing I was. I wasn't seeing much of him by that time, but he did come out to my house for a drink one evening to tell me about his son Norman, who'd got strapped for cash trying to keep that blue-blooded wife of his in style—Stephen was being asked to help out with the overdraft. And during all this time, in case you've forgotten, he was paying enormous school fees; Pip's not a scholar at Winchester and Elizabeth has no bursary at Roedean. Stephen's first family was cheap to educate because everyone got some sort of useful hand-out, but that second family eats money—and now there's more expense coming up because Elizabeth wants to be a deb and do the season. Can't you just see Dido chafing to organise a ball at Claridge's?"

"So what you're saying is—"

"My theory is that in 1963 a number of circumstances combined to drive him deep into debt. And at the end of 1963—"

"The West Front Appeal was launched and money began to pour in at a great rate. Then once he had sole control of the fund—"

"It would just have been a loan, Charles. He would have had every intention of paying it back."

"How? If he had no capital and spent every penny of his income—"

"He would have created a scheme," she said at once, "a brilliant scheme for repayment." She picked up her empty glass again and looked at it. Then: "The stock market," she said firmly, looking straight at me with her limpid green eyes. "He would have tried the stock market. He would have gambled, won, put a bit back, gambled again—"

"—and finally made the trip to the well once too often."

"Not necessarily! But he'd need some time to work off such a large debt. That's why I'm sure that if you gave him the extra time it would be the most sensible thing you could possibly do."

After a pause I said: "And this is all just an unproved theory of yours."

"Oh yes," she said. "Wholly unproved . . . Can I have another drink?"

I refilled her glass before saying: "I'm not sure I find the theory plausible. For a start, I happen to know Stephen presented some acceptable accounts last year. If he was in debt, as you suggest, I don't see how he could have squared the accounts unless the whole debt had been repaid, and if it had indeed been repaid, why is he now apparently still working to make everything come right?"

"He might have borrowed a sum from somewhere else in order to set the accounts straight and then returned it after the accounts were approved."

"If he borrowed money, what did he use as collateral? He doesn't even own his own home! And if he was able to raise money from another source, why didn't he go there in the first place instead of filching money from the Appeal?"

She was still staring at me blankly when the telephone rang, and as if welcoming the chance to escape she turned aside. "I must go."

"I'll see you out," I said, no longer bothering to hope the call was from Michael and fearing only that it was from Sheila, finally losing patience as she waited at the Staro Arms.

"If you want to answer that—"

"They'll ring back if it's important." As I opened the front door and stepped out with her into the porch I said suddenly: "I can't help noticing your stress on Stephen as a hero. It's as if he's reminding you of a hero you've lost."

The telephone finally ceased ringing as Harriet stopped to stare at me.

"Perhaps," I said, "I should say *the* hero you've lost. Captain March certainly cut a heroic figure."

"How very perceptive of you." She hesitated for a moment before saying: "Donald was quite different from Stephen physically, of course, but yes, he too was an idealist, and yes, he too had his naive side and yes, in spite of all his *Boy's Own* fun-and-games he too was capable of a genuine heroism." And turning aside she added over her shoulder: "We were well suited. I made love to my sculptures and he made love to his mountains and we met when we had nothing better to do. I'm sure most people think the marriage was a failure and that I've forgotten him."

"But you haven't."

"No, he haunts me. I keep looking and looking for him in other men, but although sometimes I seem to catch a glimpse of him he's never really there . . . It's all guilt, of course. Silly of me, isn't it? But I'd so like to tell him I'm sorry now that I always put my sculpture first. In the end we had so little time together."

She began to drift over to her car and I drifted with her. The night air was very cold and the grass on the front lawn was white with frost. Our footsteps crunched on the frozen gravel.

"I think he would have forgiven you," I said. "After all, you understood about his mountains."

"Bloody mountains! After they killed him I wanted to emigrate to Holland and never see so much as a molehill again." Opening the door of her car she paused to look back at me. "Maybe you're not such a thug after all," she said, changing the mood of the conversation by speaking lightly. "Maybe I could even be tempted to do a small model of your head some day. Your bones are really very well arranged."

"So glad they meet with your approval."

We smiled at each other and it was not until she was sitting in the driving-seat that I added: "Let me know if you change your mind about telling me the whole truth."

She slammed the door so that the light inside the car was extinguished, and when she wound down the window her face was just a white blur in the darkness. All she said was: "Just give him the chance to make everything come right."

Then she drove away very fast down the drive.

10

RETURNING TO my study I telephoned my brother.

Peter was two years my junior, a solicitor who worked in London and lived in Surrey. Priding himself on being a phlegmatic philistine, he never became passionate unless cricket was discussed, but this at least made him a restful companion and we had a not unaffectionate relationship which flourished best when we were at least fifty miles apart. He thought that the Church of England, like the Royal Family and the Conservative party, needed to be supported for the good of the nation, and he loyally went to church once a year to hear the Christmas carols. His wife Annabel, whom I could only endure in very small doses, told him what to think on all important issues and I had no doubt that this was a great relief to Peter, who was happiest when he did not have to think at all. His three children, all older than mine, were thoroughly conventional and well-behaved. ("Very boring," Lyle had commented acidly when our own children had been torturing us during their adolescence.)

"Poor old Charley," said Peter, who was the only person who still called me by the name now reserved for my son. "I've been meaning to phone you. Hope you're keeping your chin up."

"Oh yes, soldiering on . . ." For some reason Peter and I regularly communicated in this obsolescent patois of the British Empire. Perhaps we were reflecting the fact that one of the few things we had in common was our childhood memory of England in its imperial prime.

"By the way," I said after we had exchanged the usual banalities about our offspring, "there's something I want to ask you." And having outlined Harriet's theory about the Appeal Fund I asked: "If this man did succeed in putting all the money back, is he still liable to prosecution for embezzlement or could the whole manoeuvre be classed as a repaid loan which can be conveniently forgotten?"

"Well, for a start he's not guilty of embezzlement."

This seemed almost too good to be true. "Are you sure?"

"Positive. It's forty years since I opened a criminal law textbook, but I'm certain embezzlement only applies to servants who cheat their masters. There's a difference, you know, between embezzlement, larceny and fraudulent conversion."

"Then what's this?"

"If a fiduciary relationship's involved, I think it must be fraudulent conversion, but I'd have to look it up to be sure. Do you know for a fact that this man's appropriated the money for his own use?"

"No. But he's very reluctant for anyone to inspect the accounts at the moment, and the circumstances do seem to suggest—"

"Oh, that sort of reluctance is very common! It usually means the chap's made a stupid investment and he's waiting for the market to perk up, but don't forget it's not a crime to be stupid. What are his powers of investment under the deed of trust?"

Unwilling to disclose Aysgarth's identity I could not tell him that the Dean and Chapter were governed by medieval statutes which had not envisaged the complexity of twentieth-century society. I merely said: "He has the power to invest money entirely as he likes while acting on behalf of the other trustees, but there's not much written down on paper. The trustees have verbally given him carte blanche."

"My God, trust the Church to set up something really amateurish and then send the chaps on their way with a prayer instead of a watertight legal arrangement! But never mind, with a bit of luck you should be able to survive this particular clanger if the chap's merely made a dud investment and is now too embarrassed to come clean—and even if the worst is true and he's had his hand in the till, you'll still be all right so long as he puts everything back. In theory he'd be liable for abusing the fiduciary relationship, but in practice you'd have the option of forcing him to resign from the trust without pressing charges. I'd have to double-check all this, of course—I'm speaking purely off the cuff without knowing the exact details of the case, but—"

"Supposing he doesn't put the money back. Could he go to prison if he was convicted?"

"Oh yes, but if he's a decent chap with a good reputation they'd pop him into one of those open prisons which are like hotels and let him out on probation after six months. Unless the crime was really rather frightful."

"When does fraudulent conversion become really rather frightful?"

"When a clergyman has his hand in the till. Judges don't like that sort of thing at all."

"Bishops aren't too keen on it either."

"Glad to hear it. Bishops are keen on some very odd things these days. Annabel heard the Bishop of Radbury on the wireless the other day and he said—"

"I know."

"The whole country's going to the dogs, if you ask me—and talking of going to the dogs, be very careful with this rogue of yours, Charley. You're all right so long as he talks to you in your role of clergyman, but don't try and do more than listen or you could wind up as an accessory after the fact."

"You mean that if he puts the money back and confesses to me afterwards I'm allowed to keep quiet, but if he doesn't put the money back and turns to me to bail him out—"

"Don't touch him with a barge-pole. Would you like a discreet chat with an expert on criminal law?"

"Not while the theory of misconduct is still non-proven," I said, but after we had finished our conversation I wondered if this was the most sensible of replies.

I slumped back in my chair. Obviously I had to stop Aysgarth's criminal career, save the Church of England from scandal and avoid winding up in the dock as an accessory, but how this trio of miracles was to be accomplished I had no idea. I also found myself wondering how much I should tell Nigel and Malcolm; I did not want them to wind up as accessories alongside me in the dock, and I could see this was the kind of catastrophe which tainted all those who came into contact with it. I remembered Bolingbroke's famous words about the sooty fate of those who wrestled with chimney-sweeps.

Having indulged myself in this manner by imagining the worst, I then cheered myself by reflecting not only that Harriet's theory was non-proven but that I myself had found it unconvincing. Something unsavoury was going on, I was sure of that, but what exactly was it and did it constitute a crime? Peter had reminded me that it was not a crime to be stupid. I now reminded myself that a business manoeuvre could be thoroughly shifty yet still fall within the law.

The telephone began to ring, but again I made no attempt to answer it and by the time the noise stopped I found I was staring once more at Miss Peabody's note which was still lying on my desk. "Mrs. Preston . . . in Starbridge for a little holiday . . . would like to see you, if convenient . . ." The sinister words, rendered all the more sinister by the genteel phrases which they formed, began to batter my brain like a battalion of miniature hammers, and suddenly I realised that my professional and private lives were now so fraught that I could only deal with them by being ruthlessly pragmatic. The Aysgarth mystery could wait. Sheila could not. It was Sheila who was the real emergency and Sheila who had to be tackled without delay.

That was the moment when I finally allowed myself to remember her firm refusal of my invitation to Starbridge and to ask myself why she had changed her mind. From my point of view was this revised decision a mere embarrassing inconvenience or a career-threatening emergency? The more I struggled to convince myself that it was an inconvenience, the more I thought of Lyle saying in her dryest voice: "I always believe the worst because the worst is usually true."

A feeling of dread settled with leaden precision in the pit of my stomach. I glanced at my watch. The time was half-past eight. Telling myself that the truth, no matter how hideous, would be better than such agonising uncertainty, I began to dial the number of the Staro Arms.

XXI

"Happy is the man who learns from his own failures. He certainly won't learn from anyone else's."

AUSTIN FARRER
Warden of Keble College, Oxford, 1960–1968
LOVE ALMIGHTY AND ILLS UNLIMITED

1

"SHEILA!" I said, gripping the telephone receiver with one hand and the arm of my chair with the other. "What an unexpected surprise—welcome to Starbridge!" As I succeeded in sounding delighted I remembered with nausea my remark to Martin and Harriet that priests too could display a talent for acting.

"Oh Charles, you must think I'm being very erratic, first refusing your invitation and then dashing down here on an impulse—"

"I always admire spontaneity!" By this time my true self was watching the slick performance of my glittering image with an appalled fascination. "Have you dined yet?"

"Well, no, but—"

"Neither have I. Why don't I join you at the Staro Arms in twenty minutes?"

"That would be lovely, but are you quite sure it's convenient?"

"Can't wait to get out of the house and relax!" I declared. "See you soon!" And then I let the receiver slide stickily from my sweating hand.

2

UPSTAIRS I shed my shabby clothes and put on a black suit, purple stock and pectoral cross. For a moment I thought of a knight, donning the suit of armour which would keep him safe, but I knew that this was far too romantic an image and that the truth was far shoddier: the actor was merely making the required quick change before playing the next nerve-racking scene. Retiring to the kitchen I began to polish my shoes in order to delay the moment of departure.

The minutes crawled by. My shoes were now glistening glassily, but I was still trying to dredge up the strength to leave the house when once more the telephone started to ring.

Desperate for any excuse to delay my ordeal I hastened back to my study to take the call. "South Canonry," I said, sinking thankfully into my chair.

"Dr. Ashworth?"

"Loretta!" I shouted. "How wonderful!" Dimly I was aware that this was my real self talking. "Where are you? Have you slipped in an extra visit to Starbridge?"

"After a greeting like that I'm tempted to rewrite my schedule! No, Charles, I'm still in London—I just thought I'd give you a quick call before I fly home tomorrow."

"Maybe I'll join you at the airport. I feel in the mood to emigrate."

"Things are really bad, are they?"

"Not while you're around. What have you been doing?"

"Thinking of you, of course! What else?"

"Continuously?"

"Well, I did take time out to talk to Dido Aysgarth who invited me to shop at Harrods with her tomorrow—she'd forgotten when I was leaving. My, how that gal makes me laugh!"

"I doubt if Stephen will laugh when he gets the bills," I said without stopping to think.

"Oh, there's no financial problem at the Deanery! Enid Markhampton tells me Dido has a private income and Stephen inherited money from a rich uncle."

I stopped lolling in my chair and sat up straight. "When did that happen?"

"Some time back in the fifties, Enid said—when he was a canon of Westminster."

"Ah, that would explain my ignorance. Stephen and I saw little of each other before we wound up in Starbridge . . . How did Lady Markhampton know?"

"The Flaxtons told her—and of course they've known Stephen well for years. But forget Stephen for the moment because there's something important I want to say and that's this: get back to your writing, and *get back soon.* If you do something you really enjoy, something you find particularly fulfilling, you'll start feeling more integrated and that'll make it easier for you to cope with the bereavement."

"I'd start feeling more integrated if only we could have dinner tonight. How I wish I could cancel my dinner-engagement, charter a helicopter and bear you off to the Savoy Grill!"

"Is your dinner companion young and female? I feel I need someone to hate."

"What makes you think I'm not on my way to another of Dido's little dinner-parties for sixteen?"

"If you were, you truly would cancel the engagement, charter a helicopter and bear me off to the Savoy! So long, Charles. Stay gorgeous, avoid being kidnapped by anything under forty and *get back to that book.* Okay?"

"Okay." Heaving a sigh I wished her a safe journey home and said goodbye with extreme reluctance.

The telephone rang again as I was dragging on my glassy shoes in the kitchen, but I knew I could delay my departure no longer. Opening the front door at last I hurried outside to my car and left the phone still ringing in the dark deserted house.

3

AT THE junction with Eternity Street I was thinking so hard about Aysgarth that I almost drove through a red light. If he did indeed have capital then Harriet's theory became wholly implausible, but how large had been that legacy? The uncle could only have been a bourgeois Yorkshire businessman, and I had no idea how much such a person could be expected to leave. The North was a foreign country to me; I knew very little about what went on there.

So absorbed was I in these speculations that I compounded my bad driving by failing to signal that I was turning right into the courtyard of the Staro Arms, and the driver behind me hooted in fury. This rebuke made me pull myself together. Parking the car neatly, I got out, restrained myself from fidgeting with my cross in the manner which Aysgarth found so intolerable, and walked briskly into the hotel.

The Staro Arms was a former medieval coaching inn which nowadays conjured up images of a favourite slipper: shabby but comfortable. I liked the place far better than the Crusader, Starbridge's smart hotel which overlooked St. Anne's Gate by the Cathedral. Currently owned by a national hotel group, the Crusader catered for wealthy tourists; the Staro Arms, owned and run by a local family for several generations, catered for the natives and had changed remarkably little since I had taken Lyle to dine there soon after our first meeting in 1937.

As I entered the hall the old porter touched his cap and said: "Good evening, my lord!" Here at least it had never occurred to anyone that the old order might be obliged to yield to the new, and seconds later the proprietor himself appeared to welcome me in pre-war style. Despite the ordeal which loomed ahead I could not help but feel greatly soothed.

"I'm afraid I've been very absent-minded and forgotten to make a reservation," I said to Mine Host, but at once he contrived to imply that the best table in the dining-room was perpetually mine for the asking.

Having explained that I first had to meet my guest, I ventured into the main reception room, a long medieval chamber where the oak-beamed ceiling curved in unexpected places and the faded carpet was strewn with armchairs upholstered in worn chintz. A log-fire blazed in the huge fireplace, but since most of the heat escaped up the chimney the air was still crisp—a fact which I could only regard as a blessing as I began to feel much too hot under my clerical collar.

There were only three people in the room; I judged the other guests were by this time at dinner. Sheila was reading a copy of the *Lady,* but when I entered the room she closed the magazine and stood up. She was wearing a beige woollen dress with a piece of plain gold costume jewellery, and looked so irreproachably seemly that for a moment I could not quite believe we had ever shared a bed. I also found it hard to believe she could ever have reminded me of Lyle, and because I could no longer find Lyle in this alien mirror, I found my loss was violently underlined.

"Sheila!" It occurred to me as I gave her hands a quick clasp that hell was not, as Sartre had proclaimed, other people. Hell was being obliged to pretend to be someone quite other than one's true self.

"I suggest we eat straight away," I was saying, and seconds later we were entering the dining-room which overlooked the garden—the famous river-garden of the Staro Arms where on fine summer evenings it was so pleasant to sit at one of the white tables and watch the water flow lazily through the city to the meadows. I could remember sitting there with Lyle on that first evening out together long ago, and at once in my memory I saw her as she had been then: thirty-five years old, slim and small, her hair reddish-brown, her dark eyes sultry, her whole being exuding that subtle air of mystery which had ensnared me from the beginning and enchanted me to the end.

The waiter was saying: "Good evening, my lord—this way, if you please," but I barely heard him. I was still remembering that first evening when Lyle and I had dined together; I was picking out that same table where we had sat, and as I did so the present seemed to veer away from its course and double back in a great loop towards the past—and as the present disintegrated beneath the weight of memory I heard Lyle's voice say: "I don't like that woman, Charles. Get rid of her."

I halted.

We were standing by the table, that same table where Lyle and I had dined, and the waiter was drawing out the chair so that Sheila could sit down in Lyle's place.

"Is something wrong?" I heard Sheila say to me suddenly, but the only words I could utter were: "Sorry. Not well. Excuse me."

Then I blundered from the room.

4

SHEILA JOINED me as I came to a halt outside in the courtyard. So shattered was I that I rejected the possibility of being other than truthful in an effort to be diplomatic. I said: "I'm sorry, but I couldn't take that dining-room. Too many memories of Lyle," and at once Sheila responded: "Let me drive you home in my car."

I said this was quite unnecessary, but I knew I could not afford to give her the impression that I was wholly rejecting her company. "We'll go to the Crusader instead," I said. "I'll be all right there."

"Charles, there's no need to go to a lot of trouble to give me dinner. Why don't we drive to the South Canonry, you in your car, I in mine, and then I can make my own way back here after I've cooked us a meal?"

"I wouldn't dream of asking you to cook for me!"

"I'd enjoy it."

"Yes, but . . ." Automatically I glanced around but there was no one in earshot. "For various reasons," I said, "I don't think that would be a good idea."

"There's nothing for you to worry about, Charles, I promise you. I'll go as soon as we've finished the meal."

I feared that to protest further might be dangerous, even more dangerous than embarking on a difficult dialogue with her in my own home without any of the witnesses who would have ensured my safety if our evening had been spent in the hotel dining-room. With an effort I said: "It's extremely good of you, and at least you won't have to do much more than light the oven. There's a well-stocked deep-freeze."

"In that case what are we arguing about?" she said, and smiled at me.

I smiled back, parted from her and slid behind the wheel of my car.

As soon as I arrived home I wanted to pour myself a double-whisky but again I restricted myself to sodawater. Even if I had not promised

Jon to abstain from alcohol, the extreme danger of my situation would have encouraged me to remain stone-cold sober. I felt I needed the clearest of heads to survive.

"Just show me where the kitchen is," she said on her arrival two minutes later. "Then you can relax in the drawing-room."

I showed her to the kitchen. But in the drawing-room all I could do was sit on the edge of the sofa and watch the large hand of the clock on the chimney-piece move with excruciating slowness from one minute to the next. The time was now after nine.

As soon as Sheila had rejoined me I embarked on a more articulate apology to reassure her that I had regained my equilibrium; I was afraid that if she thought I was still in a state of distress she might become too compassionate. "... and it seems so odd," I concluded with a finely judged air of bemusement, "that Lyle's memory should overpower me at the Staro Arms yet now be manageable in her own home."

"Grief isn't always logical."

"Apparently not . . . Can I get you a drink?"

She requested a gin-and-tonic, and when we had our glasses in our hands I said warmly: "Let's drink to your surprise visit to Starbridge!"

This pleased her. She took a small, ladylike sip.

I was just reflecting that sodawater had never before tasted so prickly and unpleasant when she said: "I'm sure you want to know why I changed my mind about the visit, so I mustn't irritate you now by beating about the bush. What happened was that after you left the flat I felt how selfish I'd been, moaning about my trivial problems when your own must be so very much worse, and it suddenly occurred to me that I might be able to make amends by offering you some help."

There is something peculiarly fascinating about watching one's worst dream come true. I did realise that some form of encouraging response was required but I found I was too mesmerised by the nightmare to speak.

"After all," she said reasonably, "I've been a bishop's wife so I know exactly how I could make myself useful. Why don't I take a flat in Starbridge for, say, six months? I could easily run the South Canonry for you, and I'd be very happy to act as your hostess at dinner-parties."

I knew that just as I could not afford to display a single sign of horror, so I could not afford any pause which would imply reluctance. At once I said: "How very kind of you! And what an enterprising idea!"

She smiled, still perfectly self-possessed, her fingers curled around the glass in her hands. I noticed that her nails were covered in a colourless varnish which gleamed in the light.

"Naturally," I heard her murmur, "there'd be no obligation of any kind."

This time I was unable to avoid a pause, and in order to distract her from its implications, I embarked on a series of trivial movements: I set down my glass, smoothed my hair and adjusted the position of my pectoral cross. I was trying to decide how I should deal with her. It was tempting to postpone all further discussion of her proposal as gracefully as possible and change the subject, but I had a strong suspicion that this, the easiest course of action, would in the long run make matters more difficult. I sensed it was important that I gave her no chance to hope. Once she started to think she had succeeded, her disappointment when I finally rejected her pipe-dream would be far greater and the risk of unpleasant consequences much higher.

With difficulty I said: "I see we've reached the point where we have to refer to what happened last Sunday."

"No, there's no need to mention that."

"Even if we never mentioned it again it would still remain a reality which has altered how matters stand between us. After all, if we hadn't been intimate, you'd hardly be making this very special offer now."

"That's true. But—"

"I quite understand that you're motivated by a commendable desire to make my life easier, and please believe me when I say I'm grateful, but I'm afraid that if you came to Starbridge to live you wouldn't ease my current distress; you'd enhance it. Close feminine friendship which falls short of physical intimacy is a luxury I'm not designed to enjoy."

To my relief she remained calm. She said simply: "I'd worked everything out—how I could let my flat, which firm I should use to store my best pieces of furniture, what arrangements I'd need to make at the bank. I was feeling so excited about escaping from London and giving my life a purpose again."

"I'm all for your life having a purpose, but—"

"It all seemed so meant," she interrupted strongly. "The way you turned up out of the blue and the way we got on so well and . . . well, I daresay this sounds pathetic to a sophisticated theologian, but I really did feel as if all my prayers had been answered and God had come to my rescue at last."

I said equally strongly: "No theologian, sophisticated or otherwise, should treat the subject of prayer with contempt. But Sheila, although you may well be right about God coming to your rescue, you may nevertheless be wrong about how that rescue's going to be achieved. After all, what's actually happened here? You've suddenly come to see that the way forward for you is to leave London for a while. Now, that can certainly be construed as a God-given enlightenment, but it doesn't necessarily follow that I'm to play any part in your new future."

She stood up. Automatically I too rose to my feet and we faced each other across the hearth.

"You think I'm trying to entrap you into marriage," she said abruptly, "and you're backing off. But I quite see it's ridiculous to talk of marriage when you're newly bereaved so let's just forget about it."

"In view of what happened last Sunday I hardly think amnesia is an available option."

"Obviously you're horribly embarrassed about last Sunday, but you needn't be. It seems to me that shorn of all embarrassment the situation's simply this: I'm extremely efficient and I can be very useful to you at the present time. I quite understand that your duty is to be celibate, but I also quite understand that one can't always live up to one's ideals. So if from time to time you did find celibacy impossible—"

"My dear Sheila," I said, sweating as the scene finally began to spiral out of control, "it's vital that we should be realistic here. I won't even begin to go into all the moral arguments. I'll just take a strictly pragmatic line and say your suggestion is an invitation to disaster. Someone would eventually find out what was going on."

"But surely if we were both scrupulously careful—"

"Someone would eventually find out. I know they would. I know."

I saw curiosity flicker in her eyes. "You sound as if you'd seen it all before. But surely as Bishop of Starbridge you'd be quite above suspicion?"

"Just because I'm above suspicion doesn't mean I'd remain there if I were to make a move which gave rise to gossip! If you came to Starbridge everyone would put our friendship under the microscope and we could only survive that kind of scrutiny if the friendship was completely above board."

She was silent, but just as I was daring to hope that I had persuaded her to be reasonable she said: "Very well, if I can't help you by coming to Starbridge, at least I can still be of use in London. I can't see how anyone would ever know, if you visited me occasionally in Pimlico, that you were paying more than a pastoral call."

Once again I found myself unable to avoid a pause, but this time my expression must have betrayed my horror because she began to blush. The atmosphere of embarrassment was now almost tangible.

At last she said in a low rapid voice: "I'm sorry, I know I'm not talking like a bishop's wife, but you didn't exactly behave like a bishop last Sunday, did you?" and after another terrible interval I answered: "I know you wouldn't be speaking along these lines if I hadn't behaved as I did. I'm not blaming you for anything you've said, and I'm certainly not passing judgement on you either."

"Thanks a lot!"

This sarcastic response gave me such a fright that I redoubled my efforts to open her eyes to reality. I could feel the polite veneer of the conversation disintegrating in a web of cracks like bruised glass. "Look," I said, "just think for a moment, just think what would happen if we embarked on a prolonged affair. It wouldn't just be Sunday night happening over and over again. It wouldn't just be a safe, comfortable, static relationship which would fill in the time while we waited until it was socially acceptable for me to remarry. Love affairs are dynamic, not static. They grow, change, become more complex—and once powerful emotions are generated, obvious hazards appear. For instance, supposing we found after six months that you'd had enough but I wanted to marry you—"

"How tactful! Of course we both know it's far more likely that I'd want to marry you and that you'd be the one chafing to walk away." She turned her back on me and began to walk stiffly towards the door.

"Sheila—"

"You're right to regret last Sunday. If we hadn't slept together we wouldn't be having this vile, humiliating scene." She stumbled out of the room.

I caught up with her in the hall. By this time I was in such a state of guilt, pity, shame and sheer panic that I hardly knew what I was saying, but I felt I could not afford to let her leave in a hostile frame of mind.

"I'm not saying this scene hasn't been painful," I said, speaking very fast, "but don't lose sight of that idea you had of leaving London and seeking a new life."

"It was just a stupid dream."

"But you could have a whole range of possible futures!"

"What rubbish—widows of fifty-two are lucky if they have anything that resembles a future at all! The truth is that you've increased my unhappiness a hundredfold by giving me a glimpse of what might have been, and now you think you can put everything right by talking a lot of drivel that has no relation to reality! I—" She broke off as we both heard the sound of a car in the drive.

Feeling dizzy with relief that I was about to be rescued from my ordeal, I could only say idiotically: "That's odd. I'm not expecting anyone."

Then it dawned on me that the car was not merely murmuring but roaring up the drive.

I knew that engine.

Abandoning Sheila I flung open the front door just as Michael's MG screeched to a halt on the gravel.

5

WHEN I hurried out into the drive to meet him I saw he had a pale drawn look, as if he had not slept for some time. In the hard light from the porch, the planes of his face were outlined in such a way that his eyes seemed more deepset, his cheekbones more prominent, the cleft in his chin more like the scar of an old injury. He was not drunk but I did not think he was entirely sober either; although in control of his movements he had the aggressive air of the drinker obliged to stand his ground in a world which had become alien and hostile.

"I phoned before I left London," he said, "and I stopped to phone twice on the way down but no one answered. I thought you'd dropped dead."

"Not quite." I almost held out my hand but was too afraid of rejection; he did not seem to be particularly friendly. Desperate to say the right thing but unable to work out what the right thing was, I could only ask: "Is something wrong?"

"Why should there be?"

"Well—"

"Why shouldn't I come home if I feel like it?"

"Please don't think I'm not delighted to see you—"

"And *don't slobber over me* just because I've chosen to show up. If you go all slobbery, like the father in the prodigal son story, I'll bloody well vomit." He suddenly caught sight of Sheila in the hall. "Who's that?"

"Bishop Preston's widow."

"Oh God!"

"It's all right, she's just leaving." Hastening back into the house I said to Sheila: "It's Michael and he appears to be very upset. Will you forgive me if—"

"Of course." To my relief I realised she had used the brief moment on her own to recover her self-control. The two words, crisply spoken, formed the competent response of the clerical wife who was able to cope unflustered with any emergency. "I'll just turn off the oven," she added with admirable presence of mind. I had entirely forgotten that we were supposed to be having dinner.

"No, don't do that," I said, trying to be equally practical. "Michael might be hungry."

"Well, if he fancies steak-and-kidney pie it'll be ready in twenty minutes." She picked up her coat from the hall chair.

"I'll phone you tomorrow, of course."

"It doesn't matter."

"On the contrary, it matters very much," I said, but by this time

Michael was entering the hall and no further private conversation with her was possible. Turning to him I said: "You remember Mrs. Preston, don't you?"

He made a big effort. I saw him draw on his "glittering image" like a glove. Smiling with great charm, he held out his hand and adopted his most winning manner. No one, not even Lyle, could have understood him as well as I did that moment, when the gap between his confident public persona and his troubled private self was so painfully wide and deep.

"Of course I remember you, Mrs. Preston!" he said. "How are you?" And barricaded behind defences which were quite as impressive as his own, Sheila assured him she was very well and remarked how nice it was to see him again. Another short conversation followed during which we all toiled to preserve the social niceties, but at last I was able to escort Sheila outside to her car. As I opened the driver's door for her I said: "Whatever you do, don't go back to London before we've talked again." By this time I had had the chance to worry about what would happen if I threw her no life-line of any kind, but Sheila remained self-possessed and even seemed amused by my words. "You don't have to handle me as if I was a tricky pastoral case," she said dryly. "I'm not about to put my head in the nearest gas oven."

This remark certainly indicated that my anxiety for her welfare was misplaced, but unfortunately it also indicated that my anxiety for my own welfare should double. I felt I was still very much in the presence of a woman scorned, but before I could attempt a reply she got into the car, slammed the door and drove away.

Staring after her I allowed myself one long moment of pulverising anxiety. Then shoving all thought of the scene from my mind I hurried back indoors to Michael.

Of course I had already realised that he was bringing news of the disaster which the final entry in Lyle's journal had foretold.

6

I WAS sure Michael had come to seek my help but I was equally sure he had no idea how to tell me about what had happened. When two people have for a long time been unable to conduct even the most innocuous conversation without winding up in a fever of furious pain, the possibility of having a profitable discussion becomes remote. The onus was obviously on me to establish a quiet, calm atmosphere so that he had the chance to intuit my willingness to listen sympathetically, but quiet, calm atmospheres are hard to establish when both parties to the conversation are already on an emotional rack. When I found him drinking neat whisky in the drawing-room I wanted to shout at him: "You stupid young fool, how dare you wreck your life like this!" and although I managed to keep my mouth shut, the effort exhausted me. Outwardly expressionless but inwardly awash with rage and fear, I removed my collar, lit a cigarette and tried to decide where I should sit down. He was occupying one end of the long sofa. Hardly daring to make the move for fear I was doing the wrong thing, I sat down at the other end.

"What was that woman doing here?" Michael demanded morosely.

"Oh, just having a quick drink."

"I never want to see another woman again. As far as I can see the only solution to the problem of sex is to be either past it or castrated."

I decided I was being invited to comment. In my mildest voice I murmured: "I assume that means your current romance has taken a wrong turn," but unfortunately I was in such a state that again I could not remember the name of the new girlfriend, the nice girl who had been with him at the funeral and had been such a welcome contrast to Dinkie. This was a distressing pastoral slip. Remembering names made a difference, implied concern, demonstrated a genuine interest. Clergymen always needed to remember names.

Staring down into his glass of whisky, Michael was either unable or unwilling to reply.

The silence began, the silence of estrangement, and although I knew I had to end it I could not decide what to say. I could only think how odd it was that in my professional life I should be so articulate and adroit while in my private life I had so often lacked the words to express my deepest feelings.

"I wish Mum was here," said Michael.

This was a signal. I knew it was a signal. I was a clergyman with a long experience of dealing with distressed people, and I could recognise the moment when someone signalled a willingness to talk on an intimate level. But the thought of Lyle, absent when she was so desperately needed, proved almost too much for me to bear. I was unable to respond.

After a moment Michael added: "It was terrible to arrive here tonight and know she'd never be here again."

I told myself that if I now failed to utter even the feeblest sentence I deserved to remain estranged from Michael for the rest of my life. I managed to say: "I'm glad you came. I wanted to see you. I meant every word I said in that letter."

"What letter?"

I was so disorientated by this question that I could only answer stupidly: "I posted it last weekend."

"Oh, *that* letter. I didn't open it. When I saw your writing on the envelope I wanted to puke. Sorry."

I was silenced again.

"I felt I couldn't cope with you," said Michael. "Not without Mum. She shouldn't have died like that, it wasn't fair. I don't believe in God. All this pain—all this mess—I mean, where is he, for Christ's sake, where is he, and what the hell does he think he's doing?" And he gave a sudden, violent shudder as his eyes at last filled with tears.

7

AT ONCE I stood up to move closer to him, but he said fiercely: "No, don't slobber over me!" and hurtled across the room to pour himself another whisky.

"Aren't I allowed even to apologise for being too preoccupied by my own grief to be of any use to you recently?"

"I didn't want you being useful. You might have slobbered. You either slobber or you're incompetent. Look at that mess I got into with Dinkie! It was Mum who sorted everything out while you just went into hiding with your archdeacon."

"At least I didn't slobber." I wondered if the mention of Dinkie was a hint that he was now ready to talk of what I could only assume was the sad end of his brief new romance. I still could not recall the name of the girl. All I could remember was that she had been one of the two girls who shared a flat with the dangerous Marina Markhampton.

Meanwhile Michael was saying bitterly: "You never understood about Dinkie. Never."

"Your mother thought I did. She thought I understood far better than I was ever willing to admit."

"What on earth do you mean?"

I thought: I can't talk about this, it's impossible, it's out of the question.

But then I thought of Lyle, taking her great spiritual journey without me, and I knew I was again being called to prove that not one word of that journal had been written in vain. Off-handedly, casually, rather as if I were reminiscing about a round of golf I said: "I'd have liked to live with a girl like that when I was your age. But I never got the chance."

Whisky slopped on the carpet as Michael's glass slipped in his hand.

"Of course I could never admit that to myself," I said, now sounding almost bored. "It wasn't a truth I was willing to face, but your mother quite understood how jealous I was. In fact she understood a lot of things which had entirely eluded me, and she wrote them all down in an exercise book which I found after the funeral. You can read the book one day, if you like. Jon's got it at the moment. It's rather interesting." I might have been talking of a library book which had helped while away an unimportant hour or two. Moving to the sideboard I siphoned myself some more sodawater and sipped it slowly. "I'm sure I would have tired of Dinkie's obvious attractions after six months," I added as an afterthought. "But the less obvious attractions would have entranced me for much longer."

Michael could hardly have looked more stunned if I had confessed to keeping a brothel. Now it was his turn to be speechless. Taking another sip from my glass I said: "I was always attracted to curing women who had been emotionally damaged."

The room was now utterly silent. I watched the soda-siphon for a moment and then turned my attention to the gin bottle which was standing next to it. "That was one of the reasons why my first marriage wasn't a success," I said. "Jane wasn't damaged. There was no challenge. I got bored." By this time I was examining the label of the Tio Pepe. "I should have guessed what was going on in your life when you told me Dinkie had had an appalling childhood," I added, "but since I'd condemned you as immoral I was determined not to identify myself with you in any way."

I heard Michael set down his glass, and when I turned to face him at last I saw he had even pushed it away across the coffee-table as if he no longer needed the scotch that remained. All he said was: "Why did you always want to cure women who are messed up?"

"My mother was a very unhappy woman. So was yours, when you were very young. I should have remembered." I sighed at the memory of the troubled early years of my second marriage before adding: "Of course the heal-the-sick syndrome isn't uncommon among clergymen, particularly those who are interested in the Church's ministry of healing. If I hadn't been a clergyman I'd have been a doctor."

"I knew you wanted me to be a doctor as soon as you realised there was no hope of me being a clergyman," said Michael, "but I just found illness was boring—and all that science was so tedious—"

"I wish you'd told me."

"I thought you wouldn't let me drop out. I thought you'd say I had to soldier on and play the game. That was why I messed around with nurses on that epic scale—I couldn't see how else to escape."

I said: "I messed around a bit when I couldn't face telling my father

I didn't want to go on reading law." I paused to examine the unfamiliar memory before forcing myself to add: "Of course it was all very different in my young day. Girls of one's own class were taboo, illicit sex always had to be covered up, the post-war syphilis epidemic was scaring us out of our wits—"

"Wait a minute," interrupted Michael, sounding as confused as if I had been talking in a foreign language. "When you say you messed around a bit, do you mean you just had a kiss occasionally?"

"No."

"You mean—"

"As a matter of fact, it was all very sordid and frustrating. No wonder I was jealous of you and your good times."

Michael whispered: "Good times!" and looked sick.

At once I realised this was a cue, curving the conversation back to his present crisis and inviting me to ask a direct question about what had gone wrong, but I still could not remember the girl's name. One of the girls who shared Marina Markhampton's flat was called Emma-Louise, but this was not the girl who had accompanied Michael to Lyle's funeral.

Meanwhile Michael was pushing the crisis away again by embarking on another diversion. "This exercise book where Mum wrote down you were jealous of me—what was she doing, writing down things like that?"

"Keeping a journal. It's a well-known spiritual exercise, and as time went on it clarified her thoughts so that she could pray more effectively."

"Effectively? All God did was turn around and vomit all over us! What a complete and utter waste of time all that praying was!"

After a moment I said: "In the beginning she did think it was rather a waste of time, particularly since she was praying for the most unlikely things to come true. She prayed, for instance, that I would come to understand my mistakes. She prayed that I would stop being so 'utterly stupid'—her phrase—about you. And I'm quite sure she prayed that one day in a future quite impossible to imagine we would sit down and have an honest conversation with each other."

I did not wait for him to speak; his silence was the only reply I needed to hear. Setting down my glass on the sideboard I said: "It was after I read the journal that I knew I had to talk to you. That's why I wrote you the letter which I posted last weekend, the letter you didn't open. I thought—"

"I did open it," said Michael.

8

AS I stared at him he fumbled for a cigarette and made a great business of lighting it before he said: "I'm sorry I lied but I was in such a state that I felt I couldn't cope if you tried to stage a prodigal son scene."

Mystified I asked: "Would that have been such a difficult thing to cope with?"

"Yes, because I don't deserve any big welcome. All I deserve is castration, disembowelment and hanging."

"Michael—"

"The Dinkie business was bad enough—God, what a mess! I was so sure that I could save her, just as you saved Mum, but we kept having rows and sleeping with other people—Dinkie said she had to hedge her bets in case I left her—so then I thought marriage would be the answer—but I knew deep down it wasn't, so I panicked and ran home to Mum and she fixed everything, but Mum didn't really understand Dinkie, not really, she just thought Dinkie was a gold-digger, but Dinkie's insecure. If only she could find someone who really cared, she wouldn't be so money-fixated, but she'll never find a man who could stand it, they'll get bored, just as I did, and she'll keep sleeping around to hedge her bets and eventually there'll be some sort of bloody ending—"

"I doubt it. I see her as a survivor."

Michael said: "You can't always tell who's going to survive," and suddenly he became so pale that his skin assumed a greenish tinge. Producing a Kleenex paper handkerchief from his pocket he blew his nose and added unevenly: "If only I'd had more foresight I'd never have got involved with Dinkie no matter how much I wanted to cure her unhappiness. It was hell."

With enormous relief I remembered the name of the girl. My memory was jolted by the word "foresight," and at once I thought of Holly, one of the characters in Galsworthy's *Forsyte Saga.* "No wonder you turned to Holly," I said quickly. "She must have seemed such a refreshing change."

"She did. She was. But she's dead," said Michael, and began to tear the tissue to shreds.

9

I SAID slowly: "I'm very, very sorry. What happened?"

Dropping the last fragment of Kleenex on the shredded pile Michael said: "It was never really much of a romance." He picked up his cigarette from the ashtray before adding in an odd monotonous voice: "I thought I'd enjoy a girl who had a reasonable IQ and no problems, but I knew right after the first night that it was no good sex-wise so I decided to give her the push, not violently, not traumatically, not unkindly, I mean just a little push, a sort of it's-been-great-you're-fantastic little push, a push that implied I hoped we'd always be good friends—because after all we're both in the same crowd and I knew I'd be seeing her again and again at Marina's parties, so I wanted to part on good terms with her, why not—hell, I *wanted* to be friends, and that's the great thing about the 1960s, isn't it, everyone knows you can have a fling and then stay friends afterwards, you can do your own thing free from guilt, everyone knows that, everyone knows we're all liberated now—and I said that to Holly, but she couldn't seem to understand. She just said: 'If this is liberation, why do I feel I'm bleeding to death in chains?' And then she told me she'd been in love with me for ages, long before I'd ever taken her out, and that was when I realised that as far as she was concerned the one-night stand wasn't just a fling.

"She called it a grand passion. She'd always kept her deepest feelings hidden, she said, because she was afraid I'd find them too much—and she was right, I did find them too much, I was horrified, I thought: my God, this is the last thing I need, a heavy emotional scene! After the mess with Dinkie I felt I wanted someone light and bright and amusing, not someone who said she felt she was 'bleeding to death in chains,' not someone who was going to flounce around playing the tragedy queen and being a bloody bore. I wanted to run a mile. But in the end I found I couldn't. I may be a bastard but I'm not a complete bastard. I didn't want to plough her under.

"I decided to abandon all idea of making a quick clean break and detach myself very gently, but oh God, that didn't work out at all, she just got keener and keener and began to talk of marriage and . . . well, I knew I had to end it, had to, and I did try a day later, but she started threatening suicide . . . Not that I believed she'd do it, of course, but when she started ranting on about 'bleeding to death in chains' I couldn't take it, couldn't cope, so I said okay, I'd stay with her—anything for a quiet life—but I really resented the way she'd piled on the emotional blackmail.

"Well, the next night I got in such a state, knowing I had to finish the affair but not having the bloody guts to do it, that I got drunk and went to bed with a girl called Nadia who'd been angling for me for ages—and hey presto, there I was, involved with yet another woman who wasn't going to let go without a fight. Holly hadn't actually moved in with me—she was too afraid of what her parents might say—so I did have the scope to entertain Nadia at my flat, but although I thought I was being so discreet someone found out. I think it must have been Marina's other room-mate, Emma-Louise. She was the one who introduced me to Nadia. They were at school together.

"Anyway last night Holly turned up, banging on the door of my flat, crying, screaming, completely hysterical, and said she knew about Nadia—and suddenly I found I couldn't take her any more, something in me snapped and I yelled at her to get the hell out of my life—which was quite the wrong approach, I knew it was, but—"

"What was Holly's reaction?" I said, trying to help him as he faltered.

"She stopped screaming, became very quiet. Then she said: 'I'm going to cut my wrists and bleed to death.' "

"And you said—"

"I said: 'Don't forget to put on your chains!' " Tears began to stream down his cheeks but he managed to go on speaking. "I didn't take her seriously," he said. "I thought: doesn't that stupid girl know that those who threaten suicide never do it? Everyone knows that, I thought to myself. Everyone."

By now I was beyond speech. Eventually Michael ground out his cigarette, wiped his eyes with his cuffs and said: "This afternoon at the BBC, around five, I got a call from Marina. She said: 'You've got to come. There's been a catastrophe.' Then she hung up. I went to her flat. Emma-Louise had got back from work and found Holly dead. Marina had arrived seconds later and called me straight away. Holly was stone cold. Obviously she'd never been to work that day and had killed herself after the others had left that morning.

"Well, I get there and I'm in shock, can't think, can't speak—we're all in shock, in fact, but suddenly Emma-Louise loses her cool and calls me a murderer. She even starts screaming before Marina shuts her up. It was funny how Marina took charge, fixing everything. I was sort of reminded of Mum . . .

"Emma-Louise was pointing at me and screaming, 'I want that bastard crucified at the inquest!' but Marina said: 'If Michael's crucified in court, we'll all end up crucified in the gossip columns, and personally I've never fancied being nailed to a piece of wood.' Then she said our best hope of avoiding scandal was to keep quiet to the police about my affair with Holly—the affair was still so new and few people knew how deeply Holly had committed herself—she hadn't wanted word to get back to her strait-laced parents. Marina said everyone in the Coterie—our crowd—would keep quiet. 'United we stand,' she said. 'Divided we fall.' Then she asked me which of my friends knew I'd been so heavily involved.

"I said I'd told my best friend but I could trust him to keep quiet. The real problem was Charley. He knew about Holly because he'd called at my flat unexpectedly and caught her wandering around in my dressing-gown—bloody Charley, always checking up on me so that he can tell tales to you! But Marina said: 'Blood's thicker than water—he'll keep quiet too,' and just as I was thinking that I really might be able to survive the mess without being slammed by the coroner, the penny dropped and I realised I hadn't followed Marina's line of reasoning at all. I said: 'But if we cover up the affair we leave Holly with no motive for killing herself.' And then Marina told me. She said: 'She doesn't need one. She's been unstable ever since she had a breakdown in her teens, and so the coroner has the perfect excuse to write her off as a neurotic who couldn't cope with life.'

"I was struck dumb. I thought how I'd assumed Holly was a nice normal girl with no problems. I didn't know about the breakdown. I suppose she didn't tell me because she was afraid I'd be put off. I thought I knew everything about her yet I knew nothing, *nothing* . . . I'd just wandered along and smashed her up and—" But he could not go on.

I tried to rescue him with a plain, factual question. "What happened when the police arrived?"

"I don't know. Marina sent me away. I know I should have stayed but I was so wiped out that I just did what I was told. Marina gave me a brandy before I left. We all had brandy, and afterwards Emma-Louise apologised, said she'd only lashed out at me because she felt so guilty. That was when it dawned on me that she must have been the one who told Holly about Nadia—I can just see Nadia bragging away to Emma-Louise in some bloody coffee-bar—but Marina interpreted the remark differently; she thought Emma-Louise felt guilty because she hadn't taken Holly's suicide threats seriously. Marina said: 'We're *all* guilty of that, but now's not the time to wallow in guilt. We've got to stay cool, stick together and survive.'

"The strange thing was that as she spoke I felt I was seeing her for the first time—I felt as if I'd previously known her no better than I'd known Holly. Marina always gives the impression of being such a dizzy society girl, but the truth is she's so smart, so loyal, so *strong* . . . And the moment I recognized her strength, I realised what a farce all my relationships with girls had been because of course *I* was the damaged one who needed curing, *I* was the one who couldn't get my act together, and what I really needed wasn't a weak woman but a strong one, someone I could always trust, someone who'd stand by me whatever I did, someone like . . . But I'll never get anywhere with Marina. She's only interested in men who aren't available for marriage, but never mind, I don't deserve her anyway, I don't deserve anyone, I ought to be locked up, I feel absolutely unforgivable."

It was the crucial moment. How strange it was that I should then think not of Lyle, writing in her journal, but of Harriet, pouring herself out into her sculpture and toiling ceaselessly to "make everything come right."

Abandoning my position at the sideboard, I moved back to the sofa and sat down at last by Michael's side.

10

"I KILLED her," Michael was saying, but I answered at once: "No. Suicide doesn't inevitably follow a failed love affair. There's always a choice, even for neurotics."

"But if she hadn't been having an affair with me—"

"She might have been having an affair with someone else. Or she might have remained chaste and still wound up killing herself."

"But I feel so guilty—"

"Of course. If you felt no guilt at all I'd be very worried about you, but it's very important that you shouldn't feel guilty about something that didn't happen and you did not kill that girl. You've got to get this whole disaster absolutely straight in your mind in order to master it and make sure you never make such a tragic mistake again. Did you see the body?"

He nodded, shuddering.

"Good. If you hadn't seen it, you'd now be torturing yourself by imagining it and that would be much worse. Did she, in fact, cut her wrists?"

"In the bath, yes. The water . . . Oh God, I'll never forget it, never—"

"You shouldn't be aiming to forget it. If you push it underground in your mind, it'll drive you to drink and destroy you. You've got to face it and learn to live with it."

"I don't see how I can. I want to go completely to pieces."

"And compound the tragedy? What use would that be either to you or to anyone else? Why throw your life away when you've now at last got the opportunity to live more fully than you've ever lived before?"

"How do you mean?"

"If you learn from your mistakes you reshape yourself and redesign the future. If you learn nothing and remain the same then the future is just the past repeating itself."

Michael said in despair: "Those are just words. I can't connect with them."

"In the war," I said at once, shifting tack, "I found out that what people couldn't stand was meaningless suffering. If they were able to give it meaning, they survived. Meaning generates hope, and hope generates the will to live."

"Yes, but—"

"You can choose to give Holly's death no meaning; you can block it from your mind, probably with disastrous results. Or you can give her death a malign meaning; you can go to pieces, certainly with disastrous results. Or you can give her death meaning by bringing something positive out of it; you can use it as a torch to illuminate your own life and as a tool to alter what needs to be changed."

Michael thought about this for a while. He produced another Kleenex tissue and shredded it. The glass of whisky remained unfinished on the table.

Finally he said: "Maybe this is a call to chuck up the Beeb, go into the Church and make you happy after giving you hell for so long."

"If you went into the Church just to make me happy I'd be miserable."

"But—"

"Michael, if God really wants you to be a clergyman, I've no doubt he'll make his wishes perfectly clear in due course. In the meantime you'll make me happiest if you continue as a drama producer."

"But if I stay at the BBC aren't I just being selfish by doing what I like best?"

"Not necessarily. It's a complete myth that people can only serve God by doing what they hate and making themselves miserable. All they're doing is serving the demon guilt which makes them want to punish themselves."

"But Christianity drones on and on about suffering—"

"The spiritual director Somerset Ward used to equate that use of the word 'suffering' with effort. Christianity's about effort—about expending blood, sweat and tears to be what you've been designed by God to be and do what you've been designed by God to do. That's certainly not incompatible with personal fulfilment and lasting happiness—quite the reverse. What's incompatible is not bothering to find out who one is, settling for something less or something other than what one should be, trampling on others in order to realise a self designed by the ego instead of valuing and caring for others in order to realise the true self designed by God."

Michael sighed and looked more despondent than ever, but he stopped sitting tensely on the edge of the sofa and no new Kleenex appeared for shredding. At last he said: "I wish I could believe in God permanently. I hate these long intervals when I'm either a dithering agnostic or a rampant atheist."

"Perhaps all the uncertainty sets up the tension which enables you to work more creatively."

He failed to hear this. "I just feel that we'd get on so much better if I was a fanatical believer like Charley—"

"I think not. I want to talk to you about Charley, Michael," I heard myself say. "I want to say how sorry I am that I got so many things wrong in the past." And as Michael gazed at me in amazement again I knew we were at last emerging from the dead desert of estrangement in which we had been so painfully trapped for so long.

II

"THE BIGGEST mistake I made," I said, "was that I refused to face up to my ambivalent feelings about the adoption and in my efforts to repress them I've been treating Charley in a way which did him no favours."

"But you slobbered over him continuously!"

"Yes, it was very unnatural. Real fathers get angry with their children sometimes. As you well know."

"Lucky old Charley, being spared all the screaming matches!"

"On the contrary, Charley wasn't lucky at all. He sensed the ambivalence and became chronically insecure. You should feel sorry for him."

"How can one feel sorry for someone who's so nauseatingly priggish? I can't even begin to describe how he carried on when he caught Holly wearing my dressing-gown! He even took Emma-Louise out to a coffee-bar later and tried to pump her for information about how long the affair had been going on."

"I'm afraid he's anxious to curry favour with me by being a model of chastity."

"Well, at least I was never tempted to do that!"

"No, but that's because you've always known that blood was thicker than water. Have you ever spent a single moment agonising about whether or not I regarded you as a son?"

"Well, no, not exactly . . . I mean, no, of course not. But don't think I haven't done my share of agonising! The main problem was that you never listened. You never listened when I tried to explain why I liked pop music, why I liked Marina's Coterie, why I was interested in the theatre and television. Pop music was just 'rubbish' to you, my friends were a 'fast set,' going for a career in the arts was 'not the done thing'—"

"I'm sorry."

"—and you never grasped that pop music's full of the joy of life, you never acknowledged that my friends are intelligent and amusing and bloody good fun, you never saw that a career in the arts can be . . . Hang on, there's a smell of burning coming from somewhere. Could the house be on fire?"

I remembered the steak-and-kidney pie and rushed to the kitchen.

12

"NEVER MIND," said Michael as we surveyed the charred remnants in the oven. "I'm not hungry."

"But we should both try and eat. Think of the meal as an aid to survival in a time of danger."

"I'd only vomit."

"In that case we'll eat here in the kitchen and you can sit next to the sink." After inspecting the larder I selected a large tin of baked beans and set it down on the counter.

"And Spam," said Michael behind me. "I can't have baked beans without Spam." Presumably this yearning for the drab post-war diet of his childhood represented a desire to regress to happier days.

I was just reaching for the tin of Spam when we both heard the sound of the front door bang far away in the hall.

"Who's that?" whispered Michael startled.

"It's either one of the chaplains or Miss Peabody. No one else has a key except Charley." I abandoned the larder. "Roger?" I called sharply. "Is that you?"

There was no reply. I hesitated, not only surprised by the silence but unnerved by it. "Who's there?" I shouted again, but even before the footsteps sounded in the hall I knew what had happened.

I froze, and although beside me Michael hissed urgently: "Who is it, who is it . . ." I did not answer. I was too busy remembering the scene last weekend when Charley had told tales to me of Michael. I could hear Charley's voice clearly, and as soon as I remembered him mentioning Nadia's name I grasped the hidden dimension of Michael's narrative, the dimension which now made Charley's arrival at the South Canonry inevitable.

The door opened. We stood facing each other beneath the stark kitchen lights, and when I saw his expression I knew I had not misunderstood what had happened. Contrary to Michael's belief, it was not Emma-Louise who had told Holly about Michael's new affair. And it was not Emma-Louise who had felt driven to go on a crusade against fornication with a fervour which was a distorted reflection of my own.

XXII

"The old women like to say that what happened was all for the best. They are probably wrong . . . It is a special revelation of God's divine power that he is able to bring some good out of evil. But his use of evil for good ends does not immediately sterilise it; it continues to breed after its own kind."

AUSTIN FARRER
Warden of Keble College, Oxford, 1960–1968
LOVE ALMIGHTY AND ILLS UNLIMITED

I

"CHARLEY!" EXCLAIMED Michael. He, at least, was astonished.

Charley seemed equally amazed to see him, and I realised that Michael's presence, as unforeseen as it was unwelcome, had confused him so much that he was uncertain what to do next. All he said in the end was: "You've told him?"

"Yes. But hang on—" Michael too began to look confused. "Told him what?"

"About Holly. Emma-Louise phoned me."

"But why should Emma-Louise—" Michael broke off. As the expression in his eyes changed I knew I had to intervene. "Sit down, Charley," I said. "You look as if you're about to pass out. Michael—"

But Michael was already saying to Charley with horror: "It was you, wasn't it? It was *you,* not Emma-Louise, who told Holly about me and Nadia—"

"I was only trying to help."

"You were only trying to *what?"*

"I meant it all for the best—"

"I could kill you!" shouted Michael. The chance to expel his guilt on to another made him sound almost delirious with the anger which masked his subconscious relief. "And you killed her as surely as if you'd slashed her wrists yourself!"

I expected to hear the retort that if Michael had behaved more responsibly Holly might still be alive, but Charley was too shattered to attempt a reply. Taking control of the conversation I said without raising my voice: "The way forward isn't to make accusations of murder. The way forward is to find out exactly what's happened. Michael, get the brandy, please."

Michael was clearly unwilling to allow his anger to be defused but the thought of brandy diverted him. He departed for the drawing-room, and as soon as he had gone Charley whispered to me desperately: "I can't talk about it in front of him, I can't. It's too shaming."

"He's got to know."

"You tell him for me!"

"He'll still want to discuss it with you. Much better to tell him yourself now when I'm here to keep order."

"But I can't—look, you've just got to let me off the hook—"

"No."

"But—"

"No. That's what I'd say to Michael if he stood now in your shoes. That's what I'd say to my own flesh and blood and in future I'm going to treat you as I'd treat him."

He stared at me. His eyes, normally such a pale shade of brown that they often seemed golden, were now the colour of dark wet sand. His white face had a pinched look. He was very still.

"No need to panic," I said, feeling panic-stricken, "but we can't go on as we are. There's got to be a change."

"I don't understand. Are you saying—"

"You've always wanted me to treat you as a son, haven't you? Well, this is it. I apologise for the lack of sentimental dialogue and soaring violins. Now sit down, show some guts and let's all try to survive this tragedy instead of using it to beat each other to pieces." And producing two glasses from the cupboard I slammed them down on the kitchen table.

Michael, who had returned in time to hear my last sentence, sat down opposite Charley. I poured out the brandy for them; how I kept my promise to Jon and resisted the longing to pour a measure for myself I shall never know. Finally I said to Charley: "Now explain exactly what happened so that we can understand the way your mind was working and make allowances for you." And to Michael I added: "Every time you feel like hitting him, remind yourself that other people might feel like hitting you—but make sure you remember too that ultimately no one's unforgivable."

The newly lit cigarette began to tremble between Michael's fingers. Charley began to speak in a rapid voice.

2

ADDRESSING HIS narrative to me as if he could not bear to accept that Michael was present, Charley said: "I knew Michael was having an affair with Holly because I found her wearing his dressing-gown at his flat. I thought it was quite wrong that he should treat Holly as he treated Dinkie. Holly was . . . different. I began to worry about her. I thought that maybe, as I was a clergyman, I had a moral duty to do something."

Michael made a disgusted noise but I said sharply: "Be quiet," and he obeyed.

"I arranged to meet Emma-Louise for coffee," said Charley. "I felt I needed to find out if Holly wanted to marry Michael. The affair itself might be brand new, but as long ago as Venetia's party last November I'd noticed Holly looking at Michael as if she were in love with him—and in fact Emma-Louise said yes, Holly was madly in love and marriage was definitely on the cards because Michael was exhausted by the Dinkie mess and probably ready to settle down. But I knew Michael wouldn't be interested in marrying Holly. He'd just picked her as a rest-cure. She wasn't really his sort of girl at all.

"I was still thinking about what I could do to save Holly when Emma-Louise suggested another meeting in the coffee-bar. She was upset because she'd found out that her friend Nadia was also carrying on with Michael, and she was very worried about the effect this might have on Holly—she asked me to have a word with Michael to try to get him to see sense and behave decently.

"But I knew Michael wasn't interested in behaving decently.

"I told Emma-Louise I'd have a word with him, but in fact I had no intention of doing so. That was because in my view it wasn't Michael who had to be severed from Nadia but Holly who had to be severed from Michael." With his elbows on the table he pressed his hands against his cheeks as if he could push back his shame, and fell silent as if unable to phrase what had to be said next. Opposite him Michael might have been carved in stone, and it was I who finally said to Charley: "No doubt you thought you had to be cruel only to be kind."

Charley managed to nod. He seemed relieved by my neutral tone of voice. "I knew I'd hurt her by telling her what was going on, but I honestly thought that if she did want to marry Michael I'd be doing her a favour by pointing out that fidelity wasn't his strong suit."

Michael abandoned his role of stone statue. "Why, you priggish, self-righteous—"

"Be honest, Michael," I interrupted, not unkindly, as I moved to muzzle this explosion of unhelpful rage. "Do you really think a disinterested observer would declare fidelity to be your strong suit?"

Before Michael could reply Charley said to him defiantly: "I thought it was my moral duty as a priest to wean her from this grand illusion which was distorting her judgement."

"You mean you were determined to smash up your brother's affair with this girl and you succeeded," I said, again speaking not unkindly. "As for your moral duty, I think it best to set aside for the moment all discussion of your motives. Just concentrate on completing your story."

Charley's defiance evaporated. He whispered: "I'm not sure I can bear to describe it."

"Think of it as something you can do to help Michael come to terms with what's happened. Think of it," I said colourlessly, "as your duty as a priest."

At once Charley said in an uneven voice: "I phoned Holly and asked if I could come round to her flat to talk to her—she'd said that Marina and Emma-Louise were out. In the end I just said that Michael was 'seeing' Nadia. Holly said did I mean 'sleeping with' and I said it seemed likely, in fact very likely, in fact certain. I was trying to break the news gently to her—like one's supposed to break news of a death—"

"You make me want to vomit all over you," said Michael.

"Before you get too angry," I said, "remember that you were rather less tactful to her later. Go on, Charley."

"She seemed to take it quite well. Of course I did realise that she'd need support in building a new life, so I invited her to St. Mary's and . . ." He faltered but drove himself on. ". . . and I gave her some pamphlets."

"Pamphlets?" said Michael with revulsion as if Charley had confessed to infecting Holly with some unmentionable disease. "What kind of pamphlets?"

"Just some stuff I'd written and mimeographed . . . about Christianity . . . and how Jesus saves . . . by bringing new life . . ." He finally ground to a halt.

"God Almighty!" exploded Michael. "You mean you smashed up this girl and then sent her on her way with a bunch of bloody clichés?"

"Shut up!" bawled Charley, covering his face with his hands in a paroxysm of grief and shame.

"Charley certainly made a catastrophic pastoral error," I said to Michael, "but we all make catastrophic errors, pastoral or otherwise, as I'm sure you'd be the first to agree."

"I got it wrong," said Charley, rubbing the tears from his face. "I got it wrong. I should have ditched the pamphlets, stayed with her, given her the support she needed—"

"You should never have bloody meddled with her in the first place!" yelled Michael, and Charley, losing all control, yelled back: "And you should never have bloody meddled with her either!"

"Since you're both being so refreshingly honest," I said, "I hardly think I can do less than acknowledge my own part in this disaster. I was responsible for your upbringing. If I'd brought you up a little better no doubt we wouldn't now be sitting around this table and putting one another through hell."

They were dumbfounded.

3

AT LAST Michael muttered: "This is our mess, not yours," and Charley said horrified: "You're not responsible."

"No?" I poured them some more brandy and said: "We're all interlinked. Who can say with confidence where the responsibility for this tragedy begins and ends?" They tried to argue with me again but fell silent when I held up my hand. "Holly killed herself," I said. "That was her decision, not ours, but we all have our reasons for feeling guilty and distressed, and that guilt and distress must be faced, acknowledged and owned. It's no good denying those feelings or trying to project them on to someone else. That's no solution. That's the road to neurosis and dislocation. The guilt and distress have to be owned so that they can be regretted, because only regret can ensure the changes which will mean our failures here won't happen again."

"What Dad's talking about," said Charley to Michael, "is confession, repentance, redemption and renewal. Jesus said—"

"If you mention Jesus one more time," said Michael, "I'll smash your teeth in."

I too felt exasperated with Charley for wrecking my attempt to phrase the reality of the situation in language which Michael could accept, but I knew my exasperation had to be concealed. In an effort to take control of the scene again before it could be entirely destroyed by all the anger and pain which was on the loose, I said very mildly, very pacifically: "Charley, Michael's not uneducated in Christianity. He doesn't need to be reminded that Jesus accepted people as they were, forgave them their errors, wiped out their guilt and restored their sense of self-worth so that a new beginning was possible. I merely wanted to underline to you both that this healing process is as relevant today as it was two thousand years ago. Modern psychological studies have made it very clear that one can't embark on a new life with any real success if one's carrying around a crippling load of unacknowledged guilt from the past."

Charley murmured something about the difficulties of atheists, but I barely heard him. I was too busy replaying that last sentence in my mind and listening to it. I had the odd feeling that it related to some other matter of importance, but I could not remember what that matter was. I was reminded of the *déjà vu* experience, in which a scene appears familiar even though one cannot identify the occasion of the previous viewing.

I suddenly realised that Charley's remark must have been diplomatically inept because once again Michael was seething with rage.

"How dare you imply I'm incapable of understanding the need for forgiveness!" he shouted. "Do you think I want to go on feeling as if I'm about to die of remorse about Holly? Do you think I want to go on wearing myself out wanting to smash your teeth in for what you yourself did to her? Why, you stupid, bigoted old bugger, if you think I can't see I've got to forgive you for being such a shit over Holly just as I've got to forgive myself for being an even bigger shit over her, then you ought to be lugged off and bloody crucified! Now for God's sake stop crashing around like a religious maniac before I go mad and bloody kill you!" And having delivered himself of these extravagant and cathartic statements, he leapt to his feet and bolted at top speed from the room.

4

AS SOON as the door had slammed Charley said in despair: "Obviously I'm a complete failure and should resign from the priesthood straight away."

"What melodramatic rubbish! All that's happened is that you've discovered you're not quite so wonderful as you thought you were at pastoral work, but most priests discover that at some time or another. It's not unusual."

"Yes, but—"

"At least you had the guts and the humility to say: 'I got it wrong.' That shows you still have the potential to be a good priest." Levering myself to my feet I added: "We must eat before we collapse. Fetch a second tin of beans, would you? There's not enough here for three." I almost reached for the brandy decanter, but I felt that if I broke my word to Jon about abstaining from alcohol the grace of God would be withheld and all hope of redemption would be lost. To distract myself I said to Charley: "No, I'll get the beans. You go and see if Michael's all right. Don't say anything to him. Just find out what he's doing and report back."

Charley departed. I opened both cans of baked beans and prised out the Spam on to a plate. When Charley returned he said: "He's being sick in the lavatory."

"Leave the kitchen door open so that we hear him when he comes out." I pushed the Spam at him. "Carve that."

Charley drew a sharp knife from the drawer of the dresser but merely stood looking at it. At last he said: "You know, don't you? You know all I couldn't bring myself to confess in front of Michael."

I emptied the first tin of baked beans into a saucepan before I answered: "Whenever someone says in an attempt to justify a dubious action: 'I thought it was my moral duty,' I always want to ask some very hard questions."

"I was lying. My decision to try and take Holly away from Michael had nothing to do with any moral duty."

"No."

"I wanted her for myself. I really liked her."

"Yes."

"Michael could easily have got someone else—he can always get any girl he wants." The knife slipped from his fingers and fell on the dresser with a clatter. He rubbed his eyes before whispering: "You did guess, didn't you?"

"As soon as you started talking about your moral duty I certainly remembered you speaking of Holly with approval during our tea at Fortnum's. It was unusual for you to approve of a girl who was available for marriage."

"And you do see, don't you, why I couldn't possibly admit all that just now?"

"I'm sure it would have been hard for you to admit you weren't driven by the purest possible motives, but frankly I think Michael would find a simple jealousy easier to understand and forgive than a complicated priggishness."

"But I couldn't possibly have confessed to jealousy! Priests aren't supposed to get jealous. After all, think of yourself! You never get jealous, do you?"

"I'm ashamed to say the answer to that question seems to be: 'Frequently and unpleasantly.' "

"You're joking!"

"Not according to your mother, whose spiritual journal I've recently read. She wrote down a whole string of very devastating home truths, including some remarks about you and me."

Charley turned a shade paler. "But what did she say?"

Across the hall sounds indicated that Michael was leaving the cloakroom. I heard the faint murmur of water as the lavatory plug was pulled.

"We'll talk about it later." I started to spoon the second can of baked beans into the saucepan.

But Charley was now very disturbed. "Maybe she got it all wrong!"

"Yes, I thought that at first." Suddenly I heard myself say: "She thought we should talk more about Samson."

Charley looked appalled. "Oh no!" he said at once. "No, that's quite unnecessary! I can't have you being constantly upset, and in fact I think that now Mum's dead we should forget about Samson entirely. We ought to wipe him out once and for all—expunge him, eliminate him, exterminate him—"

"Is this a sermon?" demanded Michael, finally returning to the room. "Because if it is I'll go and shut myself in the lavatory again until you've finished." He turned to me. I was standing now by the dresser. I had picked up the sharp knife which Charley had dropped, and I was fingering the shining blade.

"You look like Macbeth remembering Duncan's murder," Michael said fractiously, and taking the knife from my hand he cut himself a sliver of Spam before demanding: "Can I have another drink?"

I pulled myself together sufficiently to say: "We'll all have another drink: water. Fill a jug, heat the beans, carve the Spam and call me when everything's ready."

Then I left the kitchen at top speed.

5

I SAT in my study in the dark and waited. Nothing happened. I listened to my quiet, shallow breathing, and eventually I realised that I was waiting for Lyle to come and say: "Don't worry, darling, I'll take care of it." But what she had to take care of, I found I did not want to know.

Eventually Michael called my name in the hall and I returned to the kitchen. Both boys were now watching me anxiously as if fearing that my sudden withdrawal might be an advance symptom of some new disaster.

"Sorry," I said in my most normal voice. "Delayed shock." Looking down at our unappetising meal I announced: "I'll say grace," but to my horror I could think of no grace to say. Panic made my skin prickle. "Charley, could you—"

Charley said the necessary sentence. We all muttered "Amen," even Michael, who was evidently so worried about me that he was willing to go to unusual lengths to make a friendly gesture. A silence fell as we all attempted to eat, but less than a minute later Michael was pushing away his plate.

"I feel terrible," he said. "I want to go upstairs and pass out, but I'm afraid something might happen when I'm not here."

Charley said: "Like what?"

"He might die of that delayed shock he mentioned."

They turned to eye me speculatively. The sheer bathos of their behaviour was so absurd that I began to laugh but of course this made them more nervous than ever. I could see them thinking that if death did not claim me, insanity certainly would.

Trying to keep a straight face I said robustly: "For heaven's sake, Michael, go and pass out before you utter another idiotic word!" but the moment he had obediently left the room I thought of all I still needed to say. I hurried out into the hall. "Michael"—I caught up with him at the foot of the stairs—"I'm very glad you came down here to see me. No matter how terrible this evening's been you mustn't think I'm not very glad you came."

"Oh, come off it, Dad, you're bloody miserable and wishing you were childless!"

"Yes, but I'm still so glad you came."

Michael said kindly: "You must be nuts," and began to haul himself up the stairs.

"You won't try and leave without saying goodbye, will you?"

"Why should I?"

"Well, if you suddenly felt you couldn't stand being here a moment longer—"

"Dad, stop twittering around like a demented hen and let me pass out in peace, there's a good chap. Go and twitter around that twerp in the kitchen."

These orders certainly put me in my place but I was not dissatisfied with the conversation.

With reluctance I trailed back to Charley.

6

"I THINK you should go and pass out too," said Charley, who was still pushing some baked beans around his plate. "I'll clear up here."

"Before I pass out I'd like your assurance that you're not still thinking of giving up the priesthood."

"God knows what I'm thinking."

"Charley, just because you've made one very bad mistake—"

"If that was the only problem I could cope, but it's not, is it? The real trouble goes much deeper than that. After all, here I am, having slaved for years to model myself on you, and all that's happened is that I've wound up in this disgusting mess. Doesn't that prove beyond dispute that there's something radically wrong with me?"

"No, what it really proves is—" I broke off. My mind had gone blank again. Obviously my diagnosis of delayed shock had been correct and I now had to go to bed without delay. "I'm sorry," I said. "I've got to rest."

"Of course. Don't worry about me, I want to be alone for a while. I've got to think."

I picked up the knife again and took it to the sink where I carefully washed the blade until it was clean.

Then I went to bed and dreamed of disembowelment.

7

IN MY dream I was facing the unmarred west front of the Cathedral and exclaiming: "Radiant, ravishing Starbridge!" But as I stepped forward I stumbled over the disembowelled corpse of my doomed predecessor, Alex Jardine, and when I looked at the Cathedral again I saw not only that the west front was in ruins but that Sheila was walking towards me with a knife shining in her hand.

I awoke in a cold sweat. The room was still dark but the birds had begun to sing in the garden, and knowing that any further attempt to sleep would be futile, I left the bed and drew back the curtains. The Cathedral, dark, dense and devoid of all embellishments in the dim pre-dawn light, seemed as if waiting to crush me, but of course that was a fancy generated by my nightmare. I turned away to concentrate on the task of getting dressed.

But when I had finished shaving I found I had to go and look at the Cathedral again. The sky was now lighter but this only made the Cathedral seem more opaque. I could not stop looking at it. I did move to the dressing-room but still I had to return to the window. I felt as if the building were trying to hypnotise me, but I knew that was nonsense; one could not be hypnotised by an inanimate object, a black lump of stone and glass. Nor could one tell oneself that it was waking up, as I had done, with the advent of dawn. Nor could one stare at it as one might stare at some strange and savage animal encountered at the zoo.

Willing myself back to sanity I finished dressing, went downstairs and brewed myself some tea. An impulse to pray was filtering through my mind. Taking the tea back upstairs to my dressing-room I set the tray aside and sank to my knees, but I found I had to take yet another look at the Cathedral; I knew the compulsion was irrational, but that made no difference. Back I went to the bedroom. Beyond the window the Cathedral was now not merely black but pitch-black against the lightening sky, and the spire reminded me of the tapering blade of that kitchen knife which had featured so prominently in my nightmare.

The impulse to pray was by this time not merely filtering but streaming through my mind. I thought of Lyle, wondering if she should pray for the Cathedral, and as I remembered those lines in her journal I suddenly knew what I had to do. I had to pray not in my dressing-room but in the Cathedral itself, before my episcopal throne.

I felt almost as if I had been lassoed, like an animal in a Hollywood western, and was now being hauled from the house towards the churchyard.

I said aloud to the Cathedral: "I'm on my way. I've found my excuse." But of course these words made no sense at all; I was talking as if the powerful urge to pray in the most hallowed place available to me was some sort of bizarre smokescreen, covering up unjustifiable behaviour, whereas I knew very well that after all the traumas of the past hours, a desire to make an extravagant spiritual gesture was not only understandable but necessary to restore my equilibrium.

Yet I felt embarrassed that I had talked to the Cathedral as if it were a person. What a lapse for a former professor of divinity to make! But perhaps it had not been the Cathedral I was addressing.

Telling myself that I deserved to wind up in a straitjacket if I continued to indulge in this form of irrational speculation, I went downstairs to my study and retrieved from my desk the key of the Dean's door, the clergy's private entrance on the north side of the Cathedral. In the hall a moment later I put on my heaviest overcoat to ward off the chill but the cold air still made me gasp as I opened the front door.

I hesitated for a moment on the threshold.

Then the Cathedral seemed to pull again on the invisible rope, and I found myself moving down the drive like an automaton.

8

THE CATHEDRAL, still pitch-black against the dawn sky, rose from its pale lawn like a monstrous tidal wave frozen in ice. I stopped for a moment once I had passed through the gates of the South Canonry, and as I stared at that pattern of dark serrated lines ahead, the sun pierced the horizon to shine right through the transept from the east, and the glass began to glitter as if the tidal wave were on the move.

Superstitious dread stirred in me suddenly, but I repressed it. I walked up Canonry Drive towards the Deanery, but once I turned to face the west front the scaffolding reminded me again of the ruin in my nightmare and suggested a swathe of bandages which concealed some gross deformity. The west front itself was in deep shadow, a fact which rendered the maimed facade even more unfathomable. Beyond the roof of the nave, the tower, foreshortened by the angle from which I was observing it, suggested primitive myths and threatening archetypes. The spire was as lean as a lance.

I began to cross the churchyard, and the Cathedral seemed to come to meet me, its shadow billowing out from the dark, dour, dew-soaked stones. At the north porch I touched the wall and it was icy. My fingers tingled; the muscles in my arm flinched; I moved through the darkness which enveloped the north wall west of the transept, and the Cathedral seemed to ripple past me as if it were a living creature, a monster from some medieval bestiary, a Leviathan hostile to mankind.

Reaching the Dean's door I groped for my key. By that time I had stopped telling myself how pathetically overwrought I was; it seemed more sensible to acknowledge that the building would inevitably look eerie in that particular light, and that I was witnessing nothing which was either sinister or unusual. To reassure myself I glanced over my shoulder to see the picturesque view of the Close, but the houses on the North Walk were ghost-pale in the unearthly light, and the Theological College, high-roofed and multi-windowed, lay lifeless as a mausoleum by St. Anne's Gate.

I fitted my key in the lock. So conscious was I by this time of the Cathedral's resemblance to a monster that I almost expected it to roar with rage as I breached its outer skin, but of course there was no noise, just the click of the lock as the key turned and the creak of a hinge which needed oil. Moving at once to the panel which controlled the alarms I pulled the switches which guarded not only the Dean's door itself but the choir, transepts and nave. I hardly wanted to be interrupted in my prayers by the police and firemen of Starbridge, all rushing to respond to my arrival.

I moved on into the Cathedral.

By this time I was wishing I had brought a torch; I had underestimated how dark the Cathedral remained when the sun was low on the horizon. Huge shadows infested the nave, and the shafts of light from the windows seemed insignificant in comparison. A pool of blackness drowned the choirstalls, but I lit one of the candles in the front row and even before my lighter snapped shut I found my eyes were adjusting to the gloom. The candle, flickering in the faint draught, at once conjured up images of haunted houses. Automatically I leant forward and blew out the flame.

Turning to face the high altar I inclined my head in respect, just as I always did, but not before I had noticed that the cross was barely visible in the darkness; the screen behind the altar was cutting off the light from the east window.

I stood motionless in the gloom, and after a while I realised I was listening. The silence had a quality which I could not identify. I felt as if I were being watched by someone who was holding his breath.

But that, I told myself without hesitation, was nonsense.

Eliminating from my mind all pictures of the Devil, pitter-pattering around in the side-chapels and pausing every so often to peep at me, I returned to sanity by walking to my "cathedra" at the east end of the choir and sitting down on the embroidered cushion which made occupying a throne less uncomfortable during long services. But I was still troubled by the deep shadows around me. Leaning forward I found I could now see all the way down the nave, but the choir was still very dark. I wondered whether to relight the candle but decided that this would be pandering to my neurotic uneasiness. I also reminded myself that when my eyes were closed in prayer it would hardly matter whether the candle was alight or not.

Kneeling down I crossed myself, clasped my hands and resolutely embarked on the task of arranging my thoughts in a suitable pattern. I decided that before I prayed for my sons—certainly the most urgent item on my agenda—it would be fitting to pray for the Cathedral, by which I meant all those employed there. The most natural way to do this seemed to be to start at the top of the organisational pyramid and work downwards, so I started by recalling Aysgarth and his difficult private life. I remembered that despite all his flaws he was a devout Christian, and I resolved that I would pray hard that he might be enabled to overcome all his difficulties, no matter what they were.

I then recalled the three residentiary Canons and decided to pray for the discernment which would enable me to see how I could be more useful to them as they struggled with their arduous Chapter meetings. After that I skimmed down to the base of the pyramid, past the Chapter Clerk, the Clerk of the Works, the Master-Mason, the Architect and the Accountant—past the Organist, the vicars-choral and the choirboys, past the vergers, the guides, the cleaners . . . Having wound up remembering the old man who picked up the litter from the churchyard lawn, I mentally patted the intercession into a satisfying shape by resolving to pray that the entire staff of the Cathedral might be rescued from the current discord and finally achieve a new harmony.

This was all very "edifying," as clergymen used to say in my young day, and having designed this splendid scheme I felt ready to lay the pattern before God and talk to him about it.

People pray in different ways and one must pray as one can, but most people find it easiest to pray in words and pray as if talking to a person. I prayed in words, but although I addressed God, according to Christian convention, as "Father," this was not the easiest way for me to think of him because I was often reminded too distractingly of the strict parent who had brought me up. However, since I was a traditionalist I was not about to start addressing God as "Almighty Monad" or "Almighty Ultimate Concern." I addressed him as "Almighty Father," the theological equivalent of "Dear Sir," and tried to project my thoughts beyond all anthropomorphic images to Goodness, Truth and Beauty. I usually pictured them as three flames springing from one torch, which was Love, but I had other images. I am not saying I did not think of God as personal. I did. But he was ultimately beyond images, beyond the limits of the human imagination. I could only address him as "Almighty Father," focus on those Platonic forms which reminded me of his essence, and then lay out my prayers as simply as possible as I tried to align my will with his.

I must make it clear—if indeed it is not already obvious—that I am not a great spiritual athlete and in no way superior to the uneducated person who knows nothing of Platonic forms and just gets on with the job of praying without going through any intellectual hoops. In fact I envy such a person. My busy over-educated brain is a positive hindrance to prayer, and far too often my thoughts speed off on tangents which are intellectually fascinating but quite irrelevant to the task of praying in an acceptable manner.

I have gone to some lengths to describe how I pray because in view of what happened next I think the processes of my brain at that moment are important. Perhaps I can draw an analogy between them and the processes involved in tuning in to a wireless programme. First of all one looks in the *Radio Times* to see what programmes are being broadcast; that would be the equivalent of my survey to see what prayers are necessary. Then one switches on the set; that would be the equivalent of the moment when I close my eyes and begin: "Almighty Father . . ." Next one tunes in to the right station; this would be the equivalent of the point where I conjure up my image of God. And finally one sits back in one's armchair and concentrates on the programme; this would correspond to the phase where I visualise the subjects of my prayer and offer my requests to God. Sometimes the wireless crackles, blighting the broadcast, and in very bad atmospheric conditions one has little choice but to switch off the set, but normally one tunes in to the chosen programme without too much difficulty.

Having devised my prayer-scheme, I now clasped my hands in the conventional position, closed my eyes and began as usual with the words "Almighty Father"; I was not speaking aloud, but each word was clearly formed in my mind. I then conjured up my favourite image of the three flames blazing from a single torch, superimposed on it another image, a triangle which represented the three persons of the Trinity, and placed in that triangle the image of Aysgarth as I prepared to offer up my prayers on his behalf.

It was at that moment that the distortion began. In my analogy of the wireless broadcast, this would have been the moment when "the ether began to play up," as we used to say in the old days, and I found that although I had placed the image of Aysgarth in the triangle, it was the wrong image. I saw not the devoted husband and father—the picture I had planned to see—but the lecherous drunkard who had trouble controlling his weaknesses, the shady priest who took scandalous risks. In revulsion I forgot my prayer-scheme. I could only shout silently to God: get him out of my life, crush him, destroy him, punish him—and all the while I was shouting these violent orders in my head, my mind was ravaged by a voice which whispered: "A senior churchman—degraded—disgraced—*disgusting.*"

I began to shiver. The air had turned intensely cold and the temperature was still sinking. With a gasp I opened my eyes and at once the pollution assaulted me, stifling my breathing as it poured itself down my throat. I began to retch. Staggering to my feet I saw that the cross was now visible on the altar and I stumbled towards it. I knew I had to grasp that cross to restore my spiritual balance, and as I thought of Jon saying: "No demon can withstand the power of Christ," I found I was no longer the sophisticated theologian who regarded with amusement those who used old-fashioned images to describe huge black psychic forces which raged beyond human control. I forgot my intellectual snobbery; I forgot my education; I forgot that I had once been a professor famous for his lucid thinking and his talent for rational analysis. All I knew at that moment was that the building was infested with demons, crawling with them, and that the Devil himself was on the point of smashing me to pieces with a flick of his cloven hoof.

I staggered to the altar-rail but remembered just in time that I had not switched off the alarm which protected the altar itself and the treasures which stood there. I backed away, stumbling, nearly falling, and blundered down the choir. On reaching the steps which led up to the pulpit I suddenly realised I could grab a cross from one of the side-chapels nearby, and it was then, as my glance travelled wildly from the great west window towards the south transept, that I saw someone was watching me from the far end of the nave.

He wore a frock-coat and gaiters, the traditional uniform for a bishop, and although he stood in the shadow of a pillar I saw the unmistakable gleam of his lambent, amber eyes.

Shocked beyond measure I whispered: "Jardine—"

But he had vanished.

I stood there, trembling from head to toe, and as the sweat pricked my forehead I told myself I was the victim of an illusion caused by the rising sun beyond the long slim windows. I found I was clutching my pectoral cross. How absurd that I should have chased around trying to grab a cross from an altar! I had been protected all the time by the cross on my chest—which explained why I was still alive—but no, that superstitious thought had to be firmly rejected because the metal itself had no magic properties, the power sprang not from the symbol but from the reality to which that symbol pointed—but at that moment I could not see beyond the symbols, they were crowding in on me, and the symbol which now dominated my mind was not the cross but the cloven hoof.

The chain of my cross snapped. I gasped, and as the polluted air began to pour down my throat again I scooped up the cross from the floor and ran outside as fast as if the Cathedral had vomited me into the churchyard.

XXIII

"To say that the psychically weird belongs to the bottom of the soul is not of course to deny that it may be made the instrument of noble acts and purposes."

AUSTIN FARRER
Warden of Keble College, Oxford, 1960–1968
THE GLASS OF VISION

I

AS SOON as I reached the South Canonry I telephoned St. Paul's vicarage in Langley Bottom. I never even hesitated before lifting the receiver. Possibly I was so shaken that I hardly knew what I was doing. But possibly too I had reasoned at some subconscious level that since Hall had already seen me at the end of my tether he was unlikely to be shocked by anything I might say. There was no question of me going to see Jon. I did not trust myself to drive.

Having dialled the number of the vicarage I made an effort to breathe evenly. It seemed remarkable that I should be breathing at all. At any moment I expected to suffer sinister chest pains.

I was still considering the likelihood of a heart attack when Hall picked up the receiver. "Vicarage," he said curtly, but as if realising that only desperate people made calls at such an early hour, he added in a more agreeable voice: "How can I help you?"

"It's Ashworth." To my astonishment I sounded casual. "I want to see you. Urgently. About the Cathedral. Something rather inconvenient's happened." Even in my distress I found myself boggling at this bizarre understatement, so I forced myself to be less elliptical. "There's been an unacceptable incident," I said. "An optical illusion. Of course I don't believe for a moment that it was real, but I want it dealt with straight away." As I spoke I realised I was talking nonsense. How could one "deal" with an unreality? Fighting my way out of this metaphysical conundrum

I ordered rapidly: "Come to the South Canonry at once." I sounded like a nervous sergeant-major, attempting to restore order to the parade ground.

"Yes, Bishop," said Hall smartly. He too had been in the army during the war.

I hung up and wondered if he had already decided I was certifiable.

2

BY THE time he arrived I had toasted myself lightly on both sides in front of the electric fire and was drinking a cup of very strong tea. I believe I would have broken my promise to Jon about alcohol if it had not occurred to me that a bishop simply cannot reek of brandy early in the morning unless he is the victim of an accident and the brandy has been forced down his throat to keep him alive. Besides, I was anxious to appear sane, normal and composed, not a pie-eyed victim of panic. I did realise that the rational explanation of my ordeal was that I had gone off my head, but the trouble with this diagnosis, which so comfortingly absolved me from all need to enquire further into my paranormal experience, was that I did not quite believe it to be true.

While I waited for Hall I tested my ability to appear sane, normal and composed by telephoning the head verger and advising him not to worry when he entered the Cathedral that morning and found that some of the alarms had been switched off. Fortunately bishops are not obliged to explain themselves to vergers. Congratulating myself on the calm manner in which I had delivered this mysterious piece of information, I returned with relief to the task of drinking my tea.

Hall arrived wearing his cassock, a choice of attire which I found helpful; I was certainly in no mood for denim and sandals. When we were seated facing each other across the desk in my study, I did hesitate but only for a moment. Then I cleared my throat and announced: "There's something very wrong with the Cathedral." I sounded as severe and chilly as a nanny much put out by the wilful behaviour of her charge, and just as a nanny might have recommended a large dose of cod-liver oil I added briskly: "It needs to be exorcised."

"Fine," said Hall equably, never batting an eyelid. "I can do that for you. But there's a problem."

"What's that?"

"It's the Cathedral."

"What about it?"

"It's very big."

"Oh."

We paused to ruminate on this curious dialogue. After a moment I opened my mouth but closed it again as I realised I had no idea what to say next. I was out of my depth. Nothing like this had ever happened to me before. Paranormal experiences always happened to someone else, usually to people who were peculiar in some way. One sent in the exorcist—I had been accustomed to use Aelred Peters, a very trustworthy old monk from Starwater Abbey—and he mopped up the mess with the appropriate ritual, the required pastoral care and absolutely no scandal. I took no risks; Father Peters only exorcised places. During the years of my bishopric I had received two requests for the exorcism of people but I had referred both cases to a psychiatrist.

"The difficulty with exorcising the Cathedral," Hall was explaining as I struggled to adjust to this bizarre interview, "is that I'd have to go all the way through it and I'd need enough holy water to fill a small lake. I'm not saying an exorcism couldn't be done, but I certainly couldn't do it before the Cathedral opens for Matins at seven-thirty."

"Then you must do it tonight."

"Fine," said Hall equably again, "but there's always the possibility that an exorcism isn't necessary. Can I start asking some basic questions?"

"Such as?"

"Well, how many people were involved, for example, and what kind of phenomena were experienced—are we talking about a manifestation, a materialisation, the movement of objects, a cold spot, unexplained noises—"

I held up my hand. He stopped. Very politely I enquired: "Can't you just do an exorcism with no questions asked?"

"I could," said Hall equally politely, "but I feel bound to say that in my experience exorcism has a much greater chance of being effective if the exorcist knows not only what he's doing but why he's doing it. If you perform an exorcism with your mind on ice you're descending to the level of superstition, and in the twentieth century that's no longer acceptable."

"Certainly not!" The implication that I might be willing to descend to superstition shocked me into making a new effort to appear *compos mentis.* "Let me make myself clear," I said crisply. "I don't see exorcism—a serious exorcism performed by an experienced priest—as a dabbling in Mumbo-Jumbo. I see it as an aspect of the ministry of healing, and the pastoral after-care is as important as the rite itself. All I'm saying is that in this particular case you can leave the pastoral after-care to me and just focus on performing the rite."

Hall did not argue with me directly. He merely said: "I can certainly perform the rite and I can certainly leave you to attend to the pastoral after-care, but I still have to know what I'm supposed to be exorcising. Then I can tailor the rite accordingly."

"I see." But I found myself becoming muddled. "The problem is that nothing actually happened," I said, "in reality. It was an optical illusion. But because the optical illusion could be classified as a paranormal incident and because it took place in a church, I have to follow this particular procedure. One always has to follow the correct procedures, stick to the rules, respect tradition. There has to be order. There have to be certainties. I can't have any chaos here." It dimly occurred to me that I was no longer sounding like a composed bishop but like a disorientated general dispatched to some unknown front line. "It was an optical illusion," I repeated, sounding very obstinate and more than a little fractious. "That's all you need to know."

"Splendid!" said Hall. "I'm an old hand at sorting out optical illusions. No need for you to worry at all."

I immediately felt so much better that I was able to confess: "If I seem a trifle confused it's because this sort of thing doesn't normally happen to people like me."

"Let me cheer you up by saying that it might not have happened to you at all—by which I mean you might just possibly have misinterpreted the incident. Were there any other witnesses?"

"No, I was alone. And anyway, no one could have seen what I saw."

"Why do you say that? It's perfectly possible for two people to see the same phenomenon."

"But since I was obviously hallucinating—"

"What makes you so sure? You seem very keen to rush to conclusions, Bishop! Shouldn't a former professor be displaying more intellectual rigour?"

I said grandly: "I'm displaying intellectual rigour by insisting on a scientific explanation."

"But there are large areas of human experience which can't be interpreted scientifically because they involve matters which lie beyond the scope of a scientific enquiry. For instance, the key to understanding this experience of yours probably lies in the value and meaning you attach to it, and that's something which lies beyond scientific measurement."

"But if the optical illusion is the result of illness—"

"Okay, since you're so keen on this idea, let's take a closer look at it. Do you normally suffer from hallucinations?"

"No."

"Are you an alcoholic?"

"No."

"Had you nonetheless been drinking steadily for some hours before the experience?"

"No."

"Had you been taking drugs?"

"Don't be absurd!"

"I meant medically prescribed pills which might have reacted sharply with something you ate or drank last night."

"Oh, I see! No."

"Have you been fasting?"

"Not exactly. I did skip lunch yesterday but I had a cooked breakfast. And I had a snack last night."

"Right. We've established that you, a bishop, a man of unimpeachable integrity, stone-cold sober, not taking drugs, not subject to hallucinations, not light-headed through prolonged fasting, saw something so abnormal in your cathedral that you reached for the phone and—despite your extreme caution about the ministry of deliverance—called in an exorcist. What a remarkable case! But I would dispute that this is a hallucination in the conventional sense of a delusion generated by illness, and although you may be under stress I would dispute that you're having a nervous breakdown. You strike me as being baffled, shocked and very anxious but still well in control of yourself."

"You think so?"

"Are you sobbing, screaming, drinking triple-brandies and banging your head against the nearest wall?"

"Not quite."

"Exactly. Now . . . dare I extend my enquiry by asking just what it was you saw?"

I hesitated but not for long. Reassured by his willingness to believe I was not a lunatic, I finally found I could talk about what had happened.

3

"*I HAD* this sudden impulse to pray in the Cathedral," I said. "Never mind why. Jon Darrow had advised me not to go there, but in fact this morning I never even thought of him because this impulse drawing me to the Cathedral was so strong. And if indeed I'd remembered his advice I'm sure I'd have discarded it. I'm not a psychic, as he is. I'd have thought it reasonable to assume that whatever bothered him when he attended Lyle's funeral wouldn't bother me . . . although I confess I did become a trifle disorientated at Evensong the other night. But that was just a passing attack of nerves, inconvenient and embarrassing but not dangerous. Or was it a forerunner of . . . no, never mind that. I must stick to the facts and not indulge in speculation . . . I'm sorry, where was I?"

"You went to the Cathedral—"

"—and as I approached I thought it was looking exceptionally sinister. But I may have been influenced by a nightmare I had just before I woke up. I . . . no, forget that, I'm speculating again. Let's just say I was in a very overwrought state."

"In what way were you very overwrought? Were you breathing hard?"

"No."

"Sweating?"

"No."

"Crying?"

"Good heavens, no!"

"Then why do you insist that you were so overwrought?"

"Last night both my sons arrived home. There'd been a catastrophe in which they were involved and I had to try to help them endure the aftermath. The evening was extremely distressing."

"Did you sleep at all afterwards?"

"For some hours, yes."

"Then I assume your ministrations must have met with some degree of success. Otherwise you'd have been too disturbed to sleep at all."

"True, but—"

"Okay, I accept you were still strained as the result of the evening, but on the other hand you were exhibiting none of the physical symptoms of extreme distress. When you said just now that the Cathedral looked exceptionally sinister, did you mean that the whole landscape had an air of unreality? Did you feel, for instance, that you were moving in a dream?"

"No, I wouldn't put it like that. Everything seemed completely real. Anyway, I reached the Dean's door, I went in, I—"

"You weren't tempted to change your mind and beat a quick retreat?"

"Certainly not! I'm not a coward and I'm not superstitious. I don't believe in—" I tripped on the unutterable word but recovered. Austerely I insisted: "I felt required to pray in the Cathedral. I told myself the eerie atmosphere was entirely the product of my overwrought mind."

"If it had been seriously overwrought I doubt if you could have forced yourself to enter the building. But I do accept that you were tense, strained and uneasy. What happened next?"

"I went to my episcopal throne and began to pray. Almost at once I was aware of an atmosphere which was . . ." I reached for an adjective but found none. "Simultaneously," I said, hurrying on, "the temperature fell sharply and I felt as if I were suffocating. I also wanted to retch. I regret to say that at that point I panicked, moving towards the head of the nave, and I then saw by one of the pillars . . . I then *thought* I saw by one of the pillars . . ." Words finally failed me.

"You knew him?"

"Yes."

"How long has he been dead?"

"Twenty years."

"What did you do?"

"Stopped. Muttered his name."

"Did he answer?"

"Don't be absurd, of course he didn't! He'd vanished in a flash."

"There's no chance that you mistook his identity? No chance that this was a real person you saw and he vanished merely by stepping behind the pillar?"

"I tell you I recognised this man, there was no question of mistaken identity, he was absolutely unmistakable—"

"Okay, what happened next?"

"Then I have to admit I did beat that quick retreat you mentioned a moment ago. In fact it was so quick I didn't even stop to switch the alarms back on."

"I think you made a smart move. If Hamlet had made a quick exit the moment he first saw his father's ghost he might have settled down with Ophelia and lived happily ever after."

The unutterable word had finally been spoken but I was almost too irritated to notice. "I'm sure in normal circumstances I'd laugh at that joke," I said, "but at this particular moment—"

"I assure you I'm speaking seriously. One should never meddle with what Father Darcy used to call 'discarnate shreds of former personalities' unless one's an experienced exorcist."

"But I really can't believe I saw a—" I baulked at the word again. "Yet I know I saw that man who died in 1945. So the question is—"

"Bishop, the important question here is not whether you saw a ghost or not. The important question is why you saw what you thought you did see."

"But—"

"Let's shelve the word 'ghost' for a moment and keep this very simple. There were actually four abnormal things which happened to you in that Cathedral. One: you experienced extreme cold. Two: you felt as if you were suffocating. Three: you felt sick. And four: you saw so clearly that there's no question of mistaken identity a man who died in 1945. I think we can accept as a working hypothesis that all four are related, but the first three events interest me more than the last. That's because although the sighting could have been some form of optical illusion, there was nothing illusory, was there, about the cold, the suffocation and the nausea?"

"Nothing. So what was going on?"

"I'll be quite frank and say I've no idea. But I've no doubts about the correct way forward. We need to stage a reconstruction tonight when the Cathedral's empty again."

"But the light won't be the same—the shadows will be different—"

"Normally that would be important, but I'm much more interested in what you didn't see than what you did."

"And after the reconstruction—"

"Then I believe I'll be in a position to decide whether an exorcism of all or any part of the Cathedral is required . . . What are you planning to do today? And don't, please, even think of giving me the answer: 'Work.' "

"I have to look after my sons. And then there's a friend I have to see at the Staro Arms—"

"I quite understand that you can't ditch your sons, but do please ditch the friend and try and spend the time between now and the reconstruction as quietly as possible."

"Are you saying all that because you think I'm on the brink of going mad?"

"No, I'm saying it because I want you to be in good shape for the reconstruction. The more frazzled you are, the harder it becomes for me to make an accurate diagnosis about what's going on."

"If only I had some idea what this incident's about I'd be less likely to wind up frazzled!"

"The odds are that it ties in with your bereavement in some way. When the mind's been rubbed raw by suffering, it's more susceptible to psychic disturbances in the atmosphere."

"But are you saying . . . No, you can't be! You don't really believe in ghosts, do you?"

" 'Ghost' is just a word, just a symbol for a complicated phenomenon which in the end we can't describe properly because we don't have enough information. But if I believe in the Communion of Saints, departed souls who have found their way after death to God, why shouldn't I also believe in departed souls who have lost their way home and left discarnate shreds of their former personalities here on earth to cause trouble?"

"One concept reflects the doctrine that after death we find eternal life with God," I said, now very austere indeed, "and the other concept is a dualistic fable which embodies an inadequate doctrine of salvation and which is primarily used to explain the mental aberrations of the living."

"Yes, Bishop. Of course I wouldn't presume to argue with you about theology, but you're not a doctor, are you, so I feel entitled to argue that a phrase like 'mental aberration' doesn't even begin to come to grips with the reality you experienced here."

"There was no reality. What I saw was all in my mind."

"What we all see is all in the mind. What comes to the mind via our five senses is popularly known as 'reality,' I agree, but Jung thought the reflections of our unconscious minds could be as much a part of reality as our normal self-censored perception of events. And anyway, surely you're not going to try to tell me that absolute truths are confined to what we can see, touch, taste, hear and smell?"

I drummed up the grace to say: "Touché!" before venturing the comment: "I think what I'm trying to say is that the sort of paranormal incident I experienced this morning belongs to the bottom level of the psyche and can't be said to have any spiritual significance—true reality—whatsoever."

"It's been my experience," said Hall, "that all things can be worked by God into his creative and redemptive purposes, even the most unlikely psychic incidents and paranormal phenomena."

"I'll let you have the last word." Too exhausted for further debate I stood up and began the task of ending the conversation on a practical note. "I'll meet you at seven o'clock tonight by the Dean's door on the north front," I said briskly, "and I'll ask Miss Peabody to make sure no one's arranged to visit the Cathedral after hours. By the way"—I decided it was more than time to remember my pastoral responsibilities—"how's Desmond?"

"Standing by with a box of matches. The Archdeacon's due to deliver the porn this morning."

This seemed a suitably bizarre sentence to end a most bizarre interview. I led the way out of my study into the hall.

4

CHARLEY, FULLY dressed and clean-shaven, was coming down the stairs as we left the study. I saw him hesitate, realise there was no escape and move on reluctantly towards us. After he had greeted Hall he asked politely: "How's Rachel?"

"Gone home. Down here for long?"

"Probably not."

"Too bad. Come and have breakfast with me some day," said Hall surprisingly, "and I'll prove I don't eat Evangelicals on toast. A tame Anglo-Catholic never did anyone any harm and can occasionally even be useful." Without waiting for Charley to reply to this extraordinary speech he added to me: "Until seven, Bishop," and disappeared outside to his car.

"What on earth was that oddball doing here at this hour?" demanded Charley mystified as soon as the front door closed.

"There was a private matter which needed to be discussed." I moved towards the kitchen before adding over my shoulder: "How are you feeling?"

"Terrible. Do you think Father Hall guessed and was being friendly to cheer me up?"

But I was remembering belatedly how I had told Hall that my sons were struggling with the aftermath of a catastrophe, and I realised his off-beat pastoral gesture had not been based on any psychic intuition. Guardedly I said: "Perhaps," and changed the subject. "What are you going to do today?"

Charley followed me into the kitchen and began to fill the electric kettle. "I thought I'd sit in the grounds of Starwater Abbey and try to figure out what on earth I'm supposed to do with myself."

"If you wanted to talk to Jon—"

"I'm sorry, I know you think Father Darrow's a genius who can fix anyone up, but to be honest I've never felt comfortable with him. I always feel he knows too much about me."

"What do you mean?"

"Well, he knows, doesn't he, that I was fathered by a bastard who wrecked my mother, betrayed his ordination vows and gave you hell. He knows I've got a terrible inheritance and my only hope of survival is to model myself on you—a hope which now seems to be in ruins. He knows the whole truth."

Suddenly unable to stand without support I leaned against the door-frame and wiped the sweat from my forehead. At that same moment Charley turned away from the refrigerator after retrieving the milk, saw my expression and nearly dropped the bottle.

"For heaven's sake, Dad, what's the matter?"

I said: "This situation's destroying you, destroying your life. I can't let it go on."

"What on earth do you mean?"

"I've got to tell the truth."

"What truth?"

"The absolute truth. I've got to set you free."

"But—"

"Everything you said just now—everything you said just now—everything you said—" But I could not get the words out, so overwhelmed was I by the thought of what had to be done.

Charley said, trying to help me along: "About Father Darrow knowing the truth?" and suddenly, in a miraculous infusion of strength, the adrenaline started to flow.

I shouted: "It's not the truth! It's a lie! It's an *absolute* lie!" And as I spoke I knew that in that other dimension of reality which I could neither see nor hear, Lyle was exclaiming: "THANKS BE TO GOD!" and willing me to have the guts to go on.

5

"I DID a terrible thing to you," I said to Charley. "I deprived you of your father. But that's all over now, all quite finished, because this is the moment when I give him back." I sank down on the nearest chair. My hands were shaking. My throat was tight. My eyes were hot. But my mind was very clear.

"But Dad—"

"Shut up. Just listen. I lied to you. I fed you a series of half-truths, omissions, evasions and distortions because I'm a jealous man and I didn't want to share you with him, I wanted you all to myself, I wanted you to be my reward—oh God, how utterly revolting all that sounds when it's finally spoken aloud—"

"Dad, honestly there's no need to say any more. If you were to go upstairs and have a little rest—"

"Be quiet. Listen to me, *listen to me,* LISTEN TO ME—"

"All right, all right—"

"Your father was a great man—and he was a *good* man. If you're like him, you can be proud."

"Proud?"

"PROUD!" I shouted. I reached out and pulled him down until he was sitting in the chair next to mine. Then I repeated: "He was a good man."

Charley, who still looked as if he might be witnessing a nervous breakdown, said faintly: "But how can you possibly say he was good when he betrayed his ordination vows like that?"

"He loved your mother. He would never otherwise have betrayed them."

"But surely it was unforgivable! A married priest—all that sin—"

"We have to forgive. We have to forgive because in the end we all need to be forgiven."

"Yes, but—"

"I couldn't forgive him," I said, "and look what it did to us all."

He was silenced. Now indeed I had his full attention. He had realised I was not having a nervous breakdown. He had recognised the ring of truth. Hardly breathing he sat bolt upright on the very edge of his chair.

I said: "After Lyle and I were married I knew she still loved your father. I hated that. I hated him. I suspect too that I had hated him ever since I found out she was his mistress, but I refused to own up to it because good priests don't go around hating people. I told myself I still liked him, I told myself I felt sorry for him, I even told myself I'd forgiven him, but that was all lies. Reality lay quite elsewhere.

"One can't forgive by an act of will in order to affirm one's self-esteem. The power to forgive comes from God, and in this case I made no effort to align my mind with his so that the power could connect and flow. I just aligned my mind with my own ego. I thought: *I* want a reward for all I've been through, *I* want compensation, *I* want to be hero-worshipped by this child—I retreated into a self-centred nest feathered by my jealousy and hatred, but I didn't acknowledge it, couldn't acknowledge it, it was too shaming—and how very easy it is to bury unpalatable truths which we're too ashamed to own.

"Lyle did love me by the time I got back from the war, and once I was more secure I did become more aware that I wasn't lined up right with the past. I began to talk to Jon about Samson. I had to convince us both that I'd forgiven him and that no ambiguous feelings existed, but although I brainwashed myself into believing Samson was just a fading memory, I still wasn't at peace with him. I longed to forget him altogether, but how could I when you were always around? Poor little Charley! I vowed over and over again that I wasn't going to take it out on you . . . But of course I did, in my own convoluted way. I can see that now.

"Lyle saw it clearly at the end. She saw I wasn't behaving like a father to you but like a benign guardian. And why? Because you were the ward who had to be handled with kid gloves so that you never suspected the truth—all my ambiguity, all my hostile feelings—but I did you no favours, did I, because unconsciously you sensed there was a side to me which I was hiding from you and you began to be afraid about what the concealment meant.

"I should have sorted out the mess when you were eighteen, but by that time I'd tied myself up in such a knot that I was incapable of an honest conversation with you on the subject. In fact I had the most dishonest conversation with you; I distorted the truth because I was so afraid you'd turn away from me to him. It was so gratifying for me to be idolised by this dutiful son who shared all my opinions and could hardly wait to follow me into the Church! I thought: I'm not letting go of this, it's owing to me after all I went through, picking up the pieces after that bastard almost wrecked my wife's life.

"When I was thinking those sort of thoughts I forgot that back in 1937 I'd felt called by God to take you on. I should have known that if the call was genuine—as of course it was—I didn't have to carve out a reward for myself; I could trust God to reward me in his own way and in his own time. But the trouble was my jealousy and hatred of Samson cut me off from God in this particular area of my life, and I lost touch with reality.

"Of course your fanatical attempts to make me happy sprang not from hero-worship but from insecurity. You knew things weren't right—and what a script I handed you, didn't I, on your eighteenth birthday, what an appalling role I gave you to play! Signalling that you should reject this villain who had fathered you—underlining the importance of modelling yourself on me—riding roughshod over the person you were in order to convert yourself into the person I wanted you to be . . . It was intolerable. No wonder everything's ended in disaster, but now listen to me, Charley, listen. When I told you Samson was a weak man doomed to make a mess of his life, a moral failure and a blighted individual, I spoke out of hatred, jealousy and self-centredness. How I slandered him! But I'll lie about him no more. I'm going to tell you the truth, the whole truth, the ABSOLUTE TRUTH about this man I've wronged for so long.

"For a start he wasn't weak. He was very strong, as tough as they come, of course he was, he'd overcome a difficult background and worked hard to enjoy a successful career. And he wasn't weak in his personal life either; there was never any suggestion that he and his wife might part, even though they were fundamentally mismatched. Perhaps he felt he had a moral obligation to stay with her after the disaster with Lyle, but whatever he felt, he never finally turned his back on that marriage, and the decision to stay must have required considerable strength of character.

"And so we come to your mother. Charley, he wasn't just a foolish man, going through a crisis of middle age by becoming infatuated with a much younger woman. He was a clever, perceptive, truthful man who had to face the fact that he'd met the right woman fatally late. The solution he devised to this agonising dilemma was the wrong one, but it was *his* decision, his alone, and if you ever face such a dilemma—which God forbid—you might well decide to resolve the problem in a very different way. The tragedy which overtook him wasn't something that can be inherited. It was particular to that man in that particular situation. I must also tell you—and this is hard, but I know Lyle would urge me on—that Samson didn't create the tragedy single-handed. Your mother was a very determined young woman and she wanted him. I can quite see how Samson found her irresistible. I found her irresistible myself.

"So let me repeat: there's no way you can inherit his tragedy. But let me speak up now about what really was there to be inherited—let me speak up at last about all those attractive qualities about which I've been so silent for so long.

"He had great vitality, immense zest, a first-class brain—he had wit and style and charm. He was fun! I did like him at first, and I admired him too. It was true he had a volatile temperament; he could be tactless, hot-tempered and downright rude, but we all have our faults and he was certainly not unaware of his.

"He was a devout Christian—I know I've always referred to him dismissively as a liberal and a Modernist, but in fact he didn't like labels and thought of himself as independent of any Church party. If he often seemed radical it was because his passion for truth led him to explore even the most dubious theological avenues, but what he believed at the end I'm not sure; Lyle said he became more conservative when he was dying. Perhaps he was always at heart conservative but enjoyed shocking the ecclesiastical establishment into rethinking their entrenched views. I believe he would have approved of you being an Evangelical—but he wouldn't have approved of an Evangelical with a narrow mind who paid too much attention to conformity and not enough to intellectual and spiritual adventurousness. He would have wanted you to hold fast to the truth by stepping outside rigid religiosity and being flexible, forward-looking and bold.

"He would have been proud of your gifts for preaching and teaching—those great gifts you've inherited from him. He would have been proud of *you,* and if he'd brought you up you would have been proud of him for being a very gifted man who did a lot of good in his life—no, don't judge him only for his faults! That wouldn't be doing him justice. That wouldn't be right at all."

I paused. I was so exhausted that I had to pray for a final burst of strength but my prayer was immediately answered. I looked straight at Charley and said: "You see what he was really saying in that letter he wrote you? You see how much he cared? He didn't want to upset you further, so he praised me, exonerated your mother and took the blame upon himself. A lesser man would have tried to justify himself and emphasise the claim he had on you, but he didn't want to tear you apart so he put your happiness before your good opinion of him—he did everything right. It was I who messed everything up by putting my welfare before yours.

"So don't waste any more time emulating me. It was Samson who showed the courage while I took the coward's way out, Samson who was self-sacrificing while I was self-centred, Samson who put his faith in truth, no matter how damaging to himself, while I retreated into lies and self-deception. And yet you mustn't waste time trying to emulate him slavishly either. You must accept him and own him—but not in order to copy him; you must accept him and own him in order to be at peace with him and so win the freedom to become yourself. He and I were clergymen for yesterday. You have to be a clergyman for tomorrow—for 'The old order changeth,' " I said with my last ounce of strength, " 'yielding place to new,' and we know that 'All things work together for good to them that love God.' "

I stopped. There was a profound silence. Then I heard myself murmur vaguely as an afterthought: "How strange that the tragic death of a young woman should give me the chance to put right my past mistakes." I could no longer look at him by this time. Levering myself to my feet I took a glass from the cupboard and moved to the sink for water, but my grip was so uncertain that the glass slid from my hands to smash upon the floor.

"Sit down," said Charley. "I'll clear everything up."

"Such a mess—just look at it—how could I have been such a fool—"

"Just sit down. Don't fuss. Don't worry. Leave it all to me."

He found a dustpan and brush. He swept up every fragment of glass. He made some tea and even put a teaspoonful of sugar in my cup as if he were treating the victim of shock. "There, there," he said, stirring the tea for me and sitting down again at my side. "There, there." He lit my cigarette when I was unable to hold my lighter steady.

And then another profound silence began as we struggled to find our bearings in the strange new world we found ourselves inhabiting.

6

AT LAST Charley said: "What a wonderful thing you did, taking me on like that! I used to think it was all easy for you, effortless, a manifestation of divine grace. Now that I know it was blood, sweat and tears and a crucifying ambiguity, I can see just what a hero you are—and better still I can see you're a hero I can be at ease with. All that agony makes you human, makes you somehow digestible—no, I'm sorry, wrong word, that makes you sound like a sort of biscuit, but it's been difficult, you know, having such a hero for a father, and I was always so afraid I'd never measure up, particularly if I took after the person I imagined to be Samson."

I managed to say: "I'm sorry—such terrible mistakes—" but Charley answered: "All that matters is that you've given me the chance to make everything come right."

He poured me some more tea. Then he took one look at my face, fetched the tea-towel from the draining-board and said: "Here, take this, I don't have a handkerchief . . . Damn, is that Michael coming down the stairs?"

It was.

Having used my substitute handkerchief I spread it on the table and carefully examined the picture printed on it of Starbridge Cathedral just as Michael, unshaven and under-dressed, padded groaning into the room.

"Don't slobber over me," he said automatically as I looked up. "I feel terrible. Oh God, isn't there any coffee?"

"Instead of worrying about him slobbering over you," said Charley sharply, "why don't you try slobbering over him?"

"What an obscene suggestion!" He turned to stare at me. "You don't want to be slobbered over, do you?"

"Not particularly."

"What do you mean—'not particularly'! Why don't you just say no?"

"All right. No."

"Why do you sound so unconvincing? Why are you looking at that tea-towel as if you've never seen a picture of Starbridge Cathedral before? Why has no one made coffee? And where the hell's the Alka-Seltzer?"

I staged a modest recovery. Relieved to hear a simple question which required a simple answer I said: "There isn't any left. I've been taking a lot of Alka-Seltzer myself lately."

"Disgusting!" said Michael before drinking a tall glass of water.

Charley began to make coffee. Michael dumped himself in the chair next to mine and helped himself to one of the cigarettes from the packet I had left on the table. I folded the tea-towel into a small square and sat looking at it.

Dimly I realised that this state of companionable hell could be classified as a form of survival.

7

WHEN CHARLEY had finished making the coffee he disappeared in the direction of the lavatory, and as soon as we were alone Michael said: "I've got to go back to London."

I hastened to answer: "It's all right. I didn't expect you to stay."

"But you do see, don't you, why I've got to go back? You never criticised me last night for anything, not even for running away, but I know now I can't leave Marina and Emma-Louise to cope on their own. And we've got to tell the truth to the police."

After a moment's hesitation I said: "If you help the police, perhaps the police will help you. Inquests can be handled discreetly, and I'm sure Holly's family won't want a scandal."

"Even if there is a scandal I've still got to be there with Marina—I can't let my friends down . . . Are you all right?"

"More or less."

"What was that fool going on about just now when he suggested I should slobber over you?"

"He was worried. I'd been a trifle emotional."

"Oh, I see . . . How typical of Charley! He always jumps to the wrong melodramatic conclusion, but I knew straight away you didn't want to be slobbered over. What you want's very simple: you want me to stop messing around and get my act together; you want me to be the best possible television producer because you think that's what God wants and if God wants it, you're happy; you want to be visited occasionally but you don't want to be buttered up by someone who's pretending to be what they're not; you want to play golf with me twice a year, give me dinner in London now and then, and be friendly towards me all the year round. You see? I know exactly what you want. I understand you better than he does." He stood up as Charley returned to the room. "I must get dressed and hit the road."

Charley demanded at once: "Where are you going?" but Michael merely said to me: "You explain," and retreated upstairs.

Having given the required explanation I said to Charley: "Don't feel you have to stay with me. If you want to go to Starwater, just as you planned, I shall be all right."

"That plan was made in another era." He sighed before adding: "I just want to do the right thing but I can't work out what the right thing is. I'd like to help Marina and Emma-Louise, but I don't want to get in Michael's way and muscle in where I'm not wanted. I'd like to stay and look after you but you might not want me fussing around. I'd like to go to Starwater and arrange all that's happened into a pattern I can manage, but I'm afraid of wasting time and being self-indulgent . . . What do you really think I should do?"

"No idea. Only you can decide."

"But what would you do if you were in my shoes?"

"The wrong thing probably. Whatever the wrong thing is."

"But—"

"Charley, you don't need me to tell you what to do. Pray, think, act. Then if you do make the wrong decision at least it won't be for lack of trying to make the right one."

"But if you could give me the tiniest push in the right direction—"

"God knows the right direction. Take the matter up with him and leave me out of it. I'm just an ordinary man who makes mistakes, and besides . . . Think back to when you were eight and went away to prep school for the first time. There came a point when you had to let go of my hand and I had to step back and watch you moving away."

"Like launching a ship."

"Yes, but there's no need for you to look as doomed as the *Titanic!* You're going to stay afloat. And whenever you return to port, you can be sure I'll be waiting on the quay to hear about the voyage."

"Well, if you've got the faith to wait on the quay," said Charley, "I've got the faith to believe I'll stay afloat." And having glanced at his watch he decided he could no longer postpone telephoning his vicar to arrange a day's leave.

I waited, still worrying about him, but when he returned to the kitchen his mind was made up. "I'm going to visit Starwater," he announced, "and cook you dinner afterwards. I don't have to choose between re-arranging my head and looking after you. It's the London scene that I must leave to Michael."

I was so relieved by this sensible decision that I could only say bathetically: "There's some duckling à l'orange in the deep-freeze." A second later I remembered that this gourmet treat had ceased to exist when Harriet, Martin and I had eaten it, but Charley was already declaring that reheated French rubbish wasn't good enough for me and that I had to be fed freshly cooked British steak.

Ten minutes later he set off for the station. He was carrying one of Lyle's string shopping-bags, and inside it was Samson's bland, evasive, unsatisfactory autobiography, reclaimed from its tomb amidst the books bequeathed to Charley long ago, and brought out at last into the light of day.

8

MICHAEL DEPARTED soon afterwards. He said: "No slobbering. Don't die. I'll phone," and trudged outside to his car.

After I had waved him goodbye I decided I needed to be prone for ten minutes, but the moment I lay down on my bed I started thinking about my optical illusion in the Cathedral. I had hoped that by this time I would find it less distressing, but to my dismay I found myself still recoiling in horror from the memory. It was a relief when Malcolm telephoned.

"I can't be with you this morning," he said in the voice of one who bears bad news, and added as I was suppressing a sigh of relief: "Not only do I have to call at Langley Bottom to fuel Desmond's bonfire with you-know-what, but I have to go up to Starrington Magna where a frightful row has broken out about the Maundy service. Apparently the vicar's threatening to wash everyone's feet, and . . ."

I ceased to listen. Eventually he said goodbye and the call ended. Sinking back on my pillows I began to replay in my mind the conversations with my sons.

After a while I got up and went to Lyle's sitting-room. I said to her: "It's all right now. You can rest in peace." Yet still I clung to her. It was so very hard to let go.

I sat mourning her death, my third catastrophe, yet slowly I realised that it looked different, felt different; I realised that it had changed subtly from the last time I had confronted it. This delicate hint of a reshaping reminded me of a passage in a book by Austin Farrer. Moving downstairs to my study I found my copy of *Said or Sung.*

"The skill of the divine potter is an infinite patience of improvisation," I read when I found the right passage. "No sooner has one work gone awry than his fingers are pressing it into the form of another. There is never a moment for the clay, when the potter is not doing something with it. God is never standing back and watching us; his fingers are on us all the time."

I closed the book and thought of Harriet, talking of the creative process. I realised I had never fully understood that passage by Farrer until I had met Harriet—and even then I had only understood it intellectually.

But now I saw with my heart as well as my mind that out of my first catastrophe had come not only my second marriage, which had brought me so much happiness and fulfilment, but the self-knowledge which had enabled me to be a better priest. I also saw that out of my second catastrophe had come my career as a theologian willing and able to speak out with authority on the nature of evil, a career which had ultimately led me to the Starbridge bishopric. Out of both my previous catastrophes had come the radical change which had led to a broader, deeper, richer life, and I had aligned myself with God not by blocking that change but by embracing it.

I knew then that it was again time to embrace radical change. This was the reality which Jon had grasped after Lyle's funeral when he had advised me to assist the redemptive process by aligning my mind with God in prayer. It was no use clinging to the past. That only impeded the creative will of God. I had to have the faith to let go of the past, that much-loved world, in the belief that there would be not only another life to come, but a life as full and rich as God could possibly make it.

I thought of Harriet again. I knew the analogy with the sculptor had now broken down, since the clay, unlike me, was inanimate, unable to assist in the redemptive process, but I was not dismayed. All analogies involving God eventually break down because God can never be wholly encompassed by our limited imaginations, and the breaking down does not mean that the analogy is invalid, only that God is indescribable. So I continued to think of Harriet as I struggled to find the courage to move on, and when I remembered how she had caressed her sculpture, I knew I was being called to believe in a creator who never gave up, a creator who suffered alongside his creation, a creator who was driven by "an indestructible sort of fidelity," by an "insane sort of hope" and above all by the most powerful form of creative love to bring order out of chaos and "make everything come right."

"The old order changeth . . ." I replaced Farrer's book on the shelf and left my study. One had to be active. One had to cooperate with one's maker. I was not just a lump of clay. I was a living, conscious human being.

"The old order changeth . . ." The words were going round and round in my head as I re-entered Lyle's sitting-room. I looked at the sofa and remembered all those hours which I had spent sunk in passive misery as I clung to the past. But those hours were over now. Those times were gone.

I thought of the new order which I could not see and the future which I could not imagine. Then I said to my Creator, just as I had said to him long ago in 1937: " 'Let thy will, not mine, be done.' " And it seemed to me at that moment that some mysterious circle had been completed, and that in this ending was the new beginning which I now had the faith to embrace.

I moved to the exact spot where Lyle had died. I had to wait a moment to summon up all my courage but then I prised my clinging fingers loose from her image and let her go. Aware of the need to mirror this mental act of farewell in a physical movement, I stretched out my clenched fists and opened my hands and held the position for a full minute.

Into my mind came a picture of Lyle, writing in her journal about Julian of Norwich. "All shall be well," Dame Julian had written, "and all shall be well and all manner of thing shall be well . . ."

But it was still terrible to have to say goodbye.

Tears blinded my eyes.

I grieved and grieved.

9

AFTER A while I washed my face and tried to refocus my mind on the present. I thought of Loretta in her pink trouser-suit, but although I felt cheered for a moment, despondency reclaimed me when I remembered she would be on her way to the airport.

Then I thought of Sheila and felt not merely despondent but despairing. I knew that despite Hall's advice I had to see her; I dared not do otherwise, but no matter how hard I tried I found myself unable to frame a speech which was remotely utterable.

Minute after agonising minute crawled by. Then at last, having prayed feverishly for help, grace, salvation—anything which could possibly be on offer from God—I forced myself to set out for the Staro Arms.

XXIV

"I suppose that . . . I felt the need to expel from myself certain evils by condemning them in him . . ."

AUSTIN FARRER
Warden of Keble College, Oxford, 1960–1968
THE BRINK OF MYSTERY

I

ON MY arrival at the Staro Arms I dealt with the inevitable enquiries about my health from the proprietor and quickly toured the public rooms. There was no sign of Sheila, but since I had given her no notice that I intended to call I hardly expected her to be waiting for me downstairs. I observed that although there were several people in the main reception room, the little writing-room beyond was empty. Taking a sheet of hotel stationery from the drawer of one of the desks I wrote: "Any chance of seeing you for a moment? C.A." This seemed a suitably neutral communication. Having sealed the envelope I gave it to the hall porter to deliver to Sheila's room and waited, pretending to study the notice-board which displayed information for visitors to Starbridge. I was still staring at the brochure on the Cathedral when Sheila came downstairs.

She was wearing a brown tweed suit with a mustard-coloured jumper and a row of pearls. As usual she was perfectly made up, perfectly groomed, perfectly composed. Trying not to quail at the sight of her and acutely aware that the receptionist would be listening to every word I uttered I said: "I'm so glad you're here—I was afraid you might be out. Shall we go and sit down?"

This suggestion allowed us to escape to the seclusion of the little writing-room. Sheila settled herself on the window-seat, her back to the cobbled courtyard, while I pulled up a chair so that I could sit facing her. The door was closed. The window was shut. I now no longer had to worry about eavesdroppers but instead I had to fight the feeling that I was locked up in a prison cell with this woman whom I so fervently wished never to see again.

"I apologise for calling on you without warning," I said, "but after making such a hash of our meeting last night I felt too embarrassed to phone. I felt it was best to come here in person to say how sorry I am that I upset you."

Sheila looked bemused by this onslaught of contrition but not, so far as I could tell, annoyed. I ploughed on.

"I've been thinking a lot about our conversation," I said, "and it occurred to me that I was being altogether too unimaginative in considering your plans for the future. I shouldn't have dismissed them so abruptly."

Another pause ensued but again, so far as I could judge, it contained no element of hostility. It seemed that Sheila merely could not make up her mind how to respond.

"Perhaps this is all very offensive to you," I said in desperation. "If you'd prefer to forget our conversation last night—"

"Not at all. I actually found our talk helpful."

"You did?"

"Yes, I was struck by your suggestion that although God might now be coming to my rescue he might not be doing so in quite the way I'd supposed. I even went to Communion this morning at the Cathedral—I hadn't been for months, but I thought I must try and make a new start."

This sounded promising but I did not dare allow myself to hope for too much. Tentatively I said: "The Cathedral didn't remind you too painfully of all you'd lost?"

"It certainly reminded me of all I'd lost. But it also made me feel I'd come home."

My heart sank but I managed to maintain a sympathetic expression.

"So I think I'll definitely go ahead and take a flat here for a few months," she said tranquilly, "but I assure you there's no need for you to be involved with my new life."

I remained silent, not knowing what to say. I could not help but think the last person I wanted in Starbridge was Sheila, reminding me of my appalling lapse, but on the other hand if the only penalty I now had to pay was to see a benign Sheila occasionally, I supposed I could consider myself lucky. However, I did not believe she had abandoned her marriage plans; she had merely shelved them and nothing had been solved.

"Well, of course if you come to Starbridge I'll do everything I can to help," I heard myself say, speaking as warmly as possible to gloss over the negative impression given by the pause, but Sheila had apparently been using the pause to come to some decision and she took no notice of my belated response.

"Charles"—she hesitated but only for a moment—"let's be honest because we're getting nowhere by being exquisitely polite. First of all, I know exactly how you're feeling so there's no need to pretend. I've lived with a clergyman who made that sort of mistake occasionally."

I stared at her. First of all I thought I had misheard. Then I thought I had misunderstood. "You're surely not saying—" I began, but stopped. I had realised that I had neither misunderstood nor misheard.

"I know you won't believe it," she said. "I know Derek's views on sexual licence were as strict as your own and that was one of the reasons why you got on so well, but he had his problems and I not only learnt how to live with them—I learnt how to be a sympathetic friend whom he could trust. So please—don't think of me as a harpy on the make! If you could only trust me as Derek did, then this situation wouldn't be such a nightmare for you."

But by this time I was no longer thinking of myself. I was thinking of my friend Derek, who had crusaded against homosexuality as militantly as I had crusaded against fornication. I was remembering our shared lunches and our shared committee work, our shared views and our shared sense of humour. I thought of our little trips to Lords to see the cricket and to Twickenham to see the rugger and to the London theatres with our wives to see the latest plays by Rattigan. I thought I had known Derek better than any other bishop on the bench. I had thought I had known him almost as well as I knew my old friend Jack Ryder. It was so very painful to realise that I had never truly known him at all.

"Of course he couldn't tell you," said Sheila, reading my thoughts.

I said: "I failed him." And I shielded my eyes for a moment as if the light in the room had suddenly become too bright to bear.

All she said was: "You've guessed what was wrong, haven't you?"

"Now that I know something was wrong it all seems so obvious. But at the time . . . No, it never occurred to me. He seemed so—" But I could not utter the word.

"Normal," said Sheila, and added equally bluntly: "You shouldn't reproach yourself, Charles. Derek wouldn't have reproached you—and he wouldn't have wanted to discuss it with you either. By the time the two of you became friends he was a bishop and his lapses were all in the past. He just wanted to forget about them."

"You're saying that when he became a bishop—"

"He did a bargain with God—well, he didn't put it as crudely as that, but he was just so grateful that he'd been made a bishop in spite of everything that he vowed he'd stay chaste for the rest of his life."

"But he wasn't called to celibacy! We used to talk about it. He always said—"

"I know. It was hard for him to do without sex. But believe me, Charles, he wouldn't have wanted you to know the truth about him. He liked you so much. He wouldn't have wanted to embarrass you in any way."

I felt as if this sentence were a long knife, revolving in my gut. I could not speak.

"I didn't know the truth when I married him, of course," said Sheila casually, rather as if she were discussing a somewhat unsatisfactory purchase at the grocer's, "and he didn't know either, he hadn't faced up to it, I think he thought the problem would go away. We did consummate the marriage, but we never slept together after the first year, it was too awful, we both felt it was better to give up." But she spoke without bitterness, and suddenly I had forgotten Derek. I had finally remembered that every disastrous marriage has two victims and that this was her tragedy as well as his.

"I wasn't really a wife," she said. "I was a business partner in a joint enterprise. That's why I was so devastated by his death. The career was all I had. It made up for not having a normal marriage with children." And still she spoke without bitterness.

"I suppose nowadays we would have got divorced," she added, "but before the war . . . well, you can remember how it was. I stayed not because of my religious beliefs—they were no use to me then, they weren't real, they were just a set of stories I'd acquired in Sunday school—but because I couldn't see how I'd manage if I left him. I had no money and no qualifications, and besides . . . a divorce would have ruined Derek, and I couldn't have lived with the knowledge that I'd destroyed the life he was called to lead."

"But didn't you feel . . ." Again I could not utter the right word.

"Bitter? Resentful? Cheated? Yes, of course. I went through all the inevitable emotions, including a hatred of God, but in the end they burnt themselves out and I just felt sad. He was such a good man, Charles. That's why all my misery eventually vanished. The goodness soaked it up, like blotting-paper."

"Nevertheless—"

"Oh, of course I'm describing a process that took years, and of course the lapses were hard to bear, but when they began to happen my prime emotion was fear, not anger—fear that he'd be found out. However, they didn't happen often and he took great care to be discreet; nothing ever happened in the parish. He used to go to London. Fortunately there was no question of boys, just consenting adults. I couldn't have coped with paedophilia—all those young victims—but as it was I found I coped rather better than he did—he was so slaughtered by guilt afterwards, whereas I took a more pragmatic line. Poor Derek, he was so grateful to me! No doubt that was why we were able to become genuine friends and why he was so very happy when he became a bishop. He wasn't just happy for himself. He was happy for me. Perhaps that vow of chastity was less a bargain with God and more of a thank-offering."

"So his faith in God—"

"—never wavered. Extraordinary, wasn't it? 'It's men who make the rules and decide what are disabilities,' he said, 'but I know God accepts me as I am.' Oh, how angry I used to get! I wanted to slap God in the face for not organising the world so that men like Derek didn't have to suffer so much."

"If you wanted to slap God I suppose that at least means you still believed in him."

"Yes, but he didn't seem to be of any use to me. It was only later that I was able to look back and see that by staying with Derek I'd saved myself as well as him. In the end we had such a fulfilling life that I was able to think: yes, maybe God's been there all along, even when it seemed he was absent . . . And for the first time in my life I became genuinely religious. But it didn't last. After Derek died I began to be angry with God all over again. I resented being left with nothing, not even a child—although it was Derek who most missed not having a family. He so much wanted to be normal."

"You never thought of adoption?"

"We did, but I could never get keen enough. I could have made time for a child of my own, but . . . Perhaps the truth was it took so much strength to survive that marriage that I had no energy left to hanker after motherhood."

"I'm just surprised you did survive."

"Perhaps I did it to spite the Church! I couldn't bear the thought of it breaking us both in two and winning. I remember screaming at Derek once: 'How can you be so forgiving to the Church when it's forced you to suffer in order to be the priest you're clearly meant to be?' but he just said: 'I wouldn't be the priest I am now unless I'd gone through all that.' Oh, and he talked about redemption and all that sort of thing, but I didn't understand, I'm no good at theology. But what I did understand was *him.* He forgave. He'd been through hell and he still suffered from depressions right up to the day he died, but he knew how to forgive and he knew how to love—and he did love me, Charles, although of course I shall always feel sad that he couldn't love me in the way I wanted. And now perhaps you can understand why last Sunday was so wonderful for me: I'd never been to bed with a normal man before. It just seemed such a miracle to be given a glimpse at last of what a normal married life must be like." And still speaking quite without self-pity she added: "I suppose it's all rather pathetic really."

I was just realising with amazement that this brave, honest, vulnerable, resolute, remarkable and even heroic woman was exactly the kind of partner I needed to accompany me through the rest of my life when I heard the door of the writing-room open. I thought: damn!—not the most charitable of reactions, but I was in no mood for an interruption. I had my back to the door, but when I saw Sheila smile I realised that the interloper was known to her.

I swung round abruptly, but the next moment my simple irritation had been replaced by a far more complex range of emotions, for the intruder was none other than the Cathedral's wife-hunting residentiary Canon, Paul Dalton.

2

"AH, I see you've been purloined by the Bishop!" said Paul good-humouredly to Sheila as he moved into the room to join us. "Sorry I'm a little late for that coffee I promised you, but my meeting at the diocesan office took longer than I thought it would . . . will you join us for coffee, Charles?"

Since this was obviously a question which expected the answer no, I said: "Thanks, but I must be off." However, curiosity welded me to my chair. "I didn't realise," I said lightly, so lightly that the words seemed to waft around the room instead of falling into the conversation with a succession of dull thuds, "that you two knew each other."

"Mrs. Preston was at Communion this morning," explained Paul, and added with a little laugh so carefully manufactured that it seemed almost a spontaneous expression of joviality: "I know you think we Canons are pretty slow off the mark sometimes, Charles, but I assure you we do know how to make a visitor feel welcome!"

"I knew Canon Dalton had been at theological college with Derek," said Sheila sedately. "So naturally after the service I introduced myself."

"Naturally." I made some idiotic remark about it being a small world. Then I realised that they were waiting for me to leave so I unglued myself from my chair and bestowed upon Sheila some cliché about keeping in touch. Sheila said simply: "Thanks, Charles. I'm so glad we were able to talk this morning," and after that, since there was apparently nothing left for me to say, I withdrew very thoughtfully to my car.

In the driver's seat I examined the nature of my deliverance. I hardly dared believe that I could have been rescued from such a hell of anxiety, but the more I thought about not only Paul's arrival but Sheila's revelations, the more convinced I became that I was safe. I felt Sheila would no more make trouble for me than she had made trouble for Derek, and besides . . . I was sure I could wholly rely on Paul Dalton to pursue his pipe-dream to its inevitable romantic conclusion.

3

AS THE vastness of my relief became apparent to me, I began to suffer a reaction to all the profound stress I had been enduring. I felt exhausted. I had told the truth to Hall when I said I had slept for some hours the previous night, but I had not slept well and the hours had been few.

I did eventually manage to drive the half-mile back into the Cathedral Close, but even that small journey seemed to consume my remaining strength. I was just wishing fiercely that Lyle was at home to fend off everyone who wanted to see me, when I turned through the gates of the South Canonry and found Charley walking back up the drive to the front door.

I halted the car beside him and wound down my window. "What happened?"

"I realised I'd made the wrong decision—I was acting on the assumption that secretly you didn't want me around. Then I saw the light. Last weekend you didn't want me around because you didn't have the strength to play the benign guardian, but now you don't have to play-act any more, so if you want me to get lost you can just say so. But this morning you didn't say so. Which meant . . . well, anyway here I am. What can I do for you?"

"Protect me from suffragan bishops, archdeacons, chaplains, devoted Cathedral ladies, the entire population of the Close and Miss Peabody. I'm retiring to bed."

"Good decision. Leave everyone to me."

"And I'd better eat something before I enjoy the luxury of passing out."

"Such as?"

"Two poached eggs on toast with a large mug of instant coffee, and make sure the mug doesn't have a picture of the Cathedral on it."

"Black coffee?"

"Show it the milk-jug. And when you deliver all that don't speak to me."

"Okay."

Finally rendered inarticulate by gratitude I parked the car and we went indoors.

4

I DID feel better after eating. After I had put the tray outside the door with a note of thanks, I lay down on my bed and started to think of Derek Preston, the friend who had felt he could look to me for neither help nor sympathy, but it proved too painful to think of him for long. I thought: I shall talk to Jon about him later; Jon will know how best to pray, how best to deal with the pain. So I put all thought of Derek aside and escaped instead into the soothing fantasy that I might run away to London to see Loretta. But of course by this time she had already left. Or had she? Yes, she had; a mad telephone call to Brown's Hotel confirmed that she was no longer registered as a guest; more mad calls to BOAC, TWA and Pan Am confirmed that the morning flights to New York had left on time. At that point the energy received from my dose of caffeine ran out and the desire to sleep became irresistible.

I lay down again and closed my eyes.

5

I SLEPT for a very long time, and when I awoke it was five o'clock in the evening. For a full minute I lay inert and savoured my deliverance from Sheila. Then I remembered my appointment with Lewis Hall at the Cathedral. I also remembered that I had forgotten to ask Miss Peabody to check that there would be no other visitors after hours, so I telephoned the Chapter Clerk myself to make sure that Hall and I would be alone.

"Can't you cancel this meeting with Father Hall?" demanded Charley when I emerged from seclusion at six and told him of my plans.

"I could, but it wouldn't solve anything. This is something I have to do."

Charley put aside the book he had been reading. It was the first book I had ever published, the ruthless rebuttal of the Arian heresy which had made my academic reputation in the 1930s. There was another book on the coffee-table in front of him: Samson's autobiography. Charley placed both books side by side but not touching, and aligned them with the edge of the table.

"I'm not sure I entirely approve of Father Hall," he said.

"I'm not sure I entirely approve of him either, but God isn't always going to work through people whom you and I entirely approve of."

Charley sighed, moved the two books together until they touched, and remarked: "That child of Father Hall's hardly goes to church at all. Maybe she's like me: temperamentally unsuited to Father Hall's brand of Anglo-Catholicism."

"Maybe she is."

Charley placed my book on top of Samson's, straightened the corners so that the books formed a single shape, and said: "It's a pity she's quite so young."

"She'll grow older. Possibly at great speed."

He sat considering this prospect. It seemed to interest him but he made no comment on it. Instead he gathered both books into his arms, stood up and said: "Shall I make you a sandwich before you leave?"

I said I felt this would be a good idea. But as soon as he had gone I thought of the Cathedral and knew I was in no mood for food of any kind.

6

WHEN I reached the north front I saw that Hall was already waiting for me by the Dean's door. He was wearing a black raincoat over his cassock, and as he stood motionless in the shadow of the walls he seemed a sinister figure, as sinister as the Cathedral which was so ferociously floodlit that it seemed to be erupting from the white sward into the pitch-black starless sky.

"How are you feeling?" said Hall casually as if I had complained of suffering from a head-cold.

"Rested. I've just slept for five hours."

"Good. Got the key?"

I handed it over. I can see now that this request was his way of taking control of the scene, but at the time I was merely relieved that I did not have to attempt to fit the key in the lock. I was feeling nervous again.

The door swung open. We stepped inside.

"Turn off all the alarms this time," said Hall, switching on a torch.

My hand travelled down the row of switches, and afterwards we entered the north aisle together.

The floodlighting was streaming through the windows but unlike natural light it was slanting upwards so that the entire floor was in deepest shadow. Hall said at once, "We need to see the nave," so I led the way to the panel which controlled the lights and we spent some minutes working out which switches to pull.

"What about the choir?" I said once we could see down to the great west door.

"No, we'll light the candles there." Hall removed his raincoat. He was wearing his enormous crucifix again, and as soon as I saw it embarrassment displaced my nervousness. I could hardly believe I was creeping around my Cathedral with an exorcist. I pictured Jack Ryder chortling with delight as he concocted an unprintable headline for *The Church Gazette*.

"Don't worry, Bishop," said Hall, uncannily sensing my thoughts. "A twentieth-century professional like me bears as much resemblance to the popular idea of an exorcist as the modern detective bears to Sherlock Holmes—and like the modern detective I find that most of my work is mere routine investigation." Having folded the raincoat into a neat square he placed it on top of the nearest tomb and led the way into the choir.

We both paused to face the altar, I making my customary nod, he indulging in his customary genuflection. Then we lit the candles in the front rows of the choirstalls. He finished his side before I finished mine; I was aware of him walking west to the pulpit steps and staring down the nave. The Cathedral seemed so quiet that I was tempted to think it had recognised his presence and was transfixed by the implied challenge to its will.

"Beautiful, isn't it?" said Hall vaguely as I joined him. "I like the lack of clutter." And when he patted the nearest pillar I was reminded absurdly of a trainer caressing an outstanding race-horse.

I was unable to resist saying: "You don't find it sinister?"

"Do you?"

"Well . . ." Not all the lights were on in the nave and below the level of the floodlighting there was a certain dimness. The candle-lit choir was shadowy. It occurred to me that although there was plenty of light in the building, the effect was uneven, ambivalent, disturbing.

"After your experience this morning," said Hall comfortably, "it would be only natural if the place still seemed slightly out of alignment with normality. Okay, let's begin—I want to know exactly what you did after you arrived."

We retired to the Dean's door. "I came in," I said. "I switched off the appropriate alarms. I went on . . ." We moved into the choir again ". . . and I bowed to the altar, just as I did just now, but that was unnerving because I could barely see the cross. Although I'd lit one of the candles . . ." I moved to the spot ". . . I'd blown it out because the flickering flame reminded me of haunted houses. So the light was poor, but of course the sun was rising all the time and the visibility was improving with every minute that passed."

"Let's just recap a moment," said Hall. "You told me this morning that you found the Cathedral extremely sinister as you approached it. You're now implying that this feeling continued once you were inside. Would you say you were even more ill-at-ease by this time?"

"Yes, I would. I even had the ridiculous notion that someone was watching me. Of course I knew I was alone, but—" I broke off.

"The impression was strong."

"Yes. Obviously what happened was that the image of the cross being almost blotted out by the darkness was triggering superstitious thoughts."

"What's so superstitious about feeling that you were being watched? It's a very common sensation, and for all you knew there might have been an intruder who'd managed to get himself locked in overnight."

"No, I knew rationally that there was no one else there. But I kept picturing the Devil pitter-pattering around in the side-aisles and pausing every now and then to take a peep at me. Obviously I was overwrought."

"For someone overwrought that's a very dainty, discreet version of the Devil you've conjured up! Well-mannered, concerned, anxious not to give you too much of a fright by a direct manifestation—in fact that doesn't sound like the Devil to me at all."

"Doesn't it?"

"It doesn't even sound demonic. More like a disturbed psychic presence who was basically benign . . . What happened next?"

"I pulled myself together by going to my chair and sitting in it." I suited my action to my words.

"Very sensible," said Hall, following me. "You took refuge in one of the most hallowed spots in the Cathedral. And then?"

"I knelt down and got on with the job of working out a prayer-scheme." I sank down on the hassock.

"Were your eyes open or closed?"

"Open while I worked out the scheme."

"May I ask whom you decided to pray for?"

"The Dean and Chapter and all those employed at the Cathedral."

"Did you have any trouble in planning this prayer?"

"None at all. I had the right pattern arranged in no time and was able to embark on the prayer itself. I closed my eyes, opened my mind—and it was then that the trouble began."

"Who exactly were you praying for at that moment?"

"The Dean. It's hard to describe what happened, but my mind resembled a car which had gone into a long skid. Simultaneously—or almost simultaneously, about a second later—I was aware of the temperature falling and I became intensely cold."

"Did you also notice an unusual smell?"

"Are you trying to explain why I wanted to retch?"

"No, I'm just trying to grasp what happened."

"Well, I certainly didn't notice any smell. There's been a recurring problem with the lavatory which was built on the cheap at the back of the sacristy, but—"

"I think we can pass over the Cathedral's sanitation arrangements. Were you holding your cross?"

"No, I had my hands clasped in the conventional position. The stupid thing was that when I panicked I forgot I was wearing a cross and I blundered around trying to find one."

"Let's just walk through those movements."

"I got up from my knees," I said, rising to my feet as I spoke, "and headed for the cross on the altar, but when I remembered that the alarm was on there, I hurried down the length of the choir"—we were both moving west as I spoke—"until I reached the pulpit steps. I had some idea of grabbing a cross from one of the side-chapels, but I never reached the transept. As I glanced down the nave I saw—or thought I saw—watching me intently—" I broke off.

"Are you going to tell me who it was?"

At once I said: "I'd rather not."

"Okay." Hall turned to face the altar. "Let's go back to your prayers for a moment—back to the point where the image of the Dean was at the forefront of your mind. Were you praying in words?"

"I would have done, but I never got that far. The trouble began when I held up the mental image of Aysgarth." I paused, struggling to recall the exact quality of the experience. "The atmosphere seemed to infuse the image with evil," I said at last, "and the next moment the evil seemed to be everywhere. When I felt I was suffocating, the evil seemed to be pouring down my throat. I'm sorry, I know that sounds absurdly melodramatic—"

"The fact that it sounds absurdly melodramatic doesn't mean it's incapable of happening. Bishop, I'm sure you've already thought of this, but could this experience of yours be classified as an example of fragmentation during prayer? I mean," he added, tactfully giving me time to think as he saw the possibility had not occurred to me, "the phenomenon which occurs when the psyche can't cope with the images rising up through the prayer-channel from the unconscious mind."

"But that's an internal dislocation," I said at once. "What I experienced was a dislocation which came from without: the drop in temperature, the thickened atmosphere, the sense of an evil which was quite external to me. Besides, why should Aysgarth cause such a cataclysmic fragmentation? I'll admit he isn't my favourite clergyman in the Church of England, but I can't believe this experience could have been generated by a mere antipathy."

"I agree." By this time we were standing by the episcopal throne again. "Okay, let's set Aysgarth aside for the moment and refocus on this appearance in the nave. There was no question, you said, of mistaken identity. But how good is your eyesight?"

"I need glasses for reading and my distance vision isn't as keen as it used to be, but—"

"—but you were convinced, despite the distance involved and the uncertain light, that you saw this particular man. That suggests you must have known him well."

"My acquaintance with him was actually confined to a few months in 1937, but yes, I did feel afterwards that I knew him better than most people did."

Hall made no comment but stood gazing at the throne for a long moment. Then he said to me: "Sit down here again for a couple of minutes and call out at once if you feel any change in the atmosphere. I'm going to take an exploratory stroll around the nave."

"Don't you want to know the exact spot where the appearance took place?"

"Oh, I'll know that when I get there," said Hall, cool as a confidence trickster, and moved casually away down the choir.

Resuming my place on the throne I clasped my pectoral cross and watched his progress. The Cathedral seemed quieter than ever. Evidently Hall was wearing rubber-soled shoes.

I waited in a state of increasing tension, but I found there was no change in the atmosphere and I was soothed by the fact that Hall, far from performing any embarrassing ritual, was wandering around like a vacuous tourist. I did lean forward to see if some psychic twinge would compel him to stop at the right pillar, but he ambled past it without pausing. It interested me that although so many people were sceptical of psychic powers they were usually always disappointed when a psychic failed to display the magical cognition attributed to him, and certainly I was no exception to this general rule. I was disappointed by Hall's failure. And having admitted my disappointment to myself, I felt greatly irritated by it.

Eventually Hall stopped at the centre of the wide space where the north and south transepts faced one another across the head of the nave. It was the centre of the cross formed by the Cathedral; he was now standing directly under the spire. As I watched he removed his crucifix and suddenly thrust it high above his head. This, obviously, was the start of one of the embarrassing rituals I had dreaded, and at once I looked away, just as I would have done if a friend had committed a faux-pas at some elegant social gathering. However, so gripped was I by curiosity that I almost immediately looked back. Facing west down the nave, Hall was still maintaining his melodramatic pose. Then he lowered his arm, turned to face the north transept and thrust his crucifix upwards again for a further ten seconds. As far as I could see nothing whatsoever happened—and nothing whatsoever happened either when he faced the south transept and repeated the movement. By this time I was wondering what he hoped to prove by this showy behaviour. His antics were so theologically "not the done thing" that I gritted my teeth, but still I found I had to keep watching him.

Finally he turned to face east; he turned to face the Bishop's throne; he turned to face me, and all at once I jumped up as if jerked to my feet. "Stop!" I shouted. "I command you to stop! Stop at once!" My legs were unsteady.

Hall ran towards me and almost before I realised what was happening he was shoving the crucifix into my hand. Speaking with such authority that it never occurred to me not to believe him he said: "It's okay, there's nothing here which can't be put right."

I sank down on my seat again. "Just tell me what on earth's going on."

"Well, for a start I think the ghost was benign. He certainly gave you a tremendous shock, but he didn't try and harm you, did he? He was watching you, you said. That implies interest, maybe even sympathy, but not hostility; if hostility had been present I'm sure there would have been a clear manifestation of it, probably in the form of an aggressive gesture."

"So what you're saying is—"

"I'm saying we have here a presence which is disturbed in the sense of being worried and concerned but not disturbed in the sense of being violent and dangerous. I was just wondering . . . could he have been identifying with you in some special way as you knelt before your episcopal throne?"

I stared at him. "You sound as if you know who he is, but that's impossible, I've told you nothing, given you no clue."

"Well, I could be wrong," said Hall, "but I believe you saw a man of medium height, slim build, between fifty and sixty years of age, straight grey hair, unusual eyes, a wide mouth, not classically handsome but definitely striking in appearance, probably a dynamic personality and a great success in his profession."

By this time I was dumbfounded.

"I remember him well," said Hall. "His photograph was regularly in the papers before the war. My mentor Father Darcy used to say that a priest who courted publicity so relentlessly was bound to come to a sticky end, but as a teenager I was fascinated by that glamorous image and racy reputation." He glanced down the nave. "Second pillar from the end on the left, wasn't it?" he added casually. "He was wearing the traditional frock-coat and gaiters but with no hat to shadow his face, and he was—of course—none other than that legendary Bishop of Starbridge, Dr. Adam Alexander Jardine."

7

WE MUST have been a curious sight: I, the Bishop, rigid with shock on my episcopal throne, and Hall, the exorcist, motionless before me, while around us billowed that haunted Cathedral, writhing beneath the spears of artificial light yet still maintaining its shadowy ambiguity. A long silence passed before I was able to say: "Yes, it was Jardine. And if we were living in another century I'd send you to the stake for witchcraft."

To my astonishment he laughed. "My dear Bishop," he exclaimed, "of course there's a rational explanation! But I suggest that before I give it we adjourn to the choirstalls so that we can sit down together and relax."

I hardly thought that relaxation was a plausible possibility in the circumstances, but I made no attempt to argue with him. Handing him back his crucifix I left my throne with relief and followed him to the bench illuminated by candles on the north side of the choir.

"Before we go any further," said Hall, "let's clear up the question of language or else we'll almost certainly get in a muddle once we start to work out what happened. The problem is that there are two languages which we have to take into account. There's the classical paranormal language in which the word 'ghost' is used, and there's the modern psychological language which talks of a projection from the unconscious mind. But no matter which string of verbal symbols we use, the phenomenon you encountered remains the same: you experienced, very keenly, the presence of a dead man. This was a real experience; there's no doubt that it happened to you. Whether you call it the appearance of a ghost (something external which isn't normally accessible to your senses) or whether you call it a projected image from your unconscious mind (something internal which also isn't normally accessible to your senses) isn't fundamentally important at all."

Realising that I was expected to comment I said dryly: "Thank you for handling the over-educated theologian with kid gloves."

"Let me now peel off the gloves by suggesting that if you can bear to think of the paranormal language as a kind of old-fashioned shorthand which at least has the advantage of brevity, perhaps we can both use the word 'ghost' without cringing."

"Very well, may I now ask you—without cringing—how you could possibly have deciphered the ghost's identity?"

"There were three big clues. The first was the fact that when the paranormal experience began in earnest with the sharp drop in temperature, you were kneeling in front of the Bishop's throne. This was an extraordinary thing to happen because a hallowed place like that wouldn't normally be the scene of an unpleasant experience, and I at once wondered if the disturbance, whatever it was, was somehow rooted in the bishopric. I thought it might have arisen either from your own past experience as a bishop or from the experience of a previous bishop—or both.

"The second clue lay in the fact that you recognised the ghost instantly even though he was some yards away, the light was poor and your distance vision, as you've just admitted, isn't as good as it used to be. How could you be so sure of his identity in those circumstances? The obvious answer was that if he'd been wearing the traditional episcopal uniform—minus the hat, which would have shadowed his features—just a blurred glimpse of his face would have confirmed his identity as a bishop of Starbridge who'd been well known to you.

"The third clue was that you told me he had died in 1945, and I remembered that I'd read the news of Bishop Jardine's death when I was looking forward to being demobbed. I then asked myself if there was any connection between you and Jardine—and there was, wasn't there? Desmond was gossiping to me only the other day about how your wife had once been Mrs. Jardine's companion, and when I recalled what he'd said I was able to theorise that your wife's death might have triggered some difficult memories about her life at the old episcopal palace before the war."

He paused as if hoping for an informative comment, but I merely asked: "End my suspense and tell me how you knew exactly where the ghost appeared."

"You gave the game away. As I toured the nave I noticed you were watching my progress, and when I reached the right pillar you leaned forward to get a better look."

I slumped back on the bench as I savoured my relief that the supernatural intuition had proved to be an example of earthbound common sense, but the next moment I remembered that the other mysteries had yet to be solved. I leant forward again. "So far so good," I said. "But let's now get down to brass tacks. What exactly was it that happened when I made my disastrous attempt to pray?"

"The ghost closed in and a demon erupted."

"Hall, I'm a former professor of divinity. Put your kid gloves on again and—"

"Okay, forget that last sentence. In my opinion what happened was a very unpleasant example of fragmentation during prayer. You said that when you began to pray you 'opened your mind.' That phrase sounds as if you were widening your mind, flinging open the gates, but if I understand you correctly the exact reverse was true; you were opening your mind to God, but to do so you had to narrow the channel of your thoughts in order to concentrate single-mindedly on the first person in your prayer-scheme, and because you were already in an overstrained state, this form of narrowed consciousness wasn't wide enough to contain your emotions—with the result that a rupture followed which allowed chaotic feelings from the unconscious to spill upwards on to the surface of your mind. This unexpected presentation of feelings which you normally suppressed would have been a severe shock to you.

"Now, when people suffer a severe shock, their body temperature drops and they become extremely cold. They can also display symptoms of nausea and find it difficult to breathe. My thesis is—"

"But how do you explain my earlier objection that I felt the disturbance was something external?"

"That would have been an illusion created by your ego, frantically trying to detach itself from this onslaught pouring out of the unconscious mind. You were trying to defend yourself against the danger of further fragmentation by converting the internal disturbance into an external force which could be more easily mastered."

"But why in heaven's name should praying for Aysgarth trigger this gigantic upheaval in my mind?"

"The obvious answer is that there was a link between Aysgarth and Jardine, but if you were vulnerable at that moment the upheaval could well have happened anyway, even if you'd been praying for someone else."

"Maybe I'm being very dense," I said, "but I still don't quite see what was going on. Why was I so vulnerable?"

"Not being able to read your mind like a book, I'm not sure I can answer that question, but it seems fairly clear that for some reason or other you were working yourself into a state about Jardine and this generated great tension. I think that the ghost was present to you as soon as you entered the Cathedral—and was even presenting himself to you as you approached it. He was knocking on the door of your mind, and when you knelt in front of that throne he began not just to knock but to hammer. You fought to keep the door closed, but—"

"The lock broke."

"The lock broke and he got in but you had to get him out straight away—and so you did when you reached the pulpit steps and looked down the nave. At that point you managed to eject the memory from your consciousness by projecting it on to the Cathedral—to the second pillar on the left at the back, which was the spot you happened to be looking at when the projection occurred. As soon as your conscious mind had 'seen' Jardine in this way, the pressure of the ghost on your psyche was eased and—"

"No, it wasn't," I said. "The polluted atmosphere choked me again and I rushed out of the Cathedral."

"Ah, but the polluted atmosphere didn't emanate from the ghost either then or earlier," said Hall. "It emanated from the demon."

8

I LOOKED heavenwards as if hoping for a miraculous infusion of patience and tried hard to conceal my irritation. It seemed wiser to avoid all comment.

"Before we start trying to identify the demon," said Hall hurriedly, "I'd just like to tie up that loose end relating to the ghost. Was there, in fact, a link between Aysgarth and Jardine?"

I can see now that he was trying to calm me down by asking a humdrum question, but at the time I was merely relieved to hear a sentence which could be described as rational. I answered shortly: "Aysgarth was Jardine's protégé. Jardine picked him to be the Archdeacon of Starbridge back in 1937." And as I spoke I was realising that what had linked the two men in my mind was not their professional past but their penchant for young women.

Knowing I could not discuss their shortcomings as priests with Hall I added: "I think I can see now how a prayer about Aysgarth could have opened the door to a powerful memory of Jardine. But what I can't see is why you have to drag in this metaphor of the demon. Isn't it sufficient to say that Jardine's memory, powerful and disturbing as it undoubtedly was, caused the fragmentation, generated the atmosphere of evil and nearly frightened me out of my wits?"

"You want to lay all the blame on the ghost?"

"Well, why not?"

"Because it doesn't make sense. All the evidence suggests the ghost was benign."

"But surely—"

"And all the evidence suggests his appearance allowed a demon to run amok."

"What evidence?" I demanded outraged. "I've never heard such paranormal poppycock in all my life! You've no evidence of a demon whatsoever!"

"Oh yes, I have," said Hall.

9

I HAD no intention of giving him the satisfaction of demanding an explanation; I was extremely cross and had a strong desire to sulk.

"You remember," said Hall after a pause, "what I did after my tour of the nave."

"You mean the moment when you held up your crucifix and revolved like a lighthouse?"

"Yes, I was trying to locate the demon—or if you want me to put that in modern language—"

"Is such a feat possible?"

"I was conducting an experiment to see if the disorder which manifested itself in your earlier experience would manifest itself again."

This sounded more promising. I allowed myself to show a reluctant interest. "But what exactly did you think would happen when you held up the crucifix?"

"If a malign force is present, the crucifix moves—just as a divining rod does when held by someone dowsing for water. But the trouble here," said Hall rapidly before I could begin to look disgusted, "is that in a building like this the psychic forces present are so profuse that it's hard to tell which powers are actually present. The psychic forces themselves are neutral. It's the powers they attract which can be classified as malign and benign."

"You sound like a Gnostic—and coming from a theologian who specialises in the heresies of the Early Church, that's not a compliment. Why are you apparently unable to resist dressing all this up in peculiar language?"

"Because to be quite honest, Bishop, I'm not at all certain you'd like it if I were more direct."

"I can stand anything except this paranormal chit-chat. Now tell me exactly what you were doing and why you were doing it."

"Well, let me start by saying that my prime task, when I walked around the nave, was not to locate the ghost; it was to observe you and your reactions. There's usually a connection, I find, between the viewer and the viewed in paranormal experiences, and the viewer is by no means always an innocent bystander.

"I was particularly intrigued by the conundrum that although the ghost had appeared as a concerned onlooker, showing no desire to harm you in any way, you had nevertheless suffered a most disagreeable experience. This suggested that there was some other serious problem which had to be uncovered. It seemed it was connected with the ghost—or, rather, with Jardine's memory—but rooted elsewhere.

"I thought that you might be able to tell me where to look for this problem—I thought that by watching your reactions I might crack the mystery, but unfortunately the Cathedral's quite the wrong place to attempt that sort of game because the atmosphere's so strong that your reactions mightn't be reliable; for example, you might manifest a fear that had nothing to do with the experience this morning; you're suffering from strain and you could be suggestible." He paused as if waiting for another angry outburst.

But I said: "Go on."

"During my walk around the nave you exhibited no abnormal uneasiness, only a very normal curiosity when I reached the right pillar, so I learnt nothing about your state of mind from that experiment. I then decided to conduct the experiment with the crucifix." He paused again before saying very carefully: "The crucifix reminds the healer that he must be Christ-centred, not self-centred; it protects the sufferer from possible abuse from the healer's ego and encourages humility in the healer. So using the crucifix makes good sense psychologically; it's not just a superstitious left-over from the old days."

"Quite. So you held the crucifix aloft—"

"—and faced north, south and west. Fine. No reaction from you except a certain fidgeting which suggested irritation. But when I turned to face the east—"

"I leapt to my feet and shouted at you like a maniac." I suddenly realised I was feeling sick again.

"Yes, but of course there's an obvious explanation for that," said Hall at once. "You suffered an intellectual revulsion towards what you thought was mere superstitious ritual, and your patience finally snapped."

"But the crucifix leapt in your hand!"

"There's an obvious explanation for that too: your sudden reaction startled me and the crucifix slipped."

There was a silence. In the candlelight we could see each other clearly.

Hall's eyes, sunk deep in their shadowed sockets, seemed hypnotic and as the seconds passed I began to feel he was willing me to trust him. The pressure mounted. Suddenly I said, reverting to the old-fashioned language which I had thought myself too intellectually grand to use: "You found the demon, didn't you? It's not Jardine who's playing host to it and polluting the Cathedral and it's not Aysgarth either. It's me." And as I heard myself utter these insane statements in a calm, reasonable voice, the temperature in the Cathedral once more started to fall.

10

HALL SAID strongly as I began to shudder: "You're going to be well." Leaning forward he grabbed my shoulders and wrenched me to face him. "Listen to me. I'm saying that you're going to be well. I'm saying—"

"Yes, yes, yes," said a voice which sounded absurdly peevish. "I know all that. You can stop trying to hypnotise me." I realised that this voice was mine but it seemed to be acting independently of my mind where another voice was shouting that I wanted to escape. As I clutched the cross on my chest I suddenly became aware of nausea.

"Here," said Hall, reaching out to support me as I lurched to my feet. "Didn't you mention a lavatory at the back of the sacristy?"

I just managed to reach the lavatory before I vomited.

"How sordid!" said my voice to Hall, and when the voice in my head exclaimed the same words I knew the split in my consciousness had healed.

"That's better," said Hall satisfied. "You've stopped shivering. Give the vomiting another go."

"Can't. Nothing more to come up."

But there was.

Anxiety prompted me to say: "I hope this isn't the prelude to a heart attack."

"Shouldn't think so. Got any chest pains?"

"No. But why should I vomit like that?"

"Shock. You'd glimpsed the demon."

"Ah. But not the ghost."

"No, not the ghost. I presume you can normally think about Jardine without being obliged to rush to the lavatory."

"Then what's the demon?"

"One of the emotions his memory arouses in you. It's obvious his memory arouses all sorts of emotions, but this is the one you never normally acknowledge."

"Contempt? Hatred? Jealousy? Resentment? Bitterness? Fear? Anxiety?"

"Well, you're certainly naming the demons, Bishop, but I've a hunch you still haven't hit the jackpot . . . Why isn't there a basin in this place?"

"They didn't bother to put one in. Back in the 1950s Dean Carter was more concerned with expense than hygiene."

"Maybe Aysgarth can tart it up when he's finished with the west front. Here, have a handkerchief to mop yourself up and then sit down while I try to find you some water."

"There's a tap next door in the flower-room." I wandered unsteadily back to the candle-lit choir as Hall went foraging in the tiny chamber, little more than a large cupboard, where the flower-arrangers kept their paraphernalia. He reappeared with a small vase, filled with water which tasted very cold, and one of the robes from the sacristy. I was told that I needed to be kept warm; a moment later I found myself wrapped in a cope of gold and scarlet brocade.

Eventually I managed to say: "Perhaps the demon's guilt. But it can't be."

"Can't it?"

"Not possibly. Not now. I put everything right this morning. I did feel guilty that I hadn't told the truth about Jardine to a certain person but I finally did what had to be done. So why is the demon still around?"

"Maybe there's more to be put right."

"What do you mean?"

"Only you know the answer to that. All I can see is that there was clearly very much more to your relationship with Jardine than is generally supposed, and that there were aspects of that relationship which were demonic."

I said more to myself than to him: "I think I at last see why you keep using the old-fashioned language. By projecting the trouble outwards on to coded symbols, you're protecting me. Once I start looking inwards I can't cope."

"I think you're beginning to cope. If I were to translate that last sentence of mine and say that there were aspects of your relationship with Jardine that were emotionally and spiritually destructive to you and to others, you could cope with that, couldn't you?"

"Yes. Translate some more."

"Let me tell you what happens in this kind of haunting—obsessional fixation—which takes root and flourishes over a long period of time. First of all there's someone who arouses in the sufferer a complex knot of unacceptable and intolerable emotions. Then, by what seems a great stroke of luck, this someone dies. The sufferer feels immense relief, and this illusion that the problem's been solved can last for some time, but after a while more complex feelings develop; it becomes clear that the relationship with the dead man is by no means over, and that there's still much unfinished business remaining on the agenda.

"My theory about what happened to you is that you ignored the unfinished business. You told yourself you could live happily ever after with Jardine's memory—and you may even have convinced yourself you'd succeeded. But you hadn't. You remained very troubled about Jardine. You suppressed your worst feelings about him, you refused to discuss him in depth, you split him off in your mind so that you could refer to him merely as your predecessor or your wife's former employer—maybe you even gave him a private nickname which allowed you to distance yourself from him—but in the end the more you tried to live in peace with him the more at war with him you became. If I describe that situation by saying the demon remained unexorcised and the haunting continued, I'm no longer trying to protect you; it's because I feel the old language gives a much better impression of the torment involved. The modern language doesn't convey the same sense of suffering."

I thought carefully for a moment. Then I said: "Are you saying the ghost's been haunting me for years because I refused to confront him?"

"I'm saying the ghost's been haunting you for years because you *couldn't* confront him. The demon sapped your will and made any confrontation impossible."

"The demon of guilt?"

"That's for you to say."

With difficulty I said: "I wronged him. It was a great injustice that I put right this morning."

"And was that the only injustice waiting to be put right?"

There was a long, long silence. At last I said: "The rest of the injustice can't be put right. He's dead. I can't say to him: 'I'm sorry.' And he can't say to me: 'I forgive you.' "

"Can't he? The demon must be distorting your vision. Think of that ghost who came to meet you here this morning—think how benign he was, how discreet, watchful and concerned! Wasn't he the very opposite of an avenging, unforgiving spirit?"

"Are you suggesting . . . No, I'm sorry, I can't work it out, my brain's finally seized up—"

"An act of forgiveness certainly seems to be required to kill the guilt once and for all," said Hall, "but I don't think we're waiting for the act to be performed by Jardine. From the behaviour of the ghost I'd guess he forgave you long ago when he was still alive."

"But then who has to perform the act of forgiveness?"

"You do."

"Me?" I was stupefied. "But who do I have to forgive?"

"Yourself."

I looked beyond the candles to the darkness of the far side of the choir, and it was as if I were staring straight into the black void of my guilt. I said: "I destroyed that man. I showed him no mercy, no compassion. It was as if I killed him." But when I dragged those words out of my mind as painfully as if they were knives embedded deep in my flesh, I found I could grieve at last for Jardine—who was Samson—who by his failure had become a symbol of my darker self, the self I had no wish to know.

XXV

"I should say that . . . wisdom consisted of two things: knowing how to live, in the most profound and human sense—how to make your life what your life was made for: that was one part of the wisdom. And the other was inseparable from it: to know those truths about yourself, and about the realities surrounding you, which you must know if you are to respond appropriately to the demands of your situation, and so live truly well."

AUSTIN FARRER
Warden of Keble College, Oxford, 1960–1968
A CELEBRATION OF FAITH

I

HALL SAID: "Jardine died of cancer. You couldn't have been responsible for that," but I answered: "I think he died of grief. I forced him into an early retirement. I took away what he valued most. I deprived him of what would have been a source of great joy, a compensation for his suffering. After that he lost all interest in life and never worked again—he never even preached another sermon."

"That was his choice, not yours."

"Yes, but if I hadn't done what I did—"

"And what did *he* do, I wonder, to drive you into taking that action which now makes you feel so guilty? No, don't tell me, I don't need to know. All I need to know is that you're allowing him no responsibility for his life after his enforced retirement. He didn't have to waste it. He could have gone on to a new life."

"Impossible. He was too demoralised, too devastated, and I was to blame."

"You speak with great authority, Bishop, but what makes you so sure you're right? You told me that your acquaintance with Jardine was limited to a few months in 1937, and it's impossible in such a short time to know more than a few facets of a complicated personality. How well did you really know Jardine? And what do you really know about his final years?"

I was too confused to reply.

"Maybe there were other factors which contributed to his inertia," said Hall, "factors you know nothing about. Maybe he suffered from depression—a clinical depression, which would have developed even if the two of you had never met. Maybe he lost his faith—but again, that could have happened without any help from you. Maybe there were events in his extreme past which fatally influenced his later life—but you can hardly blame yourself for events that happened back in the last century. You might have been the catalyst triggering a period of great unhappiness for Jardine, but I doubt very much whether you were the entire cause of his malaise, and I'm quite sure you shouldn't hold yourself responsible just because he apparently never received or sought the medical and spiritual help which could have transformed his final years."

It was only then that I remembered telling Michael that it was Holly's decision, not his, to end her life and that she might still have committed suicide even if she had been involved with someone else. I stared again at the dark side of the choir and thought how odd it was that one could so often see clearly what advice should be given to others even when one was incapable of applying that same advice to oneself.

At last I said: "I was so confused. I knew I had to forgive him, I wanted to forgive him, I was so keen to do the right thing and be a good priest, but somehow the forgiveness never quite happened; the version of it which I produced had no psychological reality."

"Didn't Father Darrow spot this?"

"Oh, he's often talked to me about forgiveness, but the words just bounced off the wall I'd built around Jardine's memory to protect myself from my guilt. I couldn't forgive myself, I see that now, and of course if one can't forgive oneself one can't forgive others." I sat up suddenly. It was as if I were hearing this truth for the first time; it was as if my mind was at last sufficiently uncluttered to allow the words to resonate. I said: "I begin to see—" I broke off, but I was thinking not of Jardine now, but of Aysgarth.

"I don't want to pry into your past," said Hall. "The details are none of my business, but I wonder if you could satisfy my curiosity on one point: why did you accept the Starbridge bishopric when you knew it would mean walking in Jardine's shoes?"

"There were good sound reasons for assuming it was a call from God—and one can't brush aside a call from God because one's squeamish about a man who's been dead for years. And Lyle thought we'd exorcise the past by coming here, but she only thought that because she herself was at peace with it."

"I suppose you convinced yourself you were at peace with it too."

"Yes, but I wasn't. He was waiting for me when I got here. I felt him sometimes, following me, watching me, *making me remember . . .* And when I tried to blot him out he went underground in my unconscious, I can see that now, and got mixed up with my own shadow side. No wonder I started to preach about the evil of sexual sin—of course I was preaching against *him,* the Bishop who had gone wrong—" I broke off again, shocked by the unintended disclosure, but Hall just said:

"I'd guessed."

After a moment I realised the disclosure had set me free to speak frankly so I said: "The person I was really disgusted with was myself. Jardine was just a good man who had made a bad mistake, but I had to see him as an immoral villain in order to justify my part in his destruction—and once I saw him as a villain I was able to project on to him all those weaknesses I hated and feared in myself . . . Had you guessed all that too?"

"Never mind what I had or hadn't guessed. Am I right in thinking your wife's death was like a depth-charge exploding in your unconscious mind where these unhealed emotions about Jardine were hidden?"

"Yes, I began to remember . . . I didn't want to remember but in the end I knew he was there, pressing on my mind. He pressed and he pressed and he pressed, and this morning when I woke—"

"You felt you had to face him."

"It was almost as if I felt he was trying to tell me something. I got up and I looked at the Cathedral and . . . Of course I made some excuse to myself about wanting to pray in it, but the truth was I went there to meet him, he was willing me there, and as soon as I went in he came to meet me. I knew he was there but in the end I couldn't face him—too much unacknowledged guilt—so I went to my throne and tried to blot him out by praying—"

"But as soon as you began to pray—"

"All the barriers collapsed in my mind and I saw the guilt—festering, putrid, rank, unhealed—"

"—which made you flail around for a cross—"

"—for redemption, yes, and deliverance, and *suddenly he was there,* we were face to face at last, but it was too much for me to bear because of the guilt. He must have understood. That was why he vanished at once. He wouldn't have wanted to distress me further. He liked me in 1937. I liked him too in the beginning. It was just that everything became so—"

"Diabolical," said Hall.

"—traumatic. I had such a terrible interview with him at the end when he knew he'd lost her."

"Let me just ask you this: what would have happened if you hadn't acted as you did in 1937?"

I thought of Lyle on the brink of breakdown, of Charley on the brink of abortion, of the bishopric on the brink of scandal and of the Church on the brink of shame. I heard myself say: "There would have been more than one catastrophe."

"And you put an end to all that? Then perhaps Jardine's been trying to thank you, but that demon of yours has been making so much noise you could never hear."

I suddenly saw not the darkness of the far side of the choir but the brightness of the candles which separated me from it. Each flame, small and upright, was intermingling with the darkness in such a way that a pattern of shadows, elaborate and mysterious, fell upon the choirstalls, while the great cross on the high altar glowed like molten gold.

The long haunting had come to an end.

2

"*LOOK AT* it this way," said Hall briskly in his best down-to-earth voice. "There was a mess. You were given the opportunity and the will to salvage something from it, but the job was hard work and you wound up bruised. The bruising wasn't anyone's fault. It was just a painful by-product of a rough process."

"The creative process," I said. "The redemptive process."

"Exactly. I'm sorry, I do realise I'm not telling you anything you don't already know—after all, you're a bishop and a theologian while I'm just an ordinary priest—"

I had to laugh. "Surely not ordinary!"

"—but if I can speak as a healer for a moment, I'd say your prognosis was good. If you can only forgive yourself for surviving the trauma of 1937 while Jardine went under—"

"I forgave myself for surviving a concentration camp. This ought to be child's play in comparison."

"Every act of forgiveness has its own problems, but if you can focus more on your role in redeeming Jardine's tragedy and less on your role in being a fatal catalyst—"

"I just wish I hadn't made such a balls-up of the redemption."

"Are you sure you're not judging yourself too harshly? Maybe you haven't played your part quite as perfectly as you'd wish, but human beings aren't perfect, are they, and an unrealistic obsession with achieving perfection can cause a lot of trouble."

"Perhaps even my imperfections here can in the end be made good." I thought of Charley, set free at last to evolve into the priest he was designed to be, and suddenly I saw that Jardine's tragedy was still being redeemed because the creative process was still at work; only the final pattern of all our completed lives would show the full breadth and depth of the redemption, and now I had to settle for seeing mere fragments of light, through a glass darkly.

I levered myself to my feet.

"Feeling better?" said Hall.

"Much improved." I shed the cope of gold and scarlet brocade and handed it to him. "Put that back while I return the vase."

But Hall took away the vase as well as the cope so I was able to sit down again and think of Charley, whom I had lost but gained. In relinquishing him to Jardine I had given up the doting son who was secretly so fearful of displeasing me; I had given up the self-centred "reward" which I had carved out for myself at his expense. But in giving him up I had saved him, and in saving him I would gain the real Charley, my God-given reward, the son who I knew would make me justly proud.

By the time Hall returned I was reciting aloud to myself: " 'For whosoever will save his life shall lose it: but whosoever will lose his life for my sake, the same shall save it.' "

"You must be feeling better," said Hall. "You're reciting one of your absolute truths."

"Hardly mine." I snuffed out the candle in front of me and added: "Where's that torch of yours?"

He switched it on. We blew out the remaining candles. The Cathedral was finally still.

I said: "He's gone away."

"Yes, but he might still be tempted to come back in a day or two to make sure you're all right. We'll say a mass for him later to provide the necessary reassurance and send him on his journey home."

"You felt his presence here?"

"Of course."

I suddenly realised not only that we had been talking like madmen but that we had been talking like madmen for some time. How could I have conceivably participated in such a demented dialogue? Had I really forgotten my years as a professor at Cambridge? What on earth had happened to my highly trained, rational mind? Drenched in embarrassment I managed to say airily to Hall: "Of course all this is an extended metaphor. My description of going to the Cathedral to meet Jardine was simply an attempt to express my neurosis by the use of poetic imagery. And just now when I uttered the words 'He's gone away' what I was really saying was: 'The oppressive burden of this particular emotional complex has been lifted from my mind'—and when you said you'd felt

Jardine's presence here, what you really meant was 'Your distress arising from this emotional complex was very obvious to me.' "

Hall adopted his politest expression and said with the slightly laboured air of a man employing enormous diplomatic skill: "Well done, Bishop. Splendidly phrased."

I did look at him suspiciously but decided in the end that further comment would be superfluous.

Outside the moon had risen and I knew that beyond the glare of the floodlighting the Close would no longer be the landscape of a nightmare but of a fairytale city, fine-drawn in black and silver. I began to relax, and by the time Hall had locked the Dean's door I felt sufficiently recovered from my embarrassment to say: "I'm most extremely grateful to you. Forgive me for not inviting you back to the South Canonry for a drink after all your hard work, but I must go straight to Starrington Magna to talk to Jon Darrow."

Hall was horrified. "You can't possibly do such a thing!" he said at once. "You've been through a huge emotional and spiritual crisis—you should go to bed for at least twelve hours to recover!"

"Later." I began to plough purposefully across the sward.

"Just a minute," said Hall, hurrying after me. *"Just a minute.* If you seriously think you're fit enough to drive to Starrington, you need to be certified, chloroformed and taken to the nearest mental hospital!"

"Nonsense! I'm all right now."

"But why can't you see Father Darrow tomorrow?"

"Tomorrow may never come. If I went to bed for twelve hours I wouldn't sleep because I'd be so worried that I might die before I've told him that I now understand how to make everything come right in another problem I have."

"Okay, I give up. I'll drive you to Starrington."

"I assure you—"

"Bishop, if you were to crash your car and kill yourself in a wave of exhaustion, how do you think I'd feel?"

I gave in. I was too anxious to see Jon to waste time in argument. Leaving the Cathedral behind us at last, we crossed the lawn to the North Walk where Hall had left his car.

3

AS WE reached the bridge at the end of Eternity Street I saw a telephone kiosk ahead and asked Hall to stop; I had remembered that someone was waiting for me at home, and when I spoke to Charley he was relieved to hear I had acquired a chauffeur. By an enormous feat of self-control he restrained himself from asking all the obvious questions.

The journey continued. Neither Hall nor I spoke. The little car rattled and roared like a bad-tempered mule in an ill-fitting harness, but eventually, as we passed the last street-lamp, we saw the white ribbon of the road curling up the moonlit valley towards the villages of the north. At Starrington Magna the main street was deserted except for the cluster of cars around the pub.

"Drop me at the gates of the Manor," I said. "There's a door in the wall on the other side of the grounds, but that'll be locked."

Hall halted the car, took the torch from the glove compartment and said: "I'll come with you."

"No, you won't. If you came you'd have to hang around outside the cottage because Jon only has one room." I took the torch, and leaving him wreathed in a disapproving silence I set off on my journey through the grounds.

4

THE MOONLIGHT intermingled with the darkness of the woods, just as the candles in the Cathedral had intermingled with the darkness of the choir, and as I saw the extravagantly beautiful pattern that was formed I remembered the opening verses of St. John's Gospel which described the light sent by God to shine in the darkness and guide flawed humanity along the path to eternal life, that mysterious temporal metaphor which embraced redemption and salvation and a mode of being which triumphed over time.

I thought too, as I reached the brink of the dell and saw the chapel shimmering below me in the shadows, that the more flawed one was the more difficult it became not merely to stick to that path but to see it as it unfurled towards that lasting happiness and fulfilment which human beings found so elusive—and indeed a perfect journey, ensured by the perfect alignment of the ego with the inner self where the immanent God dwelt, would have been difficult to imagine if Christ had not been sent to show us the way, yet there he still was, a timeless image, the man who was wholly human yet so God-centred that he was wholly divine, and he was himself the way to that kingdom of values, those absolute truths, which gave all creation meaning.

" 'Strait is the gate, and narrow is the way, which leadeth unto life,' " Christ had said, and as I followed the path which zig-zagged downhill into the dell I thought how my own path through life had twisted and turned during my years as a priest; I thought how I had squeezed through that strait gate only to wander from that narrow way as my damaged self steered me in a multitude of wrong directions, but now I was crawling back, my new self-knowledge forming the compass which guided my return journey.

"High and wide is the gate which leads to self-deception and illusion, but for those seeking truth strait is the gate and narrow the way and brave is the man who can journey there," Jon had said to me long ago in 1937, and now it seemed that 1937 was once more encircling me; I could almost see 1965 running backwards to meet it, because here I was again, on my way to a crucial meeting with Jon, and the narrow way was once more unfolding past his door.

The blinds were drawn so I was unable to see through the windows. Reaching the door I called out to Jon to announce myself, just as I always did before rapping on the panels, and seconds later we were face to face.

I said: "I had to see you. I had to tell you that everything's fallen into place at last and I see what I must do to make a new beginning." And as I moved past him I think I was not entirely surprised—and I was certainly not in the least displeased—to find that Aysgarth was once again sitting by the window.

5

"SORRY TO clutter up your spiritual path," said Aysgarth, hauling himself at once to his feet. "Despite the fact that I had plenty of better things to do this evening, I found I had to come out here and have my hand held. I must be finally going off my head."

Needled into taking the tough line which Aysgarth found so stimulating, Jon said tersely: "Be quiet and sit down."

"But since Charles obviously wants a private audience—"

"If Charles has a vision of a new beginning, it's not impossible that you appear in it. Maybe he has something to say to you." Turning to me he added in a mild voice: "Take your time, Charles, and don't be distracted by Neville's nervous facetiousness. We'll keep a short silence while you sit down and focus your thoughts."

In the pause that followed I was aware of a variety of small sounds—the crackle of burning wood in the grate, the creak of the cupboard door as Jon extracted the folding chair, the ticking of the clock on the shelf above the fireplace—and I found myself more conscious than ever of the room's special serenity. The crucifix over the bed glinted in the soft light from the lamps. The faded colours of the books on either side of the fireplace seemed to flow into each other in the manner of an abstract painting. Even the striped fur of the cat on the hearth merged harmoniously with the muted colours and subtle patterns. I glanced again at my companions. Aysgarth was drawn and tired, the pouches heavy beneath his eyes and the lines deep about his mouth, but Jon, standing with his back to the light, seemed little changed since the day in 1937 when we had first met.

I broke the silence. To Aysgarth I said: "Jon's right. I do have something to say to you. I want to say I'm sorry I've been a bad bishop, not helping you as you deserved, not treating you with sufficient compassion and understanding when you got into difficulties back in 1963, not making any real attempt to repair the damage which made friendship impossible. I'm sure my successor will be a lot more use to you—and a lot more Christian—than I've been."

Aysgarth said blankly to Jon: "What's he talking about?"

Jon said without expression: "Charles has apparently decided to resign the bishopric."

"But he can't do that!" In his stupefaction Aysgarth sounded as outraged as a scientist who had obtained an apparently impossible result in the laboratory. "He must be mad!"

I ignored this unflattering reaction. "There's only one thing more I want to say," I added to him, "and that's this: it's all right about Lyle. I know you regret that incident in 1945 and I do now accept your apology. I'm only sorry I've been so unforgiving for so long."

For the first time I saw Aysgarth, that killer in debate, at a loss for words. In confusion he turned to Jon, but Jon had evidently decided to adopt an iron neutrality; he gave Aysgarth no clue about a possible response.

"I mean what I say," I said in case either of them should be harbouring any doubts.

"Well, don't just sit there like a deaf-mute!" said Aysgarth furiously to Jon. "Open your mouth and tell him!"

"Tell him what?" said Jon, maddeningly obtuse. "Tell him you're grateful to be forgiven for your behaviour in 1945?"

"No, no, no—well, I mean yes, of course I'm grateful—thank you, Charles—but what I meant was you've got to make it clear to him that he can't possibly resign, he's needed, he's the one person who can look after the Chapter as they wait for the new Dean!"

"New Dean?" I shouted.

Aysgarth finally abandoned his attempt to recruit Jon to do his talking for him and said rapidly to me: "I'm resigning. I accept that I've failed at my job and that I'm unfit to run a great cathedral. I'm extremely sorry that I've caused you so much trouble, and I shall pray that after my departure you'll finally be able to establish some peace in the Close at last."

After a pause I said to Jon: "He's offered to resign."

"Yes."

Having confirmed that I had not finally succumbed to the grossest of hallucinations I turned back to Aysgarth and announced: "I refuse to accept your resignation."

"It's not being offered to you," said Aysgarth smartly, recovering a fragment of his debating skill. "Since the deanery is a Crown appointment, the person who must receive my resignation is the Prime Minister."

"I'm still your father-in-God," I said equally smartly, rising to the debate. "I forbid you to resign."

"That still sounds as if you're trying to usurp the power of the Prime Minister! Render unto Caesar the things that are Caesar's!" retorted Aysgarth, now fully recovered.

"Bugger the Prime Minister!" I turned to Jon. "You'll wear that fence out if you sit on it much longer—what's your opinion of all this?"

"I must confess I'm very surprised to hear you advocating buggery, Charles."

It then proved impossible not to laugh. The atmosphere lightened. Finally Jon declared: "You've both made the most splendid progress and I'm no longer ashamed to be in the same room with you!" And he beamed from ear to ear before announcing his intention to make us some tea.

"I've drunk enough of your tea to launch Noah's ark," said Aysgarth pithily. "Is there really nothing else on offer?"

"Since I'm now feeling exceptionally indulgent," said Jon, "and since you both look a trifle exhausted, I shall prescribe some medicinal brandy. Charles, don't dream of refusing it," he added, temporarily releasing me from my promise to abstain and giving the release in an oblique manner which respected the privacy of the confessional. "I know you'll want to refuse but I shall overrule you." He pottered away to the kitchen.

"I suppose it's too much to hope for Rémy Martin," muttered Aysgarth to me, "but I do hope the brandy's not Spanish."

"Fortunately I'm not in the mood to be snobbish."

"On second thoughts neither am I."

We waited. Eventually Jon returned with a tray of three glasses, all barely bigger than thimbles. Each glass contained a very small measure of brown liquid.

"What are we supposed to do with that?" demanded Aysgarth. "Inhale it?"

"Thank you very much, Jon," I said hastily. "A splendid symbolic gesture."

"I'm by no means opposed to alcohol," said Jon severely, "but it has to be drunk at the right time and it must be drunk in moderation. Father Darcy used to say—"

Aysgarth and I both sighed gustily.

Jon was too surprised to complete the sentence.

"If you've got to rattle on about that hero of yours," said Aysgarth, having knocked back his brandy in a single gulp, "tell us how he would have resolved this impasse which Charles and I have apparently reached. Should we both resign? Or should neither of us resign? Or should only one of us resign—and if so, which one should it be?"

Jon staged a quick recovery. "Father Darcy," he said at once, "would without doubt have reminded you both that you're here to serve God, not yourselves—and so the question becomes not simply: what should we do? But: what does God now require of us?"

We all contemplated one another.

Of course no one answered the question.

As Dean Inge once wrote: "The silence of God has always been a great trial to mankind."

6

AS JON sat down again at the table with us I thought how mysticism always streamed forth in a tide of renewal whenever the liberals and the conservatives of the Church had fought themselves to a standstill.

"You should each explain your decision to resign," he said, "so that the other can fully understand it. Then if understanding is present I doubt if discernment will be denied us."

Aysgarth said cautiously: "Shall we toss another coin?"

"Not this time, I think. As your bishop, Charles does have the right to know exactly why you wish to resign."

I said to Aysgarth: "I'm not interested in passing judgement on you. I just want to understand."

Aysgarth fidgeted with his empty glass but I thought he was no longer reluctant to confide; it seemed more likely that he was unable to decide where to start.

"Try revealing to Charles that you've been considering resignation for some time," said Jon at last.

This certainly surprised me. To Aysgarth I exclaimed: "But I always took it for granted that you'd never resign!"

"No, I knew after the mess I'd made of everything in 1963 that I ought to go, but the trouble was that I couldn't see how to do it without upsetting my wife and triggering another of her breakdowns." He lapsed into silence again.

Jon murmured delicately, steering him on: "This could be the moment to explain why your determination to care for her is so powerful. If Charles is fully to understand your story—" But Aysgarth did not wait for the end of this sentence; it seemed he was already of the same opinion.

"A long time ago," he said, looking straight at me with his tired blue eyes, "I did a great wrong to a woman who loved me, and later, at the beginning of my second marriage, I came to understand that by never treating Dido as I'd treated that other woman, I could put everything right. It was atonement—redemption—insanity—call it what you like, but it enabled me to be at peace with myself and continue my work as a clergyman. Indeed I worked much better as a clergyman once I realised I was called to look after Dido and care for her."

There was a pause while he decided what to say next. In the end, adopting a studiously casual voice which masked his feelings, he added: "That was why 1963 was a disaster for me. I lost touch with reality and failed to look after Dido. Of course I can see now I was suffering from years of strain—but I don't want to make excuses for myself, and I don't want you to think I'm complaining about my marriage either. It's the proof that even my most horrific mistakes can be redeemed and transformed into something of value. I have my children and I have a wife who loves me. I'm immensely fortunate and privileged.

"However, having said all that . . . well, it would be foolish, wouldn't it, to pretend my private life's overflowing with unalloyed bliss, particularly when you know about my bouts of hard drinking. Sometimes life's not so easy, but no matter how difficult it is I know I have to do whatever's necessary to make sure Dido's all right. Which is why I'm currently in a slightly tighter corner than usual." He had ceased to look at me and was gazing at the leaping flames in the fireplace.

"He's been a hero, hasn't he, Charles?" said Jon, giving him time to gather strength for the next stage of his explanation. "Standing by that difficult marriage, doing his best not only for his wife but for all those children, toiling away at the Cathedral—"

"Oh, don't drivel on in that sentimental fashion!" interrupted Aysgarth crossly. "What an old Victorian you are sometimes! Of course I'm no hero—think of all the times I've fallen short of my ideals!"

"But think of all the times you've tried to live up to them."

"Well, what on earth's the point of having ideals unless one tries to live up to them? One might as well be a mindless bundle of fur like that cat over there!"

I said hastily before Jon could take offence: "Now that you've set the scene by explaining why Dido's welfare is so crucial to you—" But Aysgarth needed no further prompting.

"Now that I've done that, you can see why I didn't resign in '63," he said. "We were already living on a knife-edge at the time as the result of my mistakes, and she was displaying all the breakdown symptoms: the migraines, the erratic moods, the spending sprees in London . . . I just didn't dare risk depriving her of her home in the Close and her role as the wife of the Dean."

"That role meant a great deal to her, didn't it?" said Jon. "She found it rewarding."

Remembering both Lyle and Sheila I said: "I understand."

"In the end I felt in such a muddle about the whole mess," said Aysgarth, "that I was glad when you ordered me to consult the old magician here. I trotted along in the hope that he'd wave a magic wand, and lo and behold, much to my surprise, he did succeed in helping me to achieve a valuable insight. He started off by asking what meaning could be drawn from the mess I'd made that summer, and I said: 'The only meaning I can see is that I behaved like a stupid old fool who deserved to be defrocked.' Then Jon said: 'Yes, yes, yes, but *why* did you behave in this way, flirting with Harriet March at a cocktail party, commissioning (as a result) a most unsuitable sculpture, quarrelling (in consequence) with your Chapter and your bishop, and indulging (as if all that weren't quite enough) in further behaviour which was utterly *verboten?*'

"Well, naturally I began to drone on about the strain of living with Dido, but Jon just said: 'Quite so. Clearly your private life has its shortcomings. But is your professional life as fulfilling for you as God would wish it to be?' And I was so surprised by that question that I couldn't answer it at all—in fact I'd never even dreamed that such a question could exist. When I was offered the Deanery back in 1957 I just thought: Dean of Starbridge, success, glamour, nice salary, beautiful home, splendid for Dido, perfect for me, the ideal way to serve God to the best of my ability, I'll love every minute of it. But you know, Charles, when I reviewed my position in 1963—aided and abetted by the old magician here—I came to rather a different conclusion.

"The truth is I'm at my best when I'm playing a lone hand and being innovative, and in retrospect I think my biggest success was as Archdeacon of Starbridge—not Alex Jardine's archdeacon, because he resigned so soon after he appointed me, but Ernest Ottershaw's. Bishop Ottershaw hated all administration and gave me carte blanche to do as I thought fit. There was no teamwork involved, just a boss who was perpetually benign. Teamwork was never my style. When I became a canon of Westminster after the war I quickly got bored with working as one of a team, and that boredom should have been a warning to me, but I ignored it. I was too busy with my outside activities: fund-raising, working on my own, being innovative—just up my street. And then came the Starbridge Deanery.

"Well, I was no good, was I? I hadn't the patience to deal with that ill-assorted Chapter and nurse them along so that we all developed into a harmonious team. I found myself restricted on all sides—by the Cathedral statutes, by tradition, by the prejudices of people I didn't like, until it seemed to me that every time I tried to be innovative I met resistance and every time I tried to stick to tradition—keeping Matins, for instance, as the main Sunday service—I met criticism. As for you and I . . . well, we were doomed from the start. Someone said to me once that I can really only work with bishops who are mild and pliable, like Dr. Ottershaw, and perhaps you can really only work with deans who know all about team spirit and 'playing the game.'

"It's a strain being in the wrong job, and the strain was exacerbated because for so long I refused to recognise that the job was wrong for me. It all seemed such a prize—a consolation prize, perhaps, for the difficulties of my private life—and the Cathedral itself was so very beautiful . . ." His voice trailed away. For a long moment he stared down at his clasped hands, and when at last he said simply: "I do so love that Cathedral," I saw his tired eyes shine with tears.

XXVI

"We must put our confidence in truth. *But that doesn't mean sitting back, and waiting for the truth to shine from above, as one might sit back and wait for the day to break. It means following with devoted obedience the truth* we have seen *as true, with an entire confidence in God, that he will correct, clear and redirect our vision, to the perception of a freer and deeper truth. Go with the truth you have, and let it carry you into collision with the hard rocks of fact, and then you'll learn something."*

AUSTIN FARRER
Warden of Keble College, Oxford, 1960–1968
THE END OF MAN

I

"SO AS the result of the disasters of 1963," said Jon, effortlessly taking over the conversation to allow Aysgarth time to recover, "Neville was able for the first time to face up to the fact that he wasn't suited to be Dean of Starbridge. This was a most helpful development because it enabled him to ask himself: 'Can I serve God more effectively elsewhere?' and the possibility of a new life was opened up. However, in spite of the fact that he was willing to contemplate a new life, it became clear to us as we continued to examine the situation that there were insuperable obstacles which prevented him leaving Starbridge at that time. Neville's already mentioned the difficulty of depriving his wife of a life which made her happy and tolerably stable. But that wasn't the only problem."

"I came to see," resumed Aysgarth, having mastered his emotion, "that the other problem was financial. I did think Dido could adjust to a new life, but I saw clearly that it would have to be the right new life—and the right new life would take money to establish and maintain. If Dido had no compelling reason to stay in the provinces she'd have to be either in or near London, and since a smart townhouse in Chelsea was out of the question I knew I'd have to aim for the smartest county nearby. But Surrey's not cheap. I wasn't too worried about getting a job; of course after the mess I'd made I knew I'd no hope of another top post, but I was confident that I could wangle my way on to the pay-roll of some Church organisation in London and do fund-raising. The only trouble was that I had no hope of free accommodation and no capital to use to buy a house."

Recalling Loretta's information I demanded: "What about the legacy from your uncle?"

"Oh, that's all gone! The last of it went to meet some particularly heavy expenses I incurred in 1963. I suppose I should merely be grateful that despite numerous children and an extravagant wife I've managed to avoid bankruptcy, but I really did regret not having the money to leave Starbridge after the 1963 disasters.

"Fortunately for my morale, Jon took a positive attitude, said we should regard this as a useful sign about what I was required to do, and eventually we worked out that because I couldn't afford to do anything except stay where I was, God for some reason was determined that I should remain at the Cathedral. So then the question became: what's so important that I have to remain to do it? And the answer, of course, was—"

"—running the West Front Appeal."

"Exactly! And suddenly I saw an encouraging future; I saw that although I'd made a hash of the job I was being given the chance to redeem it—and by fund-raising, the thing I do really well. For the first time in months I felt happy. I thought: I'll stay in office until the Appeal's wound up and then I'll sweep away in a cloud of glory to some nice little country cottage which Dido can convert into a *Homes and Gardens* dream—exposed beams, chintz, roses growing around the front door—"

"Most alluring," I said politely, repressing a shudder. I knew exactly what I thought of the nouveaux riches who inflicted wall-to-wall carpets and too many bathrooms on houses in Surrey's few unspoilt rural outposts, but now was obviously not the time to complain about the despoliation of my native county. "And where was the money going to come from?"

"That was the big question." Aysgarth began to gaze meditatively at a distant point on the ceiling. "I thought that with Dido's income and my own earnings we could probably live there without inducing chronic dyspepsia in my bank manager, but as I couldn't afford a high rent or mortgage payments I knew I had to have the capital to buy the place outright." After another moment of meditation he turned to Jon and said: "I'm not sure how to phrase the next bit."

Responding to this appeal Jon said carefully: "The spiritual side of Neville's nature said: 'God will provide.' But the secular side—the side formed early in life by his Uncle Willoughby, a gentleman not noted for his spirituality—said: 'God helps those who help themselves.' I'm afraid it was at this juncture that Neville thanked me for accompanying him through the crisis of 1963 and went on his way alone."

"The point to grasp," said Aysgarth hurriedly to me, "is that I did it for my wife. And it wasn't wrong. It was just a little innovative, that's all."

Striving to match Jon's delicacy I said: "Perhaps the most painless way of continuing is just to tell me in one sentence what 'it' was."

"Oh, it was nothing really," said Aysgarth, examining his empty glass as if he had never seen anything quite like it before. "After all, I never even considered embezzlement, larceny or fraudulent conversion. In fact I went to the library and read up all those crimes just to make sure I didn't commit them. The very last thing I wanted was for there to be any little awkwardness as the result of my innovative thinking."

Jon eventually said to break the ear-splitting silence: "You did actually have the power to invest the Appeal money as you thought fit, didn't you, Neville?"

"Certainly I did! The Appeal Fund was a revamped version of the Dean's Fund which I used to control in the old days. The only difference was that I used to put the Dean's Fund money into investments which paid low rates of interest but which were completely safe. With the money from the Appeal Fund, on the other hand, I was rather more . . ."

"Innovative," I said.

"Yes, but legally there was nothing to say I couldn't be as innovative as I liked! The point to grasp, Charles, is that I had *no intent to defraud*—and without that intent there can be no crime. All I aimed to do was invest the money, receive a high return and make sure the ultimate net benefit to the fund was at least as much as the interest the sum would have earned if it had been merely left to moulder on deposit at the bank. Of course I had to follow this procedure several times in order to cream off enough money for myself, but—"

"My dear Stephen!"

"—but the point is *I'm innocent!* I must be! I looked it all up in a book on criminal law!"

"But did it never occur to you that there might be other law books which were relevant to your activities? And how could you be so confident that you'd interpreted the law correctly?"

"Oh, a Balliol man with a first in Greats can always read any text-book and find out what he wants to know in double-quick time! Besides, the idea that only lawyers can understand the law is just a myth put out by the legal profession to make sure their fees don't dry up."

"But what about the law of trusts? What about the law of equity? What about—"

"All that matters," said Aysgarth firmly, "is that at the end of the day—and I'm glad to tell you the sun's just about to set on my activities—the accounts will be straight as a die and we'll all live happily ever after. I've just been living a little riskily for some months, that's all."

Finding myself speechless at this point I turned to Jon who promptly said to Aysgarth in his most austere voice: "I'm sure Charles wants to take a charitable view of your activities, Neville, but you must allow him his moment of horror. Now tell him how you set about manufacturing your cream."

"My first step was to change the accountants as soon as the new financial year started," said Aysgarth rapidly, seizing the chance to shift the discussion from the morality to the mechanics of his manoeuvres. "Possibly I would have changed them anyway—Bob Carey's never been at ease with my innovative style. Anyway I got hold of this nice little firm in London—a one-man show even though there are two names on the letterhead, and the one man himself is an old chum of mine, I met him years ago when I was fund-raising after the war, and I knew I could just say to him: 'Nothing much for you to do here, old boy—just cast a quick eye over the figures once a year, sign your name and leave the rest to me.' He knows my talent for fund-raising, just as he knows a clergyman never commits a crime, so he was quite happy to oblige. I take him out to lunch at the Athenaeum occasionally and send him some good claret at Christmas and he's been happy as a lark, I'm glad to say, right from the start. I never believe in upsetting accountants.

"Well," said Aysgarth, having embarked on a second prolonged examination of his empty glass, "having solved the problem of the accountant—I really couldn't have borne to have Bob Carey breathing down my neck and periodically having hysterics—I then got down to work. I'd dreamed up this marvellous scheme. I knew it was no good turning to the stock-market; I didn't know any broker who would give me the kind of first-class undivided attention which would guarantee success. But I did have a brilliant alternative in mind.

"I decided to play the art-market. Of course it's not a game for the faint-hearted, but if you have an eye for art—which I do—and if you have a clever accomplice with all the right connections—"

"So that's why your friendship with Harriet revived!"

"Wasn't it useful that I'd got to know her in '63? Naturally I thought of her as soon as I realised I needed someone with the inside knowledge to back up my flair. I wasn't fool enough to tell her everything; in those days I didn't quite know how discreet she was, and I didn't want word to leak to the press that the Dean of Starbridge had embarked on—" He paused to concoct an inoffensive phrase.

"A gambling scheme," I said.

"—an innovative investment policy," said Aysgarth imaginatively. "So I told her I had a little money left over from my Uncle Willoughby's legacy and that I wanted to increase it in order to realise my dream of a little country cottage with exposed beams, an inglenook fireplace, roses growing around the door—"

"I'm sure she was enchanted. So with the aid of this glamorous accomplice—"

"—I set out on the road to riches. I must say, it *was* all rather hair-raising, but I loved it, the excitement cheered me up no end, and it was such fun being conspiratorial with Harriet—what a marvellous girl! And quite safe too because she had a lover up in London—well, as a matter of fact I think she had several—so she wasn't going to waste any amorous energy on a battered old wreck like me. We bucketed along and did pretty well until a couple of months ago when I thought for a terrible moment that my flair had led me astray—"

I had to say: "You must have nerves of steel."

"A steel stomach is actually what's required. Harriet got such indigestion she thought she had an ulcer, but we soldiered on, buying and selling with terrific panache, until eventually I had an off-day and fell in love with a Brooking—"

"A what?" I said.

"What a philistine you are, Charles! Are you trying to tell me you've never heard of Brooking's seascapes?"

"I've never heard of them either," said Jon, "but that hardly matters. Go on, Neville. You fell in love with this painting—"

"I should never have let my heart rule my head. I paid too much—prices for a Brooking can range from around nine hundred guineas to over five thousand pounds and it's not always so easy to get it right when one's buying. But now, thank God, there are two Americans fighting to pay a most inflated price for it, so everything's going to fall into place—and once I've set myself straight after this sale I shall have accumulated enough cream to set me on the road to my Surrey cottage. Ideally I'd have liked a little more, but one can't have everything, can one, and since now is obviously the time to quit, I'm willing to call it a day.

"Having told you all this, I'm sure you quite understand, Charles, why I was reluctant to show you the accounts. It wasn't merely that the Brooking looked like being a big disaster. I just thought it kinder not to inform you of my innovative investment policy until we were all set to live happily ever after. After all, why should you too have to suffer from extreme nervous tension as you waited for everything to come right?

"Now, I do realise that a clergyman who takes such scandalous risks is a very depressing problem for a bishop, but let me cheer you up by saying that every cloud has a silver lining and I'm doing great things for that Cathedral! In fact I give you my word that provided you give me time to put everything straight I'll go out in a blaze of fund-raising glory which will enable us to gloss over how innovative I was. My chum the accountant certainly won't be talking, the Chapter will keep mum out of sheer fright and all the people I've dealt with in London will keep mum out of sheer ignorance because they think I've been buying and selling on my own behalf. There'll be no scandal."

I managed to utter three words. They were: "What about Harriet?"

"Oh, we can trust her. I'm sure she's guessed by now that I'm using money from the fund instead of from my private bank account, but she'll want to avoid any scandal which might affect her standing in the art world."

"Such as being charged as an accessory after the fact."

"What fact? I'm innocent!"

"Stephen, my father was a lawyer, my brother is a lawyer, I myself studied law for a short time, and I just can't believe—"

"Well, I'm no lawyer at all," said Jon, "and I wouldn't presume to make any legal judgement on Neville's activities, but nevertheless I can't help wondering who really owns that cream."

"I do," said Aysgarth. "It's my commission."

"Your *what?*" I shouted.

"Commission, Charles. C-O-double M—"

"I was wondering how you were going to square the accounts," murmured Jon, "not to mention the tax authorities."

"But this is the shadiest manoeuvre I've come across in a month of Sundays!" I exclaimed outraged. "Are you seriously trying to tell me—"

"What's so shady about it? Naturally if one invests in the art market, one pays commission to the expert who gives advice on what to buy! And since Harriet's working for no reward other than my devoted affection, all the commission comes to me for advising myself so well. The cream will appear in the accounts as 'commission to art expert' and I fear I shall have to pay tax on it, but the commission won't be illegal, just rather large."

There was another ear-splitting silence. Then suddenly Aysgarth's defences crumbled. Making a gesture of resignation with his hands he said exhausted: "All right, I'll admit it. I still don't think I've done anything illegal, particularly as I have complete power to invest the money in any way I like, but I'll admit the scheme was shady, shifty, reckless and scandalous and I'll admit you have every reason to judge me a rogue, a spiv, a wheeler-dealer and a sharp-shooter who's utterly unfit to be a clergyman. Now pass judgement on me—voice any criticism you choose. I'm sure there's no contemptuous phrase I don't deserve."

But all I said was: " 'Judge not, that ye be not judged.' " And as I spoke that sentence which had been framed so long ago in another language, I felt all my hostility dissolve and knew that the atmosphere in the room had entirely changed.

2

I SAID: "We're all capable under pressure of acting foolishly and taking scandalous risks. How can I be sure that if I'd been in your position I wouldn't have done as much for Lyle as you've done for Dido?"

"I somehow can't imagine you ever acting foolishly and taking scandalous risks—"

"Maybe imagination's not your strong point. Or maybe my imagination's just better than yours is. Certainly if I attempt now to put myself in your shoes I can see exactly what a nightmare the past few months must have been."

Aysgarth said to Jon: "Tell him I'm not asking for sympathy."

"This is empathy, not sympathy. Go on, Charles."

"You've made a good story out of this nightmare," I said to Aysgarth. "You've made it sound exciting and amusing, but the truth is that for months you've had to live with the knowledge that you were within an ace of ruining yourself, wrecking your wife and plunging the Church into scandal—and as if all that weren't enough to beat a man to his knees, you've finally had to endure this humiliating confession to me. No wonder you're trying to resign! You've reached the point where you're willing to do anything to end such an ordeal, but don't think I don't understand what you've been through and don't think I feel no responsibility for what you've suffered. I should never have washed my hands of you so completely after the disasters of 1963. I should never have treated you with such anger and contempt and turned my back. That wasn't following in the footsteps of Jesus Christ. That was following in the footsteps of Pontius Pilate."

Aysgarth's expression changed. Indeed his whole face seemed to change until I could look at him and see again the strait-laced, devout young Archdeacon, reserved and solemn, whom I had first met long ago at Jon's wedding. All the trappings of sophistication which he had acquired during his journey up the ladder of worldly success—the easy charm, the racy manner, the air of impregnable self-confidence—all disappeared. I was reminded of the moment at the end of a Greek tragedy when the hero lays aside his golden mask and reveals himself in all his vulnerability as an ordinary, fragile, suffering human being.

"I know you're sorry for it all," I said. "I know you'd far rather lead a life which is more in tune with the man you truly are. Finish the last appalling manoeuvre, present the accounts, consider the matter closed, go your way and don't punish yourself like this any more."

A stillness descended upon the room, and in the heart of that stillness was something beyond the power of mere language to describe. I felt we were being given a glimpse of the underlying unity of all things, and that this harmony—though no metaphor was adequate to describe that singing silence—was enfolding us so that we were wholly in tune not only with one another but with a healing presence at the very centre of our being. My tension was smoothed away and my aching muscles relaxed. Jon crossed himself. Aysgarth, slumping back in his chair, closed his eyes as if suddenly released from pain.

The moment passed, but I thought of the disciples on the road to Emmaus and how they had recognised the stranger in the breaking of the bread.

Finally Aysgarth levered himself to his feet, muttered an excuse and withdrew to the bathroom. Neither Jon nor I made any attempt to break the silence which followed. When Aysgarth returned he was chalk-white but his mask of insouciance was firmly in place again.

"So!" he said dryly, resuming his seat at the table. "Despite the Bishop's admirable display of Christian charity the Dean has presented the unanswerable case for his resignation! Your move now, my lord."

I prayed for the courage to speak nothing but the truth.

3

"HOW STRANGE that you weren't happy in your job," I said to Aysgarth. "I wasn't happy in mine. You said your biggest success was as Archdeacon of Starbridge, and mine, I now think, was as Lyttelton Professor of Divinity. I still feel I was right to believe God was calling me to Starbridge, but I just wasn't up to the task of responding to the call in the right way.

"I'm sure I was given this rich, powerful bishopric so that I could stand up for conservative values with the maximum effect; Jon talked the other day about how both the conservatives and the liberals need to be strong if the Church is to progress properly and not become seriously unbalanced, and since this is obviously the decade of the liberals it was all the more important that someone influential should be around to push the conservative line, but what's happened here in Starbridge? I've been debilitated by unresolved conflicts with the result that I've lost my way. I've become not a conservative bishop, concerned with truth and tradition, but a parody of a conservative bishop, concerned with making an idol of the past and tailoring the truth to fit it.

"What a disaster! I knew from the beginning that something was wrong—it was like pedalling a bicycle uphill with the brakes on—but I blamed the job and not the unresolved conflicts which were sapping my spiritual energy. I missed Cambridge. I felt lost, disorientated, lonely—yet there was hardly ever the chance to be alone, life was so busy, there was so much work to be done, so many problems to solve . . . It was a nightmare, and at first I didn't see how I was ever going to adjust.

"Lyle was very concerned. I suppose that was when she made her heroic decision to sacrifice her own welfare to the task of keeping me going. If I hadn't had Lyle, I couldn't have gone on. That's the big difference between us, Stephen. The difference isn't that you're capable of hard drinking and behaving foolishly with women. I'm just as capable of making those sort of mistakes as you are. The real difference is that I couldn't have survived if I'd had a wife who was a burden instead of a source of strength.

"How have you done it? How could you ever have survived? That demanding job, those unrelenting pressures, the terrible isolation one has to endure as the man at the top of a large organisational pyramid—so little time to *think,* to be alone with God, to be oneself . . . You must have tremendous reserves of spiritual strength—and how can I avoid the conclusion that God's constantly replenishing them, recognising your courage and pouring out his grace so that you can sustain this tour de force? No, don't attempt a denial, spare me the false modesty—"

"You're not so short on false modesty yourself—a lesser man would have given up and run back to Cambridge!"

"I nearly did. I would have done if Lyle hadn't assumed the roles of nanny, nurse and private secretary in order to keep me going."

"Let's not forget the distinction," murmured Jon, "between false modesty, which implies neither a truthful approach nor repentance, and humility, which implies both. Very well, Charles, go on. Under pressure you regressed in your domestic life to the helplessness of childhood—"

"—and allowed Lyle to sacrifice herself until her whole life was spent propping me up. I suspect a lot of men condone this sort of response when they have demanding jobs, but how sad it is for the marriages and what an unfair burden it places on their wives."

"You're exaggerating all this," objected Aysgarth. "I'd say Lyle still got plenty of enjoyment out of being Mrs. Bishop."

"Being Mrs. Bishop was fine. It was being Mrs. Ashworth which was obviously the problem—not that I realised at the time. I was too self-centred. I was too self-centred in my job too. I never really had much time for the flock—as I said to Malcolm recently, my pastoral ministry was eclipsed by my prophetic ministry; I was too ready to pass judgement, too reluctant to exercise compassion, too blind to be imaginative and understanding . . . as you know, all too well.

"And I can't close this analysis of my failures without telling you, Stephen, that since Lyle's death it's been painfully obvious to me that I'm not only unable but unfit to be a bishop. I've been drinking too much. I've got involved with a woman to a degree which can only be described as insane. I can't think, I can't work, I can't cope, I'm useless. I've failed God here. All I can do now, it seems to me, to help him redeem this disaster, is to leave as soon as possible, retire to Cambridge and devote myself to scholarship—provided, of course, that by this time I'm not intellectually over the hill and capable only of embarrassing my publishers."

I stopped. I looked at Jon but his expression was inscrutable. I turned to Aysgarth. "Well, there you have it," I said flatly. "An admission of failure and inadequacy which leaves me no alternative but to resign. I rest my case."

Aysgarth said brutally: "I've never heard such a load of balls from a bishop in all my life. Jon, give us some more brandy."

4

JON RAISED an eyebrow but withdrew without a word to the kitchen to retrieve the bottle. When our glasses had been refilled Aysgarth said to me: "You mentioned at the beginning—before you spewed out all that rubbish at the end—that you still believe God wanted you in Starbridge but the problem was that you hadn't been able to realise your full potential. Well, I don't believe God ever wanted me to come to Starbridge. I should have stayed in London and developed my gift for fund-raising by working for some large Christian organisation."

"That's something only you can know. But speaking for myself, as I recall the last eight years of my bishopric—"

"Forget the past eight years, Charles. That was just the rehearsal. This is where your bishopric really begins."

I stared at him. "How do you manage to come to such an irrational conclusion?"

Aysgarth enquired of Jon with deceptive mildness: "Is there anything to beat the sheer intellectual arrogance of a professor from the ivory towers?"

"I'm sorry," I said hastily, "I withdraw the word 'irrational.' "

"No need—simply apply it to yourself! You've delivered yourself of this dramatic and detestably gloomy argument for your resignation but it's all based on a false premise."

"It can't be."

"Try a little humility, Charles," said Jon. "Say to Neville civilly, amiably: 'Please can you tell me what the false premise is? I'm afraid I don't follow your line of argument.' "

I took a deep breath. "Please can you—"

"It's the premise that you're weak—so weak that without Lyle you're unfit for life in the real world and can only survive by locking yourself up in Cambridge with a lot of books on the Early Church. Can't you really see that by some process which I can't begin to imagine you've now been granted the enlightenment which will make you strong—strong enough to fulfil that potential of yours and be exactly the Bishop you're supposed to be?" Turning to Jon he demanded mystified: "Obviously Charles has been granted the strength and the guts to see all his faults in the light of truth, but why does he have to botch up this useful revelation by screaming that he's too weak to do anything but commit professional suicide?"

"I didn't scream. I simply said—"

"When I first met Charles in 1937," said Jon to Aysgarth, "he had a very poor opinion of his own worth. He did become more realistic about himself, but every so often, when he's under acute stress, this poor opinion surfaces and clouds his judgement."

"Are you trying to tell me he has an inferiority complex? *Charles?* The man who's always the last word in public-school self-confidence?"

"It all goes back to my relationship with my father," I said. "He—"

"Say no more!" said Aysgarth. "I know all about parents—and uncles—who mean well but cause havoc. Now Charles, be sensible for a moment. The loss of a spouse can be the most traumatic event. Of course you're going to knock back the whisky for a while until you claw your way back onto an even keel! And as for that woman you mentioned—well, no matter how far you went (if indeed you went any distance whatsoever) you should be reminded that it takes two to tango, and if the lady took advantage of you when you were in a desperate state, I don't think you should flagellate yourself too hard about what happened (if indeed anything *verboten* happened at all). Don't be so hard on yourself! Your whole life's been smashed up—do you really think you can sail breezily along with only a slight wobble or two to hint that you've suffered rather more than a minor inconvenience?"

"In other words," said Jon, "he's forgivable."

"Of course he is! Charles, try to get it into your head that you're only human. You're not a cardboard hero out of *Boy's Own* and you're not a marble statue on top of a plinth marked BISHOP. You're a bereaved man and you should be allowed to behave like one. Being overwhelmed by bereavement doesn't mean you're weak and unworthy, just as failing to be a perfect bishop doesn't mean you're an episcopal write-off. You're not required to be a superhuman ecclesiastical robot! All God requires is that you should be you!"

"Well spoken, Neville!" exclaimed Jon.

"To say to yourself: 'I'm weak and worthless,' " pursued Aysgarth, "is the false modesty of Uriah Heep. To speak the truth—and achieve true humility—you should say to yourself instead: 'Yes, I've been through hell and I've made some humiliating mistakes, but at least I've got the brains and the guts to pull myself up by my bootstraps now and serve God much better than before.' "

Instantly I suffered a Pavlovian reaction to this theologically careless statement that salvation could be achieved by a mere act of will. Like an automaton I declared: "That's the Pelagian heresy."

My companions looked at each other. Aysgarth said to Jon: "He's getting better!" and Jon said to Aysgarth: "I detect signs of recovery!" They both spoke at almost the same moment.

Clinging to my theology as a child clings to a blanket which symbolises security, I began: "St. Augustine—" but was interrupted.

"Your difficulty at the moment," said Aysgarth kindly, "is that as you're hanging on the cross all you can see is the dark. But don't forget that we look back on Good Friday in the light of Easter Day."

"The light and the dark intermingle to form the pattern of redemption and salvation," said Jon. "The dark doesn't become less terrible but that pattern which the light makes upon it contains the meaning which will redeem the suffering."

But Aysgarth was still pursuing his own line of thought. "During one of my own Good Fridays," he said, "Jon told me that when a man gets to the spiritual crossroads, he can either turn aside and go in a completely different direction, or he can go on but in a completely different way.

You could go back to Cambridge, Charles, but where would the meaning lie in that decision? You'd have a comfortable life, no doubt, but how well could you live with the knowledge that you'd never given yourself the chance to repair the flaws in your bishopric and put everything right? It seems clear to me that although we both now stand at the crossroads, we're being called to take different paths: I'm to turn aside and do something new; you're to go on but in a revitalised, resurrected way."

We were silent in that quiet room. Only the ticking clock reminded us that we were embedded in the temporal world as we struggled to interact with our Creator in eternity, and only the cross above Jon's bed reassured us that such interaction was possible. No darkness was so impenetrable that it could not be pierced by light and transformed. I thought of Harriet's hands touching the ugly mass of clay which she would transform into a statement of beauty and truth. The clay would still be clay but she would have created the pattern which gave it meaning, and in that pattern every one of her costly creative steps would be redeemed.

At last Aysgarth, my companion, my fellow-traveller, my mirror-image whom I had failed to recognise for so long—Aysgarth said to me as one old friend to another: "What are you thinking?"

And still grieving for Lyle, still confused about the future, still spiritually bruised, emotionally drained and physically exhausted after my difficult birth into a new life, I was nonetheless able to say: " 'All things work together for good to them that love God.' "

5

AYSGARTH EXCLAIMED: "The old magician here must have reminded you of that quotation just now! I was reminded of it too when he talked of the *intermingling* of the dark and the light."

"Am I allowed to be human for once?" said Jon crossly. "Am I allowed to thwart your repeated attempts to turn me into a shady psychic? Am I allowed a moment of anger? Am I allowed to say how very much I dislike being referred to as an 'old magician' and an 'old pirate'?"

"I'll always think of you as an ecclesiastical buccaneer with an over-developed taste for magic," said Aysgarth fondly. "When I remember how you bounded around back in the forties during that appalling ministry of healing—"

Hastily I interrupted: "Why did you put that heavy emphasis on 'intermingling,' and how does it link up with that sentence I quoted from Romans?"

"The correct translation of that passage is actually: 'All things intermingle for good to them that love God.' I know you think I'm a rotten theologian, Charles, but at least my New Testament Greek is sound."

I flexed my memory to recall the verb under discussion. "But what's the point of the alternative translation?"

"It gives a better impression of synergy—the process where two different things are put together and make something quite new. If you just say: 'All things work together for good'—as if the good and the bad are all stirred together like the ingredients of a cake which later emerges from the oven smelling wonderful—then the man who's dying of cancer will want to punch you on the jaw because he knows damned well you're understating his pain and playing fast and loose with the reality of his suffering by implying that his disease is in the end a good thing. But if you say: 'All things intermingle for good,' you're implying that the good and the bad remain quite distinct. There's no question of well-mixed cake ingredients which emerge from the oven smelling wonderful. The bad really is terrible and the good may seem powerless against that terrible reality, but when the good and the bad intermingle—not merge but intermingle—"

"They form a pattern," said Jon, "as I pointed out a moment ago. The darkness doesn't become less dark, but that pattern which the light makes upon it contains the meaning which makes the darkness endurable. Do you remember telling me, Charles, that when you were a POW you found that human beings could endure almost anything so long as they believed their suffering had meaning? What they couldn't endure was the possibility that there was no meaning which would allow the suffering to be redeemed."

"Talking of redemption," I said, struggling to my feet, "it's time I took an active part in the redemptive process again instead of sitting around on my bottom and feeling demoralised. I'm going to pull myself up by my bootstraps, and—"

"Do I hear the Pelagian heresy?" interrupted Aysgarth at once, greatly entertained.

"Heavens above, I must be going senile! What I meant, of course, was that by the grace of God—"

"I think you can rely on us to know what you meant!" interrupted Jon amused as he and Aysgarth also rose to their feet. But ending the meeting on a more sober note he added: "You meant that your new knowledge has given you new power, the pattern of redemption is now clearer to you, and your recent suffering will be given meaning by the new life which begins for you today."

We stood there in our ecclesiastical triangle, the conservative, the liberal and the mystic—the Catholic, the Protestant and the churchman from the Middle Way—three strands of one tradition forming a single band of light, and then as if we all became aware of our final creative alignment at exactly the same moment, we reached out to clasp one another's hands.

XXVII

"To enter into God's plan for us is to be most sovereignly ourselves; it is through giving us the power and courage to be ourselves that he fulfills his purpose in us . . ."

AUSTIN FARRER
Warden of Keble College, Oxford,
1960–1968
THE BRINK OF MYSTERY

"What is the supreme motive of a truth-seeking mind? Is it to explode shams, or to acknowledge realities? After the detection of shams, the clarification of argument, and the sifting of evidence—after all criticism, all analysis—a man must make up his mind what there is most worthy of love, and most binding on conduct, in the world of real existence. It is this decision, or this discovery, that is the supreme exercise of a truth-seeking intelligence."

AUSTIN FARRER
THE END OF MAN

I

I HAVE now reached the theological end of my memoir; I have written paradigmatically on the ontological, teleological and soteriological nature of the twentieth-century Church of England by employing the tool of Hegelian dialectic: the thesis and antithesis (I myself and Aysgarth) had clashed to produce (with the aid of Jon, the channel for the Holy Spirit) the synthesis which embodied both the substance of the Church, its ongoing purpose and its painful but not entirely unsuccessful journey towards salvation. However, since I am writing not just as a theologian but as a human being I shall end my memoir on quite another note. ("Thank God!" would no doubt be the reaction of many after reading this paragraph.)

Aysgarth and I eventually left the cottage and walked together through the woods to the house. He had left his car in the forecourt, and it was here that we shook hands before parting. My last words to him were: "I shall tell Nigel and Malcolm that I'm bound by the rules of the confessional, but don't keep us waiting too long for the accounts or they'll start to worry about what on earth it was you confessed."

Needless to say, Aysgarth, that incorrigible gambler, merely declared that the trumps were all there, waiting to be turned up. I sighed, envying him his nerves of steel, and walked away down the drive.

Outside the gates I found my chauffeur sunk in a torpor behind the wheel of his Volkswagen. As I scrambled into the passenger seat I asked: "Were you sleeping?" and he answered: "No, praying"—a response which certainly put me in my place and reminded me that even renewed bishops (perhaps especially renewed bishops) needed to be prayed for. Then he said suddenly: "It's all right now, isn't it?" and I told him that it was.

We drove back to Starbridge, and as he halted the car outside the South Canonry he said: "I think we should meet again at the Cathedral at the same time tomorrow. It's not necessary for me to go through the whole building with holy water, but I'd still like to celebrate mass on the exact spot where the ghost appeared."

I was not at all sure I approved of this very Romish proposal and I was quite sure I did not approve of my optical illusion being treated as an objective reality, but I did my best to be polite. "That's an interesting suggestion," I said. "But if you're merely proposing the mass as a psychological exercise to set my mind at rest, I assure you—"

"The mass is never just a psychological exercise to set the mind at rest! Really, Bishop, whatever are you going to come out with next?"

I reminded myself what an enormous help he had been to me in my hour of need and redoubled my efforts to be tactful. "Very well," I said soothingly, "we'll do whatever you think's best. I certainly don't want to have any more optical illusions."

"I'm sure the ghost doesn't want you to have any more optical illusions either," said Hall. "I'm sure he'd much rather rest in peace than flash upon the retina of your psychic eye."

"Quite so," I said kindly. After all, even an exorcist must be allowed his little joke, but I was unable to stop myself adding: "Now why don't you just translate that last sentence into the other language?"

"There's no translation."

I was still boggling at him when the front door of the South Canonry swung open and Charley ran down the steps to meet me. Pulling myself together I said hastily to Hall: "I'll phone you tomorrow—many thanks for your help," and unfolding myself from the cramped space I scrambled out of the car.

"What's happened?" I demanded, sensing Charley's urgency and immediately dreading that I was about to be confronted with some new disaster. (By this time I was very tired and vulnerable to all manner of wild fears.) "What's wrong?"

"Nothing!" It seemed that Charley had merely been keen to convey some unexpected but not unpleasant news. "You've got a visitor, that's all—she did wonder whether to go back to her hotel but then she decided to wait."

I supposed it was too much to hope that Sheila had called to announce her engagement to Paul Dalton. To Charley I said: "Make me another sandwich and some tea, there's a good chap. I feel I need fortifying."

"Poor old Dad!" said Charley, and the next moment I found myself clutching his hand and holding it tightly. (Of course I was *very* tired. Englishmen like me don't usually go to pieces by making tactile gestures whenever someone addresses them with affection.)

"There, there!" said Charley, as if he were the parent and I were the child—a small child who had been lost but was now found. "There, there!" His fingers curled tightly round my hand.

I staggered into the brightly lit hall, and as Charley moved away into the kitchen to prepare my sandwich I walked into the drawing-room. My mouth opened. I drew breath to say: "Sheila, what a pleasant surprise!" but the words were never uttered. My eyes registered the flash of pink trousers, my ears heard the jangle of costume jewellery, and for one wild moment I thought I had succumbed to yet another optical illusion.

Loretta said unevenly: "It was the phone call. You sounded as if you really, truly wanted to see me. So in the end I junked the plane, went back to London, drank three martinis, loaded myself on to the train to Starbridge and checked in at the Crusader. Am I crazy?"

I laughed and said: "Magnificently sane!" Then I took her in my arms and showed her how grateful I was for her courage.

2

I HAD thought that this scene would be the perfect ending for my memoir—I am always very partial to a touch of romance at the end of a story—but I find myself unable to resist producing a third ending, a conclusion which combines the theological and anthropological ("human interest") angles to form a Grand Finale—and if anyone wishes to complain about this reckless literary self-indulgence, I shall plead that I am now exceedingly old (it is, as I write, 1975—ten years after the events I describe in my narrative) and allowances should be made for venerable retired bishops.

But before I reach the Grand Finale, which takes place in Starbridge

Cathedral (where else?), I think I must say a word about what happened to everyone; I think it would be more truthful, if less romantic, to admit that we didn't all live in harmonious bliss ever afterwards following that theologically pleasing scene in Jon's cottage—and since I have been so concerned with truth in this memoir, let me pursue truth to the final line. Life is open-ended. Human beings are fallible. They crawl forward, then slip back before crawling on again. Catastrophes lurk to ambush them. Tragedies erupt unexpectedly. "The whole creation," as St. Paul wrote, "groaneth and travaileth in pain," but nothing worthwhile can be created without blood, sweat and tears, and at least we know that our Creator is alongside us, sharing our suffering and never abandoning that enormous struggle to "make everything come right."

However, these thoughts on the nature of ultimate reality were hardly in my mind during the romantic scene I have just described, and they were even further from my mind when Charley, returning to the drawing-room to ask what filling I wanted in my sandwich, discovered me in this passionate embrace with a foreigner who, despite her advancing years, was quite definitely a *femme fatale.* Charley was appalled. It took him some time to grow out of his priggishness, and even today he tends to take an austere line on matters connected with sexual morality.

I had hoped that Michael might take a more liberal line with my exceedingly stylish romance (I refused from the start to describe it as "autumnal") but I had reckoned without the bizarre fact that the young, who pride themselves on their open-mindedness about sex, become very upset when the members of the older generation display any hint that they are not quite, carnally speaking, "over the hill." Michael did finally manage to digest this outrageous manifestation, but he spent some time going through a period of behaving like a Victorian paterfamilias, obsessively concerned that his nearest and dearest should remain chaste. We even had a row in which he accused me of betraying Lyle when she was not yet cold in her grave (more Victorian behaviour) but since by the grace of God I managed to conduct my private life as a man should and as a bishop must, he realised in the end that I was being true to my principles and not letting him down. My relationship with him bumped on erratically for a while but improved greatly once he was married, and now, ten years after the crises of 1965, I can only say that he is very good, keeping in touch, coming to see me when he can and sharing his thoughts with me without constraint.

Occasionally I wonder how he endures his career in television, but he has Lyle's tough, pragmatic streak and seems to have worked out very well how to thrive in such a high-powered modern world. Perhaps it was this tough streak which enabled him to survive the amoral maelstrom of the 1960s (I remain convinced that I should have been rapidly ruined if I had been young in that decade) and perhaps too it was this tough streak which enabled him not only to outmanoeuvre all the other eager young men who chased the dangerous Marina Markhampton, but to create a successful marriage with a blonde and beautiful *femme fatale.*

I must now summon the humility to admit that I was quite wrong when I believed Marina was a mere decadent society girl. I have long since decided that she is charming, intelligent, indestructibly loyal to her husband and exceptionally kind to old buffers past their prime. She pampers me shamelessly and tells me how gorgeous I still am. (All old buffers need a beautiful young woman to peddle this kind of fantasy to them occasionally.) She and Michael have one child, a son; needless to say, I am immensely and foolishly proud of him.

Charley has two sons so far and more children are planned when his wife has finished her doctoral thesis, but although his boys are excellent little fellows they do not belong to me in quite the same way and Michael's son remains the grandchild who reduces me to being a doting old man. How fortunate it is that old men are allowed to dote! It's certainly one of the compensations of old age.

I want to say a few words about Charley's wife who, as I have already narrated, captivated me from the moment I first saw her, but I know I must choose my words with care for Rachel has hidden difficulties which are not allowed to be mentioned. She and Charley met again in 1968, when Charley had succeeded in reaching his belated maturity, and they married in 1969 after Rachel graduated from London University. Her nervous breakdown occurred after the second child was born in 1972. She still sees the psychiatrist who assisted in her recovery. I did try to ask questions, but Charley would only say that in 1968 she had witnessed a violent death and that this had had a traumatic effect on her. He also made it very clear that this subject was not to be discussed, a ban which made speculation inevitable. Loretta thought that the "violent death" explanation was a fiction and that the real trouble was that Rachel was trying to do too much.

"Women who try to be the perfect clerical wife, the perfect mother, the perfect cook, the perfect hostess *and* the perfect doctoral student are deliberately putting themselves on course for a visit to the mental hospital," she pronounced, but this is the 1970s and women are expected to be superhuman. (Lyle, I'm sure, would have had a very tart comment to make about this new social trend.) I did not argue with Loretta; indeed I thought it probable that Rachel's quest for perfection had made her overstrained and in consequence more vulnerable to the malign effects of past traumas, but for reasons which I shall explain later, I was unable to dismiss the "violent death" explanation as a fiction.

All this reticence suggests I am on uneasy terms with Charley, but in fact we get on well enough whenever we meet. I am bound to say, however, that the brash, insecure young man of 1965 has evolved into a self-assured, strong-willed adventurer who is not always so easy for me to understand. Strangely enough I see less of Alex Jardine in him now and more of Lyle; perhaps, in an ironic twist of fate, he is not the clergyman that Jardine failed to be but the clergyman Lyle never was. He has inherited from her that same tough, pragmatic streak which enables Michael to thrive in the world of television, and in addition I detect Lyle's Machiavellian ability to "fix" awkward situations by a series of ruthless manoeuvres.

I know he is a devout priest and I know I should be content with that knowledge, but he is not the kind of priest with whom I feel at ease; his approach is not quite "up my street." He is certainly a conservative, as I am, but he seems to think that anyone who subscribes to the Middle Way nowadays is shying away from what he calls the big issues. The big issues all seem to be about fighting. Apparently we have to fight the sloth and indifference of secular society, fight the decadence and idolatry of Anglo-Catholicism, and fight every one of the liberal-radical heresies. Naturally the Anglo-Catholics and the liberals don't like this militant stance at all and want to fight back. I foresee that by the 1980s the Church factions will be completely polarised and that by the 1990s the Church of England will be torn apart by open war.

"But by the year 2000 the Evangelicals will have won and saved us all!" says Charley, dismissing my doubts as the muddle-headed murmurings of someone far gone in senectitude.

Of course Charley can never resist an oratorical flourish, and no doubt it is a good thing that the old-fashioned, biblically naive, politically innocent Evangelicals are being replaced by this clever, sophisticated new breed who will perform the essential function of checking the excesses of liberal-radical theology, but all this militancy is not to my taste at all. I also cannot help but notice that when the Anglo-Catholics and the Evangelicals are jostling for supremacy they become mirror-images of each other, both of them paying far too much attention to that idol "The Church" and forgetting too often that we are called neither to lead nor to fight nor to creep around the corridors of power in Machiavellian manoeuvres, but to serve.

"Charley's just a wheeler-dealer in a dog-collar!" Michael said acidly the other day. "Imagine supporting all that stuff about speaking in tongues—what's in it for him?"

Charley is indeed very interested in the Charismatic Movement and no doubt he *is* busy calculating how far it should be supported to propagate the Gospel, but I do not say this to Michael. I say peaceably instead: "All priests have a duty to support the genuine manifestations of the Holy Spirit." But what do I really think about the Charismatics? I cannot help remembering Bishop Butler's matchless comment—"Sir, the pretending to extraordinary revelations and gifts of the Holy Ghost is a horrid thing, a very horrid thing!"—and immediately I feel not only sceptical but lukewarm. But on the other hand, what does it matter what I think? I've had my day. "The old order changeth . . ." The Church of England is no longer a gentlemen's club, conducting business according to gentlemanly rules, and I dare say it does need to throw off that outdated image in order to be more effective, but something special will be lost, something precious, some quality of elegance and innocence that I loved.

And now *I'm* the one who's making an idol of the Church. How easy it is to criticise others for the faults one cannot acknowledge in oneself! So I must not be too critical of Charley; I must accept that the Church lives and dies in every generation only to be born again in the next. It is Jesus Christ who is the same yesterday, today and forever, not the Church, which is always in the process of development.

It will be obvious by this time that Charley is doing wonderfully well, frequently getting himself quoted in the papers, making speeches in that ghastly invention the General Synod, running conferences, writing articles, publishing books. He is a very busy, very successful man, so busy and successful that he seldom has the chance to visit me, but when he does come he is always most kind and affectionate. He knows that despite all my doubts about his militancy I'm proud of him—but I think he knows too that Alex Jardine would have been even prouder.

Sometimes I mind that Charley has so little time for me these days but I console myself with the knowledge that I always have Michael to talk to, either in person or on the telephone; Michael always has time for me. The television drama which he produces goes from strength to strength. I admit to being prejudiced, but everyone says that the BBC's drama is magnificent. "British drama on Channel Thirteen," said Loretta on our most recent visit to New York, "is the only excuse any civilised American has for keeping a TV set."

I have enjoyed my visits to New York. It seems to me like some European city which I can never quite identify—or is that city merely the Edwardian London of my remote boyhood, a huge, lavish, spectacular concoction where the nouveaux riches lived cheek by jowl alongside the families with old money, and all were surrounded by the teeming hordes of the poor? But whatever city New York resembles it is certainly not Starbridge. Before I retired I used to find the contrast very stimulating.

I retired in 1970 (I think a bishop has a moral duty not to cling to office once he has lurched into his eighth decade) and after the inevitable holiday in America we indulged ourselves by settling down in Cambridge. I had forgotten that the winter wind comes straight from Siberia, but Loretta, with masterly American efficiency, solved that problem by installing the very latest gas central heating system in our house on Maid's Causeway, keeping the thermostat permanently at seventy-five (this would have horrified Lyle, always a thrifty housewife) and sealing the windows by a process known as "double-glazing." First of all I thought I would suffocate but then I found I was thriving like a hot-house plant.

Loretta says: "I'm sure British men have a certain reputation only because so many of them spend so much time being half-dead with cold," and I find myself bound to agree with her. All the heat certainly did wonders for my rheumatism and ensured my continuing agility. I still play a little golf, but not too much. Loretta says: "The other mistake Englishmen make is to waste too much energy on outdoor sport," and once again I find myself bound to agree with her.

Life in Cambridge is most stimulating. We write our books, do our research at the University Library, enjoy the theatre, the cinema, the Fitzwilliam Museum, the dinner-parties with my old friends, the guest-nights at my old college. I still preach now and then. I suppose I do miss my life as a senior churchman, but not very often. I miss Lyle sometimes, but that's natural. Loretta understands. Lyle and I were married for over twenty-seven years so of course I am going to think of her now and then—and particularly on our wedding anniversary and on her birthday and on that terrible day when she died. But the day of her death was the day I began my journey to my new life. I never forget that. It's why I can now recall her death with sadness but without bitterness or anger. In the end, in my new life—because of my new life—acceptance of her absence came.

Loretta enjoys her own new life immensely, particularly now that we have left the provincial ways of Starbridge far behind us. Settling in Starbridge was the sacrifice she made when she married me, but I made it plain from the start that she was to lead the life she wanted and that I did not expect her to convert herself into a stereotypical Mrs. Bishop. I thought of Lyle and said: "I don't want you to sacrifice your life to the task of keeping me going"—and indeed, after I had resolved the hidden problems which had so debilitated me, I had more than enough energy to do my job without being constantly propped up.

The fact that I encouraged my wife to lead her own life was felt by some members of the Starbridge clerical establishment to be somewhat shocking, and more than one person hinted that I was behaving strangely for a traditionalist bishop. Gossip even circulated that I had been so undermined by this foreigner that my mind had been affected, and when I declared robustly during a visit to the Deanery that it was the height of sanity to acknowledge that everything changed, even the role of bishops' wives, Dido was so infuriated that she declared the marriage would all end in tears. ("As I'm famed for my candour, Charles my dear, I consider it my absolute moral duty to tell you . . .") Before the Aysgarths left the Close she even had the impertinence to lecture Loretta on how to be the wife of an eminent clergyman.

"Poor little Dido!" said Loretta with a Christian charity which I myself was quite unable to summon. "Of course she's jealous of me because I'm free to be myself while she feels she has to break herself over and over again to be something she's not cut out to be—a clerical wife. Perhaps if I were to find her a really understanding therapist . . ."

Having spent years in analysis, Loretta is very keen on psychology and the highest compliment she can pay people is to pronounce them "well integrated." I love being married to an American. My command of modern phraseology has expanded enormously.

Jon remarked with interest that although a man tends to marry the same type of woman on repeated trips to the altar, I had proved to be the exception to this particular trend; not only was Lyle quite different from Jane, but Loretta was quite different from either of them. For the first time I am now married to my intellectual equal, although I believe I had to reach my mid-sixties before I felt ready to take on this challenge. In fact if I had married Loretta in the 1930s I doubt if I could have lived comfortably with either her intellect or her independent disposition. It was during Lyle's life that I travelled towards the emotional maturity which marriage to Loretta required, and it was certainly during the aftermath of Lyle's death that I saw my shortcomings as a husband sufficiently clearly to want to redeem my mistakes.

Loretta says that for a privileged Englishman of the old school I have come a long way and that I am to be greatly commended for achieving this rare degree of modernisation; of course, she adds, my consciousness will never be "*fully* raised" but this is without doubt a good thing because if I became wholly perfect I would bore her. Curiosity compels me to ask what I would have to believe in for my consciousness to be "*fully* raised," and when I receive the reply: "The ordination of women," I launch myself into a long and learned speech explaining why this most intriguing ecclesiastical step is quite impossible to take.

Loretta just laughs.

I throw a cushion at her but wind up laughing too. Loretta can always make me laugh. What fun we have together! I must say, I never in my wildest dreams imagined that old age would be so amusing.

Jon said to me before he died in 1972: "I'm very glad you're so happy in your marriage, Charles." I still miss Jon more than I can say. With his guidance I think I did finally make a success of that Starbridge bishopric—a spiritual success instead of merely a worldly one. In worldly terms it was said that I went soft, lost my edge, became fuzzy on dogma, but in fact all that happened was that I stopped proclaiming the absolute truths of Charles Ashworth and started proclaiming the absolute truths of Jesus Christ. This annoyed the liberals, since they felt that now I was less authoritarian I should join their ranks, and it annoyed the conservatives even more because they felt I had sold out to the liberals, but when I found I could live very happily with myself as a conservative liberal—or should I say a liberal conservative?—Jon suggested that God was not annoyed at all, and that God, in the end, was the one who mattered.

I daresay I shall still go down in history as a thoroughly traditionalist bishop, but in a decade as radical as the 1960s even the mildest conservative is going to look like a hardened reactionary. Certainly they continued to think of me as a traditionalist at the Theological College, that jewel of my episcopate, but I still tell myself that an ultra-conservative hand at the helm was the making of that place. Or was it? Jon's son young Nicholas shocked me in 1968 by calling the College "dead," but Nicholas in those days was such a very odd young man. I am relieved to report that although he is by no remote stretch of the imagination a conventional priest, he has settled down well and is currently rated a success as chaplain of the Starbridge General Hospital. I do wonder sometimes if he is any more talented than Jon at the delicate art of being a family man, but at least he and his wife have known each other since childhood so she must have realised exactly what she was taking on. I tell myself I must stop worrying about Nicholas, so instead I pray regularly for his welfare and hope for the best.

And that, I fear, is also all I can do for that other unconventional priest, Hall—whom, since we have grandchildren in common, I nowadays call Lewis. Desmond Wilton has long since retired; oddly enough although I always visualised that Lewis would look after Desmond, the reverse proved to be the case and in the end it was Desmond, with his prayerful life and basic spiritual stability, who looked after Lewis. Once Desmond had retired, Lewis's behaviour became more erratic and in 1973, when Rachel had barely recovered from her nervous breakdown, he turned up dead drunk at the small family dinner-party which Charley had organised to celebrate her birthday.

By chance I was there on my own (Loretta was recuperating in Cambridge from a cold) and in the disruption which followed Lewis's arrival it was I who rescued him, took him to the club in London where I was staying and sat up with him in my bedroom until he passed out. Admist all the inebriated nonsense he talked (he even insisted that Father Darcy was possessing him in revenge for Lewis's decision not to become a Fordite monk!) he embarked on a story which I soon realised was the story Charley refused to tell me, the story of the "violent death" which lay at the root of Rachel's breakdown.

I think it quite unnecessary for me to recount this florid tale. It is far more important to state that I did not for one moment believe it. Some violent incident happened, I have no doubt of that, and whatever happened was dreadful; I have no doubt of that either. Obviously Rachel had been traumatised and Lewis was now beside himself with guilt because he had decided to cover up the disaster in the mistaken belief that this would be the best thing for his daughter, but evidently the whole episode was so dreadful that even in his very inebriated state Lewis was unable to tell me the truth. He said Rachel had been visiting a country church and had disturbed a drunken tramp who had committed suicide by cutting his throat in front of her. Of all the improbable stories! And Lewis could not even remember the name or location of the church! However, summoning all my pastoral skill I told myself that the facts of the case were at that moment unimportant; all that mattered was that I had been presented with a distressed man who needed help in easing his guilt.

Firmly I said: "You did what you sincerely believed to be ethically justifiable at the time. None of us can do more than that when we have to grapple with an appalling crisis, and the instinct to protect our children from further pain after they've suffered greatly is very strong. You may now feel that the price you and Rachel have paid for your decision was high, but that still needn't mean the decision was wrong; any decision in such an agonising dilemma was likely to prove costly." And I told him of my days as a prisoner of war when I had learnt that a situation could be so difficult, so riddled with moral dilemmas, that a strict legalistic solution was inadequate. "So don't judge yourself too harshly," I urged. "Offer the incident to God, offer your repentance for your part in it, and then let your guilt go before it corrodes you any further."

To my relief Lewis found this approach helpful, but when he had sobered up he was horrified that he had disclosed even a fantasy version of the great trauma, and I have no doubt he regretted confiding in me. By that time I was wondering if the incident might have arisen from an exorcism which had gone horrifically wrong. I had forbidden Lewis to conduct the exorcism of people without my permission, but I thought he might well have disobeyed me for some reason which had seemed overwhelmingly right at the time. A botched exorcism would certainly have explained his extreme guilt about Rachel—but what on earth had Rachel been doing at any exorcism, botched or otherwise? I did tentatively say to Lewis later on: "If there's anything else you'd like to tell me about the disaster in 1968 . . ." but he looked so appalled by the suggestion that I knew I would never learn the whole truth. And perhaps that was just as well.

As the result of this drunken yarn-spinning, I found Lewis a new spiritual director (any priest who gets drunk in public needs someone taking a different approach to his spiritual life) and made a point of keeping in touch with him regularly by letter, but I was very conscious that he needed more help than I, far away in Cambridge, could provide. The main trouble seems to be that Lewis can never find a spiritual director who is quite right for him. In 1968 he finally met Jon, but although they had some enthralling conversations about Father Darcy, Jon always refused to be Lewis's spiritual director. To me he simply said: "I'm too old," and I have no doubt he was right. Lewis seems to exhaust spiritual directors in record time; I suspect he sets them huge tests of endurance and then sacks them when they fail to meet his impossibly high standards. "No one ever measures up to Father Darcy," he's said to me more than once. Sometimes I think that eccentric old monk has a lot to answer for.

Lewis is better at the moment. He tells me he has restricted his drinking and is being moderate in his eating habits, but rumour reaches me that he has been seen dining in London with a blonde divorcée. I fear he was born to live dangerously, and indeed my successor in the bishopric tells me he's consumed more indigestion tablets since he met Lewis than he had hitherto consumed in his entire ministry.

The Healing Centre is a success; no one disputes this. It has helped many people, the ethical standards are impeccable and it is a credit to the Christian ministry of healing. But the risk of scandal is always there, the worm lurking in the woodwork, and Lewis—dynamic, controversial, attractive to both sexes, capable of spiritual brilliance and spiritual instability in more or less equal proportions—Lewis lives always on a knife-edge. Malcolm Lindsay escaped, becoming Provost of Richmond, but the new Archdeacon was unable to cope with that special ministry in Langley Bottom and wound up having a nervous breakdown. "*'Après nous le déluge!'* " said Malcolm when we lunched together in London shortly afterwards, and we both experienced an agreeable shiver of *schadenfreude.*

Paul Dalton also moved on from Starbridge; I secretly coaxed a brother-bishop to offer him a canonry closer to Berkshire, Paul's home county, because I felt sure Sheila would be as anxious as I was that she should embark on her new life at a comfortable distance from me. She did promise that she would never tell a soul what had happened during that night I spent in Pimlico, and I was careful to express sincere gratitude, but of course it was in her best interests to ensure that Paul never knew about her little lapse. He had married her in the firm belief that as the ideal clerical wife she had never put a foot wrong, least of all in the company of stray bishops, and I could well imagine her saying mildly that it would have been very unkind to disillusion him.

"I find that nowadays I can remember Sheila almost with affection," I said the other day to Loretta after reading an article on the Daltons' cathedral in *The Church Gazette*. "In some ways she was a remarkably nice woman."

"Oh yeah?" said Loretta in the time-honoured manner of the American sceptic. (And in my memory I could hear Lyle sigh: "Dear Charles! Such a very Christian nature!") "I think she was a pretty tough cookie. She nearly nailed you, and she nailed Paul in double-quick time. A classic English adventuress in a twinset and pearls!"

I retorted that of course no adventuress could be taken seriously unless she wore a pink trouser-suit and talked with an American accent.

"Isn't it odd," said Loretta when we had finished laughing, "how even the shadiest incidents of the past can contribute beneficially to the present? If you hadn't got in such a muddle with Sheila she wouldn't have closed in on Starbridge like a man-eating shark—and if Sheila hadn't come to Starbridge Paul might never have found his ideal wife. And just think: if we hadn't rolled around together in the heather in 1937—"

"Bracken," I said, *sotto voce.*

"—I wouldn't have become a Christian, and if I hadn't become a Christian you wouldn't have considered marrying me, and if you hadn't married me I'd still be moseying around my New York apartment in my muu-muu trying to kid myself it was fun to spend old age alone, and if I was still alone, then we wouldn't be having such fun confounding all the doomsters who say old age is hell. So in other words, our current moral Christian bliss is all due to the fact that we fornicated amidst the *non-specific vegetation* long ago before the war!"

Since this thesis implied that we could all eat, drink and be merry without restraint in the knowledge that God would always clear up the mess, I felt obliged to point out: "You're forgetting I've had to sweat blood to try to help God redeem my mistakes as far as possible! And the fact that a surprising degree of redemption's been achieved doesn't alter the fact that my mistakes caused a lot of trouble at the time and that I paid a stiff price for them."

"But you can't deny our happy ending!"

"I'm just pointing out it didn't happen painlessly as the result of God waving a magic wand. Besides, redemption doesn't always come in the form of the traditional happy ending. Look at Aysgarth. He redeemed his remote past somehow by looking after Dido, but one can hardly say he lived happily ever after. The point was that the redemption enabled him to live with his past and gave his marriage meaning."

But Loretta had been swept away on a tide of liberal optimism. "You're making it all sound much too gloomy!" she argued with spirit. "I think Stephen gets a big charge out of that marriage. He loves all that wining and dining and socialising! I'm not saying the marriage hasn't been a challenge, but can you really see Stephen being married to a nice little wife who caused him no trouble? He'd have expired from boredom before the first wedding anniversary!"

It was strange how Aysgarth's name came up at that particular time. When I opened *The Times* at the obituary page the next morning, I saw that he was dead. Old age remains a poignant journey, even when one travels in good health and with the best of companions. The circle of friends contracts, the future slowly disappears, tales of illness and suffering multiply. The fact that I believe God will enfold me when I die and that the pattern which is Charles Ashworth will be recreated in another dimension does not alter the fact that I have had a good life which I shall be sorry to leave. I console myself with the knowledge that in every ending there is a new beginning, and that out of death comes redemption, resurrection and renewal. I lived through that great truth after Lyle died and I have never forgotten it, particularly now when I live each day to the full and give thanks to God for his mercy and generosity to me. Nevertheless, it's hard when the old companions die, and is there any companion to whom one is linked more subtly and irrevocably than an old enemy whom one forgives and befriends at the end? I see now before I close this memoir I must make some final comment upon this fellow-traveller whom I misunderstood so often during our journey through the Church of England in the twentieth century, but the right words will be hard to find. What can one say about a heroic ecclesiastical gangster who was addicted to taking scandalous risks? Yet I want to be as generous to him as I know he would have been to me if I had been the one to die first. Generous, forgiving . . . but not sentimental.

I suppose in the end it's all a question of truth.

3

HOW CLOSELY Aysgarth's life was interwoven with mine, and how important we were to each other! I cannot say we became close friends after he resigned the Deanery in 1965, but we kept in touch and during his annual visit to Starbridge he always called to see me. He made this annual pilgrimage to visit the grave of his three sons who had died at birth; the first infant had died in Starbridge and the other two were buried with him. I found it touching that Aysgarth, that tough old warrior, should keep those lost children of his so alive in his memory. How sad it was that Dido never accompanied him.

I hardly need reveal that he pulled off his final scandalous risk as Dean, produced immaculate accounts and was hailed as the most brilliant fund-raiser in the Church of England. (Nigel, Malcolm and the Chapter were all nearly felled by apoplexy when they saw the enormous fees which had been paid to the "art expert," but we were united in agreeing that in order to keep the story out of the press we had to have our apoplexy quietly, in private.)

On his retirement the ecclesiastical organisations queued up to offer Aysgarth a job and he was much courted. I hear he raised some amazing sum of money for Guildford Cathedral. Certainly he had a busy life once he was safely installed in his lavishly modernised, tastelessly extended former labourer's hovel in the most picturesque part of rural Surrey. (Roses were immediately trained to grow around the front door.)

Perhaps because of the guilt caused by his extraordinary machinations with Harriet March, he almost worked himself to death in his last months at the Deanery with the result that more money was raised for the west front than was needed. This surplus has been devotedly tended with absolute propriety by various accountants and brokers of unimpeachable reputation, and is now set to gladden the heart of the future Dean of Starbridge when the spire begins to sway in the wind in the late 1980s. (The Cathedral architect prophesied this apocalyptic event as long ago as 1963.) In fact the present Dean is so grateful to Aysgarth that he and the Chapter have voted unanimously to place a large stone in his memory in the floor of the nave, and apparently Dido has already demanded that the memorial should be unveiled by the Archbishop of Canterbury. *The Church Gazette* will no doubt squander columns of newsprint in declaring what a character Aysgarth was, and by the turn of the century he will have gone down in history as a great ecclesiastical hero.

"If they only knew what he'd got up to!" I muttered to Loretta as I ploughed through the obsequious obituary in *The Times*.

"Assuming that God knew and forgave him," said Loretta, "isn't it theologically correct that the obituary writers should reflect only the good side of Stephen's character and allow the murky side to be consigned to oblivion?"

I sometimes wish Loretta could have been one of my divinity undergraduates. What stimulating discussions we would have had! "You're ignoring the question of truth," I said benignly, "but that's because the question, as you've posed it, doesn't reflect what's actually happened. What the obituary writers are reflecting is neither Stephen's good side nor his bad side but his final pattern. As Jon would have said, all the dark episodes have been penetrated by the light so that only this extraordinary image of a rehabilitated, redeemed Aysgarth remains—but of course it only seems extraordinary to us because we can best remember him in the days long before the final pattern was fixed."

I could see this response appealed to Loretta, but being of an independent disposition she tossed another thought-provoking question at me. "How do you think God intends to redeem Stephen's family?" she said, and added regretfully: "I suppose that's one piece of fancy creative footwork which we won't live to see."

It is a sad fact that various members of Aysgarth's family were felled by tragedy in the latter half of the 1960s, and not all the disasters could be attributed to random misfortune. Loretta says it's obvious that Aysgarth was quite unable to "communicate" with the sons of his first marriage with the result that the family became malfunctioning; she attributes this fatal dislocation to Aysgarth's infatuation with Dido so soon after his first wife's death, and theorises that Aysgarth was probably so smitten with guilt about his behaviour that he was unable to discuss the situation "meaningfully" with the bewildered and scandalised children. Wary though I am of some of Loretta's more extravagant flights of fancy through the realm of psychology (complete with peculiar American jargon), I have to admit I find this explanation plausible, particularly since the children of the second marriage do not seem to attract misfortune in quite the same way as their older siblings. Both have their odd side (why does Pip have no girlfriends? Why did Elizabeth marry an elderly foreign roué when she was pretty enough to marry a decent Englishman?) but one would hardly expect Dido's children to reflect the dead norm of youthful behaviour.

It has just occurred to me that now at last I can see why Aysgarth was so devoted to those three sons who died at birth. They could not grow old and hurt him as the other boys did; he could love them devotedly in the knowledge that they would never disappoint him. Strange how that continuing devotion to the dead children still has the power to move me. The fact that they had such a special place in their father's heart gives their brief lives meaning.

After I had read the obituary I went to my study and reread the last letter he had written to me and which would now remain unanswered. He had been on a little holiday to Norfolk to visit Lyle's protégée Venetia, the daughter of his best friend Lord Flaxton.

"Naturally she was horrified to see what a battered old wreck I've become since my stroke," he had written with characteristic insouciance, "but she was so kind that she even allowed me to convince her that Holman Hunt's *Light of the World* wasn't just one big Victorian cliché! Flushed by this spiritual triumph (and God knows, one was long overdue) I then became very cosy and confidential. 'My dearest Venetia,' I said to her, 'spare a tear for poor old Dido and thank God *you* haven't wound up yoked to a decrepit old crock!' She refused to shed a tear for Dido, but she did give me a kiss, which is a very delightful treat for a man of my age and condition to receive, and I venture to hope that everything will come right for her now that she understands about *The Light of the World.* Not that I shall live to see things come right for her, but at least now I have absolute faith that they will.

"Talking of death and speaking as one clergyman to another, I have to admit that despite my decrepit state I'm not too keen on dying, but never mind, I can't complain, I've had a good life and despite all the difficulties and sadness I can still say with sincerity: THANKS BE TO GOD! I only hope that when the end does come it's sudden and I drop straight into God's lap. Quite what he'll do with me is, I realise, open to debate, but since I shall always remain until my dying day a good Liberal Protestant Modernist, I can't help but be an incorrigible optimist and I believe that God will be as merciful to me as you were, back in 1965, when you discovered the full extent of my passion for innovative fund-raising . . ."

The telephone rang on my desk just as I had finished rereading these lines, and when I picked up the receiver I found myself speaking to Charley. He had been informed by the lawyers that there was to be a big funeral service for Aysgarth in Starbridge Cathedral, and Aysgarth himself had left Charley a letter which asked him to give the address.

"I suppose the situation has a certain inexorable logic," Charley was saying as I struggled to digest this startling information. "He preached at Alex's funeral in 1945 and he died still believing that fable that I was Alex's grandson. None of his sons became clergymen. Alex was the friend and mentor who gave him a helping hand at the start of his career. Aysgarth himself always took an interest in me. The request really isn't so surprising."

All I said was: "Do you have his letter in front of you?"

"The lawyers enclosed it with their own letter which arrived this morning. Strangely enough Aysgarth asks me to consult you about the text on which I'm instructed to preach. He says you alone know exactly how he believed it should be interpreted."

I said: "It's Romans eight, isn't it?"

"Verse twenty-eight, yes. 'And we know that all things work together for good . . .' "

And so I come to the very end of my story, the third ending, the ending which will leave me with nothing more to write. For here I am, once more, in Starbridge Cathedral, and here, at last, is the Grand Finale.

4

JUST AS I wrote in my memoir of 1937: "I came at last to Starbridge . . ." so now I write nearly forty years later in the other half of the twentieth century: we *all* came at last to Starbridge, radiant, ravishing Starbridge, and we all took our seats in the Cathedral, all of us, the living and the dead, the echoes from the past mingling with the flesh and blood of the present to foreshadow the shimmering possibilities of the future. We came to the Cathedral to mourn the dead, but in our mysterious world of being and becoming, death and resurrection are perpetually linked; the present falls away into the past in a succession of timeless moments, but the future opens up ahead of us even as the present dies before our eyes.

The funeral service opens with the famous words "I am the Resurrection and the Life," the words of the Eternal Christ of St. John's Gospel as he begins to define the absolute truths of human existence. We die; indeed we have to die in order to be resurrected, restored and renewed. We die and we die and we die in this life, not only physically—within seven years every cell in our body is renewed—but emotionally and spiritually as change seizes us by the scruff of the neck and drags us forward into another life. We are not here simply to exist. We are here in order to become. It is the essence of the creative process; it is in the deepest nature of things.

"But no matter how firmly one believes that death is always followed by renewal and resurrection," Aysgarth had written in his funeral instructions, "there can be no denying it's sad to say goodbye in this life and this sadness shouldn't be glossed over. So please—don't give me one of those ghastly memorial services where everyone exudes false jollity and behaves as if they've just dropped in on a Saturday matinée! On the other hand I don't want a funeral which is one long dirge from beginning to end. Let's have a suitably sombre start, please, but let the final hymn be 'Thine Be the Glory,' and before Charley gives the address let's get the choir to sing one of the great anthems written not for a funeral but for a coronation—let's rejoice in the coronation message that an ordinary man can become someone special, sanctified by God for a new life—let's raise the Cathedral roof with 'Zadok the Priest'!"

The organ began to play the anthem's long introduction, and as I listened to the pattern of the notes forming and re-forming the cadence which led to the mighty entry of the choir, the Cathedral began to come alive, no longer a sinister animal from some medieval bestiary but a radiant city from some medieval book of hours, pointing beyond itself, as all great works of art do, to the ultimate values and absolute truths of our being and our becoming and our journeying into eternity.

I looked up the nave. I looked at the vaulted ceiling far above me, but in my mind's eye I saw the whole Cathedral; I saw the transepts and the chapels, the choir and the sanctuary, the vestry and the sacristy, the chapter house and the cloisters, the library and the cloister garth; I saw the tower vault, the black Purbeck marble pillars, the triforium, the clerestory, the pulpit, the lectern, the high altar; I saw the statues and the carvings and the tablets and the glass—stained glass, plain glass, dim glass, clear glass—and I saw the arches, narrow arches, perpendicular arches, pointed arches and most arresting of all the strainer arches, which supported the great weight of the spire—and beyond the roof of the nave, above the massive block of the tower, the spire itself was rising and rising and rising, yard after yard, foot after foot, inch after inch, upwards and upwards and upwards until at last it had tapered to the point which supported the cross.

And as in my mind I saw the cross on the top of the spire, my eyes saw the cross on the altar and the cross formed by the transepts and the cross hanging on the wall behind the pulpit. Everywhere was the cross, the intersection of the temporal with the eternal, the symbol of suffering redeemed and horrors forgiven and darkness conquered by the Lord and Giver of all life, the Creator of all things.

The organist was almost at the end of the anthem's long introduction, and as the crescendo increased the Cathedral began to glitter before my eyes until I felt as if every stone in the building was vibrating in anticipation of the sweeping sword of sound from the Choir.

The note exploded in our midst, and at that moment I knew our Creator had touched not only me but all of us, just as Harriet had touched that sculpture with a loving hand long ago, and in that touch I sensed the indestructible fidelity, the indescribable devotion and the inexhaustible energy of the Creator as he shaped his creation, bringing life out of dead matter, wresting form continually from chaos. Nothing was ever lost, Harriet had said, and nothing was ever wasted because always, when the work was finally completed, every particle of the created process, seen or unseen, kept or discarded, broken or mended—*everything* was justified, glorified and redeemed. Then I thought, as I looked around the Cathedral, of the pattern our Creator had made of us as he had toiled to shape the dark with the light in such a way that our suffering was given meaning, the meaning which gave value to our lives.

"Reality is a kingdom of values," someone had written long ago before the war, but I could not quite remember who it was (Charles Raven? Dean Inge?) and in the past I heard Jon say more than once: "Reality is spiritual." Then the thought of Raven and Inge took me back to the world of the Church of England before the war, and as I looked up into the pulpit I remembered Alex Jardine declaiming there in 1937: " 'For what shall it profit a man, if he shall gain the whole world, and lose his own soul?' " I could see him clearly in my memory, and I could hear his voice too—and the next moment I was back in his episcopal palace, in that old-fashioned drawing-room, and my hostess Carrie Jardine was talking about the weather.

The memories streamed on. I saw Carrie Jardine's brother Colonel Cobden-Smith; he was listening to his dogmatic wife who talked so much about India, and out of the corner of my eye I could see Lady Starmouth, who had taken such a benevolent interest not only in me but in Aysgarth, and beyond Lady Starmouth I saw her husband the Earl—at which point my memory of the Jardines' drawing-room was replaced by my memory of the Earl fishing by the river which flowed past the end of the palace garden, and as my mind shifted from scene to scene I saw Lyle saying: "Dr. Ashworth? I'm Miss Christie, Mrs. Jardine's companion," while on a Surrey hillside Loretta talked of a painful past—and the thought of painful pasts reminded me then of my father, talking in his greenhouse of his past suffering—which enabled me to see my parents through new eyes—and the next moment I was meeting someone else who was to be so important to me. "Dr. Ashworth," said my friend Alan Romaine as we came face to face for the first time, but before I could hear my reply the scene shifted yet again so that I found myself confronting another stranger, and Jon, dressed in his monk's habit, was sweeping into the visitors' parlour at his Grantchester monastery to make his grand entrance into my life.

I suddenly realised that the anthem had ended and that Charley was standing at last in the pulpit where his father—both his fathers—had stood before him.

" 'And we know that all things work together for good . . .' "

My memory changed gears and moved on; the recent past eased the remote past aside, and I heard Lyle asking me why I had formed the habit of scribbling on my blotter that same quotation from St. Paul's Epistle to the Romans. Then I heard myself repeating those words automatically in the seconds after her death, and I remembered how I had recoiled from them in horror by flinging the bottle of whisky against the wall.

But the recent past vanished again as Charley began to speak in Jardine's strong, harsh voice, and again I could see only the memories of 1937, the good memories still good, the bad memories still bad, but intermingling together now to form a pattern which had transformed my life.

" 'And we know,' " declared Charley, translating the passage just as Aysgarth had wished, " 'that all things *intermingle* for good . . .' "

Then suddenly the pre-war years disappeared over the horizon in my mind as I saw myself officiating in 1940 at Jon's marriage to Anne Barton-Woods—and later Jon was giving me his blessing before I went overseas—and after the war there he was again, recurring in my life as the bearer of the light which would eventually create a meaningful pattern out of the vile darkness of my prison experiences—and thinking of those war years reminded me how physically debilitated I was afterwards—which called to mind my visit to a London doctor for a check-up—which in turn reminded me of the call I had paid afterwards at the headquarters of the Fordite monks.

I saw myself talking to Francis Ingram, meeting Aidan Lucas, hearing (of course!) about Father Darcy, and suddenly Aysgarth was there, visiting the Fordites at the same time as I was—which was so very odd (and I could remember the exact quality of my surprise) because Aysgarth was such a Protestant that he normally had no time for the monks of the Church's Catholic wing—and the next moment I was remembering my row with Aysgarth in the dining-room of Starrington Manor when I had smashed my glass in the grate . . . Yet it had been Aysgarth, my enemy, who had helped me to come to terms with God's apparent absence in the prison-camp by offering a denial of that absence, a denial which had made me think afresh and set me on the road to recovery.

" 'All things work together for good . . .' " Charley was performing the oratorical trick of allowing each line of thought to reach an identical end in order to hammer home his text, but I hardly heard him because my memory had jumped forward to 1957, the year Aysgarth and I had received our preferments to Starbridge, and I was meeting him again at Lord Flaxton's London townhouse in Lord North Street. I could remember Lady Flaxton talking about her plants and Lord Flaxton insisting that

the country was going to the dogs—and there was Lyle, I could see her so clearly in one of her little black dresses, and she was talking to her protégée Venetia whose unhappiness was to generate the prayer-group.

How interlinked we all were, moving in and out of each other's lives—and often getting into such unchristian messes . . . and I saw myself confronting Aysgarth in 1963 as we argued about the sculpture he proposed to instal in the Cathedral churchyard—an argument which had taken me to Harriet's studio where I had at once decided that the sculpture was capable of a pornographic interpretation—which I had outlined to my old friend Jack Ryder who had chortled: "Anti-Sex Ashworth rides again!"—and finally 1963 flowed into 1965 so that I was again viewing sculpture with Harriet in her studio.

At that point, as I allowed my gaze to wander around the congregation, I saw Harriet herself, still remarkably alluring despite her advancing years. Chastely dressed in a smart black suit she saw me looking at her and remained poker-faced both before and after she had given me a wink. That sculpture of Aysgarth's hands is generally considered to be her masterpiece. Strange to think that if Aysgarth had never renewed his friendship with her in order to pursue his innovative fund-raising, that magnificent work of art would never have been created.

"*'And we know that* ALL THINGS WORK TOGETHER FOR GOOD . . .' "

Having succeeded in mesmerising his congregation Charley was battering them rhythmically with each syllable of the quotation. I was sure his amber eyes were glowing as he reached his peroration but I was no longer watching him; my glance was travelling on around the Cathedral as I recognised the familiar faces, seen and unseen, the living and the dead, those present in the spirit and those present in the flesh. I saw the people from the days of my bishopric: Malcolm and Nigel, all my chaplains, Miss Peabody, the Cathedral Canons, all my clergy, the Chancellor of the diocese, the Lord Lieutenant of the county, the Mayor of the city—the faces streamed on and on—and Lyle was there, of course, and both Michael and Charley as their past selves, everyone was there, all woven into the texture of my life in a pattern of multi-coloured threads, and some of those luminous strands, old friends such as Jack Ryder and Lady Markhampton—and Jon—kept recurring and recurring, but now I could see in my mind a later generation springing up around them—Martin Darrow, amusing us all in *Present Laughter,* Lady Markhampton's granddaughter Marina, Aysgarth's doomed sons, that tiresome feminist Primrose—and there was Primrose's former best friend Venetia, recurring yet again—and young Nicholas Darrow, who had been so very odd (how *could* he have believed in 1968 that the Theological College was "dead"?)—and beyond Nicholas I saw Lewis Hall, the latecomer to the scene, with his crucifix held high in his hand.

" 'ALL THINGS *INTERMINGLE* FOR GOOD . . .' "

Charley was delivering the text yet again and pouring even more power into it so that every word crackled with life, and as he raised his voice he sounded more like Jardine than ever—so that I even wondered for a fanciful moment if he *was* Jardine, but no, that was nonsense, and now that I was so old I had to be very careful not to sink into senile and sentimental thoughts which would be quite unpardonable for a former professor of divinity. Charley was not Jardine reincarnated. But Charley's present was reshaping Jardine's past. Jardine's tragedy remained tragic, but Charley's life was creating upon it a pattern in which the terrible errors became so much less important than the great gifts which had survived.

The truth was that out of all the suffering and despair had come a gifted man willing and able to preach to a new generation the Gospel of hope, faith and love. I could look at Charley and see redemption—which made me realise afresh that reincarnation is just a belief which allows us to cling to this imperfect world for fear of moving on. I certainly believe God has a far better fate in store for us than endless returns to earth, but how little we know, how limited we are, how puny are our words as they strain to describe the truth which lies beyond all truths, the final truth which is God. Indeed in the end there are no words, only Christ on the cross symbolising God's agonising involvement with his creation, Christ rising from the dead symbolising God's creative promise to redeem and renew, Christ enacting in flesh and blood the absolute truths for all mankind to see.

Charley paused. There was a moment of complete silence as if the entire congregation were holding its breath. Then as he declared for the final time: " 'WE KNOW THAT ALL THINGS WORK TOGETHER FOR GOOD TO THEM THAT LOVE GOD!' " I felt as if I were clasping hands yet again with Jon Darrow and Neville Aysgarth as we completed our great twentieth-century spiritual journey out of darkness into light.

Author's Note

ABSOLUTE TRUTHS is the final volume in a series of six novels about the Church of England in the twentieth century. Each book is designed to be read independently of the others, but the more books that are read the wider will be the perspective on the multi-sided reality which is being presented.

The first novel in the series, *Glittering Images,* was narrated by Charles Ashworth and described the events which took place in Starbridge in 1937. *Glamorous Powers,* narrated by Jon Darrow, opened in 1940, *Ultimate Prizes* was narrated by Neville Aysgarth after the war, and *Scandalous Risks* viewed the Church in 1963 through the eyes of Venetia Flaxton. In *Mystical Paths,* Nicholas Darrow set his story in 1968, three years after the events described in *Absolute Truths.*

AUSTIN FARRER, whose writings Charles Ashworth so much admired, was one of the most distinguished intellectuals of the Church of England in the twentieth century. Born in 1904 he was educated at St. Paul's School in London where he became School Captain before winning a scholarship to Balliol College, Oxford. Here he obtained a first in Classical Moderations, a first in Greats and a first in Theology. It was at Oxford too that he became a member of the Church of England. He was ordained deacon in 1928 and served as a curate in a Yorkshire parish.

In 1931 he returned to Oxford as chaplain and tutor at St. Edmund Hall. Soon afterwards his friendship began with Katharine Newton who in 1937 was to become his wife; she was an undergraduate, and after she had taken her degree they became secretly engaged. In 1935 he moved from St. Edmund Hall to become chaplain of Trinity College, and in 1945 he took the degrees of Bachelor of Divinity and Doctor of Divinity on the same day. He was happy at Trinity but at last he felt the time had come to move on, and after failing to be appointed the Regius Professor of Divinity he became Warden of Keble College in 1960.

During his twenty-five years at Trinity Farrer taught both philosophy and theology. Moreover, he lectured not only on the philosophy of the past but on the philosophy of modern times and was well acquainted with those systems hostile to religion. He became famous as the result of his Bampton lectures (published as *The Glass of Vision* in 1948) and during his last years he wrote a succession of acclaimed works including *Faith and Speculation, Saving Belief* and *Love Almighty and Ills Unlimited.* The latter, which seamlessly blended his philosophy and theology, was concerned with providence, evil and suffering. His biographer points out that Farrer was no stranger to suffering in his home life, for his wife became addicted to alcohol and his only child, Caroline, had learning disabilities. He died of a coronary thrombosis in 1968 after months of strain and overwork, but his reputation remains high and his admirers rate him a religious genius and even a saint.

REGINALD SOMERSET WARD, whose work is also quoted in this book, took a degree in history at Cambridge and was ordained in 1904. For a time he was secretary of the Church of England Sunday School Institute and in 1913 he became rector of a Surrey parish, but two years later he gave up the security of this conventional job in the Church and embarked on a peripatetic ministry of spiritual direction. This meant visiting fourteen city centres three times a year and seeing people by appointment for spiritual direction and, if necessary, for confession and absolution. Married with children, he lived in a house provided by an anonymous group who supported his work.

He believed in a rule of life which enabled people to get the best out of their souls, bodies and minds; the first priority was prayer, the second rest and recreation, and the third the God-given work which they were put in this world to do. His concern was with a God-centred wholeness, and in his desire to help people overcome the disabilities caused by sin and fear he welcomed the best insights of psychology. He wrote several books, including a guide to spiritual directors; he also wrote a monthly "instruction" on prayer for several decades and corresponded with hundreds of people, many of them clergy, about the spiritual life which he called "The Way." He died in 1962.

PERMISSIONS ACKNOWLEDGEMENTS

Grateful acknowledgement is made to the following for permission to reprint previously published material:

Doubleday: *Excerpts from* Love Almighty and Ills Unlimited *by Austin Farrer, copyright © 1961 by Austin Farrer. Reprinted by permission of Doubleday, a division of Bantam Doubleday Dell Publishing Group, Inc.*

The Austin Farrer Estate: *Excerpts from* Said or Sung *by Austin Farrer (Faith Press, UK, 1960). Reprinted by permission of The Trustees of the Austin Farrer Estate.*

Hodder & Stoughton Publishers Limited: *Excerpts from* A Celebration of Faith *by Austin Farrer. Reprinted by permission of Hodder & Stoughton Publishers Limited, London.*

A NOTE ON THE TYPE

THE text of this book was set in Bembo, a facsimile of a typeface cut by one of the most celebrated goldsmiths of his time, Francesco Griffo, for Aldus Manutius, the Venetian printer, in 1495. The face was named for Pietro Bembo, the author of the small treatise entitled De Aetna *in which it first appeared. Through the research of Stanley Morison, it is now acknowledged that all old-face type designs up to the time of William Caslon can be traced to the Bembo cut.*

THE present-day version of Bembo was introduced by the Monotype Corporation, London, in 1929. Sturdy, well balanced, and finely proportioned, Bembo is a face of rare beauty and great legibility in all of its sizes.

COMPOSED by ComCom, a division of
Haddon Craftsmen, Allentown, Pennsylvania
Printed and bound by The Haddon Craftsmen,
Scranton, Pennsylvania
Book and ornament designed by Margaret Wagner